PRAISE FOR TH

"Penelope Douglas show... central characters and th... [They] deliver a multilayered love story that strikes every emotional chord along the way—a story that is beautifully complicated, infinitely angsty, and completely impossible to put down."

—Natasha Is a Book Junkie

"Beyond addictive! Visceral and cuttingly edgy, *Punk 57* will own you from the first page to long after you turn over the last. Penelope Douglas slays it!"

—Katy Evans

"Douglas launched this series and held nothing back. They delivered a medley of emotions I never thought I could feel at once. I was afraid, intrigued, anxious, and enamored. A must-read!"

—B.B. Reid

"*Credence* consumed me with its sinfully unique taboo story and gorgeous imagery. Truly a one-of-a-kind book that I can't recommend enough."

—Carian Cole

"The seductive tug highlighted by the character-driven storyline held me in its grasp until the very end. Douglas's ability to draw such powerful emotions from the reader is truly fascinating."

—Abbi Glines

"Misha and Ryen's fiery romance will have your heartstrings twisted in knots and have you wanting a pen pal of your own. They're fire and ice, and I couldn't get enough."

—H. D. Carlton

"Penelope Douglas does many things very well. One of the best of those things is their ability to make something taboo seem irresistibly satisfying. With *Birthday Girl*, they twist the older man / younger woman taboo and make it compelling, sensual, and a wonderful treat."

—Eden Butler

PRAISE FOR THE NOVELS OF PENELOPE DOUGLAS

TITLES BY PENELOPE DOUGLAS

The Fall Away Series

BULLY

UNTIL YOU

RIVAL

FALLING AWAY

THE NEXT FLAME
(includes novellas *Aflame* and *Next to Never*)

Stand-Alones

MISCONDUCT

BIRTHDAY GIRL

PUNK 57

CREDENCE

TRYST SIX VENOM

The Devil's Night Series

CORRUPT

HIDEAWAY

KILL SWITCH

CONCLAVE
(novella)

NIGHTFALL

FIRE NIGHT
(novella)

NIGHTFALL

DEVIL'S NIGHT 4

PENELOPE DOUGLAS

BERKLEY ROMANCE
New York

BERKLEY ROMANCE
Published by Berkley
An imprint of Penguin Random House LLC
penguinrandomhouse.com

Copyright © 2020 by Penelope Douglas LLC
Bonus Scene copyright © 2024 by Penelope Douglas LLC
"Dear Reader" letter copyright © 2024 by Penelope Douglas LLC
Penguin Random House supports copyright. Copyright fuels creativity, encourages diverse
voices, promotes free speech, and creates a vibrant culture. Thank you for buying an authorized
edition of this book and for complying with copyright laws by not reproducing, scanning, or
distributing any part of it in any form without permission. You are supporting writers and
allowing Penguin Random House to continue to publish books for every reader.

BERKLEY and the BERKLEY and B colophon are registered trademarks of
Penguin Random House LLC.

Library of Congress Cataloging-in-Publication Data

Names: Douglas, Penelope, 1977- author.
Title: Nightfall / Penelope Douglas.
Description: First Berkley Romance Edition. |
New York: Berkley Romance, 2024. | Series: Devil's night; 4
Identifiers: LCCN 2023042108 | ISBN 9780593642030 (trade paperback)
Subjects: LCGFT: Romance fiction. | Novels.
Classification: LCC PS3604.O93236 N54 2024 | DDC 813/.6—dc23/eng/20231011
LC record available at https://lccn.loc.gov/2023042108

Nightfall was originally self-published, in different form, in 2020.

First Berkley Romance Edition: May 2024

Printed in the United States of America
1st Printing

Book design by George Towne
Map © Pink Ink Designs

This is a work of fiction. Names, characters, places, and incidents either are the product
of the author's imagination or are used fictitiously, and any resemblance to actual persons,
living or dead, business establishments, events, or locales is entirely coincidental.

For Z. King

You need not be sorry for her. She was one of the kind that likes to grow up. In the end, she grew up of her own free will a day quicker than the other girls.

—J. M. Barrie, *Peter Pan*

DEAR READER,

This book deals with emotionally difficult topics, either on-page or mentioned, that include sexual assault, rape, violence/assault, domestic abuse, bullying, incest, and murder. Anyone who believes such content may upset them is encouraged to check reviews before deciding whether to continue reading.

AUTHOR'S NOTE

Nightfall is the final novel in the Devil's Night series. All of the books are entwined, and it is recommended to read the prior installments before starting this book.

If you choose to skip *Corrupt*, *Hideaway*, or *Kill Switch*, please be aware you may miss plot points and important elements of the backstory.

Onward!
xx Pen

PLAYLIST

"99 Problems" by Jay-Z

"#1 Crush" by Garbage

"A Little Wicked" by Valerie Broussard

"Apologize" by Timbaland, One Republic

"Army of Me" by Björk

"Believer" by Imagine Dragons

"Blue Monday" by Flunk

"Devil Inside" by INXS

"Down with the Sickness" by Disturbed

"Everybody Wants to Rule the World" by Lorde

"Fire Up the Night" by New Medicine

"Hash Pipe" by Weezer

"Highly Suspicious" by My Morning Jacket

"History of Violence" by Theory of a Deadman

"If You Wanna Be Happy" by Jimmy Soul

"Intergalactic" by Beastie Boys

"In Your Room" by Depeche Mode

"Light Up the Sky" by Thousand Foot Krutch

"Man or a Monster (feat. Zayde Wølf)" by Sam Tinnesz

"Mr. Doctor Man" by Palaye Royale

"Mr. Sandman" by SYML

"Old Ticket Booth" by Derek Fiechter and Brandon Fiechter

"Party Up" by DMX

"Pumped Up Kicks" by 3TEETH

"Rx (Medicate)" by Theory of a Deadman

"Satisfied" by Aranda

PLAYLIST

"Sh-Boom" by the Crew Cuts

"Teenage Witch" by Suzi Wu

"Touch Myself" by Genitorturers

"White Flag" by Bishop Briggs

"Yellow Flicker Beat" by Lorde

"You're All I've Got Tonight" by The Cars

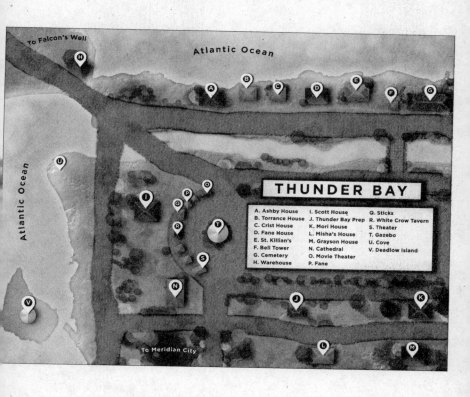

THUNDER BAY

A. Ashby House
B. Torrance House
C. Crist House
D. Fane House
E. St. Killian's
F. Bell Tower
G. Cemetery
H. Warehouse

I. Scott House
J. Thunder Bay Prep
K. Mori House
L. Misha's House
M. Grayson House
N. Cathedral
O. Movie Theater
P. Fane

Q. Sticks
R. White Crow Tavern
S. Theater
T. Gazebo
U. Cove
V. Deadlow Island

Atlantic Ocean

To Falcon's Well

To Meridian City

NIGHTFALL

CHAPTER 1

EMORY

Present

It was faint, but I heard it.

Water. Like I was behind a waterfall, deep inside a cave.

What the hell is that?

I blinked my eyes, stirring from the heaviest sleep I think I've ever had. Jesus, I was tired.

My head rested on the softest pillow, and I moved my arm, brushing my hand over a cool, splendidly plush white comforter.

I patted my face, feeling my glasses missing. I rolled my eyes around me, confusion sinking in as I took in myself burrowed comfortably in the middle of a huge bed, my body taking up about as much room as a single M&M inside its package.

This wasn't my bed.

I looked around the lavish bedroom—white, gold, crystal, and mirrors everywhere, palatial in its opulence like I'd never seen in person—and my breathing turned shallow as instant fear took over.

This wasn't my room. Was I dreaming?

I pushed myself up, my head aching and every muscle tight like I'd been sleeping for a damn week.

I dropped my eyes, spotting my glasses folded and sitting on the bedside table. I grabbed them and slipped them on, taking inventory of my body first. I laid on top of the bed, still fully clothed in my black skinny pants and a pullover white blouse that I'd dressed in this morning.

If it was still today, anyway.

My shoes were gone, but on instinct I peered over the side of the bed and saw my sneakers sitting there, perfectly positioned on a fancy white rug with gold filigree.

My pores cooled with sweat as I looked around the unfamiliar bedroom, and my brain was wracked with what the hell was going on. Where was I?

I slid off the bed, my legs shaky as I stood up.

I'd been at the firm. Working on the blueprints for the DeWitt Museum. Byron and Elise had ordered takeout for lunch for them-selves, I went out instead, and—I pinched the bridge of my nose, my head pounding—and then . . .

Ugh, I don't know. What happened?

Spotting a door ahead of me, I didn't even bother to look around the rest of the room or see where the two other doors led. I grabbed my shoes and stumbled for what I guessed was the way out, and stepped into a hallway, the cool marble floor soothing on my bare feet.

I still went down the list in my head, though.

I didn't drink.

I didn't see anyone unusual.

I didn't get any weird phone calls or packages. I didn't . . .

I tried to swallow a few times, finally generating enough saliva. God, I was thirsty. And—a pang hit my stomach—hungry, too. How long had I been out?

"Hello?" I called quietly but immediately regretted it.

Unless I'd had an aneurysm or developed selective amnesia, then I wasn't here willingly.

But if I'd been taken or imprisoned, wouldn't my door have been locked?

Bile stung my throat, every horror movie I'd ever seen playing various scenarios in my head.

Please, no cannibals. Please, no cannibals.

"Hi," a small, hesitant voice said.

I followed the sound, peering across the hallway, over the banister, to the other side of the upstairs where another hall of rooms sat. A figure lurked in a dark corridor, slowly stepping onto the landing.

"Who is that?" I inched forward just a hair, blinking against the sleep still weighing on my eyes.

It was a man, I thought. Button-down shirt, short hair.

"Taylor," he finally said. "Taylor Dinescu."

Dinescu? As in, Dinescu Petroleum Corporation? It couldn't be the same family.

I licked my lips, swallowing again. I really needed to find some water.

"Why am I not locked in my room?" he asked me, coming out of the darkness and stepping into the faint moonlight streaming through the windows.

He cocked his head, his hair disheveled and the tail of his wrinkled Oxford hanging out. "We're not allowed around the women," he said, sounding just as confused as me. "Are you with the doctor? Is he here?"

What the hell was he talking about? *We're not allowed around the women.* Did I hear that right? He sounded out of it, like he was on drugs or had been locked in a cell for the past fifteen years.

"Where am I?" I demanded.

He took a step in my direction, and I took one backward, scrambling to get my shoes on as I hopped on one foot.

He closed his eyes, inhaling as he inched closer. "Jesus," he panted. "It's been a while since I smelled that."

Smelled what?

His eyes opened, and I noticed they were a piercing blue, even more striking under his mahogany hair.

"Who are you? Where am I?" I barked.

I didn't recognize this guy.

He slithered closer, almost animalistic in his movements, with a predatory look on his face now that made the hairs on my arms stand up.

He looked suddenly alert. *Fuck.*

I searched for some kind of weapon around me.

"The locations change," he said, and I backed up a step for every step toward me he took. "But the name stays the same. Blackchurch."

"What is that?" I asked. "Where are we? Am I still in San Francisco?"

He shrugged. "I can't answer that. We could be in Siberia or ten miles from Disneyland," he replied. "We're the last ones to know. All we know is that it's remote."

"We?"

Who else was here? Where were they?

And where the hell was I, for that matter? What was Blackchurch? It sounded vaguely familiar, but I couldn't think right now.

How could he not know where he was? What city or state? Or country, even?

My God. *Country.* I was in America, right? I had to be.

I felt sick.

But water. I'd heard water when I woke, and I perked my ears, hearing the dull, steady pounding of it around us. Were we near a waterfall?

"There's no one here with you?" he asked, as if he couldn't believe that I was really standing here. "You shouldn't be so close to us. They never let the females close to us."

"What females?"

"The nurses, cleaners, staff . . ." he said. "They come once a month to resupply, but we're confined to our rooms until they leave. Did you get left behind?"

I bared my teeth, losing my patience. Enough with the questions.

I had no idea what the hell he was talking about, and my heart was pounding so hard, it hurt. *They never let the females close to us.* My God, why? I retreated toward the staircase, moving backward, so I didn't take my eyes off him and started to descend as he advanced on me.

"I want to use the phone," I told him. "Where is it?"

He just shook his head, and my heart sank.

"No computers, either," he told me.

I stumbled on the step and had to grab the wall to steady myself. When I looked up, he was there, gazing down at me, his lips twitching with a grin.

"No, no . . ." I slid down a few more steps.

"Don't worry," he offered. "I just wanted a little sniff. He'll want the first taste."

He? I looked down the stairs, seeing a canister of umbrellas. Nice and pointy. *That'll do.*

"We don't get women here." He got closer and closer. "Ones we can touch anyway."

I backed up farther. If I bolted for a weapon, would he be able to grab me? Would he grab me?

"No women, no communication with the world," he went on. "No drugs, liquor, or smokes, either."

"What is Blackchurch?" I asked.

"A prison."

I looked around, noticing the expensive marble floors, the fixtures and carpets, and the fancy, gold accents and statues.

"Nice prison," I mumbled.

Whatever it was now, it clearly used to be someone's home. A mansion or . . . a castle or something.

"It's off the grid." He sighed. "Where do you think CEOs and senators send their problem children when they need to get rid of them?"

"Senators . . ." I trailed off, something sparking in my memory.

"Some important people can't have their sons—their heirs—making news by going to jail or rehab or being caught doing their dirty deeds," he explained. "When we become liabilities, we're sent here to cool off. Sometimes for months." He sighed again. "And some of us for years."

Sons. Heirs.

Then it hit me.

Blackchurch.

No.

No, he had to be lying. I remembered hearing about this place. But it was just an urban legend that wealthy men threatened their kids with to keep them in line. A secluded residence somewhere where sons were sent as punishment, but given free rein to be at each other's mercy. It was like *Lord of the Flies* but with dinner jackets.

But it didn't exist. Not really. Did it?

"There are more?" I asked. "More of you here?"

A wicked smile spread across his lips, curdling my stomach.

"Oh, several," he crooned. "Grayson will be back with the hunting party tonight."

I stopped dead in my tracks, lightheaded.

No, no, no . . .

Senators, he'd said.

Grayson.

Shit.

"Grayson?" I muttered, more to myself. "Will Grayson?"

He was here?

But Taylor Dinescu, son of the owner of Dinescu Petroleum Corporation I now gathered, ignored my question. "We have everything we need to survive, but if we want meat, we have to hunt for it," he explained.

That's what Will—and the *others*—were out doing. Getting meat.

And I didn't know if it was the look on my face or something else, but Taylor started laughing. A vile cackling that curled my fists tight.

"Why are you laughing?" I growled.

"Because no one knows you're here, do they?" he taunted, sounding delighted. "And whoever does meant to leave you anyway. It'll be a month before another resupply team shows up."

I closed my eyes for a split second, his meaning clear.

"A whole month," he mused.

His eyes fell down my body, and I absorbed the full implication of my situation.

I was in the middle of nowhere with who knew how many men who'd been without any source of vice or contact with the outside world for who knew how long; one of whom had a great desire to torture me if he ever got his hands on me again.

And, according to Taylor, I had little hope of any help for the next month.

Someone went to great lengths to bring me here and make sure my arrival went undetected. Was there really no attendant on the property? Security? Surveillance? Anyone with control of the prisoners?

I ground my teeth together, having no idea what the hell I was going to do, but I needed to do it fast.

But then I heard something, and I shot my eyes up to Taylor, barks and howls echoing outside.

"What is that?" I asked.

Wolves? The sounds were getting closer.

He shot his eyes up, looking at the front door behind me and then back in my direction. "The hunting party," he replied. "They must be back early."

The hunting party.

Will.

And how many other prisoners who might be just as creepy and threatening as this guy . . .

The howls were outside the house now, and I looked up at Taylor, unable to calm my breathing. What would happen when they came inside and saw me?

But he just smiled down at me. "Please, do run," he said. "We're dying for some fun."

My heart sank. This wasn't happening. *This wasn't happening.*

I backed up as I headed down the stairs, keeping my eyes on him as he stalked me, liquid heat coursing in my veins.

"I want to talk to Will," I demanded.

He might *want* to hurt me, but he wouldn't. Would he?

If I could just talk to him . . .

But Taylor laughed, his blue eyes dancing with delight. "He can't protect you, love." And then the floor creaked upstairs, and Taylor tipped his head back, looking at the ceiling. "Aydin is awake."

Aydin. Who?

But I didn't care to stick around and find out. I didn't know if I'd really be in danger with these guys, but I knew I wouldn't be in any if I ran.

Leaping down the staircase, I swung around the banister and bolted toward the back of the house, hearing Taylor howl as I disappeared down a dark corridor, sweat already cooling my forehead.

This wasn't happening. There had to be surveillance. I refused to believe Mommy and Daddy sent their heirs and assets here without some kind of insurance that they'd be safe. What if someone were injured? Or gravely ill?

This was a . . . a joke. A vastly inappropriate and lavish prank. It was almost Devil's Night, and he was dealing me in. Finally.

Blackchurch wasn't real. In high school, Will hadn't even believed this place existed.

I passed rooms, some with one door, others with two, and some with none at all as the hallway splintered off into other hallways, and I didn't know where the hell I was going. I just ran.

The rubber soles of my sneakers squeaked across the marble floors, and a tickle hit my nose at the stale scent of age. Nothing was warm here.

Walls changed from cream to maroon to black, rotting wallpaper fading in some areas and ceilings a mile high, as well as drapes falling down windows that were eight times my height.

But the light fixtures shone, casting a somber glow in every office, den, parlor, and game room I passed.

Stopping short, I took the second right and dashed down the hall, thankful for the silence, but also unnerved by it. They were outside the door moments ago. They had to be in the house now. Why wasn't I hearing anything?

Dammit.

My muscles burning and my lungs tight, I couldn't hold back the groan as I stumbled into the last room at the end of the hall and ran to the window. I lifted it open, the crisp air rushing in and breezing through the drapes. I shivered, seeing the vast green forest, almost black in the night beyond the window.

Hemlocks. I looked out, scanning the terrain. There were red spruces and white pines, too. The moist scent of moss hit me, and I hesitated. I wasn't in California anymore. These trees were native to land much farther north.

And we weren't in Thunder Bay. We weren't anywhere near Thunder Bay.

Leaving the window open, I backed away, thinking twice. The chill in the air blew through my short-sleeved white blouse, and I had no idea where I was, how far from civilization, or what kind of elements I'd run into unprotected.

I ran back out of the room, pinning myself to the wall and quietly stepping down the corridor, keeping my eyes peeled. *Think, think, think* . . .

We had to be close to a town. There were paintings on these walls, priceless antiques, massive chandeliers, and a hell of a lot of money that went into furnishing and decorating this place.

It hadn't always been a prison.

No one would spend this kind of money on something a bunch of little frat shits were going to trash. It was someone's home, and they wouldn't have built it leagues away from town. A home like this is for entertaining. There was a ballroom, for Christ's sake.

I wrung my hands. I couldn't care less who dumped me here. Right now, I just needed to get somewhere safe.

And then I heard it.

A call—a howl—above me. I stopped, my blood freezing. Tipping my head up, I followed the sound as it drifted from my left to my right, my pulse skipping a beat as the floorboards above whined with weight.

Simultaneously. In several places.

They were upstairs, and there was more than one. Taylor saw me run this way. Why would they be upstairs?

And then I remembered what else was upstairs. Aydin.

Taylor spoke of him like he was a threat. Were they going to him first?

An echo of a voice traveled down the hall, and I trained my ears, the window behind me beckoning.

Another cry echoed farther down, possibly from the foyer, and then another howl somewhere around me.

I twisted around, dizzy. What the hell was going on? The nerves under my skin fired, and I forced myself to swallow as bile churned in my stomach.

They were spreading out.

Wolves. I paused, remembering the howls outside. It was like wolves. A pack separates to surround its prey and test for weaknesses. They flank the sides and the rear.

Tears hung at the corners of my eyes, and I lifted my chin, pushing them away. *Will.*

How long had he been here? Where were his friends? Did he have me brought here as revenge? What the hell?

I told him not to push me all those years ago. I warned him. This wasn't my fault. He got himself put here.

I dove into a billiards room, grabbed a cricket bat off the wall, and crept back out, hugging the walls with my back and darting my eyes all around for any sign of them. Chills spread up my arms, and despite the cold, a light layer of sweat covered my neck. Training my ears, I listened as I took one quiet step after another.

A thud hit the floor above me, and I sucked in a breath, shooting my eyes to the ceiling again as I trailed behind the stairs.

What the hell was going on?

A blue hue, like moonlight streaming through a window, lit the dark marble floor down the hallway, and I followed it, heading to the back of the house.

I inhaled, a sting hitting my nose. Sterile, like bleach. Taylor said the cleaners and staff just left.

My knees shook, and my heart hammered in my chest. I felt like I was already walled in, and I didn't even know it.

"Here!" someone shouted.

I gasped, flattening myself to the wall as I slipped around a corner.

Peering back around it, I spotted shadows moving along the wall as they found my open window.

"She's running!" one of them shouted.

I exhaled, fisting my hands. *Yes.* They thought I crawled out the window.

Their footfalls pounded across the floor, racing back toward the foyer, hopefully, and I clasped my hand over my mouth as they faded away.

Thank God.

I didn't wait another moment. I ran and ran, finding the kitchen in the southwest corner of the house. Leaving the lights off, I dashed for the refrigerator and swung it open, racks of fruits and vegetables shifting with the motion.

I looked around, gaping at the size for a moment. It was a walk-in. I thought Taylor said they had to hunt for their meat. There was a shitload of food right here.

I stepped inside the space, the immediate temperature change making me shiver as I scanned the shelves of food, all looking freshly stocked. Cheeses, bread, deli meats, butter, milk, carrots, squash, cucumbers, tomatoes, grapes, bananas, mangoes, lettuce, blueberries, yogurt, hummus, steaks, hams, whole chickens, burgers . . .

And this wasn't counting the pantry they probably had, too.

Why would they have to hunt?

Wasting no more time, I grabbed the netted bag hanging inside and dumped out the produce it stored, quickly stocking it with two bottles of water, an apple and some cheese. Maybe I should bring more, but I couldn't take the weight right now.

Diving back out of the fridge, I tied the bag closed and raced to the window, inching up on my tiptoes and seeing flashlights dance across the vast lawn.

I almost smiled. I had time to find a coat or sweater and get the hell out of here before they got back.

Spinning on the ball of my foot, I took a step, but then I saw him standing right there, a dark form leaning against the doorframe to the kitchen, staring at me.

I halted, my heart leaping into my throat.

At least I thought he was staring at me. His face was hidden in shadow.

My lungs froze, aching.

And then I remembered . . . *wolves.* They surround you.

All except one. He came at you from the front.

"Come here," he said in a low voice.

My hands shook, knowing that voice. And those exact words he'd said to me that one night.

"Will . . ."

He stepped into the kitchen, moonlight casting a dim glow on his face, and something inside me ached.

He was big in high school, but now . . .

I swallowed, trying to wet my dry mouth.

A light spatter of raindrops glimmered on top of his messy but trimmed head of chocolate hair, and I'd never seen him with scruff on his face before, but it made him look harder—and more dangerous— in ways I didn't realize would look so good on him.

His chest was broader, his arms in his black hoodie thicker, and he brought up his hands, using a cloth to wipe off blood that coated his fingers. Tattoos adorned the backs of his hands, disappearing up the sleeve of his sweatshirt.

He didn't have any tattoos the last time I saw him.

The night he was arrested.

Where was the blood from? Hunting?

I backed away as he slowly advanced, but he wasn't looking at me as he approached, just gazing at his hands as he cleaned them.

The cricket bat. Where was it?

I blinked long and hard. *Shit.* I'd set it down on the fridge floor when I packed the food.

I flashed my eyes to the refrigerator, gauging the distance.

Searching the counters, I spotted a trio of glass apothecary jars and reached out, swiping one onto the floor between us. It crashed, shattering everywhere, and he paused a moment, a smile in his eyes as I continued to back away, making my way for the fridge.

"This won't end with you in my sleeping bag this time," he warned.

I grabbed another jar and shoved it to the floor, backing up some more and closing the distance. If he charged me, he'd slip on the glass.

"Don't make promises you can't keep," I taunted. "You're still not the alpha."

The dark eyebrow above one of his eyes cocked, but he didn't stop, continuing toward me.

The pulse in my neck thumped, my stomach swimming, but . . . as the glass crunched under his shoes and his gaze held mine, the pulse between my legs throbbed, and I almost cried.

"Do you know why I'm here?" I asked.

"Have you been bad?"

I locked my jaw, but I remained silent.

A wicked smile spread across his face, and I knew this was it. I didn't think it would happen like this, but I always knew it was coming.

"You know," I said. "Don't you?"

He nodded. "Don't you want to explain?"

"Would it matter?"

He shook his head.

I gulped. *Yeah, didn't think so.*

He served two-and-a-half years in prison because of me. And not just him. His best friends, Damon Torrance and Kai Mori, too.

I dropped my eyes for a moment, knowing he didn't deserve it, but I also knew I wouldn't have done anything differently if I could. I'd told him to stay away from me. I'd warned him.

"I wish I'd never met you," I said, almost whispering.

He stopped, glass grinding under him. "Believe me, girl, the feeling is fucking mutual."

I backed up, but my hand brushed my leg, and I felt something in my pocket. I continued making my way for the fridge, but I reached into my pants and pulled out the hunk of metal, seeing a folding knife with a black handle.

Where did this come from?

I didn't carry knives.

I dropped the net and unsheathed the blade, holding it out in front of me, but he shot out and grabbed my wrist, prying my fingers open. I fought against it, trying to keep the weapon, but he was too strong. I cried out as I couldn't hold it anymore and it fell to the floor, clanking on the marble.

Whipping me around, he fisted my collar and brought me in, pinning me between his body and the counter.

He looked down into my eyes, and I breathed hard, a lock of hair brushing against my mouth.

"You like alphas?" he challenged me.

I sharpened my eyes on him. "We want what we want."

He glared, those words far more familiar than he wanted to remember, and if I weren't so fucking scared, I'd laugh.

Growling, he picked me up and threw me over his shoulder. "Time to meet one then," he said.

CHAPTER 2

EMORY

Nine Years Ago

Why are you quitting?"

I stood there, avoiding my coach's eyes as I gripped the strap of my book bag that hung across my chest.

"I don't have time," I told her. "I'm sorry."

I risked a glance, seeing her gaze hard on me under the short blond hair hanging just over her eyes. "You made a commitment," she argued. "We need you."

I shifted on my feet, a curtain of self-loathing covering every inch of me.

This was shitty. I knew that.

I was good at swimming. I could help the team, and she put a lot of work into training me over the last year. I didn't want to quit.

But she'd just have to deal with it. I couldn't explain, even if not explaining meant that she'd misunderstand my silence as being irresponsible and selfish.

The voices of all the girls outside the office filled the locker room as they got ready for practice, and I felt her eyes on me, waiting for a response.

It was useless, though. I wasn't going to change my mind.

"Is there something else going on?" she asked.

I squeezed the strap across my chest, the fabric cutting into my hand.

But I drew a deep breath and pushed my glasses back up the bridge of my nose, straightening my spine. "No one's giving me a scholarship for swimming," I spat out. "I need to spend my time doing things that will get me into college. This was a waste."

Before she could fire back, or the look on her face made this hurt worse, I spun around, pulled open her door, and left her office.

Tears lodged in my throat, but I pushed them down.

This sucked. I was going to pay for this. It wasn't over. I knew that.

But I had no choice.

The ache in my back fired up as I stalked through the locker room, and I slammed my hand into the door, feeling the pain in my wrist shoot up my arm before stepping into the hallway.

But I pushed through it, ignoring the discomfort as I headed down the nearly empty corridor.

I was glad I got out of there before she asked why I wasn't quitting band, too. Band wouldn't get me into college, either. I wasn't that good.

It was just all I had left now that got me out of the house, and I didn't have to wear a swimsuit to do it.

I chewed on my lip, a ten-ton truck sitting on my shoulders as I stared at the floor. I headed for my locker without looking where I was going, because I'd walked this path a million times. *Just keep it together.* Time would pass. Life would move on. I was heading in the right direction.

Just keep going.

A few students milled around the halls early, because of clubs or sports, as I reached my locker and dialed in the combination. It was still a bit before the first class started, but I could go hide in the library to kill time. It was better than being home.

Emptying my bag of my math and physics that I'd finished last night, I pulled my binder, my lit book, my copy of *Lolita*, and my Spanish text from my locker, holding everything in one arm as I dug on the top shelf for my pencil bag.

He is going to find out I quit. Maybe I had a few days' peace before that happened, but a knot tightened in my stomach. I could still taste the coppery cut in my mouth from two days ago.

He was going to find out. He wouldn't want me to quit swimming, and pointing out why I had to would only make him angrier.

I blinked a few times, no longer really searching for my pens or pencils as the searing pain under my hair from the other night raced across my scalp again.

I hadn't cried when he pulled it.

But I retreated. I always flinched.

Laughter went off somewhere down the hall, and I glanced over, seeing some students loitering against the lockers. Girls in their school uniforms, skirts rolled up much shorter than the three inches above the knee we were allowed, and blouses too tight under their navy blue jackets.

I narrowed my eyes.

With heads together and smiling as they joked around with the guys, the whole group looked about as shallow as a rain puddle. Never deep enough to be more than what it was.

Shallow, boring, tedious, ignorant, and insipid. All the rich kids here were like that.

I watched Kenzie Lorraine lean into Nolan Thomas, her mouth moving over his like she was melting into him. She whispered against his lips, and his white teeth flashed through his little grin before he slid his hands around her waist and leaned back against the lockers. My heart skipped a small beat, and I felt my pencil bag, absently sliding it into my satchel without taking my eyes off them.

Shallow, boring, tedious, ignorant, and insipid.

I blinked, my expression softening as I watched them.

Happy, excited, brave, wild, and in heaven.

They looked seventeen.

And suddenly, for a moment, I wished I was them. Anyone other than me. No wonder hardly anyone at this school liked me. I was even tired of myself.

Wouldn't it be fantastic to be really happy for just five minutes?

Her friends hung around, talking to his, but I only saw him and her, wondering how it felt. Even if it wasn't true love, it had to feel good to be wanted.

But just then, Nolan opened his eyes. He looked over at me, meeting my gaze head-on as if he knew I was there the whole time. The vein in my neck pounded, and I was frozen.

Shit.

He didn't stop kissing her, though, holding my eyes as they moved together. Then . . . he winked at me, and I could see his smile through the kiss.

I rolled my eyes and looked away. *Great.* Emory Scott was a pervert. That's what he'd say. Just what I needed.

I turned back to my locker, embarrassed, and slammed the door.

Everything ached, and I arched my back, trying to stretch the muscles, but just as I turned around to leave, a fist came down and knocked my books out of my arms.

I sucked in a breath, startled as I retreated a step on instinct.

Miles Anderson glared at me as he passed, but a smirk curled his lips, too.

"See something you like, stupid?" he taunted.

I clenched my jaw, trying to get control of the pounding in my chest, but the sudden fright made my stomach roll as his friends followed him, laughing.

His blond hair laid haphazardly over his forehead, while his blue eyes trailed down my form, and I knew exactly what he was taking stock of.

The outdated plaid pattern of my secondhand skirt.

The missing button on the cuff of my blouse that was two sizes too big.

My faded blue blazer with little pieces of thread sticking off the patch-ups I had to do from the previous owner.

My worn shoes, from all the walking because I had no car, and how I never wore makeup or did anything with my dark hair that just hung down my arms and in my face.

So much different than how he looked. How they all looked.

Little shits. I let Anderson have his pathetic fun, because it was the only time he had any power. One thing I could be grateful to the Horsemen for.

I hated how this school was their own personal playground, but when they were around, Miles Anderson didn't pull shit like that. I could bet he was probably counting the days until they graduated so he could take over the basketball team.

And Thunder Bay Prep.

Clenching my jaw, I crouched down and gathered up my books, stuffing everything into my bag.

But a light sweat covered my face all of a sudden, and I felt sick. Pushing myself to my feet, I blew out a breath and hurried for the bathroom, the closest one up the stairs and down the hall.

My stomach filled with something, the burn of the bile rising up my throat growing stronger. Throwing my weight against the door, I pushed through and dove into a stall, leaning over the toilet and heaving.

I lurched, the vomit rising just enough to taste the acid, but it wouldn't come up any further. I coughed, my eyes watering as I gasped.

I pushed my glasses up on top of my head, holding the sides of the stall as I drew in breath after breath to calm down.

I rubbed my eyes. *Shit*.

I fought back sometimes.

When it didn't matter and when I wasn't really threatened.

I wiped my brow and flushed the toilet out of habit, exiting the stall and walking to the sink. Turning on the water, I dipped my hands underneath the faucet, but then I paused, my energy to even splash water on my face now gone. I just turned it off and left the bathroom, wiping my hands dry on my skirt.

I was too tired, and the day had barely started.

But as soon as I opened the door, someone stood there, and I stopped short, looking at Trevor Crist. He smiled at me as I fisted the strap of my bag, staring at him.

He was only a freshman, two years my junior, but he was already my height and looked absolutely nothing like his brother. Fake, plastic eyes that didn't match his smile, and dark blond hair that was as perfectly styled as his tie was positioned.

He looked like his name should be Chad. What the hell did he want?

He held out a blue notebook, and I recognized the frayed notes and loose papers inside, highlighted with scribbled yellow marker. I darted my eyes back down the hall toward my locker.

I must've left it behind when that jackass knocked everything out of my hands.

I took the notebook, stuffing it into my bag. "Thank you," I mumbled.

"I got it all, but I can't be sure it's in order," he said. "Some of the papers fell out."

I barely heard him, noticing the hallways filling with more students, and Mr. Townsend making his way toward my first class.

"Trevor Crist." The kid held out his hand.

"I know."

And I walked past him, ignoring his hand.

Heading a few yards down the hall, I held open the door, following another student inside, and scanned the classroom for the safest seat. In the corner, at the rear and near the windows, an empty desk sat surrounded by students at every available angle—Roxie Harris next to me, Jack Leister in front of me, and Drew Hannigan kitty-corner.

I ran for it.

I slid into the seat, the legs of the desk skidding across the floor as I dropped my bag to the ground.

"Ugh," Roxie groaned beside me, but I ignored her as I dug my materials out of my bag.

And she started to pack up her things.

The classroom filled, chatter and laughter pouring in as Mr. Townsend stood, hovering over his desk and going through his notes.

But Roxie didn't even have time to clear out of her seat before they were there. Drifting through the door, tall, magnetic, and always together.

I turned my head toward the window, closing my eyes behind my glasses and holding my breath as I quickly pulled my earbuds out of my jacket pocket and stuck them in my ears.

Anything to look unapproachable.

Please, please, please . . .

The prayer was too late, though. I could feel Roxie's, Jack's, and Drew's eye rolls as they sighed and grabbed their shit, vacating their seats without even being asked, like it was my fault these guys insisted on completely crowding me no matter where I sat in this damn room.

Kai Mori slid into Jack's seat ahead of me, while Damon Torrance took the seat diagonally from me.

I didn't have to look up to see their dark hair, and I could always tell who was who without checking because Kai smelled like amber musk and the ocean, while Damon smelled like an ashtray.

Michael Crist had probably planted himself somewhere close, but it was the last body, passing me in the aisle and planting himself in the seat next to me in what should've been Roxie's seat, that made my heart beat faster.

I could feel his eyes on me as I stared out the window.

If I knew we were going to share classes when the administration decided to move me to senior English a few weeks back—a year ahead of schedule—I would've said no. No matter what my brother wanted.

I was pretty sure they only moved me, because I was "difficult" last year and they thought challenging me would put a cork in my mouth.

They were all finding out that wasn't true.

"You're out of uniform," I heard some girl whisper.

Then I heard Will Grayson's voice heating the back of my neck. "I'm in disguise," he told her.

"That piece of shit has a hard-on for you or something," Damon added. "Every time he sees you, he wants to get you alone."

I clenched my fingers around my notebook and pencil.

"In his defense," Kai chimed in, "it was you who put the 'Sorry, I hit your car' notes on people's vehicles all over town with his phone number on them."

Damon snorted and then burst out laughing, while Will breathed out a self-satisfied chuckle.

Assholes. My brother's phone rang all damn night last night because of that prank. And when he's aggravated, he shows it.

"So, what do you say, Em?" Will prodded, finally engaging me like he could never stop himself from doing. "Is your brother hot for me? He's certainly on my ass enough."

I remained silent, absently opening my notebook as people got situated in their seats and talked around us.

Everyone in this school hated my brother. Their money and connections had no effect on his willingness as a police officer to hand out speeding tickets, parking tickets, investigate noise complaints, or shut down parties and drinking as soon as he got a whiff of anything going down.

My brother was a jerk for doing his job, and when they couldn't come at him, they came at me.

I saw Will dig something out of his pocket, and I watched him unwrap a piece of candy and lift it to his mouth, peeling the sweet off the paper with his teeth.

His eyes never left me.

"Take out your earbuds," he ordered me as he chewed.

I narrowed my gaze.

"And stop acting like you're listening to music and that's why you can't be bothered to deal with the people around you," he bit out.

Every muscle in my body tensed, and when I didn't listen, he tossed his wrapper onto the floor and leaned over, yanking the cord and pulling the earbuds out of my ears.

I startled, sitting up straight.

But I didn't shrink. Not with him.

Now . . . he had my fucking attention.

Grabbing the cord from where it hung down to the floor, I rose from my desk, picked up my notebook and bag, and started to leave.

But then his hands were on me, pulling me down into his lap.

Everything in my arms tumbled to the floor, and liquid fire coursed under my skin.

No.

I gritted my teeth and shoved at him as Kai sighed and Damon snickered, neither one stopping him, though.

I struggled against him, but he simply tightened his hold, turning his face away from my attack.

Will, Kai, Damon, and Michael. The Four Horsemen.

I just loved the nicknames the little wannabe gangsters gave themselves in high school, but someone should really tell them it wasn't scary when you had to tell everyone how scary you were.

Every school had these guys, too. A little money, some connected moms and dads, and pretty faces without hearts to match. None of that was really their fault, I guessed.

What was their fault was that they took full advantage of it.

Wouldn't it be fun if anyone ever said no to them? If one of them ever paid for a mistake? Or ever said no to a drink, a drug, or a girl?

But no. Same story. Shallow, boring, tedious, ignorant, and insipid.

And while others may give in or pathetically protest before finally giving in, I wasn't interested.

And he hated that.

I could scream. Get the teacher's attention. Make a scene. But he'd only get the laughs he craved, and I'd get the attention I didn't.

"Wipe that fucking glare off your face," he warned.

I locked my jaw, not doing a damn thing he said.

He dropped his voice to a whisper. "I know I may seem like the nicest one, and you probably think I regret the shit I give you sometimes, and someday I'll wake up and reevaluate my life and its purpose, but I won't. I sleep like a baby at night."

"You wake every two hours and cry?" I asked.

There was a snort behind me, but I didn't look away as Will's eyes sharpened on me. School was always the one place I had a reprieve.

Until I got to high school.

I rolled my wrists inside his fists, trying to pry him off. "Let me go."

"Why are your cuffs wet?"

His gaze fell and he forced my arm up, so he could look closer.

I didn't answer.

He looked back up at me. "And your eyes are red."

My throat tightened, but I gritted my teeth together and yanked my wrists free.

But before I could escape from his lap, he grabbed my chin in one hand and wrapped his other arm around my waist, pulling me in. Against his body, and whispering so softly no one could hear him but me.

"Don't you know that you can have anything you want?" His eyes searched mine. "I'll hurt anyone for you."

The weight on my chest was too heavy, it almost hurt to breathe.

"Who is it?" he asked. "Who do I have to hurt?"

My eyes burned. Why did he do this? He'd soften and tempt me with the fantasy that I wasn't alone and maybe—possibly—there was hope.

His scent hit me. Bergamot and blue cypress, and I looked up at his brown hair, perfectly styled and rich against his perfect skin and dark brows. Black lashes framed eyes that looked like the leaves surrounding a lagoon on some stupid island somewhere, and for a moment, I was lost.

Just for a moment.

"God, please," I finally said. "Get yourself a life, Will Grayson. You're pathetic."

And his beautiful eyes instantly hardened as he lifted his chin. He pushed me off his lap and shoved me back toward my desk. "Sit down."

He almost sounded hurt, and I nearly laughed. *Probably disappointed I'm not stupid enough to fall for his shit.* What was he planning? Gain my trust, lure me to Homecoming, and watch as they dumped pig's blood all over me?

Nah, not original enough. Will Grayson had more imagination. I'd give him that, at least.

"All right, let's go ahead and get started," Mr. Townsend said, clearing his throat.

I grabbed my bag and notebook off the floor and slid back into my chair, tucking my earbuds into my pocket.

"Take out your books," Mr. Townsend instructed as he took a quick sip of his coffee and flipped a paper on his desk.

Will just sat there, staring silently ahead, and I faltered for a moment as I watched the muscle flex in his jaw.

Whatever. I rolled my eyes and dug out my copy of *Lolita* as the rest of the class found theirs. Except Will, because he hadn't bothered to bring a bag or books today.

"We've talked about Humbert being an unreliable narrator in the book." Townsend took another drink of coffee. "How we are all the righteous heroes of our own story if we're the ones telling it."

I heard Will draw in and release a breath. I focused on the back of Kai Mori's neck, usually fascinated by how precise and clean the lines of his trim were.

I was having trouble concentrating today.

Townsend continued, "And how often a matter of right or wrong is simply just a matter of perspective. To a fox, the hound is the villain. To a hound, the wolf. To a wolf, a human, and so on."

Oh, please. Humbert Humbert was derailed.

And a criminal. Fox, hound, wolf, whatever.

"He believes he's in love with Lo." The teacher circled his desk and leaned against the front, his paperback curled in his fist. "But he's not completely ignorant of his crime, either. He says"—he flipped open his book, reading from it—"'I knew I had fallen in love with Lolita forever; but I also knew she would not be forever Lolita.'" He looked up at the class. "What did he mean?"

"That she'd grow up," Kai answered. "And no longer be sexually attractive to him because he's a pedophile."

I smirked to myself. Kai was kind of my favorite Horseman, if I had to pick one.

Townsend considered Kai's thoughts, but then prompted another student.

"Do you agree?"

The girl shrugged. "I think he meant that we change, and she would, too. It's not that she's growing up. It's that she'll outgrow him, and he's scared."

Which was probably what Humbert actually meant, but I liked Kai's assessment better.

The teacher nodded and then jerked his chin at another student. "Michael?"

Michael Crist looked up, sounding lost. "What?"

Damon snorted at his friend, and I shook my head.

Townsend hooded his eyes, looking impatient, before restating his question. "What do you think he meant when he said she wouldn't be forever Lolita?"

Michael remained silent for a moment. I almost wondered if he would answer.

"He loves the idea of her," he finally told Townsend, sounding finite. "When she eventually faded from him, the dream of her would still be there, haunting him. That's what he meant."

Huh. Not an entirely poor assessment. And I thought Kai would be the only one of them who'd actually read the book.

Townsend shifted, flipping to another page and read, "She says, 'He broke my heart. You merely broke my life.' What is she telling him?"

Everyone kept silent.

The teacher scanned the room, looking for a flicker from any of us. "'You merely broke my life,'" he repeated.

Needles pricked my throat, and I dropped my eyes. *You broke my life.*

A student sighed from a seat near the door. "She willingly indulged him," he argued. "Yeah, it was wrong, but this is an issue today. Women can't just decide after the fact that they were abused. She was willingly sexual with him."

"Minors can't consent," Kai pointed out.

"What, so you magically become emotionally and mentally mature when you turn eighteen?" Will replied, suddenly entering the conversation. "Just happens overnight, does it?"

"She was a child, Will." Kai turned in his seat, debating his friend. "In Humbert's head, he demands sympathy from us, and most readers give it, because he tells them to. Because we're willing to forgive anyone anything if they're attractive to us."

I stared at my desk, not blinking.

"He doesn't have a thing for Lo," Kai continued. "He has a thing for young girls. It's not an isolated incident. She was abused."

"And she left him to go shack up with a child pornographer, Kai," Will spat out. "If she were being abused, why didn't she have the sense to not put herself back in that situation?"

I rubbed my thumb over the paperback cover, hearing it skid across the gloss. My chin trembled, my eyes stinging a little.

"I mean, why would she do that?" Will asked.

"That's what I'm saying," another student chimed in.

Words hung on the tip of my tongue, telling them that they were oversimplifying. That it was easier to judge a girl you knew nothing about than to allow someone the dignity of their process. That it was more convenient to not consider that there were things we didn't know and things we'd never understand, because we were shallow and entitled and ignorant.

That you stayed, because . . .

Because . . .

"Abuse can feel like love."

I blinked, the voice so close that my ears tingled. Slowly, I raised my eyes to look at the side of Damon Torrance's face, his shirt wrinkled, and his tie draped around his neck.

The whole class fell silent, and I glanced at Will next to me, seeing his eyebrows pinched together as he looked at the back of his friend's head.

Mr. Townsend approached. "'Abuse can feel like love . . .'" he repeated. "Why?"

Damon remained so still it didn't look like he was breathing.

He looked at the teacher, unwavering. "Starving people will eat anything."

I stilled as his words hung in the air, and for a second, I felt warm. He wasn't completely devoid of brain cells maybe.

Feeling eyes on me, I turned my head, seeing Will's gaze focused on my leg.

I looked down, finding my fingers curled around the hem of my skirt, the scratches and part of a bruise visible on my thigh. My pulse quickened, and I yanked my skirt back down to my knee.

"Flip to the last chapter, please," Townsend called. "And take out the packet."

But the bruise pounded with pain, and I suddenly couldn't breathe.

Don't you know that you can have anything you want? I'll hurt anyone for you.

My chin trembled. I had to get out of here.

Abuse can feel like love . . .

I shook my head, stuffing my materials back into my bag, standing up, and hooking it over my head as I charged down the aisle and toward the door.

"Where are you going?"

I turned my head toward the teacher. "To finish the book and the constructed responses in the library."

I kept walking, blinking away the tears hanging in my eyes.

"Emory Scott," the teacher called.

"Or you can explain to my brother why my SAT scores will be shit," I said, walking backward with my glare on him, "because they're dominating ninety-eight percent of every conversation in this class." I gestured to the Horsemen. "Text me any additional assignments, if we have them."

I pushed the door open, hearing whispers go off in class.

"Emory Scott," the teacher barked.

I looked over my shoulder at Townsend, seeing him hold out a pink slip.

"You know what to do," he scolded.

Strolling back in, I snatched the referral from his fingers. "At least I'll get some work done," I retorted.

Dean's office or library, it made no difference.

Walking out of the room, I couldn't help but glance back at Will Grayson, seeing him slouched in his seat, chin on his hand, and covering a smile with his fingers.

He held my eyes until I left the room.

Walking down the sidewalk, I didn't raise my eyes as I turned left and headed up the walkway toward my house. I blinked long and hard for the last few steps, my head floating up into the trees as the afternoon breeze rustled the leaves. I loved that sound.

The wind was foreboding. It made it feel like something was about to happen, but in a way that I liked.

Opening my eyes, I climbed my steps and looked right, not seeing my brother's cruiser in the driveway yet. The heat in my stomach cooled slightly, the muscles relaxing just a hair.

I had a little time, at least.

What a shit day. I'd skipped lunch and hid in the library, and after classes were done, I struggled through band practice, not wanting to be there, but not wanting to come home, either. Hunger pangs rocked my stomach, but it took the edge off the pain everywhere else.

I looked back at my street, taking in the quiet avenue, decorated with maples, oaks, and chestnuts, bursting with their finale of oranges, yellows, and reds. Leaves danced to the ground as the wind shook them free, and the scent of the sea and a bonfire somewhere drifted through my nose.

Most of the kids like me were bussed to Concord to attend the public high school there, since our population in Thunder Bay was too small to support two high schools, but my brother wanted the best for me, so TBP was where I stayed.

Despite the fact that we weren't wealthy, he paid a little, I work-studied a lot, and the rest of my tuition was waived as my brother was a public servant. The wealth and privilege my private high school matriculated was supposed to be a better education. I wasn't seeing it. I still sucked at literature, and the only class I really enjoyed was independent study, because I could be aloooooone.

On my own, I learned a lot.

I didn't mind that I didn't fit in, or that we weren't rich. We had a beautiful house. Turn-of-the-century, three-story (well, four if you counted the basement), redbrick Victorian with gray trim. It was more than big enough, and it had been in our family for three generations. My great-grandparents built it in the thirties, and my grandmother has lived here since she was seven.

Opening the door, I immediately kicked off my boots and jogged upstairs, throwing the door closed behind me as I went.

Passing my brother's room, I pulled off my schoolbag and dropped it just inside my door before continuing down the hall, softening my steps just in case.

I stopped at my grandmother's door, leaning on the frame. The nurse, Mrs. Butler, looked up from her paperback, another wartime thriller from the looks of the cover, and smiled, her chair ceasing its rocking.

I offered a tight smile back and then looked over to the bed. "How's she been?" I asked the nurse as I stepped quietly toward my grandma.

Mrs. Butler rose from the chair. "Hanging in there."

I looked down, seeing her stomach shake a little and her lips purse just slightly with every breath she expelled. Wrinkles creased nearly every inch of her face, but I knew if I touched it, the skin would be softer than a baby's. The scent of cherries and almonds washed over me, and I stroked her hair, smelling the shampoo Mrs. Butler used for her bath today.

Grand-Mère. The one person who meant everything to me.

For her, I stayed.

My eyes dropped, noticing the wine-colored fingernails the nurse must've painted today when she couldn't convince my grandma to go with a nice, gentle mauve. I couldn't hold back the small smile.

"Had to put her on oxygen for a bit," Mrs. Butler added. "But she's okay now."

I nodded, watching her sleep.

My brother was convinced she'd go any day now, the occasions she was able to get out of bed fewer and fewer.

She was sticking around, though. Thank goodness.

"She likes the records," Mrs. Butler told me.

I looked over at the stack of vinyls, some stuffed haphazardly back into their sleeves lying alongside the old turntable. I'd found the whole lot at an estate sale last weekend. Thought she'd get a kick out of it, fifties baby that she was.

Well, she wasn't born in the fifties. She was way older than that. But she was a teen in the fifties.

Mrs. Butler gathered her purse, pulling out her keys. "You'll be okay?"

I nodded, but I didn't look at her.

She left, and I stayed with Grandma for a bit longer, making sure I had her pills and shot ready for later, and I opened the window a few inches, letting in some fresh air, which Mrs. Butler asked us not to do, since the allergens in the air could aggravate her breathing.

Grandma said, "To hell with it." This was her favorite time of year, and she loved the sounds and smells. I didn't want to make her miserable merely to continue a life of misery.

Bringing up the room's camera on my phone, I left the door open a crack, grabbed my bag from my room, and headed downstairs, starting the water boiling on the stove. I set the phone on the kitchen table, keeping an eye on her in case she needed me, and laid out my books, going through the easy stuff first.

I logged onto my laptop, requesting all the books I'd need from the public library, a few from Meridian City that Thunder Bay didn't have, all for my history report, and drew up my outline. I finished the WebQuest and packet for physics, completed my reading for Spanish, and then stopped to chop and sauté vegetables before starting literature.

Literature . . . I still hadn't done the constructed responses and they were due tomorrow.

It's not that I didn't like the class. It's not that I didn't like books.

I just didn't like old books. Third person, wonky paragraphs a mile long, and some dumb academic trying to force me to believe there's profound meaning in the author's overwritten description of a piece of furniture I don't give two shits about. I'm pretty sure the author doesn't even know what they were trying to do in the first place, and they were probably just high on laudanum when they wrote it.

Or soothing syrup or absinthe or whatever the kids were doing in those days.

They push this shit down our throats as if there were no quality stories being written anymore, and this was it for us. *The House of the Seven Gables* is what Caitlyn the Cutter, who sits three seats down from me, was supposed to find relevance in? Got it.

Of course, *Lolita* wasn't that old. It just sucked, and I'm pretty sure it sucked in 1955, too. *I'll ask my grandma.*

I soaked the pasta, cooked the peppers and onions, and fired up the meat, mixing everything together before popping it in the oven. After making a salad, I set the timer and pulled out the worksheet, reading the first question.

But then lights flashed, and I shot my gaze up, seeing a car turn into our driveway from out the window. Rain glittered in front of the headlights, and I jumped to my feet, closing my books and piling my papers, stuffing everything into my bag.

Heat curdled my stomach.

Shit. Sometimes he pulled a double shift or got caught up with a matter or two, and I was blessed with a night without him.

Not tonight, it seemed.

I pinched my thighs together, feeling like I was about to pee my pants, and threw my book bag into the dining room where we never ate. I quickly set the table, and as the front door opened, I spun around and pretended to fluff the salad.

"Emory!" Martin called out.

I couldn't stop my stomach from sinking like it did every day, but I plastered a bright smile on my face and peeked my head through the open kitchen doorway and down the hall.

"Hey!" I chirped. "Is it raining again?"

Just then, I realized I'd left my grandmother's window opened. *Dammit.* I'd need to find a minute to run and close it before it soaked the floor and gave him an excuse.

"Yeah." He sighed. "'Tis the season, right?"

I forced a chuckle. Droplets flew everywhere as he shook out his coat, and I watched him hang it up on the coatrack and head down the hallway toward the kitchen, his wet shoes squeaking across the wooden floor.

I had to remove my shoes at the door. He didn't.

I pulled my head back, straightening and blowing out a steady breath. Picking up the salad and tossing forks, I spread my lips in a smile. "I was thinking of going jogging around the village later," I told him, setting the bowl on the table.

He stopped, loosening his tie and giving me the side-eye. "You?"

"I can run," I feigned, arguing. "For a few minutes."

He breathed out a laugh and walked to the fridge, taking out the milk and pouring himself a glass.

"Smells good." He carried his glass to the table and sat down. "Is your homework done?"

His silver badge glinted under the light of the overhead bulbs, his form in his black uniform seeming to grow larger and larger by the second.

Martin and I were never close. Eight years older than me, he was already used to being an only child by the time I came along, and when our parents passed away about five years ago, he'd had to take care of everything. At least he got the house.

I cleared my throat. "Almost. I have some lit questions to double-check after dishes."

I hadn't completed them at all, actually, but I always embellished. It was like second nature now.

"How was your day?" I asked quickly, taking the pasta out of the oven and setting it on the table.

"It was good." He served himself, while I doled out salads into our bowls and poured myself some water. "The department is running smoothly, and they offered to move me up to Meridian City, but I—"

"Like it clean and tidy," I joked, "and Thunder Bay is your ship."

"You know me so well."

I smiled small, but my hand shook as I picked up a forkful of lettuce. It wouldn't stop shaking until he left for work in the morning.

He dug into his meal, and I forced a bite into my mouth, the silence filling the room louder than the sound of the drops hitting the windows outside.

If I weren't speaking, he'd find something to say, and I didn't want that.

My knee bobbed up and down under the table. "Would you like more salt?" I asked, lacing my voice with so much sugar I wanted to gag.

I reached for the shaker, but he interrupted. "No," he said. "Thank you."

I dropped my hand and continued eating.

"How was your day?" he inquired.

I looked at his fingers wrapped around his fork. He'd stopped eating, his attention on me.

I swallowed. "Good. We, um . . ." My heart raced, the blood pumping hot through my body. "We had an interesting discussion in lit," I told him. "And my science report is—"

"And swim practice?"

I fell silent.

Just tell him. Get it over with. He'll find out eventually.

But I lied instead. "It was good."

I always tried to hide behind a lie first. Given the choice between fight or flight, I flew.

"Was it?" he pressed.

I stared at my plate, my smile gone as I picked at my food. He knew.

His eyes burned a hole into my skin, his voice like a caress. "Pass the salt?" he asked.

I closed my eyes. The eerie calm in his tone was like the feeling before a storm. The way the air charged with the ions, the clouds hung low, and you could smell it coming. I knew the signs by now.

Reaching over, I picked up the shaker, slowly moving it toward him.

But I knocked his glass instead, his milk spilling onto the table and dripping over the side.

I darted my eyes up to him.

He stared back, holding my gaze for a moment, and then shoved the table away from him.

I popped to my feet, but he grabbed my wrist, yanking me back down to my seat.

"You don't rise from the table before me," he said calmly, squeezing my wrist with one hand, and setting his glass upright before taking my water and moving it in front of his plate.

I winced, my glasses sliding down my nose as I fisted my hand, the blood pooling under the skin because he was cutting off my circulation.

"Don't you ever leave this table without my permission."

"Martin . . ."

"Coach Dorn called me today." He stared ahead at nothing, slowly raising my water to his lips. "Saying you quit the team."

The unbuttoned cuff of my white uniform shirt hid his hand, but I was sure his knuckles were white. I started to twist my wrist because it hurt, but I immediately stopped, remembering that would just anger him more.

"I didn't say you could quit," he continued. "And then you lie about it like an idiot."

"Martin, please . . ."

"Eat your dinner, Em," he told me.

I stared at him for a moment, reconciling my head, once again, to the fact that it was going to happen no matter how hard I tried to stop it.

There was no stopping it.

Dropping my eyes to my plate, I lifted the fork, less sure with my left hand than with my right, and scooped up some rotini noodles and meat sauce.

"You're right-handed, stupid."

I paused, still feeling his fingers wrapped tightly around that wrist.

It only took a moment, and then I felt him guide my right hand over, prompting me to take the fork. I did and slowly lifted it to my mouth, his hand still wrapped around that wrist as the dull points of the silver utensil came toward me like something I'd never been scared of until now.

I hesitated, and then . . . I opened my mouth, almost gagging as he forced the silver in deep, almost brushing my tonsils.

Taking the food, I pulled the fork back out, feeling the resistance in his arm as I did.

We refilled the fork for round two, my lungs constricting.

"What *is* the matter with you, exactly?" he whispered. "Nothing can be done right. Ever. Why?"

I forced the bite down my throat just in time for another forkful to be shoved in. He jerked my hand as it entered my mouth, and my heart stopped for a moment, a whimper escaping at the threat of the prongs stabbing me.

"I thought I'd walk in the door, and you'd sit me down and explain yourself, but no." He glared at me. "As usual, you try to hide it like the candy wrappers under your bed when you were ten, and the three-day suspension when you were thirteen." His words quieted even more, but I almost winced at how it hurt my ears. "You never surprise me, do you? There's a right way and wrong way to do things, Emory. Why do you always do it the wrong way?"

It was a double-edged sword. He asked questions he wanted me to answer, but whatever I said would be wrong. Either way, I was in for it.

"Why is nothing ever done how I taught you?" he pressed. "Are you so fucking stupid that you can't learn?"

The fork moved faster, scooping up more food and rising to my mouth, the prongs stabbing into my lips as I opened them just in time. My mouth filled with food, not swallowing fast enough before more was pushed in.

"Dead parents," he mumbled. "A grandmother who won't die. A loser sister . . ."

Dropping my wrist, he fisted my collar instead and rose to his feet, dragging me with him. I dropped the fork, hearing it clatter against the plate as he backed me into the counter.

I chewed and swallowed. "Martin . . ."

"What did I do to deserve this?" he cut me off. "All these anchors pulling me down? Always constant. Always a weight."

The wood dug into my back as my heart tried to pound out of my chest.

"You wanna be ordinary forever?" he bit out, scowling down at me with my mother's green eyes and my father's shiny, dark brown hair. "You can't dress, you can't fix your hair, you can't make friends, and, it appears, you can't do anything impressive to help yourself get into a good university."

"I can get into a good school," I blurted out before I could stop myself. "I don't need swimming."

"You need what I tell you that you need!" he finally yelled.

I tilted my eyes to the ceiling on instinct, worried my grandmother could hear us.

"I support you." He grabbed my hair with one hand and slapped me upside the head with the other.

I gasped, flinching.

"I go to the teacher conferences." Another slap sent my head jerking right, and I stumbled.

No.

But he pulled me back by the hair. "I put food on the table." Another slap, like a wasp sting across my face, and I cried out, my glasses flying to the floor.

"I pay for her nurse and her medicine." He raised his hand again, and I cowered, shielding myself with my own arms as he hit again and again. "And this is the thanks I get?"

Tears filled my eyes, but as soon as I could catch my breath, his hand would come down again.

And again. And again. And again.

Stop. I wanted to cry out. I wanted to scream.

But I clenched my teeth instead.

I hissed at the pain. I winced, and I cowered.

But I didn't cry. Not anymore.

Not until after he was gone.

He grabbed me by the collar again, fisting it tightly, the fabric chafing my neck. "You'll go back," he breathed into my face, "you'll apologize, and you'll rejoin the team."

I couldn't meet his eyes. "I can't."

He threw me into the counter again and backed away, unfastening his belt.

A lump swelled in my throat. *No.*

"What was that?" he asked. "What did you say?"

Anger twisted his face, and his skin boiled with rage, but he loved this. He complained about my grandmother and me—spit in my face all the time about what a burden I was—but he didn't actually want me gone. He needed this.

"I can't," I whispered, unable to do more, because my voice shook so badly.

He yanked his belt out of the loops, and I knew what was coming. There was no way to stop it, because he didn't want to.

"You will."

I stood there, halfway between wanting to cry and wanting to run. It would only make the punishment sweeter for him if I made him work for it. Screw him.

"I won't."

"You will!"

"I can't wear a swimsuit because of the bruises!" I blurted out.

He paused, the belt dangling from his hand, and I couldn't even hear him breathe.

Yeah.

That was why I quit swimming. My face wasn't the only thing we had to worry about people seeing. My back, my arms, my thighs . . . People weren't stupid, Martin.

I almost wanted to look up, to see what—if anything—played across his face. Worry, maybe? Guilt?

Whatever he felt, he had to know we weren't coming back from this. It was real now. No matter the apologies, the presents, the smiles or hugs, I would never forget what he did to me.

So why stop now, right, Martin?

Darting out, he grabbed my wrist, growling as he threw me into the table. I squeezed my eyes shut as I bent in half over the top, my palms and forehead meeting the top.

And when the first strike came down, I fought the tears.

But I couldn't fight the cries coming up from my throat as the strap landed again and again. He was angry now and going harder than normal. It hurt.

He wouldn't fight the issue again, though. He knew I was right.

I couldn't wear a swimsuit.

After he left, I laid there for a moment, shaking with the pain slicing through my back.

God, just make it stop.

I whimpered as I shifted, thankful that I hadn't cried out, and I reached over, picking up my cell phone and turning it to see my grandmother still asleep on the screen.

Tears hung at the rims of my eyes.

She was lucid less and less, so it was getting easier to hide this shit from her. *Thank God.*

His shower ran upstairs, and he wouldn't be back down for a long time. Tomorrow, we'd wake up, pass each other silently before heading to work and school, and he'd be home early in the afternoon, being the one to make us dinner for a change. He'd be gentle and quiet and then start some topic of discussion at the table about touring a college that I was interested in, which he normally wouldn't indulge and had no intention of indulging in by the time the weekend road trip was set to happen. I might be able to breathe for a week before I knew the novelty of our "wonderful sibling relationship" would wear off, and he was primed to relapse again.

Like an addict.

Like a disease.

But now, I didn't know. This week had been bad. There had been less breathing room in between now and last time.

In a daze, I found my glasses and slowly cleaned up the mess we'd made, finished the dishes, and put all the leftovers away before turning off the light and grabbing my bag.

I slipped my phone into the satchel, but as I rounded the stairs and took the first step up, I stopped.

She was still asleep. Maybe for the rest of the night. I could watch her on my phone from anywhere.

I shouldn't leave, though. My back hurt, my hair was a mess, and I still hadn't changed out of my uniform.

But instead of going up to finish my homework, I backed away, as if on autopilot. Picking up my shoes, I slipped out the door and ran, not even stopping to put on my sneakers. The rain pummeled my hair, my clothes, and my legs, my bare feet splashing through rain on the sidewalk as I raced back up the street, around the corner, and toward the village.

I didn't care that I'd left her window open. She loved the rain. *Let her hear it.*

I didn't care that my bag and books and homework were probably getting soaked.

I made another right and saw the glow of the square ahead and stopped running, finally able to breathe. I drew in breath after breath, the cool air in my lungs and the rain plastering my clothes to my skin almost making me smile.

The movie theater's marquee shone ahead, and I knew before I could read the words that they were having an all-night monster marathon. *Kong, Frankenstein, Killer Ants, The Fly* . . .

During October, the theater was only ever closed between eight in the morning and noon for cleaning and restocking, showing new releases and old favorites the other twenty hours of the day in celebration. Sort of a monthlong horror fest.

Jogging up to the ticket booth, I slipped on my shoes, now soaked with my shoestrings dangling, and reached into my bag, pulling out some cash.

"Just give me the all-night pass," I told the girl, slipping her a wrinkled ten through the little hole.

I wouldn't be here all night, but I could be here as long as I liked, at least.

Grabbing my ticket, I hurried inside the door and passed the concession stand, heading upstairs to theater three.

Walking fast, I opened the doors, keeping an eye around me in case my brother had found out I'd left and followed, and then I slipped off my bag as I made my way down the aisle. Some animal screeched onscreen, and quickly, I dropped into a seat, looking around to make sure I was safe.

Not only was I safe, but I was alone. There was no one in here, except me.

I relaxed a little.

It was a weeknight and a school night. Made sense that the place would be empty. It was weird that they still ran the film even if no one bought a ticket, though.

I set my bag on the floor and reached inside, thankful that the contents were still dry, and pulled out my phone, checking on my grandmother again.

She still laid in the dark, on her bed, the monitor in the room beeping steadily and raising no alarms. Sometimes I worried about leaving her alone with Martin, but he really didn't care to deal with her more than he had to.

I clutched the phone in my hand and sat back in the seat, wincing at the pain I forgot was there as I looked up at the screen and saw Godzilla.

A small smile turned up the corners of my lips.

I like Godzilla.

And before I knew it, I had popcorn and sat there staring at the screen, my eyes attached to every frame as my brother faded away, school faded away, Will Grayson faded away, and lit class faded away.

Because Godzilla was great.

And *Lolita* hurt my head.

CHAPTER 3

EMORY

Present

W ill?" I climbed up on my hands and knees, patting the stone floor and feeling the grime under my hands.

Where had he taken me?

I blinked in the darkness, trying to see, but it was so black. I touched my face. Where the hell were my glasses?

Shit.

I could see decently without them or the contacts that I sometimes used, but not with the darkness making it even more difficult. I rose up off the ground, the uneven stones under my shoes curving into my soles.

I looked around, shoving my hair behind my ear. Nothing pierced the darkness. No sliver of light. No moon. No lamps. Nothing.

I'd fought and thrashed and hit, and the next thing I knew, we went through a door, down some stairs, turned a corner, and everything suddenly went dark.

Will, my God. It had been years since he got out of prison. Why had he waited until now?

I breathed in the cold air, the scent soaked with soil and water, as I spun around.

He'd changed. He looked exactly the same and worlds different at the same time.

His eyes . . .

Was he going to let something happen to me?

"I told you I wasn't lying," someone said, and I stiffened.

It sounded like Taylor Dinescu's voice in the room, but I couldn't see anyone or anything.

"I knew you weren't," another man said on the other side of me. "Girls smell different. She was all over the house when we walked in."

I twisted around, facing the new voice.

But then another one spoke up from my left. "I say let her run," he taunted. "She'll die out there anyway."

I spun toward him, breathing hard and holding out my hands. Where were they?

Where the hell were they?!

"Before we've gotten acquainted, Rory?" the other one I didn't know asked. "Come on. I'm bored. She's welcome to stay as far as I'm concerned. Aren't you bored?"

"No," Rory replied in a clipped tone. "I like things just the way they are."

Laughs echoed around the room, Taylor joking, "You may have all you need here, man, but I sure don't."

"Where's my glasses?" I yelled. "Turn on the fucking lights!"

"You got it," the one who wasn't Taylor, Rory, or Will said. "Here."

A glow suddenly brightened a few feet away from me, and I blinked several times, adjusting to the light as a dark form lit a candle. Brick walls came into view, and someone was in front of me, holding something out.

I stumbled back, sucking in a breath, but then I noticed my glasses in his hand and grabbed them. "Get away from me," I said, moving away.

"Relax, baby," he cooed. "We were just afraid you'd break them. Don't want you to not see this."

A snort went off somewhere, and I slipped my glasses on, jerking my head left and right and taking it all in.

Ceilings made of wood hung low, water dripped down, wetting the brick on the walls, and wooden barrels sat around the room as empty wine racks, taller than me, filled the rest of the space. Stairs led up to a set of doors in the ceiling behind me, and a furnace ran, grumbling in the corner. We were in a basement. This house might have several.

I eyed the doors.

"Micah." The guy who gave me my glasses approached me again, holding out his hand. "Moreau."

I quickly backed away, shooting a glare from his hand up to him.

Micah Moreau? I took in his shaggy black hair hanging down his neck and around his ears, piercing blue eyes and a dimple in his left cheek when he smiled. Maybe early twenties.

Moreau, Moreau . . .

"As in Stalinz Moreau?" I inquired, unable to catch my breath.

Was that his father?

He just smiled tightly and shrugged.

Shit. How bad does a kid have to be for a career criminal to not even be able to stand his own son?

He pointed behind him to a lanky blond with hollow cheeks and better skin than mine. "Rory Geardon," he pointed out. "And you've met Taylor."

I looked over at Taylor who sat on a stack of crates behind Will, leaning over his shoulder, smirking at me.

I locked eyes with Will. He leaned against the crates, his hands tucked in the center pocket of his hoodie.

A door was next to him, and I ran for it. He shifted away from the crates and grabbed me, and I shoved at his body, feeling something in his pocket.

I paused and then it hit me. *My knife.*

Or the knife I had on me when I woke up. I'd never seen it before, and I had no idea how it got in my pocket, but I wanted it back.

I dove into his sweatshirt, pulled out the knife, and backed away, unsheathing it again as I looked around me.

The other guys chuckled under their breaths.

"Did you bring me here?" I yelled at Will.

How long had *he* been here?

But I didn't expect an answer.

I just screamed. "Let me out!"

I sucked in air, the small space, the darkness, and no place to run making my blood chill. I choked back my sob.

I knew he couldn't be trusted. I told him that. I knew it.

"I hate you," I said. This had everything to do with him.

Taylor jumped off the crates and came at me, and I lunged for him, only to have someone from behind grab my wrist.

I whipped around, swiping the blade, and Micah stumbled backward, hissing.

Blood dripped from his arm, and I backed away, holding the knife and keeping them in front of me.

"Fuck," Micah cursed.

"I told you to let her die out there," Rory bit out, taking Micah's arm and elevating it as it bled.

"Let me out of here!" I screamed again.

But then all of them looked up, staring behind me as they stopped in their tracks.

I straightened my spine. *What?*

But I didn't have time to wonder. Someone grabbed my hand with the knife, squeezing it as he fisted my throat with his other hand.

I gasped, crying out as I dropped the knife to the floor.

He turned me around, still clutching my neck, and I tipped my head back, looking up and seeing golden brown hair, slicked back, and high cheekbones framing amber eyes.

Young but older than the rest of them. Maybe Will's age.

His lips curled at the corner, and my heart pounded so hard it hurt as I took in the broad shoulders, the five-o'clock shadow, and the vein bulging in his neck.

"I would think they'd have a separate facility for the young women," he joked, letting his eyes fall down my body. "Are they trying to make sure we keep misbehaving?"

Snorts went off behind me, and I planted my hands on his chest, trying to push him away as I heard a scrape on the ground, probably someone picking up my knife.

My hair hung in my face, over my glasses, and I was so thirsty.

He released me and I darted backward, putting distance between me and every one of them.

"Forgive me," he said. "Just a joke."

He walked around me, stopping at Micah Moreau and lifting the guy's arm, inspecting it.

I flashed my gaze to Will, but he just stared down, absently scraping the blood out from under his nails with my knife as if I weren't here.

"It'll be okay." I looked back at the guy talking to Micah, seeing him raise his arm back up to stop the flow of blood. "Just keep it clean."

Who was this guy? Was he . . . ?

Was he the one "in charge"?

I scanned his clothes, seeing a smooth-looking white Oxford, perfectly pressed and tucked into some black dress slacks with a shiny leather belt. He wore black leather shoes, and everything fit him perfectly, as if it were tailored especially for him.

A little better dressed than the other guys, but he did say "we." *Are they trying to make sure* we *keep misbehaving*, he'd said.

He was a prisoner, too. He was the alpha Will spoke of.

Micah nodded at him before tossing me a scowl, and the alpha came back, regarding me.

"My apologies for them." He pressed a hand to his chest, coming in. "Sincerely."

But I shoved him back before he got any closer, his pressed white shirt now smudged with my dirt. "Get away from me." And then I looked to Will. "Will!" I barked.

He just stood there, his gaze rising to meet mine without a care in the world.

"Will!" Jesus, snap out of it!

To hell with this. I ran for the stairs, jiggling the double doors to get out.

"I wouldn't try that," the alpha said. "It's cold, I'm guessing you don't know how to hunt, and believe me when I say you can walk a day in every direction and see nothing but your own footprints when you finally give up and drag your freezing ass back here because you have no other choices."

I growled, pushing and slamming my body into the doors, but all I could hear were chains on the other side, holding it secure.

"Give it back to her," I heard him say behind me.

I looked over my shoulder, seeing him speak to Rory who now held my knife, turning it over in his hands and inspecting it.

He narrowed his eyes. "She sliced Micah," he argued.

The alpha stepped up to him, looked down into his eyes and didn't say another word. Rory tightened his lips and stalked over, tossing me the knife, now sheathed.

I caught it, stepping down off the stairs and holding it firmly in my fist.

"I'm Aydin," the alpha said, looking at me. "Aydin Khadir. No one will touch you again. You have my word."

"Your word . . ." I almost laughed. "Does that mean anything when all I know about you is that you were despicable enough to get locked up in here?"

He quirked a smile, walking over to a small steel door on the wall and opening it.

Flames burst inside, and he reached down, taking a couple of logs and tossing them inside the oven. "You may know me," he retorted, taking the poker and churning the wood. "My family probably owns one of the many sweatshops in Vietnam where your cheap Target blouse was manufactured."

Taylor laughed, and I steeled my spine.

I watched as Aydin unwrapped a cut of meat from the same white butcher paper I saw on lots of the fare inside the refrigerator upstairs.

Picking it up with his fingers, he slapped it on a metal tray and slid it into the brick oven. I flinched as the flames engulfed it, the oven looking deep enough to hold a whole damn person.

I tensed.

"No one will touch you," he said, staring at the flames before turning to look at me. "Until you want us to."

Snickers filled the room, and I licked my lips, unnerved.

"Why am I here?" I demanded.

But he just taunted me. "Right?" he said. "Why are any of us here? We're all innocent."

Rory and Micah laughed, and I inched forward, the knife clasped in my hand.

"I'm not a prisoner," I told him. "I don't come from wealth. All I remember is leaving my office in San Francisco for lunch and waking up here. Where are we?"

Aydin just stared at the flames, the light dancing across his face.

"She knows Will," Taylor said.

"Does she?" Aydin looked over his shoulder at Will. "Is she family? Please say it isn't so."

Will hung back, his hands in his pocket again as he leaned into the crates. The fire reflected in his gaze as he stared at me.

"Will," I pleaded.

But he remained quiet.

"He doesn't seem to know you," Aydin teased.

I shook my head. "There must be some way to get a hold of security or the people who run this place or—"

Aydin pulled out the steak, sizzling on the tray, and set it on the wooden table, grabbing a knife and fork and cutting the meat.

"We have a kitchen, of course, but the meat is so much better cooked down here." He looked at me, bidding me over. "You must be hungry. We're not completely uncivilized. Come here."

He took a pitcher and poured a glass of water, and my mouth dried even more, seeing how good it looked.

"Your name?" he asked, pushing the glass and pan toward me.

I clamped my mouth shut.

But Will spoke up for me. "Her name is Emory Scott," he answered.

I shot Will a glare. A smirk danced across his eyes.

"From Thunder Bay, as well?" Aydin asked him.

Will nodded.

Taylor took back his spot, sitting on the crates behind him and hanging over Will's shoulder again as everyone watched me.

I stepped a little closer to Will, too angry to care right now.

"Always following," I taunted him. "Never the leader, and always latching on to anyone who loves you."

He stared at me.

"Your friends have moved on," I told him. "Buying up Thunder Bay. Starting families. Probably happy to be rid of their weakest link." My eyes burned on him. "Even Damon seems happy, judging from the news I catch from home. No falter in his steps as he does just fine without you."

The muscles in his jaw flexed, and I smiled a little.

Yeah, he didn't like that.

"Damon . . ." Aydin murmured, looking over to Will. "Torrance?"

Will remained silent.

"And Michael Crist and Kai Mori, right?" Aydin continued. "I would be jealous you have people who care enough to send help if it weren't a female a year too late."

Everyone chuckled.

No one sent me. Someone kidnapped me.

"Took them long enough," Taylor added. "And we've been here the whole time, taking care of him."

"He's ours now," Aydin told me. "The senator's grandson has elevated his company, my dear. We're not toys playing at war."

"No, you're prisoners playing like you have *any* power."

He nodded once, unfazed. "We'll revisit that topic again another time. Eat."

The food sat there, the smell permeating the air, and I saw Micah staring at it more than once.

Aydin dug into his steak, taking a bite. Where was their food? I looked at Will, but he still just stared at me.

"I'm not staying here for a month," I said.

Aydin continued eating and took a drink of water, washing it down.

"Things happen fast in the wild," he said, cutting another chunk. "Hunting, fishing, hiking, remote as we are . . . a simple injury can mean death." He raised his eyes to me. "A simple injury can leave you in a lot of pain."

He chewed his food and then pushed his plate away, swallowing.

"Micah had an anxiety attack when he first arrived," he explained, looking at the guy. "Remember that? We had to put him down here for a whole day, because his hysteria was driving us insane."

I shot my eyes to Micah, his gaze on the floor now. They locked him in here? Because he had a panic attack? He could've died.

I begged Will with my eyes, but he wasn't looking at me anymore. He wasn't looking at anything anymore, staring at the floor, same as Micah.

"I'd hate for that to happen to you at the wrong time," Aydin said, approaching me. "When the crews show up again, you could be down here, in the tunnels, undetected until they come again the next month."

My heart sank to my stomach, and while I had no clue why the rest of them were locked up in here, I had a very good idea about what made him such a threat.

He stepped up to me, and now the guys behind him weren't laughing so much anymore.

"You'll stay with us," Aydin whispered. "We'll take care of you until they arrive."

I looked up at him, the dark brown in his amber eyes sharpening with the threat.

"I want to see Will alone," I said, trying to keep my tone calm.

Aydin looked over at Will. "Is there anything you can hear that we can't?"

Will's eyes darted from me to him, hesitating a moment before replying, "No."

Aydin turned, smirking, and I knew.

I knew . . .

I couldn't stay here. There was a town nearby. If I had to walk for three days until my body nearly expired from dehydration, I'd find it.

Slowly, I circled around Aydin, backing up and keeping my eyes on the boys as I made my way toward the door. "You want some fun?" I asked Taylor. "Five-minute head start then."

He grinned wide, looking to Aydin and then back to me. "Two," he cooed.

He hopped off the crates, Will, Rory, and Micah turning to face me as Aydin stood in the back, waiting.

And then . . .

I launched for the door, swinging it open and racing through, charging up the old stone stairs and through the door at the top.

They howled behind me, lighting a fire under my feet, and I swung around, not knowing where the front door to the house was from here, but I saw the kitchen and ran for it.

Swinging around the large island, I bolted for the back door and charged through, leaping onto the grass, immediately stumbling to my knees and rolling down the small wet hill, darkness looming everywhere.

Ice seeped through my skin.

He was right. It was cold.

Scrambling to my feet, I dug in my heels and ran. I ran and ran, not risking a look back as I made for the cover of the trees ahead.

Gasping for breath, I glanced to my left, seeing a huge ass waterfall gushing over a cliff. I slowed, widening my eyes as it rose high above and the balconies of the house overlooked it.

My God. I kept running, not believing what I was seeing. Where the hell was I?

The waterfall spilled into a ravine I couldn't see, but I just shook my head and ran so hard my body screamed. Diving into the darkened woods, I raced through the brush. I wished I wasn't wearing a white shirt.

I rounded trees, deciding to stay close to the edge of the forest where the land spilled off to the side. Good chance there was a river below that carried the water from the fall, and where there was water, there were towns.

Stumbling over rocks as branches whipped at my arms, I barely even bothered to look ahead as I pushed my glasses back up the bridge of my nose, the knife still in my hand as I struggled for air.

It was fucking cold. Where were we? It was only mid-October, there was a waterfall in their backyard, and trees that didn't belong anywhere I'd ever lived.

Canada? There were hemlocks, spruces, white pines . . . These trees were partial to the northeastern part of North America.

I had been part of a design team right out of college that renovated an old house in St. John. The owner was adamant about reintroducing native flora to the property.

God, how did I get here?

Hollers went off behind me, hitting the air, and I whimpered. They were coming.

I dug in harder, sweat coating my back despite the cold as their howls got closer and closer, and I could almost feel their hands on me as I raced. I hit the ground, scurrying behind a bush to hide myself.

I couldn't stop gasping for breath, my heart about to beat out of my chest. I wasn't going to make it, outrunning them.

I'd hide until they gave up, and then I'd make a run for it.

Leaves rustled and footfalls pounded past. I didn't see them through the bush, but I could hear them.

They ran, their steps fading away, and I stayed rooted in my spot.

"Em-ory!" they called, but their voices were nowhere near me.

I smiled.

"Emmmmmoryyyyyyy!" they sang.

And still, their voices sank farther and farther away.

Slowly, I slipped the knife into my pocket, got my feet under me, and rose enough to look over the edge of the bush, just to sneak a glance at their position.

I didn't see anyone. *Yes.*

I'd hide here—or somewhere else if I had to—and make my escape when they were gone. The grounds were huge. They couldn't cover every inch.

I was getting out of here—rain or shine.

I squatted back down to maintain my hiding place, but then I caught sight of Micah, racing right for me.

"Boo!" he shouted.

I screamed and lost my balance, flailing my arms and flying backward. I rolled down the small incline and grappled at the ground to stop myself, but I just kept slipping.

Shit!

I cried out, my legs falling over the edge of something, and I tumbled over the side of the cliff, a hand grabbing my wrist just in time.

I kicked and looked down, seeing the river far below as I swung my other hand up, grasping for whoever had me.

"Rory!" Micah shouted, sliding on his ass with me as he held on. "Taylor!"

I whimpered, feeling us slide. He was coming with me. He couldn't hold on.

Another body dropped down next to him, and Rory grabbed my other arm.

I hung there as they held on to me, knowing they could let go at any moment, and not so sure anymore that I'd rather risk starvation or dying of exposure out in the wilderness. *Don't let me go.*

Taylor, Will, and Aydin slid down the hill behind them and came to stand over the three of us. Aydin looked as calm as he did inside the house, like he didn't even have to break a sweat to come out here after me.

He cocked his head, watching me dangle there. "Put her in my room," he told them.

CHAPTER 4

EMORY

Nine Years Ago

hat did you do in lit class yesterday?"

Elle Burkhardt pulled on her uniform trousers, staring at me while I pulled off my necktie and started unbuttoning my shirt.

My long-sleeved white T-shirt underneath remained on as I snatched my band jacket off the hanger dangling on the outside of my locker.

The girls' locker room was packed—cheerleading, band, and the field hockey team all vying for space, either trying to get out to the court or to go home.

"I finished reading *Lolita*," I mumbled to her.

"You know what I mean."

I shot her a look.

I'd skipped lit this morning, no doubt another confrontation with my brother waiting to happen tonight once he found out, but I just couldn't face Will and his merry band of morons this morning after my outburst yesterday.

I'd hid in the library, instead.

"Let them do their worst while they can," I said, pulling on my coat, the heavy fabric grazing my back and burning the skin. "Life will eventually knock them down to size, like it does to us all."

It wasn't that I was scared of the Horsemen and the repercussions of calling them out in class yesterday. I just knew another outburst from me couldn't happen again quite yet, so rather than give them the satisfaction of seeing me shut up and sit there, I just didn't show up at all.

Gathering all of my hair, I pulled it into a low ponytail and picked up my glasses off the bench, slipping them back on. The poster across the locker room came into view more clearly.

VOTE FOR ARI!
HOMECOMING QUEEN

Homecoming. I groaned. Pretty sure slamming my nipple in a car door would be less painful.

Or joining a gym.

Or reading *The Bell Jar* in between bouts of banging my head on a wall.

Elle reached into her locker and took out her deodorant, rolling it on. "You're coming to Sticks tonight, right?"

Kicking off my sneakers, I pulled my newly pressed pants off the hanger before unzipping my skirt and letting it fall to the floor. "What do you think?"

"Too school for cool?"

I nodded, slipping my pants on and fastening them. The girl knew me.

Leaning over, I jerked my chin at her and opened her locker door, gesturing to the Trojan bumper sticker she had plastered inside. "Some of us don't have parents with the admissions office at USC on speed dial."

We buttoned up our navy blue and white coats, but I could feel her eyes on me as she braided her blond hair and I slipped on my black shoes.

"You're allowed to relax once in a while." Her voice was calm but firm. "The rest of us aren't less because we like to have fun, you know?"

"Depends on your idea of fun, I guess."

I sat down and started tying my shoes, but then I saw her stop. I paused, realizing how that came out.

I looked up at her, kind of wincing. "I'm sorry," I said. "I didn't mean that."

Damn, I was rude. Why was I so awful? Elle and I weren't friends, but we were friendly. She tried, despite how hard I made it.

"And I have fun," I teased. "Who says I don't have fun?"

She continued braiding her hair. "Depends on your idea of fun, I guess," she shot back.

I laughed, thankful she was playing back. I knew how I was. Judgy, rude, and close-minded, but I also knew why.

I was jealous.

Happy people didn't hurt others, and while I didn't dwell on my behavior in lit yesterday with Will and his friends, people like Elle didn't deserve it.

I wanted someone to understand me.

"Have you ever seen a Lamborghini commercial on TV?" I asked, looking over and meeting her eyes.

She shook her head.

"They don't make them," I told her. "Because people who can afford Lamborghinis aren't sitting around watching television."

"So, you want a Lamborghini someday, and that's why you work so hard and don't have any fun?"

"No." I chuckled, gathering my school uniform scattered on the floor. "My own private jet will get me out of this town a hell of a lot faster than a car. I'll wave goodbye and let it all disappear in my wake."

The cheer team ran by our aisle, everyone starting to make their way out to the gym. The football team was on a bye week, but the basketball team had an exhibition game against Falcon's Well.

"I'll try not to take that remark personally," Elle replied.

I shot her a smile, hoping she didn't take it personally. I wanted as far away from this town as possible for several reasons, and once I left, only one thing would ever bring me back.

"Is there nothing you love in Thunder Bay?" she asked.

I dropped my eyes for a moment and then looked over at her. "Why do you think I'm still here?"

Then I opened my locker and flashed her the inside of my door, but instead of my own Trojan bumper sticker, or any bumper sticker, it was a single, three-by-five snapshot of my grandma and me at my eleventh birthday picnic in the park.

My skin in my blue tank top was darker than my usual olive from all my time in the sun that summer, my cheeks rosy from smiling and not having a care in the world other than what I was going to do for fun the next day, and no matter what size glasses I wore, they always looked too big for my face. I was geeky and happy. Remembering that the woman in the picture no longer resembled the woman who was lying in bed at home right now made my throat prickle with tears.

But I looked at Elle and smiled small, my grandma the one thing I'd come back to town for.

In fact, the idea of leaving for college and leaving her if she was still alive by then was almost unbearable.

I rubbed my eyes under my glasses and then stuffed my school clothes into the locker.

I looked up, noticing something.

What was that? I narrowed my eyes, reaching up and taking the stuffed animal off the top shelf.

I paused in confusion. How did this get in here?

I looked around for anyone watching me and met Elle's eyes, holding it up.

"Did you put this in here?"

She looked at it and then me, shaking her head. "Nope. I don't even know what that is. A Komodo dragon?"

I studied the gray plush toy, taking in his claws, teeth, tail, the scales down his spine, the angry snarl on his face . . .

"It's Godzilla," I murmured and then laughed.

Who put this in here?

And then my face fell. I watched *Godzilla* last night. I thought I was alone in the theater. Did someone see me?

It was coincidental, wasn't it?

"What's this?" Elle picked up the paper and granola bar tied to its leg. She read the note, "'Sunset is at 6:38 p.m.'"

I flashed my gaze to hers.

She shrugged. "It's from someone who knows it's Yom Kippur," she said.

In a town like this, everyone knew who the Jewish kids were.

And the black kids. And the poor kids.

We were in the minority in Thunder Bay, so we stood out.

Anyone could've sent this, and I was tempted to keep the snack bar. I hadn't checked what time sunset was to know when I could eat, and I'd forgotten to bring anything for after the game. I was hungry.

But then, I saw a black strip of cardstock tied to Godzilla's tail and ripped it off the ribbon.

Admit One
Emory Scott
L-348

My hand shook as I read it over and over again, recognizing the black paper with the ornate silver border and the serial number identifying every ticket sold. It was an annual event.

It was—

"Are you serious?" Elle blurted out, snatching the ticket from my hand and staring at it. "An invitation from a senior?"

I opened my mouth to speak, but no words came out. The senior lock-in was held every October, and it was tonight. After the basketball game. Non-seniors could attend only if they secured an invitation from the graduating class, and even then, the seniors were only allowed to invite one person each.

One senior used their only pass to invite me?

It had to be a mistake.

"Take it," I told her.

There was no way I was going. This was a trap waiting to happen.

She held it for a moment and then sighed, handing it back to me. "As tempting as that is, you need this more than me."

I crumpled it in my fist, about to toss it onto the floor of my locker, but Elle plucked it out of my hand and stuck it inside my jacket, slipping it in between two buttons.

"Line up!" our director called.

But I was swatting Elle's hand away. "Stop, dammit," I gritted out. "I'm not going."

"In case you change your mind," she chirped. But then she dropped her voice to a whisper. "I mean, what's to worry about? It's not like you're really locked in with them."

Them. She meant the seniors.

But when she said it, only four came to mind.

I side-eyed her, tossed Godzilla into my locker, and pulled out my flute.

He's so cute!" Elle said, but it came out in a little growl like he was a baby and good enough to eat.

I chuckled under my breath. I wasn't sure which one she was talking about, but I could guess.

Will Grayson jogged down the court, dribbled the ball, and passed it to the center before racing ahead again, catching it, and shooting it straight into the basket.

It slipped through the net, the scoreboard added two points, and the crowd cheered. Michael Crist shot him a five and charged down the court, sliding in front of the other team's forward and stealing the ball again, passing it to Kai.

"Whoo!!" everyone screamed around me.

I wiped the sweat off my forehead, watching Will lift his shirt up and use it to do the same.

I couldn't help my eyes falling to his bare stomach, the shorts making his skin look more golden with the ridges and dips tight and visible from here.

Heat covered my face again, and I looked away. Navy blue was absolutely his color.

I tried to space off like I did with the football games, but even when I wasn't looking at the court, I wanted to look at it. Will Grayson was the best shooter we've ever had, better than Crist who was already in talks for an athletic scholarship he didn't need for college next year.

Why wasn't Will vying for one? How lucky it must be to have a talent like that to get you in the door, but then again, he didn't need help opening doors, did he? He was probably a legacy somewhere, his future already planned.

The final buzzer blared, and I checked the scoreboard, making sure of what I already knew. We won. By a lot.

Too bad it wasn't a real game. Just a little show before the regular season started in November.

Hesitantly, I raised my eyes again, finding him on the court. He talked to Damon Torrance as he wiped the sweat off his face, the wet hair at the back of his neck darker than the hair on top.

Then . . . he looked over his shoulder and locked eyes with me.

A smile spread across his face, like he knew I'd been watching him the whole damn time, and my face fell, heat rising to my cheeks.

Ugh. I looked away.

Such an ass.

Everyone descended the bleachers, the crowd dispersing, and

I looked up at the clock, seeing it was just after seven. The hunger pangs had stopped, but my mouth watered for that granola bar, and now I could eat.

I wasn't stupid enough to eat food from someone I didn't know, though. Hopefully Martin left me alone so I could get some food in me before he went to town.

"Scott!" someone called.

I looked up to see Mrs. Baum, the director. I slipped through the crowd of students, walking over to her.

She leaned in. "Change and put your instrument away," she told me quietly, "and then hurry back into the gym to help clean up the mess before the lock-in."

"Yes, ma'am."

I was grateful she didn't shout that across the room. No one needed reminding that I was a work-study kid.

Heading for the locker room, I passed Elle as she talked to two of our band members. "Have fun tonight," I told her.

She smiled. "Better hurry and make it out in time before they lock the doors."

And then she wiggled her eyebrows.

"They don't actually lock the doors," I retorted. "It's a fire hazard."

She stuck her tongue out playfully, and I smiled, spinning around and heading for the locker room.

After changing back into my school clothes, I hung my band uniform back up, stored my instrument in my locker, and started to close the door, stopping when I spotted the granola bar.

I twisted my lips to the side, slipping it off the red ribbon around Godzilla's foot and checking it for holes like I used to do with Halloween candy.

It looked safe.

My stomach hollowed, and suddenly, I was hungry again.

I stuffed it into the center pocket of my black hoodie. *I'll throw it away in the gym.*

Slamming the locker door shut, I started walking but looked down and saw the crumpled ticket on the floor.

Crouching down, I picked it up and looked at it again. *Must've fallen out of my uniform.*

For a moment, I was tempted. I wanted to be that girl. The one with a lock-in and cute boys and music and friends to look forward to.

The longing coursed through me and eventually out, and I stuffed it into my hoodie pocket, as well. I'd throw that away with the granola bar, too. Definitely before Martin saw it.

I hurried back to the gym.

"Okay, one!" Bentley Foster called out. "Two . . . three!"

An hour later, the gym was clean of soda cups and popcorn boxes, the bleachers stored, the hoops raised, and the floors quickly swept. Two of us each picked up the ends of several mats, and on the count of three, pulled them open, spreading the hardwood basketball court with a cushion for sleeping bags and blankets.

In no time, the floor was covered in blue wrestling mats, and my stomach ached at the smell of burgers and nachos wafting in from the kitchen.

I checked the clock in the wall. *After eight.*

Looking over, I caught the director's eyes. "Are we good?" I asked her.

"You walking?"

I nodded.

"Then go on and go," she told me. "Have a good weekend. Be safe."

"Thanks." I backed away as they rolled the coolers full of soda and juice out. "You, too."

I jogged toward the locker room door to collect my uniform and backpack when I heard her behind me, "Open the doors!" she called to someone.

Students had no doubt gathered outside, having packed and stored their sleeping bags in their cars since this morning, probably leaving after the game to eat before they came right back here for the lock-in.

I pushed through the locker room door as the main entrances swung open, letting in the crowd.

"Scott!" Baum shouted.

I stopped, turning around.

She still stood where I left her, muttering into a walkie-talkie and then turning her attention back to me. "Coach Dorn is up in her classroom," she said. "She wants to see you before you leave."

I hesitated a moment and then sighed. "Okay," I called out and spun back around, pushing through the door with a hard shove.

I needed to get out of here. It was dark, I was starving, and they didn't really lock the doors during a lock-in, right? I mean, I was pretty sure that was illegal, but now I didn't know.

Skipping the stop at my locker, I exited the locker room, swung open the door, and stepped into the hallway, slipping through the students who were trying to get into the gym. I turned left and jogged up the darkened stairs, their footsteps and chatter fading the farther up I climbed.

Mrs. Dorn was not only the swim coach, but she also taught biology on the third floor. I took biology two years ago, though. What did she want?

Was this about me quitting swimming?

Fear cooled my blood. She knew something didn't sit right about why I'd quit. I could see it on her face.

Reaching the top floor, I grabbed the door handle and pulled it open, entering the silent third floor and looking around.

No lights shone except for the lanterns that glowed outside, and tiny droplets of rain spattered the windows that peered into the courtyard below.

Great. Now I was going to get soaked walking home.

The door closed behind me, and suddenly, the lock-in was miles away.

"Coach?" I called out, walking down the hall toward her classroom.

Heading up to the door, I stopped and peered inside. Stools sat upside down on top of the long, black worktables, and I looked to the teacher's desk, seeing her computer off, her chair pushed in, and the classroom pitch-black.

"Coach?" I said louder this time. "It's Emory Scott."

Stepping back into the hallway, I turned, looking around. "Hello?" But there was no answer.

I dug in my heels, charging down the hall and glancing into classrooms as I passed, all dark and not a soul to be found. Everyone was either home or downstairs on the first floor.

I rounded the corner and then the next, coming up on the teachers' lounge and found the door cracked.

Creeping up, I pushed it open a sliver more. "Hello?" I said. "Coach, are you in here?"

Every hair on my arms stood on end, and all I could see was dark. What the hell?

Then, a shadow suddenly moved across the wall in my view, and I sucked in a breath.

I swallowed. "Coach?" I choked out.

Rain tapped the windows behind me, and I knew someone was in the room.

I almost pushed the door open, but whoever was in there heard me. And they weren't responding.

To hell with this. I tried. She could talk to me Monday.

Jetting off, I ran to the end of the hall and threw my body into the door leading to the other stairwell.

But it didn't budge.

I grabbed hold of the bar and shoved again, the door jiggling but not opening.

"No, no, no . . ." I pushed again and then tried the other one, kicking at it and growling. "They don't really lock the doors," I mocked myself.

Shit!

Running back the way I came, I bolted past the teachers' lounge and whoever might be in there, heading back toward the lab, passing it, and trying the doors I had come through when I arrived.

I shook the handles, yanking and shoving, but they wouldn't open. Dammit! Did they lock behind me automatically or . . .

I shook my head, not wanting to think about the other option.

I slipped my hands inside the pocket of my hoodie, but when I pulled out the items inside, all I had were the granola bar and the lock-in ticket.

"Where's my phone?"

I breathed hard, my hair tickling my nose as I searched my brain. *My locker.* I'd left my phone in my backpack inside my locker.

I couldn't call home anyway. Not yet. Martin was a last resort.

I could call the office.

Or Elle.

I closed my eyes. "Shit." I didn't even know her number. I didn't know anyone's number. *A friend would be useful right now, loser.*

There had to be speed dial on a classroom telephone for the front office. Please, please, please, let someone be in there.

I rushed back to the biology lab and swung inside the door, grabbing the receiver off the wall and squinting at the keypad.

I couldn't see shit. I flipped the light switch.

But nothing happened. "What?" I breathed out, confused.

I flipped the switch up and down a few more times, looking up at the lights and hoping for a flicker, but they were dead. The room was black.

I gritted my teeth and clenched my thighs, because I felt like I was about to pee my pants. I pushed my glasses back up my nose and squinted at the keypad again, trying to make out the writing.

Before I could dial, something glinted to my left, and I looked down on the floor, seeing a large, wet footprint.

I stopped breathing, following the trail, but it disappeared out the door and into the hallway. Whipping around, I dropped the phone, seeing the window on the other side of the room open with rain pouring across the roof outside, splattering the windowsill.

I was just in here, looking for Dorn. That window wasn't open.

I dropped the phone and backed into the hallway, keeping my eyes peeled.

"This isn't funny!" I barked. "And I'm not scared!"

Twisting my head left and right, I continued retreating to the wall of windows that wrapped around the third level, glancing over my shoulder to see if I could signal anyone outside in the courtyard.

There was no one, though. Just dark and rain and trees below.

So the lights were cut off. The doors were suddenly locked. Someone creepy was playing around, probably the same creep who sent me the invite to the lock-in.

Fucking Will Grayson.

I squared my shoulders, looking left and then right. "How flattered I am that you have nothing better to do with your time than this," I bit out. "Come on. I'm almost excited. Let's go."

This was bullshit. I had things to do. I had to get home.

But no. Everyone was at their disposal for their entertainment. No one else's time was important.

"You think you can scare me?" I said, not yelling anymore, because I knew he was close. "You're boring."

I didn't know anything about fighting back or protecting myself, but I knew that nothing surprised me.

I might not win, but I wouldn't scream.

Dashing back into the biology lab, I reached around the doorframe to grab the receiver I'd left dangling, but I only caught air. Patting the wall, I searched for the phone and looked up, seeing the receiver and its cord gone.

What . . . ? My heart skipped a beat. I just had it in my hand.

I quickly scanned the room, knowing someone was in here. I tried to spot them in one of the darkened corners, or their eyes peeking through one of the bookshelves . . .

Maybe Michael Crist's red mask, Kai Mori's broad shoulders, Damon Torrance's stupid smirk, or Will Grayson's black hoodie.

But I wasn't waiting around. Leaving, I ran back toward the teachers' lounge and darted into the girls' bathroom, hopping up onto the radiator and unlatching the window. Flipping it up, I hung my arms over the side and stuck my head out.

I tried to lift myself up, my legs flailing as I tried to get some traction against the wall to push myself up more, but my back ached, and the muscles in my stomach burned as I struggled.

If my spaghetti arms could lift more than a blueberry, that would be fantastic. *God, I was pathetic.*

I grunted, using every ounce of strength to pull myself up, but I heard something and stopped.

Looking over the gym roof, I saw Michael Crist on the outdoor basketball court dribbling a ball and shooting baskets in the rain.

He was outside.

He wasn't inside.

Were they all outside? If it wasn't the Horsemen up here with me, freaking me out, then who . . .

The bathroom door suddenly whined behind me, and I didn't know if someone was leaving or coming in, but I scrambled, hopping down off the radiator and whipping around to face whoever it was.

The door swung closed, no one in front of me, but then a click pierced the silence, and my eyes flashed to the stall door.

The closed one.

Someone was in here. Someone's . . .

I couldn't swallow.

If it wasn't Will and his pals, then that changed things.

Running past the stall, I threw open the door and dashed into the hallway, making my way for the chemistry lab. It had a window like the bio lab, and I could crawl out onto the roof—flail, scream for help, whatever. I was safer in the open than stuck up here with God knows who.

Laughter broke out from somewhere, echoing down the hall, and I noticed more wet tracks on the floor, some leading back to the bathroom where I had been and some moving alongside me.

Tossing a look over my shoulder, I saw a dark shadow moving through the glass in the other hallway and the door to the bathroom swing open, another figure emerging.

My stomach rolled. What the hell?

Racing into the chem lab, I closed the door, locked it, and pulled the shade down on the window.

Rain fell all around, pummeling the roof and tapping the windows, but I heard it louder in here.

I narrowed my eyes.

It was loud. *Just like in the bio lab.*

Looking over my shoulder, I saw that one of the windows was open in here, too—rain bouncing against the roof outside and drenching the countertop along the wall.

I dropped my eyes to the floor, my heart sinking as I saw more wet footprints.

Only this time, they weren't leaving the room. Following the trail around the desks, I walked toward the back of the room and stopped as they disappeared into the dark corner.

I tried to inhale a breath, but I couldn't stop shaking.

Grabbing a pair of tongs off the tray on the table, I kept them in my fist before picking up a flask, rearing back, and launching it into the corner.

It shattered against the bookshelf, missing the corner by a mile, because I suck, and I picked up a beaker next, throwing it at him—whoever it was—and hitting the wall this time.

I kept going, picking up a cylinder and loading my arm, but then . . .

He stepped out, his dark form somehow much bigger than I was expecting.

I took a step back but released a breath, looking up.

Jeans, black hoodie, and a white paintball mask with a red stripe down the left side.

Will.

I almost relaxed. Until I dropped my eyes and noticed the gloves. Black leather. He balled his fists, making them grind and whine as he stretched the material that glinted in the moonlight.

I glanced at the door, but it was no use. Kai and Damon, I assumed, were out there somewhere still.

I glared at Will as he took a slow step toward me.

"I'm not scared," I told him.

He cocked his head.

"I'm annoyed." I clenched my weapons in my hands. "I have to walk home in the rain now."

I threw the cylinder at him, damn near hitting him, but he whipped out his arm and swatted it away before it hit his face.

It crashed to the floor, and I backed away, snatching another flask off a table as he stepped closer. "You got a problem with my brother, then you take it up with him. Don't be a coward."

He stalked toward me, and I launched the flask. It hit him in the chest, making him stumble, but it didn't break, tumbling to the floor instead, the glass finally shattering.

He walked, the glass cracking under his boots, and I watched as he laid his gloved hand on the black lab table, gliding it over the top as he moved.

My heart pounded in my chest, my stomach swirling as the fear took root, and I looked up at his face, his eyes through the little holes in the mask barely visible in the darkness.

I stopped, suddenly lost in those voids for a moment.

He took another step, and a jolt hit my heart, my whole body warming.

Still, I didn't move.

I couldn't.

Another step. He was almost at me.

Why wasn't I moving?

My pulse raced more by the second, and the feeling almost made me smile because I kind of liked it.

Something built inside me, stacking one brick on top of another until I was a wall, and every second more that I stood there, the more the room started to spin around us like a storm.

And he and I were the eye.

What was I doing? What if this wasn't a joke?

Just another second. Just one more second. I wanted to push it.

With every moment that passed, my lungs worked faster to take in air, and I just wanted him to take another step—one more step— to be closer to me. Until . . .

Until he was there, two inches from my body and looking down at me—so close that if I spun around to bolt, there was no way I'd get away.

My stomach swirled, and my knees shook.

I tried to swallow, but I couldn't. "Is this the part where I giggle?" I said, trying to sound tough but failing. "Or beg?"

He cocked his head to the side again, like he was studying me.

I forced a smirk despite my hands shaking with fear. "Stop it, you're scaring me," I whimpered, imitating one of his Barbie dolls. "Oh, no. Whatever will I do? Don't be too hard on me, Daddy." I batted my eyelashes. "But I admit, I like it when you're hard on me. Sooooo hard." And then I moaned for good measure.

Then I dropped the smirk and cocked an eyebrow. Is that what he expected from me?

"You . . . don't scare me," I repeated.

Shooting out my hand, I grabbed a set of test tubes and reared my arm back, throwing them through one of the windows. I growled as it crashed through, all the glass hopefully falling on top of the sky-light of the gym below and alerting someone I was up here.

The sound of rain filled the room even more, and cool air rushed in, the wind blowing my hair. I looked up, glaring into his eyes, hoping that that did it and he'd stop now.

But he just stared down at me.

And then, as if accepting a challenge, he reached out and swiped an entire stand of beakers, flasks, and funnels off the countertop and onto the floor.

The crash ached in my ears, but I didn't flinch. Reaching out, I grabbed hold of another stand and pulled it onto the floor, every empty vial and container shattering between us as I backed away and he advanced.

Passing the next student worktable, he reached for the left and pulled the chemistry set onto the floor, and I reached right, yanking another between us as he continued walking, the glass crackling under his feet.

We moved faster, him reaching left and me reaching to the right, metal stands clanking to the floor between us as glass crashed and filled the room with chaos after chaos.

Again. Left, right, left, right. We kept going, him getting faster and me stumbling back to grab the next table's stand as something filled up in my stomach, my muscles charged, and I started to smile.

He moved into me, and I stumbled back, tripping on my foot and losing my balance. I fell backward, but he followed, his arm circling my waist just in time as his other grabbed the table for support.

I looked over my shoulder, seeing bits of glass on the floor where I would've landed.

Turning back to him, I stared up into his eyes as my fingers clutched his shoulders.

And then I felt it. The smile still on my face.

I was smiling. A little.

Shit.

Slowly, I let it fall, but I couldn't take my eyes off his. Guilt washed over me at the mess we had made, knowing I couldn't pay for it, but the worry left as quickly as it came, because all I could feel was the here and now.

The rain and wind blew through the room, and I reached up, my hands shaking as I lifted his mask off his face and dropped it to the floor.

He just held me as I slipped the hood off his head and looked up into dark green eyes.

"I was never trying to scare you," Will said, rain glistening on his face and wet hair. "I just wanted to see something."

I stared at him, because I couldn't speak no matter how hard I tried. I didn't know what was wrong with me, I . . .

I wanted to go, but . . .

I didn't want to leave.

I liked this.

But I twisted out of his hold, stumbling backward and landing on my hands away from the glass. A smile glinted in his eyes, and he dropped to his hands and knees, too, watching me with mischief.

My heart raced again, hearing the glass crunch under his palms, and I held his eyes, scooting back slowly as he moved toward me.

But just then, he moved with the speed of light, barreling right at me, and I yelped as I leapt to my feet and so did he, but before I could run, he crashed into me and pinned me to the wall.

I exhaled hard, trying to keep the smile off my face, but I couldn't help the small laugh that escaped. My heart was beating so fast.

His body pressed into me, and I could feel his eyes on me as he tipped his chin down, his nose nearly brushing mine.

"Get . . . get . . . get away from me," I stammered, because I was trying not to laugh.

A drop of sweat trickled down my back, his body on mine making it too unbearable to even breathe.

He took my chin in his hand and lifted it up, trying to get me to look at him.

His heat surrounded me, and the pulse between my thighs throbbed.

I didn't want him to go anywhere.

And I hated that.

Blinking long and hard, I swallowed the lump in my throat and looked up into his eyes, hardening my gaze. "You're all assholes," I said, grabbing his wrist. "Boring and predictable, and maybe that shit works on everyone else, but not me."

I yanked his fingers off my chin and shoved him in the chest, stepping away.

He didn't want me. He wanted to use me, and no matter how much I wanted to indulge a fantasy of fun and excitement, I'd be the one to pay later. Not him.

Getting me into bed, so he could get laughs when he told everyone what a lousy lay I was or rub it in my brother's face that he'd gotten me to spread my legs, were the only things he was interested in.

No. He wasn't going to win.

"Unlock the doors," I told him.

But he just stared at me for a moment, and instead of heading to the hallway and toward the stairwell doors that had been locked, he walked for the wall of windows, the wind and rain barely staying at bay beyond the broken glass.

"Unlock the doors," I said again, walking over to his side.

"Why?" he asked.

I scowled. "Why?"

What do you mean, why?

"I wasn't trying to scare you," he said, staring out at the rain pummeling the roof, "but why wasn't I?"

"Real monsters don't wear masks, William Grayson III," I retorted. "They look like everyone else."

He kept staring at the rain, but he didn't respond.

"Now, unlock the doors." I turned around. "You're pathetic, and you've wasted my time."

I walked for the classroom door, but then I heard his voice behind me.

"They won't let you walk home in this weather," he said.

"They can't stop me."

"*I* won't let you walk home in this," he clarified. "You'll sleep here tonight."

I glanced over my shoulder at him, placing my hand on the door handle. "Make me."

And before I could even turn the doorknob, he reached into his pocket and pulled out his phone, tapping the screen.

"'Stop it, you're scaring me,'" I said on the recording. "'Oh, no. Whatever will I do? Don't be too hard on me, Daddy.'"

I stopped breathing for a moment, every muscle in my body losing strength. My hand dropped from the knob.

"'But I admit, I like it when you're hard on me. Sooooo hard.'"

I closed my eyes, hearing myself moan on the phone. *Shit*.

I turned around, meeting his self-satisfied little smile and knowing he'd recorded his prank. They always documented their dumb crap on that stupid phone.

I almost walked out. My feet almost took that step, and they could post that online for everyone to have a good laugh. My brother would get angry, because his mind would make up whatever story was the easiest to go along with what he thought was happening in that recording, too.

No skin off my nose because I was used to it.

But then Will said, "Door's unlocked. Go get some pizza." And he picked up his mask off the floor. "We'll clean up here."

I hesitated, looking around at all the broken glass and how much trouble I'd be in if my brother found out I'd helped make this mess. Even though I was kind of defending myself, I still didn't want him to have any idea of what happened up here because he'd just blame me.

I blinked long and hard. *Fine.*

I walked out, charging down the hallway and through the doors to the stairwell.

I should be at home. I should be with my grandma.

He just wanted to play with me to prove he could.

But . . . a night away was rare. At least I could relax, knowing Martin wouldn't be here. I had my earbuds and a book.

I still wasn't giving Will another inch tonight, though. The lock-in was filled with witnesses. Let him try.

I kicked rocks all the way back down to the gymnasium, ignored the pizza, and planted my butt on the bleachers.

Opening my phone, I tapped the app and tried to continue reading *The Night Eternal* as the music and activity went on around me.

But after ten minutes, I'd barely absorbed a paragraph.

And when he and his friends finally came back downstairs, I forgot about the book as I waited for him to come over and try something.

Engage me. Annoy me. Tease me.

But he didn't.

He left me alone.

I faltered for a moment, a little confused. I expected him to try to piss me off or coerce me into the scavenger hunt they were having or something.

But he just left me sitting there, the minutes stretching into an hour, and the hour stretching into two.

Just as I thought. *To prove he could . . .*

The band director called my brother and asked if I could put in more work-study hours by helping in the kitchen tonight. Then they'd keep me over since it would be too late to go home.

Martin was probably fine with it since I was "working," but I didn't for one second think the director came up with that lie herself.

Because I didn't help in the kitchen at all.

I just sat there, trying to read on my phone. Will glanced over every once in a while as he spent time with his friends or slow danced with some girl to make sure I was where he'd left me.

He just liked making me sweat. That's what this was about.

Control.

Before I knew it, the lights were dimming and Will was shoving me toward his sleeping bag smack-dab in the middle of Michael, Kai, and Damon.

I groaned. Did I really have to be here?

"Take it." He pushed me again, and I stumbled. "I'm warm enough without it."

Like I care about your comfort. Seriously.

He laid down on the mat next to his sleeping bag—black with red-and-black-checkered lining—and I stood there, scowling.

Keeping my shoes on, I climbed inside the sleeping bag, seeing Crist on my right, Torrance lying at my feet, and Kai above me. Michael pulled off his T-shirt, his long, toned torso spread out next to me like he didn't know we were still in public no matter where we were sleeping.

I quickly turned away, heat rising to my cheeks.

I scooted up toward Kai—the safe one—but something grabbed my feet and yanked my ass back down. I glared at Will, but he just smiled to himself as the lights in the gym went off and everyone settled in, giggles piercing the air and chaperones patrolling to keep peoples' hands off each other.

Yes, let's lock up more than a hundred hormonal teenagers in one space. What a stupid idea.

My stomach growled, and I shot a glance up at Will, seeing his eyes closed, his arm propped up under his head as a pillow, and his lips curled with a smile.

He'd heard that. Someone brought me pizza earlier as I sat on the bleachers—maybe at Will's behest—but I told him to screw off.

Now, I regretted it. I hadn't eaten in over twenty-four hours.

The minutes passed, the chatter started to quiet, and Bryce started to snore from the other side of the gym. Arion Ashby slipped on her sleep mask and some students put on their expensive headphones to cancel out the noise.

I was too hungry to sleep, and the granola bar in my pocket called to me.

I turned my head, looking over at Will. His hair had dried, and even though I'd never seen it looking so messy, he still pulled it off, because he was born with it. Stern brown eyebrows, a sharp nose, but soft lips and the most beautiful eyes I'd ever seen behind those sweet, sleeping eyelids and long lashes.

Why couldn't guys this cute ever be nice?

I blinked, dropping my gaze. Of course, he did give me his sleeping bag.

And probably the granola bar and Godzilla, too, even though he broke into my locker to leave it for me.

"So, what were you trying to do?" I asked in a low voice.

"When?"

I looked up to see his eyes still closed. "You said you weren't trying to scare me upstairs," I told him. "So, what were you trying to do?"

His chest rose and fell in steady breaths, hesitating a moment. "I was trying to see if you liked it," he whispered.

If I liked what? Him?

The chase? The danger? The risk?

Well, I didn't.

But I couldn't help but ask, "And? What conclusion did you come to?"

The corner of his mouth curled into a smile, but he didn't open his eyes, and he didn't answer. "Go to sleep."

I turned my eyes back up to the ceiling, seeing the rain still hitting the skylight.

He needed to leave me alone. Just give up. If he kept pushing me, I'd do something stupid because I could feel it coming.

I clenched the sleeping bag in my fingers.

There were moments I wanted to do something outrageous. I mean, sure, I wanted a boyfriend. I wanted fun.

But I couldn't bring someone into my life. It was a nightmare, and I needed to keep it together for my grandma.

Just mess with someone else, Will Grayson. I don't want your attention.

Unable to stop myself, I turned my head again, taking in the peaceful look on his face as he slept. The way his neck looked so smooth and soft, and what would've happened upstairs in the chem lab if I hadn't pushed him away.

I would've regretted it, but I would've liked it, I think.

I stared at his lashes and the way they draped over his skin underneath his eyes.

My own burned with tears I refused to let loose.

I guess I understood people letting themselves be used, even for just a night if it meant not being alone for once.

I turned over on my side, watching him sleep, but then my eye caught something, and I looked down, seeing Damon lying on his stomach and watching me. His head was propped on his hand, his eyes sharp as he brought up his fingers and dragged his thumb across his throat, not blinking once as he stared at me.

I clenched the sleeping bag tighter at the small scowl in his eyes.

Rolling over, I stared at the ceiling again, getting the message. *You're not special, so don't get confused, girl.*

I reached into my pocket and fisted the granola bar.

But I was no longer hungry.

CHAPTER 5

WILL

Present

I stared at her through the two-way mirror as she stood on the other side, moving her gaze left, right, up and down, taking in Aydin's bedroom.

Noticing the bathroom, she hurried through the door and turned on the faucet, filling up a glass with water. She tipped her head back, gulped down the whole thing, and refilled again, drinking that, as well.

I finally blinked, balling my fists as I watched her in her tight, cropped black pants, and her sweet little, fitted white blouse with the collar buttoned right up to the neck. She might look like the grown-up architect she was if it weren't for the white Adidas sneakers instead of heels.

Amusement curled the corners of my lips, remembering over-hearing her words in class once. "It doesn't matter if I arrive in style if I can't arrive at all."

She hadn't changed a bit. Why the fuck was she here?

I let my eyes fall down her body, knowing she couldn't see me as I took in her dark hair, kinky and wild from the tumble. The heat on her cheeks, rosy against her golden skin, was still so beautiful, and I'd bet her slender neck could still fit in my hand.

My mouth watered, and my cock started to swell.

Coming back in the room, she carried a newly filled glass of water and set it down on the chest of drawers before walking around the room. Mud smeared her clothes, and a leaf stuck in her hair as she wrung her hands.

Micah and Rory dumped her in there an hour ago, while Aydin and Taylor went off somewhere.

Aydin would be back, though. I looked over at his bed, the largest in the house, with his fresh white sheets and luxurious, feather-down comforter.

Walking over, she lifted the pillow to her nose and inhaled his scent.

I narrowed my eyes, a knot tightening in my gut.

She pulled back, and then dove back in, drawing him in again. I clenched my teeth.

She dropped the pillow to the bed and continued around the room, opening drawers and closets, sifting through the medical notes and drawings on his desk and leaning down to inspect the jars of dead animals floating in formaldehyde.

Then, she picked up one of the bones strewn on his desk and lifted it up, turning it over.

She hissed, realizing what it was and threw it back onto the table. I smiled.

She took out the knife Aydin let her keep and gripped it in her fist before she downed another glass of water and then walked to the locked door, yanking on it.

It didn't give, though.

What did she think she was going to do?

What was I going to do? She was on my agenda, but not yet.

This changed things.

She paced and paced, breathing heavier and getting worked up, but then she stopped.

And she looked over at me.

I cocked my head as she thinned her eyes and stepped slowly over to the mirror on her wall, stopping directly in front of it.

The square mirror was about three feet on all sides, and she seemed to look through it, but her eyes never really found mine.

She couldn't see me, but she clearly knew it was more than a mirror. You could never get much over on her.

She peered around the edges of the mirror, trying to take it off the wall or pry it away enough to see behind, and I stepped closer until I couldn't step anymore.

Standing up straight, she held out her index finger and touched her nail to the surface, leaning in close to see if the reflection touched the tip. A little test to determine if a mirror was two-way or not.

The corner of my mouth curled up in a grin.

Her chest caved and she froze.

Uh-oh.

She stayed there a moment, and then . . . she rose up and stared through the glass, searching for whoever was watching her.

I raised my fingers to the mirror, less than a foot from her face as I stared into her stunning eyes. I swallowed the bitter taste in my mouth.

Nine years. Nine years, and I still wanted to fuck her.

Only now I wouldn't give her sweet and gentle. Shit had changed.

"You have to take," she said, staring through the mirror.

I trained my ears, listening.

"Because you're too weak to know how to win what you want. That's why you're in here."

She backed away and then shot out her foot, kicking the glass with a snarl on her face.

I stared.

"Come on, Will," she begged. "Stop the waiting and come on."

She kicked the glass again and again, baring her teeth, and I almost smiled again, remembering that night in the lab. How she challenged us, so ready to face danger.

So tough. So cocky. I liked stubborn. I liked women who took control.

But then she spoke up again, inhaling hard and shallow. "It's not my fault," she bit out. "It's not my fault that you wrapped your entire happiness up in some delusion you'd cooked up in your head where I loved you and life would be right as rain if we were together."

My amusement fell, and I flexed my jaw.

"I did what I had to do, and I'd do it again," she growled, her voice cracking. "I'd do it again."

She gasped for breath and closed her eyes, dropping her forehead into the mirror and punching the glass. "I'd do it again," she choked out, her voice thick with tears.

I moved my palm to hers, staring down at her, centimeters away as I rubbed her cheek with my thumb.

"No worries, baby," I murmured. "I intend to deserve it this time."

Excitement fluttered through my stomach, and I curled my fist, almost feeling her in it.

A knock sounded on the door, and it opened wide. Aydin entered carrying a plate.

My heart hammered, and I watched as he stopped and looked at her, his golden brown eyes dark with mischief.

"Are you hungry?" he asked her.

She shot her head up and whipped around like she hadn't heard him knock. Unsheathing the knife, she held it tightly at her side, backing up to put more distance between him and her.

He set the plate and silverware down and looked up at her as he slipped his hands into his pockets. "I said I wouldn't hurt you."

"I don't remember you saying that."

"No?" He smiled. "Well, I meant to."

He said no one would touch her. They weren't synonymous, I'd learned here.

He gazed at her, and I folded my arms over my chest, watching him watch her and waiting for any movement.

But he simply drew in a deep breath and turned around.

"Eat," he said, walking to the door. "And bathe. You're filthy."

He pointed to the white porcelain tub in the corner of the room.

"Or I'll bathe you," he warned over his shoulder. "And there are five of me to hold you down."

He closed the door, locking it, and she stood there for a moment, glancing from the door to me and back to the door again. Taking the chair at the desk, she fit it underneath the door handle—as if that would keep us out—and then she walked over, lifting the plate up to her face.

She sniffed the pasta.

He wouldn't poison her food. What fun would that be?

He was just getting started with her.

I closed my eyes, turning away.

I clenched the window frame on both sides, staring out into the vast, silent night high above the rest of the house.

Michael.

They'd sent her here. I knew it. But why? To motivate me?

It had to be them, and if they could get someone in, why not one of them?

I had my plans for her, but there were bigger things at play right now, and it wasn't the time.

Fuck.

I squeezed the frame, hearing the wood crack in my fist.

Did they know what she did? They would've had to in order for Rika, Banks, and Winter to be on board with this.

It was kind of cool, I guess. I figured they'd find me, and never doubted they'd look, at least, even if it did take them forever.

Unfortunately, none of it was necessary. I knew exactly what I was doing, and even though it pissed me off, I couldn't blame them for doubting that I was in control.

The stairs creaked, and I heard a voice behind me as someone entered my room. "Can you finish it?" Aydin asked.

I glanced over my shoulder, seeing him stand at the top of the stairs leading into my attic room. He walked over, carrying his shirt in his hand and holding my gaze like a snake.

Always like a snake, coiled for the kill, and when it struck, you didn't even know what had happened until it was over.

I nodded, pulling off my T-shirt and tossing it on my bed. I grabbed my kit and joined him at the leather bench I had sitting against the wall.

Setting his shirt down, he laid on the bench and tucked the other arm under his head as I poured the rest of the black ink I'd siphoned into a small dish.

I sat down and picked up the needles I'd tied to a pencil and dipped the tool in the ink. I approached him, leaning down to his right shoulder.

"So, what should I do with her?" he asked.

I faltered for a moment but then pressed the three-needle tool into him, breaking the skin as the ink seeped immediately into the wound.

I didn't answer, because I knew better than to answer.

"You didn't help her," he mused, unfazed by the pain. "She clearly expected you to."

I pressed again and again, redipping the needles into the ink every few moments as I tattooed the final line and colored it in.

His chest rose and fell in steady breaths, not missing a beat. I had some professional ink on my body, but a lot of mine was homemade like this, and I knew well it hurt.

Like Damon, though, it was the pain or it was nothing with Aydin.

"She's a fighter," he said.

He gazed up at the vaulted ceiling of my little hideaway that I'd moved into after my first night here. The white rooms and white rugs and white everything chilled me downstairs. I wanted my space, and I wanted it dark.

Plus, the windows opened up onto the roof up here. I liked the view.

"I love that about her," he continued. "As long as she doesn't hang herself with what little rope that I'm giving her. Did you notice that?" He looked at me. "It was like she didn't actually realize the gravity of her situation. Trapped—and no way to survive if she leaves—with five men who want to have the kind of fun we've been deprived of for so long. And if she complains, a simple matter of money can make it go away."

I clenched my teeth, pressing the needles in hard. His muscle jerked under my hand, but still, he stayed fixed on me.

"What was her name again?" he asked softly. "Emory?"

My arms burned until I realized every muscle in my body was tensed. I forced the lump down my throat.

"Those eyes . . ." he murmured. "Brown with flecks of gold. They're beautiful. I wonder what they look like staring down at you in the heat of it."

I stared so hard at his shoulder and the design he'd instructed I tattoo that I was surprised his skin didn't catch fire.

"How do I make her come?" he asked, watching me.

I tightened my hold on the instrument.

"Some women need a thumb on the clit when you're inside them, you know?" he taunted. "Does she like men to do that to her?"

I gritted my teeth, punching a hole in his skin and hearing the little *pop*. He hissed under his breath but then smiled, pleased he'd gotten to me.

"Our fathers didn't send us here to learn how to behave, Will. They would enjoy her, too, with or without her permission." He paused and then continued, "They sent us here as punishment for not being more mindful of discretion. To learn how to not be sloppy," he explained.

My father didn't send me here. I didn't understand how any father could send his child to a place like this, because one thing would be for certain if they ever got out: Blood isn't love, and love is the only thing that begets loyalty.

I looked at Aydin, who now stared at the ceiling again. In my time here, I'd figured out Micah, Rory, and even Taylor, but Aydin . . .

He'd been here the longest, and by this point, he might've come too far to go back anymore.

"When I was twenty, I was at a resort wedding," he told me, a faraway look in his eyes, "and I watched one of my father's business associates drug his own wife, lay her down on a bed, and back away as he let my father climb on top of her and fuck her to seal a deal."

I paused, something like pain crossing his eyes. But then it was gone.

"After a while, you know you'll never escape it," he said, "so you can either keep fighting the ugly, or you can reinvent it." He turned his eyes on me again. "The biggest difference between my father and me is I just didn't care if anyone saw the blood on the walls."

I couldn't move for a moment.

Em . . .

I dropped my eyes and finished the design, scratching in the last of the color.

"Don't worry," he told me. "I'm nothing like my father. Or Taylor, or Damon Torrance. I don't force or coerce." He dropped his voice. "It'll hurt you more if she wants it."

Then he reached down, kneading his cock through his pants, and the needles in my hand shook for a moment as the temptation sat there in my gut.

I had Micah and Rory. Taylor could be controlled.

No one would touch Emory if I ended Aydin right here and now.

He laid there, watching me and waiting for it, giving me my chance—daring me, but . . .

Finally, he just smiled and sat up, taking a clean cloth from the table and patting the blood off his shoulder.

"Everything is part of a bigger plan," he said. "Whether it's God or fate or something else, I honestly believe that, Will." He tossed the cloth and looked at me. "We were always going to be important to each other."

I raised my eyes, unable to hide the scowl.

He grabbed the back of my neck, giving me his reassuring little pat, and then nodded to the black garbage bags I had sitting close by to wrap up his tattoo.

"Finish me up," he said. "It's going to be a night."

CHAPTER 6

WILL

Nine Years Ago

I should've touched her.

I took a drag off the cigarette and dumped Damon's lighter back into the cup holder, blowing smoke out the driver's side window.

But no. She wouldn't have wanted me to.

I rubbed my temple and closed my eyes. She was killing me. Had been killing me for years.

Real monsters don't wear masks, William Grayson III. A smile pulled at my lips. She was unpredictable, though, wasn't she? I couldn't stop thinking about last night and the lock-in.

I took another drag and blew out the smoke as I squeezed the steering wheel under my fist.

"Is this pissing you off?" Michael asked next to me, and I could hear the humor in his voice as he relaxed his ass in the passenger side seat of my truck.

I looked over, seeing him stare at my white-knuckled fist wrapped around my steering wheel.

"Nothing pisses me off," I mumbled, seeing his head tilted back and his eyes hooded. "Except when I drive, it's Damon and me up front," I pointed out. "On the rare occasion you *let* me drive for the night."

"The only reason you're driving is so we can cart the keg to the church," he told me. "If you didn't have a truck—"

"Then I might be useless?" I finished for him.

He laughed.

But he didn't argue, did he?

"That three-pointer from the wing sure wasn't useless," Kai joked from the back.

I shot him a look in my rearview mirror, but his face was buried in some booklet.

I shook my head and turned my eyes out the window. I had my talents. At least I was on for the game last night.

"About fucking time," Michael grumbled.

I blew out a puff of smoke and followed his gaze, seeing Damon finally jog out of the cathedral and across the street.

Switching the cigarette to my left hand, I started the engine again.

"Get out." Damon opened up the passenger side door and jerked his thumb at Michael. "Now."

But Michael just sat there, looking amused.

Damon cocked an eyebrow. "I will put you in my lap if you want," he told him, "but I'm sitting there."

I laughed under my breath. Michael knew the rules. When he drove, which was almost always, Kai rode shotgun. When I drove, Damon and I were the ones in charge.

After twiddling his thumbs for a moment, Michael finally gave in. He hopped out of the truck, both of them trying to stare each other down like it was a pissing contest.

"I was almost hoping you'd put up more of a fight," Damon taunted.

Michael teased back. "Make ya hard, do I?"

Damon smiled and climbed in, while Michael circled the truck and got in behind me.

"What took you so long?" I griped, shifting the truck into gear. "What the hell do you do in there so long?"

"He's in there every Saturday night," Kai pointed out. "They got some meeting of the over-eighteen female chastity club or something?"

"Come on," Damon whined. "That's way too easy for me. They don't have to be eighteen."

"Or female," Kai added.

I snorted as Damon whipped around and threw a playful punch at Kai. "Bastard."

Kai just laughed, trying to shield himself.

I shook my head, pulling away from the curb and steering back onto the street.

But then Damon shouted at me. "Wait, wait, stop."

I slammed on my brakes, seeing Griffin Ashby, the town's mayor, dart in front of my truck.

Shit. That was close.

He looked over at us, dressed in his gray suit and yellow shirt and tie, narrowing his eyes on Damon as he crossed the street. Damon stared back, but when Ashby's gaze twisted into a scowl, Damon stuck up his middle finger, taunting him.

Ashby looked away, stepping up onto the sidewalk and disappearing into the White Crow Tavern.

I hit the gas, taking off down the street. "What is it with you and him?"

Damon sighed, taking a cigarette out of his pack and sticking it between his lips. "I ruined his daughter."

"Arion?" Michael asked. "Thought you said she had the brain power of a Pringle."

"Not that one," Damon mumbled, lighting his cigarette.

Ashby's other daughter had to be only fourteen or so. I'd never seen her and Damon together.

But his gaze was turned out the open window now as he smoked, and if I knew anything about Damon, it was that if he was vague, it was on purpose.

Heading up into the hills, I drove down the darkened highway, the sun having set an hour ago and the sky nearly black now.

Kai flipped a page in his booklet. "What is that?" I asked.

"Course catalog." He flipped another page, harder this time. "A fucking course catalog."

"Come to Westgate with me," Michael said.

"Or UPenn with me," Damon added.

I smiled. "Or Fiji with me."

"You're coming to UPenn with me," Damon told me.

Fat chance.

I flicked the ashes out the window and took another drag. College was months away, but decisions needed to be made soon. If I weren't a Grayson, I'd never be able to get into Princeton, but the fix was in, and I was off to Jersey next summer whether I liked it or not.

I couldn't think of anywhere I wanted to be less, but I also couldn't think of anywhere better to be. That was my problem. As my dad said, "Until you can make a decision, we'll make it for you."

Apparently, a beach bum in the Polynesian islands wasn't a lofty enough goal.

Kai tossed the catalog down on the seat next to him. "My father wants me on my own. He thinks we all need space."

"From all of us, or just Will and me?" Damon asked, humor lacing his tone.

Yeah, Katsu Mori didn't think much of us. Damon was trouble, and I was . . . nothing. At least Michael was ambitious. He was a leader, and Kai's father respected that as a viable influence for his son.

But Kai just joked back. "Don't be like that," he cooed to Damon. "He was really flattered you approved of his taste in women when you adjusted yourself right in front of him at the sight of my mother."

"In a bathing suit, Kai!" Damon pointed out, looking at Kai over his shoulder. "I mean, what the fuck? Jesus."

I shook with a laugh, remembering that day last summer when we were all at Kai's house.

"And you all think I don't have any shame," Damon said. "If she weren't your mom . . ."

"My father would still rip your dick up through your stomach and out your mouth?" Kai retorted.

Damon quieted, settling back into his seat and sticking his cigarette into his mouth. "Daddy's boy."

Kai shook his head, but I saw the smile fade as he looked out the window.

"Maybe we'll stay in the area and go to Trinity instead," Michael said, "so we can all be close to Kai's mom."

I snorted, all of us laughing as Kai rolled his eyes.

I took a puff off the cigarette, realization starting to dawn. It was months away, but it was coming. Different schools. Different states.

New people.

And that's what scared me the most. People change us. Others become important, while others become less, and soon, we'd be gone.

She'd be gone.

I turned my eyes out my window, the inevitable sitting on my shoulders like a house.

"Okay, Devil's Night . . ." Michael cleared his throat. "Probably the catacombs, but keep the cemetery in mind," he told us. "I'm thinking about changing it up this year. There are some tombs, and that Bell Tower through the woods. What are you guys thinking for your pranks?"

I couldn't think of anything yet. Nothing good anyway.

"I'm kind of thinking about getting out of town," Kai answered. "Meridian City. The Whitehall district, maybe. Or the opera house? Maybe book a floor at a hotel?"

"The whole point is to be here with our people," Damon told him. "On our turf."

Kai was silent, and I saw him open up his course catalog again, mumbling, "Just an idea."

I watched the both of them, kind of enjoying how they hardly ever got along. Kai was ready for tomorrow. Damon never wanted to leave today.

I had no idea where the hell I was half the time, let alone where I wanted to be.

An idea occurred to me, though. "The Cove," I said. "After hours."

Damon nodded. "That might be an idea."

I looked over at him. "I heard a rumor the place might not be open much longer."

"Even better."

"Too much of a liability," Michael interjected. "Drunk people get stupid, and stupid people on roller coasters will piss me off."

Come on. It would be fun. Just us and a few others—invitation only.

But as usual, my ideas were tabled.

"I'll think of something," Kai told him. "Something that lets us end the night in one piece, and between the sheets with something pretty."

"Hell yeah," Damon replied. "That's all you had to say."

I shook my head, remembering what our real priorities were. I rounded the bend, climbing toward the cemetery, but just then, blue and red lights flashed in my rearview mirror, and I spotted headlights charging me from behind.

"Ugh, fuck," I growled. "That son of a bitch."

Dammit.

Pressing the brakes harder than necessary, I jerked my truck over to the shoulder and halted, hearing the gravel kick up underneath.

"Will . . ." Kai started.

"I'll hold my tongue," I assured him, already knowing what he was going to say. I pulled the weed out of the center console and slipped it to Damon. "Get rid of this."

"Dude, what the hell?" Kai barked.

But I ignored him. "Get rid of it now," I told Damon again, turning off the engine. "And don't toss it out the window. His dashcam . . ."

"Goddammit," he grumbled, stuffing it into the glove compartment and slamming it closed.

"Lock it." I threw him the keys.

"You think he knows?" Damon looked at me as he quickly locked my glove box.

I peered into my side mirror, seeing Officer Scott walk up to my side with his flashlight beaming.

"I think Em is smarter than that," I said.

She wouldn't complain about last night and the lock-in. Tattling would dent her pride. Not sure how I knew that about her, but I did.

"Think he knows what?" Michael pressed. "What did you guys do? Dammit. You're always pulling shit when I'm not looking."

"We didn't hurt her," Damon assured.

"Just made her pee her pants a little," Kai added.

I bit back my smile just as Scott tapped on my glass.

I rolled down the window and flicked the butt of my cigarette out onto the highway, missing him by just a hair.

He stopped, turning his eyes toward the cigarette burning its last embers and back to me, flashing his light inside.

"Here to see that picture of me again?" I teased.

But he wasn't laughing. "License and registration, please."

I hesitated a moment for good measure, and then reached into the console, pulling out my registration and insurance card holder, and then my license out of my wallet.

I handed him both. "I promise you, they haven't changed since last week, Scott."

He didn't seem to hear me as he flashed his light on my license, like he hadn't seen it a dozen times in the past three months, and then my registration and insurance, as if he didn't already know that they don't expire until my next birthday.

"You know how fast you were going?" he asked, studying my insurance card.

"It wasn't fast."

"Have you been drinking?" he inquired, unfazed.

"No."

He paused, still looking over my material. "You on drugs?"

"Sometimes," I replied.

Damon snorted, and Michael cleared his throat to cover up his laugh.

Scott straightened and took a step back, looking down on me. "Step out. I want to look around the truck."

I couldn't stop myself. "Well, my glove compartment is locked, so is the trunk in the back, And I know my rights, so you go'n need a warrant for that," I sang.

Everyone started laughing, Damon shaking next to me, and Kai hunching over in my rearview mirror, his head in his hands to cover it up.

I always loved that Jay-Z song. At least I was good for a few laughs.

Officer Scott looked down at me, chewing the inside of his lip like he'd just love to have a reason. This was the kind of guy who would discharge his weapon on someone, claiming the cell phone in their hand looked like a gun.

The laughter calmed down, and I turned my eyes on him again.

"I'm sorry," I told him. "I'm an idiot."

I bid him to come closer, softening my voice.

"I know how you see me," I said. "Ignorant, arrogant, frivolous . . . I want to be good. Honestly. Goal-oriented, a hard worker, honest, righteous . . ." I paused. "Like Emory. Your sister, right?"

He narrowed his eyes on me, and I could see his shoulders tense.

"You know," I continued, "it's amazing that given the years your family has been in Thunder Bay, I don't know her as well as I'd like." I turned to my friends. "You hear that, guys? A girl I don't know."

Some laughter went off inside the truck.

I turned back to him, seeing the threat start to register.

We were starting to understand each other.

"All the hours we walk the halls together at school," I taunted. "All the hours on that bus to away games and back. All the late nights at basketball practice and her at band practice."

"Plenty of time to get to know someone," Kai added. "Turner didn't even need five minutes to get Evie Lind pregnant."

"Some of us have better longevity," I joked over my shoulder.

"We know you do." Michael patted my shoulder.

Hell yes, I do.

I turned my gaze back on Scott, seeing the corners of his eyes start to crinkle in a glare.

I hooded my own. "I promise you . . ." I growled low. "However much you don't like me, there is still so much more to come if you don't . . ." I pulled my license and card holder out of his hand, whispering, ". . . Stop pulling me over."

I was normally a happy boy, but his hard-on for me was fucking with my patience. He didn't pull over Michael, Damon, or Kai constantly. He messed with me because he assumed I didn't have a brain.

They thought that because I liked being nice, that I didn't know how to be mean.

And believe me, I was capable.

Snatching my keys from Damon's hand, I started the truck, cast Scott one last look, and took off, pulling back onto the road and cranking up the music as the wind blew through the cab.

"Be careful," Michael said after a minute. "That was entertaining and all, but men like him are shortsighted. I don't think he's going to have the sense to stop. Watch for his next move."

"Fuck him." I gripped the steering wheel. "What the hell's he going to do to me?"

No one said anything more as we pulled up the drive and through the open gates of the cemetery. My interest in Emory Scott had nothing to do with her brother, sadly. I wish it were that easy.

But I wasn't averse to killing two birds with one stone, either. How much would he lose his mind if he couldn't find her one night, and then found her with me?

The thought made me smile.

Winding around the avenues, I spotted cars ahead and flashlights and headed toward them, pulling up behind Bryce's black Camaro.

We hopped out of the truck. Michael and Kai grabbed a cooler out of the back and all of us walked over the grass, past trees and hedges, and up to the rest of the team already gathered around the grave.

"Hey, man," I greeted Simon and tipped my chin at the others.

More "heys" went off around the circle, and Michael and Kai set down the cooler, some of the team immediately digging in for a beer.

I looked down. "What the hell?"

Marker flags were stuck in the ground, lining the grass-covered gravesite, making a rectangle the width and length of a casket.

"They're digging him up," Bryce said, cracking a beer. "They're actually doing it."

I glanced over my shoulder, frowning at the newly finished, brand-new, piece of shit McClanahan tomb, complete with the arrogant columns and pompous stained-glass windows.

"He wouldn't want this," Damon said.

I looked back down at Edward McClanahan's grave, the old marble headstone green with age, rain, and snow, the years of his life barely visible anymore. But we knew his age: 1936 to 1954.

Eighteen. Young, just like us.

He'd be eighteen forever.

His surviving relatives wanted his legend to die, and the notoriety of the family name with it, so they built themselves a tomb, thinking they were going to hide him behind stone walls and a gate.

"They're not moving him anywhere," I said.

Michael caught my eye, a knowing smile curling his lips. Pulling the cell phone out of my pocket, I turned it on and started recording, documenting our annual pilgrimage to McClanahan's grave every year since freshman year.

Damon threw me a beer, and the rest of us cracked ours open.

"To McClanahan," Michael called out.

"McClanahan," everyone joined in, raising our cans in the air.

"The first Horseman," Damon chimed in.

"Give us the season," another said.

Michael, our team's captain, looked around. "Offerings?" he teased.

Jeremy Owens reached behind him on the ground and whipped out a pink tulle dress with a cheap silky bodice. It looked like a ballet costume.

"Close enough." He tossed the replica of McClanahan's girlfriend's Homecoming dress on the grave.

Simon took a swig of his beer. "All I want to know is what that bitch looked like splattered all over the rocks."

"We'll never know," Michael told him. "Only that when push came to shove, he did what he had to do. He sacrificed for the good of the team. For the family. When it comes down to it, would any of us do the same? He was a king."

Not *was* a fucking king. *Is* a fucking king, because to us, he was a living, breathing part of this town.

"Give us the season," Kai chanted, raising his beer.

"Remind us what's necessary," someone added.

And then everyone chimed in.

"For the team."

"For the family."

I moved the camera around the circle, taking everyone in.

"Give us the season," they called out.

"Give us the season."

And again.

And again.

Some poured a beer onto the grave, and all over the dress; the candles were spread out in devotion, flickering in the light breeze.

We didn't explain this to anyone ever. It was kind of like the people who didn't really believe in God but still went to church.

There was something to be said for tradition. Ritual.

It was good for the team.

The basketball team had been coming here for decades at the beginning of every season. We would never not come.

An hour later, a small bonfire burned inside the ruins of St. Killian's, the keg already half empty and laughter and shouting coming from down in the catacombs.

Damon sat in some dilapidated lawn chair, staring at the flames as two girls talked and kept an eye on him from near the sanctuary.

Waiting.

"I wish he'd gotten to grow up," I said, tossing a stick into the fire. "I wonder what he'd be like now."

"McClanahan?" Damon asked.

"Yeah."

He waited, the flames glowing in his eyes. "He wouldn't be special if he didn't die."

"He was special before that." He was a captain, like Michael. He was a leader, selfless, a fighter . . .

No one really knew what happened that night.

"He wouldn't be special," Damon repeated. "Everyone changes. We all grow up."

"Not me."

He breathed out a laugh. "You're going to have to be someone someday."

"I'm going to be Indiana Jones."

He just smiled, but kept his eyes on the fire. He never tried to drag me into reality as hard as Michael and Kai did. I had no clue what I wanted or who I wanted to be. I just wanted my people, and I wanted the girl of my dreams.

The girls giggled again, and Damon's eyes flashed up, seeing them. "Are you coming?" He sighed.

I followed his gaze, eyeing the legs and hair and how easy it would be to have some fun and get off, but . . .

"I don't know," I told him. "You ever think of doing this shit in the comfort of your bed?"

I was tired of playing in the catacombs, but Damon didn't like to play alone. He needed me.

I liked someone needing me.

"Why does no one ever get to go into your room?" I asked. "Not me. Not Michael. Not Kai. Definitely no girls. Can't we all go somewhere comfortable?"

"You wanna see my bed?" Damon teased.

"I'd like to make sure it's not a coffin."

He snorted, but still . . . he didn't answer the question. What was he hiding in there anyway?

I looked up at the girls again, but my gaze went right through them like they weren't even there.

I didn't want that tonight. I didn't want to play here.

I'd rather relive last night, even though all that girl and I did was fight.

I smiled to myself. She'd fallen asleep with her glasses on last night. I took them off. I loved the way her tie was always tightened half-assed, her cuffs were too long and never buttoned, and her skin was my fucking religion lately. Especially the skin on her neck.

I hated school, but I was dying for Monday. She was gone when I woke up this morning, and I wanted to see her look at me after last night.

Would anything have changed? Would the sharpness in her eyes have softened at all?

"You're not good enough for her," Damon said, breaking the silence.

I stared at him. How did he know what I was thinking?

"You'll never be good enough for her," he pointed out. "Best you hear it now."

"A friend would help me get what I wanted," I told him.

He fell silent, and I studied him.

"You don't want me to have what I want, though," I said. "You don't want Michael or Kai to have what they want."

"I shouldn't have everything I want, either," he argued. "Getting what you want risks losing what you already have, and nothing can come between us." He looked up, meeting my eyes. "Nothing will be as perfect as this. I don't like change."

He turned away again, gazing into the fire.

"Michael is always in so much control," he continued, his voice growing harder. "I'd love to show him what he really needs. I'd love to see Kai troubled and confused. Really fucking unhinged, so nothing I have can ever escape me. They act like they don't need us. I wish they knew that they did."

I knew what Damon did to sink his teeth into those around him.

"You wanna fuck me, too?" I said in a low voice, a soft smile tilting the corner of my mouth.

He grinned, still not looking at me.

But surprisingly, he replied, "Sometimes."

I stilled.

"Sometimes I think about her watching us," he went on. "I think she'd like it, but she'd hate that she liked it."

With Damon, he didn't see the person. He was attracted to control. Making people do things they wouldn't normally do. It was all about the turn of the screw. Like a fishhook, he burrowed his way into heads and stayed there, long after he'd gone.

And his friends were the most valuable thing to him. He'd die for us, but the scary part was, that might not be the worst that could happen.

"She'll never be to you what we are," he told me, "because she's too scared, too proud, and too boring." He stopped and finally turned to me. "She'd never love you like you deserve, because she doesn't respect you. You're too shallow to her."

And I felt my insides fold in on themselves, over and over, creating this hole in my gut, because I knew he was right, and fuck him.

What would she see in me?

And why the hell did I care? I was William Grayson III. The grandson of a senator. The best shooter on our basketball team, and she'll be coming to my company in ten years, begging for a grant to fund her stupid theory on the viability of rooftop farms with their own microclimates or some such shit.

I didn't need her.

I dug my keys out of my pocket, not caring where Kai and Michael had disappeared to. Everyone would find their way home.

I turned around. "I gotta go."

"Will."

But I didn't stop. Heading outside, I jumped into my truck and sped out of there, charging back onto the highway, and I didn't care if that asshole pulled me over again.

I rubbed my hand over my face, shaking my head as that whole conversation replayed in my mind.

Emory Scott hated me, but she hated nearly everyone. So, she was making me work for it. So what? I'd be disappointed if she didn't. She didn't respect Michael, Kai, or Damon, either. It shouldn't hurt.

But it did.

I always liked her. I always looked for her.

And over the years, passing her in the halls and feeling her in the classroom next to me, she got hot as fuck in ways no one else seemed to notice but me.

God, she had a mouth on her. I loved her attitude and her anger, because I was always too warm and I needed the ice.

It made me smile.

But I also saw things no one else did. The cute way she'd trip over a sidewalk slab or walk straight into a mailbox, because her eyes were lost in the trees over her head instead of watching where she was going.

How she'd push her grandmother in her wheelchair down to the village, both of them smiling and eating ice cream together. Emmy would hold her hand the whole time they sat.

The way she worked so hard, all by herself, without anyone to keep her company on her creative projects around town.

There was so much there that people didn't see. She shouldn't be alone all the time.

But Damon was right. She'd never be on my arm. She'd never let her guard down.

I turned, going past her street, and straight to the village, stopping at the gazebo she had started building before the school year started. Some project she'd convinced the city to let her build in the park at the center of the square.

She seemed to be here working if she wasn't at school or band practice. I stopped along the curb outside of Sticks, looking up into the park and the beams rising up toward the sky but no roof yet.

She wasn't there.

It was Saturday. She'd probably been there all day, but I'd missed it.

Pulling back onto the street, I drove past the cathedral, about to head home, but just then, I saw her.

She pulled the hood of her hoodie over her head, her long brown hair spilling out as she gripped the bag over her chest.

I kept driving but kept glancing behind me, watching her.

Her glasses made her eyes hard to see, but she had them buried in her phone anyway.

Damon was in there two hours ago. Was she? How long had she been in there tonight?

I thought she was Jewish. If not, I was going to feel stupid for the Yom Kippur gift I left in her locker.

I continued driving, watching her disappear in my rearview mirror, and I wanted to go back to find her, but I knew she wouldn't take a ride from me.

She wouldn't take anything from me.

I was nothing, and she knew it, and in ten years, she'd be amazing, and I'd be nothing.

She would never need me.

Within minutes, I was descending the steps of the catacombs, hearing whispers below and knowing which room Damon liked best.

I leaned on the doorframe, seeing him toss his shirt onto the floor before lifting his mouth off the girl he had laid on the table.

His eyes met mine, the other chick still in her clothes and straddling a stool in the corner.

Damon smiled, standing up straight. "Get your ass in here."

CHAPTER 7

EMORY

Present

I popped my head up, my eyelids heavy with sleep and my head pounding.

White filled my gaze as I jerked my head left and right, realization settling in.

It wasn't a dream. I was at Blackchurch.

Checking the door across the room, I saw it closed and the chair still fixed underneath the knob. I exhaled, pushing myself up from where I'd crouched in the corner to keep all angles in view.

I hadn't meant to fall asleep. I looked around for a clock, but there was nothing.

How long had I slept? I rubbed my eyes, pulling open a curtain and seeing that it was still dark outside. The forest laid beyond the tree line, the great expanse nearly pitch-black under the cloud-covered moon.

Would I still be alive if I were out there now?

Releasing the curtain, I eyed the two-way mirror to my right, wondering if they were watching me. Did all the rooms have those?

And why?

The floor above me creaked, and I shot my eyes up to the ceiling, the floorboards whining with someone's weight.

Where the hell were we? *Think, think.* The foliage outside, the trees, the moss on the rocks, and the air, heavy with moisture . . . Maybe Canada?

And we couldn't be as secluded as they thought. Checking out the fancy woodwork, ornate doors and fixtures, and the chandeliers I'd noticed in the house, I knew one thing for certain. Blackchurch wasn't always a prison. It wasn't functional as one.

Someone built it as a home, and a home this size was built for more than a family. It was built for entertaining. A place this size didn't run without support from a local population—servants, craftsmen, farmers . . .

My stomach ached with hunger as I looked at the pasta Aydin Khadir had left me on the bench at the bottom of his bed. The sauce had settled, and the noodles had yellowed, less opaque, but my mouth still watered looking at it.

I'd refused to eat it on the chance it was drugged—which was an entirely reasonable concern, since I must've been drugged when I was first brought here, but . . . I'd also slept without incident, so they clearly weren't waiting for me to be less on guard to attack.

This was his room, he'd said. He would've come back here to sleep if it was that time of night. Where was he?

Leaving the food behind, I twisted around, looking for the knife, and I grabbed it off the floor where I'd dropped it when I was sleeping. Taking it, I dashed into the bathroom, filled a glass of water, and downed a cup before wiping off my mouth and heading past his treadmill for the door.

I only hesitated a moment before pulling the chair away and slowly twisting.

The pulse in my neck pumped hard, even though I knew I wasn't in any more danger outside this room than in. If they had wanted to get in, they would've. I only put the chair up to give myself a warning before they broke through.

But I needed food not made by someone else, and I needed a better look at my surroundings.

Peering into the hall, I glanced left and right, half expecting to see a guard posted at my door, but the night outside the windows around the foyer darkened the floors and walls, the beautiful glow of the glass chandelier the only thing lighting the empty second floor.

There was no one.

That was weird. Were they that confident I wouldn't try to run again?

I looked right, scanning the wall and seeing the crack in the paneling. Doing one more sweep to make sure I was alone, I stepped out into the hall and dug my nails into the crack, trying to pry the panel away.

I knew it opened. Maybe someone hadn't been watching me in that mirror, but I knew the room was here, dammit.

After it didn't give, I planted both hands on the panel and pushed instead, hearing the springs snap and watching as the door immediately opened.

My heart skipped a beat, and I almost smiled.

I swung the door wide and looked inside the small room, seeing a chair sitting on a concrete floor, surrounded by concrete walls. I stepped inside and walked to the glass, turning to look into Aydin's room, the view spanning the entire width.

I shook my head. *Unbelievable.* Was Will here hours ago? Watching me?

Was someone else?

So many questions, but mostly . . . Were there more secret rooms and were they here when Blackchurch was someone's home?

Or were they installed when it became a prison?

Because if so, that meant there was indeed some kind of surveillance. Someone might be checking up on them more than just every thirty days. If there were hidden chambers, then there were hidden ways for people to get in and out.

I backed out of the room and closed the door, scanning the landing again. The shadows of the leaves on the trees outside danced across the railing that loomed over the foyer, and the water falling outside surrounded the house like a metronome—steady and constant.

Inhaling, the scent of old books and burning wood hit my nose, and I clutched the knife tightly at my side as I descended the staircase.

I wanted to go everywhere. See every room, inspect every closet, and get the lay of the land, but I had no idea what time it was, or which rooms would be occupied at this hour.

Stepping off the staircase, I walked through the foyer, passing a dark and empty drawing room, as well as a dining room on my right, and a ballroom and library to my left.

Candles flickered on antique silver candelabras that stood as tall as me around the foyer, and I stopped at one, staring at it for a moment.

The place had electricity. Why the ambience?

I picked up the matchbox on the nearby table and stole a couple of matches out of it, sticking them into my pocket.

Lightly stepping through the house, I sneaked right, toward the kitchen, but a cry echoed down the hall from my left.

I stopped and looked, the hair on my arms rising as I heard a grunt.

"Just leave it, Will!" someone growled.

I narrowed my eyes, inching toward the voice even though I should just run.

I passed a sitting room and an office, and kept walking down the hall, seeing movement on my left.

I turned and looked into a home gym, much like the wrestling room back in my old high school. A wide open-area mat surrounded by equipment—treadmills, ellipticals, free weights . . .

Taylor Dinescu did push-ups on the mat, his eyes darting up and locking with mine.

His sweaty brown hair stuck to his scalp as his naked chest and back glistened. My stomach dipped at the look in his eyes as his push-ups got faster and faster, and he continued to stare at me like I was something on his plate.

My heart beat in my throat, and I turned away, hearing a grunt from farther down the hall.

"Goddammit!" And then there was a crash.

I jumped, fisting the handle of the knife. What the hell? Following the noise, I stopped near a cracked door and peered inside.

"Just leave it!" Micah growled, falling into a dark wooden secretary, the books on the shelves tumbling out behind him.

Tears wet his cheeks, but fire blazed in his eyes as he pushed Will away.

I inched closer.

Blood was dripping out of Micah's nose. He was dressed in black pants while Will wore jeans, both shirtless, their forms lit only by the glow of a small lamp.

Will grabbed the back of Micah's neck and brought him in, forehead to forehead as Micah shook.

My heart ached a little, despite itself. What was wrong with him?

Will stared at him as their deep breaths fell in sync, harder and louder like they were getting ready for something, and then Will took hold of Micah's arm, grabbed the side of his neck with his other hand, and shoved hard, a low, hollow *pop* sounding as Micah cried out.

"Ah!"

I winced.

"Motherfucker!" he shouted as his shoulder was snapped back into its socket, choking on the pain and shoving the secretary over until it crashed onto the floor.

Jesus. How the hell did that happen?

Sweat coated Micah's black hair, which hung over his eyes, ears, and down his neck, and he leaned into the wall, gasping for breath as the color drained from his face.

I wasn't sure how old he was, but right now, he looked twelve and helpless.

Will handed him a bowl of something with an eating utensil.

But Micah pushed it away. "I'm gonna be sick."

And at that moment, he grabbed the copper wastebasket and leaned over, spilling whatever was in his stomach.

I looked away for a moment, but then I heard more growls and grunts coming from farther down the hall and looked toward it, but couldn't see anything.

Micah wiped off his mouth and set the wastebasket down as Will set the bowl on the little table.

"Eat it when you're ready," he told him.

"I can't take your food."

Will picked up an elastic bandage and started unraveling it, probably meaning to wrap up Micah's arm.

But Micah pushed that away, too. "Don't," he said. "I don't want him to see."

Who? And see what? That he was hurt?

Just then, Micah looked up and met my gaze, finally seeing me hiding behind the door.

I straightened as Will followed his gaze, noticing me, too.

Walking over, he kicked the door, slamming it in my face, and I blinked, startling.

Prick.

Ruckus sounded from somewhere down the hall, and then a growl, and I looked toward the kitchen and back again, gauging my choices as my knee bobbed.

I should get back to the kitchen. No one was paying attention, and for all Aydin knew right now, I was sleeping. I could grab some provisions and be two miles downriver before he realized.

But . . .

Another cry pierced the air, and my curiosity got the better of me.

Continuing down the hall, I followed the sounds and rounded a corner, seeing white and blue ahead, as well as steam rising into the air through the open door down the hall.

Hiding behind the frame, I peered inside, taken aback by the sight of an indoor pool.

And heated, judging by the steam rolling off the surface.

I scoffed. *Rich boys . . .*

Two men rolled around on the mat laid out on the white-tiled pool deck, and I inched in, hearing Aydin talk to Rory as he pinned him to the mat.

"Ask for it," Aydin taunted him. "He can have it. All you have to do is ask."

Rory Geardon shot up, grabbing Aydin by the neck and trying to throw him over, but Aydin flipped him over, his naked chest on Rory's bare back as he whispered something in his ear.

Rory bared his teeth, pain in his blue eyes at whatever Aydin was saying. And déjà vu hit me, remembering a similar wrestling match I'd seen with Will.

Wood creaked next to me, and I tore my eyes away from the match and looked at the wall, feeling a vibration behind it on my shoulder.

It sounded like the movement I heard upstairs.

I stood up straight, ready to lean in and listen some more, but then I saw shadows fall behind me and turned my eyes to see Taylor, followed by Will and Micah, heading for the pool.

They stalked past me, each one throwing a look before stepping inside the room. I hung back, watching as Rory growled under Aydin's attack.

"All the pleasure you got from their pain," Aydin told him. "You knew it was going to cost something someday, didn't you?" He bit his ear, pulling it as every muscle on Rory's body tensed.

Aydin released it.

"But no," the alpha continued, "you only dish it when you're sure you can win. On girls who couldn't even tell you were coming for them. You knew that wasn't going to last forever, right?"

What was he talking about? Was that why Rory was here?

Taylor smiled, clearly enjoying the scene. Micah stood at the edge of the mat, looking helpless as he stared down red-eyed.

Girls who couldn't even tell you were coming.

What did that mean?

"Say it, socio." Aydin leaned into his ear again. "'I'm. So. Fucked. Up.'"

Rory resisted, trying to turn away—find a way out—but the cut on his brow dripped blood into his eye, and he just remained silent.

"'I'm,'" Aydin recited, egging him on, "'so fucked up.'" And then he dropped his voice to a hard whisper we all could hear. "In the head."

A sob escaped Rory, and he squeezed his eyes shut like he was afraid it was true.

I looked over at Will, his gaze locked on the scene playing out.

But he must've sensed me watching because he looked over at me, his expression unwavering but his eyes hard.

Why aren't they helping him? The only person who seemed to be enjoying the show was Taylor. Was this how Micah got injured? Fighting Aydin?

"They're never going to let you out," Aydin told the man under him. "I'm your family now."

Rory gasped, not looking happy about it, and Aydin shot off him, standing up and walking to the small table at the edge of the pool.

Taking a bottle of Johnnie Walker Blue, he poured himself a glass of Scotch and threw it back, everyone watching him.

I thought Taylor said they didn't have liquor here.

Will walked over, and Aydin set his glass down, telling him, "Just ask."

But Will just grabbed for the bottle, and Aydin grabbed him, a hand at the back of Will's neck and the other squeezing his throat.

"Look at me," he told Will, their noses almost touching.

And then, Aydin's gaze flashed over to me, a bitter smile playing on his lips and a sinking feeling hit my gut.

He controlled everything.

Shoving Will away, he brought his hand down hard, slapping Will in the face.

"Ask," he said again.

Will stumbled, his back to me, but after a moment, he rose again, standing tall.

Aydin shook his head, charging up to him and slapping the same side again and again, pushing Will back until he lost his footing, spun around, and dropped to his hands and knees.

Tears filled my eyes. I stared down at Will as he took a moment to catch his breath, and then he rose back up, facing Aydin and steeling his spine for more.

What the hell was he doing? Will could fight. He wasn't even trying.

What had happened to him?

Aydin stepped up, nose to nose, and gazed into Will's eyes. "He's hurting," he said to him. "Ask me or beat me, and you can have the whole bottle."

The bottle. I eyed the Scotch whisky.

And then to Micah. Rory and Will were trying to get Aydin's liquor to soothe Micah's pain.

The muscles in Will's jaw flexed, and Aydin didn't wait for his answer. Balling his fist, he reared back, swung, and slammed Will across the jaw, then grabbed his head and brought it down on his knee.

I gasped as blood spurted from Will's nose and he fell to his knees again. I started to rush toward him, but he shot out his hand, stopping me without a look in my direction.

He sucked in air, eyes squeezed closed as he wiped the blood away from his mouth and knelt there, trying to get his legs under him again.

Finally, shaking, he rose to his feet.

But Aydin just chuckled and walked away, pouring himself another drink.

"I can't trade with someone who doesn't play," he said.

Will stood there bleeding, and I moved a little, trying to catch his eyes.

But just when I thought he was going to look at me, he looked away instead and walked off the mat.

What had happened to him? He wasn't the leader in high school, either, but he never let anyone treat him like shit.

"Sleep well?" Aydin asked.

I blinked, realizing he was talking to me.

"Taylor thought for sure we'd have to pry you out of that room," he mused, taking a towel and wiping the sweat off his face.

He tossed the towel on a nearby chair, his gaze falling to my hand and the knife in it.

"You may as well relax," he told me. "You're not leaving."

"I'm not staying."

He laughed, unfastening his belt. "Denial. The first phase. I remember it well," he mused, dropping his pants to the floor and leaving him in his boxer briefs. "Dealing with the loss of freedom and choice are exactly like dealing with the loss of a friend or parent. 'This isn't happening. This isn't my life now. There has to be some way out of this . . .'"

He stared at me, amused, and then he peeled down the rest of his clothes, leaving him completely naked.

Heat rose up my neck, but I clenched my jaw and kept my eyes dead center on that stupid smirk of his as the others stood around, remaining silent.

"You're dirty." He sighed, throwing back another swallow of liquor. "I warned you that we'd bathe you if you didn't do it yourself."

"You're going to have to, hotshot," I fired back. "I don't listen to you."

"Oh, what a delight." He smiled, turning and dropping waist deep into the pool. "I was so hoping you were going to make this hard."

I glanced at the doorway I came through, wishing I'd gone for the kitchen like I was supposed to.

"Are there more people in this house?" I asked.

He splashed water on his face, coating his chest, as well. "Why would you think that?"

"I heard movement above me in your room a few minutes ago," I told him.

Maybe if I got them distracted, searching the house, I could get to the kitchen. I might not get out of here tonight, but I could hoard some food.

"And again, in the walls down here," I said. "But you're all in here."

I didn't pass anyone on my way downstairs, and it appeared they were all already down here when I arrived.

"You've never heard anything before?" I asked.

The surveillance room, probably one of many, and movement in areas of the house where there weren't supposed to be people?

But he knew where I was going with my train of thought. "There's no help for you here."

He sank below the surface, submerging his body, and rose up again, swimming to the other side and then smoothing his dark hair over the top of his head as the steam billowed around his body.

Unable to stop myself, I dropped my gaze. The curves and dips of his tight stomach, the bronze skin that looked like he was loved by the sun on some Mediterranean island instead of a cold, desolate house in the middle of nowhere, and looking at the V of his hips that disappeared down into the water would make lots of women—and men—happy.

And I had no doubt he was well aware of it.

"Come here," he said softly.

I darted my eyes to his, seeing him tread through the water to the edge closest to me, looking like a god on Earth.

Too bad for him, I worshipped no one.

"Why do you control the food?" I demanded, staying right where I was.

"Why *would* I control the food?" he challenged and then looked behind me. "Taylor?"

I looked over my shoulder, seeing Dinescu approach. I moved away.

"Because we're surviving," he answered for Aydin. "When you can't run to the supermarket or get takeout from a restaurant, you have to make sure people don't overeat."

"Or maybe controlling basic necessities helps you control the people," I retorted, shifting my gaze from Taylor to Aydin.

It was a basic tactic common amongst dictators. When people spent their days fighting for food, shelter, and safety, they didn't have the time or energy to fight for anything else. Keep them poor, hungry, and dumb.

"In any case," I said, looking him up and down, "you don't seem to be underfed."

Unlike Will, who gave his rations to Micah—and how often was he doing that anyway?

But Aydin simply smiled. "Stay on my good side, and you won't be, either."

I'd rather eat razors.

He walked out of the pool. Taylor tossed him a towel, and I watched him dry off his face as he stood there naked, because he could.

"You want to walk out of here with a bag of food and water, right?" he guessed. "Maybe a sweater?"

Yes.

"Tell you what, then . . ." he said. "We earn what we eat here. You can fight for it. If you win, you can leave. Or try to," he added. "But if you lose, I'll show you to your own room with a private bath and some clean clothes until the restock team arrives in twenty-nine days."

He wrapped the towel around his waist and approached me.

"Or, if you prefer, we can come up with another arrangement." His eyes drifted down my body. "Women have their uses, after all."

Taylor laughed under his breath to my left, and I stared at Aydin, trying to keep my nerves in check, even though my insides were bouncing off the walls.

Fight for it? Jesus, he was so nervous about how the size of his cock measured up against everyone else here that he made them fight him—or beg—for whatever it was they wanted or needed.

Did he expect me to have a chance?

"Ready to give up?" he asked, a smile ghosting his lips.

But I stood there, thinking about my options. I could hunker down, earn his trust, hoard supplies when no one was watching, and then make my escape some night when they'd lowered their guard.

That would be smart.

But I also had no idea I wouldn't be put through hell in this house if I stayed, either. I couldn't risk it.

"All I have to do is win?" I pressed.

Will lurched forward before he could respond, his whole body tight and flexed.

"One more step," Aydin growled over his shoulder to Will, "and the choice is no longer hers. We can explore a whole slew of other arrangements to help her earn her freedom."

Will halted, breathing hard, and the first glimpse of worry in his eyes I'd seen since I got here darted between Aydin and me.

"Isn't that right, Micah?" Aydin prodded. "And Rory?"

Both boys stood off to the side, bleeding, sweaty, and defeated. "Right," they murmured with their eyes downcast.

Taylor stepped forward, throwing off the towel around his neck and circling me in his black sweatpants.

I took in his wide chest, thick arms, and the ridges of his stomach, flexing as he stepped around me.

I spun around slowly, following him.

All I needed was one good hit. The jaw was the knockout button. If I hit his jaw, he'd go down like a dead deer.

"If you're lying," I said, turning my gaze to Aydin, "they'll know your word means nothing."

He nodded once. "You win, you walk." And then he waved his hand, signaling us to start. "Taylor?"

"No, me." Will pulled up next to Aydin. "Let her fight me."

"But then how can you watch?" he retorted.

He didn't really want Will to answer the question. He knew—love me or hate me—Will would go easy on me, and I was starting to get the feeling that Aydin wanted this to hurt Will, too.

Hands slammed into my chest, and I flew back, the wind knocked out of me as I landed on my ass.

Shit.

Pain shot through my tailbone, and I sucked in a breath, déjà vu washing over me.

"Instead of winning, maybe you should worry about just staying on your feet," Taylor teased, followed with a laugh.

It sounded like Martin, though, the dark sound burrowing through my stomach like a screw.

I pushed myself to my feet, feeling Will off to the side, the energy in his legs ready to move at any second.

But I didn't need him.

I reared back my fist, aiming straight for Taylor's jaw, but he caught it, squeezing my wrist with one hand and throwing the other across my face.

"Ah," I gasped, my cheek bursting into flames.

Grabbing the back of my hair and making my scalp scream, he threw a fist into my stomach, and I collapsed to my knees before another hand flew across my face again. Blood filled my mouth, my eyes watered, and I could barely see.

No.

I clenched my teeth to keep the cry in, but then I remembered my grandmother wasn't upstairs to hear anything.

"Enough!" I heard Will yell.

I flexed the muscles in my thighs, forcing my legs to stop shaking. Will had never seen me get hurt. He didn't know what I could take.

And Taylor Dinescu was nothing.

Opening my eyes, I saw his groin right in front of me, and I shot out the palm of my hand, roaring and using every ounce of strength as I slammed my hand into his dick and then quickly rolled backward, out of his reach.

He howled, falling to one knee, and I threw off my glasses and charged for him while he was down. I jumped onto his back, locking my arm around his neck and squeezing as hard as I could, paying no mind to the whispers or chuckles going off around the room.

Taylor hunched over with my weight on him, but pushed himself to his feet, breathing a mile a minute and no longer at ease.

"I went easy with those hits," he gritted out.

"And believe me when I tell you I know how to take one," I replied.

He popped up, flying backward, and I cried out, seeing the ground rush us over my shoulder. I landed on my back with his weight crashing into me on top, and I coughed and gasped for air, my ribs aching with pain.

"You fucking bitch," he muttered.

He rolled over, shooting off me, and I opened my eyes in time to see his foot come in for my head.

I widened my eyes and rolled away, my heart in my throat just as the toe of his foot hit me in the eye.

Fuck.

I squeezed my eyes shut, and I could feel the blood dripping over my cheekbone.

"Goddammit," Will yelled. "Enough!"

"Is that enough, Emory?" Aydin chimed in. "You giving up?"

I didn't have a chance to respond. Taylor straddled me, slapping me once and then again, and I barely had time to catch my breath before he planted his hand over my mouth and plugged my nose.

I inhaled, blood coating my face, but I couldn't get any air in. My lungs constricted, my brain shut down, and all of a sudden, I was home with Martin like it was yesterday. I thrashed, flailing my hands as my body screamed for oxygen. I slapped Taylor's chest, scratched his face, and clawed his neck, kicking and squirming under his hold.

His thighs tightened around me, and I twisted and twisted, trapped. I couldn't breathe. I couldn't move. Tears filled my eyes as my pulse flooded my ears.

No, no, no . . .

He leaned down next to my ear. "I could be inside you in three seconds," he whispered. "And I will be when—"

I pounded my fist, slamming it right into his jaw, and his head bobbed, his whole body going slack.

He loosened his hold just enough, and I pulled his hands off my face, sucking down air as I pushed him off me.

Scrambling to my feet, I spun around and backed away, seeing him sitting on the mat and holding his jaw, glaring at me.

But he wasn't moving for me yet.

I pivoted, staring at Aydin. "Open the door," I demanded.

He cocked his head but didn't budge.

Spotting the bottle on the table, I snatched the hem of my shirt, tearing it at the seam and ripping off a chunk as I raced for the bottle.

Grabbing it, I stuffed the cloth in, backed up toward the door, and pulled out one of the matches from my pocket, dipping down to swipe the tip over the dry grout between the tiles.

I faced the room full of boys as blood dripped down from my eyebrow and the corner of my mouth.

I met Will's eyes, hoping he noticed the symmetry in the Molotov cocktail. He knew this trick well.

"Stay back!" I ordered them, holding the bomb and the fuse.

Aydin still inched forward, drawing close. "You think I won't handle you myself if I have to?"

"I think you want something from me, too, so . . ." I stated. "Better stay on my good side."

He laughed. "Oh, phase two," he mused. "Anger. I was so looking forward to this one."

Instead of being worried I could burn down their entire shelter with this one bottle, he was excited. Taylor rose from the mat, all five of them facing me and moving toward me as I drifted down the hallway.

Was I really doing this? Leaving now? No food, no clothes, no help? He wasn't backing off. They weren't going to let me run.

Whatever I did, I had to do it now.

I lit the cloth, raised the bottle over my head, hearing the liquid slosh around inside, and they stopped, looking halfway between charging me or retreating.

Fuck it. I launched the bottle, the glass crashing and flames bursting forth, consuming the hallway as they scrambled back, and I swung around, charging for the front door.

They'd have to go around. There was a back door in the natatorium for them to get out, and I couldn't believe I'd done that, but that was me. Given the chance to run, I always ran.

Digging in my heels, I raced for the front door and swung it open, but then suddenly, Taylor was there, pulling me to a stop right on the front stoop.

I gasped, stumbling back, and he charged toward me, the rest of them shouting from outside, too.

They . . . they were already rounding the house. *Shit.* It only took a moment to decide. Twisting around, I scurried up the stairs, remembering that I saw a balcony overlooking the waterfall somewhere on the second floor. If I could get to it, I could shimmy down a pipe and run.

With Taylor on my tail, and the rest of the boys barreling into the house, I raced across the landing on the second floor, someone grabbing my hair from behind and yanking me back.

I whipped around, shoving Taylor away, but I lost my footing and tumbled over the railing, his fists gripping my collar and holding me as my legs flailed fifteen feet off the ground.

"Ah!" I cried out, grappling for his arms. I met his angry blue eyes as he just held me there. The fire extinguisher went off downstairs, putting out the fire, and the fabric of my shirt started to rip.

I gasped.

Taylor growled as he tried to raise me, but then . . . he lost hold, shooting out his hands and trying to catch me again. Rory appeared, diving for me just as I fell.

I slipped, descended, and Rory toppled over with me, both of us flying through the air to the floor below.

I screamed, crashing to my side on the hard, marble surface, and I looked up, seeing the blond boy fall through the air right for me. He hit the ground next to me, his head whipping back, and I shot out my hands, catching his skull right before it cracked against the floor.

We both breathed hard, his head cradled in my palms next to me, and he blinked, finally meeting my eyes.

Then he closed them, relief falling over his face.

"Jesus Christ," Will said, rushing over.

He took my head in his hands, inspecting me.

"Fire's out," Micah called. He rushed over to Rory, holding his face and gliding his hands over his torso and arms. "Anything broken?" he asked him.

Rory shook his head, and I watched Micah's thumb rub across Rory's cheek.

I moved my eyes around, trying to reconnect with my body, but I couldn't tell if I was in one piece. Everything hurt.

"Emmy, Jesus . . ." Will glared at me, his eyes drifting down my body.

But before he could say more, Aydin dove in and swept me into his arms, something between a scowl and worry playing in his eyes, too. "Get her some food and water," he ordered someone. "And get my kit, some clean bandages, and some alcohol."

He carried me up the stairs, and I watched Will and Micah sling Rory's arms around their necks and walk him, following us.

Will met my eyes over Aydin's shoulder, and while I couldn't tell what he was thinking, he didn't look away.

"You're a fighter," Aydin said. "I like you."

What? I gaped at him, in too much pain to even roll my eyes.

"You saw the bones in my room today?" Aydin asked.

I didn't reply.

"That was someone else who thought he could run," he explained. "We found what was left of him three months later when we were out hunting."

Another prisoner tried to escape?

It was definitely a human bone. A femur. I knew it the moment I picked it up.

I'd dropped it just as quickly.

I didn't know if an animal got him or the elements, and I didn't ask.

And then I remembered something else he'd said. *His kit. Bandages.*

Then there was all that stuff in his room. Biology. Drawings. Notes.

"You're a doctor?" I said, finally realizing.

"When I want to be."

"How long have you been here?"

He met my gaze. "Two years, one month, fifteen days."

I swallowed the lump in my throat. The idea of Will being here that long hurt.

"Use your head," he told me, carrying me into his room as if I weighed nothing. "You'll need it to stay alive, because this is not how we end, Emory Scott."

Despite myself, I almost smiled.

But I didn't.

No. This wasn't how I ended.

I had twenty-nine days.

CHAPTER 8

EMORY

Nine Years Ago

I lifted one book after another, loose papers flying everywhere as I searched for my *Lolita* packet at the bottom of my locker. Old math papers, tattered and crinkled, blanketed the floor, and I held out book after book, fanning each one for any sign of my missing homework.

Shit.

That packet was more than a week late. Where the hell did it go?

Tears stung my eyes. I couldn't believe I was about to cry over this. I should've just done it when it was due instead of dragging my feet. *This is what I get.*

I knew I lost shit when that asshole Anderson knocked my books out of my hands yet again last week. Everything scattered over the floor of the crowded hallway, passing students kicking my crap as they went.

I'd lost it. Townsend wasn't going to give me another one.

Sifting through the mess, I quickly gathered up the old papers that had spilled onto the floor and stuffed them back into my locker, rising off my knees and pulling out the books on the shelf. I searched those pages as well, one last-ditch effort for hope that it was still somewhere.

"You okay?"

I glanced over my shoulder, seeing Elle walking toward me with a backpack on one arm and a trumpet case in another.

"Fine," I said, turning my attention back to my search.

"Well, everyone is about gone," she said. "It's getting dark."

She kept walking, but spun around to watch me as she spoke.

"Need a ride?" she asked.

"No, thanks."

"'K, see you tomorrow."

"Night," I told her, not bothering to look.

What was I going to do? School had ended two hours ago. The teachers were gone, and band was gone, practice having ended over twenty minutes ago. It was too late to find my bandmate Joseph Carville who shared that class with me to see if I could make a copy of his on the printer in the library.

But of course, he'd probably turned his in last week anyway.

I slammed my locker shut. The silence of the empty hallways only made the thoughts in my head louder.

This was my fault, and I wouldn't even be able to blame Martin for getting upset when he saw the missing assignment on my records. It was almost as if I enjoyed provoking him.

I was stubborn to the point of being self-destructive. I was asking for it.

Diving down, I swiped my bag off the floor, but instead of heading out the doors toward home, I went back the way I came—down the stairs, down the hallway, and toward the locker room.

"Come on," I heard someone suddenly say. "You can do better than that."

It sounded like Damon Torrance. I passed the wrestling room and peered inside, seeing him pin another kid to the mats as the basketball team worked on the weights nearby and his friends stood around, watching with amusement.

I kept going.

But then I heard another voice. "Why don't you pick on someone your own size?"

I slowed and then . . . stopped, tingles spreading up my arms at hearing his voice. I hesitated a moment and then retreated, hearing thuds on the mat as I peeked around the corner.

Will grunted, plastered to Damon's back and pinning him to the ground as the poor kid from before stood by, smiling that the jerk was getting a dose of his own medicine.

Damon jerked, freeing his arms, but Will grappled for them, quickly securing them again between their bodies and using his weight to keep them there.

"I'm letting this happen," Damon gritted out.

"Sure, you are." Will's body shook with a laugh behind his friend, and his grin just looked so happy and easy. I started to smile, too, but stopped, remembering myself.

He must've sensed me, because he looked up and met my eyes.

The pulse in my neck throbbed, but I didn't run.

It was weird. He'd left me alone since the lock-in. Days and not a single word in lit class or a single look in the halls.

I was glad for it. I didn't want his attention.

Turning around, I continued on my way to the locker room and pushed through the doors, turning on the lights.

I slipped into my black swimsuit bottoms and matching, long-sleeved rash guard and then pulled my hair into a low ponytail. Grabbing a fresh towel off the cart, I headed to the indoor pool, leaving the lights off because the emergency track lighting was always on and that was enough for me. I didn't want to alert anyone on the outside that I was in here when it was supposed to be empty.

Setting my towel down on a bench, I kicked off my shower shoes and walked up to the edge of the pool, stretching my arms and shoulders as I hopped up and down to warm up my muscles.

The chlorine in the air tickled my nostrils, and my blood coursed hot down my legs in anticipation.

I'd missed this. I loved the water.

Climbing up on the riser, I pulled down my goggles and bent over, gripping the end of the platform and blowing out a few quick breaths.

Drawing in one large gulp of air, I pushed off, diving into the pool and fishtailing as I cut through the water.

The icy cold was like a needle in every pore of my skin, but I exhaled out of my nose and then shot out, one arm after the other, freestyling at a nice, steady pace to the other end.

I wasn't here to race, but I wanted to sweat, too. Keeping my eyes down, I tilted my head to take in air every three strokes before putting it back in the water.

Spotting the black marker on the tile below, I took one more stroke and flipped over, pushing off the wall and heading back the way I came.

I could say band and swim were an excuse to be out of the house. That my project in the park was something else I used to avoid going home. That all these activities were things I could do relatively alone without too many others, especially peers, interfering in my role.

The truth was, I liked showing people what I could do. To the town with the gazebo. To the few students and parents who had showed up to cheer us on at swim meets when I was on the team. To the whole school when I walked the football field and played the flute.

Every little thing you could do made you feel stronger. *I have this, so I don't need you. I have that, so I don't need you.*

Sometimes I was able to kid myself into believing that having this or being able to do that made me too busy and too important to possibly care about everything that I didn't have and everything I'd never be.

Like a smiler.

Like friends.

Like having someone who loved to tickle me and kiss me all over my face, not just on my lips.

Nah. Being able to swim the hundred-meter freestyle in forty-eight seconds was really what life was all about. That made me happy. I didn't need that other shit.

Charging toward the other end, I flipped, pushed, and headed back the other direction, deep in my rhythm now and the worries and stress burning away like fog in the sun.

I tilted my head, took a breath, and stuck my face back in the water, but just then there was another face looking straight up at me from the bottom.

I screamed, bubbles pouring out of my mouth like a goddamn geyser. What the hell?

I halted and scrambled to get my head above water.

But before I could get to the surface, something wrapped around my ankle and yanked me back down.

I screamed louder, my submerged cries muffled as I flailed.

Then, I inhaled. A gulp of water lodged in my throat, and I shot out my foot, kicking the prick so hard pain fired through my toe and straight up my leg.

Gasping and sputtering, I broke through the surface, coughing as I tried to escape.

But then . . . someone else took hold of me. "Whoa, whoa, whoa," he said, pulling me to him and holding me with one hand around my waist, and the other under my thigh. "Calm down."

I coughed, only managing short, shallow breaths as my lungs cleared, and I wiped my eyes.

"Piss . . ." I choked out, blinking and seeing Will Grayson holding me. "Off."

But I was coughing too hard to sound stern, and he just snorted, laughing.

I pushed away. "Get off me."

"They're just fucking around, Emmy."

He let me go, and I looked over, seeing Michael and Kai waist deep in the pool and talking to Diana Forester, while Damon slammed his fist in the water and shot daggers at me with his eyes. Blood poured out of his left nostril as he reached onto the deck for a towel.

Asshole. I could've drowned.

A blonde came up behind Will, watching us before taking his hand. "I have to be home by ten," she said. "Come spend time with me."

His eyes stayed fixed on me. "You okay?"

I shot him a snarl as I walked for the edge.

"Then go home," he ordered me, turning away.

I whipped around, still trying to catch my breath. "I was here first."

He looked from the girl back to me, a smile playing in his eyes. "Suit yourself."

Leaving her, he stalked toward me again, and I backed up until I hit the edge of the pool. He stopped and fiddled with something under the water.

In a moment, he leaned over and pulled the black mesh shorts he was wearing in the wrestling room out of the water and threw them over my head, onto the pool deck.

I stopped breathing.

Whistles and hoots echoed in the room, and I stared up into his eyes, the moments stretching to an eternity as he waited for me to do something, and I almost thought he wanted me to.

Instead, I turned around and grabbed the ladder.

But he took my arm and pulled me back, my body slamming into his chest.

I whipped around and shoved hard against his chest, but he barely moved.

Anger boiled in my gut. His hand was still wrapped around my arm, and for a moment, I almost let my eyes drop down to the water to see if he really was naked.

Raising my hand, I slammed it across his face again and shoved him in the chest, pushing him away. The girl was gone. I had no idea where.

"You grab me again, and I won't care about the consequences," I growled low.

Turning around, I started to climb the ladder.

But then he said behind me, "Stay."

"No." I climbed out of the pool, water dripping down my body as their patronizing whistles went off around the room.

"Why not?" he called out.

"Because you're disrespectful." I looked at him over my shoulder. "I was working out here. Your mansions all have pools. Get out and go home, why don't you?"

He stared at me, and I was just about to turn away and leave, but then he yelled, "Guys!" His eyes stayed on me. "Do me a favor? Get out and go home."

"Huh?" someone said.

"What?" came another voice.

"I mean it," he told them. "Go home. Now."

I narrowed my eyes. *Aw, what a gesture.* Flexing his muscles to prove he had the strength of a playground bully and the moral compass of a tube sock.

I rolled my eyes and walked over to the bench, picking up my towel.

Water sloshed behind me, and grumbles continued, slowly fading away as the locker room doors opened and closed.

When I turned around only Will remained, staring at me from where I left him in the pool.

"Why don't you like me?" he asked.

I ignored him, wringing out my ponytail.

"And what happened to your legs?" he questioned next.

I tensed, but I didn't look down to see what he was talking about. Minor bruises dotted my legs, but my arms, torso, and back were worse. I'd made sure to cover those with the rash guard.

I slipped on my flip-flops, but I heard movement in the water and looked back to see him leaning over the edge and gazing up at me.

"Why were you coming out of the cathedral last Saturday night?"

I cocked an eyebrow. *Stalker.*

Throwing the towel over my shoulder, I took the goggles off my head and started for the locker room.

"Stay," he said again.

And something about how he said it made my insides shake a little. Slowly, I stopped.

Stay.

I had no doubt I'd love everything about staying with him for an hour. If he went slow, then maybe two hours.

I'd let him mess with my head and take me away, because every day more and more of me needed my head messed with. I needed away.

But . . .

"What are we going to do?" I asked quietly.

When he didn't answer, I turned around.

"Will we play?" I inquired. "Will you make me smile?"

He didn't reply, just watched me, his chest rising and falling harder.

"What did you want to happen?" I pressed. "How would it go if I stayed with you here?"

I dropped my towel and goggles, and I approached him, crouching at the edge of the pool and staring down at him.

"Maybe I'll joke around with your friends, and we'll all laugh," I told him, imagining things that would never happen and he knew it. "You'll touch me and whisper things in my ear. They'll take the hint and leave us alone, and I won't be able to resist you. I won't want to, right?"

His eyes sharpened on me, but he listened.

"You'll press me against that wall"—I jerked my chin to the one near the girls' locker room door—"and I'll let you have me, because your attention feels so good."

I had no doubt that part would be true.

"And tomorrow, we'll walk down the hallway, hand in hand, and everyone will know we're in love, right?"

He cocked his head and hooded his eyes, knowing what I was up to now.

I breathed out a laugh. "Come on, Will," I said. "I have nothing you want. I'm not a happy person. Ever. We don't mesh. Your life is trite to me, far removed from reality, and I thought your views on *Lolita* were repugnant, and worse, dangerous."

His jaw flexed, his green gaze turning defiant.

"I hate your friends," I continued. "I don't want to be around any of them. Except Kai, maybe. One of three Asian kids in a school full of WASPs, he, at least, has some clue what it's like to be me."

Pretty sure the only other Jewish kid graduated last year.

"And you have nothing I want," I went on. "You coast through everything, so where does your character come from? I don't want to have fun with you, because there's nothing and no one you don't use. I don't respect you."

He tipped his chin down, looking angry now as he glared.

"In twenty years, you'll all be your fathers—powerful, wealthy, and with a string of mistresses your wives will be drugging themselves in order to forget that you have." I stood up, looking down on him. "But even as a master of the universe, Will Grayson III will never forget that I was one notch on his belt that he could never get. I'm not going to let you win this one. At least I'll have that."

I started to walk away, but before I knew what was happening, he'd jumped up, grabbed my arm, and yanked me down into the pool.

I screamed and splashed, but he didn't let me go under, pulling me into his body and wrapping his arms around me instead. I looked up at him, breathing hard, and he looked down at me, our lips inches from each other.

Drops of water glistened in his hair and wet his eyelashes, and for a moment, I had no will. I lowered my eyes to his mouth. Supple and strong and most amazing when he used it to smile.

Tears pooled in my eyes. I couldn't stop him.

Don't. Please.

I wasn't a happy person. Not ever. *I won't be able to stop you.*

He pulled me in, and I opened my mouth to protest, but instead of a kiss, he just pulled me into his arms, pressed my head to his shoulder, and wrapped his arms around me so tight, it felt like he was the one about to break, not me.

I stilled, not sure what to do, but I could feel every muscle in his body flex as he held me and took deep breaths.

And slowly, I closed my eyes, every ounce of fight draining out of me, feeling his embrace.

It had been so long since I felt this. My grandmother was hardly lucid enough to hug me much anymore.

My arms itched, wanting to touch him. God, I wanted to hold him.

But before I could work up the courage to pull away or hug him back, he whispered, "I'm not like that." And he pulled up, staring down at me almost nose to nose. "And I'll see you on the bus tomorrow night, Emory Scott."

He released me and swam for the edge, leaving me cold in the pool. What?

The air chilled, and I watched as he pulled himself up the ladder, and I spun around just in time, giving him my back as his naked body exited the pool.

Shit.

Unable to help myself, I surrendered to the pull and glanced over my shoulder.

But it was too late. He was fastening a towel around his waist, the cords and muscles in his back intimidating and everything about him was perfect. Without sparing me another glance, he opened the boys' locker room door and disappeared inside.

Ugh. What was he doing? Why wouldn't he just stop? I swam for the edge of the pool, picked up my shit without bothering to dry off, and stormed into the girls' locker room.

Why couldn't he just leave me alone? Didn't guys like him want . . . something else? Or someone else?

He was getting to me. Making me think I was wrong about him or something. For years, he'd had this whole "what you see is what you get" vibe, and now he wanted to convince the world that we were wrong.

I didn't need the trouble. I had much bigger problems than him, and I didn't need this.

I dressed, stopped at my locker to grab my bag, and before I knew it, I was halfway home already, lost in my thoughts and replaying every frame with him in my head.

My throat swelled with a golf ball–size lump, and I couldn't stop feeling his arms around me.

It was nice.

I didn't want to want more. Everything I said about him was true. He was shallow, and he was using me. Bottom line. I couldn't forget that.

There was a moment, though, when he held me, where he was me, and I was him, and we weren't alone. It felt like I was supposed to be there.

I closed my eyes as I walked, tears wetting my lashes.

I was looking for meaning where there wasn't any because I had nothing else. It wasn't real, and he didn't feel it, too. *Remember that, Em. Don't forget it.* For a few seconds, I saw what I wanted to see.

Heading into the town square and up the small incline into the park, I gazed at my gazebo that I was building, the beams still wet from rain, but the smell intoxicating. I loved the smell of wood.

Circling the structure, I saw it was still in pristine condition, my foundation holding up and no vandalism so far.

Tires screeched on the street, and I looked over to see Sticks crowded with people and four black vehicles racing up to parking spots on the curb, Will's truck bed loaded with people.

Tires peeled, smoke billowing into the air, and people shouted as car stereos blared.

"How's it going?"

I looked over my shoulder, seeing Trevor Crist holding a football. He tossed it back to his buddy down on the sidewalk.

"Hey," I muttered, looking back at Sticks.

Will climbed out of the driver's side, grabbing the black T-shirt out of the back of his jeans and pulling it on as Damon came up behind him and appeared to be whispering something in his ear. I couldn't see their faces.

People cleared the sidewalk as they crossed it, walking into Sticks.

"Look at it this way," I heard Trevor say. "Once they graduate, Devil's Night is dead. Thank-fucking-God, right?"

I turned to him. "Not going to carry on the family tradition?"

Trevor was three years behind his brother Michael. Plenty of time left in high school.

But he just scoffed. "You mean the once-a-year beef fest where my brother and his friends get the whole town to suck their cocks because they're too stupid to remember how to be men the other three hundred sixty-four days of the year?" He shook his head. "No."

I snorted. I may have misjudged him. The silver spoon in his mouth was salty.

"When everyone grows up and realizes they're nothing," he continued. "I'll laugh and celebrate then. Or when they finally get arrested for all the dumb shit they pull."

"Some brother you are."

He shrugged, but I smiled a little. He might not be so bad, after all.

And I understood where he was coming from. I wouldn't cry if my brother got into a little trouble.

In the distance, Will took out a cell phone as he stepped into the hangout, looking like he was filming a couple of the guys roughhousing.

"That is true, though, isn't it?" I thought out loud. "About the risk of getting arrested, I mean. They film everything with that phone. It's pretty careless."

Trevor followed my gaze; everyone knew that the Horsemen recorded their escapades. There was proof of all the petty crimes and pranks they'd pulled.

"If anyone had half a mind to," I went on, "there would be no way to ignore their behavior if someone shared those videos in the right place, you know? Can you imagine the embarrassment?"

The places they'd robbed? Vandalized? The underage girls—maybe guys, too—or, hey, maybe there were even married women on that phone. The town would go crazy.

He was silent for a moment, and when I looked back at him, his gaze was still on the crowd in Sticks, but his expression was serious as the wheels in his head turned.

"They're too comfortable in their surroundings, that's for sure," he added.

I nodded. "False sense of safety and all that."

They took video—probably pictures, too—because they knew they were invincible. Even if anyone found it, would it amount to any more than a slap on the wrist and some very embarrassed parents?

Money solved all problems.

Trevor still stood there, gazing after them in the billiards hall.

"Learn a lesson from this," I told him. "Don't document your shit. The Internet lives forever. Got it."

But I didn't think he heard me as he absently nodded.

"See ya," he said, finally turning away and heading back to his friend.

I gazed across the street, hearing the music from here and knowing I'd made the right decision. I wouldn't belong in there with them. Could you imagine? Me? Like, having fun?

I'd be wondering what the point was the whole time. I couldn't not be serious, and he was never serious.

Turning, I picked up my bag, but the flap flew open, and I spotted a packet of papers inside.

Pulling them out, I turned it over and saw "*Lolita* Study Guide" written on the front.

"Huh?" I mumbled. I'd looked everywhere for this! Including this bag, both of my lockers, my house, the garbage . . .

What the hell?

But as I looked over the packet, my name written at the top, I saw the questions already completed. All of them. Neat, block lettering in pencil.

I flipped through, inspecting every page and reading every answer, seeing that it was all completed, the answers impressive, even for me, although a couple of the responses kind of pissed me off.

I dropped my hands, staring off. I thought for sure Godzilla and the granola bar was Will, but this was snuck into my locker, as well. And it was done tonight. This wasn't in my bag before I went swimming.

There was no way he'd done this. Unless he buttered up a girl to do it for him.

It did look like a guy's penmanship, though.

I raised my eyes, making out his black T-shirt and chocolate-colored hair as he stood near a pool table inside Sticks.

He wouldn't have to look for me, because I had a question that needed answering.

See you on the bus tomorrow night, Will Grayson.

CHAPTER 9

EMORY

Present

I blinked my eyes open, the blurry room in front of me slowly coming into view. The weight of a truck sat on my back, and I rolled myself over, peeling my face off the pillow.

My arm draped over the other half of the empty bed.

It was just a dream.

I stared at the ceiling, still feeling him next to me in bed, but I knew he wasn't there. He was closer than ever now, but I felt his absence more than I ever did.

Tears ached behind my eyes, remembering how he felt and how much I really wanted to feel that again right now.

He barely looked at me yesterday. He always looked at me.

God, who put me in Blackchurch? My brother wouldn't have the clout for this. I'd heard he'd married, but it had been years since I'd seen him. Why now?

No, it had to be someone else. Someone who wanted to give Will his revenge and didn't give a shit about me.

There were lots of possibilities.

Sitting up, I winced at the soreness in my stomach, and I reached out, tonguing the cut on my lip. It was funny, and I wasn't sure why, but I didn't mind the pain. I actually kind of liked it. It was familiar. It reminded me that I was alive.

Strange as it was the past several years—free and on my own—I hadn't felt that in a long time.

Climbing out of bed, I found my glasses on the nightstand and slipped them on, looking down at my boxers and tank top. Aydin had undressed me when he put me to bed, offering me some bottoms from his drawer. I looked around the room, not sure where he'd slept, but he'd stayed out after he patched me up last night.

Walking to the mirror, I turned and looked at myself.

My hair had coiled and ratted, wild and messy as it fell around my face and down my chest and arms. Dried blood coated my left nostril, and the skin on the inside corner of my right eye was purple. My cheek was red from where he'd slapped me, a cut adorned my bottom lip, and a white bandage was wrapped around my upper right arm.

Reaching out, I touched my reflection in the mirror, feeling it. Remembering.

Every hair on my arms rose. Every inch of my skin hummed. The air coursed through my fingers, and the muscles in my legs flexed, standing tall and strong.

I curled my fingers into the mirror, alive.

I was a fighter once.

Closing my eyes, I flattened my hand against the mirror once more, feeling warmth from the other side.

Was one of them in there keeping an eye on me? Was Will in there?

"Hi," someone said.

I opened my eyes and turned toward the door, seeing Micah standing there in black cargo pants, his hands full of stuff.

I backed away from the mirror, grabbing the sheet on the bed to cover myself as he entered the room in his bare feet.

"Some clothes," he said, gesturing to the pile in his left hand. And then he set down a plate. "And in case you're hungry."

I looked at the juice, fruit, a small baguette, and a wedge of what looked like brie, my stomach growling. Aydin had soup brought up to me last night, but I couldn't remember the last time I ate anything substantial, and I was starving.

Dropping the sheet, I grabbed the bread, broke it in half, and cut off some cheese with the butter knife, smearing it on the bread.

Lifting it to my mouth, I ripped off a piece with my teeth and chewed.

Jesus. My mouth salivated, and I almost felt nauseous at the taste because I was so hungry. I groaned, loading on more cheese and then drinking the juice.

"You want a bath?" he asked.

I looked over as he pulled his T-shirt over his head. His abs flexing and his hair hanging in his eyes, all messy-sexy.

I choked, coughing with my mouth full. "With you?"

He just chuckled, stuffing his T-shirt into his back pocket. "I'll draw you one. You look rough," he explained. "How do you feel?"

I opened my mouth to say *Fine* or *I'm hanging in there*, but surprisingly, I just nodded. "Good."

I took another bite and stuffed a piece of apple in, too.

I felt good.

Weird.

Walking to the tub in the corner of the room—that wasn't in the bathroom, maybe because the previous owner of the house liked his wife to bathe in full view of the bed—he started the water, dipping his hand in the stream and adjusting the temperature.

"Rory told me what you did," he said, sitting on the edge of the tub and looking over at me. "Thank you."

I'd seen enough in my twenty-four hours here to know all wasn't what it seemed. Rory was the one who'd spoken in the cellar yesterday. The one who didn't want me here, hoped I'd die out there, and liked things just as they were because he had all he needed here.

"Are you and him . . . ?"

I didn't finish, just letting him figure it out.

He smiled and looked back at the water, but I caught the blush on his face.

I ate some more fruit and the rest of the bread before finishing the juice he'd brought me. Everything tasted so good, probably because I knew it was safe. If they'd wanted to drug me, they could've already done it.

"What time is it?" I asked.

"Maybe noon." He shrugged. "I don't know. Time isn't relevant here."

I wiped my mouth with the napkin, studying him. "Do you know how long you've been here?"

"A little over a year, judging by how many times the crew comes to restock us and clean," he told me. "We've all been here a while. Rory was the last to show up, about seven months ago."

No clocks. No calendars. No connection to the life outside. The only way to count the months was to count the resupplies.

It was like constantly waiting for something you weren't sure would ever happen, much less when.

"You don't seem like you should be here," I told him.

He scooped some bath salts into the tub and pulled a towel and washcloth over from the nearby table.

With Stalinz Moreau as a father, I thought Micah would be different.

He stared at the water. "My father hasn't been seen in public in nine years," he explained. "He lives on a yacht that's constantly moving from port to port, and the only way my five brothers and sister can see him is when we take a helicopter to follow whatever coordinates he sends us."

I'd heard that somewhere. It was actually pretty smart. When you supplied weapons to terrorists and competing factions in third-world countries, upsetting the "consistency" of the tyranny already in power, many people would want you dead.

"People think wealth means choice and freedom," he continued.

"But oh, how I envied those filthy, barefoot kids running around some of the worst neighborhoods I drove through growing up." He looked up at me, finally. "It's nice not starving, but I don't want to live like he does. I don't want power. I don't give a shit about money. I've had it, and now I'd just rather have peace of mind."

I approached him. "So, you're the black sheep?"

He flashed a sad smile. "'Who needs to learn a lesson about family loyalty and not being a pussy,'" he recited—his father's words, no doubt.

So, we were all stuck here. Maybe I wasn't so alone then.

Keeping my bottoms and top on, I stepped into the tub, the hot water instantly spreading amazing, glorious chills all over my body.

He smiled at my attempt at modesty by keeping my clothes on, but I really just wasn't ready for him to leave.

I sat down, letting my eyes fall closed at how good the water felt. Taking the bait, he tipped my head back and water poured over my scalp, wetting my hair as he filled the cup and did it again and again.

I opened my eyes, looking at the mirror across the room as water cascaded down my back, over my chest, and soaked my tank top.

"What happens when the resupply team shows up?" I broached.

"They resupply."

Yeah, duh.

"You know what I mean," I told him.

If I were stuck here for the time being, I'd use that time wisely. I needed to map the house, explore the land, and start stocking food, water, and maybe another weapon.

Micah held up his wrist, showing me his bronze-colored bracelet.

I studied it, just realizing they all wore one. It hadn't struck me yesterday, but now that I was seeing it, I remembered they all had one on.

"It tracks us," he said. "And it doesn't come off. Believe me, we all try."

I didn't have one, though.

"It vibrates when the team is coming," he explains. "Security arrives first, and if we're in our rooms like good little boys, they simply flip a lock to keep us secure. If we're not, then they'll find us and lock us in our rooms themselves. When the doors open again, they're gone, the fridge is stocked, the toilets are clean, our wardrobe is replenished, and every piece of furniture is shining. Almost like we get a do-over every month."

"A whole new chance to not break, spill, or bleed all over the floors again, huh?"

He snorted. "Yeah."

"Can you talk to them when they arrive?"

"We can try." He removed the now-soaked bandage on my arm. "But ultimately, the ones in charge aren't the ones we see. The team is just doing a job."

He soaped up a washcloth and gently cleaned off the blood on my arm.

"And while Aydin is correct that you should stay put, because you won't make it out of here alive," he went on, "I wouldn't trust that they'll be the ones to save you when they come."

I tensed. "Why do you say that?"

"Well, they had to have noticed you being brought here in the first place, right?"

My heart skipped a beat, and I paused, thinking.

It was safe to assume they saw me brought in or helped bring me in. He was right. If Aydin didn't lock me in the cellar and keep me undetected like he'd threatened to do, they might not care anyway when they came in a month. They still might not rescue me.

"Like I said," he repeated. "It's a job."

Well, I wasn't going to sit here and do nothing. Someone had an agenda bringing me here, and it wasn't Will.

I looked over at the glass again, imagining he was watching as Micah slipped the cloth inside my tank top and washed my back.

"How do they know when you're 'fit' to go home?" I asked. "I mean, people have gone home since you've been here, right?"

"One," he said. "But he got sent back."

The floor creaked, and I tipped my head up, seeing Rory lean against the doorframe, watching us as he ate an apple. His gaze moved between Micah and me, something loaded happening behind them.

"And I wasn't unhappy about it," Micah added, humor in his voice as he looked at the other man.

I glanced between them, the vibe making my blood warm.

I was pretty sure these two might just be happy staying here for the rest of their lives if they had each other.

"Would Rory mind if you helped me with my hair?" I asked Micah.

He grinned, kind of devilishly, and picked up the shampoo, pouring some into his hand.

I closed my eyes as he spread it across my hair, lathering it up, and I knew Rory was watching us as I imagined Will watching me through the glass.

I let my head fall back, and he poured water over my scalp again and again as it rinsed my hair and coursed down my body. The fabric of the white tank top chafed the hard points of my nipples.

His fingers trailed down my hair, squeezing the water out, and I almost shivered, it felt so good.

All I could feel were the eyes behind the glass on me, and I gripped the sides of the tub, liking it.

"I think I better go," Micah finally said.

I opened my eyes to Rory still leaning against the doorframe, but he'd stopped eating and stared at Micah, his gaze piercing.

"He needs me more than you do right now," Micah joked.

My thighs hummed. *Damn.*

"Thank you." I sighed, not ready to give up the attention.

But I totally understood.

"Anytime."

He walked toward the door, his T-shirt still dangling out of his back pocket, and then he turned to close the door.

"Oh, and the gift is from Aydin," he said, pointing to the floor next to the tub.

I peered over the edge, finding an old, rectangular wooden case and picked it up, opening the rusted clasp. Flipping the lid, I saw mechanical pencils, a French curve, a T-square, an eraser, a compass . . .

I darted my gaze to Micah. These were drawing tools.

"You can walk freely about the house," he told me. "No one is to touch you, Aydin says." And then he smiled, adding, "Unless you invite us to."

He closed the door, Rory's laugh echoing down the hall.

CHAPTER 10

EMORY

Nine Years Ago

Five hundred pairs of feet stomped the bleachers, cheering their respective teams, and I watched Will shoot another two-pointer from the top of the key.

Howls filled the air as the ball fell through the net, and we raised our instruments, playing a few notes to celebrate the moment.

Elle's arm pressed into mine, and I shifted to keep my balance. The whole place was packed, and I looked across the court to Morrow Sands's cheer section, seeing it filled with a lot more girls than guys.

It was funny how good-looking basketball players could suddenly spark an interest in just about anything for teenage girls. Everyone was a basketball fan now.

The center passed the ball to Michael Crist, and he dribbled it, running the rest of the way down the court, passing it to Damon Torrance.

Damon caught it and bounced it up and down on the floor, two girls waving to him to where he stood in the wing. He shot the ball, and it bounced off the rim, spilling over.

Will caught it, jumped up, and dunked it, the buzzer blaring through the auditorium as it fell through.

I smiled, catching sight of his grin.

Everyone was a basketball fan now.

Cheers filled the room, and I glanced at the scoreboard: 59–65, Thunder Bay.

A close call.

The coaches and players on the bench swarmed the floor, and I lifted my flute as everyone else raised their instruments. We belted out the school song, all the attendees on our side singing along.

I watched Will, smiling as he hung on to his friends as the auditorium echoed with noise, chatter, and music, celebrating the win.

Not that I cared. I barely ever paid attention, only knowing it was my moment when the others around me stood up or readied their instruments.

Will pulled off his shirt, sweat glistening on his back and darkening his chocolate hair as he swung the shirt over his shoulder and nodded to whatever some guy from the opposing team was saying to him. I let my eyes trail down his spine.

I paid attention to the game tonight, though. He was good.

And he was fun to watch.

I followed the rest of the band off the bleachers as everyone started to clear the gym, and we made our way into a spare room to put our instruments away.

But then some girl yelled, "Emmy, catch!" I spun around just as a cup of something ice-cold crashed into my chest.

I sucked in a breath as cola spilled down my navy and white uniform, seeping through my pants, down my legs, and coating my flute.

I shot my eyes up. *Are you kidding me?*

Maisie Vos hung over the railing of the bleachers, feigning a look of surprise before breaking into a laugh.

"I thought you were the trash!" she explained, jogging down the bleachers and rounding them to approach me. "I mean, you clear our trash at school, so I thought you'd help me out here. That's what I meant. Sorry."

Air poured in and out of my lungs, but I still couldn't catch my breath. She did that on purpose.

Elle stopped at my side, gaping, while others tiptoed around us, laughing under their breaths. A couple of guys followed Maisie, all seniors at my school, and I wanted to spew every dirty word in the book at them and their stupid faces.

But I just swallowed it down, because if not, then they'd win. They'd know that they mattered.

This was just my weekly reminder that I wasn't one of them.

"What's going on?" Will said, coming through the crowd with his shirt still hanging over his shoulder.

Maisie bit back her grin, while the two guys she was with made no effort to hide their amusement.

Will looked me up and down as the soda dripped off my clothes and flute, and then he turned his narrowed eyes on the two guys.

"Cover me," he gritted out.

They stopped laughing, and I watched as Michael, Damon, and Kai took up position, surrounding Will as he stepped up to Hardy Reed and Silas Betchel.

The two boys straightened, looking suddenly uncomfortable, and no one said anything as the Horsemen shielded Will's body from our view.

What . . . ?

I looked around Michael to try to see what was happening, but all I could catch was Will staring into Silas's and Hardy's eyes, doing something with his hands, but I couldn't see what.

Then, Will froze, blinked once, and I heard it. The steady stream, almost like something was being ripped in a slow, constant line.

A wicked smile spread across Damon's lips as Silas squeezed his eyes shut, and Hardy's chest moved up and down faster as he turned his head away and cursed under his breath, "Son of a bitch."

But whatever Will was doing, they stood there and took it.

After a moment, Will shifted again, never breaking eye contact as the Horsemen backed away and Silas and Hardy came into full view.

The whole place erupted in hoots and laughter.

My eyes fell, seeing the streams of piss wetting their jeans all the way down to their shoes, and Maisie dropped her eyes, heat rising to her cheeks as everyone made fun of her boyfriend standing there in a mess.

I clenched my teeth. They weren't fucking laughing now.

Will bent down and swiped the cup off the floor and tossed it in the trash, but before he could meet my eyes, I spun around to leave.

The muscles in my throat ached as I struggled to keep back the tears.

But someone shouted behind me again, "Emmy, here."

I tensed, but then a cheerleader rushed up and dug inside her backpack, taking out some clothes and handing them to me. Band came here in our uniforms. I didn't have anything to change into.

I was tempted to toss it back at her and choke on my pride, but Martin would drill me if I came home like this.

I nodded once in thanks. "I'll bring them back Monday."

And I made my way for the bathroom to wipe up and change.

My chin trembled, everything threatening to spill over, and I didn't know why. Stuff like that had happened before. It was no big deal. It wasn't like it happened all the time.

I could've shoved Maisie if I wanted to. Yelled at her, maybe. Definitely bit back a little.

This time I just wanted to run. I didn't want anyone to see me, like I was so embarrassing I wanted to erase myself from people's memories and cease to exist.

Just disappear.

I cleaned and stashed my flute, changed clothes, and stuck in my earbuds, carrying my instrument and bag to the bus. It was an hour drive back to Thunder Bay, and I wished I could damn well walk it.

Hanging my head, I charged toward the back of the vehicle, slid into an empty seat, and dumped my case and clothes on the floor. I held my phone in my hand, my playlist on *Teenage Witch* as I stared out the window.

People passed me, quiet and not a snicker to be heard, because Will Grayson had cast his net, letting them all know I was off-limits.

It was actually okay. Scared or not, most of them weren't going to sit down next to me anyway. They never did.

The bus filled up, and I waited for the seat next to me to dip, but as the doors closed, the lights dimmed, and the engine started, I remained solo.

I chewed the corner of my mouth to hide the tremble. What did I care? What did it matter that I'd been humiliated again? What did it matter that he saw that in the gym?

The tears welled.

He saw me. He saw that happen to me.

He saw what the whole world thought of me, and now he . . .

Now, he . . .

A hand slipped under mine, warm and smooth, and I snapped my head left, seeing Will in the seat next to me.

What . . . ?

A lump filled my throat as I gaped at the side of his face, wanting to be raging mad that he was there and touching me again without my permission, but . . .

He curled his fingers, gripping me, and . . . and it took a moment to get a hold of myself.

Finally, I forced a scowl and yanked my hand away.

Or tried to.

He wouldn't let go. Or look at me. He just tossed his black hoodie over our hands and chatted to the guy in the next seat like I wasn't there.

My heart pounded in my ears, drowning out the music from my earbuds, and I had to force my breathing to slow down.

I closed my eyes and turned toward the window. Why was he doing this?

And why was I just sitting here? The warmth from his strong fingers seeped into mine as he held me, and I looked over at him again, seeing him slouched in the seat, long legs stretched into the aisle as the players, cheerleaders, and band carried on around us.

He just stared at his phone now like there was nothing going on underneath the hoodie between us. Like he wasn't completely aware that he was holding me.

It took three tries, but I eventually swallowed, wetting my dry throat as I pulled his sweatshirt over us more, making sure our hands were covered. Maybe he thought I didn't want anyone to see. Maybe he didn't want anyone to see. Either way, I didn't care anymore.

The bus jostled side to side, taking us back onto the highway, and I fisted my hand, too, a fire burning low in my belly at the feel of his skin.

Movement caught my eye ahead, but I didn't look up because I knew what it was. Desi Castro sat in Ram Miller's lap, reverse cowgirl, and through the dim moonlight and shadows, I was pretty sure they were being fairly fucking stupid—albeit quietly—in the seat in front of us.

Her long, red locks draped over the back of the seat, and I finally raised my eyes as she leaned back against him, their lips barely touching as their bodies moved slow but rhythmic in the darkness.

Will rubbed his thumb across my finger, and my stomach flipped, the gesture comforting.

My phone beeped, and I turned over my right hand, unlocking the screen with my thumb. The phone lit up my place by the window, rain pummeling the bus as we drove through the dark night.

Let me take you home, it read.

I clicked my music off, glancing over and seeing his phone in his hand, too—the same text visible.

No, I typed back.

I couldn't let him take me home. Not ever. I tried to pull away from his hand, but he clasped it tightly.

Let me take you home, he typed again.

I clenched my teeth and turned my eyes out the window. I tried to pull my hand away once more, but he grasped it, forcing it instead onto my thigh, his fingers grazing my skin there.

A bolt of lightning shot through me, but instead of being angry, butterflies swarmed in my stomach and I squeezed my eyes shut. Leaving him there.

My phone beeped, and it took a moment to look at it. I want to hold you like that, it read.

I glanced up at Miller and Desi again, his arms wrapped around her, and I pictured myself in Will's lap, parked off some dark road in the rain, and it took everything I had not to look at him, because if I did, he'd know . . .

He would know that I didn't always hate him. A sliver of my brain was starting to believe there was more to him.

But I shoved his hand off, biting the corner of my mouth to keep the emotions away.

"Cops came to the warehouse and took all the tappers," someone said loud enough to pierce my earbuds.

I turned my head enough to see a cheerleader, Lynlee Hoffman, across the aisle, looking back at Will.

He sat there, his hand still under the hoodie, acting like everything was completely normal. "Oh, yeah?" he said.

But he didn't give a shit.

Lynlee shot me a look, narrowing her eyes and lifting her chin, because if they found out there was a party, it was because I had told my brother, right? As if the cops had to be geniuses to figure out a win always equaled a kegger at the warehouse. Duh.

I turned up the volume on my music again, drowning out any other sounds and tapped my thumbs, typing out a message. Take her home. She'll drool all over your dumb haircut and extensive knowledge of microbrews and penis jokes.

I mean, he was a jock.

I felt him shake with a laugh next to me.

He typed, letters flashing on his screen. I take you home, or I take you in my lap right here. Decide.

I ground my teeth together.

Everyone would see that. If my brother heard about it, I'd . . .

Jesus.

Damon leaned up from behind us, squeezing Will's shoulders and talking in his ear. Will laughed at whatever he said, no one the wiser.

My phone beeped again. Almost there, he warned.

I shook my head. People will see, I typed out.

Then make sure they don't.

He pulled the hoodie off us and slipped it over his head, covering his white, sleeveless T-shirt and his tan, toned, beautiful arms that always made my mouth hang open like an imbecile.

We entered Thunder Bay, heading back to our campus where everyone would pick up their cars and head to parties, but I'd be walking and heading straight home, as always.

I stared out the window, seeing the village breeze past, the twinkle lights of the park, and my neighborhood before we got up into the cliffs where Will and the wealthy resided. Part of me wanted it. Part of me loved how good his attention felt, because he was cocky and confident and good-looking and smooth. He was popular, looked great in everything he wore, and I liked his smile.

He was untouchable, and he wanted to touch me.

Tonight, anyway.

My eyes dropped to my lap. Even if I wanted to, though, my brother would never tolerate it.

The phone vibrated in my hand once, and then again and again, but I just bobbed my head to the music like I didn't notice. The school came into view, and liquid heat rushed my chest, but I ignored it. I was almost out of here, and he could spend the rest of the night taking whomever he wanted home, for all I cared.

We were nothing.

Another text came in, and I finally looked.

When the bus stops, get in my fucking truck.

I breathed out a bitter laugh. *Aw, someone's lost his temper.*

Why? I asked.

The next thing I know, the bus stopped, he yanked the earbuds out of my ears, and I sucked in a breath as he leaned into my face.

"Because you're mine," he growled in a whisper.

And all at once, the Horsemen rose from their seats, grabbed their bags, and charged down the aisle, leaving the bus first.

My heart hammered. What the—

Seriously.

Because you're mine. I ignored the flutter in my chest as I grabbed my bag and fumbled for my dangling earbuds.

I mean, for Christ's sake. What was his deal? Was I on some scavenger hunt he was doing or something? Nail the Nerd?

I rose with everyone else and stepped into the aisle, getting ready to leave the bus.

I'm not yours, Will Grayson.

And I'll walk, thanks.

The bus emptied, engines out in the parking lot already firing up and headlights glowing in the night. I walked to the undercarriage to see if anyone needed help with their equipment, but it was empty already, the band and players quickly clearing out.

I turned to bolt and make my escape before he saw me, but Elle clasped my hand.

"We're getting a ride home," she said.

"Huh?"

"Will," Elle explained, pulling me along. "He's taking us home."

"Um, no." I yanked my hand away. "He's not."

"You don't want me riding alone with him, do you?" She planted her hands on her hips. "A mature guy, used to getting what he wants?"

"Then you shouldn't have agreed to it."

Pivoting back around, I headed toward the gates to go home.

"But tomorrow I can say I rode in his truck," she whined, jogging up to the side of me.

So? "No."

He was only offering to give her a ride because it included me. It would only encourage him.

Elle fell back, and I kept walking.

"It's nice to be nice, Emmy," she called after me. "Please?"

I slowed, her pathetic whine making me feel guilty. I stopped and rolled my eyes, sighing. Him giving her a ride would make her year.

And who was I kidding? He wasn't going to give up if I refused a ride tonight. The creepy-stalker-weirdo would follow me in that damn truck. Right up to my front door.

I turned around, seeing her already heading back into the parking lot, a morose slump to her shoulders.

"Wait," I bit out.

She spun around, smiling ear to ear.

I joined her again, and we both walked over to Will's truck, still parked.

"You're sitting up front," she told me. "My house is first."

Huh—?

But she shoved me at the door of the huge, black Ford Raptor and pulled open the back door, climbing into the truck before I could utter an argument.

Seriously?

I yanked open the door and stepped up into the truck, ignoring Will's eyes as I plopped my ass down and slammed the door.

Just then, the back door opened again, and I shot a glance over my shoulder, watching Elle quickly exit the truck again and close the door.

"What are you . . . ?"

She walked past my window, swinging around and moving backward as she winked at me. "Have a safe ride!" she singsonged, doing a taunting little wave.

What the . . . ? I stopped breathing as realization dawned. This was a trick. Dammit.

The locks clicked, the parking lot still swarmed with people, and I was officially done for the day, shaking my head as I watched her disappear into the crowd.

"That's what I get for trying to make a friend," I grumbled.

I pulled my seat belt on, glaring over at Will as a smile curled his lips and he started the engine.

So clever, wasn't he? Must've worked that out with her in the thirty seconds it took for me to get off the bus.

He pulled ahead, driving through the empty space ahead of us, and exited the parking lot, turning up the volume as "In Your Room" played on the stereo.

We drove down the road, heading back toward the village, and I clasped my hands in my lap as my bag and flute sat on the floor.

It smelled good in here. The leather seats cooled the backside of my thighs, and my stomach dropped a little as he went over the bumps and dips.

The darkness of the cab engulfed us, hiding us, and it felt private. Like we were alone somewhere we shouldn't be.

Sneaking a glance, I watched his long fingers drape over the T of the steering wheel and then looked up to his face, seeing his eyes narrowed on the road ahead and the unusually stern expression on his face.

His chest rose and fell, steady and controlled, and if there was one thing I knew about Will Grayson III, it was that when he was in control you *should* worry.

Like in the pool last night.

When he got serious, he got to me.

I looked back down at my lap, breathing hard and feeling a little sick because my body was raging with a lot of different things.

I liked it.

We crawled closer to my house, and he hadn't said a word, but I didn't care. I just soaked up the feeling for as long as I could. Feeling him next to me. Riding with him. Goose bumps on my legs because I felt kind of pretty in the skirt now. Did he like it?

He turned onto my street, and I clutched the hem of my shirt, seeing my house ahead, but I didn't want to leave him.

He drove too fast, though. Why was he driving so fast? He had to stop in a second.

But we passed my house, not stopping or even slowing, and I popped my head up, looking back at my place through his back window.

He maintained speed, not slowing as my house came and went, disappearing again.

I swallowed the lump in my throat, despite my heart leaping a little. "You have to take me home," I said. "I can't be late."

I couldn't muster any more than a soft voice, because I really didn't want to go home. I just knew I had to.

Finally, he glanced over at me. "What are you afraid will happen? You're good at saying no to me, right? You can stay with me for another hour."

I arched a brow. What the hell was he going to try that would make me need to say no?

I checked the clock on the dash. It was only 9:19. As long as I was home by ten, Martin probably wouldn't ask questions. Probably.

He would know the bus had arrived already, though.

Will drove us through the neighborhood and pulled onto Old Pointe Road, heading toward Adventure Cove.

I tensed. What was he up to? The place closed at eight, and there was nothing else out here.

He turned and pulled into the parking lot of the theme park, the whole place empty for the night. He stopped the truck, not really bothering to fit into any particular space, but he kept the engine running and turned down the radio.

I let my eyes trail around the deserted lot, the empty ticket booths and darkened rides looming beyond the entrance gates. One single overhead light shone on the parking lot.

I looked at him out of the corner of my eye as he leaned back in his seat, staring out the window as the weight of the silence made my heart skip a beat.

"Do you see the Ferris wheel?" he finally asked.

I followed his gaze, looking out my window and finding the Ferris wheel to the right, on the edge of the theme park.

"If you head past it," he said, "about five hundred yards east, you'll come to Cold Point."

Cold Point was a part of the cliffs that jutted out into the sea a little more than the rest of the coastline between here and Falcon's Well. With the theme park in the way, it was nearly inaccessible now.

And for good reason, given its history.

"Do you know that story?" he asked me.

"Murder-suicide," I muttered.

He was quiet, and then I heard his soft, "Maybe."

I turned my eyes to him as he leaned his head on his hand and stared ahead.

"In 1954, Edward McClanahan was my age," he told me. "Senior, basketball star, bit of a bad boy, but only where it counted . . ." He smiled, teasing me. "He was good to people. He showed up for people, you know?"

I didn't know much about Edward McClanahan, other than the basketball team made an annual pilgrimage to his grave. I never really cared.

But I stayed quiet.

"That season was supposed to be their greatest," he said. "They had the team, the coach, the years of training . . . They could anticipate each other's moves, even their thoughts." He met my eyes. "That's what years of playing together had brought them to. They were a family. More than family. They were in perfect symbiosis."

Like the Horsemen. Watching them sometimes, the other players didn't exist. Michael, Kai, Damon, and Will were like the four limbs of a single body.

"And that rarely happens," he continued. "They relied on each other and would do anything for each other, and they were going all-conference. Everyone was hyped for what was coming that season. The games, the parties, the celebrations . . ."

I wondered how true all of that was. He painted a nice picture, but we believe what suits us to believe, and nothing more. Everything seemed better in hindsight.

He smiled. "Elvis had just hit the scene, everyone wanted a Chevy Bel Air, and 'Sh-Boom' by the Crew-Cuts was the number one song in America." His face fell a little, and he continued, "Homecoming night, a girl from Falcon's Well—one of our rivals—showed up at our high school dance. Alone and wearing a pink dress of lace and tulle. The twinkle lights above the dance floor glittered across her hair and bare shoulders as she walked in, and no one could take their eyes off her. She was so nervous, knowing she didn't belong there." He paused, turning his head and holding my eyes. "Feeling like a mouse in a snake pit. She kept holding her stomach like she was going to throw up or something. But she was pretty. So pretty. *He* couldn't take his eyes off of her."

McClanahan.

I looked off, past the Ferris wheel and toward Cold Point, seeing her in my head. The strapless pink dress that poufed out the way dresses in the fifties did, while young men wore suits.

"They say she came to cause trouble," he told me, his soft, low voice drifting into my ear. "That the rival team sent her to sow discord. They say she taunted our whole team. Tried to get them to do things to her that night so she could play the victim the next day."

Why was he telling me this?

"No one knows how they knew where to find the body, or if she even screamed, but she was found through the morning fog hours later, broken on the jagged rocks below," he said. "Her pink dress was stained red and the waves plastered her hair to the stones as her dead eyes stared up at the cliff above. The last thing she saw was the person who pushed her."

I tried to lick my lips, but my mouth was too dry.

"They say the team was going to have to forfeit the season under all the media scrutiny and investigation." He drew in a long breath and exhaled. "They say all the guys who didn't come from wealthy families were going to have to forego their hopes of athletic scholarships because of it. They wouldn't go to college." He paused. "They say the coach would have to be fired and move his family, the prospects of finding another job after such a scandal not high."

I didn't know all that. I listened as he went on.

"All I know is." He sighed. "A week later, Edward McClanahan left a confession on his parents' kitchen table and then followed her over the cliff. The last line of the confession read: *We want what we want.*"

I turned my eyes on him as sweat cooled my pores.

We want what we want.

"They say McClanahan sacrificed himself so the season could go on."

Like he took the blame? He didn't do it?

"That's what they say, anyway," he mused, a gleam hitting his eyes. "But the whispers tell of something else."

A flutter hit my stomach, and I barely breathed, waiting for him to continue.

"They say she was caught between two best friends—McClanahan, who was in love with her, and A.P., her boyfriend. He wasn't wealthy like McClanahan, but he was clever. And ambitious. Not someone to be underestimated."

My interest was piqued even more. A mystery.

I liked mysteries.

"They say she was pregnant," he told me. "They say she jumped." And then he looked at me again. "They say Edward . . . didn't."

Didn't jump? So the rumors say Edward was pushed instead?

A smile played on his lips. "They say the note on the kitchen table was a confession, but not his."

He took another breath and looked out the front windshield again. Everyone revered Edward because they thought he took the fall to save the team's season. Save some kids their college scholarships and a coach his job.

I always thought it was moronic. Edward clearly didn't understand all that life could throw at you. He had far bigger things to survive than a scandal.

But I liked the way Will told it. Like nothing was what it seemed, and there was a story waiting to be unearthed.

After all, no one really knew what happened out at the Point all those decades ago.

"I like it here," he almost whispered. "I like mystery. Sometimes I'm dying to know what happened that night, and other times, I hope I never find out, because it's more interesting this way. Reality always disappoints." He turned to me. "I think that's why I've always liked this time of day best. People hide in the dark. They quench their thirsts in the dark. They build their secrets in the dark. We're more ourselves here than anywhere else. I get to be me"—he swallowed, staring at me—"when nightfall is coming."

I gazed into his dark green eyes, his whole face shadowed in the cab of the truck, and I wanted . . .

Every nerve on my lips hummed, feeling the weight between us like each end of a string tied around him and me, and it kept getting shorter.

I want . . .

"We want what we want," he whispered.

I dropped my eyes to my lap, curling my fingers into fists.

And then his voice came again, barely audible, "Come here," he said.

My heart dipped into my belly, and I could feel him in my hands. I looked at him, seeing him grind the steering wheel under his fist and breathing hard.

"Come here," he said again.

I absently shook my head. "Why?"

"Because I'm your man."

My heart cracked and splintered, aching with the warmth of those stupid words. Who the hell was he, huh? He didn't get to decide that someone belonged to him just because it struck his fancy.

And that's all I was. A passing fancy. He didn't listen, and he didn't take no for an answer.

If I let this happen—let him love me and protect me and all that shit he spewed—I'd just be trading one abuse for another.

He'd use me, dump me, and I'd be worse off for it.

I'd be shattered.

"Take me home," I demanded.

He blinked but didn't move otherwise.

I unlocked my door, yanked the handle, and pushed my door open, jumping out.

I'd walk then. *Fuck you*.

Slamming the door, I heard his open on the other side, and he'd rounded the car and stopped me in my tracks before I even made it to the tailgate.

"Why are you afraid of me?" he barked, backing me up.

"Why did you tell me that story?" I retorted.

"Why do you think?"

"To prove again what I already know?" I yelled. "That Thunder Bay boys always get away with it."

I stopped, and so did he. "You think Edward McClanahan got away with anything?" he fired back.

I didn't give a shit about Edward McClanahan! *I just . . . I just wanted . . . I just wanted to go home!*

"I told you, because I like this place," he finally answered. "I wanted you here with me, because . . ." He searched for words, his hand shooting to his hair and gripping it. "Because we want what we want, Em! Jesus!"

"Take me home."

He inched in, his eyes on fire. "No."

I chuckled once, aghast. Was he kidding?

"This isn't happening," I spat out, getting back in his face. "I'm not going to be the one all over you in the school hallways tomorrow in front of everyone. I'm something dirty you hide!"

"Speak for yourself," he growled. "I think you're the one ashamed of me. That you want me. That you want this."

I laughed. "And who told you that? Your secret society of date rapists who advised that me walking away from you the last fifteen times was a 'signal.'" I held up my hands, doing air quotes.

He snarled and advanced on me, but then backed away and turned around. He ran his hands through his hair again, and I could see him breathing hard, the veins in his neck bulging.

"I would never stop touching you," he said, his voice almost tired. "And I would touch *only* you."

He turned and looked at me, and he was so beautiful I wanted to believe him.

Raindrops started to fall again, lightning flashing across the sky, followed by thunder cracking overhead.

Out of all the boys in school, Will was the biggest threat. Not because he was handsome or because he was one of the only ones who was ever somewhat interested in me, but because . . .

He never gave up. Deep down, I loved that, because I was going to be an effort for anyone, and he wasn't easily discouraged.

Right now, I wanted him to pick me up.

But instead, I circled the truck and climbed in the driver's side, immediately locking the doors. If he wasn't driving me home, I'd drive myself.

Rain tapped against his window, and I watched him come around and stand there, a glint in his eyes at my challenge.

I waited for him to try to stop me, but . . . he didn't.

Shifting the truck into gear, I punched the gas and sped off, pulling a quick U-turn as the tires screeched against the pavement.

I sped past him and headed out of the parking lot, not even taking one last look in my rearview mirror.

I turned onto the dark road and pressed the gas pedal to the floor, speeding back to Thunder Bay and gripping the wheel like it was his damn neck.

Who did he think he was? Did every girl just roll over and thank her lucky stars for his attention? Is that where he got such confidence?

I just wanted to go home. Study. Graduate. And leave this town.

I didn't want anything else!

"Ugh!" I growled, turning up the radio and inching up in my seat because I could barely reach the damn pedals, and it was too dark to try to figure out how to adjust the seat in this stupid truck.

God, where did he get off? He's all like "Hey, babe. I'm"—insert hair flip and surfer boy tone—"Will Grayson. Should we, like, maybe get together and mate? We can totally honeymoon in Hawaii. I'll put a stamp in your passport and make all your dreams come true."

Which, of course, we wouldn't need our passports, because Hawaii was still in our own country!

I growled under my breath, breathing hard as rain fell harder, blurring the road in front of me.

I turned on the wipers, my brain calming a little.

Okay, okay. He wasn't *that* dumb.

He wasn't dumb at all. He would know Hawaii was in America.

And he didn't say *like* and *totally*.

I hooded my eyes, sighing. *And he could be kind.*

And sweet.

I hesitated a moment, watching the rain really come down now before I slowed on the empty highway and pulled another U-turn, heading back to him.

He was persistent to the point of exhaustion, but . . . I couldn't let him walk home in this. I couldn't do that to him.

Speeding back to the Cove, I turned into the parking lot again and spotted him kicked back on a parking stump, hood up and ankles crossed.

I pulled up next to him, rolling down the window.

He peered up at me, batting his eyelashes against the rain.

"I really don't like you," I said nice and loud so we were clear.

He smiled and pushed himself up, coming up to the truck and climbing up on the step, peering down at me.

"I like that you don't like me," he taunted.

He pushed his hood off, and I watched streams of rain cascade down his face.

"So, I'm a challenge then?" I asked. "That's what all this is really about?"

"No." He shook his head. "You just make me want to be . . ."

"Better?" I rolled my eyes at the cliché statement.

But he paused a moment. "More," he finally said. "No one ever expects more from me."

I studied him, not having anything to say to that.

I looked down at the phone in his hand instead. "Is someone coming to get you already?"

"No." He stuffed the phone in his pocket. "I was getting ready to call your brother to report my stolen car."

I widened my eyes and almost screamed, but I just clamped my mouth shut and gritted my teeth.

Son of a bitch.

"Scoot over," he said.

I huffed and crawled over the console into my seat, and he opened the door, climbing in.

C an I pick you up for school Monday morning?" he asked, turning onto my street.

I unfastened my seat belt. "No."

"I just asked to be nice," he said in a stern tone. "I'm picking you up. I don't like you walking."

"Please . . ." I shook my head, ready to plead. "Please don't."

We approached my house, and I grabbed my bag and flute off the floor.

"Stop here," I told him.

"I'm not afraid of your brother, Em."

"Please just drop me here," I bit out. "Stop the truck, Will. Please."

"Okay." He quickly pulled over to the curb, sliding behind Mrs. Costa's Buick.

I opened the door, but he grabbed my hand.

I looked at him over my shoulder.

"I'll be right here," he said. "At seven."

I stared at him for a moment, wondering if saying no again would do any good, but I just took my stuff and jumped down from the cab.

I met his eyes once more before I closed the door and then jogged down the sidewalk, turning up my walkway. I looked around for anyone who might've seen us, but thankfully, it was late and the street was quiet.

I climbed my steps and twisted the door handle, my heart dropping a little because that meant Martin was still up.

I stepped inside and heard Will's truck finally pull off, breezing past my house. I closed and locked the door, my lips twitching with a smile.

He actually waited until I was inside to leave.

Dishes clanked in the kitchen, and I dropped my bags to the

floor, heading in to face the music. I had no idea how late I was, and I hadn't checked my phone for missed calls.

Hands in my jacket pockets, I stopped just inside the dark kitchen.

Martin stood at the sink, prewashing dishes before loading them into the dishwasher. He turned his head, eyeing me over his shoulder.

"Dinner is there." He gestured to the plate on the table.

But I rushed up to his side instead, taking the plate out of his hand. "I can do it. You worked all day."

He let me take over, grabbing a towel and drying his hands as he stepped away. I took the dish brush and scrubbed the crust from our breakfast this morning.

"You know," he said. "Funny thing. When you didn't make it home by ten, I tracked your phone."

I faltered, feeling the hair on my arms rise. He could track my phone? How long had he been doing that?

"It told me that you were at the Cove." He walked away and leaned against the counter, his eyes on me. "Funny thing is, the Cove closed at eight tonight, and when I drove out there, all I saw was Will Grayson's truck in the parking lot."

I rubbed circles on the plate, pressing hard so my hands wouldn't shake.

"I support your education, Emory," he told me, "your extracurricular activities, and your projects, because I want you to make something of yourself, and I know that all looks good on your college applications."

I put the plate in the dishwasher and picked up another one, avoiding his gaze.

I wished I was still in Will's truck.

"And while you're off playing, I'm working or I'm here." He inched closer. "No woman wants me with you in this house. No one wants me because I can never give her the Thunder Bay life, because I'm paying for Grand-Mère's nurse and for you."

He stopped at my side, and I couldn't stop shaking as I washed the dish.

"And you're off playing," he said, pushing me in the head.

I stumbled to the side. "Martin . . ."

"You don't listen to anything I say." He dug the tips of his fingers into my skull and shoved again, and I almost dropped the brush. "Is it so hard? Just doing what I tell you to do?"

He pushed me in the head again like I was stupid, and I fell to the side, dropping the dish and brush into the sink. I waited for the slap, but he just grabbed my wrist and yanked me to the table.

Pushing me down in the seat, he grabbed a handful of the spaghetti and stuffed it into my mouth.

Tears swelled my throat, and I squeezed my eyes shut, holding them back.

"As if we don't have enough problems, you go and get a reputation for being one of their little whores," he said, stuffing another fistful into my mouth. "Thinking you're going to be one of them. Thinking you're better—and them thinking they're better because they get to play with you like a toy!"

Spaghetti flew in my face, dirtying my glasses as he stuffed handful after handful at my mouth, the noodles pressing down my throat so hard I couldn't breathe.

Silent tears streamed down my eyes. I twisted my head away, trying to spit it out, but he grabbed my face and squeezed my jaw to open me up again.

I couldn't stop crying as I gasped for air. I couldn't breathe, and I gripped the sides of the table, my teeth cutting the insides of my mouth.

I tried to think of my gazebo. If Will helped me build it.

How nice that might be someday.

Will and the gazebo . . . Will and the gazebo . . .

The breeze on my face was warm, and the leaves in the trees smelled like summer.

But as Martin yelled, and I gagged, spaghetti choking me, I couldn't muster another single coherent thought.

I couldn't think. I couldn't remember what Will looked like. What my gazebo looked like.

I didn't have a gazebo. There was no Will Grayson.

There was nothing but this.

There was nothing but this.

CHAPTER II

EMORY

Present

Wrapping the towel around me, I ignored the eyes I felt through the glass and grabbed the clothes Micah had brought, taking them to the privacy—hopefully—of the bathroom. Of course, there could've been a two-way mirror in there, too.

Stripping off my soaked boxers and top, I dried my hair as best I could with the towel, brushed with the brush I found on the sink counter, and dressed, pulling on my clean underwear I'd washed out last night and hung to dry on the shower door, someone's clean boxers over them, and their button-down white Oxford.

I rolled over the shorts to make them fit and buttoned the shirt, rolling up the sleeves. If I had to guess, I'd say these clothes were Rory's, since he was the smallest.

I still swam in both pieces of clothing, though.

Heading back into the bedroom, I sheathed my knife and stuck it into my breast pocket. I still had no idea how I got the knife. Whoever brought me here might've wanted me to be able to defend myself, but if they didn't want me hurt, why the hell dump me here in the first place?

I had so many questions.

Turning my head, I spied the wall of antique sporting equipment

I'd vaguely noticed but hadn't inspected. Plenty of weapons on that wall. Cricket bats, old blades from rowing teams, and . . .

I walked over, grabbing the shadow box of old fishhooks. Flipping it over, I pried out the backing and set it on the table against the wall, picking out four hooks and taking them to the dresser where Aydin had left the bandages.

Sticking each hook through the gauze, I wrapped the bandage around my knuckles, fitting the ends of the hooks between my fingers to pinch them in place, while the sharp, curved ends reached out like claws.

I bit back my smile, wrapping the gauze around my hand like a glove, ripping it free from the rest of the roll, and tucking the slack into the bandage over my palm.

Balling my fist, I lashed out, hearing the claws cut the air. I wanted a weapon I didn't always have to carry. Freddy Krueger glove, it was.

With my wet head, weapons, and glasses on, I left the room, keeping my eyes peeled in all directions.

I passed the secret door and kept walking around the landing, treading quietly down the hallway that I saw Taylor come out of yesterday when I'd awoken.

I hadn't heard any more movement above me or in the walls since last night. Maybe it was critters.

I passed a couple of rooms—a bedroom and a nursery—and then I walked past an office before I came to a closed door, quietly reaching for the handle as I debated.

I wanted to know which rooms were what, which ones had windows, and who was settled where, but I also didn't want to draw notice.

To hell with it.

I needed to know.

Gently, I twisted the handle, but then I heard grunts from the other side of the door and stopped, leaning my head in to listen.

Another grunt followed by a groan with muffled whispers, and I took a step back, releasing the handle.

That was undoubtedly Micah and Rory's room.

Noted.

I trailed around the second floor, finding another dark bedroom with the sheets mussed, clothes on the floor, and a couple more rooms freshly made up by the cleaning crew yesterday.

I stepped into one with a massive bed, an ornate hardwood headboard and footboard, and a large cushioned chair in the corner. Unlike most of the other rooms, this one wasn't white or black. Earth tones and decorative lamps dressed the room, and I instantly felt cozy and warm.

If it wasn't already taken, then it was mine if I was still here tonight. I checked the handle for a lock, but there wasn't one, same as Aydin's room, and there was also a mirror in here, too.

I could secure the door with a chair and hang a sheet over the glass. Just in case.

Walking to the window, I peered through the curtains, taking in the run-down courtyard below with dead leaves covering the patches of grass, the remnants of a fallen tree, and a fountain in the center of the drive that held a couple inches of rainwater that had now turned brown.

It was a mess compared to the inside of the house. There may be outdated décor, torn drapes, and peeling wallpaper, but it was clean in here.

For now.

I left the room and closed the door behind me, trailing around the rest of the second floor, opening every door, every closet, and looking out every window to get the lay of the land.

I headed for the stairs to explore the rest of the first floor, but a floorboard creaked above me, and I stopped, looking up to the ceiling.

Footfalls moved from my left to my right, the wooden floor whining under the weight of whoever was up there, and I swallowed the lump in my throat, turning around instead.

I followed the sound, checking the ceiling for an entrance to the attic, thinking perhaps Will was up there. I guessed that messy room I found was either his or Taylor's, but that meant there was one bedroom still unaccounted for.

But I couldn't find an entrance to an attic or one to a third floor.

Hmm. I was pretty good at finding a secret room. I still had one in Thunder Bay, now that I thought about it.

Heading downstairs, I inspected every inch of the bottom floor, spying Taylor in the gym again, but I scooted away before he saw me.

Walking into the natatorium, heat rolling off the surface of the pool and fogging the windows and glass ceiling, I gazed at the water, tempted to dive in. I was alone, and it had been ages since I swam, but I wasn't here to play.

I spotted a half wall about fifteen feet beyond the other side of the pool and headed over to inspect. Probably some sort of dressing area or something.

As I got closer, though, I heard water running, but it wasn't until I'd rounded the wall that I saw it was showers.

I stopped, seeing Will—naked, wet, flexed, and . . .

My stomach dropped.

And hard.

I quickly backed up, dashing back behind the wall.

Shit.

Pool showers.

What the hell? Aydin was naked in plain sight yesterday. Will was naked in plain sight today.

I breathed hard, but I didn't move, remembering the last time I saw so much of him. He had been fit, his body unmarked back then, but before I could stop myself, I peered around the corner again, taking in the sight of him now, years later.

He'd changed on the outside, too. I let my eyes fall down his body, soap spilled down his skin and little bubbles dotted his stomach and arms.

I gazed, heat rising up my neck as he tipped his head back, smoothing hot water over his hair, steam billowing around his golden, wet skin. Tattoos covered both arms, drifting onto his chest and back, and they lined his collarbone and hands, but I couldn't see them well enough to decipher everything.

I made out his basketball number on the back of his right hand, his Devil's Night mask on his left arm against the backdrop of Thunder Bay, the cemetery, the Ferris wheel, and St. Killian's easily visible. His other shoulder and arm featured a cascading vine of leaves surrounding a skull, words written on the forehead I couldn't make out, and the rest of his body was covered in big and small pictures as well as words, some even draped around his collarbone like a necklace.

I wanted to see everything. I wanted to touch him.

He had shaved, and every muscle on his body had doubled in size since the last time I'd seen him, too.

I dropped my eyes and froze, staring at the other hard muscle standing damn near upright, long and thick between his legs.

My lungs emptied, and he turned around, leaning on the wall with his hand as the water cascaded down his face, and he grabbed his cock, stroking it slow and tight.

I gripped the wall for support, heat pooling between my legs as I chewed the inside of my mouth.

I stared at his hard-on, and in the not-so-far recesses of my mind, I wondered what he was thinking about.

Me?

Or her?

A whisper hit my hair. "You want him?"

I sucked in a breath and whipped around, swiping my fist with the claws.

Aydin jumped back, slivers of red opening up on his chest where I'd caught him with the hooks.

He looked down and then up at me, reaching out and grabbing

me by the throat with one hand, and my wrist with the glove in the other.

I whimpered.

Slamming me into the wall, the showers on the other side, he pressed his body into mine, staring down at me hard.

"You said you wouldn't hurt me," I told him.

"I'm not hurting you," he cooed as the shower ran behind me. "I'm scaring you."

He pressed my wrist to the wall out to our side, and he looked over, studying my glove.

He grinned. "It's clever."

Staring down into my eyes, he breathed across my lips and sweat covered my stomach and back. I needed air.

"What happened between you two?" he asked. "It's not a coincidence that you're here, you know?"

I studied him. *Yes, I knew that.* It had something to do with Will. "So, you think whoever dumped me here is giving Will a present?"

"Perhaps." He eased his grip on my neck. "They are definitely no friend to you, though."

Spinning me around, he forced me to the edge of the wall, both of us leaning in and watching Will.

"Do you think he'll protect you?" he whispered.

I tried to jerk out of his hold, but he held tight. Will fisted his cock, leaning into the wall, eyes closed, and breathing hard.

"Does he have to?" I asked, my eyes trailing down his body again. "Why are we watching this?"

"You're watching this," he explained. "I'm watching you."

"Why?"

He didn't answer, and I turned my head, looking up at him. His amber eyes watched Will and his brow knit, troubled.

"I don't know," he finally answered. "Maybe to remember what it feels like when you weren't alone. When you weren't the only one looking out for yourself." He looked down at me. "Maybe to remember what we left behind. And to remember what we didn't."

What was he talking about?

"Will and I are about the same age," he said, "but I think we were probably very different in high school. He was the talker, right?" He smiled at me. "I was the quiet one."

Now it was the other way around, it seemed.

"I wasn't always like this," he told me. "I was miserable. Six feet of weakness, fear, and cowardice." He gazed at Will again as he talked. "'You'll be a doctor,' they said. 'You'll study that. Work there. Go here on vacations. Spend your free time doing this. Marry her. Have three children. Live up there in that house after the honeymoon tour of London, Paris, and Rome.'"

I tried to picture him as he described himself, but I couldn't. I couldn't imagine him docile.

"Until one night, buried in my books, I saw her," Aydin continued.

I listened, but I turned my gaze back on Will as Aydin spoke in my ear.

"It wasn't her body or her face," he told me. "It was how everything with her was effortless. Every movement. Every look."

Will sucked in air between his teeth, his strokes harder and faster and the muscles in his arm tight.

"She loved to love," Aydin said. "She loved to touch and to feel and to wrap her every breath around someone and hold them with it, because she was an artist."

Everything warmed, and I envied how he described her. Whoever she was.

What would Will say about me?

"It wasn't her job," Aydin said, "but it was her calling."

He paused, and then he dropped his voice as if thinking out loud. "It *wasn't* her job," he said again. "Then."

It was like Will. He loved to love. He loved to be happy.

He'd wanted to make me happy once.

"I'd never wanted anything more in my whole life," Aydin went on, "and I was studying to be a surgeon who would've gladly cut off his own hands to have her."

Will squeezed his eyes shut, and I dropped my gaze to his cock again, my breathing nearly in sync with his strokes. What was he thinking about?

"Maybe I'm to blame," Aydin told me. "In the end, I didn't claim what was born to be mine because I was a shit twenty-two-year-old kid who knew nothing." He trailed off and then continued, his voice lower again, "But later, when I could finally stand up and claim her, I spit on her instead, because every effortless breath she wrapped around everyone else became another nail through my heart, and I couldn't look at her."

My chin trembled, and I wasn't sure why. He wasn't special. We'd all suffered loss.

But one thing was pretty clear. She was the reason he was here. Much like Will could saddle me with that honor, possibly, as well.

A woman happened to them both.

"I couldn't look at her, much like he can't look at you," Aydin said.

My stomach coiled, and he released me, backing away.

I turned and looked at him.

"I just wonder . . ." Aydin said. "If he ever decided to run from here, would he care to take you?"

He turned and walked away, leaving me there and feeling more alone than I ever had in my life.

Will would leave me, and he would be right to.

I stood there next to the pool for I didn't know how long, Aydin's words hanging in the air even after he'd left the room.

Was Will planning on running? What would happen to me if he weren't here? Or if he were sent home?

Would he fight for me?

I'd left him once. I'd let him be arrested and sent to prison, and in his head, I hadn't cared at all. Maybe I deserved the same.

I walked to the pool's edge, descended the steps into the water, and jumped in, sinking my entire body below the surface.

The water held me, warm and weightless, and I drifted back up to the surface, floating on my back.

The saltwater stung the cut on my lip, but the pain filled me with anger and memory, and I knew this was coming. I always knew.

I just figured it would've come after he got out of prison, and as the subsequent years passed, it didn't. I got comfortable.

Where would both of us be if he had just left me alone like I told him to?

I stood up, walking to the side of the pool as the shorts and shirt stuck to me like a second skin and tears hung in my eyes.

I used to think that if I got out of Thunder Bay and lived my life for me, doing what I loved and inviting only the people into my life whom I wanted, everything would be perfect someday.

But I hated everything I had, and loved nothing as well as what I'd given up, all of it tainted from the moment he was charged seven years ago, because I knew I didn't deserve to be happy.

Despair sat on my heart as warm tears streamed down my cheeks, and I didn't even realize the shower had stopped running until I noticed him standing there.

I looked up, seeing a towel wrapped around his waist as he stared at me. The air thickened, I almost couldn't breathe, and I was torn between wanting to run to him and run away from him.

Just go.

I begged him in my head, meeting his hard eyes with my blurry ones, and there was so much to say, but if I didn't explain, then maybe I wouldn't have to feel him spit on me and throw me away for good.

Please just go.

He charged over instead, not going, and I gasped as he reached down, grabbing me by the collar and hauling me out of the water.

"Will," I cried.

He picked me up under my arms and lifted me up, nose to nose with him, glaring at me as he dug his fingers into my body.

Another cry escaped.

My legs dangled, and I wanted to look away, but I couldn't.

I was frozen, waiting for what was to come.

I could see it inside of him, ripping him apart, his lips tight and his brows narrowed.

But instead of spitting, he shook me hard, growling like he was frustrated with himself more than me, and I broke into more tears.

"I'm sorry," I cried.

I was so sorry for all of his pain.

But when I thought he was going to throw me back into the pool, he brought me in instead, wrapping an arm around me and pressing his forehead to mine.

His hard muscle nudged my thigh through the towel, and he took my face in his hand, breath pouring out of him as he hovered over my mouth.

"Will . . ." I started.

But he lifted my thighs up around his waist and backed into the shower again, slamming me into the wall as he took my bottom lip between his teeth.

I opened my mouth to argue, but the heat of his breath made my whole body shiver, and I sucked in a breath, tightening my thighs around him.

He ripped open my shirt, and a whimper escaped me as he pressed his chest into my bare breasts and thrust up into me, grinding hard.

I dug my nails in, but when he came in for my mouth, I turned away.

"Get off," I told him. "I— We can't."

He wrapped his fingers around my throat and squeezed. "This is how it should've gone," he whispered up to me, cutting me off. "You were a hot little piece of meat, and I know you liked it."

He let my neck go and grabbed my breast instead, plumping it up and out for him as he dipped down and covered my nipple with his mouth.

I moaned as the heat of his tongue covered my skin, my clit throbbing as I grinded on him.

"We should've just kept it this simple, huh?" he said. "But you didn't want people to know the shit we did."

His mouth covered mine, stealing my breath as he slid his tongue inside and completely took me over, moving across my lips like I was a car he was shifting into gear.

"Why did you do it?" he asked. "Ashamed of what you liked me to do? There was still so much more to come, but you cut us short. We didn't even do half of everything I had planned for you."

I rocked into him again, panting. *Yes.*

But then suddenly, he dropped me to my feet, and my knees shook, everything going cold.

Huh? I opened my eyes.

I barely even registered him peeling my bottoms down my legs and taking my panties.

What?

"And now that you're here," he said, grabbing the back of my hair.

I gasped as he brought me in nose to nose again, slipping his hand between my legs and caressing my pussy.

"We have all the time in the world."

Then . . . he turned and left, his threat echoing through my ears as it took a moment to realize what had just happened.

I blinked, locking my knees under me as I quickly closed my shirt and covered myself.

Dammit.

Aydin was right.

Will wasn't an ally.

CHAPTER 12

WILL

Nine Years Ago

Arion Ashby's having a party," Damon told us, lying on the hood of his car and blowing a stream of smoke up toward the sky. "Her parents will be out of town."

Kai groaned, and Michael laughed at him under his breath.

"What?" Damon taunted. "Are you bored, Kai? Restless? Need a new kind of fun?"

"Me?" Kai retorted. "Never. I'm perfectly content. Loving life."

Damon smiled to himself, taking another drag off his cigarette, looking like he didn't believe Kai for a second.

The school parking lot swarmed with students, all of us hanging out and trying to soak up the rare, warm October morning before classes started. A calm breeze swept through the trees, clouds rolled in, the air charged, and I looked around for any sign of Emmy Scott.

Without looking like I was looking for her.

It wasn't that I didn't want my friends to know that I was into her, because they already knew I was, but if she got the slightest attention for it, she'd get scared off, and she was already constantly bolting away from me.

My eyes lifted, covertly scanning the crowd.

She wasn't waiting for me this morning.

I mean, of course she wasn't, but still. Pretty sure I would've died, seeing her waiting on the corner of her block for me, but as much as I wished I didn't know, I did.

She would *never* make anything easy.

Or maybe she couldn't. Something kept bugging me about Friday night. Dropping her off at her house, I could hear it in her voice when she demanded I stop a couple houses down, instead of right in front of her driveway. It was fear.

Almost like she was panicked.

I tied my tie, keeping it loose around my collar, and watched cars enter the gates, parents drop off their freshmen, and some students head through the parking lot on foot.

I was one of the first here this morning. Where the hell was she? Was she already inside?

"Same parties. Same girls," Michael mumbled. "I'm fucking bored."

"I know." Kai let out a sigh. "I'm feeling it, too. I need something to happen."

"Something to obsess over," Michael added.

And then Damon chimed in. "We should kill someone."

Michael snorted, Kai rolled his eyes, and I plucked the cigarette out of Damon's mouth, taking a drag and shaking my head.

Michael whipped his uniform blazer at Damon. "I was thinking I need the season to start, you fucking psycho."

"Or maybe you need to fall for someone," Kai told him, pulling his jacket out of his Jeep and slipping it on. "I'm ready to have my guts twisted into knots."

But instead of looking at Damon or Michael when he said that, Kai met my eyes, a knowing smile playing behind them. I flipped him off, and he just laughed silently.

"Blood would be better," Damon pointed out, plucking his cigarette back, taking a drag, blowing the smoke up to the sky, and then flicking the butt somewhere. "Come on. We'll pick someone. Someone who deserves it. Stalk her—or him—watch them, plan how we're going to get away with it, dispose of the body . . ."

I shook my head, only half listening as I scanned the parking lot again for Em.

"And then watch this town lose their minds at the danger lurking right under their noses," Damon said. "It'll be fun."

I heard someone breathe out a laugh again, but then silence fell, and no one said anything.

Because while no one was ready to do more than entertain the idea as a joke, not one of us doubted that Damon was somewhat serious.

He might even already have someone in mind.

"I'm so glad you're on my side sometimes," Michael told him.

Damon just took out another cigarette and lit it, musing out loud. "We'd be bound together in the secret forever."

"Yeah, well, there's no one I want to kill," Kai said.

Damon just stared up to the sky before bringing the cigarette toward his mouth again. "Lucky you," he murmured.

I looked down at him, his gaze still on the clouds, and I couldn't help this feeling in my gut.

Michael and Kai needed something to happen, and I . . . I already felt it coming.

The first bell rang, and we all headed indoors, students racing up the steps and trying to maneuver their way down the halls.

She'll be in class. She never misses school.

After stopping at the lockers and dodging conversations the others got tangled in on the way down the hall, I finally dove into lit class with my book and binder, looking to see who she planted herself around, so I knew whose ass to move.

But as I looked, I only spotted Chase Deery and Morgan Rackham in the classroom. No one else.

I stopped for a moment, faltering. *Fucking great.* This was what I got for rushing and trying to pretend like I wasn't rushing. Now I got to sit here like a dumbbell. And if she came in and sat far away, I couldn't move, or else she'd know I was waiting for her.

And I didn't want her to know I was waiting for her.

Continuing to a seat toward the windows, I took out my phone, pretending to look busy.

People drifted in, filling the seats, but I didn't look up as Kai, Michael, and Damon surrounded me.

As the minutes passed, I barely registered the teacher talking, the papers shuffling, or the nudge on my shoulder to pass the new packets back.

There was only one thing I was aware of as I sat there.

She wasn't here.

Maybe she was taking her time. She hated this class, after all.

But as the class wore on and she was nowhere to be seen, I barely heard a fucking word the whole time.

We started a new book. The teacher passed them out and finished his lecture, and something was due by the end of the week, but if it wasn't tomorrow, then I didn't care.

I didn't give a shit. Where the hell was she?

The bell rang, and everyone rose from their seats, piling out of the classroom, but instead of turning left outside the classroom, toward my next class, I turned right.

"Hey, where are you going?" Michael asked.

He and I shared government and economics.

"I'll be at practice," I assured him.

And I spun around and headed toward the library.

Coach would make me run laps once he found out I'd skipped classes, but I'd run so many laps the past few years, I was kind of perfect at it.

I couldn't sit in class right now. My head ached and heated up like a fuse, and I refused to look for her, because even though I told myself it would be just to make sure she was safe—make sure everything was okay—it was because I was pissed.

She really went to any length to avoid me, didn't she?

Rushing into the library, I made my way through the tables of students working and jogged up the open stairwell all the way to the third floor. I tossed my binder and books onto a table and pulled the group phone out of my pocket, heading down the long aisle and turning right down the fifth row. I reached up to a line of books and pulled out a fat, navy blue text, titled *Data Entry and Transcendental Curves of Non-Regular Polytopes*, something we know no one on this planet would even be interested in touching.

Opening the cover, I punched in the combination to the lockbox inside, stuck the phone in, and closed it, placing it back onto the shelf. The communal phone that recorded all our pranks had to be hidden somewhere no one would look and all of us could have ready access to it. Not sure why since I ended up being the one to fetch it and record most of the videos.

Then I heard someone's voice. "That title makes no sense."

I turned my head over my shoulder, seeing a glimpse of brown hair through the bookcases.

I clutched the disguised lockbox in my hand, pausing. Had she seen what I put in there?

I let go, peering through the bookcase and seeing Emory lean against the back wall, her head down with her hair and glasses covering her face.

"You weren't in class," I said.

Her chest shook, and I thought I saw her lip tremble.

But then she cleared her throat. "Wasn't I?" she snipped. "Wow, you're outstanding. Maybe for your next trick you can make fire and draw stories in the dirt about those funny holes in the sky that let the light in."

Huh? Holes in the sky?

Oh, stars. Was she calling me a caveman?

Little shit. I mean, I did do her literature assignment for her. Did she have any idea how hard it was to try to sound like an angry teenage girl with zero sense of humor?

Then a tear fell down her cheek, and she quickly swiped it away.

I dropped my eyes down her body, taking in the worn and cracked gray Chucks, and the skirt two inches too short with the green and navy blue tartan pattern that was two years outdated. The glowing olive skin of her beautiful legs, interrupted with the occasional bruise or scrape, which I actually kind of loved because she probably got them from constructing that gazebo and being amazing at something most of us could never do.

Her shirttail and cuffs hung out of her navy blue cardigan because it was too big, and her tie was missing, her blouse laying open an extra button. A lock of hair was caught inside her shirt, laying against her chest.

She was here and dressed for school, but she was hiding instead of going to class?

"What happened?" I asked.

But she just shook her head. "Just leave me alone," she whispered. "Please."

Please? God, she must be desperate if she was using manners.

"We started a new book in class," I told her.

She remained quiet, chewing on her lip.

"We had a choice," I said. "*The Picture of Dorian Gray, The Grapes of Wrath,* or *Mrs. Dalloway.*"

A little snarl peeked out, and I bit back my smile.

"I chose for you."

She gently pushed off the wall and started walking, dragging her satchel slowly down the aisle of books as I followed on the other side of the bookcase.

"I have your paperback in my binder," I told her. "Don't you want it?"

She didn't answer.

"Don't you want to know which one I picked for you?"

She kept walking, but she was going so slowly. Like she wasn't in her body.

"I picked something good."

"There's nothing in that selection that's good, so just give me *The Grapes of Wrath* paperback, because things can always get worse, and that choice will really make this day complete."

Seriously? How the hell did she guess which book I picked?

Dammit.

I knew she'd hate all the choices. The first week of school she went on some rant about the lack of diversity and relevant topics on our reading list and how the "classics" were only "classic" because novels written for a broader audience weren't getting published in the old days. The whole system was rigged and damn the man, et cetera.

I just wanted her to smile. It would be one thing if I were the one making her miserable, but I had a feeling I wasn't.

"Em, look at me a minute."

She stopped, looking like the whole world sat on her shoulders. What the hell was wrong?

I knew if I asked, she wouldn't tell me, though.

"Em?" I murmured.

Just look at me.

Still, she wouldn't turn. She was right here but miles away, and my chest ached.

"I grabbed you a study guide, too." I reached into my pocket and pulled out the folded packet. "Here."

I reached through the books and handed her the guide. It only took her a moment to reach out and finally take it, but when she did, I let it go and grabbed her hand instead.

She sucked in a breath and tried to pull away.

But I whispered, "Look at me."

She stopped resisting, but still refused to meet my eyes.

What was wrong with her? As far as my friends were concerned, there'd always been something wrong with her, but she looked . . . defeated. Like a broken vase barely held together with glue.

Emory Scott never looked like that.

She looked down, probably at our hands, and I didn't tighten my hold or caress her fingers. I just held her hand.

"Look at me," I whispered.

But she choked out a sob, turning her face away so I wouldn't see. "Don't," she demanded. "Please, don't be sweet. I . . ."

But all she did was shake her head, the words lost.

Rage boiled my blood, and I wanted to know what happened. Who hurt her? The sight of her crying was like a knife in my gut.

But she wouldn't talk to me. Not yet.

Maybe never.

"Knock knock," I said.

She just sighed but stayed silent.

I knew I was being annoying. I'd punch me if I were her.

"Come on, knock knock?"

She shook her head and dried her eyes, ignoring me.

I hardened my tone, demanding, "Knock knock."

"Come in," she snapped, cutting off my joke.

I stood frozen for a moment. How did she always do that?

Contrary to popular belief, it's not often I could be outsmarted, let alone repeatedly.

But that was clever. I broke out into a laugh, and after a moment, I noticed a small smile playing on her lips that she tried to hide.

Releasing her hand, I rounded the bookshelves and approached her, staring down at her bowed head and eyes that still avoided me.

"Look at me," I repeated.

Slowly, she shook her head, but it seemed more to herself than an answer to me.

"Emory . . ."

She stared at the floor and then retreated a step, but I grabbed her face, bringing her in close and rubbing my thumbs underneath her eyes. I wiped away the tears, but more just streamed down.

And in that moment, I wanted to do nothing else with my life more than change her world, so she'd never feel like this again. God-dammit.

She tried to pull away, but I couldn't let go. I wrapped my arms around her and pulled her in, hugging her as she gasped. Sobs wracked through her as she tensed, but I just held her tight, keeping her standing so she didn't have to even worry about that right now.

I couldn't stand this. She had to stop crying.

Finally, her arms relaxed, and every bit of fight inside of her melted away. She let her cheek fall into my chest, her arms hanging limply at her sides as she leaned into me, letting me hold her.

People passed behind us, but I didn't care what they saw as long as they kept going.

I stroked her hair with my hand, my fingers humming at the feel of finally touching her. Such a big mouth and attitude on a person who was really so soft and small.

I dipped my nose into her hair, the scent making my head buzz and the feel of her warming every muscle in my body.

"Let's go," I told her, taking her hand in mine and her bag in the other. "We're getting the fuck out of here."

I pulled her, not waiting for a reply.

She dug in her heels, suddenly alert. "We can't."

"Watch me."

I pulled her out of the library, leaving my shit on the table because I knew it would still be there later, and walked down the hallway and out of the school, hearing her nervous breaths behind me as she looked around frantically for teachers or surveillance cameras.

For some reason, though, she didn't protest more.

Heading to my truck, I tossed her bag into the bed and opened the passenger side door for her.

She finally met my eyes, looking so tired. God, the circles around her eyes I was finally able to see in the light of day . ... When was the last time she'd slept?

She opened her mouth, like she might argue, but then, she just climbed in. I slammed the door, rounding the truck and climbing in on my side.

I almost wanted her to fight. Emory Scott was letting me take her off school grounds during school hours, and she wasn't even demanding to know where.

I didn't like this dead look on her face. What the fuck was going on?

Starting the truck, I pulled out my phone and dialed as I drove out of the parking lot, turning to head toward the village.

She absently pulled her seat belt across her body, fastening it.

Roger Culpepper answered on the other end. "Hello?"

"Hey, it's Will. Can you open the doors?"

"It's nine a.m.," he told me.

"Just open the theater," I told him again. "Then you can go back to sleep."

I hung up before he had a chance to argue and looked over at Em, who just stared out the window. She'd stopped crying and just relaxed back into the seat, looking sad but comfortable.

I stared out at the road as we headed back into town, unable to help the smile peeking out. *Sorry, D. That's her seat now.*

R oger had the movie theater unlocked for us when we arrived, and I parked in the alley so no one would spot my truck off school grounds. Emmy didn't ask any questions as I parked her in one of the theaters and left to grab snacks.

Culpepper managed the theater and had been here for the nightly festival until a few hours ago. I felt bad about waking him up and dragging his ass in, but ever since my impromptu birthday party last

May after prom, my parents took my keys to the theater so I couldn't let myself—or others—in.

Roger relaxed when he saw it was just one girl. He loaded the film, dimmed the lights, I made the popcorn, and after he left, I locked the doors again and carried a handful of junk food into theater three.

"Hungry?" I asked, slipping her drink into her cup holder.

She looked up at me, her eyes still red but always beautiful. She shifted nervously in her seat and looked behind her toward the doors, probably scared we were going to be caught.

"It's gonna be okay." I set down the rest of the snacks and picked the popcorn back up as I sat down. "I know a kid who works in the office. I already called and told him to mark you present in every class today."

Plus, I had her turn off her cell phone in the truck, since I knew her brother might be tracking her. My parents threatened me with that from time to time.

I stuck some popcorn in my mouth and offered her some, the credits rolling on the film in front of us.

But she just stared at me.

"You know a kid?" she repeated, her usual snark painted all over her face with a big fat brush. "Of course, you have the whole school wired, because—"

"*Thank you* would be the correct response," I said, mid-chew.

She gaped at me.

"Try it out," I told her.

She closed her mouth, straightening her shoulders, but after a moment she dropped her defiant little chin and mumbled, "Thank you."

Sitting back in her seat, she took her Coke and held it between her legs, and after a few minutes, I offered her some popcorn. She took it, pecking at her handful like a bird.

It was a rotten breakfast, but it was better than eating nothing, and I wasn't sure she'd eaten yet today.

The trailers ran, and slowly, I felt her relax next to me, her eyes focused on the screen.

The opening scenes began, but instead of watching the movie I'd already seen, I watched her instead. Her eyes moved up and down and all around, mesmerized by the action, and her hand with a piece of popcorn stopped halfway to her mouth as she forgot all else.

"What is this?" she asked, but she didn't take her eyes off the screen. "Is this . . . ?"

The corner of my mouth lifted in a smile.

"*Underworld: Awakening*?" she finally said and looked over at me. "This doesn't come out until January. How do you have it already?"

I cocked an eyebrow, and she rolled her eyes, remembering who I was.

"Of course," she retorted. "Must be nice to—"

I looked back at the screen, clearing my throat extra loudly.

She halted whatever insult was on the tip of her tongue and let out a little laugh. "Thank you," she told me. "Thank you, thank you, thank you."

"Yeah, shut up," I teased. "Just watch the movie."

She focused her bright eyes back on the screen, a smile still spread across her mouth that I had a hard time ignoring. I'd seen her in the theater by herself from time to time, so I figured this was her happy place.

We watched, and as the movie played, she started to change. Her eyes got bigger, her color came back, and I even heard her laugh once.

I held out the Twizzlers and Milk Duds, giving her first choice, but when she picked the Milk Duds, I opened the carton and spilled half in my hand before giving her the rest of the box. I gave her a choice to be nice. I didn't actually want the Twizzlers.

I ate and she ate, and I snuck peeks at her throughout the film, watching her more than the movie.

She noticed, because she finally glanced over at me, catching my eyes. "What?" she asked, turning her eyes back to the screen.

"You're not what I expected," I said. "You like action movies, huh?"

"You don't?"

I laughed. She was back to shaming my antifeminist remarks. Yay for normal.

After a moment, she spoke up, her voice soft. "I don't think about anything else when I'm watching them," she explained. "They take me away. It's an escape. I like the survival aspect in some of them, too. Ordinary people becoming extraordinary. Being called to do great things." She rolled a Milk Dud between her fingers, watching the screen. "Hell hones heroes, you know? I feel it when I watch them."

What did she need to escape, though? I didn't ask, because that would only put her on guard, and I didn't want her to run.

"Well, I prefer the classics," I told her. "Arnold Schwarzenegger, Sylvester Stallone . . ."

"Jean-Claude Van Damme," we both said at the same time.

She turned to me, and I laughed.

"Yes," she said, smiling.

"Fuck yes." I nodded. "I mean, the Muscles from Brussels? Hell yeah."

"*Bloodsport*," she added.

"*Kickboxer*," I chimed in.

Great movies. The eighties were the golden age. Ordinary people going to war—battling for honor. I mean, you just don't get movies like *Lethal Weapon*, *Beverly Hills Cop*, and *Cobra* anymore.

You're the disease, and I'm the cure. Booyah.

But then, Em started laughing, her pearly white teeth gleaming in the biggest smile I'd ever seen on the smart-ass little shit.

I pinched my eyebrows together. "What?"

What was she going to make fun of me for now?

"*Kickboxer*," she said between giggles. "That scene where his teacher gets him drunk in a bar to see if he can fight intoxicated, and he starts dancing. Just the thought reminded me of you there for a minute."

"Why?"

She shrugged. "Big guy, super happy, having fun . . . I don't know." She stuck a piece of candy in her mouth. "Just seems like something you would do."

She sat back in her seat and looked up at the movie again.

"Hang around more and maybe you'll find out," I taunted.

I could dance. I could dance really well.

She licked her lips, the smile falling, but her breathing quickened.

We fell quiet again, the surround sound blasting every fight and explosion, but I swore I could only hear my heart beating with her next to me.

The minutes stretched, and I didn't even know what movie we were watching anymore.

"Why do you like me?" she finally asked.

I looked over at her, repeating Edward McClanahan's words, because it was the only way to explain. "We want what we want."

Her chest rose and fell harder, but not an inch of her moved anywhere as she sat there and seemed to sink into her seat.

I looked down at her hands, the yellow box in one and the other clenching her skirt.

What would she do if—

"Do you still want to hold me?" she suddenly asked me.

I shot my eyes up to hers, but she just stared at the seat in front of her. My heart hammered in my chest, and every inch of me warmed.

Fuck yes.

Leaning over, I put her cup in the holder and dumped her Milk Duds into the popcorn container on the floor, taking her hand and pulling her up. I watched as she came over and lowered slowly into my lap.

I slid down in the seat, folding her into my arms as she tucked her head into my neck, neither of us giving a damn about the film anymore.

I closed my eyes, savoring the feeling of finally having her in my arms. I had to fist my hands to keep them from roaming, or else she'd probably slap me.

But God, she felt good. Like everything was lighter when I held her.

"Don't tell you I said this," she whispered in my ear, "but you smell good."

I shook with a laugh, unable to help myself. "Keep being, like, pleasant and shit, and I'm going to find it really hard to keep being nice, Em. What are you trying to do?"

She shook with a chuckle, but then she slipped a hand around the back of my neck and whispered against my throat. "Remember what you said about nightfall?" Her lips grazed over my skin, feeling me. "You don't have to be nice. Not until the end of the movie."

The end of the movie. When the lights came up.

My dick swelled and hardened, and I threaded my fingers through the back of her hair, fisting it as I nuzzled into her mouth. "Em, Jesus."

She came up, both of us tightening our arms around each other as the heat of her lips fell over mine. "Just until the end of the movie," she whispered.

Sweat cooled my pores, and my cock twitched. I wanted everything at once, and my hands shook so fucking bad, I was afraid I wouldn't be able to control myself. I didn't want to scare her.

We held each other, our mouths centimeters apart as I came in and she inched away, and then she came in, and I held back, playing.

And then finally . . .

I caught her bottom lip with my teeth, she whimpered, and her mouth sank into mine, every nerve in my body firing as her warmth hit my tongue and her taste filled my head.

God, I'd waited for this, but as soon as my mouth moved over hers and her body filled my hands, I wasn't in a hurry anymore. I slowed everything, slipping my hand under her skirt and squeezing her thighs as she repositioned herself and straddled me.

I wanted this to last forever.

"So soft," I panted over her mouth.

God, her lips were soft.

I kissed her, both of us getting faster and harder, and when she came in for more and more, I was high. My dick strained against my pants, and I gripped her thighs, pressing her down on me.

She moaned, diving down to my neck and yanking my tie looser so she could get to more of my skin.

My head floated, the feel of her mouth blazing through my body with the sweetest pain. We nibbled and teased each other, and I wanted to take things off and see her. I wanted to touch her and kiss her in other places.

But I had to go slow. I didn't want this to be over, and she scared easily.

My cock bulged, and I felt it almost there. I grabbed her head, holding her to me and stopping her from moving, but not letting her go.

I . . .

She grinded on me, nibbling and licking my mouth.

I sucked in a breath. I . . .

"Shit." I gasped.

I dug my fingers into her thighs, the theater spinning around us. *Kissing. Only fucking kissing, and I was about to come already.*

She breathed hard into my neck, and I could feel her heart racing, too.

I hated it when things ended up being exactly how you hoped they'd be.

I leaned in and kissed her gently, starting slow again and taking my time.

She might regret this tomorrow. She was in a weird mood today, and maybe I was an action movie, here to help her escape, but that wouldn't fly when I finally took her into bed.

I wanted inside her head first.

Because contrary to whatever she thought, this shit wasn't ending when the lights came up.

CHAPTER 13

EMORY

Present

H e'd changed. And I didn't like it.

It had been over a day since he took my underwear in the pool shower, and he still hadn't spoken to me. Will was never so angry. Not that I was an expert on him, but I was the temperamental one. He was the lover.

I might've been able to get help from him eventually, but I didn't have time to wait for it.

Aydin's mind games. Taylor's leering. Rory's scowls.

I wasn't sure why I'd remained protected, but I wasn't counting on it lasting.

Will could get revenge on me all he wanted. Back in Thunder Bay. It was time for a plan.

I walked down the hallway and entered the game room, spotting the pool cues on the wall. I took one down, pausing as I looked at all the paintings adorning the maroon wallpaper on the walls.

This place was like Dracula's castle with all its nooks and treasures. But sad and dying, too. Why would people send their kids here? Why not a beach, with sun and warmth? Depression only made moods worse. Was this place really supposed to help?

I gazed at the paintings of ships and pirates, of sea battles and sea creatures. What was the connection? Did the person who previously owned the house enjoy the ocean?

Or were we close to one?

A sudden weight anchored me to the ground, a new possibility I hadn't considered.

If this was an island, I was fucked.

I needed to get to the roof. It was the best view I was going to get.

I shook my head. There were too many problems, and I wasn't solving any of them. It was Thursday, and my coworkers at the firm would've reported me missing by now, right? Missing one day would be odd for me, but three?

I wasn't friendly with any of them. No one had a key to my apartment. But they'd contact the police if I wasn't showing up to work or answering my phone. Right?

Not that it would do any good. No one would find me here anyway.

"You walk around bold as brass, don't you?" someone said from the dark corner in the room.

I startled, turning around and searching for the source.

"Like you have nothing to fear," he added.

I twisted my head right again, finally seeing long, black-clad legs. He slouched in the chair at the far corner behind the chess table. His face was in shadow.

I inched around the pool table, toward the door, but kept my eyes on him.

"But you forget," he panted. "We're all in here for a reason."

Taylor.

There was movement, and I stepped closer, my heart starting to hammer. He'd been sitting there the whole time. Watching me. Why was he out of breath?

My grip tightened on the pool cue as I approached.

"Ask me what I did," he said. And then continued with a loaded tone, "Ask Rory what he did. The underwater wax museum at his parents' lake house. It was *soooo* lifelike."

A shiver ran up my spine. A wax museum? *Lifelike.* What the hell did that mean?

And then I saw him.

I dropped my gaze, seeing his cock in his hand as he jerked it.

I sucked in a breath, rearing back.

He stroked up and down, quicker and quicker, and then I spotted my blue panties.

They were wrapped around his dick as he masturbated.

My heart sank into my stomach, and I glared at him as he moaned, his eyes falling closed as my lace rubbed against his skin and the muscles in his arms flexed.

What the . . . ? I stepped back, sickened.

"We want to leave," he told me, "but we'll never really be free, Emory." He looked at me again. "You can take him home, but he can never go back."

And he zoned in on me, jerking harder and harder. My stomach rolled, but I couldn't move, completely paralyzed as I watched him.

Until he begged in a whisper, "Suck on your finger. Deep throat it for me. Suck it hard."

I couldn't make my legs move, and I didn't notice I wasn't breathing until my lungs ached.

I bolted from the room, hearing his deep, dark laughter echo behind me as I ran.

I wasn't even sure where I was going until I found myself in the gym, ignoring Micah on the weights as I jumped on the treadmill, starting the machine and running in my bare feet.

I needed to run. I needed to be too exhausted to care.

Will gave him my underwear? I gnashed my teeth together, my nausea turning to fury.

Micah popped up his head, watching me for a moment, but then left the weights and started sparring with the dummy.

My body cooled with sweat, and I upped the pace faster and faster until I thought I couldn't keep up just to work off the steam and worry and rage.

I wasn't just going to sit here for four weeks.

I wasn't going to count on anyone to protect me.

I may not be able to run, depending on the elements, so I couldn't count on that as my only option, but I could do something.

Nine years ago, I decided to sit and wait. Ride it out and then run.

I wasn't doing that anymore.

I hit the emergency stop button and jumped off the treadmill, panting as I walked over to Micah.

"Show me some moves?" I asked, breathing hard as I removed my glasses.

He stopped and straightened, scowling at me. "Why would I do that?"

"What do you want in return?"

He grinned, and I arched an eyebrow at him.

I was pretty sure he didn't want *that*.

"A sandwich," he said.

I snorted, not missing the intended insult about a woman's place.

But it wasn't a horrible idea. I'd have an excuse to be in the kitchen with access to the food.

Even if someone kept an eye on me, I could hoard away something. It might come in handy if I needed to run or hide for an extended period of time.

"A *Philly cheesesteak* sandwich?" I clarified, upping the ante.

It wasn't kosher, so I couldn't eat it. It was one of the few rules I followed.

But I'd make it for them. That kind of sandwich would take longer than ten minutes to cook, giving me plenty of time in the kitchen.

His face lit up. "Really?"

I held up fists, widening my stance as my answer.

He smiled and took up position opposite of me, bidding me to attack. "Let's do this."

Two hours later, and I was sweaty and hot but not tired, strangely. I felt energized, and I wiped off my face to cover up my smile.

Incredible. Stranded for two days with five men—four of them strangers—and you'd think I would feel some danger.

It wasn't that I didn't. I just wasn't unaccustomed to it. It was familiar.

I walked toward the door, glancing behind me at Micah and Rory wrestling on the mat. Micah pinned him down, laughing, but one look from Rory, and Micah let his guard down. The skinnier guy grabbed him, flipped him over, and tried to choke him, but they were both laughing as they tried to get a hold of each other.

I shook my head, continuing out the door. "Have fun, survive . . ."

And then I stopped, remembering.

Lord of the Flies. A disturbing classic novel and one of the only ones I actually enjoyed in high school because it was so dark and . . . possible.

The boys who crash-landed on a deserted island without any adults had three rules. Have fun, survive, and . . . keep a signal fire going.

It only took a moment to decide. Shooting off, I glanced around me to make sure I was alone and headed outside to the driveway.

The empty fountain sat in the middle of the circular drive, and I looked overhead, seeing a clear sky for once.

I wasn't sure this would last, especially if rain soaked the wood, but I had to try.

Gathering sticks, branches, and even twigs, I hauled armful after armful to the empty fountain and threw them in, creating a massive pile. I returned to the edges of the driveway, gathering more, and built the pile higher, so it blazed bright and big, the light hopefully visible in the dark and the smoke visible in the day.

I ran farther to the tree line, picking up more kindling, and ran back, throwing it in.

But an arm shot out and grabbed my wrist.

I jerked my head, seeing Will in his jeans and T-shirt, green eyes void of the boy I remembered.

I yanked my wrist away and pushed him back. He grabbed my arm, and we both fought, me trying to escape and him trying to stop me.

"Someone is bound to notice it," I growled.

"No one will notice it," he told me. "And you're mistaken if you think he's going to let you light that in the first place."

Struggling, I pushed him away from me, and he let me go.

Yeah, I know. It was a long shot, and maybe without Mommy and Daddy's money, there was no point in them even trying to escape, because if they left here, they could only go home to the very people who sent them here in the first place. They weren't going to give up their names, hide in Brooklyn, and be pizza delivery boys.

But I didn't belong here. I had a job, and I didn't need anything from anyone.

"What did you do to get sent here?" I asked him. "I mean, your parents actually sent you here? Aren't you their favorite or something?"

He just held my eyes, refusing to answer.

It had been a while—maybe a year or more. Micah said Rory was the last new arrival seven months ago, and even he had already been home once, only to be sent back.

What was Will doing with himself? He was going to have the life.

"You're twenty-six," I told him. "What comes after this? Where do you go? Do you suddenly grow up?" I searched his eyes. "If it hasn't happened by now, it's not going to. You do you, and I'll do me."

He stepped in, looking down at me. "I hear you're making dinner," was all he replied with. "We're hungry now. Go cook."

I flashed a glare. Excuse me?

I shoved him in the chest, pushing him back.

I'm not serving you.

I'm not sitting at your table.

You can go and screw up your life without a care.

And also . . .

"You gave that sleazebag my underwear," I said.

You son of a bitch.

A grin teased the corners of his mouth, but he simply turned back to me, holding back his smile.

"But then you didn't need them, right?" I taunted, calming my voice. "Still have my pink ones from after Homecoming? Have you used them a lot, or did you just lube up with your own tears over the years?"

He crouched down and got in my face with his eyes on fire. "What makes you think there weren't lots of hot, wet panties over the years?"

Spinning around, he left, and I burned a hole in his back as he disappeared into the house.

Believe me, Will Grayson. I know exactly where you've been.

CHAPTER 14

EMORY

Nine Years Ago

They have mac and cheese, burgers, turkey tetrazzini," Erika Fane told some girl ahead of me in line, "and chicken potpie today, but I'd recommend the chicken sandwiches. They're good and spicy."

No. They aren't. The freshmen were the only ones who still hadn't realized where those cramps in the middle of fifth period were coming from.

The other blonde who looked like she could be her sister—except Erika Fane didn't have a sister—just stood there, not looking over the selections that Fane listed off.

"It all sounds fine," she replied. "Whatever you recommend."

Fane grabbed the chicken sandwich wrapped in foil and brought it to her. The other girl held out both hands, feeling for the item.

I narrowed my eyes, watching her. Slowly, and keeping her eyes focused ahead, she took the item and set it on her tray herself, albeit a little clumsy.

Like she couldn't see.

Realization dawned. This was Winter Ashby. Bitchy Arion Ashby's kid sister.

She was blind, I'd heard.

Well, hopefully, she was nicer than her sister. When did she start here? I rarely ate lunch, and we weren't in the same classes, so I hadn't seen her before.

They moved down the line, but not before an attack of conscience hit me and I plucked the chicken sandwich off her tray, quietly replacing it with a burger without her or Fane noticing. She wouldn't know who to thank, but that was okay.

I grabbed a burger and a banana before reaching over and taking a bottle of water, adding it to my tray.

An arm came around me and took my necktie, threading it through long, beautiful fingers, veins bulging through the back of his hand.

"Nice tie," he whispered close to my ear.

My heart leapt, and I stopped breathing for a moment.

His breath tickled my hair. "Thank you for wearing it."

I couldn't turn around and look at him because I was sure my face was ten shades of red. He'd put his tie on me after the movies when he'd dropped me at home, and I wasn't going to wear it, but . . .

He'd taken another bad day and made it good. I liked wearing something that reminded me of it.

He dipped down, slipping his hand around my waist and breathing into my neck.

"Emmy . . ."

Heat covered my body, hearing him say it just like he'd said it when I straddled him in the theater.

"Please," I begged, throwing off his hand, "just . . . go back to your table." I looked over to their regular seats, seeing Damon watching us while pretty girls loitered around. "Lots there to keep your attention."

"That's not what I want," he taunted, squeezing my waist again.

I moved down the line, looking around to see if anyone else was watching us.

"Don't worry," he said, letting me go and adding a brownie and chocolate milk to my tray. "All they see is me fucking with you. They'd never suspect—"

"That you were serious?"

He grinned to himself and dumped a bag of pretzels and some French fries on my tray. "No, that you like me."

He reached around my other side, his cheek on mine as he reached for a pudding and fruit cup.

He blanketed my back, pressing into me, and my heart beat so fast. I turned my head, feeling his lips close to mine.

"Please, just . . ." *Go sit down.*

But the words were lost, and I didn't finish the sentence. Sweat cooled my neck, and I finally clenched my tray, getting a hold of myself.

"Just go sit down," I snapped and then blinked, seeing all the shit on my tray. "And stop putting all this food on here! You're not eating with me."

"It's *for* you," he told me, taking out his wallet. "You're pale. All of that's kosher, right?"

I growled, starting to put the food back, but he grabbed my tray and handed the cashier the money.

"I'm going to need my tie back," he said. "Tonight."

"I can't," I told him.

"You will." He took his change and handed me the tray. "I'll pick you up at the end of your block at eleven."

"I can't," I said, louder this time.

But he came in closer, looking down at me. "And then I'm taking you to my house. Just us. I want to have a *Mission: Impossible* marathon with you tonight."

A *Mission: Impos* . . . ? I snorted, despite myself, and quickly looked away, trying to hide my smile. God, he was an idiot.

I wanted to go, though.

I stood there, shaking my head absently. *I can't*, I mouthed.

Martin would find out.

My grandmother would need me.

We had school tomorrow.

I'd let things happen he'd only make me regret.

But he came in, taking his tie around my neck and rubbing it between his fingers. "You come to me," he said, "or I'll come to you."

I got an A on that *Lolita* study packet. Over a week late, and I still got an A. And the best part was, I didn't even turn it in. I was tempted to.

I just couldn't do it, though. Every educational success I would've had after would've been marred. The rest of my life would've been over.

A fraud. A cheat. A lousy example to my children.

All because I faked one English assignment. That was how neurotic I was.

Unfortunately, the long arm of Will Grayson stretched all the way into the teacher's gradebook and changed my zero to a hundred percent, despite the missing assignment.

Not very inconspicuous. I would've been fine with a ninety-eight. Safe with a ninety-two, even.

I'd inform Mr. Townsend tomorrow that the grade was wrong.

If I don't forget.

I walked across the empty locker room and opened the shower curtain, stepping in and hanging my towel on the hook. Turning on the water, I dipped my already wet head under the spray, my skin breaking out in goose bumps at the feel of the hot water.

It was only four thirty in the afternoon. I still had hours before I was supposed to meet Will, and even though I'd spent the rest of the day—and my private time sneaking into the pool for a workout afterward—trying to tell myself I wouldn't care when eleven rolled around, and I'd left him waiting at the end of my block, it hurt inside a little at the idea of blowing him off.

It shouldn't hurt, right? I never agreed to go to his house tonight. He never even asked. Just another guy making you feel obligated to show him how grateful you are for his attention.

I pumped some shampoo into my hand from the dispenser on the wall and washed my hair, trying to hurry. I still had to make dinner, do homework, and I'd promised my grandma we'd watch a movie in her room tonight.

And I still wanted to get to the gazebo tonight to get some work done.

Will could come to me. If he found me.

I rinsed my hair and conditioned, pumping some soap into my hand and scrubbing the pool off my body. But I stopped, feeling the nubs on my legs.

Maybe I should shave again. *I mean, if he found me, I . . .*

Then I shook my head and stood up straight. *For Christ's sake. Get it together.*

I finished washing and ducked my head under the water again, rinsing the conditioner out of my hair as I stared ahead.

But then a shadow moved on the other side of the shower curtain, and I froze.

It stopped, standing there, the dark form looming just outside.

My heart skipped a beat. Only the emergency lighting remained on since there wasn't supposed to be anyone staying after school for any sports or band today, so I blinked as if that would clear my vision.

Shit, I needed my glasses. I could see okay without them, but I was nearsighted.

"Hello?" I called out. "Who is that?"

Forgetting to turn off the shower, I reached over and grabbed my towel, holding it up to my body.

"Martin?" I said.

The shadow peeled back the curtain slowly, and a lump swelled in my throat as Damon Torrance stepped into the shower with me.

"What the hell?" I barked.

But he just came closer, closing the curtain and approaching me with a towel around his waist, his smile coming into view.

"Martin?" he repeated. "Why would your brother be stalking the girls' locker room?"

"Why are you?"

I backed into the wall, the shower spilling over my shoulders and drenching the towel I clasped to my body.

He shrugged. "Practice just ended. I needed a shower."

"The team isn't practicing tonight." I shoved him in the chest, pushing him away. "You've been here. Were you waiting for me?"

But he just came right back in, pinning me to the wall. "Shhh . . ."

He stroked my hair, pressing his body into mine as he breathed down on me.

My knees started to tremble, and I clenched my thighs, suddenly feeling like I was going to wet myself.

I jerked away, pushing at him with one hand and holding my towel with the other. "What do you want?"

He pinned my wrist to the wall at my side as he smiled down. "I want to know what he sees in you. Maybe I'll see it, too."

My stomach twisted into a knot. I'd rather fucking die.

I looked up into his black eyes and smelled that shit he smoked, a scream lodged in my throat.

Just scream.

Scream.

There was no one here to hear me, and even if there were, Martin Scott wouldn't believe me. I was going to pay for this either way.

"Get out," I gritted through my teeth. "Get the hell away from me!"

"I thought you'd have more fight," he said, studying me. "You're kind of disappointing."

What, you can only get hard if I'm scared?

I was scared.

"Leave." I glared up into his eyes and then slapped him, but he shot out for my hands, trying to get a hold of them as I fought.

My towel fell, and he caught both my wrists, bending my arms at the elbows and holding my hands between our chests, using his weight to keep them pinned.

"Leave!" I growled.

"Then scream," he demanded instead.

I locked my jaw, pretending I was tough, but I was breathing a mile a minute.

He looked into my eyes, the water falling over both of us as he searched my face. "Why don't you scream?"

You wouldn't understand.

I gathered it was new for him. He preyed because it got him off, but it ruined his plans when he wasn't the victim's first rodeo, didn't it?

Because it wasn't the blood he was after, but the fear.

It wasn't the sex, but the power.

His eyes trailed down my neck and slowly down my arm, narrowing.

I don't scream, because . . .

"Because screaming doesn't help," he murmured. "Does it?"

My heart thundered in my chest, but I remained frozen, staring up at him as he looked at my body and the bruises in the shapes of fingers wrapped around my upper arm. The scrapes on my legs and the blue and purple on my shoulders.

"Because you get tired of being the victim," he said, like he was thinking out loud, "and it's easier to just let it happen."

He raised his eyes, meeting mine again, and my throat stretched painfully as his words burrowed into me.

He loosened his hold, but I didn't run.

"To just pretend we're in control of everything happening to us," he told me.

He blinked a few times, his demeanor completely changed, a troubled set to his brow.

My chin trembled.

"Until you can't remember who you were before you started lying even to yourself," he added. "Until you can't remember ever smiling when it didn't fucking hurt."

Tears filled my eyes, and I ground my teeth to keep my shit together.

Abuse can feel like love.

I remembered his words from lit class.

Starving people will eat anything.

His eyes fell down my body again, his head cocking and taking the purple and red on one side of my torso and the others on my thighs.

He didn't have any marks that I could see, but there were other kinds of pain.

"Will is like that," he said, his voice softening, somber now. "Isn't he?"

Like a smile that doesn't hurt. I nodded.

"Easy, normal, peaceful . . ." he told me. "The only thing in my life untouched by anything ugly. Nothing has tainted him. He's the one thing that's still beautiful and thinks the world is beautiful and believes people are beautiful and all that shit."

Yeah. But I couldn't say it out loud, because it was hard enough holding back the sob.

"You can't take him away from me," Damon told me, stepping back and letting me go.

And in that moment, I understood exactly what his problem was. He didn't dislike me. He resented Will liking me so much.

One day of wearing his school tie, because I loved the way he made me feel and I had to have a piece of him with me every moment, was nothing compared to the years Damon had relied on Will to be his little beacon of hope that the world was still a pretty place.

"You know it won't work anyway," Damon pointed out. "His family is one of the wealthiest in the country, Emory. His life is so far beyond your understanding, and vice versa. You know you have no place in Will Grayson's Homecoming picture."

I dropped my eyes, slowly sinking down and picking up my soaked towel, holding it over my body.

"I know," he continued. "Hurts to hear it, but it's true, and you know it. And what's more? It's pointless because you know how you are. Even I know how you are. The whole school knows. He won't fit, because you're committed to being miserable and you'll just drag him down."

I fisted my hands, wanting to scratch him up good.

I was not miserable. I was . . .

My heart sank, and I looked away.

He was right. What had I done since the beginning but push Will away?

I knew how it would end, so I knew better than to let it start.

"He wore you down," Damon went on, "and you need a release. I get it."

He approached me again, water spraying over his body as he hovered over me, imposing in a different way now that still scared me, but didn't frighten like before.

"So, take it for what it is," he whispered. "And release with me."

My stomach swirled. Huh?

"His infatuation will end, so pretend you're the one in control," Damon taunted. "Call it for what it is, because it's sure as shit not love. It's a crush. Hormones. Instant gratification. Acting out."

No. It wasn't.

Was it?

I mean, was he right? Was Will just a scratching post? Would he ever be anything more? I knew he wouldn't.

I could do it with anyone. I could do anything I wanted to. Will wasn't the only person I could escape with.

"You feel it, don't you?" Damon asked. "That need kids like us feel that Will never will? That need to destroy anything good, because every man for himself, and if you can't beat 'em, then join 'em." He came in and caressed my hair, and my chest ached, like something wanted to tear out of it, and I just wanted the pain to end.

Even for a minute.

I wanted the control.

"That tingle between your thighs," he panted, "that's telling you to just let it happen, because in the back seat of my car is where you'll be in charge."

I trembled, tears pooling, but when he pressed his body into mine, I gasped, my eyes falling closed.

"And when you're done with me," he breathed out over my mouth, "you'll get to be the first to walk away from something that was never going to happen anyway. You can do that with me. Don't play with his heart. Use me, instead."

I'd be in charge because I'd never love Damon.

I'd never be broken.

"I'm good," he whispered, holding my eyes. "I'm really good, Emory, and I'll make it worth it and save you the pain of him. As long as you quit now."

I planted my hands on his chest, entertaining what it would be like.

What it would be like to feel him on top of me.

What it would be like to kiss that mouth.

I thought about what it would be like . . . for a moment.

And then I blinked long and hard, clearing my throat.

He was good. I'd admit that. No wonder he got as much ass as he got, because if all anyone wanted was sex, Damon Torrance was gifted at manipulating someone's mind. Putting the right glasses over someone's eyes to make them see the world how he wanted them to see it.

God help the woman who ever fell in love with him.

I was tempted. I was tired of myself, and it was alluring—the prospect of not being me for a night.

But Will liked Em. I'd rather live in that memory of the movie theater forever than ever make another one with anyone else.

I pushed Damon away. "And you call yourself his friend."

He stood there, faltering for a moment, but then he chuckled, recovering. "His best friend," he pointed out. "Maybe he sent me to test you."

I rolled my eyes, wrapping my towel around me and shutting off the water.

"Or maybe not," he said, and I looked over to see his eyes falling down my body slowly. "You would've liked it, you know? I think I might've liked it, actually. It certainly wouldn't have been a chore."

Asshole.

"Get out," I said.

He nodded, turning around. "Well, I tried." And then he looked back at me over his shoulder. "Has Will seen the bruises?"

I tensed.

"Be prepared for what's going to happen when he does," he warned. "And what can happen to him if he goes up against a cop."

He walked out, and I stood there, my shoulders slowly slumping with the weight of his words.

Will could never see the bruises.

The moon hung low, casting the only light into the kitchen as I unloaded the dishwasher. I stacked the glasses and sorted the silverware, refusing to look at the clock that chimed on the wall, the pendulum inside ticking away the seconds.

"You should get to bed," a voice said.

I faltered, hearing Martin behind me.

He approached my side and reached down, picking up a couple of plates out of the washer and handing them to me.

I took them, bracing myself. "I will after this," I murmured. "Promise."

I turned and put the plates in the cabinet, waiting for his temper. Always waiting.

"Your grades are looking good," he told me instead. "And the gazebo is coming along. People compliment me on it."

He loaded the dirty bowl and fork into the dishwasher, and I rinsed out the sink and wiped off the counters.

"You still have a year to start applying, but I'll try to help with anywhere you want to go to college," he said. "Okay?"

I blinked away the sudden burn in my eyes, nodding. These moods were harder to take sometimes than the violence.

I wiped down the stove, setting the spoon rest back in place and waiting for him to leave.

But then, I felt his fingers brush my hair, and I stopped, standing there but still not looking at him.

"I'm sorry, you know?" he choked out, and I could hear the tears in his throat.

I locked my jaw, trying to keep it together.

"I do love you, Emmy." He paused. "That's why I want you to go. You'll be the one thing in this family that's not a fucking failure."

I closed my eyes.

Please, just go. Please.

"It just builds up," he explained at my back, "all day, every day, until I can't see straight, and I'm confused and blinded and ready to jump out of my skin. It's like I can't stop it."

And when he comes home, he takes it out on me, because I won't tell and I won't run.

"I don't even know what I'm doing when I do it," he mumbled. "I just can't stop."

A tear fell down my cheek, but I didn't make any noise.

"You know this isn't me," he said. "Right?"

I nodded, finishing the stove.

"Remember when I used to let you ride in the front seat?" he said, laughing a little. "Even though Mom said you were too little, so I'd wait until we got out of the driveway, and then I'd let you crawl up front?"

I forced a laugh. "Yeah." I looked at him over my shoulder. "As long as I promised not to tell Mom you were running a casino night in the basement while they were in Philadelphia that time."

He chuckled. "Is it strange that someone who loved breaking the rules became a police officer?"

"No," I told him. "They make the best cops. They know all the tricks."

He grinned. "True."

And what better place for a criminal to hide?

I didn't say that out loud, though.

"I got you something today."

He turned and dried off his hands, walking to the table where a brown bag sat. Reaching in, he pulled out a large, hardcover book and came over, handing it to me.

"It's used, but it caught my eye today when I walked past the library's sidewalk sale."

Greatest Deep Sea Dives.

I smiled and started flipping through it, evidencing my interest. "It's great," I chirped. "The photography is so beautiful."

"I thought you'd like it."

He turned and grabbed his thermos and lunchbox, and a glimmer of relief hit me, knowing he was getting ready to leave for the night shift. I drew in a welcome lungful of air.

"I love coffee-table books," I assured him. "Thanks for remembering."

He came over and kissed my forehead, and I stilled, only relaxing again when he'd backed away.

"Lock up tight," he said. "And sleep well. I'll be home at seven."

"Bye."

He left, heading to work, but it wasn't until I heard his car engine fade away down the street that I finally moved.

Putting the grocery bag in recycling, I carried my book, checking the doors and making sure lights were off before heading upstairs to my room. I left the lamp off and trailed to my bookshelf, pushing the row of books upright again and slipping in the newest addition to my collection.

Barcelona: An Architectural History

101 Most Amazing Caves

Always Audrey: Six Iconic Photographers. One Legendary Star

West: The American Cowboy

History of the World Map by Map . . .

I backed up, reading all the other spines on the two shelves, heavy with more than just the weight of the hardbacks. I liked to put them on the shelf whenever he gave me one. It pleased him to see me display his gifts, but also . . . it was like I'd accomplished something. It was like a trophy.

When the bruises faded, and I had nothing else to show for what would never fade in my head, I had this.

One book for every time I stood back up.

Again.

And again.

And again.

He'd bought me other things over the years, presents every time he'd spent his anger and the guilt crept in, and those things were also set about the room. Things I'd leave behind when I left, so that when he came in here, he'd see and remember everything, but I'd be gone.

I dropped my eyes.

At least, that's what I told myself.

My grandmother slept down the hall, the record player in her room working its way to the end of side A, and I wanted her to live forever, but sometimes . . .

Martin would be so much worse if she weren't here. She was the only person who loved me. I needed her to stay alive.

But she was in pain.

And if she were still alive when I was supposed to go to college, I couldn't leave. I couldn't leave her with him, and I'd have to stay here.

I hated myself for that thought, but . . .

While I didn't want her to go, I needed to get out of here.

What the hell was I going to do?

I hugged myself in my cardigan, only wearing my sleep shorts and tank top underneath, and turned around to close my curtains.

But someone sat there, in the corner of my room in my chair.

I gasped, jumping back.

"Hey," Will said.

My eyes widened, and I breathed hard, my heart still lodged in my throat. "What the hell?" I dashed to my window, plastering my cheek to the pane to get a view of the driveway and make sure my brother was gone.

"No candle in your window tonight?" he asked.

But I wasn't listening. "Are you insane?"

I scanned as much of the street as I could see through the tree outside, but I didn't see Will's truck. Hopefully, he'd parked it far away.

How the hell did he get in here? My brother just left. He could've seen him.

"You have to light a candle, Emmy."

"I never light a candle!" I growled in a whisper so my grandma wouldn't hear. "I don't give a shit about EverNight. You have to leave."

He sat there, wearing jeans and an Army green T-shirt that brought out the color of his eyes even from here. His hair was relaxed, the gel from the day about gone, and laying across his temples so beautifully.

"What did I say?" he said in a low voice. "If you don't come to me, I'll come to you."

So I didn't show up down at the end of the block. As important as a *Mission: Impossible* marathon was, I had other things to do, and he neglected to ask if I was free tonight.

He stared up at me, his arms resting on the chair, and I forced a scowl, despite the shot of excitement through my body at seeing him.

"I can't believe Emory Scott has a poster of Sid and Nancy on her wall," he joked. "A couple of obnoxious junkies, one who could barely even play his guitar."

"Please," I asked, ignoring his teasing. "You can't be here."

He rose slowly, never taking his eyes off mine. "Or maybe you have a thing for doomed romances."

I stepped back as he stepped forward. "Just leave," I told him again. But he kept coming. "You're so pretty," he whispered.

I shook my head, curling my fingers into fists.

"But I'm getting really tired of you looking at me like that," he said, his expression suddenly serious. "Like I can't be trusted."

Well, could he? And even if I could trust him to have good intentions with me, I wasn't ready for this. I didn't want him involved in my life. I was doing him a favor.

I loved the theater, and I'd treasure the memory forever.

But Damon was right. Yesterday was fun. We were done.

"You need to leave," I said again.

His eyes sharpened on me. "And I'm getting really fucking tired of you saying that." His jaw flexed. "What's the problem? Yesterday was amazing. Why do you always have to think so much until you've twisted something that was good into something bad?"

"I don't owe you anything," I bit out, "and I didn't invite you in, so just leave! Get out."

He stopped, the glare in his eyes almost as heart-stopping as his smile. "You know, I was nicer to you than I had to be." He squared his shoulders. "You know how many girls I can get like that?"

He snapped his fingers, and the funny, laid-back, sweet protector from the last several days was gone.

Believe me, I was well aware that he could get any piece of ass he wanted and had already. I wasn't the first to touch or kiss him.

"Well, I should just thank my lucky stars that all my relentless, hard work following you around like a pathetic puppy just to get your attention actually paid off!" I yelled, calling him out fucking good.

He chased me! Not the other way around.

He took a step toward me but then someone called my name, and he stopped, both of us glowering at each other.

My blood boiled, and I could see his neck glowing with a light layer of sweat already.

Everything was hot. It was dark, we were close, and my bed was right there.

My clit throbbed once, and I stopped breathing.

"Emmy," a small voice called again.

I blinked, releasing the breath I didn't realize I'd been holding.

"Emmy?" my grandmother called again.

Will's rigid stance relaxed a little, and his eyes softened.

I dropped my gaze and shook my head, managing no more than a whisper. "Please, just leave."

I left the room, turned right, and headed to my grandmother's bedroom, the late evening breeze making her white curtains billow.

She tried to push herself up in bed, her bulky pink robe wrapped around her.

"Hey, hey," I said, rushing up and lifting the cord to the oxygen mask so she wouldn't snag it. "I got it. I'm here."

She sat up further, leaning back on her pillows as I helped her take off her mask.

I put it up, listening to her breathe and making sure she was all right for now.

"Are you okay?" I asked.

"I just need water."

I picked up her cup and refilled the water, handing it to her as I held the straw in place.

"You forgot to light my candle," she said as she took a sip and peered up at me.

I stared at her, my brow still tense from a moment ago. Everyone was out to try my patience today, it seemed.

"Don't give me that look," she warned. "Go light it. It's my last, no doubt."

I pursed my lips, knowing there was no way to argue with that. She may not be here next EverNight.

Fine.

I turned and walked to the mantel, grabbing the matches we kept for the fireplace she no longer used and took one of her midnight patchouli-scented candles to the windowsill. I set it down and lit it, making sure the flame was visible through the glass.

Such a stupid tradition.

Although, there was something more alluring about it now since Will told me more of the story. Every October 28, since 1955, a year after the Cold Point murder, the residents of Thunder Bay lit candles in their bedroom windows for Reverie Cross on the anniversary of her death.

While the basketball team made their annual pilgrimages to Edward's grave, everyone else honored his victim, convincing themselves that if they didn't, not even death would withhold her vengeance. If your candle was still lit by morning, you were in her favor.

If not, something bad would befall you before the next EverNight.

It made about as much sense as throwing salt over your shoulder to ward off bad luck.

I watched the reflection of the candle flickering in the window and then reached over, closing her other window. If she wanted the candle to stay lit, then she'd have to do one night without her beloved wind.

I cast one quick glance out the window, wondering if Will had left.

Walking over to her side, I took the cup and set it down, smoothing her hair away from her face. Eighty-two years old, and she looked five hundred.

Except for the eyes. In her eyes, she still looked sixteen and secretly planning to steal the old man's car for a joyride with her friends.

"Do you have a boy here?" she asked.

I stilled. "No, Grand-Mère."

"Menteuse," she retorted, calling me a liar in French. *"Qui c'est?"*

"Who's who?"

She jerked her chin behind me, and I whipped around to see Will standing in the doorway.

Dammit. I told him to leave.

But he just walked in, smiling gently. *"Allô,"* he said. *"Je m'appelle Guillaume."*

I gaped at him, hearing French spew out of his mouth like it was nothing. *Guillaume* was the French variant of William.

Seriously?

Frankly, I'd been surprised he even spoke English. Figured him for someone who communicated solely in emojis.

But my grandmother smiled. *"Parlez-vous français?"*

"Un peu," he said, measuring about half an inch with his fingers. *"Très, très peu."*

She laughed, and that same smile that made him look like he was built for hugs spread across his face.

He looked down at her, and I rolled my eyes.

Un peu, *my ass.*

My grandmother had been born here, but her parents came from Rouen in France. They fled in the thirties under the growing threat from Germany, and even though she'd grown up speaking English at school here, her parents made sure to preserve her heritage.

In turn, she raised my mother to speak French, as well. I didn't speak it as well as I'd like, but I understood it.

More French poured out of Will's mouth as he talked with her, and I listened.

"I hope we didn't wake you." He looked thoughtful. "Your granddaughter was giving me the verbal beating I deserved. I apologize."

My heart pitter-pattered a little, but then my grandma laughed.

"Perhaps deserved," she said. "And perhaps she has my short temper."

I leveled her a look.

Settling back down into her bed, she took her mask off the hook, holding it. "It was a long time before I met someone who could take me," she explained. "That's the thing about broken people, Guillaume. If we ever give you our heart, then you know that you deserve it."

Tears welled in me, but only for a moment.

"He was patient with me," she told him, a far-off look in her eyes.

My grandfather.

Long since passed, but they were well and truly in love. At least she was happy for a while.

"Now go," she told us, starting to put on her mask. "I'm tired."

Like hell she was. We could watch a movie or something.

"Grand-Mère . . ."

But she shouted, "Go! Be young!"

I wanted to laugh, telling her that I was forty-three at this point and just over it, but it would make her happy if she knew I was happy, so . . .

She put her mask on, and we left the room, me leading the way back to mine.

Once inside, I closed the door and watched Will set a candle on my windowsill. It was the one that sat on my grandmother's dresser. He must've swiped it.

He pulled out a lighter from his jeans and lit it, positioning it in the center as the small glow came to life, burning against the black night.

He turned, the light of the flame flickering in his eyes as he looked over at me.

"No movies tonight then?" he asked, walking around my room.

I shook my head, not meeting his eyes.

"And I think," he continued, moving toward me, "even if you could leave, you wouldn't anyway."

Taking a step, I moved away from him, both of us circling each other.

Again, I shook my head.

"Because you're suspicious of everything good," he told me.

I remained silent, continuing to move away as he moved in.

"And it won't end when you go to college or leave this town, Em. Nothing will change. You still won't have good things."

I tried to swallow through the lump in my throat, but I couldn't.

"Because you'll still be you," he said.

I breathed in and out a few times, and then the words spilled out before I could stop them. "I want to let this happen," I told him, finally looking up and meeting his eyes. "Part of me really does, Will. You know why?"

He stared, and I barely noticed that we'd both stopped moving.

"Because as soon as it was over, I know I'll never have to hear from you again."

I didn't blink as I held his eyes, his beautiful greens sharpening and his spine straightening.

Yes, fucking you would be the one way to get rid of you. It was almost tempting.

But then I watched his lips tighten as his eyes glistened.

He fell silent, looking taken aback, and I faltered, watching my words work their way through his head, slicing a bloody path that I immediately regretted.

He dropped his eyes, stuck the lighter into his pocket, and let out a resolved breath. "Why are you so mean?"

But he didn't really want an answer. Turning away, he left my bedroom and headed down the stairs, and in that moment, my insides crumbled, because I knew I'd gone too far.

I didn't want this.

I didn't want him to go because I'd never hear from him again. I'd go to school tomorrow, pass him in the halls, but this time, he wouldn't look back at me.

I'd gone too far.

Racing after him, I jogged down the stairs, leapt over the last few steps, and pushed the front door closed again just as he was opening it.

"I'm sorry," I blurted out, gripping his T-shirt at his waist and dipping my forehead into his back. "I'm not . . ." My voice shook. "I'm just . . . not a happy person, Will. And you're right, I never will be."

Tears lodged in my throat, and I blinked long and hard to keep the tears away. I didn't want to cry in front of him again.

He stood there, still, only the beat of his heart pulsing through his body.

"I'm not right for you," I told him.

And not because he was rich and popular and I wasn't, but because he made my life better. I looked forward to him.

What did I give him?

"Noted," he replied coolly. "Now let me go."

I squeezed my eyes shut at his cutting tone.

He wouldn't be back.

And something started to come over me, like a curtain falling— or lifting—and for once in my life, I refused to stop myself. I was so cold.

And he was so warm. It was like an invisible rope pulling me to the edge that it was beyond me to control.

"You wanted your tie back," I whispered.

His back moved with each breath. "Keep it," he told me. "Or throw it away."

He reached for the door handle.

"You want something of mine instead?" I blurted out.

He stopped, gripping the handle but not turning it.

My heartbeat raged, and I knew I was going too far again. I'd regret this. I'd hate him later. He'd hate me. My brother could drop by on his rounds to check on me . . .

But . . . I didn't give a shit.

I wanted to be here now.

Pushing my cardigan over my shoulders, I pulled it off my arms and held it out in front of him.

"This, perhaps?" I asked softly. But then I let it slide off my hand to the floor. "No, it won't fit you, I guess."

He stared down at my discarded sweater, and I could barely breathe, but he wasn't leaving, and I kept going.

Taking the hem of my tank top, I pulled it over my head, the air hitting my bare breasts, every inch of my body alive with awareness. "Or this?" I murmured, holding my white top in front of him.

His chest rose and fell harder, and it was like he was frozen, unable to move.

I leaned in, pressing myself into his back, and dropped the shirt, whispering up into his ear, "That's too small, too. I told you, Will Grayson. We . . . don't . . . fit."

He exhaled hard, looking over his shoulder. "There's a part of you that's my size, I'll bet," he teased.

I bit my bottom lip to keep my excitement in check. I slipped my hands inside his shirt and circled his waist, running my fingers over his stomach and up his abs.

Heat pooled between my legs, and I nearly groaned, feeling his soft, tight skin, the muscles and curves of his body and things I wanted my mouth on now, not my hands.

There was nothing about Will Grayson that wasn't perfect. God . . .

"I want to take off your shirt," I told him.

He planted his hand on the door to steady himself, and I could see the sweat on his temple.

He looked exhausted. I almost smiled.

After a moment, he straightened, and I took that as my cue. Lifting up his T-shirt, I pulled it over his head, dropped it to the floor, and came in, circling my arms around his waist and pressing my skin to his as I took a chunk of his back between my teeth.

He gasped, slamming his hand into the door again, and I grinned.

I dragged my teeth across his back and then licked his skin before kissing him. He moaned, and I held him, closing my eyes and feeling his body quiver. His smell—warm and heady—seeped into my brain.

I wanted him to know he deserved better. I wanted him to know that if I were someone else, I'd be his and I'd love him so good.

Running my hands up his chest, I traced the ridges of his collarbone, down the dip between his pecs, and trailed kisses on his back.

Reaching over, I pulled a silk paisley scarf off the coat hanger and brought it up to wrap around his eyes.

He inched away, trying to turn around, but I stopped him.

"What's this for?" he demanded.

Every bruise on my body throbbed, and it took a moment to answer. "Rules," was all I said.

He didn't understand, but he didn't argue, either. I tied the scarf around his eyes so he could face me and not see everything.

His breathing quickened as he lost sight of the world around him, and I turned him around, looking up at his face.

"Can you see anything?" I asked.

"No."

Inching up on my tiptoes, I pressed myself into him, guiding his arms around my body and then wrapping mine around his neck. "And now?"

The corner of his lips lifted into a smile, his hands immediately roaming and taking hold of me. He ran his fingers all over my back, the pressure growing as he learned the terrain, and then he slid his hand up my stomach, taking one of my breasts in his palm as he leaned down and took my mouth with his.

I sucked in a breath, whimpering at the heat and nerves firing over every inch of my body. Lifting me off my feet, he moved over my mouth, slipping his tongue between my lips, and I groaned, feeling it down to my toes.

A sound pierced the air, but I barely noticed as I wrapped my legs around his waist, lost in his body.

His lips trailed to my neck, sucking, and I tightened my arms around him, trying to get closer and closer as I felt my eyes roll into the back of my head.

"Will . . ."

He squeezed my ass in both hands as I found his mouth again, almost too hungry to register the far-off sound when it happened again.

He bit my lips and slipped my glasses off my head, setting them on the table.

The sound—a ringing—perked my ears, and I finally blinked my eyes open.

My phone. I pulled away from his mouth, turning my head over my shoulder toward the kitchen, hearing the special ringtone I had designated for Martin.

Shit.

I tried to push Will away. "I have to answer it."

"Don't."

He pulled me in tighter, kissing me softly as he rubbed his thumb around my nipple again and again.

"Please." I moaned, not wanting to let him go. "It's my brother."

"And I'm your man now." He took off the blindfold, looking up into my eyes. "And I'm asking you for tonight."

He started to carry me up the stairs to my bedroom, but the phone rang again.

That was three times he'd called.

I squirmed out of Will's hold, running back down the stairs. "If I don't answer, he could come home to check on me. He could find you here."

He grabbed my arm, pulling me back. "Then let him." He glared down at me. "I don't give a shit. He won't keep me away from you, so the sooner he knows the score, the better."

My naked body, except for my bottoms, seemed to scream, and even though it was dark, and he wouldn't see much, he might still notice the bruises. I had to cover up.

"Let me go," I gritted out, anxious.

But he didn't. Pulling me in, he lifted me into his arms again and looked up into my eyes. "Look at me," he said.

I did, the softness in his voice making me forget my brother and my body for a moment.

"I . . ." He trailed off, struggling for words. "I . . . like you."

It sounded like "I love you," and my chin trembled.

"I've liked you forever," he said. "If you talk to him, the spell will break and the night will be over because you're not the same in the sun. You'll have all kinds of reasons again tomorrow about why I can't have you. Stay with me tonight. Don't talk to him. Don't let anything between us tonight."

Sobs swelled in my chest, and I held his shoulders, wanting to just wrap my arms around him because he was probably right.

"Or you can come to Homecoming with me," he said, giving me a choice. "Tomorrow night."

Homecoming?

The phone rang again, but we just stared at each other, me in his arms and my legs dangling.

I couldn't go to Homecoming. I didn't have a dress. I didn't dance. I didn't want to be around his people.

Martin would never allow it.

People would just laugh.

I pushed against his hold, diving down to the floor for my cardigan as the phone rang and rang. I looked back up at him, covering myself with the sweater.

"No," I said. "You can go now. I'm sorry I stopped you."

He advanced on me, but I turned and ran, slipping on my sweater as I dashed into the kitchen for my phone.

I answered. "Hello?"

"What the hell were you doing?" Martin snapped. "I've called four times."

I almost turned to see if Will was behind me, but my heart was beating so fast, I was afraid Martin would hear the shake in my voice.

"I'm sorry. I . . ." I stammered. "I fell asleep with my phone downstairs."

"Of course, you did." His tone was clipped. "We're expecting wind tonight. Make sure the windows are closed, the garbage cans are stored, and the . . ."

But my mind trailed off as he barked in my ear the same orders I'd heard a hundred times.

I licked my lips, still tasting Will and feeling the emptiness grow and grow behind me as I heard the front door click shut.

I wanted to cry.

Martin eventually hung up, and I came back to the foyer, seeing that Will was gone.

I stood there for a minute, sick of the guilt and self-hate. I'd done it again. I was a bitter, condescending coward, and hopefully, he'd move on to someone like him. Happy and bubbly and . . . fun.

At least I wouldn't be at Homecoming to see him enjoy someone else.

Taking myself upstairs, I checked on my grandma one more time and then entered my room, closing the door and plugging my phone into the charger.

Walking over to the window, I watched the candle flicker, debating for a moment to leave it alone.

But I didn't believe in anything.

Least of all, Reverie Cross.

I blew out the candle, the room going dark.

Except for the two headlights that came into view, shining outside my window. I straightened, looking out to the curb and seeing a matte black car suddenly speed off, its tires peeling and screeching as it raced away.

I squinted, but I couldn't see well without my glasses that were still downstairs where Will left them.

It wasn't a truck—I don't think. It wasn't Will.

And then I saw it. The glimmer of gold coming from the tree outside.

It shook and jingled in the light breeze, the bronze chain draped over a branch that was empty before.

I inched closer. What the hell was that?

CHAPTER 15

WILL

I jerked as Aydin grazed me with the scissors, the small blades slicing through the thread.

A cigarette hung from his mouth, and I pulled it out, taking a drag as I sat on the table in the kitchen and he stood next to me, removing the stitches at the top of my arm where it met my shoulder. Just a small cut from taking a tumble in the woods last week before Emmy arrived.

I stared off, watching her as he worked.

She was sly. I'd give her that. Spending years getting the shit kicked out of her had taught her how to hide.

Emmy moved around the kitchen, back in the black pants she'd arrived in, but wearing one of Rory's white T-shirts as she fried up meat and added peppers, onions, and cheese.

She stole glances over at me every now and then, and I kept my gaze locked on her.

A piece of bread here, a wedge of cheese there. Some cheesecloth to wrap it up, as well as an orange and then some more bread.

I fought not to smile, admiring how she deflected attention from the hand stealing food to the hand reaching up to grab a plate or snatch a fork out of a drawer.

Aydin hadn't noticed because he had Taylor watching her and

Taylor was an idiot. He stood in the corner, under the dead clock, peeling the label off his water bottle and only glancing up at her every now and then.

But the glances lingered, drifting down her body as she reached to grab some utensil or bent over to pull out a pan from the cupboard.

Aydin was the only thing keeping that one on a leash. If Aydin weren't here, I knew exactly what Taylor would try to do with her.

"Have you ever requested anything other than liquor and cigarettes?" I asked quietly, taking another puff before sticking the cigarette back into his mouth.

He inhaled one last time and then dropped the butt into his cup of coffee. "Yes."

"Like what?"

He didn't answer, and I shot him a look, seeing a smile playing on his lips. Somehow, he got a connection—someone to bring him contraband every month, and while he was a brutal fighter who would go to any length, the alcohol and tobacco were the only other means he had to control us.

Or them, at least. Micah and Rory might be with me, but we wouldn't get far if I didn't have Taylor or Aydin. I still needed one of them with me before I could leave.

This shouldn't have taken so long. I just didn't expect him to be so tough to crack. I had no idea where he was hiding his contraband, and after over a year, I had yet to find it.

Taylor walked behind Emmy at the stove, picking up a lock of her hair and smelling it. I clenched my jaw, watching her jerk her head around and move away.

"So, did you get it?" I continued, prodding Aydin. "The other thing you asked for?"

He finished cutting the stitches and picked up the tweezers, pulling the thread out of my skin. "Yes."

"Then you can get her out," I stated. "I want her gone."

"You want her safe. She is safe."

I thinned my eyes on him. She wasn't, and even if she were, she was messing up plans and accelerating my timeline. I didn't need the distraction.

"She thinks I arranged to bring her here," I told him.

"And your pride hurts."

Yes. Right now, she thought I was still obsessed and small-minded, every moment we spent together vivid and tantalizing in my memory.

I didn't want her to know that was true. Ever.

I was supposed to be somebody by now. I was supposed to make her regret not wanting me, and this was humiliating. She shouldn't be here.

"I'll arrange it," he told me.

I looked at him.

"When we're done with her," he clarified.

Rain tapped against the kitchen window over the sink, the sun already set as Rory and Micah walked into the room, dressed in their best as Micah rushed over to her side and smelled the food.

She didn't smile back at him, but she didn't move away, either.

"Did she ever mention what kind of alcohol she likes?" Aydin asked. "Vodka, rum . . . ? Might help her loosen up. I was thinking of sharing tonight."

I turned my gaze on him, straightening my spine at the threat.

Get her drunk. Get everyone drunk.

No.

He yanked out the last stitch, and I hissed, drawing everyone's attention as they looked over at us.

Aydin leaned into my ear, whispering, "You think I don't know you're planning something?"

His breath ran down my neck, and fear coursed through me. I hated having him so close.

"You've spent a year whispering in their ears, trying to turn them against me," he gritted out, "but you'll never be able to do what's necessary to take power, here or anywhere in life, William Grayson." He dropped his tool, meeting my eyes. "You have no idea what it takes to be me."

He moved away, and I held Emmy's eyes as she watched us, paused in her stirring.

I remembered similar sentiments from her years ago, and a similar feeling around my friends even.

Nothing had changed for me here.

Not yet.

Thunder cracked outside, rain pummeling the windows, and I glared at Emmy as everyone sat at the dining room table and dug into their sandwiches. Her presence made everything harder.

I was going to kill Michael when I got home. I was going to drench his fancy, fucking suit in his own blood for sending her here.

"How do you know I am an architect?" Emmy suddenly asked.

I shot my eyes to Aydin.

He stared at her, looking confused.

"The gift," she reminded him.

What gift?

"I . . . didn't," he answered. "There's not much to do here. Figured you'd enjoy drawing."

He gave her drawing pencils? Where did he get drawing pencils?

He sat there in his expensive black suit and black shirt, all of us dressed and shaved at Aydin's insistence.

I had to admit, nice clothes made me feel human again, but I didn't appreciate this prelude to whatever he was planning. Micah, Rory, and Taylor enjoyed the bourbon Aydin gifted to the table, chowing down on their sandwiches and sucking down shot after shot.

Emmy scooped up some soup she made with the entrée, sipping spoonfuls, while I tried to resist the sandwich as much as the alcohol.

I eyed the bottle of liquor, my tongue like sandpaper in my mouth.

I wanted the burn of the drink in my throat. I'd been clean for almost two years, but only sober for one, and it was still hard.

I was sure Aydin knew that, and corrupting me was part of his plan.

I pushed the glass he'd offered away toward Micah.

"What kind of work do you specialize in?" Aydin asked her. "Homes? Skyscrapers?"

"Restoration," she murmured. "Churches, hotels, city buildings . . ." And then she looked at me. "Gazebos."

I forced a slight smirk, letting her know that I knew that she knew what I did to hers.

She may not have deserved it, but . . .

Okay, yeah, she kind of deserved it after she laid waste to my fucking heart. I wanted to break something of hers, too.

Fuck it. I was drunk and pissed that night.

"Well, you've come to the right place," Aydin told her.

She half smiled, looking around the room. "Think they'd mind if I cleaned the place up a bit?"

"You already do."

She laughed, and I swore I saw a blush cross her cheeks.

She continued drinking the broth, and I cocked my head, studying her.

She was flushed. Why?

"So, did Will ever tell you about Devil's Night?" she asked him. "We celebrate it in Thunder Bay. It's coming up, actually."

Then she looked at me, leaned back against her chair, and pulled at the collar of her shirt like she was hot.

I tensed. Something was off about her right now.

"In fact, I hear one of his best friends is getting married that night," she said to him, but really to me.

Michael and Rika? Didn't know that, but she didn't need to know that. I hid my surprise.

"He doesn't talk about home much," Aydin replied.

Because when people know what you love, they know your weakness, and I didn't trust Aydin. I was here to gain strength. Not bring more enemies down on my family.

Emmy continued, "It's an annual festival of sorts, but it basically boils down to local rich kids basking in the gloriousness of their privilege."

He laughed. "Yes, I know the type. Too stupid to set the bar higher because they've never been challenged."

Her eyes glowed bright, her skin glistening a little. What was going on?

"It happens the night before Halloween," she said, explaining her vast knowledge of something she barely knew anything about, "and it's common to pull a prank as part of the ritual."

"Did you join in the festivities?" he asked.

"Once." She met my eyes.

Once? When?

"Didn't he ever tell you, Will?" she asked me.

I narrowed my eyes. Who? And tell me what? She had gone out on Devil's Night? With who and when?

But I sat there, acting like I knew exactly what she meant because I wasn't fucking asking.

She laid her forearms on the table, leaning in. "Did you ever find what I had buried under the gazebo when you burned it down?" she asked. "Or is it still there under the dirt?"

I balled my fists.

"All the shit you don't know," she said. "So clueless. It's almost comforting how you don't change."

I shot out of my chair, my limit reached and my control gone. I swiped my arm across the table, shoving my plate and shit onto the floor.

"You don't get to waltz around this house, shooting off your mouth as if you've been through even half of what I've been through!" I shouted.

She stared up at me, her eyes piercing. "This is your life, and it's not my fault," she said in a hard but low voice. "Drugs and alcohol and more drugs and alcohol, mixed with how many women over the years?" And then she looked around the table, stopping on Micah first. "I know your story." Then she flicked her gaze to Taylor. "And I can only assume you're plagued by every vice in the book, judging from the leering and creep factor. What happened? Accidentally almost kill a girl when you kept the plastic bag on her head too long during sex?" She shook her head and gazed around at all of us. "You're not monsters. You're jokes."

No one moved, her words hanging in the air, because everyone was waiting to see what Aydin would do. No one talked to him like that.

But this was how Emory was. Quick to judge because it felt better to push everyone away. If she didn't understand us, she didn't have to surrender a single piece of herself.

Was she drunk right now?

And then it hit me. Flushed skin, sweat . . . I found her bowl of spilled soup on the table and picked it up, smelling it.

The bourbon was faint, but it was there. I darted my eyes to Aydin, and everything was written behind the mild amusement in his. He'd spiked her dinner.

Motherfucker.

But before I could do anything, Rory spoke up.

"I killed a girl," he said.

We looked at him as he sat there, calm and relaxed.

"Three, actually." He took a gulp of his bourbon and set the glass back down. "And four men, as well. I drugged them and took them to the lake." He paused, his gaze falling. "In the dark. At night. Deserted. Alone."

Em stared at him, unmoving as she listened.

"At first, I hurt them," Rory went on, the memory playing in his head. "Burned them, waterboarded them, cut them . . . just to see if it would make me sympathetic enough to not kill them. To see if I could stop myself from crossing that line."

Emmy's brow knit, and her breathing turned shallow.

I'd heard bits and pieces of what he'd done here and there, but never from his lips. I'd kept my distance when I first arrived, feeling him out, but after a while I'd realized not everything was as it seemed.

"By the third one," he continued, "I just started tying them up and throwing them off the boat."

His voice was almost a whisper now.

"Someone saw me one night," he told us. "Luckily, it was the hillbilly sheriff my parents owned."

He took another drink, emptying the glass and rising from his chair.

Emmy tipped her head back, not taking her eyes off of him.

"And believe me, they deserved exactly what they got," he said. "I'm just ecstatic no one caught me until I was done with all seven of them."

He buttoned his suit jacket and drew in a long breath, exhaling it.

"Thank you for dinner," he said, leaving the table.

He walked out of the room, and Micah sat there for less than a moment before he followed him. Em dropped her eyes, probably feeling like an ass.

Would she ever learn?

"I want her gone," I told Aydin again.

He shot me a look. "I can't help you."

Turning to her, he continued, "You're right. We're not monsters." He reached across the table, taking the bourbon and pouring more into his glass. "Evil doesn't exist. That's just an excuse for people who want quick answers for complicated questions that they're too lazy to deal with. There's always a reason things are as they are."

"I want her gone!" I growled.

He ignored me, taking a drink and holding my eyes.

I shook my head, turning to Em. "You know why he likes it here? Because if not for this place, he'd be alone."

Whatever this friendship was forming between them, it wasn't genuine on his end. Aydin Khadir didn't want to leave, and now that he had a woman in the house, there was no reason to. This was his dominion, and I could feel the shitstorm coming.

"You couldn't take the shame, could you?" I said to him. "People finding out the things you liked. The kink and the various ways you like to fuck. Everything was a secret in your rigid family, and that was fine, until . . . until you were done hiding it."

He said nothing, his expression unreadable.

"I know someone like that," I told him. "He couldn't fight for the life he wanted until he was forced to fight alone. He held on to his friends and to his sister so tightly, he almost killed us, because in that moment, he couldn't bear to see us leave, and he would've rather seen us dead."

Aydin's gaze faltered, and I knew something was finally cracking in there. If he wasn't careful, he was going to die here. Alone.

"Did you ever forgive him?" he asked, his tone gentle for once.

"Family does."

He blinked, something churning in his head. "But he had to submit."

The corner of my mouth quirked. "Family does."

Damon learned. He'd fucked up, but he learned.

He'd hurt so many people so badly that he lost everything, but it was only then that he realized his pride was less important than everything he loved.

I felt Em's eyes and looked down at her, almost shaken at how she stared at me, unblinking. Like a tiny crumb of the wall inside of her had suddenly peeled away.

Silence filled the room. Taylor was at my side, quietly drinking, while Aydin and Em just sat there.

I wanted to fight. Him, Taylor . . . something to get rid of this steam rising up my goddamn neck.

Lightning struck the sky, flashing through the windows and followed by thunder. Then, the lights all around us went out, the room falling into darkness except for the single taper lit on the table.

"Shit," Taylor grumbled. "Not again."

Aydin rose from his seat, jerking his chin at Taylor to follow, and they both left the room. Probably to check the fuse box or generator.

But I still stared at her as I sat down, leaning back in my chair.

"You weren't that fucking great," I said. "You were a huge hassle that I indulged in for far too long."

She held my eyes. "I know."

"There were girls who were nicer."

She nodded, her tone softening. "I know."

I ground my thumb against the insides of my fingers. "Friends who were kinder."

"Yeah."

"I haven't called you," I pointed out. "I haven't contacted you in any way in nearly nine years."

She opened her mouth but then closed it, breathing a little shallower.

"I don't care what you went through," I said.

Again, she nodded.

"There were people who loved me, and I wasted time on someone who didn't."

My heart hammered as I dropped my gaze to her neck. Her olive skin glowed with a light layer of sweat.

"I understand," she said.

Fucking bitch. My dick swelled and hardened as I got angrier by the second.

"You had years to reach out, but you didn't," I told her. "Believe me, I had time to become well aware you didn't give a shit, and now, neither do I."

I saw the lump in her throat move up and down.

"I moved on." The candle flickered, a draft hitting us from somewhere in the house. "I kissed others, touched their faces like I touched yours, and spent time with them like I never did with you."

You don't matter.

Her jaw flexed, and I gazed at her pretty little throat, my fingers humming with the urge to pin her to this table and eat her out until she screamed.

"Years of nights," I said, and I wasn't sure if I was saying it more for her or me anymore, but I kept going. "Years of not thinking of you. Nearly an entire life of memories and history that doesn't include you. You were nothing."

She stared at me, no longer responding.

"She took care of me." My voice dropped to nearly a whisper, and I didn't care that she didn't know who I was talking about. "She listened to me. Made me smile."

No movement.

"Stood next to me," I gritted out. "Fit in with my friends. She's smart, clever, resourceful, and she took the shitty hand life dealt her and still knows how to love people, unlike you."

Her eyes blazed, a fire kindling behind them.

"She's hot in the shower," I taunted more, "on the beach, against the wall, on the hood of the car in the rain, and in my back seat—"

She growled, flying out of her chair and swiping a hand at the candlestick, sending it tumbling to the floor where it extinguished.

I couldn't hold back my shit-eating smile.

Charging around the table, she made for the door, but I grabbed her and backed her into the wall.

But before I could rub in my escapades a little more or wrap my hand around her pretty little neck, she shoved me hard in the chest.

I stumbled and fell into the chair, and then she was on me—glaring down and squeezing my neck in her fist.

I gasped, fully fucking hard now.

She breathed fast and shallow, seething like she wanted to end me with her teeth.

Holy shit.

I groaned. *God, straddle me, please.*

She glowered, and I searched her eyes, waiting for her to lose control. To show that she grew up, wasn't afraid, and was willing to admit she liked it and she might like it a lot if I bent her ass over this table right now, fucked her, and used her hair as leverage.

She didn't. Growling again, she whipped around and stalked out of the room, and it only took two seconds to bolt after her.

I threw open the dining room doors, storming into the hallway, and spotted her, running away from me.

I raced for her.

She glanced behind her, saw me, and bolted, hurrying away, but I caught her.

I took her in my arms, hearing her squeal as I pressed my chest into her back. I forced her into the darkened doorway of the drawing room and reached around, taking her jaw in my hand.

She tried to wriggle out of my hold, but I didn't give a shit if she drew blood or ripped out my throat. I was seeing this through.

I had questions. Like, why didn't she tell me what was happening at home? Or why couldn't she trust me?

I was patient. I would've understood.

I wouldn't have disappointed her.

But not only did she not trust me, she attacked, and I didn't give a fuck about the why anymore. We all went through shit.

I leaned into her ear, ready to finish everything I was saying at the table and make her listen, because it was the least of what she owed me, but . . .

Panting and moaning hit my ears, a thud hitting the wall, and I darted my gaze through the cracked door into the drawing room. I saw Micah pressed into the bookshelves, Rory behind him and thrusting into him in the dark.

"God, fuck." Rory gasped, fisting the back of Micah's hair and biting his neck.

Em's chest caved, and she collapsed back into me as I pressed my cheek to hers, both of us watching the scene ahead.

Hell, if they wanted privacy, they'd be in their room.

Both of them shirtless, Micah gripped the shelves in front of him, his black hair in his eyes as Rory gripped the curve of his leg where it met his thigh with one hand and his shoulder with the other, driving into him, their pants hanging around their asses.

Emory had frozen, tense but having completely forgotten she was resisting.

Sweat glistened across Micah's back as Rory's normally well-groomed hair laid in disarray across his forehead, his brow etched in a mixture of passion, pain, and uncontrollable need as his mouth drifted across Micah's skin, biting and breathing as he rode him faster and faster.

I exhaled, snaking my arm around her tighter and watching the looks flash across Micah's face.

Looking at them, you'd assume Micah was the one in control. He was bigger, taller, more muscular, and he had that whole dark and dangerous vibe.

He wasn't. Rory was the dominant one, and Micah loved every second of it because all he wanted was love.

I was like that. Emmy was like Rory.

Perfect for me.

When she let herself be.

We watched Rory reach around and dig Micah's dick out of his pants, already long and erect, and stroke it as he thrust faster and harder. He threw his head back, growled, and Micah shook the shelves, books falling to the floor as Rory came, pumping his dick and spending himself.

He barely took a moment to catch his breath before he shoved Micah onto the couch, pulled down his pants, and dropped to his knees, taking his dark-haired boy into his mouth and returning the favor.

Micah's abs and arms flexed as he slouched in his seat and stroked Rory's head, drawing him down again and again onto his cock.

"You ever do that to a man?" I asked Emory.

She tried to pull away, as if just waking up and realizing I was here.

"I never did that to you," she retorted.

I spun her around and slipped my hand straight down her fucking pants, diving into her cunt—hot and wet just like I knew it would be.

She whimpered, the feel of her tingling up my arm, and I snatched her bottom lip between my teeth, so turned-on and hard at how much I'd missed this.

All my friends loved the control. Loved to hold them down and make them beg for it like Rika, Banks, and Winter were their toys.

Not me.

She dominated me, and I didn't want it any other way. In the classroom, in the library, in the movie theater, in my truck . . . Watching her cash in on my ass was better than actual sex.

I could be a bad boy, and I needed to be disciplined.

She growled, trying to push me away, but I brought my hand up, rubbing my glistening fingers in her face.

And then I crashed down on her mouth, kissing, nibbling, sucking, and tugging her sweet flesh and hearing a moan escape before she tried to push me away again.

"I know you know how to take a beating," I told her, whispering over her lips, "but this isn't the kind you're used to."

Crashing through the doors to the drawing room, I pushed her back onto the other sofa, ignoring Micah and Rory still going at it a few feet away, and fell on top of her, ripping open her shirt before grabbing her bra between her tits and yanking with full force, hearing it tear apart, baring the golden skin of her beautiful breasts.

She struggled, swatting her hands at me as I came down on top of her, smiling as her legs fell open.

"Hit me," I whispered over her lips before diving in to kiss her. "Hit me for all the tail I fucked after you. For all the nights I forgot about you, ridden to kingdom come by tits and ass ten times hotter than you."

"Ten?" she taunted me. "Really? Come on. You can afford hotter than that! Maybe twenty times hotter! Still got their numbers?"

I laughed bitterly, rising up and pulling down her pants, but she wasn't wearing any panties, because I took those yesterday. I came back down, molding my mouth to hers and thrust against her.

I glided my hands all over her body. God, she was so damn hot.

"Damon was right." She pushed at me. "You are smaller than him."

My heart pounded against my chest, fire filling my lungs, and I rose up, yanking her ass down and diving into her pussy, covering it with my mouth.

She cried out. "Will . . . Ah!"

I was not smaller. And I didn't need reminding of how the hell she knew what he looked like naked.

Sucking and tugging, kissing and biting, I ate the bitch with no hesitation and no mercy. I licked up the sides, nibbling her skin and flicking her clit with my tongue as she squirmed under me, trying to crawl away.

She gasped for breath, a sweet sweat glistening across her tight stomach as her nipples hardened to little rocks.

Then . . . moans filled the air, her body quivered, and her thighs fell wide as she lifted her head and watched me lick her pussy.

"Will . . ." she panted, threading her fingers through my hair.

Rising up, I threw off my jacket and glanced over my shoulder, seeing Micah grin as he watched us. Rory was swallowing his cock, servicing Micah like I was doing to her.

Dipping back down, I slowed a bit, kissing her flesh and licking her before sticking my tongue inside, tasting her so warm and wet.

Her back arched off the sofa, and she threw her head back, shuddering and clawing my shoulders.

Flicking her clit with my tongue, I sucked it into my mouth again and again, her tits bobbing back and forth as she sought it, trying to grind into it and ride my mouth.

"That feel good, girl?" Micah called out to her.

She nodded, panting with her eyes closed. "Yeah."

"Be sure to park his ass next to me when he's done with you," he told her, sucking in air between his teeth. "You drop to your knees like Rory, and I can watch both of you swallow us down."

Cum leaked out of my dick as I pulsed with need.

"Yeah," she whimpered.

I placed my hand on her stomach, feeling her shake and her breaths grow erratic. When she sucked in air, holding it, again and again, I knew she was right there.

Aching and boiling with heat, I tore myself away and stood up, sweat cooling my brow.

I wanted to bring her there. I didn't want to ever stop.

And the old me wouldn't have.

It took a moment to catch my breath as I stared down at her. She blinked a few times, opening her eyes when she realized I'd stopped.

"Wha . . ." she breathed out.

I leaned down, getting in her face. "When you're ready for me to finish that," I said. "You come to me."

She dug in her eyebrows, gaping.

"My bed is on the third floor." I rose up, grabbing my jacket. "Come and ask me for it."

And I left, the appendage between my legs trying to tear a hole in my pants as Micah's laugh followed me up the stairs. Along with the shatter of whatever vase Emmy threw in the drawing room that crashed two seconds later.

That was the hardest fucking thing I'd ever had to do.

Like harder than prison, detox, and the Doris Day double feature at the drive-in my mother asked me to take her to when I was seventeen.

Combined.

CHAPTER 16

EMORY

Nine Years Ago

Here you go." Mr. Kincaid handed me a pack of college brochures, secured with a rubber band. "When you apply, though, your acceptance letters will come to your house."

He winked at me, and I gave him a tight smile.

Reaching over his desk, I took the booklets. "Thanks."

Believe me. I knew I'd have to deal with this sooner or later.

I left his office and walked through the main office, heading out to the hallway. My brother expected me to go to college. It was one of the only areas we agreed and where I didn't experience resistance from him, but that might change if he learned my choices. I wasn't ready for his opinion on the matter, so I asked the dean to request the brochures for me for now. I still had a year to apply and face the fights.

I pushed through the doors, opening the top booklet as a few students made their way down the hall.

"Ooooh, Berkeley." Someone snatched the booklet out of my hands.

I turned my head to see Elle flipping through the brochure. "Hey," I scolded, reaching for the brochure.

She pulled away, looking at it. "You couldn't get any farther away from here," she said. "But I guess that's what you want."

I stole the booklet back. "Yep."

Berkeley was at the other end of the country, and I could afford maybe two years with the college fund my parents had put in a trust for me.

I wasn't planning to use any of it, though.

I'd barely slept last night after Will left, spending much of the night replaying him in my head, part of me sure I should've just let him leave when he tried the first time, and the other half of me sorry that I let him go the second time.

But I did decide on one thing that had been troubling me. If my grandmother was still alive when I left for college, my trust would be more than enough to pay for a year at the best convalescent home in Meridian City.

That would get her out of my brother's house, and I'd be able to go to school without worry.

All I had to do was earn a scholarship—or ten—to pay for my education.

I looked ahead, hearing a group of students laughing.

Will stood against the lockers, surrounded by his friends, his arms wrapped around Davinia Paley as he lifted her off the ground and stared into her eyes. She smiled at him.

My heart sank, and my mouth went dry.

I faltered for a moment, blinking and looking quickly away. *Looks like he found his Homecoming date.* What a prick.

Elle stopped at my side, following my eyes as I looked up at him again. He held Davinia like she weighed nothing, talking to her and looking playful and happy, while everyone around them, with their clothes and their cars and their friends, looked like a *Teen Vogue* ad I'd never belong in.

He looked over at me, and I dropped my eyes, turning away. It was just as well.

I continued down the hall, feeling his eyes on me as I passed, and Elle and I rounded the corner, stopping at my locker.

"Will I see you in class?" she asked.

"Ugh."

She snorted because she was well aware I hated literature class. Touching my arm, she continued, "Maybe see you at lunch then."

"See you."

I stuck the brochures into my locker, hiding them at school for now, and pulled out my notebook, *The Grapes of Wrath*, and the rest of my materials for the morning, stuffing everything into my bag.

The bag grew heavier, though, as Will and his friends' laughter escalated around the corner, my patience and silence spent. I couldn't sit in class right now.

I wish I could. Show him that he didn't bother me. That Davinia didn't bother me.

He should see me as tough and unaware of all of it.

It was a game I knew well.

But I slammed my locker door shut and walked down the hall, passing lit class and taking one flight up to the art room.

It was always empty first period, and Mr. Gaines didn't arrive until he absolutely had to. I'd have the room for another hour.

Dropping my bag at my usual drafting table, I pulled my rolls of paper out of my cubby and slid onto my stool, spreading everything out and getting to work.

The bell rang, students raced down the halls outside the doors, but soon everything quieted, and all I could hear were the teachers beginning their lessons beyond the dark, quiet walls of my little hideaway.

Using my rulers, I continued the redesign of the Bell Tower, the one near the cemetery that had fallen to ruins when St. Killian's was abandoned so many years ago. I measured the gables, as well as drawing lines for each of the small decorative dormers I was adding. It was an assignment, but I'd love to see it come to fruition someday.

Despite my hatred of this town, I loved this place. Its history. The allure of its secrets and traditions. The mysteries that survived the years and the architecture. So many nooks and crannies to get lost in, not only with places like the catacombs or the Torrance garden maze that used to be open to the public once a year when I was a kid, but the way every avenue and piece of coastline seemed to have a story.

A building out in the world was a building out in the world. Designing something in Thunder Bay wouldn't just stand on its own. It would be a part of something bigger.

I worked on my design, getting close to finishing, even though we still had weeks left. I wanted to raise the Bell Tower again, make it taller, so you could climb it and take in more of the sea, and I wanted to add more bells.

And maybe a light. A flickering light at the top.

"'Hang a lantern aloft in the belfry arch,'" I recited as I sketched. "'One, if by land, and two, if by sea . . .'"

But it wasn't "Paul Revere's Ride" poem that popped into my head next. I stopped, thinking.

Or maybe . . . like a candle—albeit electric—perpetually lit for Reverie Cross up at the top.

I rolled my eyes, shaking my head clear of the idea and dropping my pencil down.

Stupid.

I looked down at my school bag, reaching down and taking the strap.

I lifted it up, digging in the pocket and finding that shiny, bronze bauble someone left tied to my tree last night.

Pulling it out, I dropped the bag and leaned my elbows on the table, inspecting it.

Studying the skeleton key, rusty and worn, I looked again for any markings that might give me a clue as to what it was for, and then I threaded the chain through my fingers, taking a look at the key chain attached.

It was some kind of pot. Or an incense burner, maybe?

I turned it over in my hand, confused. Why would someone give me this and then not tell me what it was for? I didn't think it was Will who'd left it. He would've just given it to me when he saw me last night.

And that car parked outside my house . . .

The only other thing I could think of was that this was evidence and someone was planting it on me, but that was reaching.

Then I noticed it.

The slits on the key chain. In the incense burner.

Like vents.

This was a thurible. They were used in churches.

The cathedral in town had one. A big one that swung like the clapper of a bell.

I rolled up my blueprints, stuffed them into my cubby, and grabbed my bag, running out of the classroom.

I stepped into the cathedral, my eyes going up every time I entered this place. I always liked coming here. It was peaceful, and you didn't feel weird about being alone in a public place here. It was expected.

Of course, I'd love it if Thunder Bay had a temple on the rare occasion Martin, my grandmother, and I attended, but no such luck. We had to drive to Meridian City for that.

It worked for me, though. If I needed to hide for a while, Martin would never look for me in a Catholic church.

"Emory?" someone said behind me.

I turned, seeing Father Beir. Everyone knew him.

"Here for confession?" he teased. "I'll need to baptize you first."

I chuckled, gripping the strap of the bag over my chest. "I'm still working out how to be an agnostic Jew, Father. Let's not complicate things." I smiled at him. "Good to see you, though."

He came to stand beside me. Some devotees were kneeling in the pews, while a couple of others sat in thought, the candles lit in devotion flickering at my side.

The stations of the cross lined the walls around us, and I tipped my head back, admiring how the columns seemed to split into the ribbed vaulting and flying buttresses the way a tree trunk spread into branches. A fantastic mural adorned the ceiling.

"You're in here a lot," he told me.

"It's the architecture." I kept my eyes on the ceiling. "And it's quiet."

He sighed. "Sadly, yes."

He sounded unhappy about that, and I realized it would be better for him—and the church—if it were busier.

He patted my shoulder. "Roam," he said. "And take your time."

"Thanks."

He left, and I took out the key again, studying the kind of lock I was looking for. Rolling the miniature thurible between my fingers, I looked up and took stock of the big one, probably half as tall as me and twice as wide. It hung from a rope and was secured to the side of the church, near a pointed arch above the chancel.

Then I lifted my gaze, seeing the gallery above it. There was a door up there.

I clutched the key in my hand, looking around me to make sure no one was paying any attention.

Then I headed across the nave to the side aisle, past the bay, and turned left at the transept.

Climbing the steps, I wound around the spiral staircase and came to the balcony landing, overlooking the nave.

To my right, an arched wooden door sat as buckets and tarps laid on the floor, repairs looking like they'd been abandoned long ago, and the gallery no longer used for seating since Father Beir barely filled the pews downstairs anymore.

No one and nothing was up here, except the light streaming in through the stained-glass windows, glimmering red and blue on the old carpet.

Opening my palm, I looked from the key to the lock on the door.

My pulse rate kicked up a notch, worry and excitement coursing through me.

But in a way that made me sick.

I walked over to the door and slipped the key in, but when I grabbed the handle and twisted, it opened without me unlocking anything.

I pulled out the key and shoved it in my school jacket, opening the door wide and wincing at the screech of the old hinges.

Shit. I cast a nervous glance around me, still seeing no one around.

Finally, I peeked inside the door, spotting another spiral staircase.

I narrowed my eyes. This might lead to a spire.

Taking out my phone, I turned on the flashlight and stepped up the stairs, the stone under my shoes gritty with dirt. I rose more and more, seeing a door on the right.

I took out the key again, the tunnel vision in the small, tight space making my hands shake.

I coughed, the dust tickling my throat.

This was probably stupid. I didn't know who the key came from, and I didn't know what was on the other side of that door. Whoever gave it to me played hard-to-get just enough by not explaining, so I would be intrigued.

I stuck the key in and twisted it, but the door wouldn't give. I jiggled it some more, turning the handle, but it wouldn't open. I spun around, looking left and then right, spotting one more door at the top of the stairs.

Holding up my flashlight, I climbed to the top, felt for the lock and stuck the key in, the click giving way as soon as I turned the key.

Butterflies swarmed in my stomach, and I hesitated for a moment, smiling.

I'd found it.

There could be someone in there, but I pressed forward, opening the door and finding my way with the flashlight. But as soon as I opened it, light swarmed me immediately. I stepped into a room, rafters coming up through the floor and stretching all the way to the ceiling, and I looked around at the windows and the sunshine falling across the floor.

What was this?

I turned off my phone, dropped that and the key into my pocket, and softly closed the door behind me.

Trunks and boxes laid about the perimeter of the room, underneath the windows, and I saw old church paraphernalia strewn here and there—altar cloths, candleholders, and those things that hold holy water . . . There was even a set of doors that looked like the ones downstairs for the confessionals.

I walked farther into the room, but I stopped, my eyes locking on the bed.

White comforter, white sheets on the pillows—everything looking clean and crisp and big enough for ten.

What the hell?

Then I dropped my gaze, seeing a scrap of paper on the comforter. I walked over and picked it up, the fresh scent of the linens making my nostrils tingle.

I read the note, the paper yellowed and nearly falling apart at the creases where it had been folded a thousand times.

It's yours now. Use it well.

No one else knows, do not tell.

When you're done, pass it on.

The Carfax Room hides us

from what we want gone.

I read it again, but I still didn't get it.

"The Carfax Room?" I said to myself.

The writing was in black cursive, a little faded, and I folded it up, sticking it in my pocket.

This was silly. Someone gave me a key to a room, didn't explain why, and I had no idea if I was the only one who had access to it.

I got some of the message. Keep the room a secret, but how did it hide me exactly? And obviously someone else knew about it because someone gave me the key.

And if it was something I passed on to someone else, then the person who gave it to me got it from someone else, too, right?

Why me?

I drifted around the room, picking through boxes that contained everything from lamps and tools to clothes, costumes, and theater makeup. I stepped slowly and then spotted something that caught my eye. Hesitating, I moved toward a trunk on the floor and pulled out a pink dress, strapless and fluffy with a tulle skirt underneath.

I smiled, loving the fifties style of it. Trim waist, little roses in the pattern, the kind of Pepto Bismol pink that was in fashion decades ago . . . Why was this here?

I guess it isn't so odd. There was also a top hat and a waffle iron in one of the crates.

Oh, the stories this room could probably tell.

I laid it back in the trunk, folding it gently and closing the lid before walking to the bed and lifting a pillow to my nose.

It smelled clean, like detergent and spring. There was a record player with some records nearby and candles on the nightstand.

There was no way I'd stay here, not knowing anything about this place or whether or not anyone else had a key, but it was kind of cool. Another nook. Another cranny.

Another story.

Taking one last look around, I left, locking the room again and leaving so as not to press my luck. For all I knew, this was Father Beir's secret place to be the real him and that dress was his.

Clutching my bag, I jogged down the stairwell, slipped the key into my pocket, and stepped into the gallery, closing the door behind me.

I'd missed three classes, but if I hurried, I'd make the fourth.

Taking the stairs, I walked through the church and out the doors, taking the path to the street and turning right. Leaves rustled in the trees, yellows, oranges, and reds fluttering to the ground, and a drop of cool rain hit my cheek. I breathed in the autumn breeze, the key light in my pocket.

Do not tell.

Part of me thought this was a prank. Otherwise, I would've gotten some real instructions.

But I wanted it to be real. Having my own hideaway made me feel like I was finally part of a town I'd lived in my whole life.

Like I belonged here now.

Walking down the sidewalk, lost in my head, I barely noticed the car pulling slowly up next to me on the street.

I did a double take, seeing the cruiser. My chest tightened.

Shit.

"It's starting to rain," Martin said through the open passenger side window as he drove. "Get in."

"I'm getting back to class," I assured him, inching down the sidewalk. "I said I would help with the decorations for Homecoming after school."

I started to walk again.

But he called out behind me. "Emory, I want to show you something. Now."

I stopped, hesitating.

It was no use. He'd tracked my phone. I was out of class during school hours. He came for me.

Knots coiling inside me, I stepped off the curb and opened the car door.

I slid into the front seat and shut the door, my body tense and ready.

"Music?" he asked.

But he didn't wait for an answer. Turning on the radio, he tuned to some oldies station with the volume almost too low to hear.

Turning the car around, he headed away from school and took me up into the hills, past the mansions, St. Killian's, and the Bell Tower. I kept my bag on my body, just needing to hold it.

Martin pulled into the cemetery, slowing as we descended the drive and wound around the path to a sea of headstones plotting the land-scape on the right and left. Rain hit the windshield, and he pulled off to the side, stopping the car.

I let my eyes drift around the grounds, fisting my hands to keep them from shaking. There wasn't a soul in sight.

All my excuses came to mind. Which tone of voice might work best? Or maybe I just needed to be quiet. Sometimes if I just let him talk, the yelling would relieve him.

He lifted his arm, and I flinched, but then I noticed he was reach-ing into the back seat for something.

Setting a white bag down next to me, he reached into the cup holder and pulled out a soda with the straw already in it.

"Eat," he said. "It's lunchtime soon."

An ounce of relief hit me, but I knew it meant nothing. He liked to toy with me.

"Edward McClanahan," he said, gesturing out the window ahead of us. "They're moving his body, Em."

I saw the small digger and that the excavation had already begun, but there were no workers with the rain right now. Just a pile of dirt and a blue tarp over the hole.

"Family wants him safe and sound inside their new tomb," he told me. "They're hoping the town will forget the dead girl, and in all likelihood, it probably will. Out of sight, out of mind."

I clasped my hands in my lap, only half listening.

"Every year, those arrogant little losers make their pilgrimage here like they're going to fucking church," he continued. "But next year, it won't be Edward in the grave. I bought it today. For Grand-Mère."

For my grandmother. Not his. He never gave a shit about her. She wasn't his. He did what he had to do for appearances, and he bought a woman who wasn't even dead a used grave.

A Catholic grave. Did they even allow that?

I wouldn't. It wasn't happening. I—

"Eat!" he barked.

I jumped, sticking my hand in the bag and pulling out the burger as I turned my head out my window and away from him.

I took a bite, chewing about a hundred times until I could swallow it.

"I got a deal on it," he said. "Since the plot had been used, of course. Get to keep the headstone, too. It'll be shaved down. They'll start working on her name in the next week."

My chin trembled, and I felt the bile rise.

"One down," he whispered. "And one embarrassment to go."

I sat there, the burger with one bite taken out of it lying in my lap.

"I have plans, Emory."

He unfastened his seat belt, and I closed my eyes.

"And you would fit in nicely if you stayed in school and stopped troubling me."

His hand whipped against my face, and my head hit the window. I let out a small cry, fire and pain spreading across my cheek and skull.

No . . . My body started to shake.

No matter how I read the signs and braced myself, it was always so much harder than I thought it would be.

"I didn't ask for this!" he screamed, grabbing my collar and slamming me into the door again. "I didn't want it! Why can't you help me out? Why can't you be better?"

I opened my mouth to scream, but I gritted my teeth and bared down instead as he slapped me.

"Goddammit!" he yelled, gripping my collar so tightly the skin on my neck burned.

"Just . . ." He sucked in a breath, and I saw tears fill his eyes. "Just be fucking normal! Why do you do that, huh? Why?"

"Martin, stop . . ." I gasped.

I turned and opened the door, but he grabbed the handle and shut it again. Gripping my arm, he threw another hand across my cheek.

I squeezed my eyes shut. "Not the face!" I cried out.

But he didn't listen—no longer able to think or care about who saw or knew. He'd lost his mind.

The rain pummeled the car, drowning out the sounds of his fists and curses as I dug my nails into the seat and the taste of blood filled my mouth.

Will's truck flashed in my memory—the smell and the feel of him next to me.

But after a few moments, I couldn't think of anything. I couldn't remember anything.

No green eyes. No beautiful smile. No warm arms around me.

My glasses spilled to the floor and then . . . something wet dripped into my eye.

After a few moments, I couldn't even remember his face.

I sat there, staring through the windshield and the wipers, barely mustering the motivation to breathe.

Martin sat back in his seat, lighting a cigarette as blood spilled off my eyebrow and the cuts stung in my mouth.

"It's Devil's Night tomorrow," he said as we sat at the stoplight near the village on the way home. "The little devils fancy themselves dangerous, but no one is more of a threat than the person willing to do what everyone else won't."

I cast my eyes to the side, seeing his shotgun in its holder. Sobs lodged in my chest.

I could take it. It would all be over.

I could sleep at night.

"This is my town, Em." He didn't look at me, the blessed exhaustion calming his voice now. "It will be someday. This will all seem like a dream compared to the nightmare that awaits everyone who stands in my way."

I could sleep forever.

I looked out at the rain, my vision blurry through the tears that wouldn't stop.

I was tired. And sad.

And if he didn't die, I would, and it had to be tonight. My insides screamed. I couldn't take it anymore.

My fingers balled into fists, every muscle in my body tightening, and my legs were moving before I'd even made the decision. Pushing the door open, I leapt out in the rain, hearing him bellow my name and telling me to come back, but I just ran.

I was at the edge, and I didn't want to stop.

Digging in my heels and splashing through the puddles, I ran as hard as I could, up the sidewalk and through the grass, back to the cathedral.

My hair coated my face, and I didn't look behind me, because I knew he wouldn't leave the car to chase me, and he might suspect I went into the church, but he wouldn't be able to find me.

I dashed into the church, slowing my steps to not bring attention, and made my way through the nave to the stairs again. I escaped up to the gallery, behind the door, up the steps, and back inside the Carfax Room, locking the door behind me.

Safe.

Hidden.

I walked to the trunks by the windows, found the dress, and pulled it out.

Emmy Scott was tired and sad.

But Reverie Cross was going to Homecoming.

CHAPTER 17

WILL

Present

My groin ached, and I flipped over in bed, my cock tenting the sheet.

I reached my hand underneath and fisted it, slowly stroking the hard muscle.

Fuck.

How did that girl always do this to me? She had me about ready to break and go ask her for it instead. I knew she wouldn't come to my room last night after I'd left her in the drawing room. I knew that.

I just hoped I was wrong.

God, I wanted her. I could chalk it up to being without a woman for so long, but no . . . it was Emory Sophia Scott and how good her smiles felt.

All the frowns were worth the trouble for just one smile.

Or so I used to think.

The morning light streamed through my small attic window, warming my chest as everything tingled, and my dick swelled more.

I groaned, closing my eyes and wetting my palm with my tongue, diving back down and pumping my cock faster and tighter.

From the moment I'd laid eyes on her, everything about her turned me on and there wasn't a single way I didn't dream about fucking her. It was an obsession from the start.

But why?

She was moody, intolerant, judgmental . . . and while I knew exactly where her distrust and hard heart came from, she refused to warm toward me after all this time. If she hadn't by now, she wouldn't.

Loving a guarded girl, I had realized, was a pyrrhic victory. The rare moments of happiness came at too great a cost.

But there she was, always in my dreams—beautiful and bare—letting me ride her and lose myself in her lips and scent.

I stroked again and again, my cock hard and fully erect, the images of her buried in my sheets—soft and sweet—filling my head as my cock dripped for her.

And I went with it. Fuck it.

I tried to forget her with others. I went with women who looked nothing like her, so I could get her out of my system, but at the end of the day, it only hurt me more.

I tightened my stomach, feeling myself coming, and I envisioned myself inside her, going hard and making her moan.

Because maybe if I could screw her, I could leave, and it would be like someone flipped a switch where she no longer mattered.

"Fuck me, baby," I gritted out, tugging on my dick faster and faster. "Come on, spread your legs."

In my head, there she was—plastered to the mattress under my weight and my nose buried in her hair as I drove into her. She kissed me and smiled and, God, she wanted it. The soft skin of her tight stomach sticky with sweat as I moved on top of her.

I tensed, jerked, and threw off the sheet, spilling all over my hand, cum shooting out, and I swear I could feel her tight heat over my cock. I knew exactly what she felt like.

I gasped and exhaled, melting into the bed as the orgasm wracked through me, and I grunted, letting it course.

Fuck.

Finally, I opened my eyes.

A pyrrhic victory. And here I was, pretty sure that no cost was too great to just be able to hold her. It kind of scared me what I'd pay.

Rising from the bed, I grabbed a cloth and cleaned up, tossing it down the laundry chute before yanking a towel that was hung over the chair and wrapping it around my waist.

Rory was always in the steam room before the rest of us were awake. I needed some time alone with him, and it had to be today.

Descending the stairs, I headed down the hallway, almost hesitating at her room, tempted to make sure she was fine, but I passed it by and jogged down the next set of stairs, heading through the foyer.

Taking a left in the quiet house, I walked down the dark hallway, toward the natatorium, and entered, swinging open the frosted glass door of the steam room.

As routine as a serial killer, Rory Geardon sat on the tiled bench, leaning against the wall as vapor billowed around him.

He opened his eyes.

"Hey," I said.

He jerked his chin at me. "Hey."

"Going hunting soon?"

"Yeah." He sighed. "You coming?"

"Maybe." I could use some fresh air, but I wasn't leaving her in the house alone, either.

I sat a few feet away, the heat coating my skin like a blanket.

I loved steam rooms. It detoxed me, relaxed me, and reminded me of home. The one at Hunter-Bailey in Meridian City was twice as big, and it was where Michael, Kai, and I had some of our most important business meetings. If I wasn't too hungover that day.

"So, Devil's Night, huh?" Rory mused at my side. "This Thunder Bay of yours is starting to sound like an adult Disneyland."

I grinned. "I miss it."

He grabbed an extra towel he'd brought in and wiped down his face. "Even though that's where your family is?"

He assumed I didn't want to see my family. He thought my parents sent me here, so why would I want to go back? Like Micah and Aydin, Rory didn't have any faith or trust in the ones who gave up on him. There was no going home for them.

Not really.

But my situation was different. "I didn't deserve to go to prison, but . . . I might've deserved this." It got me clean and sober. "Besides, the family I chose would never send me here. They're what I'm returning to," I told him.

"Well, I'm never going home," he replied. "I know that without a doubt. My mother won't risk it."

Meaning it wasn't a choice of going back. He never thought he was actually getting out.

And after what he did, I had to agree they weren't completely unjustified in their concern.

Rory was like the Terminator. Rule of law or not, the mission was the only thing he saw. It was like tunnel vision. Those kids deserved what they got, and maybe he seemed to enjoy himself, but whether or not he was wrong was a matter of opinion.

As the son to an ambassador to Japan, he was a liability.

To me, he was perfect.

"And if I do get out of here," he continued, "she'll give me some hotel to run on some low-population island somewhere where I won't draw notice."

"Will you draw notice?" I asked.

He breathed out a laugh but didn't answer the question.

"You're not unique," I told him, resting my head against the wall and closing my eyes. "Everyone has that point of absolute clarity where conscience isn't a factor. We are who we are, and we want what we want, and there's no question of what has to happen. The only difference between you and the rest of the population is that you reached that point, and most people will never reach it."

Not many have the opportunities to be driven to a point of despair or survival and look danger in the eye.

"What you did was calculated," I said in a gentle tone. "It needed to be done."

He'd found Micah, but he still hadn't found a home, and I had no intention of leaving him to rot here.

"I'm lucky," I said, almost to myself. "I have a family full of people who know what going over the edge feels like. They know there's a place inside of us where you make the rules instead of following them. I'm not alone."

Out of the corner of my eye, I saw him turn his head and look at me.

"They're a storm," I told him.

He remained silent for a moment, and I could feel the wheels turning in his head. He'd fit in nicely with my friends.

Leaving the thought to linger, I rose to my feet and walked for the door to go shower.

"What did she do to get sent here?" he asked before I had a chance to leave.

I gripped the handle, still.

Dread settled inside me, because she'd interrupted my plans, and things had changed whether I wanted to face it or not.

Would I proceed, considering her a factor?

It wasn't even a question.

"Just like the rest of us," I said, "she knows what she did, and no one here is innocent."

I left the room, but instead of heading to the showers, I charged back up to my bedroom, the house still asleep as I closed the door and placed a steel bar underneath the handle.

Walking to the bed, I pulled off the fitted sheet, lifted the mattress, and flipped it over. It toppled, partly on the bed and partly on the nightstand, the lamp falling over and extinguishing.

Reaching inside the tear on the bottom, I slid my hand between the springs and pulled out the black laptop, walking it over to the table near the window for some light.

I opened it, powered it up, and waited for the chat to load.

Are you there? I typed.

Copy, he wrote after a pause. **He wants you extracted. Soon.**

Not yet. There's a . . . development.

I didn't want to say too much in case someone was spying on us, and where she was concerned, I didn't know who was involved.

Is there anything you're not telling me? I asked.

Such as?

I cocked an eyebrow. **Have you sent anyone else in?**

I waited a moment for his response, and then the letters flashed in green. **No.**

You're sure?

I don't lie to you, he said.

I exhaled, relaxing my shoulders. Okay, then. It wasn't my people.

Either Michael, Kai, and Damon were working on their own, or someone else was behind this. I still knew nothing, but at least I'd ruled out anyone on my end.

More text came in. **How many and when?** he asked.

At least four, I typed.

But then I noticed Taylor outside, leaning against the glass solarium door, peering in at something.

What was he doing?

Quickly, I typed the rest, finishing my sentence. **Maybe five,** I told him. **Hold until you hear from me.**

Through the glass roof, I spotted two figures moving. I thinned my eyes, trying to make it out.

Aydin.

He was holding Emory.

I reared back, my gaze sharpening.

Are you safe? Came the next question.

But I was gone.

Closing the computer and storing it, I pulled on some sweatpants and buttoned them up before jogging down the stairs. I yanked the steel bar away and threw open my bedroom door.

CHAPTER 18

EMORY

Nine Years Ago

I walked into the school, the hallways dim and the music pounding from the gym. Prom was always held in Meridian City, at an expensive banquet hall or hotel.

Homecoming stayed at home.

The frilly pink, strapless dress I'd found in the Carfax Room brushed against my knees, cool air caressing my bare shoulders and back. My long brown hair, parted in the middle, draped around me and in my face, and I left the natural kink wild and shiny. I'd found some theater makeup in the room and used the mascara and eyeliner. Lipstick tinted my mouth.

Nothing covered the dried blood that had spilled down my temple, the blue and purple bruising around my eye, or the cut on my lip. My bare arms wore his handprints, no longer aching so much with the ibuprofen I'd taken.

I could hide in plain sight tonight because it was almost Halloween, the one time of year everyone could bring what was inside outside.

Opening the door to the gymnasium, I stepped inside, the hair on my arms instantly rising. Music blared, blue and pink lights swirling around the darkened room as decorations and balloons adorned every table.

A few dozen couples moved on the dance floor, and I could feel my heart thumping in my chest as I gazed around the room.

Was he here?

The dance had begun a while ago, the ticket takers and photographers having already abandoned their posts near the door, but I spotted a few sets of eyes turn toward me as I entered the room. Most people wore costumes, while others wore simple masks with their cocktail dresses and suits.

They stared, some leaning in and whispering to each other, and it might've been because I was here or because of how I looked, but I didn't care.

My feet moved on autopilot, taking me farther into the room as I stepped in my heels through the noise, the dancing, and the looks.

Normally, I'd run. I'd escape into my phone or a book or another room. Normally, I'd—

But just then . . . he was there.

And I stopped.

He leaned against the wall, surrounded by his friends, away from the crowd and looking amazing in a black suit with a white shirt and no tie.

He hadn't seen me yet, and I waited, suddenly paralyzed.

I wanted my phone or a handbag or something to hold. Something to not feel so alone and vulnerable, but I'd left my schoolbag with my wallet in Martin's police car, as well as my glasses which were probably lying on the floor somewhere. My phone was at the cathedral, turned off.

I walked toward him, his scent and arms and smile beckoning me like food, because I was dry and hungry and empty.

I hated home. I didn't love the gazebo anymore. I was tired of school and tired of never seeing anything that didn't drain me, no matter which way I turned.

I wanted to see him. I wanted to feel his hand in mine.

Ignoring the whispers of others as I passed, I watched him talk and nod, one hand in his pants pocket and the other holding his keys like he was getting ready to leave.

I didn't see a date anywhere.

He looked away from Kai, noticing me as he met my eyes, and stared, unblinking as he took in my appearance. The pink party dress, the blood and bruises . . . Nothing was funny about Reverie Cross's demise, as there was nothing funny about mine.

Tonight I could be seen. Let them all see.

His friends turned and looked, following his gaze.

"Wanna dance?" I asked quietly, my heart beating so fast it made the words shaky.

I saw the guys shift out of the corners of my eyes, breathing out a laugh that didn't really sound mean. Just surprised.

Will stared at me, and it took everything I had not to chew on my lip or squeeze my fists.

I'd gone too far. He might not be alone. I knew he'd probably have a date, and here I was, stalker girl. I was constantly messing with his head, sending him mixed signals, and yes, he pushed too hard and no means no, no matter how many times I'd changed my mind, but . . .

He and I both knew I wanted this. He just didn't understand why I was holding back.

And maybe he was finally realizing that I wasn't worth the trouble.

But to my surprise, he pushed off the wall, coming toward me with a soft smile playing on his lips.

He took my hand, looking down at me as he led me to the dance floor. I could see his eyes trailing over the blood dried in a stream from my eyebrow and the bruises on my body.

"Part of my costume," I explained.

I searched his eyes, unable to look away, because just the sight of him made my heart ache.

I had one night. *Just one night with him.*

"You didn't dress up?" I asked.

His green eyes held mine. "I didn't want to make it hard for you to find me."

I felt the heat rise to my cheeks, and I smiled. He had come alone then.

Walking to the middle of the dance floor, he stopped, and I turned to face him. "Mr. Sandman" by SYML began, and I started to move my arms up to his shoulders, but then I stopped.

"I actually don't know how to dance," I told him.

I'd never done this before.

Taking my waist, he pulled me in, and I gasped, my arms instinctively wrapped round his neck.

"Put your feet on mine," he said.

Without argument, I stepped up on his shoes in my pink heels, happy to just hold on. Tipping my head back, I looked up at him as he held me close and started moving, turning in a slow circle and box-stepping small enough for me to easily follow.

"You look beautiful," he said. "Despite that nasty spill you took down the rocks at Cold Point."

He touched my face, thankfully only seeing the costume. People watched us, but I didn't care what they thought. I couldn't take my eyes off him, the slow, haunting tune playing just for us.

"Reverie Cross," I mused. "She sounds like someone who had her own bathroom."

"No." He shook his head. "She was actually not well-off. And she was okay with that because he loved her anyway. Nothing else mattered to him."

I tightened my arms around him, feeling my knees shake a little.

They were young, and I understood it. In that moment, everything prevailed and nothing else mattered. Why not let them have the dream?

Will pinched his eyebrows together, studying me. "Something's wrong."

I shook my head. "Not tonight there's not."

Just one night.

And if it was just going to be one, I didn't want to share him with anyone else.

"Can we leave?" I asked suddenly.

He stopped dancing. "You want me to take you home?"

"Not unless you want to," I replied, still holding on to him. "I don't want to leave you yet."

He smiled, taking my hand as I stepped off his shoes. "Let's go," he said.

He pulled me from the dance floor, the people and the noise and every care I've ever had left behind as excitement heated my veins.

"Have you decided what you're doing for your Devil's Night prank tomorrow?" I asked as he pushed through the doors.

But he just smirked. "I have ideas."

"I have one, too," I told him.

A re you sure about this?" he asked as we dumped our goods all over the grass. "Technically, it's theft. A lot of theft. And vandalism."

"I'm shaking in my boots, Will. Really."

I set out the candles in a vigil on the step leading into the crypt, keeping my eyes peeled for the caretaker who lived on the grounds. No one was supposed to be in here after dark, but that didn't mean someone wasn't strolling around.

And it wasn't like it was irreparable vandalism anyway. I had nothing against the McClanahans.

I just wanted to freak them out a little, so they'd rethink their agenda. Will and I had the same goal, albeit for different reasons.

The grave had become a local legend. In Will's mind, Edward McClanahan belonged to everyone.

In my mind, if he stayed in his grave, my brother would be shit out of luck on buying it.

Will moved around the wrought iron fence surrounding the crypt, fitting all the scarecrows we stole from Mr. Ganz's Halloween yard display and the basketballs we also stole from the supply closet onto each head.

I stared at the McClanahan tomb, its dark, stained-glass windows and smooth, new stone, unmarred and clean. Brand-new and ready for use.

"He shouldn't be moved, right?" I asked, making sure we were still on the same page.

"Right."

After we'd left the dance, I sent him to the gym while I raced to the bio lab and stole all the dead animals floating in jars full of form-aldehyde. I put them on a cart, wheeled them to a window, and Will drove up with his truck and helped me load.

After making a couple of more stops, we were here. Ready to show the McClanahans what would happen if they moved Edward.

The vigil . . . would follow him. Year after year, unfailing, and complete with a *Children of the Corn* vibe.

If they didn't want their final resting place to become a pilgrim-age for messy, destructive, sexually active teens, they'd change their minds.

I took one more look around the cemetery, making sure we were alone as I lit the candles.

Only the shadows of the trees on the grass—blue in the moonlight—moved as the breeze shook the leaves free off their branches.

I half expected Will to try to take out his phone to film this, but thankfully, he didn't. I didn't want to wind up on one of his videos.

Adding the dead animal offerings, I checked to see that Will had finished the scarecrows, complete with basketball heads and scary faces drawn in Sharpie with forbidding eyebrows and teeth.

I laughed and rolled my eyes, hearing him snort at his own clever-ness as he moved around the fence.

I stuck in the tiki torches from Will's garage around the crypt, lighting them, and then fished some light green chalk out of one of the bags that I'd grabbed from bio lab.

Running inside the fence, I raised the chalk to the stone, about to start the vandalism part, but I looked up at the stained-glass windows once more, hesitating.

"It is empty?" I said again. "Right?"

I didn't feel bad about the vandalism or petty theft, but I would if people were laid to rest in there right now.

But he just shook his head. "They just finished it. No tenants yet."

I nodded, squeezing the chalk. *Go to hell, then, Martin.*

Hurrying, I drew triple Xs all over the wall, reading in one of my coffee-table books about a ritual where you draw the symbols on a tomb, making a wish. If the dead grant it, you have to come back and leave an offering and circle the Xs.

It was washable, and the tomb would be good as new when they cleaned it, but if the spark caught fire with the public, they'd be continually cleaning this tomb for a century.

Will grabbed a blue piece and helped, both of us smiling and rushing, because it would be no good if we got caught, especially me, and he knew it.

I grabbed the bag off the grass that I used to haul the candles, and we backed away, staring at the McClanahans' newest nightmare.

"Hey!" someone yelled.

I sucked in a breath.

"Oh, shit." Will grabbed my hand and pulled me, running down the slope. I looked behind me, seeing a man in a khaki uniform jogging after us.

Oh, my God!

I squealed, laughing as Will dragged me through the trees, around a tomb, and past the fountain.

I dug in my heels, trying to keep up as the cold air whipped across my face.

Will yanked me behind a massive headstone, and we hid, Will peering around the corner to see if we'd made it.

He'd left the truck parked just on the other side of the tree line, otherwise anyone would've known his vehicle. It was a pain in the ass, dragging all that stuff in three trips, but, man, that was worth it.

I hugged his arm, still shaking with laughter.

He turned, smiling as he gazed into my eyes. "I love seeing you laugh."

I dipped my forehead to his, my body filled with excitement and more freedom than I'd ever felt in my whole life.

"More," I begged.

He took my hand in his, caressing my jaw. "Yeah? I have just the place."

An hour later, I laughed, squeezing his hand and feeling that drop in my stomach as the pirate ship swayed back and forth.

Shit. I squealed, butterflies swarming my stomach as the ride slowed, the tires screeching against the bottom as we went up, caught air for a split second, and then fell back down, the wind blowing through my hair.

Why the hell didn't I come here more often? How many people could have roller coasters in their lives every day?

It was kind of pricey, I guess. The cost for a ticket kept getting more and more expensive as Adventure Cove struggled to stay open over the years.

The bars came up, and Will and I climbed out, laughing down the steps.

"It's my favorite ride," he said. "Nothing quite like the sensation of free falling."

Nope. It was better than the best roller coaster. I looked up at Will, seeing him pull cash out of his wallet and then take a stick of pink cotton candy, handing it to me as he took his change.

"You want my jacket?" he asked as we started to walk again.

I picked off some of the fluffy sugar. "I'm okay."

I stuck the candy in my mouth, honestly a little chilly, but I was loving the wind too much. I was like my grandmother that way.

We walked, the sounds of the park raging around us—screams and coaster tracks and bells ringing from the game booths . . .

The sea air wafted through my nostrils, and I looked past the Ferris wheel, deep into the dark where I couldn't see it, but I knew it was there.

The coast and the ocean and Cold Point—the edge that dropped off onto the rocks and into the sea.

Will leaned over and picked off some candy, and I did the same, warming when his arm brushed mine. His other hand rested on the small of my back, and I felt his eyes on me.

"Have you ever heard of the Carfax Room?" I asked, picking off more candy and eating it.

"Sure," he said. "It's like Edward McClanahan and Blackchurch and EverNight. Another Thunder Bay urban legend."

I turned my head, looking up at him. "What's Blackchurch?"

"A house." He shrugged. "Supposedly."

He paused, eating more, and we passed game booths where a few people played. The park wasn't too crowded tonight, some middle schoolers making it louder than normal.

He continued, "No one knows where it is, if it's even real, but stories abound of rich, young men who can't behave being ferried away there to be hidden."

He'd hesitated, like he couldn't think of a better word.

"'Hidden'?" I pressed.

He laughed under his breath. "Well, we can't be arrested," he pointed out, as if I should've known. "It looks bad for the family, you know? So, moms and dads will send you to Blackchurch if you become too uncontrollable. You just disappear. Overnight. Legend has it that it's remote, secluded, and wild."

I realized I'd nearly stopped walking as I stared at him. "And you get sent there forever?"

"Until we learn to behave," he said. "But for some, it has the opposite effect. They go feral. So yes, they would stay there forever."

I gaped at him. Who does that? Who sends their kid away because they're afraid of publicity?

Were they getting help while they were away, or were they just marooned and abandoned?

He looked at me and started laughing. "It's not real, Em. Just bullshit people like to spew because we're bored." He took some more candy, sticking it into his mouth. "And if it did exist, my parents would never send me there. Everyone loves me."

I shot him a look. He was too self-aware. But came off adorable.

"But the Carfax Room," he continued. "I can see that being true."

"What is it?"

"It's a fabled, hidden room somewhere in town," he told me. "Which is entirely plausible since this town has lots of hiding places. It's like a panic room, from what I understand. It's passed from one person to the next, each occupant searching for the next who has need of such a place. There are no limits on how long you can have it. Just pay it forward when you're done. Or something like that."

Now, the note made a little more sense.

A panic room. Someone who needs it.

Use it. Pass it on.

But . . .

Someone gave it to me. Out of everyone in town, someone gave it to *me*.

I opened my mouth, tempted to tell Will I had found it.

But I wasn't sure I wanted anyone to know I had it.

"So, it's like the Room of Requirement from *Harry Potter*."

"No idea what you're talking about," he replied, "but . . . if it does exist, each occupant must be carefully chosen, and the place must command a lot of respect."

"Why do you say that?"

"Because we would've found it by now." He looked down at me. "If it is real, the location would've been divulged at some point over all the years, don't you think? Whoever it's being passed on to must need it for more than just keg parties or . . ."

I caught his eyes. *Or hookups*, he didn't finish saying.

That's true. Whoever had it before me kept it quiet, and they trusted me—for some reason—to do the same.

I took another bite of cotton candy but noticed Will still looking down at me. He stared at my arm, pensive.

"Doesn't seem like makeup," he mused, reaching out to touch the bruise.

I pulled away but flashed him a playful smile for good measure. "Take me on another ride?" I rushed to change the subject. "Something dark."

He broke into a grin and took my hand, the bruise forgotten, and pulled us back around, leading me toward the back of the park.

I tossed the rest of the cotton candy into the trash and followed him past the boat races and the Gravitron, bells and whistles echoing in the night and middle school kids racing up and down the walkways.

Heading up to Cold Hill, the ghost train, Will nodded at the blond guy running the ride, the man opening the gate and signaling the next person in line to wait.

My cheeks warmed in embarrassment at cutting others in line. We could've waited our turn.

But I kept my mouth shut, glancing up at Will.

I'd never liked Cold Hill because it was dark, creepy, and you were confined indoors in a car that only allowed one vehicle per section, so by the time you pushed through the doors and entered the next theme, the car ahead of you on the track was gone. Not typically a big deal, unless you were alone. Then it was scary.

Right now, though . . . I didn't want to be anywhere else with him. Maybe his connection would even let us go around twice. Or more.

Walking past the candelabras flickering their lights, we stepped onto the moving walkway and into an empty car, settling in as the bar came down on our laps.

Leaving the last of the light behind, we traveled down the track and around a corner, the darkness and cold hitting me as I glanced side to side. Groans and howls filled the air as the wall to my right shook, a red light shining between the panels of wood like someone was banging against it from the other side. Then a shot of air blasted us as smoke drifted around and the sound of chains being wound cranked above us.

The hair on my arms stood on end, and I huddled closer to Will, keeping my eyes peeled.

We traveled through Hell, the Underworld, and Hades—masks and mirrors flashing their terror on the walls, while skeletons and beasts jumped out at us.

I laughed, squeezing his hand and gazing up at the chandelier above us. Its faux candles cast a soft light against the black ceiling, changing the darkness from frightening to mysterious in a way that made me want to live in its beauty.

I almost snickered at myself, but it was true. Will was right. Something changed in the air when nightfall came, but . . .

The allure for me was in the glow that softened the shadows. It was more beautiful than the sun.

A lantern, a candle, a—

An idea occurred to me about the gazebo and the trees around it in the park—decorating them with chandeliers. A dozen chandeliers hanging in the branches above, lighting up the canopy of leaves.

I smiled again, tipping my head back and gazing at all the lights glimmering across the crystals above me, suddenly excited to get back to work. I could do it. There had to be lots of old chandeliers collecting dust somewhere. I'd bet I could find them cheap and get it done.

I looked over at Will to tell him my idea, but he was already staring at me. He gazed down with an entranced look in his eyes like he'd just been watching something so interesting as he stared at me.

Something swelled in my chest, and all of a sudden, I could barely catch my breath as the chandeliers were forgotten. Red lights flashed across his face and then dimmed, his eyes barely visible and then lighting up again, still watching me.

I . . .

God, I just wanted to wrap myself around him and never let go.

Screams and screeches went off around us, and my fingers tightened more inside his as I hovered over his mouth, letting my eyes fall closed.

"Will," I breathed out, the torture of the centimeters between us making my blood race.

I took his hand and guided it under the bar as I tugged my dress up and slid his fingers up the inside of my leg. He exhaled hard, his nails immediately digging into my skin.

I sucked in an excited breath, my clit throbbing, and I wanted him to keep going.

Opening my eyes, I held his stare as he slid deeper between my thighs and I grew warm and wet the farther up he drifted.

A werewolf caricature jumped out of the wall on the other side of Will, and I gasped, every inch of my skin on fire. His fingers peeled my panties away from my skin and dipped inside the fabric as I reached behind my back and unzipped the dress.

I glided a hand around the back of his neck, leaning in and whispering again, "Will."

The doors in front of us opened, the room going dark again, and we entered Davy Jones's Locker as I held his eyes and slowly peeled down the top half of my dress for him.

Yes. I couldn't stop. I didn't want to.

Cool air tickled my bare breasts, making the skin of my nipples tighten and harden as his gaze fell and his lungs caved.

I loved his eyes on me. I didn't know if he liked what he saw, but I didn't care about anything right now. I knew this was over before it even started. I knew he'd lose interest eventually.

I just wanted tonight.

He dove in, grazing my lips with his, but not kissing, as I propped up my foot on the front of the car, arching my back and opening myself for him. He rubbed me, soft and slow, between my thighs, teasing again and again as he worked his fingers inside to my clit.

Reaching around with his other hand, he covered my breast with his palm, kneading and gently squeezing as his hot breath fell across my lips.

He tickled my clit, and I moaned, pleasure sweeping through me and fire pooling between my legs. I needed more. I needed everything.

He slid a finger farther down, teasing my entrance, but I grabbed his hand through my dress, stopping him.

He tensed, his brow knit in pain. "Emmy . . ."

"Not your fingers," I whispered. "You. I want you in me."

He hissed, fisting the hand between my legs, and then he let out a painful groan.

Taking both hands off me, he lifted the bars.

But they wouldn't give.

He grunted, lifting them, fighting to free us now, and I leaned in, taking his face in my hands and kissing his cheek again and again.

"Fuck," he growled, jiggling the bar harder and faster so we could climb out.

It was no use, though, and he attempted to try to slip out from underneath it, but he was too big.

I laughed in his ear as I nibbled his lobe. "Get us out," I begged. "I want you, and I'm not going to say no tonight."

"Shit," he exclaimed, fighting the bar again and growling desperately. "Goddammit."

He grabbed me and kissed me, zipping up my dress as we devoured each other.

"When we get off, we're hurrying to my truck," he breathed out. "And then to my house."

I caught his bottom lip between my teeth, his warmth and taste too intoxicating to even open my eyes. "Just to your truck," I whimpered. "I can't wait. I need you in my hands. In my arms . . ."

The next set of doors opened, and light washed over us as we held each other.

I opened my eyes, seeing we'd reached the end as the rain had started again, falling hard outside as people ran.

I pulled away from him, and when the bar lifted, we jumped out. He clasped my hand, and I ignored the attendant's eyes as I tried to right my dress again.

It was all bunched up and twisted. *Shit.*

Will led me off the ride, took off his jacket, and put it around me before pulling me in a sprint across the park.

Rain fell on us, cold and sharp, but I could still feel him on my mouth as the slickness between my legs grew warmer.

I just wanted to be someplace small with him, feeling him and stretching the hours forever, and I didn't care where.

"Dammit," he blurted out, stopping us.

I halted, following his gaze out to the parking lot. Martin circled Will's truck with a flashlight, rain coming down on him in his black uniform as people scattered to leave.

My heart sank. "My brother," I breathed out.

I didn't bring my phone. How did he know I was here?

"What the hell?" Will cursed. "Why does everything want to stop us?"

"Find us a place," I pleaded. "Hurry."

He grabbed the back of my neck, pressing his lips to my forehead, and then looked around. If Martin saw me with him, it would be over. I didn't care if it was in a game booth or in a Tilt-A-Whirl car. I needed him.

"Come on." He pulled me out of the gates and off to the right.

I threw a glance behind me, seeing Martin in the distance peering through the truck's back window, and I picked up the pace, racing with Will.

He ran up to a yellow school bus, probably the one that brought the middle schoolers here for their Mayhem till Midnight, and punched the door with his fist, prying it open.

I dove in first, and he followed, closing it behind him again.

I threw his coat onto a seat and tried peering out the windows to gauge if Martin had seen us, but Will grabbed my arm and whipped me around. I crashed into his chest, he took me in his arms, and his mouth crashed down on mine.

I moaned, opening my mouth for him and feeling his damn tongue all the way down between my legs.

Dipping low, he lifted me by the backs of my thighs, and I winced at the pain in my body, but I didn't care. I wasn't stopping this. He carried me down the aisle, my legs wrapped around him.

I took his face in my hands, tearing my lips away from his. "You have something?" I whispered. "Please tell me you have something."

He smiled. "Yeah."

I sank my mouth into his again, whimpering as I locked my ankles behind him.

I trailed my mouth across his cheek, over his jaw, and down his neck as he gasped and squeezed my thighs.

"Ah, Em," he moaned.

Reaching the back of the bus, the long bench seat in the last row looming underneath me, he dropped me to my feet and unzipped my dress, never leaving my mouth. He pulled down the top, the dress hanging at my waist as his hands ran all over my naked back and he kissed my neck, holding me to him.

"You're mine," he whispered in my ear.

I tipped my head back, savoring his warmth on my throat and ignoring the sting as his hand brushed the cut on my brow.

"For tonight," I retorted with a smile.

He grabbed the back of my neck and covered my mouth, fierce and making me tingle to my toes.

I worked the buttons on his shirt.

"I'll take care of you," he whispered. "You don't have to worry about anything."

I ripped off the shirt as he worked the buckle of his belt, and I nuzzled into him, letting my fingertips glide over his narrow waist and stomach.

"I don't need you to take care of me," I said between kisses. "I just want right now with you. I don't want to think about all the tomorrows."

He growled and pushed me. I fell down to the seat, gasping as the cool air lapped at my sensitive skin. He bared his teeth, yanking his belt open and unfastening his pants.

My nerves fired as my eyes drifted up his bare chest, my entire body throbbing for him.

Jesus. Perfect golden skin. Toned arms, tight stomach, gorgeous pecs . . .

Beautiful smile.

Soft, funny, and sweet.

Was this mine?

I clenched my thighs, but he scowled down at me, unhappy I wouldn't talk about the future, but it was kind of cute because his eyes kept dropping to my breasts as he heaved with every breath.

He couldn't stop any more than I could.

Coming down on top of me, he grabbed my throat and pushed me down. I whimpered, arching my bare back and closing my eyes as he dipped down and sucked a nipple into his mouth.

"Ah," I moaned.

He pushed up my skirt and reached underneath, taking my underwear and tugging.

The fabric screamed, tearing clear off my body, and I spread my legs wider, feeling his other hand still squeezing my neck.

"God, I wanna knock you up," he said, rising up and looking down at me as he took out a condom. "I want to ruin you for all the times you made me think you didn't want me. I want to give you a piece of me you'll never be able to escape."

His eyebrows were etched in anger, and for a moment, I wished he could. I'd love to have an excuse to drag him into my hellish life and keep him there forever.

I shot up, looking up at him as I took the rubber, unwrapping it myself as I kissed his stomach.

"Then pretend you are," I whispered. "Pretend you're going to knock me up and we're going to do this every day."

I tossed the wrapper, and reaching into his pants, grabbing his cock as a shock coursed up my arm. He groaned at my touch and helped pull down his pants enough for me to pull him out.

God, he felt so good, and my head swarmed as I looked down at his hard muscle and stroked the soft skin.

"You're going to have me tomorrow." I rolled the rubber on, trailing kisses across his abs. "After school in your truck. Against the stacks in the library at lunch. Reverse cowgirl in your lap at the movie theater."

He fisted my hair at the back of my head, his cock steel-rod straight and reaching right for me.

"My sweet little secret," he murmured.

He breathed hard and pushed me back onto the seat, looking down into my eyes as he reached between us to guide himself.

The thick head of his dick crowned my entrance, pushing inside just barely, and I shifted uncomfortably. "Will . . ."

"You'll be mine," he whispered, pressing himself deeper and deeper.

I groaned, stretching for him.

"You can ignore me. You can run," he said, grunting and tipping his head back as he closed his eyes. "You can leave. You can hide . . ."

He slid in, burying himself to the hilt and filling me so wide and deep that I cried out just once.

"But you're going to be fucking mine someday," he growled. "Come hell or high water, Emory Scott. You're my woman, and you're going to come home to me every day and sit at my table and warm my fucking bed." He kissed me. "And you're going to give me a Will Grayson IV. Mark my words."

I whimpered, shifting under him and adjusting as he withdrew and sank back in faster and harder this time.

"Oh, God," I moaned, the skin of my already sweaty back peeling off the seat as I arched it.

He gripped my neck again, propping himself up with the other hand as he stared down at me and entered me over and over.

I gripped his shoulders, the discomfort subsiding as the pleasure of stretching for him started to feel good.

So good.

"You're gonna want it," he promised, squeezing my neck. "You're gonna beg for me and love me so much you can't stand it."

He picked up the pace, my breasts bobbing back and forth as he went harder, and my eyes rolled into the back of my head, his cock sliding in and out easily because I was so wet.

I spread my legs as wide as they would go, reveling in how deep he went. *Yes, God, please.*

"More," I begged. "Harder, Will."

I held on to him, and he groaned, sucking in air as he rolled his hips into me and fucked me.

God, I . . .

Sweat seeped out of my pores, and I opened my eyes, gazing up at his beautiful face and the sheen on his chest, all for me.

Reaching behind him, I slipped my hands inside his trousers, digging my nails into his ass and helping him come faster and harder.

You're gonna want it.

I already do.

You're gonna beg for me and love me so much you can't stand it.

I . . .

"Will, I . . ." I gasped, feeling my orgasm crest and holding him as close as I could, but it was never enough. "Will, I . . ."

"Will, what?" he pressed.

But I squeezed my eyes shut, his head deep inside me hitting my spot over and over, and I cried out as the orgasm flooded me, the world spun around me, and my body wracked with euphoria and shivers.

Fuck. *Fuck, fuck, fuck . . .*

Oh, my God. I . . .

I crashed back onto the seat, and he wiped the hair off my wet face, thrusting into me again and again.

"What?" he asked again, wanting to know what I was going to say.

But I opened my eyes, unable to remember what it was.

I took his mouth with mine and hugged him close as he rode out his own orgasm, as tears hung at the corners of my eyes.

He wanted to give me a piece of him I'd never escape, but he had a part of me I'd never get back.

This would never be as good with anyone else. I was fucked, and he'd already had his revenge.

CHAPTER 19

EMORY

Present

Three knocks hit the door, and I popped my head up, slamming the drawer closed in my bedroom.

I'd already been awake for twenty minutes, scouring the closet and drawers, but there were no clothes in here. And the temperature outside was dropping by the day.

Walking to the door, I leaned my ear to it. "Who is it?"

The sun was just rising, although the clouds were brewing a storm. I thought I was the only one up this early.

"It's Rory."

My heart stopped for a second, and I straightened, staring at the handle.

What did he want?

"Thought you needed a new shirt," he called out. "And maybe some pants."

I glanced down at the boxer shorts and button-down I was swimming in because Will had ripped all the buttons off of my other shirt last night. I still had pants, but I shouldn't turn down clothes. They were what I was on the hunt for right now, after all.

I hesitated a moment and then pulled the chair away from the door and opened it. Rory stood there—a towel wrapped around his waist and hair disheveled with a stack of clothes in his hands.

He stared at me, unblinking, and heat coursed under my skin, remembering last night and what went down in the drawing room. I'd been so angry after Will left, I'd thrown a vase, fixed my clothes, and stormed out of there, more aggravated that I wanted to go ask him to finish, and I almost did. Being with him was just as good as that night on the bus, and it took every last drop of pride to drag my ass into a cold shower before I stooped to begging him for sex.

God, how I would've loved to never be reminded of how good he felt.

I snatched the clothes from Rory.

"Cut them if you want," he told me, gesturing to the black pants. "They're probably too long for you."

"Thanks."

I stood there, forcing myself to make eye contact, and he made no move to leave as he watched me.

The silence stretched between us.

"I'm going to head into the steam room for a bit, and then Micah and I are going hunting today," he said, clearing his throat. "We might take Will. I suggest you come with us or stay in here with the door secured."

It would only be Aydin and Taylor in the house with me? Not ideal, but with less eyes, I could explore.

And siphon supplies, maybe.

"I'll stay," I replied. "How long will you be gone?"

"Hours." He looked me up and down. "If you need food, get it now."

I nodded, and he just kept standing there. His pale eyes had this midnight blue circle around the pupil that made his stare pierce and made the hair on my arms rise.

I swallowed. "So, are you . . . like a . . . like a serial killer, then?"

He grinned. "Are you afraid?"

"Are you going to tell me I shouldn't be?"

He shook his head. "No."

He walked away without elaborating, and I watched him for a moment before diving back into my room and shutting the door, securing the chair underneath the knob again.

Ugh. I had felt something off about him, and while I still didn't feel like he was evil, he was definitely capable of a lot. He premeditated the murders of seven people. It sounded like there was more to the story, but if he could do it once, he could do it again.

Taylor was right about that. They were all here for a reason, and none of them were my friends.

I slipped off the shirt and boxers I'd slept in and pulled on one of his white T-shirts before cutting his black pants at the knee and pulling them on, too. I rolled them at the waist so they wouldn't fall down, and slid on my sneakers, double-knotting them.

Cleaning my glasses, I slipped them on my face and ran a comb through my hair before brushing my teeth. I wasn't sure where the soaps, shampoos, and hygiene shit came from, but it was in here when I came into the room last night, still packaged and brand-new. I wished whoever got me this stuff had cared to supply me with some underwear and another bra.

As soon as Micah and Rory left later, I'd sneak into their room and steal a hoodie.

Leaving the room, I looked around me, rain starting to hit the windows as the gray sky loomed outside, and I jogged down the stairs, heading into the kitchen.

I had bread, cheese, a couple pieces of fruit, and some granola. I'd figure out how to get it out of the kitchen cabinet I had it stored in, but I also needed water.

Approaching the kitchen, I peered inside, seeing it dark, lit only by the light over the stove as I headed around the island, toward the back door, and keeping my eyes peeled around me.

I opened the cabinet and reached behind the stew pot, feeling the cheesecloth bundle still safe and sound.

I smiled.

Now for some water. I took an apple out of the basket on the counter and started eating it as I searched the cabinets for some kind of canteen or water bottle, finally finding some stainless steel tumblers with lids.

I pulled one out and filled it, quickly storing it with the food. I'd test the waters in a bit and see if I could make it to the basement undetected with the bundle. I'd store it down there to grab if I needed to escape or hide.

Slipping the bottle behind the pot, I hit the wall and paused, the apple pinched between my teeth.

That was weird.

I pawed the back panel, feeling that it completely covered the wall, and pulled my arm out, diving into the next cabinet to check its backing.

Same thing.

These cabinets weren't as deep as they should be. I closed both and stood up, putting my hands on my hips. The countertop was at least six inches less in width than the other countertop on the north wall where the stove was. Heading left, I opened up the kitchen door to the terrace and looked outside.

The house extended at least four feet beyond the end of the wall of cupboards.

The hair on the back of my neck stood up, and I couldn't hold back the smile that peeked out as realization dawned.

Extra depth in the walls was required to allot space for wiring, plumbing, insulation . . . But not four feet.

This house had passages.

Holy shit. Did they know?

I closed the door and turned to the wall, behind which should be a secret tunnel and possibly stairs, leading up or down. Who knew where the passages went, but I wanted to find out. If they were clueless, it would be a good place to hide, and it was certainly one way that security could keep tabs on the people here without being detected.

And now was the time to find out. Aydin and Taylor might still be in bed. The others were on their way out to hunt soon.

I backed up and turned in a circle, seeing the house like I hadn't before. What if the tunnels led off the grounds? To a crew housed closer to here than the guys thought? I could get away undetected. The possibilities were endless. I needed to explore.

I passed the stove, sink, and the kitchen window, seeing the solarium next to the house. There was a garden shed on the other side of it. If it had tools—a screwdriver, at least—I could pry panels open, assuming I couldn't find the trigger designed to open them in the first place. In movies, it was always a book that you'd tilt to get the door to open, but it was more often some kind of lock mechanism or lever.

Dammit. How had I not seen this?

Opening the back door again, I stepped outside and crossed the terrace, droplets wetting my legs and arms as I dashed across the stone for the greenhouse.

Opening the door, I hurried inside and took off my glasses, cleaning the water off with my shirt.

A wave of warmth instantly hit my chilled skin as I inhaled the scent of ferns, soil, and wood, the sudden increase in humidity blanketing me.

I slipped my glasses back on and looked around, hearing the drops *tap, tap, tap,* against the glass panels that made up the roof and walls, as well as a light classical tune coming from somewhere deeper in the greenhouse.

I slowed, gazing all around at the ancient conservatory, the white paint of the metal window frames chipped and rusted. I stepped across the small white tiles, the grout black and filthy, and a spiral staircase leading to a catwalk that creaked when it thundered outside.

The plant life was in beautiful form, though. Green, thick,

lush . . . Trees reached up to the roof, palms stretching wide as too many plants to name adorned the landscapes and beds around the walkway. This place was well loved.

Did the crew also tend to this when they came in? Seemed like pointless work when these little shits wouldn't give a damn.

Water hit me from above, and I tipped my head back, seeing an open panel of glass, the rusty chain severed and dangling as rain poured in.

That would need to be fixed soon. With the temperature dropping, it would be impossible to maintain the heat needed in here.

I strolled through the greenhouse, zero clue what most of the plants were called, but it felt like another world. Not cold and dark—not dangerous—like Blackchurch. It was calm and decadent, like an island somewhere where the heat and scent got under your skin and into your head.

Like waking up from a nightmare. Or opening your eyes to presents and cake. I liked it.

The music hit my ears again, and I looked ahead, spotted Aydin, and stopped.

He sat in a pair of black pants and a white T-shirt like me, but his was filthy with dirt smudges as he leaned over the plant bed and cut something. His hair, usually slicked back, laid dry and haphazardly over his forehead and temples, and a light sheen of sweat covered his forearms.

I stared at him, unable to move, because I couldn't remember why I'd come in here, but I knew it was a secret. I hadn't wanted to run into anyone. I had thought he was still asleep.

He glanced over, dropping whatever he'd cut into the bowl and reached over, cutting some more.

I shifted on my feet, ready to turn around. I couldn't go to the shed now.

But instead, he called me over. "Come here."

I looked up at him again, seeing him concentrate on his task, and I walked over to his side, doing as he said.

He picked a strawberry out of the bowl and handed it to me, leaves, stem, and all.

I shot him a suspicious look, but I took it. He'd just cut it. It was probably fine.

Sticking it between my teeth, I bit into the small thing, pressing the chunk between my tongue and the roof of my mouth, sucking on the juice. My mouth exploded, savoring the flavor.

I nodded, swallowing and nibbling on the rest.

"Good?" he asked.

"Yeah, it's . . . sweet."

It was surprising.

"Mmm . . ." he agreed, returning to his work. "Yes."

I looked at the remnants, knowing that real strawberries were this small. His tiny garden had tomatoes, basil, peppers, lettuce . . . I wouldn't think he'd be into this, but I guess now I knew who was taking care of the greenhouse.

"Strawberries used to be sweet when I was young," I said. "I don't know. They're sour all the time now."

"Commercial strawberries the last couple of decades are bred to be big and beautiful, but that's it," he said. "They taste bad. I can barely eat any produce in the States."

I looked down at him. "You're not from here?"

He turned his eyes on me, cocking an eyebrow.

"The US, I mean."

Okay, yes. I assumed we were in the States, but we might not be.

He returned to his task. "I was born in Turkey," he told me. "My family relocated when I was fifteen."

So he was an immigrant. Was it hard for him, being different in school? Trying to fit in?

"Did you assimilate quickly?" I asked.

"Assuming I had any ease assimilating to anything to begin with?" he joked, amusement in his eyes.

I couldn't help it. I smiled.

I could relate.

I was the only kid in school who didn't celebrate Christmas. Who didn't take part in the annual winter pageants or do Secret Santa on the swim team.

But if I could've faked it, I wouldn't have. It wasn't my style to fit in. Screw 'em.

"Did you assimilate to her?" I broached, almost whispering.

The woman he talked about at the pool showers. The one made for him.

He faltered and then stilled, a faraway look crossing his eyes.

I swallowed, but I smiled to myself. I'd found his weak spot.

"Still hearing noises?" he asked, ignoring my question.

"No."

But I might know where they were coming from now.

I glanced at the phonograph near the windows, still playing Schubert.

"Why are you roaming?" he asked me.

I shot him a look, an excuse lost on my tongue.

But then I remembered.

"I, uh . . . I saw the garden shed," I told him. "I thought I'd look for tools. Maybe a ladder. That panel is off its hinges."

I pointed to the roof and the broken panel of glass.

But he didn't look, just kept working as he cut and cleared weeds. "Come here," he said and held out his arm, inviting me in.

I reared back a little, but then . . . something pushed me forward.

I inched in, and he circled my waist, pulling me down into his lap.

I protested, trying to stand back up, but he took my hands in his and pushed them forward, palms down into the plant bed and sliding them underneath the soil.

What the hell was he doing?

Turning my head, I looked at him as he squeezed my wrists, keeping my hands in the dirt. What . . . ?

"What do you feel?" he asked.

I hesitated, speechless. What did he mean, "what do I feel"?

"Soil," I said.

Obviously.

He cocked his head, looking unimpressed.

Did he really have to hold my hands down?

Sighing, I wiggled my fingers a little, indulging this as the crisp feel coated my skin.

Almost like planting your face in a fresh pillow.

"Cool earth," I finally told him. "It's soft with water. Fluffy. Like flour, almost." I looked over at him, his nose inches from mine. "Thick but . . . clean between my fingers."

He released me, but I stayed there and watched him pick up a small glass pitcher, pouring water over the soil covering my hands.

Ice hit my pores as the fluff turned to goo.

"And now?" he pressed.

"Weight," I replied. "It feels heavy. Muddy. Sticky." I stared off, almost grossed out by it. "It's suffocating. Like I'm buried."

He nodded. "There's not much that's bad for you, done in moderation. Some water is necessary for plants to thrive. Too much kills them."

Holding my eyes, he gripped my wrists again, pinning me to the dirt.

"You want tools?" he asked. "To fix . . . hinges?"

I stared at him, not liking the gleam in his eyes.

"You came out here to get tools for broken hinges you didn't see until you . . . came out here." He stared at me, the ghost of a smile crossing his face. "You can have all the tools you like, Emory. In moderation."

I swallowed the golf ball in my throat as he continued to hold my hands and my eyes.

He knew I was full of shit.

He knew it the moment I walked out here. Did he know about my stash?

I clenched my teeth, keeping my nerves in check, but he cocked his head, eyeing me curiously.

"Did you grow up with an addict?" he asked.

"Why?"

He shrugged. "I can usually spot liars fairly easily. They keep their explanations vague, fidget, break eye contact . . . You've had practice."

"I'm not lying about why I need the tools."

"You are," he retorted calmly. "But that's okay. I like being played with. In moderation."

Chills spread over my skin, and my pulse kicked up a notch in my chest, but then . . . something brushed the tip of my finger underneath the soil.

I jerked. "What was that?"

But he held me down, warning me, "I wouldn't move."

What?

Something slithered over my fingers under the dirt, and I froze, unable to breathe.

I pulled against his hold, but he pushed me back in as his piercing gaze pinned me, the smooth body under the soil thick and never-ending.

It was long. It wasn't a worm.

I gulped, whispering. "Is that a snake?"

"One of them."

One of them? I darted my eyes around the plant bed, trying to spot others. There was a clear, plastic wall around the garden, the panel in front of us removed so Aydin could work.

"Who was the addict in your family?"

"Huh?"

"Look at me, Emory," he said.

I looked up at him, worry knitting my brow. I tried to slide my hands out, but he held firm. Shit.

Where was Will?

"Who conditioned you to lie so well?" he asked, staring into my eyes and keeping his voice calm and steady.

"He . . ." I trailed off as the snake, or whatever it was, stopped over my hand, and I felt it shift or . . . start to coil. Another lump lodged in my throat. "Aydin . . ."

"Who?" He tightened his hold on my wrists.

"He . . ." I breathed hard. "He wasn't an addict. My brother had a temper," I explained.

Fuck, where was Will? Tears sprang to my eyes.

"And he got physical with you?" Aydin asked.

A flicker of something hit my pinky—again and again. Its tongue?

"Oh, my God." I gasped. "Please."

Let me go.

"Be still," he said. "Look at me."

I darted my eyes to his again.

"Like a rock," he instructed. "You're part of her terrain. She won't notice you unless you want her to. Like a rock, Emory."

"Aydin . . ."

"Don't move," he chided again.

I closed my eyes, trapped. Feeling it there. Unable to run. Any sudden movement, and . . . *God, get it off me. Please.*

"It reminds you of him, doesn't it?" Aydin asked. "Your brother."

What?

"Waiting for the danger to hit," he continued. "Knowing it was coming."

I kept my eyes closed, trying to drown it out, but my knees started shaking, and I wanted to hit him. My arms were charged, the anger there, like before, but I couldn't do anything with it. Not yet. I couldn't move.

"Unable to live, damn near wetting your pants and waiting for the inevitable as it got closer and closer to you."

Shut up. He didn't know me.

"Would you get sick right before you knew he was coming home?" he asked. "Run to the bathroom and vomit, maybe?"

I opened my eyes, meeting his through the blur.

Needles pricked my throat, remembering. "The kitchen sink," I told him. "It was closer than the bathroom. I was usually making dinner."

He nodded, a thoughtful look in his eyes.

The snake's head slid over my hand again, grinding the dirt into my skin.

"Is it poisonous?" I asked.

"Something is only poisonous if you eat it," he retorted. "Organisms that bite and inject you with poison are described as venomous."

Jesus, fuck. "Is it venomous, then?"

"They're black racers," he pointed out, as if that meant anything to me. "What if I said it's venomous, but I have antivenom?"

"Let me go."

"What if I said it's not venomous, but it can bite?"

I gritted my teeth, the snake's head nudging between my fingers. What the fuck? Why wasn't it moving on?

"What if I said it can't bite, only constrict?" he asked instead.

"What are you doing?"

"Or maybe it's not harmful at all," he told me, "but I might put some in your bed tonight? Would you fear them any less?"

"Aydin . . ." I started to pull at my arms.

He barked, "If you move, she'll strike." He glared at me. "Own it, Emory. Own this moment."

What? I shook my head, my thighs tense as I got ready to bolt and fight and run, but . . .

"Don't run," he told me, reading my mind. "Don't cry. Don't get angry. Just let go."

N . . . no. What . . . ? The dirt shifted a few feet away, and I whimpered. Was that another one?

But he yelled, "Let go!"

I startled, resisting the urge to curl my fingers into the dirt.

"Look at me," he said. "Look into my eyes."

I snapped my gaze to his. *Please* . . .

"Look at me," he urged again. "Hold my eyes. Don't fight. Don't rage. Don't scream. Don't give him your fear."

I panted, staring into his brown eyes, tunneling deeper into the flecks of honey and amber.

"I am here," he recited. "This is it, and I am not scared."

I exhaled, sucking in another breath but starting to calm.

"I am not scared," he repeated. "I am the eye of the storm. The calm in the madness."

I blew out a breath, drawing in another, slower.

"The quiet in the chaos. The patience for my moment."

My hand started to melt into the dirt, the snake shrinking and my heart starting to slow down.

We didn't blink.

"I am the eye of the storm," he murmured again, and I was transfixed. "He did not happen to you, Emory. You expected it. It was supposed to happen. It was all part of the plan. You knew it was coming."

I gazed into his eyes, his voice surrounding me like music as cool calmness swept through my blood.

"Nothing is ever a surprise," he said. "Always act as if you knew it was coming the whole time. Pretend it was part of the plan. You move with the storm, Emory. Calm, quiet, patient, and then . . . Then you happen to him."

My chest rose and fell in steady breaths as I whispered, "I happen to him."

"He may hit you again," he breathed out, "but he will never hurt you. You will smile, and then . . ."

"I will happen to him," I whispered.

Warmth coursed over my body, a curtain lifted, and my lungs opened, steel coating my skin and knives sprouting from my nails.

The racer slithered over my finger and up to the surface of the soil, moving away into the other plants, and I looked down, seeing my palms still buried, but Aydin was no longer holding me.

When had he let go?

Taking them out, I looked at him, seeing him give me a small smile. Then, he leaned over and grabbed the black snake, still fisting its body and staring at me as the reptile hissed, snapped back around, and struck the back of his hand, sinking its fangs into him.

Aydin released it, and I watched as he sucked the two red punctures into his mouth and spit the blood into the plant bed.

"Like nearly all suffering," he told me, "it bites, but you live."

Sweat cooled on my skin, and my head was in the clouds, a tremendous weight I thought I'd always feel suddenly gone.

Leaning in, Aydin kissed my temple, and I didn't even consider pulling away. His lips were warm and gentle—almost like a . . .

Like a father.

"You're Lilith," he whispered against my skin. "You can't be burned if you're the flame."

Pulling back, he looked down into my eyes, and I didn't want to smile. He wasn't off the hook for that scare, but I walked in here with something that I was going to leave without. Everything felt stronger and lighter.

How the hell did he do that?

Lilith . . . His words drifted through my head. Was he Jewish? She was in our folklore. Adam's first wife and cast out of the Garden of Eden, because she refused to be subservient.

She was dark and light. She wasn't afraid to fall or to burn too bright.

She was a flame.

Something shifted off to my right, and we both turned our heads, seeing Will standing just inside the room.

He wore gray sweatpants, hanging low on his hips, and nothing else as his hair stuck up all over the place in the most adorable way.

My heart instantly ached at the anger always in his eyes, but I was ready to do something about it now.

His gaze shot from Aydin to me in his lap, the sharpness in his scowl suddenly turning flat, like he didn't care. He just stood there, unmoving, and I rose from Aydin's lap, remembering that night on the dance floor at Homecoming.

Everyone had stared at us because we didn't belong together, but we felt nothing other than the ache of the agonizing inch between us, and suddenly Aydin wasn't even in the room.

"Micah and Rory gone hunting?" Aydin asked, leaning back in his seat.

Will nodded, refusing to look at me now. "I told Taylor to go with them."

Aydin chuckled under his breath, looking at Will over his shoulder. "Just the three of us, then," he mused, glancing at me. "You kids want to play in the pool?"

I gazed at Will, ignoring Aydin's thinly veiled request that I take off my clothes, but then Will spoke up.

"Just take her," he said. "I've had her."

I stared at him, the challenge clear, but while I would've mouthed off or walked out ten minutes ago, I felt roots sprout from the bottoms of my shoes, keeping me steady.

An oak.

The eye of the storm.

Aydin laughed to himself and rose from the chair, replacing the panel that kept the snakes confined, and ruffling my hair as he headed out of the room. "You know where to find me," he called out, "when you're ready for the next level, Miss Scott."

He left and Will looked at me, shaking his head. He wouldn't even stop me if I jumped on every dick in this house right now.

He didn't care, because he hated me.

"Nothing was going on," I told him.

"I don't care," he shot back. "And you wouldn't care if I did."

Without another word, he twisted around and walked away.

My lungs constricted. "Godzilla," I called out, taking a step forward.

He stopped. Turning back around, he narrowed his hard eyes. "What?"

I took another step, tempted to fidget or look away or shrink like it was always in my nature to do when I was scared shitless, but I kept my gaze locked on him.

No matter how much it hurt.

None of what's happening right now is a surprise. I knew it was coming. Handle it.

"You, um . . ." I swallowed the lump in my throat. "You missed a *Godzilla* movie since you've been gone. *King of the Monsters,*" I told him. "It was pretty decent, except for the plot."

He remained still, eyeing me suspiciously.

I took another step.

He could walk out any second, but I wouldn't let him. *Stay.*

"Good cinematography and action sequences," I said. "You get to see Mothra, too."

The sprinklers overhead sprouted to life, but I didn't look away as warm rain fell over the trees, plants, and garden, wetting my clothes.

I removed my glasses, setting them on the edge of another tree bed.

"I bought Milk Duds and Twizzlers." I chuckled under my breath. "I don't know why because I was on my own, and I didn't need all that candy, but I didn't eat the Milk Duds." I swallowed, staring deep into his eyes. "I couldn't help but think . . . 'Will would love this.'"

My eyes stung, but I blinked away the tears, knowing exactly why I bought the Milk Duds. They were Will's.

Water cascaded down his bare chest, and I breathed steadily, unwavering no matter how hard my heart pounded.

"I kept wondering what you'd say about the movie," I told him. "And what you'd like about it."

His eyes stayed on mine as I inched forward, water dripping down his mouth and glistening on his skin.

Please stay.

His Adam's apple bobbed up and down the closer I got, and he dropped his eyes, breathing harder.

"Mothra?" he murmured.

"And King Ghidorah, too." I nodded. "All the titans. The visual effects were amazing."

Stepping up to him, I stopped as my shirt grazed his chest. Heat pooled in my belly, feeling him so close.

"They're releasing *Godzilla vs. Kong* soon," I told him, kicking off my shoes.

His chest rose and fell in front of me, and I gazed at all the skin my fingers hummed to touch. I balled my fists.

"They're both heroes," he replied. "The ending will be ambiguous, Emory."

"No." I shook my head, pulling my shirt off and dropping it to the ground. "The directors have stated there will be a clear winner."

He stared at my body, his breathing growing ragged. "What the fuck?" he griped. "Fucking writers."

My clit throbbed, and I stared at his mouth, damn near tasting him and wanting to climb him so damn bad.

"So, it'll be Kong," I stated, unbuttoning Rory's pants around my waist. "It's more hopeful for the underdog to win."

He watched me, unblinking. "Japan will ban the film if Godzilla doesn't win."

"I guess he could win," I told him, dropping the pants to the floor as rain hit my breasts, arms, and back. "With Godzilla's arsenal, and the fact that he can fight on land and at sea . . ."

"And in the comic books, he battles God and the devil, for crying out loud," he said. "What the hell's Kong ever done?"

I leaned up on my tiptoes, our lips inches from each other. "Godzilla now also emits an omnidirectional blast."

"He does?"

I nodded. "You missed it."

Running my fingertips up his chest, I tried to swallow, but my mouth was too dry.

"Told you," he said. "How's Kong going to survive a molecular level attack?"

I pressed my body to his, my hard little nipples aching against his heat.

He shook a little underneath my hands, and I couldn't take it anymore. I curled my fists again, my body boiling, and I didn't care that I wanted to squeeze the life out of him half the time—I wanted in his bed.

But I wasn't asking for anything. I was taking it.

My heart damn near in my throat, I pushed him down into the chair to my left and hovered over his lips as I slid my hand up his chest.

He laughed, gripping the arms of the chair. "You want it?" he taunted. "You're not getting it."

I grazed my lips across his cheek, over his jaw, and down his neck, the hunger making my clit throb so hard I had to hold back a whimper as the rain fell all over my naked body.

"You don't have to do a thing," I whispered over his skin. "In fact . . ."

I slid my hand inside his pants and dived for his cock, fisting the hard muscle.

He gasped, his eyes going wide.

"You don't even have to move," I told him, pumping him slow and tight. "Stay right here, because I'm going to drain you dry."

I squeezed his neck, gentle but possessive before sliding to my knees and drawing my claws down his chest and then his thighs.

He was mine. Straightening my back, I felt his eyes on my breasts as I untied the drawstring and pulled down his pants, just enough so I could take him out.

Water sprayed my hair, my chest, his stomach, and his face as he stared down at me, a cross between anger and excitement in his eyes.

But he wasn't stopping me.

Fisting his cock, I stroked it as I kissed and licked his stomach, running my free hand around his waist, over his back, and up his chest. I nibbled and bit, dragging his skin out with my teeth before sucking it into my mouth, his body caving under me with every breath.

"Fuck," he whispered, groaning.

Coming back down, I cast him a quick look, seeing his white knuckles as he gripped the arms of the chair. Holding his eyes, I moved the head of his dick to the opening of my mouth, not slipping it in just yet as I teased him.

I flicked my tongue, tasting his heat as his eyes softened and need flashed across his face.

"Emmy," he panted.

And my heart started to shatter, hearing a younger, happier Will Grayson begging me to let him hold me again.

I closed my eyes and slid him into my mouth, pushing my lips down his shaft until the tip touched the back of my throat.

He sucked in air through his teeth, his fingers sliding into my hair and holding my head as he moaned.

I held him there, relaxing my throat and trying to take him all in, but I was hungry and I wanted to suck. Moving up and down, I drew him out slow and then glided my mouth back down his cock, taking him again.

His fingers fisted my hair, the hard muscle in my mouth getting stiffer. I dragged my tongue up and down his shaft, licking the veins under his skin and sucking the sweet drip off his tip.

He growled, glaring down at me. "Taking advantage of a man who's been in prison is low. Really low."

"You're not at Blackchurch," I whispered, kissing the length of his cock. "We're at the lock-in, and we snuck off, so I could kiss you. Down here."

He groaned, letting his head fall back and his eyes close, the fantasy hopefully taking over. Taking him back before I hurt him. Before he hurt me. Before all the shit and all the years . . .

I moved faster, sucking him harder and tighter, whimpering at his size trying to push down my throat as his hips started thrusting up to meet me.

"Will," I begged, the slickness between my legs growing.

Slipping a hand between my legs, I swirled the wetness around my clit, throbbing and aching for him as I brought my fingers back out.

I swirled my wet fingers around his tip, watching him watch me and holding his eyes as I sucked him back into my mouth and licked myself off of him. His piercing eyes caught fire as I licked off the water and covered him in warmth.

But suddenly, he grabbed my arms and pulled me up.

What?

He glared into my eyes for a moment before he spun me around and planted me in his lap.

He wrapped an arm around me, breathing into my neck and holding me close. "What else we gonna do?" he panted. "Before a teacher comes."

His dick pressed into my ass, and he grabbed my pussy, sticking a finger deep inside, and then two.

I gasped as he cupped my breast, sliding my nipple in and out between his fingers.

"Huh, little Emmy?" he taunted.

I closed my eyes, the water raining down on us in the hothouse as I pictured all the fun we could've had if I'd just dived in all those years ago.

God, I wanted him. Fuck.

Pulling away, I stood up and faced him, watching him stroke his cock, and look at me.

I didn't wait another second. I climbed on top of him, crashing my mouth to his and straddling him as I ate up his lips and clutched his throat.

Mine.

He jerked his mouth away, smirking like the cat that ate the canary, but I didn't care, because I wanted to give him this.

He positioned himself under me, crowning my entrance, and I whimpered already at the anticipation as I nibbled his jaw.

I slid down, burying him inside me.

I stretched and gasped, and he hit deep before I raised back up, coating him in my wetness before sliding back down on him and sheathing him to the hilt.

"Ah," he groaned, squeezing my ass in both hands.

I stilled, staying there and feeling the stretch and fullness.

I kissed his cheek, watching his face and his closed eyes as he let me trail my mouth over his temple and his forehead and to the corner of his lips, leaving little kisses. Sliding my hand through his hair, I dipped down to his neck, tasting the water on his hot skin as tingles spread everywhere at the memory of his smell.

Sitting back, I stared at him as I started to move slowly, arching my back and rolling my hips. I slid him out and thrust back onto him, fucking him slowly at first. He opened his eyes and gripped my hips, his eyes trailing all over as he watched my body move on top of him.

Diving forward, he sucked my breast into his mouth, and I dug my nails into his shoulders, letting my head fall back as the wave of euphoria coursed over me.

"You fucked me up," he growled, pulling my nipple through his teeth.

"And you fucked up," I argued, tipping my head back up, the water running down my face as he nibbled one breast and moved on to the other.

Part of all this shit was my fault, but not all of it.

I rolled my hips again and again, my breathing getting shallower as the pleasure built.

"I want to kiss you," I whispered. "On the lips."

"Yeah?"

"Yeah."

"Why?" he teased.

I panted, leaning back up and bouncing up and down on him as I held him close. "Because," I whispered over his mouth. "Because I want to be your girl."

He circled my waist with both arms like a steel band, stopping me. "And you remember what that means?"

I gazed down at him, trying to hide my smile as I remembered everything he wanted.

Me, coming home to him every night.

Me, at his table and warming his bed.

Me, making him a daddy.

I nodded.

"Say it," he ordered.

I swallowed, the excitement coursing through my veins as I whispered, "It means you come inside me."

We didn't have condoms here.

He grinned and stood up, taking me with him as he walked to the tree bed behind us, dropped down, and pushed me onto the soil. Rising back up, he flipped me over, and I gasped, whimpering as realization dawned.

I moaned, my clit pulsing like a jackhammer as he came down on my ass, forced my knee out, and thrust back inside my pussy, going at me hard and fast.

"Will . . ." I cried.

He wrapped a hand around my neck and whispered against my cheek, "Say it again."

He hit me deep, in and out, in and out, again and again, and I squeezed my eyes shut, taking it. "It means you come inside me."

"You want that?"

"Yeah."

The soil ground into my body, and finally, he twisted my head toward him, sinking his mouth into mine and kissing me deep, stealing my breath away.

His tongue dipped in and made my heart sink down to my toes. I whimpered.

"My little Em," he breathed out, slipping a hand underneath me and palming my tit. "My little Em likes her little secrets. Little nerd by day who likes it a little hard at night."

"Yeah," I chanted. "Yes."

My pussy tightened and constricted, and I pressed my hands into the soil, backing up into him, craving it.

My hair stuck to my back as I arched it, and all I could think about was all the time we'd lost in high school. Of how this was it, and I should've known it. I should've snuck out with him and done this with him every single chance we got, because there was nothing that I was protecting myself from that wasn't already happening at home. I shouldn't have let the fear stop me.

The orgasm started to build, and I cried out as he thrust his cock inside me again and again, fucking me on the dirt and every inch of my skin feeling all of this.

He grunted, and I could tell he was getting close. "Say it again," he said.

"Come inside me," I whimpered, feeling it coming. "Oh, God."

"Again."

"Come inside me, Will," I begged. "Please."

He bottomed out, and I exploded, the orgasm shaking my entire body as the world spun under me, and he thrust again and again, harder and harder, finally spilling inside of me as he squeezed my breast and moaned.

I cried out, every muscle burning. The orgasm wracked through me, my pussy squeezing around his cock, and he flipped over, collapsing onto the ground next to me.

"Fuck," he panted.

I closed my eyes, laying my head down and unable to swallow because my mouth was so dry. I really hoped the snakes were confined to the garden and not here.

But I couldn't muster a muscle to care.

Aydin probably watched us from somewhere, too. The guys could've come back early for whatever reason, but I didn't give a shit. I wanted a shower, and I wanted sleep, and I wanted both of them with Will.

But without another touch or kiss, he rose from the dirt and pulled up his soaked sweats, tying them closed.

I turned over and sat up, watching him as he walked over and retrieved my drenched clothes from the floor.

He tossed them to me. "Go piss," he said. "And hurry up."

I sat there, my eyes narrowing but my chin trembling a little. I clenched my jaw to stop it.

The eye of the storm . . .

I forced the lump down my throat. "That's an old wives' tale," I told him, rising and starting to dress. "I'm on the shot, so don't worry."

Asshole.

Not that I was ready for any kids right now, anyway, but he wasn't telling me that because he didn't want them. He was telling me that because he didn't want them with me.

It was just sex talk.

I swallowed through the needles in my throat, not looking up again until he'd walked out, leaving me in the wet dirt alone.

I rose to my feet and pulled on my glasses, cutoff pants, and T-shirt, and then I picked up my shoes and carried them through the quiet house and back up to my bedroom.

I secured the door, lost in my head as I showered and washed the dirt from my hair, still feeling him inside me.

I'd show him. I was strong, and I wouldn't beg for anything.

I'd get out of here and live and keep my damn chin up.

The calm in the madness. The quiet in the chaos. The patience for my moment.

I dried my hair and wrapped the towel around me, heading into my dark bedroom and collapsing onto the bed.

I closed my eyes, hearing the rain outside and trying to concentrate on the next step of my escape plan.

A little more food, a hoodie, and I still needed some kind of tool from the shed. It would make a good weapon, too, if needed.

A draft hit me, and I rubbed my eyes with my fingers, so tired all of a sudden.

But I couldn't go to sleep. Opening my eyes, I spotted a dark form looming at the side of my bed, and I sucked in a quick breath.

What the hell?

But before I could shoot up and away, she spoke.

"You let them watch while he ate you out last night?" she asked.

And then the lamp on the nightstand turned on, and I looked up at her, hair a little shorter than the last time I'd seen her and dressed like a cat burglar, complete with a black beanie on her head.

"Girl," she cooed, smiling with approval. "I knew you had it in you."

I stopped breathing, my eyes going wide. "Alex?"

She threw up her hands, striking a pose, and I popped up, grabbed her, and pulled her into a hug as we collapsed back to the bed.

Oh, my God. "What are you doing here?" I cried.

She clamped a hand over my mouth, quieting me as she shook with a laugh. "Missed you, too, little stick," she whispered.

My body shook with a quiet laugh, and I squeezed her so tight she grunted.

CHAPTER 20

WILL

Nine Years Ago

She stopped and looked around as I took the key from her and unlocked her back door.

It was after one in the morning, and I hurriedly twisted the handle and pulled her in from the rain.

"It's okay," I assured her. "The coast is clear. He's still at work."

I closed the door, locked it, and knelt down, slipping her heels off her feet. Taking her hand, I pulled her toward the stairs.

"We really need to stand up to him sometime."

She leaned her head on my arm, yawning. "He's scary," she said.

I shook my head, sweeping her into my arms and carrying her up the stairs. "He's a joke." I hugged her close as she wrapped her arms around my neck. "I'm your man now. He'll have to get through me."

She just let out a single chuckle into the crook of my neck, but didn't say more.

I wasn't trying to be funny.

"Paige?" someone called.

I froze, the weight of my footsteps halting the creaking on the floorboards.

Emmy popped her head up and shifted out of my arms, hurrying into her grandmother's room.

"Yes, Grand-Mère."

I hung back, not wanting Em to have to face questions about why she was with me so late.

"Where is your father?" her grandma asked.

I heard Em walk around the room, pour some water, and shuffle blankets.

Her father?

But Emmy answered, not missing a beat. "He had to go back to the flower shop. He got you yellow flowers, and he knows better."

"Red flowers." Her grandmother's raspy voice held a hint of humor. "How could he forget?"

"Go to sleep," Em cooed. "When you wake up, they'll be here."

Emory walked back into the hallway, yawning again as she pulled the door closed, only leaving it open a crack.

"Love you, sweetie," her grandmother called.

"Love you, too."

She gazed up at me in the dark hallway and took my hand, laying her head on my chest. She was fucking exhausted.

I led her to her room.

"Your father?" I inquired.

Adam Scott died with her mother years ago. Caught in their car when the river flooded during Hurricane Finn that hit us head-on about five years ago.

But Emmy clarified, "My grandfather. Her husband. She thinks I'm my mother sometimes."

I nodded once, not really knowing what to say to that. It was a lot for a high schooler to deal with. In this moment, I was grateful she spared me any time, considering the bigger things she had on her plate. I was too hard on her.

We entered her room, and I turned on the lights.

But she protested, "No, leave them off." She made her way for her bed. "I'm so tired."

She crashed down, not even bothering to undress, and I flipped the switch off again, the room going dark.

"But I don't want to sleep, either," she said, yawning again. "Because when the night's over, it ends. No more fun."

I walked over, unable to keep the smile off my lips. "Nothing is ending." I pulled at her comforter and then the blankets, working them out from underneath her to cover her up. "It wasn't just fun to me, Emmy. Don't you know that?"

I stared down at her as she turned on her side, and I covered her up.

We weren't done. I needed more.

"You still don't trust me?" I asked.

She remained still and quiet, refusing to look at me. Was she asleep already?

But then I heard her speak. "Part of me wishes I could have you," she said. "Part of me wishes you were my man, but . . ."

I heard her swallow, and then she sighed.

"Everything will be real tomorrow," she told me.

As if that explained everything.

Walking over to her window, I closed her drapes.

"Someday you'll be big and powerful," she continued.

I turned to see her sitting up in bed and punching the pillows behind her, trying to get them to the right fluffiness.

"Like I am now?" I teased.

"And stunning in a three-piece suit with fabulous hair," she went on, thinking out loud like I wasn't even there.

"I look better wet."

"And everyone will love you." She plopped back onto her pillows, lying on her back.

"They already do."

"And you'll be the life of the party."

I walked over, straightening her blankets and biting back my smile. "Mm-hmm."

"With little magazine-cover-looking children."

"My sperm will be the stuff of legends," I joked.

"And married . . ."

"Several times, I'm sure."

"And to all blondes."

My body shook with a laugh as I leaned over her, smelling her and me on her skin and dying to crawl into this bed with her.

But she was done for the night.

"And the only time you'll notice I'm alive," she went on, "is when you sign the checks, paying my dog-walking service for taking care of your labradoodles every week."

"Like a busy, important, fabulous god like me would be bothered with such tasks?" I retorted. "My eighteen-year-old former Playboy-bunny wife, Heidi, will sign those checks."

A snarl flashed on her mouth, and I snorted.

"You're going to remember this, Will Grayson," she said, sounding all tough. "I blew your mind tonight. Even if for just a minute."

She turned over, giving me her back, and I smiled, smoothing the hair off her face and neck.

You've been blowing my mind for forever.

"Now, get out of here," she said, nudging me playfully and closing her eyes.

I stared down at her, the shadows of the trees outside dancing across her back, and my body hummed, wanting more of her.

She was incredible, and I hated that no one saw how beautiful she was except me. I'd been dying in that bus and fucking happy for it.

Her body moved in slow, steady breaths, and I watched her lips meet, so softly time and again with each breath.

"I love you," I murmured.

She didn't shift or open her eyes, the exhaustion taking over as she sank deeper and deeper into sleep.

Standing up straight, I stepped away, but then I dropped my eyes to her back, seeing the bruises and scrapes.

How did she paint her back? Did her brother help her?

I doubted it.

Squatting down, I leaned in closer, studying the marks on her arm and back with the little moonlight streaming in through the sheer curtains.

Licking my thumb, I rubbed at the dark purple one with red around it, but . . .

The makeup didn't rub off.

I narrowed my eyes, licking my thumb again and rubbing harder.

But then she whimpered, shifting away from me like it hurt.

I rubbed my finger against my thumb, not feeling any grease or oil from the makeup, either.

I stopped and looked up at her face, studying the blood coming down from her eyebrow she said was part of her costume.

Heat filled my veins, and my pulse echoed in my ears as my mind raced.

The bruises on her legs that I saw in the swimming pool . . .

The bruise on her leg in lit class.

The overly baggy clothes and how she hardly ever showed skin.

Rising up, I stared down at her, tempted to drag her out of this bed.

But it was late, and she needed sleep.

Tonight was Devil's Night. I'd let her rest for now.

Because later today I was going to find out what the fuck was going on once and for all.

CHAPTER 21

EMORY

Present

I pulled back, staring down at her face to make sure she was real.

Alex . . . I smiled from ear to ear. "Oh, my God."

"Shh," she hissed, glancing at the door. "I know. I know. But don't start celebrating. Neither of us is saved yet."

She shot off the bed and hurried to the door, listening for something, and then whipped around, running into the bathroom.

I stared after her as she filled a glass with water and drank it down. Where the hell did she come from?

Did . . . ? How . . . ?

And then I caught sight of the portrait on the wall. The massive, framed painting of a little girl and her corgis frolicking in some garden hung open like a door.

A secret passage.

I smiled to myself. I guess I didn't need that screwdriver after all.

Walking back out, she pulled her hat off her head and smiled at me with her full lips and white teeth. She'd cut her hair. The A-line, shoulder-length bob curtained her long neck, strands hanging in her face and over her beautiful eyes, her green a shade darker than Will's.

"How are you here?" I asked, taking in her tight jeans that were a lot more practical than the dress pants I'd arrived in, and her fitted, brown leather jacket that matched her rubber-soled brown leather boots.

She was dressed to run. Dirt scuffed her jaw, and she pulled off her gloves, black gunk embedded under her nails.

And then I registered what she had said a moment ago, my spine straightening. She'd watched us in the drawing room last night?

She'd been here, hiding. For at least a day.

I shot off the bed. "Did you put me here?"

I pinched my eyebrows together, anger suddenly replacing the relief I'd just felt.

But her eyes darted to mine. "No," she said, knitting her brow. "God, no. I promise. I have no idea why you're here."

"Then why are you here?" I demanded, tightening the towel around me. "How . . . Where did you come from? How did you know about the secret passageways? Where are we?"

I had too many questions, and the confusion from when I'd arrived started to bubble up again. No one had any answers.

She opened the painting wider and leaned down, pulling out a black duffel bag. Walking over, she dug out some clothes and handed them to me, remaining silent.

I looked down at the jeans and long-sleeved black tee and . . .

Yes. Underwear and a bra.

She'd packed for this. She knew she was coming here, unlike me. I swallowed, staring at her. "Alex?"

Why wasn't she talking?

She shuffled the stuff in her bag, refusing to look at me.

"Alex."

Finally, she said in a low voice, "We're on an island. In North America."

"Canada?"

She hesitated.

"Where in North America?" I pressed. "East Coast, West Coast, New England . . . ?"

But she just spun around, taking her canteen into the bathroom and refilling it.

An island . . .

Was it deserted? Was it near the mainland? Shit. There were millions of islands out there.

"Alex?" I barked.

Goddammit.

But she whisper-yelled at me. "Emmy, shut up."

I glanced at the door again, remembering we had a house full of men on the other side who didn't know she was here.

And even though I was glad she was, she wasn't putting me at ease.

I have no idea why you're *here*, she'd said. So, she knew why she was here, then?

"How long have you been here?" I demanded.

How long had she been hiding in the walls? I heard those sounds the night I arrived. She hadn't been hiding that long, right?

But even as the thought occurred to me, I watched her eyes shift as she filled her bottle, and the fury boiled over.

"I arrived on the shipment like you," she said in a low voice.

I charged over, grabbed her water bottle, and threw it. I fisted her collar and shoved her away, growling. She stumbled backward, tripped over the toilet, and fell onto the ground, landing on her ass. She broke the fall with her hands and her eyes flew up to me.

"What the hell is the matter with you?" I gritted out as quietly as I could. "Do you have any idea what could've happened to me?"

All this time. She'd been watching all of us. What the hell was going on?

She breathed hard, but she never blinked. She knew she'd fucked up.

"You've been hiding in the walls," I pointed out. "It didn't occur to you at some point to grab me, too?"

"Of course, it did," she said, climbing to her feet again and picking up her bottle. "It just got complicated."

I closed the distance between us and swatted her about fifteen times lightly in the chest. Goddamn her.

"Are you hitting my boobs?" She batted at my hands. "Seriously."

I didn't know what was going on, and while I was momentarily grateful not to be as alone as I thought, I had no doubt she had the answers I wanted and was refusing to give them to me.

This was bullshit.

She caught her breath, and I stood there, not at all scared if she decided to hit me back.

But she didn't. She just cocked an eyebrow, saying, "Save it for the plutocrats. You need me."

I stood there, about ready to hit her again, but she was right. I had a much better chance of getting out of here with her.

She refilled the water bottle that I'd spilled when I threw it, and I stalked back into the bedroom, throwing on the underwear and bra she gave me. I didn't put on the clothes yet, because if I faced the guys again, they'd wonder where I got them.

I pulled on Aydin's Oxford and tied up my wet hair into a ponytail with a rubber band I'd snatched from the asparagus in the fridge.

"Listen . . ." Alex entered the room, stuffing the bottle into the bag and tossing the duffel into the passageway again. "We guessed Will was sent here several months ago—maybe a year or more, we don't know exactly. He'd been using and drinking, and we figured with his grandfather's reelection coming up, Senator Grayson took matters into his own hands before Will became a liability."

A year . . . So, he had been here that long. At least.

"We couldn't get him out because no one would tell us where it was," she told me, "but we could get someone in."

Me?

But no. She said she didn't know why I was here.

So, that meant they sent her?

"Michael, Kai, Damon . . ." I rattle off. "And they sent you?"

She stared at me, but the hesitation in her eyes said it all.

"No," she finally admitted. "Michael was coming. I . . . I slipped him a mickey before the pickup."

I narrowed my eyes. She roofied him? "Why?" I searched for words. "Alex, why would you volunteer for this? A woman would be in so much more danger. It's crazy."

Her gaze faltered, and she didn't answer me. Why would she put herself in such unnecessary risk when anyone could've come for Will?

Unless . . .

Unless she loved him.

That was the only reason she'd come in Michael Crist's place. She thought only she'd be able to bring Will home.

My stomach coiled and jealousy rolled through me, making my heart pound. *It is my place to save him. Not hers.*

But it was ridiculous for me to have such a thought, I knew that.

I was jealous, though. I knew their history and I liked Alex—more than I wanted to—but somehow it hadn't hurt until now, because she just had this way about her that made you all warm and want to be wherever she was. It was impossible to hate her.

And I'd been kind of glad he had her at his side. As long as I didn't let myself wonder if she was better for him. If she made him happy.

But now I couldn't keep the thought from my mind.

She'd come for him. I hadn't.

She was better for him.

I opened my mouth. "Alex, I—"

But she pressed her finger to her lips. "Shhh."

The hallway outside my door creaked, and she grabbed my hand, pulling me into the secret passageway.

She closed the painting, and we stood there quietly as she dug in the bag at our feet for something.

"Do they know about the passageways?" I asked quietly.

"I don't think so," she told me. "I've been able to skulk around undetected."

"Seems weird," I said. "There's a secret room off Aydin's bedroom with a two-way mirror. They should suspect there are more disguised rooms and tunnels."

She rose, and then I heard a winding, the rechargeable flashlight illuminating as she pulled out a large, folded-up piece of paper that looked like a map.

I dropped my eyes, noticing it wasn't paper. Not normal paper, anyway.

I grabbed it from her, the feel instantly familiar. It was vellum. This was a blueprint.

How did . . . ? Where . . . ? I snatched her flashlight and turned away to inspect the plans.

"If I'm being punked, I'm going to kill you," I hissed, studying the floor plan. "If this is someone's idea of a prank, and we're in Thunder Bay . . ."

"And they imported that waterfall you saw outside?" she spat out. "Think, Em."

She snatched the blueprints and flashlight out of my hands and walked past me, down the tunnel. I couldn't help but glare at her back as she flipped over the folded document in her hand and studied it while we walked.

No, there wasn't a waterfall in Thunder Bay. But there were plenty throughout New England and possibly more on the hundreds of islands dotting the coast.

I needed to see that blueprint again. I could read it a hell of a lot faster than she could.

A faint light caught my eye, and I stopped. "Alex . . ." I whispered, inching toward the wall and closer to the light. "What's the plan here?"

If we were on an island, she had to have a boat or someone

airlifting us out of here. I guessed she had some kind of tracker on her so they knew where to come.

"I have a satellite phone," she told me. "The cavalry is on its way."

"What does that mean?"

"The Horsemen," she clarified. "They tracked me when I was transported here. We just need to hang on."

Hang on?

"It's been days," I bit out in her face. "I could've gotten to China and back by now! Twice! Have you even talked to them? How do you know for sure they tracked you? Satellite phones use a lot of power. You would have to keep it turned on for them to track you."

"Or make a call," she retorted.

I narrowed my eyes. "You called them?"

"Yes."

"And they're coming?"

"Yes."

My shoulders relaxed a little, but still . . . something concerned me. "Have you talked to them recently?" I asked.

Her eyes sharpened, and she studied me. "Why?"

"It's been too long," I told her. "They should've been here by now. When was the last time you spoke to them?"

She shifted on her feet, looking hesitant. "The night we arrived," she murmured.

I closed my eyes, turning away. "Shit," I said under my breath.

"It's fine, Emory." Her tone was firm and decisive. "They're traveling, there's been storms, and I haven't been able to use the phone at times because I was afraid of being heard. They'll be here."

When? One day? Eight more days?

We needed to leave now. Make it to the coast and wait for the boat. Anything could happen, and I still didn't know who dumped me here, but it was only a matter of time before the shit hit the fan.

She walked down the passageway, and I spotted slits and holes in the concrete, light from the rooms on the other side streaming through.

"What do you know about these guys?" I asked.

All I knew was what they'd wanted me to know.

"Stay away from Taylor," she said, flashing her light ahead. "And stay away from Aydin Khadir."

Wow, better late than never.

I pulled her to a stop and looked at her. "Why?"

She sighed and pulled out of my hold, continuing down the tunnel. "Micah is harmless unless you hurt Rory," she told me. "Rory Geardon . . ."

"Killed people," I finished for her.

But she stopped and peered through a peephole, whispering, "His twin sister was born with cerebral palsy. She was confined to a wheelchair. One night, a small party of teenagers broke into their house and brutalized her." She peered over at me. "And I mean, brutalized her."

I stopped breathing for a moment, remembering his story. *And one by one, he sank them to the bottom of a lake and drowned them.*

For his twin.

I swallowed the lump in my throat, unable to bear thinking about the details of what they might've done to her. *My God.*

"He had a motive, but that doesn't mean it takes a lot to set him in motion, either," she told me. "Watch yourself. His mother is an ambassador to Japan, and his family is one of the biggest real estate developers on the East Coast, specifically in for-profit prisons. That killing spree wasn't his only foray into crime. They certainly had it coming, but that doesn't mean he's done, so be careful."

I frowned. He was probably unlikely to ever get out of here. That meant he had nothing to lose.

"Taylor definitely belongs in here," she continued. "He likes to take weekend road trips to college campuses, set fires in dorms and sorority houses, and then molest girls as they try to escape. When he finally lets go, they're so scared of the fire, they don't stop to fight back or try to identify him."

The image of him with my panties flashed in my mind, and I winced.

"And Aydin?"

She'd told me to stay away from him, too.

But she just blurted out, "Just stay away from him. He doesn't get to win."

Win what?

"How do you know all this?" I asked her.

She twisted around and started walking, ignoring me. I guessed she must've done reconnaissance in her search for Will, but . . .

I grabbed her, hauling her ass back. "You're not telling me something."

She knocked my hand off her arm and glared. "I don't know why you're here or who arranged for you to be brought in," she whispered, leaning in close. "But I came to get Will out, and you're going to help me."

I stared at her.

"I don't mean to be cruel," she continued, "but you better keep up and stop asking fucking questions. I like you, Em, but I'm not leaving without him, so don't straggle."

Why the hurry all of a sudden? It had been days already.

My breath shook as I raised my eyes again. "A year," I said, hardening my eyes on her. "He's been gone at least a year, and you knew that when we talked last summer."

"Well, what were you going to do?" she fired back. "Care?"

What the hell did she just say to me?

The urge to slap her hit me, but I balled my fists instead.

"This isn't my fault." I stood strong. I was to blame for some things, but not everything. "You're his friend. You saw him every day, and you knew what he was doing to himself. This is *your* fault."

Maybe she was a little right. Maybe I hated myself, because she'd come for him, and I'm not sure if I would've. Maybe it wouldn't have changed a damn thing if I'd known about this place months ago.

Or maybe she knew nothing about me and should shut her stupid mouth.

She held my eyes for a moment and then dropped her head, sighing. "I'm sorry," she said. "I didn't mean that. I'm worried about Will. I'm scared, because I haven't heard from my friends. I don't want to be found here." And then she shook her head as if clearing it. "I'm glad I'm not alone. I'm glad you're here."

I chuckled despite myself. "I'm not," I joked.

She put her hand on my shoulder, giving me a reassuring squeeze. "Nothing is going to happen to us. I'm sorry I didn't get you sooner."

"Why didn't you?"

She hesitated, searching for words. "I didn't know you were here until I saw you running for your life through the forest on our first night. I spotted you from a window as they gave chase," she said. "We couldn't get out until the crew got here, and you were already discovered, so . . ."

So you stayed hidden.

I had been sedated when we arrived because I was brought here against my will. She was smuggled in and probably awake when she entered the house. She had intel, blueprints, and supplies. She ran and found a place to hunker down, no doubt.

"I . . ." She paused and then continued, "I kept an eye on the situation from my vantage points, ready to swoop in if needed."

I studied her. That made no sense. She wouldn't have been able to stop anyone from hurting me at any moment. She could've dived in at any time, collected me, and hidden me somewhere. Why leave me in their care? Every moment that she did was a gamble.

"What if Will doesn't want to leave?" I ask her.

He wasn't even remotely content, but he'd given up. Suited to his lot in life of perpetual sidekick, whether it was to Michael Crist, Kai Mori, and Damon Torrance, or Aydin Khadir.

Alex was quiet for a moment as she looked for the entrance to the next passage. "We just gotta wake him up."

Maybe.

Maybe seeing Alex would snap him out of it.

Another wave of jealousy rushed over me. He would listen to her.

I heard a voice through the walls and some pounding, and I trained my ears.

"Shh," I told her.

"Emory?" Another knock in the distance.

I darted my eyes to Alex. *Shit!*

Spinning around, I ran back for my bedroom.

"Emory, no," she whispered after me.

I spun around, looking at her as I walked. "The chair is under the door handle," I told her. "He knows I'm in there. He's going to wonder how I disappeared if he breaks in and sees me gone."

He couldn't find out about the passageways.

I ran back to my room, calling behind me, "Go to Will. Come back for me."

Pushing the picture open, I leapt through, closed it, and ran to my door, scooting the chair out from underneath the knob.

Opening the door, I saw Aydin standing there with a stack of clothes in his hand.

I swallowed the heavy breaths pouring in and out, so he wouldn't wonder why I was out of breath.

"Why didn't you answer the door?" he asked.

"I was asleep."

His eyes thinned on me.

But he didn't argue further, handing the clothes out to me.

I wanted to take them, since everything I had was wet, dirty, or ripped, but . . .

In my clarity, I was a little pissed.

"My brother used to bring me presents, too," I told him. "After he made me bleed."

I moved to close the door, but he shot out his foot, stopping me.

I looked up, seeing his eyes crinkle at the corners. I'm sure he thought we bonded or some shit over that episode in the greenhouse—and maybe we did a little, because I wasn't afraid of him anymore—but I wasn't letting him off the hook. That was mean.

Also, the more I distracted him, the more time Alex might have with Will.

"What are you playing at?" I asked him. "What do you want from me?"

He dropped his hand, still holding the clothes, and stalked toward me, forcing me back into the room as he slammed the door behind him and never took his eyes off me.

"The clothes aren't an apology," he said, tossing them behind me to the bed. "They're respect."

He stared down at me, still dressed in his black pants and smudged white T-shirt, but instead of feeling backed into a wall or defensive, I . . .

I couldn't help the comfort I felt. I shouldn't need his respect or admiration, but something about it made me feel stronger.

Strangely, he hadn't been exactly bad for me, had he?

I grabbed the black sweatpants off the bed and slipped them on, fastening the tie and thankful these actually fit pretty perfectly, and then pulled off his dress shirt, aware of his eyes on me in my bra.

I turned around and picked up the white T-shirt, slipping it on.

I felt him approach.

"Does he know about your brother?" he said, standing at my back.

"Yes."

"And he's still so cold?"

I pulled the shirt down my stomach and fixed the neckline, straightening it.

For a moment, Alex was forgotten.

"You see Micah?" I asked him in a quiet voice. "Kind of playful, prone to smile, happy to let others lead because he's afraid of upsetting the balance in order to take his place?" I paused, feeling him pull my ponytail out of my shirt for me. "Because he's afraid of failing?"

"Yeah."

"That was Will," I told him. "The joker. He never had a worry in the world. Happy, because he didn't want to be unhappy. He was charmed."

I turned around, my mouth dry and so weary I just wanted to crawl into bed, almost as if I didn't care Alex was here.

"He hasn't smiled since I've been here," I said. "Not the same way anyway. He hasn't laughed or played or cracked a joke."

"He never does."

I nodded, Aydin and I holding each other's eyes. "I did that to him," I told him. "I killed him."

Before I could stop it, tears sprang to my eyes, and I didn't know what was wrong with me.

At this moment, I didn't want to leave. I didn't want to hurt Will anymore. I didn't want to face the world.

Aydin took my face in his hands, wiping my tears with his thumbs.

"Stop crying," he said. "You're in the company of killers now. You're not special."

More tears spilled over, but I drew in a deep breath, hearing him.

"Welcome to the tribe," he told me.

I broke out into a laugh as he wiped more tears, and I didn't know what the hell was wrong with me, but it was nice to have someone to talk to.

"Stop crying," he said again. "Shit happens, and you did your best."

I stared at him, those words like a glass of cool water on the fire in my head. I wanted to believe them.

And there was nothing I could do to change what I'd done.

But if I'd done to Aydin what I did to Will, Aydin might not sympathize with me so much.

I belonged here.

CHAPTER 22

EMORY

Nine Years Ago

I licked my lips but then bit my bottom one to keep from smiling.

It didn't work. Heat rushed to my cheeks, and my mind kept pulling me back to last night at the Cove—the feel of him, his taste and smell, and his words.

God, he was incredible. So much so that I probably wouldn't have cared if he'd knocked me up last night, after all. I just wanted to be his.

I shook my head, trying to clear it. We committed a crime at the cemetery. What was I thinking? We could've easily been seen. *Jesus.*

I woke at four a.m. to find him gone, but I was tucked in tightly, and the house was locked up. My brother still wasn't home from the night shift, so I washed out the dress, hung it to dry, and took a shower before checking on my grandma and making him breakfast.

Minutes before he was due to be home, the nurse showed up, and I grabbed the dress and my schoolbag that Martin had left inside the front door, and then I left him a note before escaping the confrontation.

Walking into the cathedral, I dug my key out of my pocket and hurried past the aisle. Rounding one of the columns, I hit something and stumbled back, looking up to see a dark-eyed girl, her mouth hanging open in surprise.

She reached out and grabbed me before I could fall.

"Sorry," she breathed out, looking in a hurry.

I laughed under my breath, tightening my arm around the dress. "That's okay. Accident."

I hesitated for a moment, taking in her worn jeans, black sweatshirt, and the tattered pair of black Vans on her otherwise bare feet. A black ski cap covered her head, but I caught sight of a low, black ponytail hanging over her shoulder and down her chest.

Pretty.

Beautiful, actually.

Definitely not Thunder Bay Prep, though. Too bad. Would've been nice to have another girl with my winning sense of style.

"'Scuse me," I said and continued past her.

I headed toward the stairs, but threw a glance over my shoulder, watching as she opened the middle door of the confessional—the cubby for the priest where he sat to listen to sins.

She looked around and then locked eyes with me, seeing me watch her. She raised her finger to her lips, telling me to keep quiet before she slipped inside with a mischievous smile and closed the door.

I laughed to myself and turned back around, jogging up the stairs to the door in the gallery. Grabbing the handle, I glanced over my shoulder one more time and saw Kai Mori.

He headed to the back of the church, and my heart skipped a beat as I watched him enter the confessional, the door to the left of the priest's chamber to make his confession.

Only it wasn't a priest in there. I snorted. *Oh, shit.*

I shook my head and opened the door, taking the hidden steps up to the Carfax Room. Not sure what she was up to, but who was I to ruin her fun? I had my own problems.

Closing the door, I looked around the room—seeing everything exactly as I'd left it. The bed still held my dent from when I'd laid there yesterday after escaping Martin, and all the old makeup still laid about the floor in front of the mirror propped up underneath the stained-glass window.

Walking over, I hung the dress up on a rafter and smoothed it out, looking at it with a flutter in my stomach, remembering last night.

Who else had worn it before me? Did their night beat mine?

Taking off my bag, I worked quickly, picking up the makeup, fixing the bed, and stuffing my clothes from yesterday into my schoolbag. My phone laid on the bedside table, and I took it, turning it on.

Fourteen percent.

The battery was almost dead, and I had umpteen calls from Martin. And a message from Will. I opened it.

Morning! Smile.

Or don't. It's completely your choice. Don't let a guy tell you you're prettier when you do. You don't need to be pretty for anyone. Your value does not rely on my opinion. Damn the patriarchy.

I laughed, shaking hard and my eyes watering. What a moron.

The smile slowly fell, though, knowing he was too good to keep. I sure liked him, though.

So much it hurt.

I typed a message to Martin, letting him know I'd be home right after school and I'd have dinner ready. Heading to class now.

Before I left the room, I walked to the window, peering through a wedge of clear glass and seeing two boys crossing the street to their cars.

Damon to his BMW and Kai to his Jeep Wrangler. Damon was in here this morning, too?

I kind of wondered what happened with Kai and that girl in the confessional, but I was going to be late if I didn't hurry.

I sighed, watching them take off and head toward school. It was Devil's Night and time to face the music, I guess.

I left the room, locking the door behind me.

D evil's Night!" someone screamed, racing down the halls and leaping into the air to snatch the Homecoming banner hanging over the hallway.

I gripped the strap of my bag in both hands, the excitement in the air raising the hair on my arms.

"Man, back off!" a girl yelled.

I turned my head to see Rika Fane pushing some guy away who had crashed into Winter Ashby. She just laughed, holding on to Erika's arm as they scurried away.

"Did you see it?" Tabitha Schultz whispered to her friends as I passed. "David and I drove past this morning. It's a mess!"

I faltered in my steps, but I kept going.

Was she talking about the crypt? My stomach churned, suddenly feeling guilty.

But . . . I wasn't sad. I was sorry for the McClanahans, but not for my brother.

Please just let me get away with it.

I turned, heading into first period, but a hand swiped under my tie, flipping it up.

Will circled in front of me, a grin he couldn't contain playing on his lips as he came down, ready to kiss me.

I nudged him away, making sure the classroom was empty. "Stop it."

He grabbed my tie, pulling me in. "I can't."

My thighs warmed, and the breath from his mouth tickled my lips.

I licked mine, taking a deep breath and tasting him.

"It was just once." I walked around him, toward a desk. "That's what we agreed to."

"I don't remember that conversation. Was I present for it?"

I arched an eyebrow, seeing other students enter the room as I set my bag on the floor next to a chair.

He leaned down, his words tickling the hair by my ear. "It's not enough," he said in a low voice. "Not even nearly enough. All I think about now is how I want last night all over again, but this time in my car, in my bed, in your bed, in the shower, outside . . ."

I exhaled, sweat cooling my forehead. Whipping around, I put a hand on his stomach, keeping him at bay.

"And you want it, too," he taunted, squeezing my tie, "or you wouldn't be carrying me with you."

Yeah, I was wearing his tie. So what?

Have a little foresight. Come on. We liked each other. I loved last night, and I hoped he did, too, but life was more complicated than that. We wouldn't make it, and at our age, it was ridiculous to expect anything more.

I'd sneak out a few more times, we'd have fun, someone would fall in love, and then we'd both fall apart as he got tired of all the things I couldn't do and constantly worried about helping me fit in.

He would lose nothing.

"Everything is a game to you," I said, about to slide into my seat.

But he took me and pulled me down into his lap as he sat next to my desk. "Not everything."

I pushed against him, seeing Michael stare at us as he took his seat in front of Will, turning just in time to hide his shitty-ass grin.

"Will," I muttered, pleading.

He took my jaw softly in his hand, giving me pause.

"I need to talk to you," he said, his eyes serious now. "The bruises on your back. Did you have an accident or—"

I wrenched my eyes away, seeing Townsend walk in. "It's time for class."

I pushed out of his lap, but he pulled me back.

"I need to talk to you," he gritted out, "and it's not waiting."

I swatted at him, my palm landing against his neck, and I spotted all the hickeys I left last night. Or maybe one of them was still from the theater. I couldn't remember.

My blood raced, seeing the evidence of how different I was in the dark.

God, what did he do to me?

He searched my eyes, whispering, "Do you like me, Em?"

Needles instantly pricked my throat. I gazed at him, not wanting to answer the question but not wanting to lie, either. I just wanted to kiss him.

I inched in, his eyes dropping to my mouth as he wrapped his arms around my waist.

"Mr. Townsend?" Kincaid called over the intercom.

I sucked in a breath, stopping and turning my head to the teacher.

"Yes?" he answered.

I jumped out of Will's lap and slid into my own seat.

"Would you be so kind as to send the following students to my office when they arrive, please?" Kincaid asked. "Michael Crist, Damon Torrance, Kai Mori, and William Grayson. Thank you."

"Ohhhhh," everyone in the class roared.

My pulse jumped, and I looked over at Will as Damon sighed and the other two rose from their seats.

He shook his head, trying to calm me. *The crypt*. I didn't even think about that. Everyone would assume it was the Horsemen. Was that why Kincaid was calling them up?

"Take your bags and books with you, just in case," Townsend told them.

Just in case of what? Expulsion? Arrest?

They trailed in a line across the front of the classroom, toward the door, every single one turning their heads and eyeing me.

A smile curled Damon's lips as he lifted his finger and wagged it at me.

Kai saw him, breaking out in a laugh as they disappeared through the door, and I didn't blink for a solid minute.

Shit!

As soon as class ended, I didn't turn right like I was supposed to, I didn't go to my locker to pick up my chem book, and I did not pass Go. I charged into the front office, tempted to go for the front doors instead to check for a police car, but I was already here.

"I need to speak with Mr. Kincaid," I told the secretary as I placed my hands on the long counter.

She glanced up from the stack of packets she was counting out. "About?"

I opened my mouth, but someone spoke up first.

"She's not getting in until after me."

I spun around, seeing Trevor Crist's hair dripping wet as he held tissues to his nose.

"I'll wait," I told the secretary.

I looked over at Kincaid's door, seeing shadows move behind the frosted glass as my stomach rolled at all the possibilities happening inside. I sat a couple of chairs down from Crist, trying to eavesdrop, but all I could hear was mumbling.

I was tempted to let them take the fall if they offered, because they'd get out of it, and I wouldn't, but I wasn't that person.

"Aren't you going to ask me what happened?" Trevor asked.

I looked over at him, a molecule of sympathy coursing through my body.

But it was just another day in Thunder Bay.

"I don't really care," I said. "Sorry."

I heard him scoff as I watched the shadows move, barely listening as he went on and on.

"Someday, all of this is going to catch up with them," he spat out.

He was talking about the Horsemen. I guessed it was them—or one of them—whom he got into it with.

"Everyone says that." I sighed.

Even me at one point.

"It'll happen," he argued. "And I won't be the only one laughing when it does."

I turned my gaze on him, seeing his jaw flex, big anger on him for a freshman.

Part of me admired the kid. He hated his brother and made no show of anything else. I understood it when maybe not everyone would.

The door to Kincaid's office opened, and I stood up, a slew of people walking out, including my brother.

He saw me, and I straightened, racking my brain for any excuse.

"You boys get back to class," Kincaid told them. "I'm letting you practice during seventh period, so you can cut out early for festivities tonight. Don't make me regret it, and I mean it, Torrance."

Damon chuckled as Martin stood off to the side, eyeing me with fire in his eyes.

"What are you doing up here?" he asked.

"Picking up college fair information," I said, shifting on my feet before finding the brochures on the wall.

I grabbed one.

What happened in there? What were they talking about? Did Martin know?

"Trevor," Kincaid said. "Come on in."

Trevor stepped toward the dean's office, coming up chest to chest with Damon and looking really brave like he wasn't a foot shorter than the senior.

"You know, someday I won't be a kid," he gritted out, "and you'll be fighting someone your own size."

"It still won't be a fair fight, princess," Damon told him, getting in his face, "but you're welcome to try. Just bring yourself some lube."

Will laughed a little, and Michael pushed Damon away from his brother. "Enough. Let's get to class."

The two just stood there, neither one wanting to give in first.

"Everyone to class . . . now!" Kincaid barked.

The boys moved away from each other, maintained eye contact for a few extra seconds for good measure before they started to filter out of the front office. I stood there for a moment, trying to figure out what had happened.

They weren't in trouble. Okay, that was good.

Should I still fess up? I paused, waiting to see if my brother would leave, but Will just nudged me out the door.

"Don't say anything," he whispered so Martin wouldn't hear.

My words, apology, and explanation lodged in my throat, and I gave my brother a tight smile as I left to get back to class. But the look in his eyes told me he knew I was up to something.

We left, Damon hitting lockers and making a ruckus as we all trailed down the hall.

"I'll see you in economics," Will told Michael as he held me back and everyone else went ahead of us.

We stopped in the empty hall, second period already begun and the others disappearing around the corner or up the stairs.

"Does he know?" I asked quietly. "Kincaid?"

"Yeah," he told me, nodding. "I mean, he thinks it was the guys and me. He can't prove it, but he has no intention of trying to, either."

So, they all just let him believe it was them? Why would they do that?

"I guess it's good to be you," I said, pretty grateful.

Will came in close, looking down at me. "They've filled McClanahan's grave back in. The family has had a change of heart." He cleared his throat, reciting the news. "'It's become a landmark.' Which basically translates to they don't want to deal with constant vandalism, so they'll leave him where he's always rested."

So, it worked.

It actually worked.

"Everything is real," he stated.

Huh?

"That's what you said last night as you were climbing into your bed," he pointed out. "Everything is real today. Am I less real at night? Is that why you're pulling away this morning?"

Yes. I swallowed over the pain in my throat.

I mean, it was fun. I would love for it to happen again, but . . .

"Who's doing that to your body?" he demanded.

I tensed, taking a step back.

"You have bruises everywhere." His eyes trailed up to my brow and the small cut I'd covered with makeup. "Is it your brother?"

My hands trembled.

He was figuring it out.

I knew he would. I blinked away the sting in my eyes.

"Emmy, stop lying to me," he said softly. "I know something's wrong. I know it. Tell me."

The lump in my throat stretched. God, I wanted to tell him.

I didn't want to lose this. I wanted to let him hold me and protect me. He cared.

As much as I wanted to pretend that he didn't, I knew he cared.

And my heart that ached to keep him hurt worse than anything Martin had ever done to me.

But I couldn't tell him. If I let this go on, he'd interfere. He'd make trouble, stand up for me, and I could be separated from her.

I could be sent away. I didn't want my grandmother alone.

My chin shook, the words on the tip of my tongue. It would feel so good to dive into his arms and look forward to more with him. I wanted to tell him everything.

But I just clenched my teeth so hard my jaw ached and backed away some more, forcing a scoff. I shook my head, my bitter smile fixed on him.

I looked at his mouth and then his hands, remembering how all of him was mine last night.

We couldn't be together.

Maybe someday. Not today.

He grabbed my elbow and pulled us close again. "Don't you know that you can have anything you want?" he repeated his words from a couple of weeks ago. "I'd hurt anyone for you. Who the hell is it?"

But I just laughed, feeling the tears well. *God, go away.*

I balled my fist and ripped my arm away from him. "Let go of me." I glared at him. "Go have fun with your friends. They're all you really have, so hang on to them. I don't love you, and I don't want you."

The words were like razors in my throat, and I wanted to throw up.

But I stayed steel as fire hit his eyes, and his heavy breath poured in and out of his chest.

"Emmy . . ."

Jesus, just go! Stop torturing me with everything I want and nothing I can have. I'd make his life horrible.

"Leave me alone," I gritted out.

"You're pushing me away. Just—"

"We're just too different." I backed away some more. "You thought this was serious? You've been on half the girls in the graduating class! If I knew that you thought last night was something more, I never would've come to Homecoming."

He bared his teeth. "Stop it," he bit out. "You hear me? Stop it. Last night was it for me. I don't want anyone else but you."

Tears sprang to my eyes, and I forced back the sob in my throat.

God, I loved him. This hurt. I had to get out of here.

I couldn't be someone he had to take care of. Someone pathetic who would just bring a shit ton of baggage on him that he'd get sick of dealing with.

Drawing in a deep breath, I forced the words out, my stomach was racked with pain.

"I wanted you, too," I said, my voice hard. "And I had you. It was fun. Even better than the gossip says it is. Now, I'm done."

"Goddammit."

"I'll be hard-pressed to find anyone better in bed," I told him. "That's for sure."

Whipping around, he slammed his fist into the lockers, and I stared wide-eyed and hot in my gut as he looked ready to kill.

Yes. Hate me.

Please hate me.

"Such a fucking . . ." He trailed off, too cowardly to say *bitch*.

My chin trembled.

He turned and looked at me. "You know how easy you *are* to replace? Is that what you want, then?" And he snapped his fingers in my face. "Because it would be that easy."

My body wracked with jealousy, because I knew it was just a threat, but I still wanted to slice him all the way to hell if he put his hands on any other girl.

But I felt myself getting stronger, feeding off the hate and the pain and the anger.

"Get on with it, then!" I snarled. "And rot in hell, for all I care."

I stalked off, back to my locker, and left him in my dust, waiting until I'd rounded the corner before I let the tears fall.

I squeezed my eyes shut, sobbing quietly as I started running.

Will.

CHAPTER 23

EMORY

Present

Aydin left my room, telling me dinner was in an hour, courtesy of Taylor. I was pretty sure I didn't want to eat or drink anything from that guy, but he said I would be served first. I guess that meant if I wanted the guys to eat at all, I needed to show up.

I nodded, kept my mouth shut, and closed my door without the chair securing it this time. If anyone came into my room, they'd just figure I'd left and they'd missed me.

Slipping into the secret passageway again, I carefully pulled the picture closed and squatted down, digging inside the duffel bag Alex had left and fishing around for another flashlight. I found a mess of clothes, granola bars, a water bottle, a blanket, a knife, and some rope.

No extra flashlights.

Were the granola bars all she had been eating? Aydin hadn't mentioned anything was missing from the kitchen, but Alex was slick. I hoped she was swiping better food while everyone was asleep.

She had to have been coming out of her hiding places to go to the bathroom, at least.

I slid my hand around the inside of the bag, feeling for the satellite phone, but no such luck. Had she hid it somewhere?

Zipping up the duffel, I started down the tunnel without a flashlight and no idea where she'd gone. The tunnels probably covered every floor, and she'd had days to explore. I didn't even know where Will's room was.

I jogged down the hidden hallway, the scent of earth and sea surrounding me like I was deep in a cave, and the echo of the waterfall outside beating around me.

Thin beams of light streamed into the dark corridor from the rooms I passed, and I quickly peered through each one to make sure Alex and Will weren't in there.

Coming to the end of the hall, I saw the tunnel continue on my left, and then looked ahead, seeing the ladder leading down.

Will showered in the natatorium. After the greenhouse, he might've gone there.

I descended the ladder, feeling it whine under my weight and instantly recognizing the same sound from the other day. In the walls in the hall leading to the pool.

Alex had been right there next to me, and I hadn't seen her. She should've made herself known. What the hell was she thinking?

I shook my head, pushing the anger back again as slivers of wood poked my palms. I stepped down, immediately jogging through the passageway.

Panels and doorways appeared here and there, outlining entrances into various rooms, and I really hoped no one else knew about this because there was so much space to hide and watch, and if I needed a shortcut to get somewhere fast, this was perfect.

I wouldn't get my hopes up, though. Aydin was smart, and he'd been here more than two years. If he hadn't found this yet, I'd be surprised.

I passed the gym, wondering how much longer the boys would be hunting and where Aydin was. I had yet to see him after he left my room.

A thud hit somewhere close, like a piece of furniture jostling, and I paused for a moment before running down the corridor toward it.

"Ah!" someone shouted, and I stopped, leaning my ear into the wall.

"Come on, you can do better than that," Taylor said.

Taylor? I thought he went hunting with Micah and Rory.

There was mumbling, and I knew they were on the other side of this wall. I scanned for the peephole, finding it a foot away and peering through it.

Taylor crouched on the other side of the pool table, only his head visible as he popped up every once in a while, someone else's hands squeezing his neck.

What the hell? I mouthed.

And then I spotted something to the right and squinted.

Alex crept up behind Taylor, already in the room with a thick, wooden candlestick in her hand. I widened my eyes, sucking in a breath.

Shit. What was she doing?

But before I could locate the opening she'd slipped through, she'd raised her arm and brought down the candlestick in a hard blow across the back of Taylor's head.

He jerked, froze, and fell over, collapsing onto the floor, and she stood there, breathing hard and staring down at him.

In a moment, Will had shot to his feet, wiping the blood from under his nose. "Alex?" He gaped at her.

She didn't look happy, though. "What the hell are you doing?" she snapped, whispering over Taylor's unconscious body on the floor. "You could've handled that guy. I've been watching you get your ass kicked for days! What are you doing?"

He just stared at her, stunned. "What the fuck are you doing here?"

She paused and then said, "That's it? That's all you've gotta say?" She waved her hand at her head. "Not a word about my hair?"

I almost snorted, despite my pulse racing. I'd never actually seen them interact together. I met Alex long after Will was sent here.

She was so comfortable with him.

He blinked at her, wiping his nose as more blood dripped out, and then he grabbed her hand. "Fuck," he cursed, swinging open the door and yanking her out of the room. "Goddamn, son of a bitch . . ."

He bolted with her, and I stilled, wondering if I should jump out and run with them, but I stayed in the walls, racing down the corridor instead.

I peered into every room I passed, afraid he was taking her upstairs to his room, but he wouldn't risk keeping her out in the open that long.

I passed the drawing room, peeked in quickly and was about to fly off to the next room, but then I saw him slip inside, pulling her behind him, and close the door, securing it with a chair.

I looked through the thin slit in the bookshelf I knew was on the other side of this wall, watching as she threw her arms around him, nearly knocking him over.

I pressed on the wall, about to open it, but . . . I stayed, watching.

His arms hung limply at his sides for a minute, but then he snapped out of it and wrapped them around her, squeezing her tight. She sobbed quietly, pressing her lips to his cheek as he closed his eyes, smiling—really smiling—for the first time since I'd been here.

My heart ached.

"I missed you, kid," he said.

She nodded, still hugging him. "We're going home."

They held each other for another few moments and then pulled away, staring into each other's eyes.

"How'd you figure this out?" he asked, pulling off his shirt to wipe down his face and the remnants of his fight with Taylor.

"I didn't," she replied.

"Rika?" he asked.

"Misha and Damon figured it out, actually."

A laugh bubbled out of him, the deep, rich sound like déjà vu. He was a teenager at the Cove all over again.

Rika. He meant Erika Fane. I'd heard she was engaged to Michael Crist, one of his best friends. Kai was married and a father, as was fucking Damon Torrance. *Shocker*.

Misha Grayson was Will's younger cousin. He went to Thunder Bay Prep, too, but that was after my time.

Alex knew all of them. She was a part of his life now. Friends with his friends.

"Damon and Misha . . ." Will mused. "Like, in the same room?"

"There may have been blood," she joked.

A knot twisted and twisted in my stomach, listening to them.

But then he grabbed her, squeezing her arms. "You want to tell me what you're doing here? Huh? This was stupid."

She looked at him, worry etched on her brow, and then he released her and walked away, tossing his T-shirt onto a chair. The black ink all over his body melted into itself in the dim light.

She approached him. "It's been a year. You had to know we were going to figure out something was wrong," she told him. "Your parents are telling everyone you're doing humanitarian work in . . . like South Sudan or something."

He started laughing as he rubbed his forehead.

She knit her brow. "Why are you laughing?"

"Because I don't know if I'm more hurt that it took you all so long to come after me, or aggravated that you had no faith that I'd be able to get myself out of this on my own?"

"At least you're not mad they sent a girl," she shot back, shrugging her shoulders.

He flashed her a look. "Oh, I know you get shit done."

He said it with almost a reverence.

I didn't know what I'd thought, but I didn't think they were so chummy. I wasn't sure why. It was like he was with one of the guys when he was with her. At ease.

She shifted on her feet, the silence stretching between them. "So, um . . . if you want to bring anything, I'd pack it now. I have an exit plan, but I can't say when it'll go down. I need you to be ready."

He didn't move, though. "How did you get here?" he asked. "Can you get back?"

"What do you mean?"

He wet his lips, finding the words. "I need you out of this house. Now. This minute."

Her brow creased with confusion. "What's the matter with you?" she whispered, but I could hear the worry in her voice. "I'm taking you home."

"No, you're leaving," he said. "And you're going to tell them I can solve my own problems. I don't need help."

"And Emory?"

He stopped, straightening his spine as he looked down at her. "What do you know? Did you have her brought here? Did Michael?"

"She just asked me the same thing," Alex blurted out. "Why would we do something so dumb? I have no idea who sent her here or why, but it was probably that brother of hers."

My brother didn't have the funds for this place, and I wasn't that important.

Will regarded her. "You know her?" he asked.

She nodded. "We met last spring."

Will's eyebrow shot up.

"Don't give me that look," she told him. "She was in Thunder Bay burying her grandmother. We ran into each other. I didn't seek her out."

"How long have you been here?" he asked.

Alex remained quiet, and a look crossed his face that said he knew the answer.

"So, you arrived on the shipment with her days ago, and you, what?" he continued. "Spotted her and decided to roll the dice and stay hidden to see this play out with her and me?"

She folded her arms across her chest, a satisfied smirk on her face.

"Get her out of here," he bit out, "and both of you fuck off."

My breathing turned shallow. That was why she left me on my own these past days. She couldn't get caught and risk stalling communication with their friends who were on their way, which I understood, but she wanted to see what would happen with Will and me. Maybe for her own interest or maybe for his.

He didn't want to leave. Why?

Alex stepped toward him, staring hard into his eyes. "Damon's second child is on the way," she said. "Michael and Rika are getting married on Devil's Night. They're getting ready to tear down the Cove and move forward with the resort. We need to leave."

"Sounds like everything is going pretty well without me, actually."

She swatted him twice, not really hard but I could hear her palm hitting his chest. He reared back.

"I almost prefer you wasted," she growled in a low voice, "because I have no idea who you are right now. When we met, what did I say to you?"

He stood there—silent, contrite, and not spouting another word.

"'I can take anything as long as I have enough lipstick,'" she recited. "I just shove it all underneath an extra coat, like you always did with your smiles. Rika, Michael . . . all of them, they're my family." She softened her voice, nearly choking on the tears. "But you . . . you're my reflection. Now, snap out of it. You're coming with me or . . ."

"Just trust me, okay?" he said suddenly, finally standing tall again and turning to face her. "I know what I'm doing. Just trust me this once."

He took her face in his hands, and I dropped my eyes, backing away, because I couldn't watch it anymore.

She was better for him. She was worlds better for him.

And even though I knew it was reckless just like all the times I did things in high school, knowing Martin would find out and knowing the consequences, I ran. The toe of my sneaker banged into a pipe, a clang piercing the air, but I didn't care if they heard. I ran and ran with every intention of getting out of here once and for all. It was time.

I didn't know where I was, where I was going, or how I would survive in the cold forest, but that was the thing about me—somehow I always made it through.

Climbing the ladder back up to my room, I bolted down the tunnel and slipped through the portrait again. I grabbed the sweatshirt Aydin brought me, slipped it on, and stuck the knife in my back pocket, leaving my claw glove and darting out of the room. Heading down the stairs, I looked quickly around the foyer, the statues and candles flickering and looming as if there were a presence I couldn't see, and I dove into the kitchen, snatching my bundle from the cupboard.

Pulling up my hood, I ran for the back door.

But just then, the panel on the wall popped open and slid over as Alex slipped through, blocking my way.

Will walked in behind me, both of them breathing hard and fast like they'd been rushing to cut me off. They must've heard me stumble over the pipe in the tunnel.

"Emmy, you have to be quiet," Alex whispered, peering over my shoulder in case anyone else came. "I won't be able to get you out if he locks me up."

He. Aydin.

"You want to leave, then?" I challenged her. "Then, let's leave now. You chose to be here. I didn't. I want to go home."

I didn't want to be here with them both. I didn't want to be here at all. I didn't give a shit if I died out there right now.

You're my reflection. The backs of my eyes burned.

She shook her head at me. "I'm not leaving without him."

"Fine."

I rounded the island, shoved the only apothecary jar left at Will, and he jumped back as it crashed on the floor.

I bolted from the room, racing back through the house and toward the front door. If he wasn't ready to leave, I wasn't waiting. I made my own choices.

I didn't know why I was so pissed, because I knew what had happened between them, and he had no obligation to me, of all people, but seeing the bond up close . . . it was stronger than I thought.

It never occurred to me it was strong at all. How could I have been so stupid.

It hurt.

Someone grabbed me, and I dropped the bag of food, staring at Alex.

"You'll die of exposure," she said, barely above a murmur. "You won't last the night."

"So, what were you planning to do here?" I barked, jerking my chin at Will as he strolled in behind Alex. "Use me as the distraction as you made your escape with him?"

"I was planning on escaping with him the day I got here and hide with him until help arrived," she retorted, "but you showed up and fucked up my plans. Now, I have two people to extract."

Aw, so sorry for the inconvenience.

Either way, I was out of here. He didn't want to leave, and she didn't want to leave without him, so screw it.

"No one is going to save you," I told him, looking over her shoulder into his eyes. "This is no one's fault but yours. It's time to save yourself, Will."

But he just stood there like an oak, his green eyes hard on me as his brown hair, still wet from the greenhouse, hung in disarray.

He didn't fight for himself. He didn't stand up for himself . . .

He never did.

"You were always pathetic," I told him, sneering. "You know that? Always so naïve and clueless and pathetic."

A smack landed on my face, the sting spreading across my cheek and blood seeping into my mouth where it cut on my teeth.

I took two breaths and slowly turned my face back, staring at Alex and her fiery eyes.

"Emmy, I'm sorry," she bit out. "I really am, but I'm not leaving without him, and you're not leaving, either, because you'll die out there. Think. You won't know where to go, and you'll cost me more time than you already have."

Like that's even remotely my fault.

I was leaving, dammit, whether she liked it or not. I wasn't important to her.

Or him.

"What do you care anyway?" I growled, shoving her back so hard she stumbled. "You'll have him all to yourself now. No competition."

And to my surprise, she just chuckled and rushed back up to me, planting her hand over my mouth to shut me up.

I slapped her back, trying to get free but to no avail.

"Is that what you are, Emory?" she taunted. "Competition?"

I stand over my grandmother's grave, the breeze kicking up as it blows through the trees.

I wipe a tear off my cheek.

I should be happy, right? She stuck around much longer than we thought she would. Like she knew she needed to be here for me.

It's been over six years—almost seven—since I've been home, and even now, I look for Martin, afraid to run into him and afraid of everything else that fills this town.

Sooner or later, I'll have to pay the piper. I just hope it isn't today.

I walk to my rental car, hugging myself against the chill still in the spring air, and slide into the driver's seat, starting the engine. My flight back to California isn't until tomorrow, so that means I have to spend the night in Meridian City, because I'm not taking a chance of being caught in Thunder Bay any longer than necessary.

Still, though . . . I've learned how to straighten my hair, and I have my prescription sunglasses and matching, pressed clothes that fit me. No one will recognize me anymore.

I drive out of the cemetery, not looking at Edward McClanahan's grave, but knowing exactly when I pass it as I exit the cemetery and turn up the music, "White Flag" by Bishop Briggs playing loud. I drive down the highway, tempted to look at the mansions as I pass—the Crists and the Fanes, the Torrances and the Ashbys—but I don't, just hoping some semblance of his life is back to what it used to be, even if I already knew he has undoubtedly changed.

I just hope he's gone. Traveling, living . . . loving, and being loved.

Tears spring to my eyes again, but I blink them away, nausea rolling through me. I did what I had to do, right? I might've even saved him from a worse fate.

But no matter how often I tell myself that, I still don't feel it.

I need to face him and come clean. This is eating a hole through me, and if he hasn't come for me yet, then he doesn't know, and he should.

I can't do this anymore.

Entering the village, I risk a drive past my old house, seeing newspapers scattered about the lawn, as well as the overgrown hedges and the garbage can lying on its side.

Does Martin still live there? There are no cars in the driveway.

After Grand-Mère passed a week ago, I emailed him and hoped for no response. He told me to let him know what my plans were.

I didn't.

I'll let him know once I'm gone. Only then can he come and pay his respects. He hasn't shown up in years to see her, thank goodness, so he isn't crying his eyes out about her death. I know that much.

I keep driving, not knowing where I'm going, but when I see the Cove ahead, I veer into the parking lot. I heard they were getting ready to tear it down. Someone on the alumni committee sent me an invite to a Throwback Celebration a while back, but of course, I didn't bother showing up.

Me, here, and near Devil's Night—yeah, not happening.

I spot a couple of cars in the otherwise deserted lot and pull into a barely outlined space where the weeds push up through the concrete and the painted lines are chipped and faded.

Shutting off the car, I step out and stick the keys into the pocket of my jeans, looking around as I stroll along and find my way inside.

The sea lay beyond the Ferris wheel, and I can smell the salt in the air as I drift past the ticket booths and toward the pirate ship. The yellow and brown paint has chipped, and I can see the rusted bolts from here as it sits silent and still, an eerie death hanging over the park that chills my skin.

I almost hear the carnival music from that night in my head as I walk closer and closer, seeing where he and I sat.

A fist squeezes my heart. I miss him. I didn't realize back then how much this would hurt and how long it would stay with me.

"Well, of course, you're not on board," some guy gripes, "because as soon as you find out what I want, you decide you want the exact opposite."

I jerk my head left and right, realizing I'm not alone.

"You're such a liar," she says. "That's not true at all. This location makes no sense, and I've had the same talk with Kai."

Kai?

Finally, I spot a trio walking by the bumper boats, and I slip behind a game booth, out of sight as I peer around it.

Michael Crist carries a rolled-up wad of papers, looking like they might be blueprints. He's walking with two women, one with black hair and the other with brown.

I squint through my sunglasses. The black-haired one looks a little familiar, but I don't think I know her.

"You can't build a marina down there," she spits back at Crist. "Guests won't have access to a beach, either. It's all rocks, remember? And when the nor'easters blow in, no one's going to appreciate a front row seat to cyclone force winds, rain, and snow. The entire coastline is eroding, and it's going to erode right up into your fucking golf course."

I bite back my smile. I've never heard anyone talk to him like that.

I like her.

"That'll take a thousand years," he whines and then looks to the other woman. "Alex, a little help here?"

"Oh, no." She taps away on her phone. "Don't let me interrupt."

He shakes his head, leading the way through the park and back toward the lot, wearing a black suit and looking even more handsome than he did in high school, unfortunately.

I haven't followed his basketball career, but I know he still plays professionally.

Great. With him around, that means the rest of the crew is close.

Who are these women, though?

"I need to talk to Kai," he grumbles.

"Yeah, run home to Daddy," the black-haired one replies, "because I'm making too much sense for you."

He rolls his eyes and keeps going, the ladies following him.

It looks like he's planning to buy the property. And for a golf course? She also mentioned guests, which sounds like a hotel of some sort.

A feeling of loss creeps in, and I'm not sure why. I have no right.

It was just a great night, and as long as this place is here, it feels like maybe not everything has disappeared.

I wait there for another minute, looking past the Ferris wheel, toward Cold Point. I'm half tempted to take a walk out there, but I already nearly got caught. It's time to go.

I head out to the parking lot again, pulling out my phone to check the time, but as I approach my rental, I see someone sitting on the hood.

It was the brown-haired woman from inside, her white tank top too short to cover her stomach. She stared at me with her sunglasses resting on the bridge of her nose and pouty, plum-colored lips.

I halt, looking around. The other cars are gone, and I don't see Michael or the other woman.

"Hi." I walk toward my car hesitantly. "I didn't mean any harm. I was just looking around."

They appeared to own the property now, and I guess I was trespassing?

But she just gives me a small smile. "You're Emory Scott."

I pinch my brows together.

"I recognize you from a photo I saw once," she explains.

"And you are?"

"Alex Palmer." She crosses her legs, leaning back on a hand. "A friend of Will Grayson's."

I tense, dropping my eyes down her form and taking in the fact that no man has "friends" who look like that.

"I saw that," she teased.

"What?"

"That little . . . eyes-falling-down-my-body-to-inspect-the-competition-with-a-side-of-judgment look," she said, rolling her neck with attitude.

Competition? Is that what she is?

I chuckle, digging in my pocket for my keys as I walk for the driver's side door. "I wasn't looking at you like that."

"Checking me out, then?"

"Yeah." I unlock the door and open it. "That's it."

"You back in town for good?"

"No."

"Just visiting?"

"Yes."

"And you stopped by the Cove?" she presses. "Why?"

"None of your business." I stand inside the door, staring at her. "Would you get off my car?"

I mean, how nosy.

"I need a ride," she tells me. "If you don't mind."

I pause. "Excuse me?"

"A lift?" she clarifies, as if I'm dumb.

"I'm not a taxi," I retort.

And . . . I don't know you.

"Saucy," she teases. "He was right about you."

He? Will told her I was saucy?

Well, if that's the worst thing he said, I suppose I'm lucky.

I open my mouth, dying to ask about him.

Is he in town? Is he okay?

Is he happy?

But I clamp it shut again, knowing she's his friend, not mine.

Hopping off my hood, she hangs over the door, peering up at me. "You give me a ride, and I'll pay for the pizza and margaritas," she says.

Pizza and margaritas . . . Is she kidding?

"What do you want with me?" I ask.

She doesn't know me, and I don't for one second believe this is anything but a trick.

But then again . . . the only thing I believe about people is the worst, so . . .

"I don't know," she tells me, her voice softening. "Do you ever have that feeling that you need something, but you just don't know what?"

She looks at me, a thoughtful look in her eyes.

"Like a drink or a good cry or to jump on a plane and see something new?" she continues. "But then none of those things are it, and you still can't figure out what it is you need?"

Her words resonate with me more than she knows. The only difference is I know what I need. I just can't have it.

"Well," she tells me, "when I saw you inside the park just before—and recognized you—I felt like we'd found it."

We?

Why would she need me?

"Sticks is still the place to be," she singsongs. "The best pizza."

"No." I shake my head. "Not there. I don't want . . ."

"To be seen?"

Pizza sounds good. And lots of margaritas sounds fantastic. My lonely hotel room back in the city seems dreadful now, but . . .

"I just don't want to run into anyone," I tell her. "Thanks, though."

She holds my eyes for a moment. "He's not in town right now. If that's what you're worried about."

I look at her just long enough for her to take that as an affirmative and run around the front of the car to climb into the passenger seat.

He wasn't in town? Where was he?

But it was none of my business. Whatever.

I sit down, seeing her pull on her seat belt. I start the car, a little weirded out, but I have a feeling she doesn't like the word *no,* and I'm not a fan of confrontation.

"Where do you live?" I ask.

I can give her a ride home, I guess.

But she just pushes her sunglasses up the bridge of her nose and replies, "Margaritas first."

B y the next morning she was dragging my hungover ass to the airport so I didn't miss my flight. We had started at Sticks and taxied to Meridian City where we drank more at Realm, and then crashed in my hotel room.

I hated her and her amazing body and her pretty face and all the times I couldn't help but think about how he'd touched her and held her. Yet I couldn't hate her because she was absolutely splendid despite how she'd struggled in life.

I'd woken up with a splitting headache, and then I hated her more for the hangover, but . . . she texted, she called, she checked up on me over the months until I was convinced that I might actually be likable.

Until I remembered she was Will's good friend, and I was keeping a secret she might hate me for.

Will stood in the foyer facing me, his eyes on fire, and I wanted to take him to my room, close the door, and hold him forever, but he knew how this would end tonight.

I wouldn't grovel, and I was leaving.

I shoved Alex away and darted for the door, but she caught me and threw me to the floor.

I crashed, my body racked with pain as I caught my breath and glared up at her from the marble floor.

I didn't waste another second. Blasting off the ground, I lunged for her, ready to tear right through her if I had to, because . . .

The only person I knew how to fight for was myself.

CHAPTER 24

EMORY

Nine Years Ago

I folded the tie slowly and stuck it in the Ziploc bag, followed by my Cove Ride-All-Day bracelet from last night, and the collapsed, empty box of Milk Duds he got me at the movie theater.

Squishing the air out of the bag, I sealed it, tears hanging at the corner of my eyes as I dropped it into an empty coffee can and capped it, setting the whole thing in the two-foot-deep hole.

I couldn't keep him close, but I couldn't throw him away, either. Maybe someday I'd dig up my little time capsule and be able to laugh at how little any of it meant anymore.

I hope.

An engine roared to my right, and I looked up from where I knelt on the foundation of the gazebo and saw Damon's BMW slide into a spot in the alley next to Sticks.

He jumped out of the car and walked inside, the whole place booming with activity.

My brother came home for a while this afternoon, finding me where I said I'd be and with my homework done and dinner ready, too. He barely said two words as he ate, showered, and redressed to go back out for another shift.

Tonight they'd need all the hands they could get, so he was pulling double duty. It was a blessing.

Grand-Mère assured me she was fine, I had a live feed of her on my phone, so I snuck out for the short walk to the village to get some work done.

Just needed to take care of something first.

I turned back to my hole, barely able to see the ground in front of me as I grabbed the gardening shovel and started filling it in. I was making the right decision, and thank God he said the awful things he said today, because I was about to break, and I needed the hurt to push through it.

I hoped he did replace me.

Tonight.

He should dance with her and slip his hands inside her clothes and love her crazy, because after that, I wouldn't be able to look back. It would shatter my heart, so there'd be nothing left to hold him with me anymore.

Tossing the shovel, I gathered the rest of the dirt with my hands and scooped it into the hole, covering the coffee can and pressing the soil firmly. I took a brand-new floorboard and lined it up next to the last one, grabbing the nail gun and securing it to the frame. I moved quickly, all eight posts rising from their anchors around me as the floor came together, each board cut to my specs.

A loud whirring sound ripped through the air, and I looked over again, seeing Damon straddle a motorbike as Winter Ashby stood next to him, fastening a helmet.

I tensed, about to wonder what the hell he thought he was doing out here with the kid.

But as she climbed on behind him, he looked over his shoulder at her, something written in his smile I'd never seen in him before.

Tenderness.

She wrapped her arms around his waist and she squealed as they sped off out of the square, disappearing down a street.

I had to smile a little, remembering the pirate ship and how I'd sounded exactly the same last night.

I loved that feeling, too, Winter Ashby.

It wasn't the ride, though, honey. It wasn't the ride.

Hours later, the square was empty and quiet, and I headed home for the second time, already having tread the shortcut through people's yards and across streets to look in on my grandmother and collect some more supplies earlier.

Sawdust coated my hands, and I stuck them in the pockets of my jean overalls, the wind breezing through the knitting of my sweater.

"Up!" someone shouted.

I stopped in my tracks, almost to the back door, and looked through a window at the back of the house.

Red and blue lights flashed, and I stopped breathing, quickly unlocking the door. Pushing through, I ran across the kitchen, dropping my tool bag on the table and casting a glance up the stairs before racing through the front door instead.

My brother stood on the porch in his uniform and thick, black jacket, and I stopped, watching paramedics load my grandmother on a gurney up into the back of an ambulance.

"Grand-Mère!" I shouted, racing down the steps. "Grand-Mère!"

They closed the doors, some guy in dark blue pants and a light blue shirt sitting with her in the back.

I pounded the doors, but he barely spared a glance before turning back to her.

I whipped around, facing Martin. "What happened?"

I had my eyes on her nearly all night. I came home earlier for a few minutes just to see if she needed anything and she was fine!

"Her oxygen levels dropped." He descended a couple of steps, his hands in the pockets of his coat. "I called the ambulance when I came home for a meal break. Get inside."

"No, we need to follow her."

"She won't wake up tonight," he told me, "and she's in good hands. We'll go in the morning before school."

The engine revved behind me, and I twisted around as the driver shifted into gear.

No.

"She's fine, Emmy."

I didn't like his tone. Why was he so calm?

"Thank you, Janice," he called out to the driver as she turned off her lights and waved to us. "Tell Ben thank you."

They drove off, and I started after them.

"Move another muscle," he warned, "and she's never coming back."

I stopped, swallowing the lump in my throat.

"Get inside now," he ordered.

I stood there, hearing his footsteps and the front door swing open, and I shook my head, wanting to run after her, but he'd find me.

I closed my eyes, the weariness of all the years and the past several days weighing heavy, because Will showing me how happy I could be if things were a little different made all this so much harder to bear.

I was tired.

I almost swayed on my feet. *I was so tired.*

A curtain slowly fell between my eyes and my brain as I went through the same rage, anger, hurt, pain, sadness, and despair I'd felt a thousand times before.

But now I understood something I never did.

Nothing made sense.

Martin, my home, the terror . . . It just was, and sometimes you were just that person to whom things happened.

I walked into the house and closed the door, not tensing or clenching or bracing, because it didn't help.

"That was for last night," he said as I entered the kitchen and watched him take off his jacket. "Just a warning."

I blinked once, staring at him. "You did that to her."

It wasn't a question. I knew the answer.

His hand curled around the chair back, and his knuckles turned white as he squeezed.

"She's the only control you have over me," I told him. "If she dies, there's nothing keeping me here."

"And without me, she'd be in hospice or some state home, neglected and in agony."

We stood on opposite sides of the table, locked in the challenge. What did he want?

Was this really all he had? He acted like he hated me, but would he suddenly be happy if I were no longer here?

Was he going to try to stop me when it was time for me to leave?

"You ran away from me yesterday," he said. "You were seen at Homecoming, and you were seen at the Cove last night." He steeled his spine, lifting his chin and tightening his lips. "And I know you know what happened to that crypt."

So, he got rid of Grandma for the night to show me how much noise he could make without her here.

My jaw ached, I pressed my teeth together so hard. People pushing me. People pulling me. People, people, fucking people . . .

I told him to deal with me. I said I was to blame.

I told them all to leave me alone and stop pushing me and pulling me, over and over again. *No one listens.*

Blood rushed to my face, something crawling under my skin with its claws. I rubbed my eyes.

"Take it out on me," I gritted out. "Leave her alone."

"But that's how I take it out on you," he replied, a smile playing behind his eyes, laughing at me. "And mark my words, there is still so much more I can do."

I let out a scream, seeing red and too furious to care as the tears filled my eyes. Grabbing the edge of the kitchen table, I shoved it across the floor, the tools in my bag clanking as the table pinned him to the counter.

He growled as I crushed his legs, and I reached into the bag, snatching out a hammer as he threw the table on its side, all the tools in the bag crashing to the floor.

"You stupid little bitch!" he yelled.

I raised the hammer, but he lashed out and grabbed my wrist, punching me across the face with the other hand as the tool spilled out of my grasp.

Fire spread across my cheek, but I whipped back around and shot up my knee right between his legs, not wasting a second.

Stop.

Just stop.

He buckled, and I shoved both hands into his chest, sending him flying to the floor. Tears blurred my vision, and I spun around, running from the house.

"Emory!" His bellow hit my back, and I let out a sob, charging down the porch, across the lawn, and as fast through town as I could race.

I hurried past the village, down the road, and deeper into the dark forest, hearing the echo behind me fade more and more as he tried to find me but couldn't.

"Emory!"

I dove through the trees, the branches whipping my face, and I fixed my glasses as the lights of the town disappeared and sweat covered my back.

My legs ached and tears dried on my face as stitches pulled at my side. I slowed to a jog, eventually falling into a walk.

I should've gone to the cathedral. The key was in my pocket, and if everywhere didn't hurt, I'd laugh at how useful that place had become when I seemed to survive fine without it a few days ago.

I squeezed my eyes shut, blinking long and hard.

What could I do? He was going to kill me.

Or worse.

My grandma would be at the hospital now. I needed to go, even to just sit in the waiting room until they let me see her, but that would be the first place he'd look, and being a minor and all, he could carry me out of there without any argument from anyone.

God . . .

I walked and walked, hearing the cars on the other side of the trees make their way up and down the road, and even though I didn't look up, I knew where I was going.

It was as far as I could go.

Crossing the bridge, over the narrow but fast river, I climbed the incline up toward the cliffs where the mansions sat: the Fanes, the Crists, the Torrances, the Ashbys, blah, blah, blah . . .

In no time at all, I'd found my way to their quiet, dark lane, lit only by the flickering gaslit lanterns hanging from their high walls and gates.

Will didn't live up here. His family owned the fortress on the other side of town, near the high school and up in the hills. The massive house that stood high above us all.

I should've met him that night he wanted to take me to his house to watch movies. Seeing that place from the inside would've surely set my stupid brain straight and solidified my resolve before it was too late.

Sleeping with him only made it hurt more now.

I followed the road past the estates, past quiet and deserted St. Killian's, and then I cut through the forest, past the Bell Tower, and into the cemetery.

I had no idea what time it was, but all that remained were the remnants of whatever party the Horsemen had had here earlier. It couldn't be any later than midnight or one, and St. Killian's was dark just now. They weren't at the catacombs anymore.

I strolled through the cemetery, seeing the damage we did to the crypt and Edward McClanahan's freshly dug grave was filled back in because he was staying right there. My brother couldn't have the discounted hole anymore.

But darkness covered every corner of the graveyard, the moonlight barely visible through the clouds.

Quiet.

Empty.

Lonely.

Was that why I'd come here? I knew they were partying here tonight. Was I looking for him?

I walked between the headstones, moving silently over the grass and barely noticing the engine that purred, growing louder and closer second by second.

I blinked, looking up, and then stopped.

A matte black car creeped down the small lane, its headlights off and the driver invisible through the dark tinting of the windshield.

My heart skipped a beat, and I darted back a couple of steps, shielding myself behind a ten-foot-tall grave marker.

They didn't speed up, turn on their lights, or stop, just kept crawling down the path toward me until it got close enough that I could tell it definitely wasn't my brother.

They stopped, and after a moment, I saw the trunk pop open and a man exit the car, the hood of his black sweatshirt drawn over his head. I watched as he rounded the car.

Who was that? The cemetery was closed.

Of course, that didn't mean anything, since the ground was littered with red Solo cups, candles, and other shit. Maybe he was cleaning up.

He lifted open the trunk, pulling something out over the edge, and I caught sight of bare feet dangling.

A cool sweat hit the back of my neck. What the . . . ?

He lifted the body out, throwing it over his shoulder, her long black hair falling out of the sheet, down his back, and her long legs bare in her outfit.

I squinted, seeing the black strapless costume—like a ballerina or something.

Was she dead? I covered my mouth with my hand, my legs fighting with the urge to bolt, but fear kept me rooted.

Walking to the grass, he leaned over and threw her to the ground, her body hitting hard right next to the already disturbed soil around McClanahan's grave.

I reached into my pocket, not taking my eyes off him as he trudged back to his car and pulled a shovel out of the trunk.

But my phone wasn't in my pocket. I blinked, feeling the key, but I didn't have my cell. I searched the other one, coming up empty, as well.

Shit.

I didn't know if I wanted to call for help or record this, but either way, I was out of luck.

He came back to the grave and started digging up the soil again, and I clutched the sides of the tall headstone, watching him.

Who was he? God, was he crazy or just stupid? We lived on the coast. Take a boat out, weight the body down, and toss it overboard, for crying out loud.

I blinked, remembering myself. It wasn't like I'd thought about it or anything.

The wind kicked up, blowing the sheet off her face, and I looked down at her, my mouth going dry. She didn't look familiar, but I wasn't really close enough to tell. At first glance, she looked my age, but the way the skin fit around certain parts of her body told me she wasn't. Maybe twenties or thirties.

I looked around, hoping the caretaker might be making the rounds or kids would be coming back to party some more, but we were completely alone out here now.

He dug for another minute and then stopped, his shoulders slumped as he stared down at the body, almost in a daze.

And all of a sudden, I was him. In his shoes, standing where he was. I'd just killed someone, and I was getting rid of the evidence.

Raising his black boot, he slowly lowered it to her neck and pressed down, watching her and baring his teeth.

Anger.

He was angry.

And despite everything in my head telling me this was a horror, I couldn't run. I couldn't stop watching.

He could be a serial killer. A rapist keeping her quiet forever. A predator of innocents.

She might not even be dead yet. I could run, get help, and save her life. At the very least, put him behind bars.

But then he started sobbing, shaking and gasping, and I was him. I would be him if I let Martin push me enough.

Someday, at some point, it was coming. I'd lose my mind and just fight. Fight until either he or I stopped breathing.

A breeze swept through the trees, his hood blew off his head, and I blinked, seeing Damon Torrance standing there with the shovel in his hand and the body of a dead woman at his feet.

I sucked in a breath and his eyes shot up, his whole body freezing as our eyes locked.

Shit.

My blood drained, and I couldn't inhale.

He dropped the shovel and headed toward me, charging hard and steady down the small hill as I stumbled backward, too scared to take my eyes off him.

Something caught my eye, and I looked behind him, seeing the woman's hand flop over and her head move.

"She's moving," I choked out, hitting the back of a crypt.

He stopped about two feet from me, holding my eyes for a moment. Slowly, he turned, looking over his shoulder at her. Her finger twitched, and I noticed the tears still hanging at the corner of his eyes.

The wind continued to glide over the headstones, the scent of his cigarettes wafting around me, and at this moment, I thought I would've liked to be him.

He was going to get away with this. What would we all do if we could get away with it?

Maybe I was lucky to never have to find out. Maybe he was because he could escape his pain.

"Who is it?" I asked softly.

I took in their hair. Hers and his. The same jet-black, so dark it almost shimmered blue in the moonlight. The same skin, pale and translucent like they were made of marble.

I looked at her costume. "Your mother?" I whispered.

I'd heard she was a ballerina back in the day.

He turned back around, guarded but trembling a little.

I tried to catch my breath. "Did Will have any part of that, Damon?"

He shook his head.

He stepped toward me, and I held my breath, closing my eyes and waiting for it.

But he didn't touch me.

He just closed the distance and hovered, and I couldn't move if I tried. My head swam.

"Not going to fight me again?" he murmured.

It took a moment, but I raised my eyes, meeting his. "It's easier to pretend that we're in control of everything that happens to us." I paraphrased his words. "It's almost peaceful. To just let it be."

He stared at me and then . . . nodded. He touched my face, and I jerked away, but then he brought up his hand, showing me the blood he'd wiped off.

I touched my face, too, patting the scratch. Was that from Martin or the escape?

"Does Will know?" he asked, rubbing my blood between his fingers. "No."

He lifted his gaze to mine. "Because he's the one pure, beautiful thing untainted by ugliness," he repeated nearly his exact words from the shower. "And we love him for it."

I remained still despite everything shattering inside and the ache in my throat from the cry I held back.

Turned out that maybe the Horsemen weren't what I'd thought, and while money may pay off the consequences, it still didn't prevent some kinds of pain.

He turned his head, looking at the body again. "She started fucking me when I was twelve," he whispered. "After a while, you get tired of pretending that you're in control of everything that happens to you." He paused, turning to me again. "And you start being what happens to everyone else."

Spinning back around, he walked over to his mother, crouched down next to her body as he faced me, and wrapped his hand around the front of her throat.

I watched as his fingers curled, tightening, and the whites of his knuckles flashed in the dark.

He lifted his eyes to mine, watching me as I watched him. My toes curled, my reflex to run, but . . .

I felt it. My hand, not his. My fingers hummed, slowly balling into fists, and I breathed heavy, feeling my heart pound and the bile rise up my throat, but . . .

God, I wanted to be him. I wanted to do it.

I liked this feeling.

I wanted to kill, and I squeezed my fists until they ached, but I didn't move until she stopped jerking and gasping and shaking, one of her legs dipping over the side of the grave.

Damon held my eyes the whole time.

The part of me that always gave in to tears was gone. Tears solved nothing.

I didn't know when I started toward him, but in a moment, I was next to the grave, holding out my foot and helping him push her into the hole. Her body hit the soil, dirt smearing her legs, feet, and arms as he grabbed the shovel. I dropped to my knees, hurriedly helping him push the earth on top of her with my hands.

We didn't talk. I didn't even think we really realized what was happening or what we were really doing, but it was too late now. Even if I turned him in for murder, I'd helped him dump the body. It was too late to panic.

And although I feared what I'd feel tomorrow in the light of day with a clearer head, I couldn't push the dirt in fast enough tonight. I wanted her to fucking die.

When we'd covered her as much as we could, Damon carried the sheet and the shovel back to the trunk, while I stepped on top of the grave, packing the soil.

I gazed at the grass around us. It was a mess. They must use a blower or something to clean up the soil scattered around the grass, but we didn't have that right now. What if they noticed?

Just then, a drop of rain hit my face, and I looked up to the sky.

A few more drops of cool water hit, and I closed my eyes, almost smiling.

Damon rushed back over, helped me finish flattening out the dirt, and then pushed me off, dropping to his knees and running his hand over the grave, getting rid of our footprints.

"The rain will muddy it," I told him. "Maybe they won't notice it was dug up."

He nodded. "Get in the car. Now."

God, he was probably going to kill me next, but I didn't think. I ran over, opened the passenger door, and climbed into his BMW.

BMW.

I'd seen this car before. Somewhere.

But I shook my head.

Of course, I'd seen it before. Everyone at school knew the Horsemen's vehicles.

Damon slammed the trunk shut and climbed into his seat, rain starting to pummel the roof, and I stared out the window at McClanahan's grave, dirt kicking up at each heavy drop.

We shouldn't have dumped her here. Where did he get that idea?

That grave was important. Damon and his pals revered it. How could he put her there? Wasn't that like desecrating McClanahan's memory or something?

I mean, I guess it seemed smart. Hide a body where no one would think it was odd to a find a dead body, especially since that grave was freshly dug and there was a good chance no one would notice it had been disturbed again, but anyone could've seen us. Maybe someone did.

I looked around, scanning the tree line and hedges. Looking for any flash of movement among the crypts and headstones.

I stuck my thumbnail in my mouth tasting the dirt on my finger and feeling it in my sweater.

I looked over at Damon, who still hadn't started the car.

He gripped the wheel, his bottom lip trembling as he stared through watery eyes out the windshield.

"I didn't love her," he said, almost to himself.

But his face was twisted in sadness and despair as tears spilled over, falling down his dirty face.

"I don't know why it hurts," he told me. "I didn't love her."

"You did," I said, but it came out as a whisper. "You learned how to love from her." I turned my eyes back out my window, staring at the grave. "This is what it looked like."

My parents raised me, but so did Martin. He shaped me.

No wonder I couldn't give Will what he wanted.

Tears finally hit my eyes until everything was so blurry that I couldn't see.

Damon took off, and I didn't know where we were going, but when he pulled into the school parking lot, I was a little relieved.

I didn't want to go home.

And I couldn't like this. I needed to find some clean clothes. The clock on the dash read 2:02 a.m.

Damon drove around the school, to the rear, and parked between the buses and the field house.

He killed the engine, reached into the back and pulled out a baseball cap, and threw it at me as he pulled up his hood.

"Put it on," he said. "And let's go."

I hesitated, my natural inclination to argue or demand answers, but . . . he seemed to have a plan, at least, and I couldn't even remember my own name at the moment.

I slipped on the hat and exited the car, following him to the door as he pulled out a set of keys.

How he had keys to the school, I had no idea, and I didn't give a shit.

He unlocked the door, and I hurried inside, following him through the boys' locker room. He grabbed two towels and led me into a huge shower with multiple heads, slinging the towels over a divider.

I looked around as he started the water.

The girls had separate stalls. Some privacy, at least.

"Clothes off," he told me. "Now."

He pulled off his sweatshirt and started undoing his pants, and I opened my mouth to protest, but I clamped it shut again.

He wasn't killing me, I guess.

He stripped off his clothes, and slowly, I did the same, just running on autopilot now.

I unhooked my overalls, pulled my sweater over my head, and discarded everything—my shoes, socks, and even my underthings, too scared of the slightest evidence.

We both dipped under our respective showerheads and rinsed,

blood dripping off his body and down the drain. I spied a black rosary hanging around his neck and down his chest. Did he wear that all the time?

I closed my eyes, shivering under the water.

"You know who my father is, right?" he asked.

I nodded.

"And you know what will happen to you if you breathe a word of this."

I opened my eyes and looked over at him, meeting his eyes through the locks of hair in my face.

"I know better," I mumbled. "I don't have your money to get out of this."

He regarded me for a moment and then dipped down, rubbing at his legs and then arms.

I couldn't stop shaking, my stomach churning as the water ran over the cut on my eyebrow, stinging.

"Maybe I'll return the favor someday." He stood back up. "When you're ready to deal with him."

His eyes fell down my body, taking in all the bruises he'd already seen.

"I'm a loose end," I pointed out. "Why didn't you kill me when you saw me see you there tonight?"

He looked like he was thinking about it.

But instead, he asked, "Why didn't you run when you saw me?"

He was right. I'd willingly inserted myself.

And why? To help him? I didn't even like him, and how did I know what he was telling me was the truth? Maybe his mom was the nicest person in the world.

I'd gambled everything on his word. And for what?

I shook my head, trying to clear it. "There's a . . ." I swallowed, raising my hand to my head. "There's a tear in the membrane today. I don't know what's wrong with me."

He stared back at me, silent.

I dropped my eyes, remembering how it felt. How I watched him and imagined what it would be like to kill someone you hated.

"I wanted to see you throw her away," I whispered.

He stood there, quiet, as if studying me or trying to figure something out, and then he sighed, rubbing the water all over his face.

He cleared his throat. "I have a sister," he told me. "Her name is Nik, but everyone calls her Banks." He met my eyes again. "If something happens, and I can't be there for her—if they arrest me for this—you need to go to my house and help her. She doesn't have anyone else. You understand?"

Huh?

"You're asking me?" I looked at him, confused. "Why?"

He had tons of people he could count on.

But he just turned around, shut off the water, and raised his arms, smoothing his hands over his hair. "I'm not sure anyone else would've helped me bury a body," he murmured.

Water poured over me as he stood there, and I looked up, noticing small scars on the underside of his arms.

Not even his friends?

"She's your age," he told me. "No one knows about her, and don't ask why. She doesn't have anyone but me. Promise me."

It took a moment, but I finally nodded. "A sister. Nik. My age. Got it."

He smiled, small but genuine, and he grabbed the towels, walking over and shutting off my shower, handing me one.

"A tear in the membrane . . ." he mused to himself, putting his arm around me and pulling me out of the shower. "Come on. Let's go find Will."

CHAPTER 25

WILL

Present

Of course.

Of course, she wanted to run, because that's all she ever wanted to do.

But rather than be hurt about it, I was pissed now. I made excuses years ago—I wasn't good enough for her or she had too many hang-ups to let herself want me, but now, there was no doubt. She was the selfish, heartless, waste of time Damon always said she was for rejecting me, and she could fuck right off.

I didn't need anyone to save me, and I didn't need her for anything.

Reaching down, I pulled her off Alex, hearing her shirt tear as I threw her back and out of the way. If she was actually going to leave without me, then she could stay here without me, too. *Goddammit.*

She lunged again, diving down for her bag of food, but I grabbed her by the collar, scowling down at her.

"You must be high if you think you're going anywhere," I said.

She shoved me, her glasses somewhere on the floor as Alex climbed to her feet.

"Didn't you ever wonder what Damon and I were doing together that night you found us at the school?"

My eyes twitched, and she chuckled to herself.

"You don't even want to know what really happened the day you got arrested, either, do you?"

"I know what happened," I growled.

She laughed again, but her eyes fell, and I saw tears pooling. "Yes. Everything except my side of the story, and maybe you would've done things differently and you would still hate me for what I did even if you knew the whole story, but maybe you'd let me say words that need to be said, but you won't. You know why?"

I heard movement upstairs, and I knew we needed to hide. Right now.

"Because you don't want to deal with things," she whispered. "Damon knew it. I knew it. Everyone knew it. You didn't have problems, because you didn't want problems. You let the current carry you and *c'est la vie*."

My fists tightened around her shirt.

"You were the child everyone protected," she went on. "Damon said you were untainted by anything bad, and that's what made you special to us. That quality needed to be preserved."

They talked about me? Together? Behind my back?

"You never thought it was odd?" she pressed. "Damon and I had hated each other. What were we doing that night? How come I was the only person to know about his sister?"

I assumed she was talking about Banks and not Rika. None of us found out about Banks until more than a year after we'd gotten out of prison.

Emmy knew about her in high school?

She held my eyes, the tears in them trembling, about to fall. "Why did you never ask these questions?"

"Because I—"

"Because you didn't want to know the answers," she told me, cutting me off. "If you didn't know what was going on, then you didn't have to deal with it."

"That's not true."

"Oh, right," she fired back. "I forgot you had a method of dealing with your problems, after all, unlike the rest of us weaklings."

I flared my eyes. What the fuck?

How the hell did she know about me using? Goddammit.

Her gaze faltered, and I could tell she saw the look on my face and maybe thought she shouldn't have said that, but I shoved her away, every muscle on fire with fight.

Alex grabbed her arm and pulled her toward the stairs. "Just shut up, Emory," she gritted out through her teeth. "Everyone is hurting. It's not all about you. We have to pull together."

She yanked her arm free and backed up toward the door, her eyes darting between us.

"You should go hide," she told Alex. "And I hope you get home safe."

She was leaving. She was actually walking out of here, to her death, because her pride took up so much room in her head that there was no space for common sense.

She'd been fine earlier. Or somewhat fine.

She couldn't stay here with both of us. She was leaving me.

"And when the crew arrives?" Alex whisper-yelled. "We're not leaving this island without you, and you're only going to delay our getaway as everyone scours the terrain for your dead body, dumbass!"

"He got sent here," Emmy argued. "It's his fault any of us are here now."

She spun around, grabbed her bag, and clutched the door handle. Alex rushed over and yanked her wrist away.

Emmy twisted around and shoved Alex, sending her body flying backward. She stumbled, spinning around, and landed on her hands and knees . . .

Right at Aydin's feet.

My lungs emptied, my gaze rising to meet his face.

Oh, shit.

He stood between the stairs and the dining room. Taylor entered behind him as Rory and Micah stood at the railing at the top of the stairs.

I steeled my spine as everyone took in our newest addition, but my gut knotted all the same. He might let me have one, but not both. I couldn't protect them both.

Alex remained frozen for a moment, staring at his shoes, but then slowly, she lifted her head and looked up at him.

He looked down at her, freshly dressed in a black suit, white shirt, and no tie. I didn't realize I wasn't breathing until my lungs started tightening.

His jaw flexed, and his eyes grew hard. "Micah?" he called. "Rory?"

"Yeah," Micah answered from above.

Aydin continued to gaze down at Alex as he said, "I want the house and grounds searched. Now."

The two stood there for a moment, and then they splintered off, searching the second floor first.

It was easy to dismiss Emmy's arrival as a lone fluke—or a stroke of luck for some of them—but Alex here, too, meant it wasn't an accident. We were being infiltrated, and Aydin still liked to behave as if we were here of our free will and this house was his domain.

Bending down, he gently lifted Alex up, staring into her eyes and wiping away the blood under her nose with his thumb.

She hesitated for a moment, but then . . . she jerked away, stepping back.

He held up his hand, staring at the blood dripping off his thumb.

Then he looked at her again and slid it over his tongue, licking it off his finger.

"Alex," he said, swallowing. "Palmer."

"You know each other?" I asked.

How the hell did they know each other? I darted my eyes to Alex, but she just stood there, her shoulders squared and her mouth shut.

"How many more are here?" he asked her. "And where are they?"

I watched them, hating how calm he seemed, because he always looked like he was expecting anything that came along and already had an agenda in place.

It was the one thing I'd learned from him. The appearance of control was just as powerful. Make a decision and act like that was the plan all along.

When she didn't answer him, he lowered his chin and shot her a small smirk. "You didn't do this on your own," he said. "How did you find this place?"

Without waiting for an answer, he drifted past her toward Emmy, who remained by the front door.

He tilted her face up to look at the bruise forming on her cheek. "Looks like you found your noise in the walls," he said.

She didn't respond, but she let him turn her face side to side to inspect the damage.

I wanted to remove his head.

"How do you know I wasn't brought here against my will like Emory?" Alex asked.

But Aydin ignored her, asking Emmy, "Why are you fighting?" He shot me a glance. "Over him?"

Again, Em kept her mouth shut, neither confirming nor denying.

"Forced to make a choice, he won't choose you," he told her. "You'll have to look out for yourself. Get used to it."

"There's nothing I'm more used to," she said in a quiet but firm tone.

He winked at her, signaling his approval of her response.

I stared at them. What the hell was he doing? Were they fucking bonding or some shit?

He dropped his arms and looked down at her feet, seeing the bag of food on the floor. He met her eyes for a moment before grabbing the black coat off the stand by the door and draping it around her.

"Taylor?" he said.

The other guy stepped up a couple more feet. "Yeah?"

"Hold Will," Aydin told him.

I tensed. What?

Before I could spin around, Taylor grabbed me, sliding his arms around mine from behind and locking his hold against my chest.

"What the fuck are you doing?" I yelled.

Aydin opened the front door, looking at Emory before he dipped down, picked up her bag of food, and handed it to her.

She paused, her gaze shifting between him and me as I struggled. "You're letting me leave?" she asked. "After all of this?"

I threw Taylor off, shoving him and hearing him tumble against the candelabras.

I shot forward.

"I wish you wouldn't," Aydin told her. "But you can."

She looked over at me, and I stopped, gauging my choices. If she ran, Alex was right. We'd just be delayed, trying to find her and make sure she didn't wind up dead, and I wasn't even sure why I cared anymore.

Goddamn them. Michael and Kai and Damon and all of them. If they weren't coming, I wouldn't be so pressed for time right now. I wasn't ready to leave yet.

Of course, they just needed to swoop in and save me.

Emmy stared at me—maybe waiting to see if I stopped her, or hoping I would—and I didn't want this confrontation with Aydin. Not yet.

Because she wasn't leaving, even if I had to fight them all and suffer every bone in my body breaking.

Something crossed her eyes, and she looked like she did that morning in the movie theater so long ago. Like she wanted to melt into my arms.

Like she didn't really want to go, because she wanted to stay with me.

But before I could take her hand, slam the door, and figure out how I was going to fight Aydin and Taylor for both of these women, he leaned into her ear and appeared to whisper something as she held my eyes.

She listened as his jaw moved, and three seconds stretched into ten, and then finally . . . she dropped her gaze as if processing and nodded to him.

He closed the door, removed her jacket, hanging it up, and took the food bag from her before flashing me a look bearing the ghost of a smile.

I straightened.

Walking past me, he left the room, Taylor following, and I stood there glaring as Emory remained silent.

She was running from me. She fought Alex in order to leave.

And now she was staying?

Because he had more control over her than I did.

"Get your shit," I told Alex, my gaze never leaving Em. "You're bunking with me."

"Will—"

"Now!" I barked as Alex protested.

Fuck it. She could grab her stuff anytime. Taking her hand, I pulled her up the stairs, leaving Emory in the foyer as I disappeared down the hallway, through the last door, and up the stairs to the third floor.

Emory was safe. She was under his protection now.

I slammed my hand into a wall as we traipsed down the hallway.

"Look, I don't know what the hell is going on," Alex said, pulling her hand out of mine, "but when we leave, she's coming with us. You can sort your shit out back in civilization. When I run, you and her are both coming."

I locked my door and turned on the lights, debating about grabbing my laptop and having my contact intercept Michael and the crew and stop them. But they needed to come now in order to take Emory and Alex to safety.

"When are they arriving?" I asked.

"Any day now."

I pulled on a shirt and walked over to the window, closing the curtains.

"You want to go home, don't you?" Alex asked.

I shot her a look.

"Will . . ."

I paced the room, feeling like I was about to jump out of my skin.

"Your parents . . ." she said, her voice softening. "The way you always talked about them. They love you. Given everything, they adore you." She approached me. "Why are you still here? Would they really have kept you away so long? It doesn't make any sense."

I should tell her. I just wasn't sure I wasn't going to fail, and I needed to do this on my own. I'd put in too much time and work.

I had to go home ten times the man. I needed to see this through.

She took my chin and tipped it toward her, stopping me. "Damon, Winter, Michael, Rika, Misha, Kai, Banks . . ." She said their names as if I'd forgotten them. "You belong home. Don't you want to leave?"

Of course, I did.

Why would she think I didn't want to leave?

K ai and Banks.

Winter and Damon.

Michael . . .

I knew what I needed to do when I came here, but Alex's words kept drifting through my head—especially now. Especially when faced with the decision I was going to have to make sooner than I thought.

Maybe I was scared.

Maybe . . . just maybe a small part of me didn't want to ever leave here. There were no drugs here. No women. I'd stayed away from the alcohol fairly easily. I didn't have to prove my worth with a career, plans, or relationships.

I just had to survive. There were no opportunities to face, so nothing to screw up.

We were all in the same boat.

And maybe I liked that. With sobriety came clarity, and I'd had time to think about my past, and I was embarrassed. I wanted everyone to trust me. To depend on me.

But that meant risking failure, and for a few minutes here and there I was content to just stay here forever.

Believe it or not, it was easier.

I headed back up the stairs to my room, carrying a bowl of stew for Alex. Micah had saved it for me, but not enough for Alex, and I wasn't about to beg Aydin for extra food. She told me she had some stuff in the tunnels, but I'd let her eat her first solid meal in days and just grab one of her granola bars for myself.

I stepped up into my room, hearing water splash on the other side of the privacy screen. I halted and watched her shadow through the cream-colored fabric.

She stood in the tub, bending over and washing. Slowly, I set the bowl down on the table, my stomach sinking as I watched her.

Alex was always easy to disappear into. I didn't have to talk or put up a front. I didn't have to seduce her or pretend.

She was my port in the storm and I was hers.

I watched her form move as she washed her legs and arms. Her hand drifted up the back of her neck, the water from the cloth dripping back into the tub.

She was the only person I'd ever felt completely safe with. The only person I never feared disappointing because the only thing she expected of me was to be there.

Why couldn't I love her? She got along with my friends. She made me laugh, and her presence was always a comfort. Always.

She fit in my life.

Watching her, I balled my fists, almost convinced I should do it. I should go and lift her into my arms and take her to bed and sink inside of her and . . .

I shook my head, sighing.

I couldn't.

Because every time I closed my eyes, I saw the girl who made me want to be better. More.

I saw Emmy Scott.

Alex was like Damon. They loved me. They indulged my dark side. They were too forgiving and too enabling.

They kept me from being lonely, but Emory taught me that not everything I wanted was going to come easy. That there were things I was going to have to fight for and there was pain in the world that my shallow lifestyle in high school kept me ignorant of.

She made me feel like a man.

Even though her words were sharp and the battle she constantly fought in her heart felt like a knife in my own, her eyes on me made me feel strong.

Her arms around me made me want to take on anything.

When I closed my eyes, I saw a girl with glasses too big for her face, and I heard the sweetest, most timid voice asking me if I still wanted to hold her.

I could still feel her cradled in my arms.

Leaving the stew, I pressed the wooden panel on the wall Alex had shown me earlier and dove into the hidden passageway, sliding the panel closed again behind me.

The guys were still up, spread out and doing their various things, but I hadn't seen Emory when I went to collect food.

Alex said she left her duffel bag in the tunnel outside of Emory's room, and even though I told myself I was just getting a granola bar and some water, I wanted to make sure she was in her own damn bed.

With the door secured.

She'd be brought back to Thunder Bay safe and sound to face the music.

I found my way through the tunnels, heading to the east wing where I knew Emory's room sat, eventually spotting the black bag on the floor in the tiny bit of light shining through the peepholes.

All this time, these tunnels were here. It was inconceivable that Aydin didn't know.

But Alex had been skulking around the house for days undetected, so . . .

I left the bag on the floor, hearing Emmy's moans before I even found the peephole to her room.

My pulse skipped, and I forgot about the bag, pushing the door open and stepping over the threshold into a pitch-black bedroom. I immediately noticed her lying in bed underneath the covers.

Her breathing shook, raspy and shallow, and she twisted under the sheets, letting out a whimper. I flashed my gaze to the door, seeing the chair propped under the handle, and then I looked back to the bed, inching forward.

She clenched the sheet in her fist, and I squatted next to the bed, gazing at her back like I did that night after I brought her home from the Cove and put her to bed. She wore a tank top and some purple lace panties I assumed she got from Alex. The sheet hung below her waist as her chest rose and fell too fast.

She let out a small cry, and I leaned over the bed, planting my hand on the pillow above her.

Her eye had bruised, and I let my gaze fall down her body, seeing more nicks and scrapes on her arms that hadn't been there before.

The tumble in the woods, the small fire, the fight with Taylor, and the fight with Alex . . . I couldn't help it. I ran my hand over her hair, smoothing it away from her face as her nightmare played out and her body shook.

I'd loved Emory since the moment I laid eyes on her when I was fourteen.

I could still see her—sitting on her bike outside the chain-link fence surrounding the school parking lot as she watched my friends and me on our skateboards that summer.

From that moment on, it seemed I was always aware of her, and everything I did, I did with it in mind that she was watching.

Every joke in class. Every strut into the lunchroom. Every new haircut and every new pair of jeans.

Even the Raptor. My first thought when my parents bought it was how she'd look in it.

This stupid fantasy of her running to my truck after school, smiling and skipping at my side, unable to keep her hands off me because I was her boyfriend and I always took my girl home from school.

I hated that she was alone. She was always alone, and she shouldn't have been, because she should've been with me.

But the older she got, the angrier she got, and the more desperate I got about trying to forget her. I just needed this to be over.

Nothing got better with her. It just decayed.

She was never going to lie in my arms in a bed that belonged to both of us.

"I love you, Will," she said in a quiet voice.

I froze, my hand paused on her temple as I stared down at her. What?

My legs nearly gave out from under me, and I gaped at her, pinching my eyebrows together and trying to see if her eyes were open or if she was still sleeping, but . . .

I knew she was awake. Her breathing had calmed, and her body had relaxed.

"Do you remember the night you snuck into my room?" she asked, still facing away from me. "When you'd had it with me and tried to walk out on me?"

EverNight. The night I met her grandmother for the first time.

She sniffled. "I warned you I wasn't a happy person, and there were so many reasons I didn't want to let you in, but . . ." She trailed off, trying to find her words. "The only time I ever loved my life was when I was with you."

My hand still lingered on her brow, unmoving.

Now? She was telling me this now?

"I was always your Em," she whispered. "No matter what I said or what I did or all the ways I let life win over the years . . . That night, I knew. I was in love with you."

The backs of my eyes stung, and I clenched my teeth.

"You can leave, and I'll survive. I always do," she told me. "I just wanted you to know that."

And just like that again, I couldn't remember why she was bad for me, and I just wanted her where she was supposed to be.

With me.

All the hate and anger and loss melted away, and I wanted to crawl in behind her and hold her the rest of the night, but I knew my eyes would be open in the morning and the light would hurt.

Everything would hurt.

I clenched my fist, just wanting to stay, but I couldn't do this anymore.

I was clean of all vices, except one, and I needed to shake her. I needed to shake her, so I could go home.

I left, too much pride to disappear into the wall again. I opened the door and walked out, closing it behind me and leaving her in the dark.

I wanted to know what he said to her—what he whispered in her ear by the front door—when I went in there, but I couldn't stay another second, or I almost wouldn't care about anything but her for the rest of the night.

She loved me.

She loved me.

The world swayed in front of me.

But it was just another example of how everyone did what they wanted to me because they thought I couldn't stay mad.

I mean, Damon almost killed me. Brutally and so badly, I could barely step foot in any body of water that wasn't a bathtub, and it didn't take much for me to forgive him.

I wasn't giving anyone else easy chances.

"Will," Aydin called as I passed his room.

I stopped, tensing.

I didn't want to talk to him right now, because whatever shit came out of his mouth would just mess with my head more. God, I wanted a cigarette. Hopefully Winter hadn't broken Damon of that completely yet, or I'd have to start buying my own packs when I got home.

Micah swiped the straight razor up Aydin's throat as he sat back in his chair, leaning his head back.

Walking in, I held out my hand, taking the razor. Micah hesitated only a moment and then handed it to me, walking out.

Standing behind Aydin, I picked up where Micah had left off, shaving the next stroke. I gave him the better shave, so he preferred me to do it.

"Do you think you'd be in charge?" Aydin asked. "If I weren't here?"

I tightened my fist around the handle, sliding up his neck again. One quick stroke right now, and I *would* be in charge.

He knew that.

He also thought he was brave, letting me shave him when he knew how easy it would be for me to end him right now in order to protect Emmy and Alex.

"I'm jealous your friends sent someone for you." He chuckled, looking up at me. "I think my people forgot about me."

"Find people who don't."

I glided the blade up over his jaw, feeling the heat of his gaze.

"I did," he said.

Us? We're not his people. Not yet, anyway.

"Demanding obedience through intimidation doesn't encourage loyalty," I told him. "Only earning it can."

He fell silent, watching me as I shaved against the grain of his cheek and chin. He knew what the hell I meant. Micah, Rory, and Taylor didn't respect him. They were afraid of him.

"I know," he finally replied. "You couldn't get her to stay in the house. I did, and I didn't have to raise a hand to do it." He gazed up at me. "I didn't even have to raise my voice. That's loyalty."

My gaze twitched.

"You have her heart, but I'm in her head now," he taunted. "With a woman like Emory Scott, which do you think she'll listen to?"

I didn't even have to think about that answer twice. My hand shook as I cleaned his upper lip.

"When you make your escape, do you think Emmy will run with you and your whore?" he asked.

I shot up straight, the blade clasped in my hand as I glared down at him.

She's not staying here with you.

"I think when I make my escape," I told him, "I'm taking a lot more than those girls."

He laughed, pulling off the towel around his neck and wiping his face clean. "She is stunning," he said. "I liked it when she grabbed your throat today. Many men don't even know how much they'd like being dominated. But it's such a turn-on. She fucked you good. I really think she's come alive here."

I locked my jaw, using every ounce of restraint to keep my temper in check.

He'd seen us in the greenhouse. He'd watched her ride me.

I dropped the blade and walked out of the room, every muscle in my body on fire.

He didn't get to have her.

I charged back to her room, threw open the door, and walked over to her bed as she shot up and looked at me in the light streaming from the hallway.

"What are you doing?" she asked.

But I didn't say a damn word.

I grabbed her glasses off the nightstand, slid my arms under her, sheets and all, and swept her up into my arms, taking her to my room with Alex and me.

There was no fucking way I was taking my eyes off her tonight.

She wrapped her arms tightly around my neck, her eyes on me the entire way up to the third floor and to my bed.

God, who the hell brought her here? She was ruining all my plans.

CHAPTER 26

WILL

Nine Years Ago

A locker slammed shut, echoing down the corridor, and I lifted the bottle to my mouth, downing another swallow of bourbon.

Motherfuckers. What the hell were they doing? How long had it been going on?

I knew something was up.

I leaned against a stack of mats in the wrestling room, hearing the locker door open down the hall as "Apologize" played low on the speaker next to me.

I swallowed another mouthful, remembering tucking her in last night in her room.

Like an imbecile.

After our fight at school today, I went out tonight, celebrating Devil's Night with my friends and a full mind to move the hell on. Get shit-faced and see if there was anyone I thought would make me feel better, because she treated me like shit, and I was sick of chasing after the girl I knew was meant for me but who didn't want me.

She gave me almost no reciprocation.

Except last night.

But today, she was back in full form, acting like I was a pity fuck. Like I wasn't good enough.

My friends and I went to the cemetery and partied.

We went to the Pope in Meridian City.

And partied some more.

I just couldn't forget her, no matter how much I drank. I caught a cab back to Thunder Bay, but instead of going home, I carried my ass to school and to our bus parked in the lot. I snuck on and plopped down in the back seat, remembering how'd she felt last night. How good her desire and love felt.

I sat in there and just got drunker, thinking about her, and then I looked out the window and saw them.

Damon and her. Walking into the school.

I blinked, not sure I was seeing right, because everything was spinning, but . . . I finally climbed off the bus and followed them.

I closed my eyes, inhaling a breath as their footsteps approached down the hall.

They weren't tough to find. In a school this old—and being nearly empty this time of night—I'd heard the water running as I trailed down the hallway. My legs went weak, my stomach rolled, and I slipped inside the locker room, seeing them as I rounded a row of lockers.

Naked in the shower together.

My fist tightened around the bottle. There was no way to misunderstand that.

That was why he left the hotel early tonight. Why she would never give in with me.

No one would choose me over Damon. Or me over Michael or Kai, either. No one thought I was worth a damn next to them.

They passed in front of the open door, Damon hearing the music and stopping. She halted next to his side, and I looked her up and down, seeing his black sweatpants hiked up to her knees, and his white T-shirt hanging on her. Their hair was wet, and he was only in jeans, no shirt.

"Did you fuck her?" I asked.

Damon paused, stepping into the dark room and finally spotting me ahead.

Emmy followed slowly.

"Really?" Damon cocked his head, trying to see me in the dark. "I'm not that boring. Come on." He approached me, gesturing to her. "Besides, she's not even pretty."

"Thanks," Emory mumbled.

I threw the bottle across the room, and it shattered against the wall as I launched out and shoved him in the chest.

He stumbled back, laughing as Em rushed up a few steps and stopped.

"This isn't a good night, Will," he warned. "Don't be stupid."

I walked around, eyeing her. "Where are the bruises coming from?"

She dropped her eyes.

I looked at Damon, shaking my head. "I knew you were rough, but I didn't think you were that rough."

He chuckled, running his hand through his hair and looking exasperated. "Tell him," he told Emmy.

I glared, my eyes shooting from him to her as she cast a worried look to Damon.

"Tell him," Damon barked again.

Son of a bitch. I reared my fist back and punched the motherfucker right across the jaw. He hit the ground, grunting and grabbing his face.

He did not get to know shit about her that I didn't. Fuck him.

"Was he good?" I turned to Em. "Did you like it?"

I knew it was odd I saw them both at the cathedral the same night. How long had it been going on?

Her eyes pooled with tears as she stared at me, looking helpless as she held her hands in front of her, like I was going to hit her or something.

What the hell did he know about her that I didn't? She was my girl, not his.

Everything ached in my chest, and I blinked away the burn in my eyes. "I told you I loved you last night," I said. "You didn't even hear me, did you?"

She stepped up to me. "Don't ruin it. Just remember it being good. Please."

"Why?" I yelled, whipping off my hoodie and working my belt as I backed her into the mats. "If it's going to fucking end, why let anything good remain? I don't want to miss you or this!"

Tears filled my eyes as I undid my belt and tore off my T-shirt, and I could hear her start crying as I pressed into her.

"Let's just ruin it for good right here!" I yelled down at her. "Remind me that I was just a fuck."

I grabbed her face, diving in, but she threw her arms around me, shaking with sobs.

"I do . . . want you," she whispered, crying. "It's all about you."

My chest shook, and I could barely breathe as I stared down at her.

"But you can't stand me, either," I gritted out. "You can't trust me, and you don't think I'll ever be anything more or ever good enough, right?"

If she trusted me, she'd tell me what the hell was going on.

She closed her eyes behind her glasses, shaking her head.

But she didn't argue with my conclusion, either.

She didn't love me.

Damon pulled me away from her, shoving me back. "You're drunk." And?

"What were you doing together?" I yelled, hooking my arm around his neck and dropping us both to the fucking floor. I swung my fist back and slammed him in the face again, blood dripping from the corner of his eye.

Growling, he threw me over, straddled me, and backhanded me

across my cheek. The sting spread across my face as I clutched his neck and squeezed his throat.

"We weren't doing that!" he shouted. "I'd rather screw a razor blade."

He threw another fist into my gut, and I shot out my hand, punching his dick.

His eyes went wide with fury, but he didn't keel over like I thought he would. He bared his teeth, slapping me over the head. "You motherfucker. You're lucky you missed."

He grabbed my wrists and pinned them to my chest, coming down and using his weight to keep them there.

"Easy to do," I bit out. I was much bigger, after all.

He headbutted my nose, and I grunted, tears springing to my eyes.

"Goddammit, D!" I growled. "Shit."

I struggled against his hold, trying to check for blood, but he wouldn't let me go.

"You gonna stop now?" he demanded. "I'm not in the fucking mood tonight, and neither is she. We've been through hell, and not everything is about you."

"Is it ever?" I opened my eyes, looking at him through the blur. I wasn't the leader. I wasn't the brains. I wasn't the passion.

My friends wouldn't be any less strong without me.

I had one thing I really liked. One thing that drove me to try. One thing that made me feel like a man.

Damon hovered over me, searching my eyes, and I could see the red in his, too. What the fuck happened tonight?

Dropping his forehead to mine, he released my hands, our chests rising and falling in sync.

"Bad shit happened," he whispered. "And I can't talk about it, but you're my best friend, so don't ever forget it."

His breath warmed my mouth, and I felt him try to hold back a sob as his eyes closed and he struggled.

"I need you," he murmured. "You don't know how much we all need you."

I bit the corner of my mouth to keep my emotions in check, but my eyes stung.

His lips hovered over mine, the heat made the room spin, and then . . . I opened my eyes, looking over at her. She was sitting against the mats and watching us. She hugged her knees to her body, unblinking as Damon's mouth ghosted mine, and . . . when I didn't pull away, he captured my lips with his, slipping in his tongue and nibbling my lip.

"We don't smile without you," he whispered. "She doesn't smile without you."

My cock hardened, and I groaned as he slid his hand down my jeans and stroked me. Emory's mouth fell open as she started breathing harder.

She wasn't running.

And every second I didn't stop him and every second she sat there, making no move to leave, I got harder and harder.

Maybe she was living last night all over again, or this was the last fucking thing I could share with her, but chills spread over my body, watching her watch us, and I fisted D's hair as he dove into my neck and sucked me dry.

"Fuck," I groaned.

I closed my eyes for a moment, pushing the worry away and just diving in. *To hell with it.*

I worked his jeans open as he unfastened mine, but before I could pull him out and show her how good my hands worked, he dipped down and sucked me into his mouth, drawing me out slow and strong.

I moaned. "Oh, God."

Curling my fingers into his hair as he moved up and down, I got stiffer, the heat of her eyes turning me on. I stared at her, the T-shirt falling off one shoulder, baring her skin, and her nipples poking through the fabric.

She liked it.

Her nails dug into the mat underneath her, and she looked so hot, almost like she wanted to come over and help him do what he was doing to me.

Let her look.

Let her know what it looks like with someone else's mouth on my dick.

I looked down at Damon, sweat cooling my pores as he pushed me between his warm lips and down his throat.

"She is beautiful," he panted, coming back up and stroking me as he bit my jaw. "And she's going to hate seeing you happy without her."

Spitting into my hand, I reached into his jeans and stroked him long and tight, kissing him back, both of us thrusting into each other's fists as his rosary draped onto my chest.

Grunts and groans filled the room as the pace grew frantic, chasing our orgasms, and I swear I heard Em moan as she watched us.

I wanted her to touch herself. I hoped she would.

"Tighter, man," Damon growled against my mouth.

"This is as tight as it gets," I told him. "You're not sticking that in my ass."

He snorted. "You're right. Your dick is smaller. You should top."

"Fuck you."

He laughed, and I smiled, thrusting up into him. Our relationship, strangely, was back to bantering.

I closed my eyes, sweat coating my back as I reached up with my other hand and choked him, both of us gasping and grunting as we pushed harder and tighter, cum spilling from my dick a moment before his.

I arched my back, crying out. "Fuck."

I moaned, tipping my head back and struggling for breath.

My muscles burned, but shivers ran through my body so good, and I tried to catch my breath.

Jesus Christ. What the fuck?

He collapsed to the mat on my side, his heat all over my hand. I kept my eyes closed for another moment, savoring the memory of her gaze on me.

But when I opened them and peered over, she stared at us with the most beautiful look of desperation and sweetness as her nails dug into her thighs.

She loved it. And hated it.

Rising up off the mat, she licked her lips and gazed at me with resolve. "I'll always want you," she said quietly.

And then she left.

I stared after her, the high of a moment ago now gone.

She wouldn't relent, and it was over, no matter how much she wanted all of this.

I closed my eyes, gritting my teeth together and wishing I hadn't busted that bottle now.

I wouldn't chase her again. She wasn't one of us. She would never fight for me.

I swallowed the lump and drew in a long breath, exhaling the pain in my gut.

Damon stood up and pulled up his jeans. "I'll be in the showers." He sighed. "Again."

CHAPTER 27

EMORY

Present

We'd never slept in the same bed.

Of course, it wasn't like we ever had a relationship. Just unbridled, stolen moments.

I looked over at him next to me, his head turned away as his bare chest rose and fell, and the morning light seeped through the drapes, making his skin glow and his eyebrows look like chocolate.

He brought me up here last night and told me to go to sleep, and I thought about arguing, but then I realized I didn't want to.

I was tired. He was tired. *Fuck it.*

My arm laid next to his, my pinky brushing his, and I almost wanted to thread them, but if I moved, so would he, and I wasn't ready for him to wake up.

Turning my head left, I gazed at Alex curled up on her side, facing me and holding the pillow under her head.

She wore one of Will's T-shirts. And while it hurt seeing them together last night and how close they were, I liked Alex. I liked her a lot.

She didn't want to hurt me. I knew that.

I couldn't help but smile a little. Her nose curled up at the end, almost like a Who, and I could see straight up her nostrils.

Not a single hair out of place on her entire body. Not a single one.

I shook my head and stared back up at the ceiling, trying to wonder if I should be weirded out that I was planted in bed between my first love and his girlfriend, but somehow it seemed like such a shallow thought in the grand scheme of things.

I rolled over, pushed myself up slowly, and climbed over Alex, gazing down at them both still asleep. Walking behind the privacy screen, I grabbed a washcloth, wetting it under the faucet of the tub.

Squeezing out the excess hot water, I pressed it to my face, closing my eyes and letting the warmth seep through and calm the ache in my jaw and on my eye where Alex had smacked me yesterday.

A bath sounded good, but I didn't want to wake them up yet.

But just then, something brushed my leg, and I dropped my arms, opening up my eyes to see Alex sitting on the edge of the tub, peering up at me.

"Sorry I woke you," I told her, reheating the washcloth under the hot water again.

"I'm fine."

I wrung out the cloth and stepped up to her, pressing it to her cheek and the nasty bruise swelling under the skin.

She tried to take it, but I nudged her away. "I wasn't going to leave without you," I told her.

In case she doubted that.

I just hated myself, and it was easier to try to disappear than face the music yesterday.

"And him?" she asked. "Were you going to leave without him?"

I inched forward, my legs on both sides of her thigh as I gently patted her face.

"The best thing for him is to be as far away from me as possible," I said.

Instead of trying to convince me otherwise, she just scoffed. "You're such a coward."

I tensed a little, but I kept my mouth shut, moving the hot towel around her face.

I wasn't a coward about everything.

"Emmy, I gotta bring him home," she told me. "Help me. I know you loved him. How can anyone not love him?"

A small laugh escaped through the lump lodged in my throat. *True.* I was glad to hear I wasn't the only one susceptible to his power.

Everyone adored that boy.

"That man last night—that temper—that's not who he is," she whispered. "You know that."

Do I? He'd been through the shit. She might've spent more time with him in recent years, but she hadn't know him in high school. That Godzilla conversation yesterday was the first glimpse of the old Will I'd gotten since I got here.

"You know how to fight," she said, sounding surprised.

I wasn't sure if she was talking about our scuffle in the foyer yesterday or if she saw my match with Taylor the other day.

But I shook my head. "I just know how to get back up."

"That's half the battle."

She studied me as I wiped her face.

"Kai owns a dojo in Meridian City," she told me. "Did you know that? It's where our family trains."

I looked into her eyes, something unsaid passing between us, but I swore it sounded like an offer.

But she was deaf, dumb, and blind if she thought I was welcome there. I had a job to get back to anyway.

Hopefully.

I tossed the cloth down and rubbed my eyes, forgetting where Will set my glasses last night.

"You need another shower," she told me.

"Speak for yourself."

Three people in a small bed . . . we were all sweating last night.

I grabbed a comb on the small table and started working through my tangles.

"Micah and Rory are all right," I informed her. "Taylor is a concern, but no one goes against Aydin's orders that we're not to be touched."

"We or you?"

I narrowed my eyes on her. "What would Aydin have against you?" Why would he protect me and not her?

But she just shrugged. "Nothing. He doesn't even know me."

"He seemed to know you," I retorted.

He knew her name. He recognized her.

She didn't say more, though, and we heard the floorboards creak, both of us spotting Will walking past and halting as soon as he saw us.

His hair was sexy-messy as his jeans hung low on his hips, the top button undone, and he just stood there, his eyes falling down and then back up again, taking us in.

I stood there in my tank and underwear, while Alex was still in his T-shirt and no pants.

"Fuck my life," he grumbled, shaking his head and continuing down the stairs to his door. "Use the tub if you want. Clothes are in the bureau," he called out. "I'll go get some breakfast. Stay here. Both of you."

The door opened and closed again, and I leaned over, starting the water.

"If you have an exit plan," I asked her, "why isn't he rushing to escape? I heard him yesterday. He didn't want to leave."

It was odd, wasn't it? You would think he'd be ecstatic to be saved, but he didn't look like he was happy she was here.

He didn't look happy either of us were here.

Prisoners sometimes got so used to being inside, that it was scarier to leave. They had a home, three meals a day, a regimen . . .

Sooner or later, the familiar hopelessness was easier than the hopeful unknown.

But that wasn't Will. He had a home, friends, money, opportunities . . .

We were missing something. Something he wasn't telling us.

Alex shook her head, looking after him down the stairs. "I don't know," she said. "But if I know anything about Will, it's not to assume anything. He knows more than we think, and he's more patient than a crocodile."

It had been days now. I still hadn't shown up to work. I still wasn't answering my phone.

A missing person's report must've been filed by now. Had Martin been notified?

Not that he'd care, but he'd probably feel pressured to deal with it, in any case.

He wouldn't find me, though. My best chance was to make my escape with Alex and drag Will out of here if we had to when it was time. I didn't like the way Aydin looked at her yesterday. Something was going on.

In the meantime, I'd stay on his good side. If it took until the resupply team showed up, I didn't want him locking me in the basement to hide me from them.

Will wanted the room to himself for a bit—to bathe, I presumed—while Alex disappeared into the tunnels to . . . do whatever it was she'd been doing in there. Will told me to go to my room and stay there, so of course, I ignored him and made my way to the greenhouse again to search for tools in the garden shed.

I no longer needed them to get into the tunnels, but they might come in handy for other things—weapons, carving out a hiding place, escaping . . .

Aydin, Micah, and Taylor worked out in the gym, and I wasn't sure where Rory was, but this was my shot.

I headed out the kitchen door, across the terrace, around the greenhouse, and into the garden shed, hearing the waterfall around the other side of the house and feeling its mist.

What was this place like in the summer? An image flashed in my mind of me sitting on the balcony with a book as the water fell in the distance.

I nearly rolled my eyes. I'd better not be here that long.

Stepping into the damp structure, I spotted a worktable and grabbed a rusty old wrench, a hammer, and a couple of screwdrivers, trying to fit them all into my pockets until I saw the tool belt hanging on the wall. I smiled, reaching over and pulling it off the hook.

Perfect.

I tied the rust-stained belt around my waist, situating the load over my side instead of at my front, because I hated walking with a clunk of crap over my thighs. I'd realized that tidbit building the gazebo all those years ago.

I scooped up some nails and pliers, pausing as I thought about that tiny gazebo. A roof like a witch's hat and constructed using aged materials that I'd salvaged from St. Killian's long after it was abandoned. I'd wanted it to look used. Like it had always been there, maybe even before the town.

It wasn't my best work, but it was my first, and finishing it was more of an accomplishment than I thought it would be.

It took so much longer than it should've because I stopped caring about everything, including my work, for so long. I went months without touching it, deliberately avoiding the village so I didn't have to see it, and eventually, I'd forced the finish, getting it done without the chandeliers I'd dreamed about, because it would've been too painful to remember him every time I looked at it.

I didn't want to build or design. I didn't want to do anything because of him.

Nothing else mattered as I mourned the loss.

But I got it done. When I finally resumed my work, it was because, once again, I'd pulled myself up to my feet. Like the coffee-table books, the gazebo was another trophy I collected for living another day.

But I'd never see it again. It wasn't there anymore.

I left the garden shed, treading through the wet grass, but instead of heading into the kitchen, I detoured into the greenhouse, pulling the ladder off the wall I'd spotted in here yesterday and propping it up underneath the broken panel in the roof.

Climbing up, I sat on the top of the ladder and started reattaching the rusted chain, using my pliers to open up the link and rethread it.

I didn't give a shit about this place. I knew I was just making beds in a burning house.

But this was who I was, and I wasn't going to wallow away my time, waiting for my heart to catch up to my head, and if it was something as simple as keeping my hands busy in order to survive Will Grayson and how much I wished I could do everything over again, then that's what I would do.

The calm in the chaos.

The only other option was to waste my time thinking about things I couldn't change. He hadn't said he loved me back last night. I hadn't expected him to, but if I had any doubt on whether or not he still did, I had my answer now.

The past was dead.

I squeezed the link closed again, pulling some wire out of my apron and reinforcing the link in case the weight of the windowpane made it split again, and then I climbed down, winding the crank on the wall. I watched as the panes lifted open in unison, and then reversed it to close them again.

A shot of pride hit me—the pleasure of solving a problem a familiar feeling that almost made me feel normal again.

This was the one part of me I'd keep. At the very least, I'd found work I enjoyed and was good at.

Setting the ladder back against the wall, I left the greenhouse, avoiding the bed of snakes hidden under the dirt on my left, and walked through the house, looking for anything else to consume my time.

Who had this house built and why? There seemed to be very few personal pieces in the décor. No family portraits or jewelry boxes or engraved clocks. Nothing that gave away the house's history, or even where we might be, based on any text I'd found. I hadn't researched the books in the library to see if they were in English, but everyone here spoke English, so . . .

Were there more Blackchurches? There had to be, right? In different parts of the world? There had to be a lot more than five sons misbehaving out there. The idea of some mountaintop house in Nepal, or cabins deep in the rainforest made my mind slip sideways. There was an army of little shits out in the world, no doubt.

I turned down the hall just before I hit the gym and passed a set of double doors that had always been closed. On impulse, I stopped and opened them.

A smaller ballroom than the one I'd seen on the other side of the house spread out before me, and I stepped onto the dance floor, taking in the red walls and the row of gold sconces around all sides.

A chandelier sat crashed on the floor, and I shot my eyes up to the ceiling, but I couldn't see well in the darkness. Walking to the window, I threw open the drapes, the dust flying and catching in my lungs, and I coughed and stepped back, examining the mess in the light streaming through now.

How the hell did that happen?

The gorgeous room of decorative woodwork, mirrors, and crystal gleamed in the light, the only thing wrong with the place being the broken light fixture and the glass scattered all over the floor.

The chandelier was wider than I was tall, leaning to one side with almond-shaped pendants strewn about. Sunlight from the window reflected in the shards, casting little rainbows over the walls, and I tipped my head back, inspecting the ceiling in the light again.

Wires were torn, the electric winch that was used to lower it for maintenance and cleaning severed. I walked over to the wall by the door and turned the dial, the lights in the sconces along the golden walls illuminating.

I tipped my eyes up again, checking out the suspension gear which seemed to still be intact, thankfully. This light fixture had been on its way down for cleaning or repair when it collapsed.

All it needed was to be raised again.

But, of course, the winch rope was ruined.

I would've heard this crash in the house. It must've happened before I came. Maybe long before I came. This door had always been closed, so perhaps the cleaning crew never got around to dealing with it.

Leaving the room, I found the breaker panels in the basement and turned off the electricity flowing to that room before grabbing some rope nearby that they'd used to tie up their deer, and then the ladder from the greenhouse, hurrying back to the ballroom. I didn't want to be stopped, and the great thing about this big place was that it was easy not to run into people if you didn't want to.

Since the winch rope was busted, and there was no way to replace that here, I checked the connections on the chandelier to make sure nothing was pried or loose before I set up the ladder, using the hand-powered drilling tool I'd found in the shed to drill a hole into the wall near the fireplace.

Placing in the bit, I wound the crank, digging into the plaster, which normally would only take seconds with a drill, but I didn't have a drill here, so it was like 1898 and churning butter for three hours so you could have biscuits for dinner.

I grunted, my muscles burning. This was for the birds.

I growled, releasing the drill and slipping the eye screw in, winding it.

I twisted and twisted, using every bit of strength I had to get it as tight as I could before climbing farther up the ladder—the full thirty-two feet—and straddling the top of it, doing the same on the ceiling, near the original output for the light.

The ladder teetered under me, and my heart skipped a beat, but I worked fast, screwing in the eye and then grabbing it and pulling, testing my weight.

It was still no indication that it would hold the chandelier, but at least it held something. I was never content to just carry the blueprints. I liked helping in the construction.

And I loved to work alone. I thought that was why I favored the small projects at the firm. The more personal renovations.

Descending the ladder, I secured the rope to the chandelier, carried the rope back up the ladder, and threaded it through the eye hook on the ceiling, and then came back down, moving the ladder to the wall and slipping the rope through the other eye again.

I stepped back down to the floor, wrapped the rope around my hand, and dug in my heels, pulling strong but slow. The shards jostled and sang as they tapped against each other, but the chandelier didn't even leave the floor.

Shit. I almost laughed at the muscles I thought I had when I thought I could do this.

It had to be a quarter of a ton. Breathing hard, I tried again, using my weight to pull and pull, but there was no way. Even if I got this off the floor, I couldn't hold it.

"No, I'm coming!" I heard Rory growl.

I jumped. "Rory!" I called, dropping the rope and standing up straight. "Rory, can you come here?"

The next thing I knew, he was standing in front of the door, shirtless and sleepy-eyed like he'd just woken up.

Planting his arms on both sides of the doorway, he cocked an eyebrow but didn't ask me what I was doing. Pretty sure he never gave a shit.

"Can you help me?" I asked, pointing to the chandelier. "It's too heavy for me to—"

I heard him laugh, and then I looked back to see him gone, not even letting me finish my sentence.

Dick!

If he and Micah helped, it would take ten seconds. Did he have somewhere else to be today?

I twisted my lips to the side and studied the chandelier, trying to figure it out. There was always a way to solve the problem.

There was always a way to accomplish something I needed to accomplish.

Or . . . I smiled to myself, a lightbulb popping on. *A way to get someone else to do something I needed done.*

I wondered . . .

Dropping my tool belt, I left the ballroom and headed to the kitchen, immediately pulling out the butter, eggs, sugar, and all the other ingredients I had memorized from when Grand-Mère had me do the baking after she got too weak. She loved the smell in the house and wanted it to be part of my memories, so that when I inhaled the scent of sugar cookies or banana bread, I'd remember the happy times with her and my mom.

After preheating the oven, I dug out a couple of pans, a bowl, and began mixing the ingredients, stirring them into glossy, chocolate heaven, the smell reminding me of most of Octobers after a morning at the farmer's market, while my dad raked the leaves outside.

I placed both pans in the oven, took an apple out of the bowl on the counter, and ate it, waiting.

The kitchen warmed, filling with the rich smell, and I could feel the hairs on my arms rising as my stomach growled.

"What the hell is that?" I heard Micah finally say down the hall.

I beamed inside but bit back my smile, hurriedly spinning around with my oven mitt as the timer went off. I pulled one of the pans out of the oven.

Setting it on the cooling rack, I stuck a knife in the middle and pulled it out, making sure it was cooked all the way through.

Micah entered, followed by Alex and Rory, and Micah's gaze locked on the pan, climbing up on the counter like a cat and sexy crawling right for the sweets. He inhaled deep, closing his eyes. "Is that . . . ?"

"Brownies?" Alex finished for him, gawking at me.

"You're making brownies?" Rory asked.

I shrugged, pulling out a fork and handing it to Micah, but he just loomed over the pan and dug in with his fingers, hissing at the hot confection before gobbling it.

Rory's mouth fell open, and I knew he didn't want to want it, but he did. He plucked the fork out of my hand and dug in, both of them hogging down the brownies with no manners and zero control.

I mean, geez. It wasn't like they couldn't make them at any time. The ingredients were all here.

Quickly, I cut out a piece before they ate it all and slid it onto a plate just as Aydin, Will, and Taylor strolled in, the scent drawing their attention.

I handed the plate to Aydin, feeling Will's eyes on me as he hung back by the door.

Aydin held my gaze, pleased, and he tried to take the plate, but I pulled it away, playing a little.

He laughed and grabbed it, immediately digging in.

I shot Will a look and turned around, shutting off the oven and reaching inside again.

"You should've put walnuts in them," Rory said.

I turned around, showing him the second pan, the surface dotted with fucking walnuts.

Micah stopped eating, staring at the other pan with chocolate covering his mouth and teeth.

He reached for it, but I pulled it away. "I need help with the chandelier first."

Rory hooded his eyes, but I could see the smile there, because he knew exactly what I was doing, and I won.

If he wanted brownies with walnuts, then . . .

He sighed. "Micah? Taylor? Help me out, please?"

Their shoulders slumped, but they went, leaving the room with Rory and heading back to the ballroom.

I cut two slices out of the new pan.

"Wendy and the Lost Boys," Aydin mused.

"And that makes you Peter Pan?" I asked.

He chuckled as I handed one slice to Alex and pushed the other plate over to Will.

But Will shot out, slapping the plate and the pan, sending them both flying onto the floor.

Every muscle in my body went rigid as they crashed and broke, the dessert splattered on the floor.

I darted my eyes to his.

"This isn't Neverland," he said, coming up to the island and glowering at me. "If it were, you wouldn't be here. Grown-ups aren't allowed."

My stomach sank a little, but I didn't blink, even though my eyes screamed to.

Spinning around, he charged out, and Alex hesitated a moment, throwing me an apologetic glance before finally going after him.

Aydin watched me, but I didn't give him a chance to insert himself. Turning around, I dug the bowl back out of the sink and began mixing ingredients again, keeping my hands busy, because that was the only distraction I had.

I got it. *You don't fit, so stop posing.*

No surprise here. It didn't bother me.

It felt like Aydin wanted to say something, but it was time to put his lesson to the test. Nothing happened to me. I happened to everyone else. Et cetera, et cetera . . .

After he left, I put the brownies with walnuts in the oven, cleaned the dishes, and made myself a sandwich that I didn't eat, because Micah and Rory walked back in, and I didn't want to be around anyone.

"Brownies are on a timer," I told them. "Take them out and turn off the oven when it's done."

They probably wondered why I'd had to make a second batch, but I was gone before they had a chance to ask.

Just put it out of your mind.

Him wanting me with him last night wasn't about us. I'd let myself enjoy it and let it mean more than it did when he swept me into his arms.

I never fit with him. I always knew it, because Thunder Bay was Neverland and the Horsemen were his tribe, and I hated to play. I didn't do *fun*.

And leaving town hadn't cured me of that.

I drifted into the ballroom, seeing the chandelier hanging high above, its lights illuminated and casting a soft glow over the floor. They'd cleaned up the glass, turned on the breaker again, and I kicked off my shoes, turning around in the big, open space with my head tipped back.

That was why I loved building and designing things. Making someone's world theirs. It was a chance to fly, and all I needed was a dumb, happy thought.

And I'd had one. Just one that I hung on to all this time.

Spotting a record player near the fireplace, I walked over and dug inside the chest underneath it, seeing a few dozen records stacked together.

There was everything from Mozart to Benny Goodman to the Eagles, but nothing from this century. It had probably been that long since this place had been inhabited by a family.

I picked one out and slipped it onto the turntable, deciding to embrace everything I hated, including this dumbass song. The stylus hit the record as it spun, and "If You Wanna Be Happy" by Jimmy Soul started playing, and I immediately smiled, remembering my mom and dad dancing to this in the kitchen when I was about seven or eight.

My body moved, and I bobbed my shoulders, hopping around as I sang along. I spun around the room, the music filling the air around me, and for a few precious moments, the guilt and everything faded away.

Fuck him for thinking I was supposed to have everything figured out at sixteen. Fuck him for demanding of me what I couldn't even give myself. He and Aydin and Martin were all dictators, and I never heard my own voice.

Ever.

And it was my fault. I should've said it louder. I should've screamed. I hated that I had to, but it was my fault I fell quiet.

I wasn't a grown-up. He was wrong. I never grew. I was always this pile of dead leaves, blowing in the wind and letting the seasons, whoever they were, come in and change me and walk on me, and I never fought for anything.

I spun and spun, the tears streaming down my face until someone swept me into his arms, and I opened my eyes to see Micah spinning me around as I wrapped my legs around his waist.

He planted his forehead to mine, smiling gently as I started laughing, the saxophone vibrating throughout the room.

"If you wanna be happy for the rest of your life," we sang, "never make a pretty woman your wife . . ."

And he spun and spun, and I started laughing so hard as I hugged him to me, catching sight of everyone else by the door watching us.

They must've heard the music, too.

God, I didn't care. I punched my fist in the air, both of us shouting the lyrics like complete idiots. No one was going to tell me how to feel. Not anymore.

No one could make me feel anything I didn't allow. I was in control.

And I was ready for an adventure.

CHAPTER 28

EMORY

Nine Years Ago

My brother stopped in front of the school, pulling off to the curb and putting the car in park.

I hadn't slept a wink last night, and while there was a cloud fogging my brain, so nothing was really clear yet, I didn't feel tired.

More like my head was floating six feet above my body, detached and delayed.

"You look really pretty today," Martin said.

I tried to smile. "Thanks."

My skirt and shirt were ironed, my hair was combed and fixed with a headband, my tie tightened, and for once, I wore the expensive navy blue blazer he bought me last year that still fit.

"I hope I find you at home when I get off work."

I nodded. "I'm sorry about everything," I said in a low voice.

I felt his eyes on me, but he remained silent for a while.

Then, his soft voice filled the car. "We have to get along, Emmy. I'm all you have." Then he ruffled my hair, laughing. "I mean, I'm nice, right? I buy you stuff and let you have freedom. I got you into this school because I want you to have the best. I try, right?"

I nodded again.

"I'll make some of that homemade caramel corn you like tonight, too," I said.

He groaned, smiling. "Sounds like a plan."

I climbed out of the car, taking my bag with me and waving goodbye before heading through the parking lot.

It wasn't often we patched things up with so little effort, but after I got home last night, I didn't even try to sleep. I showered again, washing my hair and scrubbing and shaving like a new me would be some kind of armor.

I cleaned my room, fixed up the kitchen again, and made cinnamon rolls, letting them bake as I sat at the table and completed all my homework, even the study guide for *The Grapes of Wrath* that wasn't due for another week.

I packed up my schoolbag, dressed, and even put on some mascara before Martin arrived home to find life perfect again.

I wasn't getting out of this situation. And I couldn't kill him.

I had to survive, and just like last night when I told Damon that there was a tear in the membrane, I realized as the hours passed that it wasn't going away.

Something had disconnected, and every memory of his hand across my face or his fist in my stomach over the years was like a dream happening to someone else.

I wasn't there.

I wasn't here now.

I didn't have the energy to care about anything.

The morning classes came and went, and I wasn't even sure if Will was in my first period, because the lecture seemed to end before I realized it had started.

I stared at my desk, the wrestling room playing in my head and something swelling in my heart but ripping it to shreds at the same time.

I was glad he had his friends. They loved him, and Will deserved to never be alone.

But I also hated the idea of anyone else but me making him happy.

Making Will happy was an amazing feeling.

I wished I could be the girl I was at the Cove every day, but it was gone. The weight had crushed that spark, and I couldn't muster the energy to even try anymore.

"God, I'm not ready for basketball season to start," Elle said, setting her lunch tray down next to me in line. "There are, like, two weeks where it overlaps with football, and we'll be swamped."

"Not me," I muttered, moving down the line. "I quit band this morning."

"What?"

I took some chicken tenders and ranch, not bothering to look at her.

"My grandmother is sick," I explained quietly. "Or sicker, I mean. I'm needed at home now."

I didn't even bother to talk to the director in person. I emailed her, pretty confident my brother would agree that concentrating on my studies and my architectural projects would be a better use of my time.

The less I was at school—or games or on buses—the better.

"I'm going to go sit with Gabrielle today," she said suddenly. "We have to talk about a . . . a project."

She took her tray and walked past me, toward the cashier, and I didn't look up or respond.

The one friend I might've had . . .

I didn't care.

I paid, walked to an empty section of a table in the corner of the room, and sat down, slipping in my earbuds and turning on some music from the iPod hidden in my pocket.

I raised my eyes for a split second, immediately locking gazes with Damon. He sat twenty yards away at a circular table filled with his friends. Chaos went on around him, but he remained still and calm like the eye of the storm, the tears and rage from last night almost like they had never happened.

I'd been waiting for the guilt to start eating me up, but it didn't. The worry sat there, but there was absolutely nothing I could do about it now, and I wasn't sure I would've done anything differently if I could go back to last night. He had as much to lose, and he was sloppy. There was probably evidence of him all over her.

Somehow, I felt more in control not caring than I ever did.

Dropping my eyes, I opened my milk and my ranch, starting to eat as "Army of Me" played in my ears, but then the air around me started vibrating, and I heard a different beat in my ears.

Pulling out the earbuds, I looked up and saw Will on top of his lunch table.

His friends sat or stood, looking up at him and laughing as he started dancing to some pop eighties or nineties tune, stripping off his school jacket as his shirt and tie hung on him like a god.

He was going to look amazing in a suit someday.

He jumped off the table, moving around the room as students hooted and howled, and he looked like . . .

I laughed under my breath, a smile spreading across my face.

He looked like Jean-Claude Van Damme in *Kickboxer*.

Hang around more and maybe you'll find out.

The smile slowly fell, but I couldn't take my eyes off him. This was for me.

Needles pricked my throat, watching him dance and loving the smile on his face.

I flashed my gaze to Damon again, seeing that he wasn't looking at me anymore. His head was turned and his eyes fixated on another table. I followed his gaze, seeing Winter Ashby and Erika Fane sitting and eating, surrounded by other kids.

What was he doing with her last night on that motorcycle? We might've bonded in ways most people never did, but I wasn't an idiot, either. Damon screwed, abused, used, and there was no one and nothing on which he didn't prey. I didn't know what his interest in her was, but I was pretty sure it would hurt her.

"Get down!" someone shouted.

I looked away from Winter and over to Will, seeing Kincaid bark at him as he stood on the table. The music over the loudspeakers died, and everyone laughed as he smiled and jumped down from another table.

The cloud that had been sitting in my head the last twelve hours started to fade a little, and for a moment, I missed him.

Wouldn't he love it if I made the grand gesture next? Snuck into his room tonight? Hung out at the pool every afternoon, waiting for him to show up?

Called him?

Erika Fane led Winter Ashby out of the lunchroom, both of them dumping their trays before they exited and Damon watching them. I tore my eyes away from Will, putting my earbuds back in and trying to eat.

I barely heard the music as I nibbled on my food, ignoring the eyes I felt on me and the sounds of laughter coming from his table.

The room started to clear, students getting ready to move on to their next class, but just then, the fire alarm screeched in my ears and commotion filled the lunchroom.

I pulled out my earbuds, the blaring cry and flashing lights from the alarms on the wall deafening. I winced, rising from my seat.

"Single file, everyone!" a teacher called, and I looked around, seeing Will and some friends already heading out the door.

What the hell? A fire?

He looked back at me, meeting my eyes as he walked, but I looked away and headed around the table.

Leaving my tray, I hurried to the line, a teacher leading us out while more trailed behind to make sure we had everyone. The hall crowded with students, everyone trying to get out of the building as teachers shouted for us to be calm and quiet.

"Do not run!" one told us.

While another said, "Get back here. You're not going to the bathroom."

We filed outside, students drifting to the far edge of the parking lot and waiting as the siren inside continued to pierce the air over and over again.

I looked around, seeing Will sit on the bricks lining the tree and flower bed, his elbows resting on his knees as he stared up at me.

Victoria Radcliffe and Maisie Vos sat at each side, Tori draping an arm over his shoulder, showing off her hundred-dollar cuticles as she chatted to someone else.

Will just sat there, and I shifted on my feet, turning my back on him as I crossed my arms over my chest.

"Where's Damon Torrance?" I heard someone ask.

I popped my head up, seeing the dean walk through the crowd.

"He was just in the cafeteria. Anyone see where he went?"

I scanned the crowd, looking for two heads of blond hair and finally spotting Erika, alone and frantically talking to a teacher.

"Winter Ashby's missing, too," I called out.

Kincaid looked over at me, then surveyed the crowd. Pursing his lips, he charged back toward the school.

"Why ruin the good time she's no doubt having, Emory?"

I looked over my shoulder, seeing Maisie wearing a smirk.

Everyone in their little group was staring at me.

"She's fourteen," I said.

I mean, duh.

But she just snickered. "Why don't you just go away?"

My gaze dropped to Will, heat spreading all over my body. He just sat there and stared at me, a self-satisfied smile in his eyes that he didn't let out. He didn't blink once.

Their disdain felt like a kick, and in more than two years at this school, I'd never felt so far on the outside, because while I didn't care how I looked in their eyes, I cared how I looked in his.

Twisting back around, I walked away, the cloud in my head thickening again until the pain of wanting him turned into an addiction to the pain of rejecting him.

It grew and fed me every day from that point on.

Destroying myself and everything I loved and wanted for myself became the only thing I had any control over.

I could ignore him in class. Pass him in the halls without a look. Act like he didn't exist.

Pretend I was above it all and they were nothing.

I did it all.

Time passed, seasons changed, he left for college, and a year later, so did I.

What I didn't know then was that the damage we would do to each other was only just beginning.

CHAPTER 29

WILL

Present

Micah dropped her to her feet, took her hands, and twirled her around before pulling her in and holding her close. They danced and laughed, and my chest swelled, feeling too much all of a sudden, my arms weighing a ton.

I couldn't help but smile to myself as I watched her. We all heard the music, one by one, each of us making our way down to the ballroom.

Micah couldn't resist, instantly gravitating toward her, and it wasn't until he had her in his arms that I saw the tears on her face.

She was quickly smiling, though, and it was heart-wrenching because I knew I'd made her cry. No matter how many times I told myself she deserved to suffer, this wasn't in my nature.

I'd be lost without some second chances myself. There were always two sides to a story, and everything was just a matter of perspective.

But finding out that she was the one who sent us to prison was almost a relief. It finally gave me permission to hate her and not just resent her because she had rejected me.

Micah swung her out, and she twirled, stepping on her tiptoes, and the both of them danced the Mashed Potato or some equally dumb dance, and I smiled even wider. For a few moments, we weren't in Blackchurch. We were friends, hanging out and having a good time.

Suddenly, I missed home a lot.

"Go to her," Alex urged me.

Taylor, Aydin, and Rory hung back, amusement written on their faces, and part of me wanted to go, too. It was like a whole other world to see her like this.

But years of disappointment and doubt kept me rooted in my spot.

"Ow, ow!" Emmy suddenly yelped.

I shot my gaze up, seeing her stumble before Micah rushed in and pulled her up to him, keeping her steady.

She hissed, lifting her leg off the floor, and I saw blood stream down the bottom of her foot.

I took a step, but then Aydin stormed in, heading to the middle of the dance floor, and I stopped, watching him.

"Ow," she grunted, but then chuckled, looking around the floor. "Shit, the glass."

Aydin glared at Micah. "I thought you said you cleaned it up."

"I did clean it up," he rushed to explain.

Aydin swept Emmy into his arms, a couple of drops dripping off her heel, and my blood boiled so hot I felt nauseated, seeing her in his arms.

Goddammit. If my head would just settle on one emotion where she was concerned, that would be fucking fantastic. *I hate her, but she's mine. Go away, but don't go with him!*

He carried her past us, and we followed as I zoned in on her hands locked around his neck. He took her up the stairs, to his room, setting her on the bed as we all lingered by the door.

He could've taken her to the kitchen. He had a first aid kit there, too.

She lifted her foot up, setting it on her knee, probably trying to keep the blood off the carpet, but he knelt down in front of her and took it, holding a cloth to the bottom.

"It's okay," she said, trying to pull her leg away and hold the cloth herself.

He wouldn't let it go.

Lifting it up, he inspected the damage, and I got angrier by the second. She'd stepped on a shard. She was an architect. *She's had her share of splinters, asshole.*

Aydin looked up, jerking his chin at the guys. "There's a bottle in the pantry," he told them. "Go have fun."

"Fuck, yeah," Taylor said, sliding back out of the room.

Rory slapped Micah's stomach. "Pool party."

He breathed out a laugh, and they all left, heading back down the stairs and leaving Alex and me with Aydin and Emory.

I looked after the guys as they disappeared down the stairs, a sinking feeling in my gut. They were going to be drunk in an hour.

Aydin wanted them drunk.

I stepped closer, watching her and him, bracing myself for the fact that I wasn't going to be able to stop myself.

"I want a bottle," she joked to Aydin.

He looked up at her, a smile playing on his lips. Without taking his eyes off of her, he reached over into the cabinet on the bedside table and pulled out another container and a glass, setting them both next to the lamp.

She grinned as he opened the bourbon and poured her two fingers.

"Here you go." He handed it to her.

I could smell the amber liquid from here, my tongue suddenly ash in my mouth as he returned his attention to her foot.

Alex remained near the door, and I just wanted to pull Em out of the room and get the girls away, but I had plans for Aydin, and I wasn't ready to escalate it right now.

Even though it looked like that decision was getting more and more out of my control.

Emmy cupped the glass in her lap, staring down at it. "My brother got so drunk on this stuff once," she said. "I remember how it tasted like it was yesterday."

Aydin tore open an antibacterial wipe with his teeth, his eyes darting to hers before cleaning the blood off her foot.

"I could never figure out why he hated me so much," she continued. "Like, where did the anger come from, you know? We had good parents. They didn't abuse us. He wasn't bullied." She trailed off, staring at the glass. "But he was always like that. As early as I can remember, everything had to be perfect. My hair. What I wore." She started breathing heavier as the memories played behind her eyes. "Something was always out of place, and it never pleased him. Everything I did was wrong."

She fell silent, and I forgot the others in the room, remembering her dirty, untidy cuffs, and the hair always in her face.

"So I stopped talking," she nearly whispered. "The outbursts got worse, and then the shouting started. Waking me up in the middle of the night, because I forgot to unload the dishwasher, or there were streaks on the bathroom mirror." The look in her eyes grew distant, like she wasn't here anymore. "I peed my pants one night at dinner," she said. "I was fifteen."

I frowned, imagining going home to that every day after school.

"I realized he was sick, and nothing was going to be good enough," she told us as Aydin bandaged her foot, "so I stopped trying. My clothes would be wrinkled and my hair not brushed, because if he was going to hit me anyway, then . . ." She met Aydin's gaze. "Then fuck him."

I watched him watch her, the space between them disappearing as he held her leg, but neither of them moved.

"I hardly ever saw him drunk," she told us, "but one night, he passed out with a quarter of this bottle left. I emptied it into a water bottle and took it to school."

She chuckled, but a look of sadness crossed her eyes, remembering that day. When was it? Did I talk to her that day? Mess with her? Was I nice?

"He thought he drank it all. He never knew." She paused before continuing. "It was just one time, but that was a good day. I didn't feel a thing. Not even the cracked rib."

I knit my brow, thinking about Emory Scott sucking down bourbon in math class or stumbling through the cafeteria, and how easy it must've been to hide it, because no one ever noticed her.

She'd needed that bourbon more than she needed air that day, and I got that.

God, I got that.

You smile and laugh, not just because your head and everything in it feels lighter, but because when you're drunk or high, it's like a vacation. When you're away from the same people, the same places, the same work . . . you don't think about it. It's a break from everything that worries you or makes you anxious or keeps your world small and shallow, and everyone who wants to take a piece out of you, and when you're high, it's like that. It just doesn't even matter. Suddenly, you're seeing Machu Picchu from your front porch, and you didn't even have to leave town.

She got drunk and loved her brother again.

What made her stronger than me was that she only did it once.

She closed her eyes as she lifted the glass to her lips, and I could tell by the longing on her face that she was escaping again. I charged over and grabbed the glass, the liquid sloshing onto my hand as I tossed it to the side.

It crashed against the wall, the glass shattering.

Don't. I stared down at her.

I'd rather eat my hands than see her do that to herself. If this was

who she was, I'd rather this than see her become what I became—
someone who needed to hurt myself day after day in order to fucking smile.

"Clean it up," Aydin ordered.

But I remained still. I didn't know what the hell I wanted to do
with her yet, but this—whatever this was going on between them—
was not happening. She didn't get to find herself with Aydin Khadir.
She was coming with me.

"He didn't save you then," Aydin told her. "He won't save
you now."

He watched her, and she watched me, and even though I knew
she'd told me the truth last night in her bed when she said she loved
me, I also knew Emmy was an oak. Her roots were firm, and love
would not save the day.

"Am I going to save you?" Aydin asked her.

"No one needs to save me." She kept her gaze on me. "I got it
handled."

"You do." He finished, setting her foot back down on the floor,
and then stood up, cleaning off his hands. "I can almost see it, can't
you?" he asked her as he gazed between Alex and me. "Them together? How good they look together? Him driving into her like he's
done a thousand times and looking down into her eyes as he does it?"

I tensed.

"All the times he was alone with her, inside of her, coming and
forgetting about you," he told Emmy. "You can see it, right?"

You son of a bitch.

"But we don't care," he went on. "Do we? We don't care that he'll
fall back into her bed at the first sign of trouble."

I flexed my jaw, the scent from the antibacterial wipes stinging
my nostrils. My brain was fried. I didn't know how to get what I
wanted anymore without resorting to just taking it.

"Go ahead," Aydin told me, his eyes flashing to Alex behind me.
"Take her. I want to see how it was with you two. All the things she

let you do to her, because that's how easily she forgets and moves on."
Then he gestured to Em. "We'll watch."

But before I could act, he grabbed me and shoved me onto the bed.
I fell, Emmy whimpering and jumping off the mattress as Aydin came
down on me and dug a knee into my gut. I growled as he gripped my
neck with one hand and backhanded me with the other.

I squeezed my eyes shut, the pain shooting through my jaw and
up the side of my face, but after a moment, I slowly turned my head
back to face him, ready for more.

Come on.

His eyes pierced, and he leaned down, his breath warming my
lips. "Mine," he breathed out. "All of you are mine. You're not leaving. They're not leaving. And when your little shits arrive, I'm going
to hang them in the cellar by their ankles like dead deer."

He hauled me up off the bed, and I stumbled back before he came
in and punched me in the stomach, sending me hunched over.

"Will . . ." Alex stepped forward.

But I shot out my hand. "Stay back," I told her. "Stay back."

It took a few seconds, but I rose again and faced him, taking his
shit but not taking it lying down. *I can be a team player, but I'm strong.*

He walked up to me, slamming another uppercut into my stomach. Bile rose up my throat. I hunched over again, out of breath and
my head spinning.

"You don't have what it takes to be me," he gritted out, standing
over me.

"Will," I heard Emmy call.

And then Alex. "What the hell are you doing?" she growled at
me. "Do something!"

"He can't," Aydin told her. "Because he can't lead. This is all he is.
Don't you see it?"

I rose up to see him glaring at her.

"Don't you?" he yelled at Alex again.

Aydin punched and kicked, and my eyes watered as fire tore

through my body. He knocked me down and then fisted my throat as we rolled around on the floor. I wouldn't fight back. Not yet.

Not yet.

But I wouldn't cower, either. It was the only way. Men like him needed to feel power, but he wouldn't respect me if I begged like Micah.

He needed me.

He wouldn't be able to tie his shoes without me someday.

Blood dripped out of my nose, and my ribs hurt. I barely registered the girls on us, trying to pry us off each other, but we rolled, forcing them back. Locking my elbows, I gripped his jaw and pushed him away from me. Sweat broke out across my forehead, and he breathed hard, the scratch I accidentally left on his cheekbone red and jagged.

"Entertain me," he said. "Let me watch, and let your girl watch, so she knows exactly how hard you missed her during your time apart."

"I did miss her," I whispered up at him, so only he heard. "Several times a day, in an array of fascinating places."

His eyes flared, and he growled. "Fuck you!"

I broke out into a laugh, even through the pain, because he was coming undone.

That was it. For some reason, he was jealous, and I didn't know why, but that was it. Did he want me or something? Maybe Alex?

"Come on!" I bellowed. "Hit me again!"

Break. Fucking break, because it is time.

He pulled back his fist, and I braced myself, but then something swung down behind him, slamming against the back of his neck.

He jerked, his eyes etched with pain, and then he fell over. I looked up at Alex standing there with a lamp in her fists.

He rolled over, hissing through his teeth as he locked eyes with her. "You better be ready to finish what you—"

She swung out the lamp, headbutting him, and he fell back, blood pouring down his mouth. He held his face.

"Alex . . ." I gasped.

Shit.

But the next thing I knew, the lamp hit my nose, too, a searing pain shooting through my head. I dropped back to the floor next to Aydin as the girls went to work.

My eyes watered, and I couldn't even open them, but I felt one of them pull off my belt, and I barely realized what was happening as I was dragged to the wall, catching glimpses of the girls struggling to move us.

By the time I came to and was able to open my eyes, my arms were secured, and I couldn't move.

I looked up, seeing my right wrist tied to the treadmill with one of Aydin's neckties, and my other wrist bound to his wrist with my belt. I looked over at him, seeing his left hand was also tied with his belt to the hook holding back the drapes.

I belted out a growl, yanking my arms and grunting as I glared at the girls.

"What are you doing?" I yelled. "What the fuck!"

They walked about the room, doing things and ignoring us, and I stared at Em, who wouldn't even look at me. I wasn't the one out of control here.

"Hey!" Micah said. Rory, Taylor, and him all rushing to the doorway. "What the hell's going on?"

But Emmy charged over and kicked the door shut, propping a chair underneath it.

"This is bullshit!" I shouted.

But Aydin just laughed, shaking his head. He wasn't threatened by them.

Emmy poured herself another glass of bourbon and then pulled off her T-shirt, leaving herself in Rory's cutoffs and a bra.

She tried to look over her shoulder, and I could see a red spot forming on her back. Did she get hurt in that tussle? I remembered them on us briefly, but I didn't know she'd fallen.

She took a sip of the drink as Alex inspected the damage.

"I'm okay," Em assured her.

But Alex spun around, fire in her eyes as she glared at us like she wanted to kill us. "None of this is okay!"

She wiped the sweat off her face and walked into the bathroom, turning on the faucet while Emory downed the alcohol and poured herself another shot. She stood there quietly, and I continued to yank and pull on the six-hundred-pound treadmill like I'd actually be able to free myself. What the hell was the plan here? What were they going to do? Take control? Enlist the others?

Emory looked over at us—or me—through her glasses and hesitated a moment before bringing her glass over and sitting down on the carpet in front of us, just far enough away that we couldn't reach her.

I held her eyes.

"The time you drove me home from the away game," she said, "and we stopped at the Cove, I had a thought that night."

All she did was think that night. She overthought everything.

"Part of me resisted you because I didn't want to bring you into my horrible life," she told me. "I was embarrassed and full of anger and without hope. I couldn't give you anything."

I tipped my chin up, remaining silent.

"But a part of me also resisted you because I feared I'd just be trading one abuse for another," she explained. "How you coerced me, pushed me, wouldn't leave me alone when I told you to . . . Tried to scare me."

My gaze twitched as I studied her. I wasn't abusive. I was a little spoiled and cocky, but I never wanted to hurt her.

She dropped her eyes, taking a sip. "The thought left me as quickly as it came," she added, "because I wanted you, and deep down I held so tightly to the hope of you. I needed that." She raised her gaze again. "But now, I wonder if I was right. Here I am, covered in bruises again. Maybe your world is just as bad as mine."

I shook my head, but any protest I wanted to offer back died in my throat.

"What do you want from me?" she asked, as if Aydin and Alex weren't in the room. And then firmer, "Huh? What do you want?"

Alex dropped down behind her, peering over her shoulder as both women sat there, challenging us.

"Who put me here?" Emmy asked. "Who thought I should be here with you? Damon, maybe? Michael?"

"Maybe it's someone who hates you?" I shot back. "Your brother?" She hesitated. "Why now?"

I grunted as I pushed myself up, using my shoulder to wipe off the blood dripping over my upper lip. "I think you know why."

A look passed between us because she knew what I was talking about. She was his loose end. The only other person who knew what they had orchestrated to send my friends and me to prison all those years ago.

"This place costs money," she argued.

"His new wife has a lot of that," Alex pointed out.

She does? I'd never met her.

But Emmy countered. "He'd save the money and kill me if he actually thought I was a threat."

"Would he?" I retorted. "In his head, I'm sure he thinks he loves you. Like Humbert Humbert." And then I shrugged. "Perhaps he wants to teach you a lesson. Make you suffer."

To my surprise, amusement crossed her eyes. "Because he loves me so much, right?"

Typical abuser. He never hated her, just like Damon's mom never hated him, and none of us ever hated Rika when we were stealing her inheritance, kidnapping her family, and burning down her house. The diseased mind only sees its own intentions, and everything they did and everything we did justified the end.

The path to who we want to be is winding, at best. Everything was justified because we were all the victims in our story.

"There's no one we make suffer more than those we love," Aydin chimed in.

His arm sat on mine, our fists grinding against each other as we tried to squirm our way free, but I gazed at Emmy and the valley between the olive skin of her breasts and her toned stomach, and I could almost feel her in my hands.

She was so close. *Do you still want to hold me?* I blinked long and hard, trying to push away the swelling in my groin.

"Do you want to know what I did to get in here?" Aydin asked her. "The awful shit I pulled?"

She watched him, and despite the cool air, a light layer of sweat coated my neck and chest.

"I refused . . . to get married," he answered. "That's it."

Alex's eyes fell, and she looked like she wanted to be anywhere else.

"And I can get out anytime I want," Aydin continued. "As soon as I agree."

I didn't actually know that, but it changed nothing. I knew of Aydin before I came here. He was in Meridian City frequently, and we were often at the same clubs and parties, although we never met.

"Did you think I killed someone?" he teased Emory. "Fucked my sister, maybe?"

Maybe, out of all of us, he was sent here for the least, but he was capable of the most, because he knew people almost immediately upon meeting them. It had happened with Rory, Micah, and Taylor. Even I had been here so much longer than necessary, because he proved too difficult to maneuver.

"My future wife is beautiful, smart, she comes from the right family," he said. "The handpicked, perfect spouse and mother to build my life around. And I was completely on board . . . until one night."

"The artist . . ." Emmy said.

I shot my eyes up, looking between them and seeing him nod. Artist? How did she know anything about it?

"What did she do?" Em asked.

He stared at the women, and I followed his gaze, both Emmy and Alex looking so beautiful that I swore I felt myself back in my old room in my parents' house, nestled in my damn bed as the morning light heated the sheets.

"That," he answered.

Alex's chin rested on Emmy's shoulder, and she slid her fingers around her naked waist, caressing her.

"This?" Alex taunted.

Aydin and Alex stared at each other, unblinking, as the pulse in my neck throbbed faster.

"I just watched her through the computer screen," he said, as if in a trance, "and it was like my skin had been sliced open, releasing all this pressure I'd gotten so used to feeling my entire life." His chest rose and fell more rapidly by the second. "And I could finally breathe and see color and shit. I felt hot, and the world suddenly looked so different, because . . ."

He swallowed as Alex splayed her hand across Emmy's stomach, touching her softly and gently. Em sat frozen, but after a moment, she relaxed into Alex, inviting her in.

"Because no blade cuts as deep as something that beautiful," he whispered.

Cuts . . . I dropped my eyes to the tattoo I'd done on his shoulder. Claw marks dug into his skin forever.

"She had these eyes." He stared at Alex, scared and desperate. Like the memory hurt. "I swore I could reach through the screen and touch her, the way she looked at me and made everything else disappear. I didn't care what I lost, what I risked," he told her, "I had to have her."

I gazed at Emmy, remembering how stubborn I thought she was, but really she just made sense, and I resented her for it. We were a part of two different worlds, my friends would be difficult with her, and I was outgoing and loved to be around people, and she preferred to be alone. We were so different.

But those moments, like when I had her in my arms in the theater, confirmed what I already knew.

It would be worth it.

"But when I finally worked up the courage to claim her, she had survived without me," Aydin explained. "It hurt. I'd been tearing myself apart in my head, going crazy, and she'd . . . she'd let everyone have a piece of something that was mine. I was a memory. I didn't matter."

"And she was a whore for it," Alex said.

He held Alex's eyes as she pulled one of the straps of Emmy's bra down her shoulder, and Emmy didn't stop her as her stomach rose and fell.

But Aydin answered, "No." He gazed at the girls as Emmy's other strap came down, and Alex's hands trailed over her body. "She puts one foot in front of the other, does what she has to do, and lives honestly. She's unashamed with her fucking chin up." His voice grew stronger. "She's loyal, everyone's mother with warm arms and a kind smile, a survivor, and she solves the problem without dwelling on the loss."

His eyes hardened, filled with pride.

"She's a fucking Viking," he said. "And I won't have anyone else."

My heart sank a moment as I looked at Em, because it was all true. Nothing else mattered. If it killed us, she was the one. In that moment, I didn't care about her sins, if anyone else had touched her besides me, or that we were both our own worst enemies.

That was my girl, scarred, tattered soul, and all. She was beautiful.

Alex stood up, her body rigid as she slowly backed up, and Aydin rose, too, his gaze locked on her.

Bringing his and my hands up to his mouth, he worked the belt loose with his teeth, and Alex breathed so hard I could hear it as she continued to retreat.

The belt loosened, and I pulled at it, finally freeing my left hand as both of us turned to our other arms and untied ourselves.

Aydin growled, unable to free himself, and Alex gasped as he ripped the hook out of the wall and charged for her. She scurried into the bathroom, and he grabbed her under the arms and lifted her into his.

"Touch me," he panted over her mouth.

She broke down, closing her eyes and sobbing. "Not now," she cried. "Not after everything. How could you do this now?"

He buried his mouth in her neck, holding her head to his body and squeezing her tight.

I looked at Emmy, her eyes rimmed with tears that hadn't fallen. She stood up and backed away from me, and I advanced, gazing at her naked shoulders and the straps lying lazily down her arms.

She ran, I caught her, and the next thing I knew we had all stumbled into the shower, a chaos of arms and legs as I twisted the knob. I turned on the water, drenching and trapping her as my mouth covered hers. I slipped my tongue between her lips, caressing her tongue, and the heat cascading right down to my groin as I pressed her into the wall and moved over her soft, full lips.

"Take it, Emory," Aydin told her next to us. "Let him touch you everywhere."

I stared down into her eyes, almost amused that he thought he still had any power over her. "Let him try to stop me," I challenged and then asked her, "You ready for this?"

"Unless you're telling me to fasten my seat belt," she fired back, "shut up, Will."

I grinned, ripping off her shorts, tearing her bra from her body, and twisting her around, pulling her panties down to her thighs.

She whimpered, and I reached around, cupping her throat as I took off her glasses, setting them on the soap dish, and breathed into her ear. "This isn't young love anymore," I told her, pressing her tits into the shower wall. "It's not a crush. This is a man who's long overdue in showing you what he can do."

And I slammed my mouth down on hers again and ripped open my jeans.

CHAPTER 30

WILL

Seven Years Ago

My mom shouted from downstairs, and I heard male voices as footfalls hit the stairs.

My door whipped opened, and I popped my head up, looking over my shoulder as I laid on my stomach on the bed.

I blinked several times, seeing Kai standing in my doorway in khaki cargo shorts and no shirt.

"You get in and you don't call us?" he snipped.

My head pounded, and I rolled over, groaning. College was bad for me. I'd never been so hungover.

Someone else pushed through the door, and then I heard Damon's voice. "Damn. I thought he'd at least have company."

They walked in, and I looked over at the clock, seeing it was 10:13 a.m.

"What the hell, Will?" Kai growled. "It's been months. You get into town, you let us know."

"It's been like ten weeks," I griped, reaching over for a cigarette on my nightstand. "We were all just in Miami for spring break. Jesus."

Kai came over and snatched the cigarette out of my mouth before

I could light it, and then walked into the bathroom, turning on the faucet.

I shot him a look. "And I just got in last night," I pointed out. "Late."

I hadn't had time to get in touch with anyone yet. They'd all been home a couple of weeks on summer break already, but I couldn't stomach the thought of returning until my mom called and laid on the guilt trip. Apparently everyone was lost without me, and if I didn't show up, so she wouldn't have to deal with Damon and Kai coming by every day, she'd cut off my credit card.

Of course, she was teasing. I was her good boy.

Although I'd barely made it through my first year at Princeton, and I wasn't looking forward to that conversation. I hated disappointing my parents. The letter from my advisor loomed on my nightstand, because I'd skipped too many classes and was failing a couple of gen ed classes.

It was painful, trying to care about that shit. I didn't want to be there, but I ended up staying in New Jersey even after the term had ended because Thunder Bay was a wasteland for me.

It had been almost two years this fall since I'd last touched her, and nothing was getting better. I rubbed my hands up and down my face, and then something landed on me, and I howled as Damon straddled me.

I scowled up at him, smelling this weird mixture of sunscreen and cigarettes on him.

"Going to the beach?" I asked.

"Again, yes," he said. "We were already there yesterday, but some of these chicks have aged up since the last time we saw them in bikinis." He swatted at me, yelling in my face. "It's harvest time!"

"Get the fuck off me." But I couldn't help laughing. It was good to see them.

Maybe I'd feel more human soon, being home.

He hopped off me, and Kai came back with a glass of water.

"Gotta spare toothbrush?" Damon asked, heading into the bathroom.

He didn't wait for an answer, though, before he started rummaging through the drawers under the sink.

Finding a package, he ripped it open and pulled out one of the new brushes my mom had put there. She was good about being prepared for anything.

I took the water and set it down on my nightstand as Damon wet the toothbrush and added toothpaste.

"Did you see prissy little Fane yesterday on the beach?" he asked Kai. "Girl has some swagger now. Tell me that's not going to be sweet."

Kai made a face. "God, you're a loser. What college guy comes home and continues to chase high school tail? Grow up."

"I saw you looking, too," Damon shot back, flipping him off.

They must've seen her at the beach yesterday.

"Besides, that tail is Michael's," Kai pointed out. "He just doesn't know it yet, so don't even think about pulling that shit while he's away."

I sat up, swinging my legs over the side of the bed and burying my aching head in my hands. I didn't want sun and sand today.

I didn't want to walk around this town, knowing she'd already left to start her college summer courses in California and had moved on with her life.

Kai stood over me and picked up the paper next to my lamp, reading it.

His eyes met mine and then he tossed it down, sifting through the other shit on my nightstand. Money and pills in a blank prescription bottle. A vial of coke.

His gaze sharpened, and his jaw flexed.

Opening the little drawer, I swiped everything off the table and pushed it inside, closing it.

"Get out," I told them, ignoring the judgment in his look. "I need to shower."

Damon rinsed and headed out the door, but Kai remained, the heat of his stare annoying me.

"One or both of you will be in jail by the end of the year if you don't get it together," he hissed. "I can't be Michael. I have enough on my plate. Get rid of this shit, or I will."

He left the room, slamming the door, and I flinched.

Was he actually surprised? My winning personality didn't happen on a dime.

Several hours later, Kai had gone to dinner with his parents and Damon and I were rolling up to the Cove to take in the view one last time. The sun hadn't set yet, but I was grimy and sticky from the beach—the only good thing coming out of our day there was that I had sweated out my hangover.

"This place is like a ghost town," Damon mumbled as we walked through the empty parking lot toward Cold Point. "They'll run through September, but the next time we come home, it'll be closed."

I gazed past the entrance and the ticket booths, spying the beams that held the pirate ship. I could still hear her laughing that night.

My heart ached. God, that dress. Her smile.

Emmy Scott happy was the most beautiful thing in the world.

"You're like a ghost, too," Damon said.

I turned away from the Cove, heading straight for the cliffs. "I'm fine," I told him.

I would be. Eventually.

"You're not," he retorted. "That fucking girl . . ."

"Enough."

"Fuck her."

"I said enough."

I shot him a glare, both of us climbing out to the point and up onto the rock, peering out at the gray sea, the lighthouse on Deadlow Island the only thing shining in the darkening horizon.

It was probably for the best that Adventure Cove was closing this fall. Things needed to die.

I looked down, inching to the edge and watching the water crash into the rocks.

"There's someone for you, too, you know?" I teased him, forcing a smile.

"I never said there wasn't." He blew smoke out of his mouth, flicking his cigarette off the cliff. "There's someone for me. I'll have her and my kids someday, but I'm not letting her fuck me up—or someone mess Michael and Kai up—the way Emory Scott messed up your head."

I sighed, thinking back on my last year in high school and all the times she walked past me as if I'd never been inside of her.

Pride is a motherfucker. I couldn't chase her anymore and still like myself, so I toughened up and gave as good as I got, ignoring her, too, and what do you know?

I still didn't like myself.

"I would've been good to her," I said, kicking a pebble over the edge. "I *was* good to her."

"And she didn't trust you," he added. "She's a snotty, stuck-up little cunt who thought she was better."

I looked away, his words making my blood boil a little. He was trying to be a friend. Trying to be on my side.

But I wish he'd shut up. Emmy wasn't like that.

I could be angry with her but no one else could.

In my heart, she was still my girl.

"And you're going to spend the rest of your life showing her that she was wrong," he told me. "That she missed out on the best."

Yeah. I'd try.

I inhaled a long breath and tipped my head left and right, cracking my neck.

He was right. It was long past time Will Grayson came back to life. With or without her.

"Let's do Devil's Night tonight," I told him. "I'm in the mood for the good ol' days."

He grinned, ready as always.

I wasn't sure when I'd figured it out. Damon would never tell me what had happened that night I saw them in the locker room—just that he'd run into Emory and she'd helped him.

Over time, I continued to watch her, the reality of her routine giving me all the information I needed, but was too blind to face sooner. The bruises, scrapes, and cuts couldn't have come from anywhere but her home. She didn't have friends. She didn't go anywhere other than school, the movies, or her little projects around town.

Unless she was in some underground fight club happening right under my nose, that piece of shit was brutalizing her.

I knew why she hadn't told me. I knew why she *thought* she couldn't tell me.

Martin Scott was only one of the things in our way, but it was the one thing I could beat the shit out of.

"Do we really want to do this?" Kai asked, hesitation thick in his tone. "A cop is a crime—like a real crime, Will. We all understand this, right?"

He sat in the back seat, while I sat in the front, Damon driving one of his father's SUVs.

I pulled on gloves. "Fire Up the Night" playing in the car as I stared out the windshield at Officer Scott across the street hassling a car full of kids he'd just stopped.

"Leave if you want," I told him.

It wasn't a threat. I didn't expect his help, and I didn't need it. Kai had a lot to lose, and I wouldn't judge him for walking out on this. Not that I didn't have a lot to lose. I just didn't care.

"What's he doing?" Damon said more to himself, tossing his cigarette out the window.

Martin Scott walked a girl to his cruiser, put her in the back, and climbed in the front, starting the car. We'd followed him from the station when he started his shift, and he took no time at all stopping the car full of teens that was speeding through the village.

"That's River Layton," I said, recognizing the sophomore.

She was only sixteen. What the hell was he doing?

Leaving the other guy and girl in their car, he pulled away from the curb and drove off with the minor, but instead of taking a left toward the station or a right toward the hills where she lived near me, he pulled an abrupt one-eighty and took the road toward the coast and Falcon's Well.

"Follow him," I said.

Damon shifted into gear and backed out of the parking lot, charging after him down the road.

It was after ten, and while school was out for the summer, the streets weren't too busy. All the parties were either happening on the beach, on Mommy and Daddy's boat, or in backyards with pools this time of year.

Damon hung back, far enough to be inconspicuous, but not too far that we couldn't see his taillights.

I dug into the duffel bag, tossing Kai his silver paintball mask, pulling out Damon's black one and handing it to him, and leaving Michael's red one in the bag as I pulled my white one with a red stripe on.

The brake lights in the distance lit up, and we watched as he turned into the warehouse. I didn't think there was anything going on there tonight. Why the hell was he taking the kid there?

Hanging back, Damon pulled the SUV onto the side of the road and shut off the engine as we all hopped out and pulled up the hoods of our black hoodies. It was too fucking hot for sweatshirts, but that was the routine.

The hoods and masks kept us covered—and hopefully—unrecognizable in video footage. Everyone knew who was who behind the masks, but they couldn't prove it.

Jogging into the brush and through the trees, we headed toward the warehouse we'd been to a hundred times, knowing the road in didn't go any farther than the old, abandoned factory.

Sweat already covered my back, and I couldn't see anything else outside of this moment.

It was his fault. It was all his fault, because even if it wasn't, it felt good to finally have someone to blame and give me hope that it wasn't me. That she ended it before it even began because of him and not because she didn't love me.

In any case, he'd fucking hurt her, and now that she was out from under him, I was let off my leash.

At the very least, after tonight, he'd never touch her again.

Stopping at the tree line and looking over the gravel parking lot to the old shoe factory with the ruins of its dark and dilapidated walls looming beyond, we watched as he turned off the car and remained in his seat with her in the back.

He moved his head, nodding here and there or cocking it as he talked, but she didn't move an inch.

Finally, he got out of his cruiser, walked to the back door, opened it, and climbed in beside her.

My lungs emptied.

I almost smiled. Any doubt or guilt I might've felt now long gone.

His face was going to be worse than ground beef by the time we were done with him.

"He doesn't have Emmy to push around anymore," Kai said, and I could hear the anger growing in his voice as he pulled on his mask.

I nodded, glad he was now on board. I did need him.

"Wanna bet my father is protecting him, too?" Damon told us, pulling on his. "So much in fucking common."

"Let's change his life forever." I started off, charging for the car and curling my fists as the guys flanked me.

I wished Michael were here—we were better as a unit—but we'd just have to fill him in when he got back from his basketball clinic in Atlanta.

"Don't let them hear your voices," I said, taking out my knife. "Whisper."

I tossed it to Kai who quickly unsheathed it, stabbed a tire, the air pouring out, and Damon and I ripped open each of the back doors.

River screamed as he grabbed her out of the car, and I shot out my fist, growling as I popped that scumbag in the fucking face.

I pulled him out of the car as he coughed and sputtered, the blood pouring into his mouth from his nose.

"Get home," Damon ordered her.

Her worried gaze darted between us; her face was already wet with tears from whatever Scott was trying to do to her in there.

But I could guess. *You're a minor. I'll take you home where you belong, but on second thought, I won't bring you in or call your parents about the drugs and alcohol I found in your car if you just come here next to me for a minute and don't tell anyone.*

Jesus Christ.

Diving down, I hit him again.

And again and again before rising up and kicking him in the back of the head.

Motherfucker. That motherfucker.

He wanted to hurt River like he hurt his sister—rough her up, make her cry . . .

Or worse.

And God help me, if he did anything like that to Emmy, I wouldn't hesitate. He'd be dead.

River ran off, back toward the highway, as Kai rounded the car, stabbing the rest of the tires. I whipped open the front door, kicking the radio and ripping it off its wires, while Damon tore off the dash-cam, dropping it to the ground and stomping it with his foot.

Chances were the cop already turned that shit off when he parked with the girl here, but I didn't want him being able to call for help, either.

I reached into my hoodie pocket, took out the cell phone and tossed it over the roof of the car to Damon before reaching back in and pulling out a thick cut of rope.

I walked over, planted my foot on his back, and pushed him back down on the ground.

"Don't look for us when this is over," I whispered to disguise my voice. "And don't you ever touch any woman again. Not River Layton. Not Emory. Not anyone." I leaned down, wrapping the rope around his neck. "If we find out you did, we won't let you walk away next time."

He gasped and grunted, and I rolled him over, his eyes sharpening as he met mine through my mask

Thrashing, he rolled away and tried to scramble to his feet, but in a moment, we were all on him, kicking him and launching fists.

I jerked my head at Kai, and we all picked Scott up, took him into the warehouse, and tied his wrists, securing them above his head to a steel beam.

We all backed away, the guys probably waiting to let me have first go as Damon took out the phone and started filming.

I paused. It was stupid to document this, but . . .

I licked my lips, seething and still tasting the bourbon I'd had in the car.

I wanted to watch it. To relive it. To see him suffer over and over again.

"Look at me," I whispered.

He breathed hard, and I walked over and took off his duty belt, dropping it to the ground.

"Look at me," I growled again, low.

Slowly, he raised his eyes and met mine through my mask. The corners of his gaze crinkled in recognition.

And then . . . the asshole smiled.

"You think it's my fault?" he asked in a quiet voice between us. "That she rejected you?"

I tightened my fists.

And then he laughed, despite how his teeth glistened with his own blood. "I would've been happy," he told me. "Even better if she would've gotten pregnant. Having an inside to all that money, power, and connection? Priceless. She would've finally been useful."

I stayed frozen, barely breathing.

He spit, spattering blood from his mouth all over me.

But I didn't even blink.

"She knew you were a loser," he said. "You'd just be the drunk womanizer you are now, not fit for her life."

My blood boiled under my skin.

He knew who we were, but I didn't care. The masks and whispering were for the camera, not him.

Was he right? He wasn't right. She didn't say it, but I knew she loved me. I felt it.

It was him. He made her forget about me. He made her scared.

"And this is just a reminder," he continued, "that she's long gone and fine without you, but you'll never be more than this. You'll never be enough."

I shook my head, my eyes burning.

Kai cleared his throat behind me. "We can't stay here forever, Will," he whispered. "Let's do this."

But Martin Scott just smiled, seeing what he was doing to me.

"She never looked at you again," he said. "Did she?"

I stopped breathing.

"She's never called. Even since she graduated and got free, right?"

How did he know that?

She could've called me. There was no reason not to once he was out of her life.

He laughed again. "You'll never be enough."

I swung my fist back, gritted my teeth together, and growled as I punched him across the face.

Fuck you.

A sob escaped, but I covered it up quickly.

Motherfucker.

I hit him again, hitting and hitting until long after he'd stopped laughing and my knuckles ached like they were on fire.

Tears welled and poured, and the whole world tipped on its side as I brought my fist down again and again.

Fuck you. Fuck you.

Kai came in, threatening him not to go near a minor again, and then I came back pounding, kicking, and punching some more until eventually my hands dripped with his and my blood, and I could do nothing else but laugh.

Until he passed out and they had to pull me off him.

We dumped his body on the side of the road, peeled out of the area in Damon's SUV, and used a burner phone to call the police to tell them where to find him.

I didn't care if it brought her back or not. He deserved it.

If he had any sense, he'd keep his mouth shut, too. He knew we knew he'd had River Layton out there.

Witnesses.

If she talked, she could be a liar.

But not all four of us.

Damon dropped Kai at home and then me.

"Wanna go drinking?" he asked.

I shook my head. I had better stuff in my room, but he wouldn't be down for that.

"See you tomorrow." I shut the car door, and he drove off as I made my way up the steps of my house, staring down at the blood all over my hands.

I didn't want to go inside. I looked up at my house—gray stone with three floors, a wine cellar, and a basketball court in the back.

I was a lucky boy.

And a fucking loser.

He was right, and nothing felt better.

I turned around and walked, leaving my truck and clutching the cell phone in my pocket.

I had no desire to ever watch it again.

I walked down my driveway and headed down the road, back toward the village in the black night as I took out the phone to delete the video. I wanted it gone.

I wanted to erase everything about me, because I hated me as much as she did.

"Hey, man!" someone called.

I looked up, closing the phone before I could finish and stuffing it into my pocket.

Bryce rolled up, peering at me through the open window. He had a girl in the car, and I leaned down, forcing a smile and stuffing my bloody hands into my pocket.

He studied me, sensing something. "You need a ride?"

I shook my head. "No," I told him. "Thanks, though."

He nodded slowly, still unsure. "O . . . okay."

He sped off, and I pulled out my hands, sick of this feeling inside me.

Scott was right. Nearly two years, and I was still pining while she'd been stone. Not a look, a hint, or a whisper from her.

She thought I was nothing.

I walked and walked, passing the village and the gazebo I'd heard she'd abandoned the last time I was home at Christmas.

I didn't want to see her and anything of hers. I just wanted the pain to go away.

Before I knew it, I was walking through Damon's house, up the stairs where the maid guided me, and up to the third floor where I knocked.

I faintly heard whispers and shuffling, and then he was there. In his lounge pants, freshly showered and no shirt.

His eyebrows shot to his hairline. "Here to see my coffin?" he joked.

I looked behind him, seeing the bed. "It looks comfortable."

His eyes turned warm, but then he dropped them, looking hesitant.

Tears pooled in my eyes. "I'm fucked up," I choked out.

"I know." He nodded. "But if you come in here, I'm not fixing you."

He was just as fucked up. Tomorrow wouldn't be any brighter for either of us.

"Just fix it for tonight," I whispered.

Dive and destroy and show me how to get lost. Just for tonight.

He moved to the side, inviting me in, and I closed the door behind me.

An obnoxious junkie.

At least Sid could play a guitar.

CHAPTER 31

EMORY

Present

I arched my back as Will gripped my hip and thrust against me, his dick sliding inside.

He filled me so tightly, stretching hot and thick, I whimpered, "Ah."

Twisting my head, he covered my mouth with his as the steam filled the shower and he yanked my hips back again and again, fucking me harder and harder without breaking the kiss.

I licked his tongue and took over, backing up into it as I guided his hand down between my legs.

He rubbed my clit, slow but steady, in circles. "I don't love you," he whispered in my ear before biting my lobe.

"I know."

He knocked my hand off his, slamming mine to the wall and returning his to my pussy, thrusting harder and bottoming out, going so deep.

I squeezed my eyes shut, moaning.

A hand took mine, and I closed my fingers around Alex's slender ones.

"Say you're sorry to me," Will breathed out.

"I did."

He pulled out, spun me around, and I let go of Alex's hand as he lifted me up.

"Say it," he demanded.

I wrapped my arms and legs around him as he slipped back inside. "What happens then?" I ask. "Huh?"

I trailed kisses over his face and then buried my lips in his neck as I hugged him to me.

"Once you get what you want, you'll stop," I told him, "and I don't want you to stop."

His hips moved as he gripped my ass in both hands, and I sucked the water off his skin, nibbling and dragging his skin out with my teeth.

He groaned.

"Don't stop," I panted. "I don't love you anymore. You're bad news and always have been."

"But don't stop, huh?" He chuckled. "The class reunion is next year, and I'm going to tell everyone what you really like to do when your nose isn't buried in a book. I'm going to tell them that you like me and how you let me have some fun when no one was looking."

I fell back against the wall, turning my head, my forehead meeting Alex's as I moaned. I wouldn't admit it to him, but I got off on how much he wanted me.

Aydin pressed Alex against the wall next to me, and while she faced me, he looked down at her, almost frozen except for his hand that slipped underneath her shirt so slowly. She breathed shallow, her lips close to mine, and in the blink of an eye, he'd torn off her bra and dropped the black fabric onto the shower floor, the water slowly drenching her shirt.

He was why she was here. This was why she was the one who came for Will, instead of Michael.

It was about Aydin. She was his artist, and she'd found out he was here when she was looking for Will.

Gliding his hand over her shirt, he moved up her stomach and between her breasts as the shirt plastered her skin, revealing the dark circles of her nipples through the linen.

She wouldn't look at him, and I pressed my lips to her forehead, trying to soothe her. It was almost like she was scared, and if there was anything I knew about Alex Palmer it was that not much scared her.

I turned back to Will, tightening my hold as I watched him tip his head back and start to lose it.

"I'm going to slip." I gasped.

He hefted me back up. "I got you."

I sank my mouth into his, my wet hair sticking to my face and neck, and I wished I was back in that wrestling room with him and I wouldn't have been so timid. I would've loved him and stayed there with him all night if I could do it over again.

"Kiss her on the mouth," I heard Aydin say.

I looked over to see Alex staring up at him. "I want to kiss you on the mouth."

He shook his head, his expression calm, but his breathing ragged.

He licked his lips. "Touch her on the cunt," he whispered. "Like that night I watched you on the screen. Do it."

He grazed his hand over her breast through her shirt, barely touching, and her mouth fell open, and I didn't think she was breathing.

"Touch her," he begged, hovering over her lips. "Fuck her for me in the bed."

She swallowed. "No," she whispered. "I do what I want, when I want, and nothing for your pleasure."

"Nothing?" he asked, touching her lips with his fingers. "For him but not for me?"

She glared up at Aydin. "I feel safe with him. I feel like a whore with you."

His jaw flexed, and his fingers curled over her breast like a claw. Her nipples hardened, poking through the fabric like bullets.

Will's head collapsed into my neck, breathing hard and groaning, and I could tell he was close.

But my blood rushed hot, my orgasm crested, and I was already there. I whimpered, squeezing my pussy around him and holding on for every thrust as my body bobbed up and down, moaning loud and not caring who heard.

Part of me hated Alex. She was gorgeous, tough, and everything Aydin said she was in the bedroom. She was more Will's friend than I ever was, and the hardest part was that she was stunning in every way.

She had to have been through shit, given her occupation. There had to have been days that brought her to tears, but you'd never know it.

And here the rest of us were, hurt and using it as an excuse to destroy ourselves, while she just kept trudging along day after day, getting closer and closer to what she wanted.

"What if I *want* to touch you someday?" I whispered to Alex, but leaned my head into Will, holding him close. "What if I want to kick them out and climb into bed with you, just us?"

Will grinned, kissing me without missing a step.

What if I felt safe with her, too, and she deserved better than how Aydin was treating her, and I wanted her to know that?

The lump in her throat moved up and down, and Will moved inside of me, both men watching us and holding us.

I gazed at her, droplets shimmering across her skin as Will nibbled the corner of my mouth.

"What would you do?" she asked, our heads together again. "If the boys weren't allowed?"

I couldn't hide the smile that peeked out.

"Yeah, what would you do?" Will panted in my ear.

I closed my eyes, loving the control they made me feel. "I wouldn't be able to stop myself," I told Will, loud enough for Aydin and Alex to hear. "I'd lock the door, turn off the light, and climb on top of her, sucking her tits into my mouth before spreading her legs and settling in between, nice and warm."

Will's body shook as he thrust faster and harder, losing control, and I looked over, seeing Aydin with her pants open and his hand inside, rubbing her through her panties. She clasped his hand in both of hers, like she wanted to stop him but couldn't find the strength.

"Then what?" Aydin asked me but stared down at her, brow etched in pain.

"I'd kiss her," I said. "If I were you and I had her under me, I'd kiss her and breathe her in and feel her body pressed to mine as I tasted her . . ."

"You like to taste things," Will taunted me, groaning. "Show me. Show me what you'd do with her in your mouth."

My belly pooled with heat, and I could feel it seeping out of me as he slid in and out.

"What does she taste like, Emory?" Aydin panted.

I glanced over, the cords in his forearm flexed as he worked her, and her eyes closed, the pleasure taking over.

"Warm," I whimpered. "She's warm and soft, and I love the feel of her clit against my lips as I lick between her legs."

Aydin groaned, and I could see the bulge in his pants growing larger as Alex gripped his shoulder with one hand.

"Open your eyes," he told her. "Look at me."

She opened them, holding his gaze as he fingered her.

"She widens her knees," I continued. "And holds my mouth there because it feels so good."

"Yeah," she pants, staring up at him as she bites her bottom lip.

I turn to Will. "I lick her up the sides," I tease him, gliding the tip of my tongue across his lips and flicking the top one as I looked into his eyes. "And I tug on her clit, sucking it into my mouth." I catch his top lip between my teeth and drag it out before sucking on it hard and swirling my tongue, playing with him.

He growled under his breath, and I flexed my thighs, riding him as he thrust.

"I'd lick her up and down." I mimicked it on the corner of his mouth. "And play with her for hours, licking up how hot she gets, because she likes her pussy sucked."

"Emmy," Alex moaned, dropping her head back. "Jesus, girl . . ."

"But God, you know what I really want to do?" I asked.

Will shivered. "What?"

"I want to fuck her," I panted, nibbling his mouth. "I want to drive her wild, rubbing our pussies together like animals, and screwing her until I sweat, because he needs to remember all that he'll be missing when he's sitting like a king at his dining room table someday. Alone and dreaming about his naked little Viking straddling him in his chair and fucking her man, because while he controls all, she controls him."

Alex cried out, wrapping her arms around Aydin's neck as she shuddered and came. Her head fell back, spray and steam caressing her face, and he held her head, his lips hovering over hers.

Aydin's eyes glistened, and he moved over her lips, looking like he was going to kiss her and struggling to hold himself back.

I bobbed up and down on Will, crashing my mouth down on his, unashamed and unconcerned for the first fifteen minutes of my entire life. I didn't care what else happened or how he might hold anything against me. I felt good and brave and high.

I rolled my hips, grinding and chasing the orgasm, and then finally . . . I cried out, shaking and coming, my thighs tightening and my belly consumed in a wave of tingles and shocks. I moaned, holding on for dear life as the burn in my back started to register from him rubbing my spine against the wall so hard.

But he wasn't done, and I wasn't telling him to stop.

"Say his name," I heard Aydin tell her.

I breathed hard, heat coursing down every inch of my body.

"Say his name," he told her again.

I looked over, seeing him still rubbing her and trying to make her come again.

"Please," he begged.

"Will?" she breathed out, looking confused and still dreamy from her orgasm.

"Again."

"Will," she said.

I froze, feeling Will slow as well.

"Again," he told her. "Again."

What? His muscles flexed, and I watched him, the same pain etched across his forehead.

She stared up at him, searching his eyes. "Will," she whispered.

"Moan it," he growled at her, fingering her.

She closed her eyes, gasping for breath as she started to come again. Will stopped, both of us watching them.

What was Aydin doing? It felt different when I was fantasizing about her, because I wanted him to see her through my eyes, but what did he think he was doing, turning the tables? It wasn't the same.

"Can't remember my name, just say his," he taunted, picking up his pace. "Dive deep into your head where I don't matter, because you've already done it a hundred times, and I was always watching you come, you slut."

She started sobbing dry tears, and he leaned in, moving rougher over her pussy. "Come on, moan for him. His dick feels so good."

Will softened inside me, and I dropped to my feet, suddenly cold.

"You didn't just fuck him," Aydin told her. "You were close. He feels for you."

I let my eyes fall, and Will tried lifting my chin, but I jerked away.

"Emmy," he said.

They were close. Maybe he felt for her in a way he and I could never be. That perfect trust.

Friends.

"Come on, say it," he urged. "Will, Will, Will . . ."

She shoved him away, slamming her palm against his face, and Will shoved him next before pulling up his drenched jeans.

Aydin slipped his hand inside Alex's panties, but he had pulled it back out before she could shove him off again.

He held up his glistening fingers to us, showing us how wet she was.

"While you've been buried in this," he told Will, "she's been sad and sorry."

His eyes flashed to me, and Will stood there frozen, while Alex quickly fastened her pants.

"It's plain as day who really suffered during your time apart," he bit out. "She owes you nothing."

I couldn't look up at Will.

And part of me didn't want to stop Aydin, either, not because he was going after Will, but because he always found a way to make me less entitled to my guilt.

He was like a power-up, which was a weird turn of events, because I thought for sure he would be chaining me to his bed by my neck when we met.

Maybe if I'd grown up with him instead of Martin, my entire world would've been different.

He left the shower, dropping his wet clothes on the floor and tying a towel around his waist as he walked back into his bedroom. I left my clothes there and walked out, too, throwing Will's hand off when he tried to grab me.

I wasn't mad. I didn't know what was wrong.

I just wanted to get dressed now.

Wrapping myself in a towel, I left the bathroom and walked for the door, but Aydin's voice stopped me.

"Emory, come here," he said.

I looked over, seeing him just inside his closet, pulling clothes off the shelves.

He tossed me some red boxers and a black T-shirt, and I caught them, lamenting the loss of my bra on the shower floor now.

The water stopped running, and Will and Alex walked out of the bathroom, wary with their eyes on me.

Will's eyes dropped to the items in my hands and then back up to me. "Come here," he ordered.

I darted my eyes to Aydin without even thinking.

"Don't look at him." Will scowled at me.

But I remained rooted, hearing Aydin's calm voice.

"Do what you want, Emory," he told me. "It's okay."

My heart splintered a little more, and I looked away, shaking my head. What I would have given for Will to say that just once. Or my brother.

Someone to guide me. I didn't realize how much I'd missed it from my life since my parents were gone.

If Will or Martin had given me freedom, I would've wanted them more. That was all he had to do. He just had to let me come to him. Like the Homecoming dance.

It just took me longer to figure things out. I didn't dive into anything headfirst. Aydin seemed to know that.

Had to hand it to him . . . I understood why he was the alpha now.

"Emory . . ." Will said.

I didn't move.

Aydin dressed, and I clutched the clothes, my legs charged to just head back to my room.

"Em . . ." he said again in a lower voice.

Tears filled my eyes, and I heard a quiet chuckle come from Aydin. "Micah and Rory are drunk by now," he told Will, "and you're going to leave without the only thing you want."

Me.

Aydin pulled his T-shirt over his head and met my eyes. "You happened to him."

Nothing happened to me. I wasn't a victim, and this was the last time I'd hesitate.

I pulled on the shorts and rolled them over a couple of times, and Aydin walked out of the room as Will's eyes bore a hole in my back. I didn't even have my shirt on yet before Will charged out of the room, slamming the door against the wall on his way, and I whipped my head around, looking at Alex.

A crash hit the floor downstairs, and a moment passed before she shot off, running after them.

I threw on my T-shirt, pulled off the towel, and flipped my wet hair back out of my face as I ran out of the room. I looked left and right, not seeing anything, but a scuffle hit my ears, and I leaned over the balcony, seeing Aydin with Will in a headlock on the floor of the foyer.

Shit.

Alex rushed in, but Will shot out his hand. "Don't," he yelled. "Stay back."

She halted, and I hurried down the stairs as Will and Aydin rolled over on the floor, Aydin strangling him, and Will struggling for air.

"Stop!" I shouted.

Will laid on top of Aydin and threw his head back, trying to hit Aydin with the back of his skull, but the other man jerked out of the way just in time. They both scrambled, their dark hair wet and messy as Will flipped over and tried to get a hold of Aydin's neck.

They shot out their legs, tumbling to the side, and the candelabra toppled over, the candles rolling to the edges of the room.

The men wrestled, and I shot my hands to my hair, trying to figure out what to do. Will could wrestle. What was going on?

And if he couldn't beat Aydin, why had he gone after him?

Enough. They were both getting locked in the cellar tonight.

I ran into the drawing room and pulled the longarm off the wall—an antique from World War I, it looked like—and dashed back into the foyer, stepping in and kicking Aydin off Will.

He fell back to the floor, but before he could dive back in, I pointed the gun, the bayonet pointing right at his neck.

"Enough!" I yelled.

I'd forgotten my glasses in the shower, but I could see Aydin's cocked eyebrow well enough.

Will shot off the floor, coming for him again, but Alex grabbed him by the jeans and smacked him over the head.

I fought not to laugh, because that's how funny all of this was.

Grown men . . .

I didn't have time to do more, though. Taylor, Micah, and Rory arrived on the scene, wet from the pool and their eyes darting between all of us.

Taylor's gaze finally settled on me with the gun pointed at Aydin, and in a blur, it all happened.

Will charged for Taylor, Aydin scurried off the floor and threw himself at Will, and the next thing I knew, Taylor had grabbed the gun, ripped it out of my hands, tossed it, and gripped the back of my head with one hand and threw a punch into my stomach with the other.

My insides tried to push through my spine, vomit rose up my throat, and I coughed, dropping to my knees.

Tears filled my eyes as everyone, blurry in front of me, scrambled to separate Will and Aydin. Taylor lifted me up and slammed me against the staircase, squeezing my jaw between his fingers and hovering over me.

"I've been waiting for this," he gritted.

My body wracked with pain, and I sucked in air, trying to catch my breath as the inside of my mouth cut on my teeth.

But he was pulled away, someone grabbing his hand, bending his finger back, and bringing him to his knees as he cried out. I blinked, gasping as Aydin grabbed the gun, propped it up on the floor for leverage, and shot the bayonet down, slicing off Taylor's pinky finger.

I widened my eyes as blood spurted, spilling onto the marble, and everyone stopped, their attention caught now.

Taylor screamed, but Aydin didn't waste any time. He hauled him up, threw him over his shoulder, and headed for the back of the house.

"Bring Will, too!" he shouted.

Huh?

I looked between Rory and Micah, who both looked unsure, but then Rory gritted his teeth and moved first, grabbing Will.

"No!" Alex and I shot forward, reacting, but Micah pushed us back, protecting Rory.

What the hell?

Micah helped him, both of them force-walking Will and following Aydin as Alex and I trailed. I grabbed the gun on my way, sweat coating my body as I watched Alex swipe a candlestick. We were both armed now, a trickle of blood gliding down my blade, and Taylor's finger on the floor somewhere.

Why had Aydin done that? Taylor was his lapdog.

"Aydin, please," I begged.

Where was he taking them?

He opened the door to the cellar, descended the stairs with the boys, and we chased, jogging down the stone steps to see them throwing Will on the ground as Aydin tied up Taylor's wrists and slung them over a hook above his head. Blood poured down his arm, and he breathed hard, his face twisted in pain.

Next, he moved to Will, but shot a glance to us. "Hold them!" he ordered Micah and Rory.

"No!" We raised our weapons, and they stopped in front of us, the confrontation at a standstill as Aydin squatted next to Will.

He laid there, blood dripping off the corner of his mouth, his eyes cast down, and making no move to fight more.

What the fuck is wrong with you?

Alex was right. Will could take these guys. My God. This hurt more than the pain in my gut. I couldn't watch.

"I like you," Aydin told him, unknotting some rope. "I didn't think I would. Life has a weird sense of humor, you know? I watched you with her at parties. I'd see you with her at restaurants. Then, lo and behold, you show up here, our new inmate."

Her. *Alex.*

I straightened, a thought taking form in my head. It was strange that out of all the people in the world, they wound up in the same place. Two men who both knew Alex.

One who clearly resented the other for it.

"Remember when you asked me if I could get things other than alcohol and cigarettes?" he questioned Will.

And I gulped. *No.* He had Will brought here. Either for revenge or to take him away from Alex.

Oh, my God.

But then suddenly Aydin turned and jerked his chin, gesturing to me, instead.

What?

My heart dropped into my stomach, and Will gritted through his teeth, "You son of a bitch."

I stepped forward. "Me?" I said, but I already knew the answer. "*You* brought me here?"

All the enemies and all the people who had something against me if they knew my secret, and it turned out to be someone I'd never met?

He didn't sentence Will to Blackchurch. He smuggled me in for revenge.

Aydin's eyes fell, and he tightened the rope around Will's wrist. "I want him to know what this feels like," he murmured. "To watch the one woman it physically hurts to look at, because you want her so much, give her time and loyalty and love to another." He glared over at me. "I want him to feel this."

Alex stepped up next to me, and I could hear her breathe.

"Then why not try to seduce me?" I charged before she could say anything. What was with all the big brother shit?

He just chuckled. "The only thing more powerful than the heart is the brain, and it was so much more useful to get into your head than into your bed."

I shook my head. "Or maybe you didn't want to take me away from Will, but Will away from Alex. Maybe she was the one you wanted to hurt."

He shrugged. "Either way."

The room fell silent except for Taylor's shaking. I looked over, not that worried about him, but Aydin was going to have to help him. Close the wound or something.

My hand shot to my hair. He brought me here.

But that meant he also gave me the knife. Did he think that was going to be enough protection?

The floor above us creaked—as well as the wood in the walls— and I smelled smoke in the air, but then thunder cracked overhead, the lights flickered, and I raised my weapon again, opening my mouth to speak.

But Aydin spoke first. "You both will stay down here," he told Will, "and if Micah and Rory know what's good for them, they'll fall in line."

He turned to the guys, ordering them, "Take the women to my room," he told them and then looked at us. "I'll be up to see you ladies in a while."

I tensed.

"Maybe they'd like some exercise tonight," he said, staring at Will. "I'll take them to the pool. Party of three." His voice lowered, but I could still hear the smile in his tone. "Maybe Emmy will play out that little fantasy of hers and put Alex to some good use the way everyone else has."

I lunged. "Will!"

Micah grabbed me, and I dropped the gun, shooting my palm up to his fucking nose as Alex shot out and caught Rory's arm, spinning him around and shoving him into the wall.

He headbutted the stone, and I dropped down, picked up my bayonet, rushing to Will.

But Aydin was there, stopping me and taking me in his arms, wrapping them around me like a steel band and holding me hostage.

"Wendy, Wendy," he taunted. "It's true, then. One girl *is* worth twenty boys, it seems. So glad you're on my team."

His mouth came down on mine, his scruff and sweat grinding against my lips as he moved over me, stealing my breath.

Will.

I grunted, a sob lodging in my throat as I pressed against his blood-soaked shirt and tried to twist my head away.

Oh, God.

And then . . . a whisper came in close—calm, hard, and deep. "You're not Peter," it said.

I blinked my eyes open in time to see Will standing right behind Aydin, the ropes suddenly gone.

Slipping an arm around Aydin's neck, Will grabbed his wrist, pulled him off me, and yanked his arm so far back that Aydin cried out and was forced to the ground. In one quick motion, Will brought down his foot at the joint where Aydin's arm met his shoulder, and a pop pierced the air, Aydin's howl echoing throughout the cellar.

I gaped at Will who'd just brought Aydin to his knees in less than two seconds, not even losing breath.

"What the hell?" I muttered.

Alex and I stood there as Will stared down at Aydin's form, a serrated knife in his hand and the rope around his wrists severed.

Where had he gotten that knife?

He inhaled a deep breath and straightened his back, cutting off the rope bracelets, sheathing the knife, and sticking it back into his pocket.

"Will . . ." I stepped forward.

He shook his head, telling me to keep quiet as he glared at the man on the brick floor.

Aydin shot up, but Will swung his fist down, landing right on his throat.

I narrowed my eyes, able to do nothing more than stare at him and blink.

Aydin gasped, hunching over and too disabled to speak or even breathe.

Will circled him as Taylor watched, and Micah and Rory stood frozen, clearly not sure what was happening.

"I was in prison," Will said to Aydin. "A real one. Did you actually think I didn't have any of this under control?"

Aydin looked up at him, a worry and puzzlement I'd never seen in his eyes now.

"I waited," Will continued. "I was prepared to be as patient as possible to get you to follow."

He dropped down, hovering over Aydin as he gripped the back of his head and delivered two punches to his face.

Aydin's nose spilled with blood, and he reared back and hit Will, throwing him off and crawling away until he could scramble to his feet.

They both faced each other, widening their stances, and Aydin charged Will, throwing his body into his stomach. They crashed back onto the floor, and I lurched forward, but Micah shot out his arm, stopping me.

"I want to see this," he said.

I darted my worried eyes to Will. His skin flushed and sweat pouring down his back, he rolled, hit, kneed, kicked, and did everything with rage in his eyes.

He wasn't taking it like he had been since I'd been here.

This was Will.

Bloody and breathing hard, he punched Aydin in the stomach and rose, sending a hard kick to his head.

"It would've been perfect," he growled. "You know that? Teaming up. Being equals, but I didn't want to win you over with fear. I didn't want to control you with violence."

Aydin tried to get his legs under him, but he kept falling back to the ground.

"I wanted to be important to you," Will told him. "If I were important to you, you'd follow me anywhere."

Follow him? What was Will talking about? Why did he want Aydin to follow him?

"It would've been perfect, because you're one of us," Will panted, circling his prey, "but it seems I have no more time to waste on you. It seems I didn't anticipate you had your own agenda with me."

Meaning me—and Aydin bringing me here.

He sniffled, wiping the blood off his face.

"Rory." Will jerked his chin to the supply of rope sitting on the table. "Micah, help him."

They tied up Aydin who was too exhausted and beat, barely kicking and thrashing as they secured him.

Will called us. "Alex," he said, standing back and watching them. "Emory."

Alex immediately went to his side, but I stayed rooted.

A fire lit behind his eyes. "I will raise hell and reduce this house to ash if you act like this is a choice for one more second!" he bellowed at me and then pointed to his side. "Now!"

I jumped, tingles throbbing between my legs, and I clenched my teeth, walking over to him.

"All this time?" Aydin breathed out. "All these months and all the fights. All the times you lost, it was on purpose?"

"You don't have what it takes to be me," he told Aydin, his deep tone sending chills up my spine.

Oh, my God.

He'd faked it. He'd faked everything. He was working the house for some reason, slowly turning everyone on his side, and he'd put up with months of this shit because he wanted Aydin's loyalty, but he didn't want it through force.

Micah and Rory finished and came over, standing with us as everyone stared at Aydin on the floor.

Will loomed front and center like an oak rising, and I swore I had to tip my head back to look up at him at my side.

"You can come with us," Will told him. "I don't want Dinescu, but I'll take you."

Alex stood on Will's other side, a flash of pain in her eyes as she looked at Aydin.

But Aydin just laughed bitterly. "Kill me," he said.

Will stood there another moment, absorbing his answer as the thunder cracked again, and I started to back away, everyone slowly following.

The boys turned and darted up the stairs as I watched Alex drag her feet, the distance between her and Aydin like nothing as the heat of their look grew.

"You wanted me," she told him, backing away from him.

He nodded, his hands bound to some rusty piping as he sat on the floor. "Now I just want to win."

She shook her head. "You've already lost."

"Not yet," he retorted. "I *do* know where you're going, love."

The hair on my arms stood on end, and she hesitated a few moments as his words hung in the air, but then . . . we both spun around, darted up the stairs, and slammed the door behind us.

"Alex . . ."

"Don't," she said, and I could hear the tears in her throat. "I already forgot his name."

We raced upstairs, a thick stench hitting me as we pushed through the door.

I inhaled. "What the hell is that?"

Hearing commotion, we ran back toward the foyer, instantly

halting as flames engulfed the drapes on the windows, rising to the ceiling and spreading onto the walls.

"Oh, Jesus!" Alex cried.

I looked for Will, spotting him rushing out from the kitchen with a fire extinguisher.

The heat baked my face, and I stumbled back as he tried to put out the flames.

Those damn candles must've been lit when they knocked them over.

"Will!" I cried.

We had to get out of here. It consumed the foyer, and I tipped my head back as I coughed through the burn in my throat, seeing the flames stretching so much higher than we could reach. There was no stopping this.

"Will!" I called again, but he sprayed the door, extinguishing the fire around the frame.

Alex shot past me, up the stairs.

"What are you doing?" I yelled after her, seeing flames flicker on the edges of the steps.

"My satellite phone!" she yelled. "It's in the secret passageway! We need it!"

"Alex, no!" Will bellowed.

I shot off to go after her, but then I heard a crash against the front door, and I stopped.

Alex stopped halfway up the stairs, and I turned around to see Will standing still.

Another crash wracked the walls as smoke engulfed the entire room, and I blinked my eyes against the sting, trying to see who was coming through the door.

They had to have security nearby. There was a fire alarm going off somewhere, I'd bet.

Another pound, and then . . . the door flew open, the smoke

gushing out the door, and I spotted black arms and legs coming into the room through the clouds.

"Will!" someone shouted.

I squatted down on the floor, pulling Will with me, so we could breathe, but also . . .

"Is that security?" I asked him, trying to see through the smoke.

"I don't think so."

I'd be glad if it was, but also, they might just transfer us all to another Blackchurch, too.

I wanted my weapon.

"Will!" another voice—this one also male—called. "Where are you?"

Why were they just calling for him and not the others?

"Will Grayson!" a woman shouted next, coughing.

My ear pricked, something familiar about that one, and Will sucked in a breath next to me.

"Oh, my God," he whispered.

He shot to his feet, pulling me up by the arm. "Here!" he shouted.

Alex came running down the stairs as figures dressed in black moved through the smoke, and I saw three tall men with paracord draped over their chest and carrying duffel bags.

"What the hell did we bring paracord for?" Kai Mori said, looking to Michael Crist. "Thought you told us we were going to have to scale the walls and shit."

Michael just smiled and grabbed Will by the neck, pulling him into a hug.

Will tensed like he was shocked, but after a moment he exhaled. "Came for me after all, huh?"

"Always," another voice said.

I looked as Damon stepped through the smoke, laughing as he dipped down, pressing his forehead to his best friend's.

A woman came up, her blond ponytail draped over her shoulder, the top of her head covered in a black ski cap.

Erika Fane?

"Let's get the fuck out of here," she said and then looked over my shoulder, calling, "Alex!"

Alex rushed forward, brushing past me and crashing into Rika's arms. "You made it," she breathed out in a laugh.

Erika nodded. "Worried?"

Alex chuckled. "No. Course not."

Everyone started to rush out the door, but Alex and I hesitated, looking back through the smoke, toward the back of the house.

"Wait," she shouted. "There's more back there!"

Everyone rushed back in the house, but the fire had drifted down the hall, splintering off toward the kitchen and then right, toward the pool.

We rushed up to the flames.

"Emmy!" Will yelled.

"Emory Scott?" I heard Damon say. "Alex, you didn't tell us she was here."

But no one had time to explain.

I peered through the fire, trying to see a way past, but I couldn't find a path. We couldn't leave them there to burn.

Alex and I tried, stepping left and right and trying to get through, but strong arms pulled me back.

"Take her," Will ordered.

The next thing I knew I was being swept into someone's arms and over his shoulder, and I screamed, trying to thrash my way free.

I could walk.

"And don't put her down," Will growled. "She likes to not cooperate."

Motherfucker!

"Lev!" someone called.

And then I heard someone say "David" and murmurs mentioning Aydin and Misha.

Where were we going?

We left the house, rain splattering my body as the foyer grew smaller and smaller in my vision and more of the house came into view.

The fire reached the upstairs windows, an orange glow filling the rooms behind the curtains, and I stared as far into the foyer as I could the farther away we got, hoping for Aydin to make it.

Waiting to see a glimpse of him.

I didn't want him to die.

"Give her to me," Micah growled.

I was pulled off someone's shoulder and into Micah's arms, looking over and seeing that Michael was the one who had been carrying me.

I snarled at him.

"I got her," Micah told him.

Michael nodded and ran ahead, and as soon as he was gone, Micah dropped me to my feet, holding my hand as we ran with everyone else. I looked over my shoulder, stumbling.

The greenhouse was separated from the main house. Not that I cared about the snakes, but that was a rotten way for any living being to go. They should be safe, though.

We ran through the woods, and I barely noticed the cold as the thunder roared over us and the rain spilled heavier.

"Where are we?" Will asked them.

"You'll never guess," Damon told him.

"How long will it take to get home," Will prodded.

And everyone just laughed, whatever that meant.

We raced through the trees, and I gasped for breath as my legs turned to rubber under me.

"Micah," I pleaded for him to slow.

But he just pulled me along, and then I saw it, through the trees in the distance.

I squinted, trying to blink away the blur that was always there. I needed my glasses. *Shit.*

Was that a . . . A train?

We scurried over the rocks and leaves, past the tree line to a train spanning to my left and right on tracks as far as I could see.

Did Aydin know this was here? They all must've known. We hadn't run that long—maybe ten minutes?

Maybe he thought it was abandoned.

Everyone ran to a car in the middle, and I looked at the beautiful black steam engine, old but well restored. Curtains hung on the inside of the windows, and the engine chugged a steady rhythm.

"Go!" Erika shouted. "Go now!"

Everyone climbed into the car, and I looked behind me one more time for any sign of Aydin or Taylor.

I do know where you're going, he'd said.

I didn't even have to act like I didn't know, either.

Back to Thunder Bay.

"Close the doors!" Michael shouted and hung out the door, waving, probably to the conductor.

We all piled in, some dark-haired woman grabbing Will's wrist and cutting off his bracelet with a bolt cutter. She planted a quick kiss on his cheek, and then moved to Micah and Rory, severed theirs from their wrists and tossing them all out the window.

The train moved under us, and I swayed, but before I could even look around or figure out who the other women were, someone grabbed my arm and whipped me around.

"You hesitated," Will growled, black streaks covering his body from the fire. "In the cellar . . . You hesitated! Again! And you were going back for him when you never came back for me. Ever!"

I flinched, remembering minutes ago when he'd told me to come to him.

He saw it as me taking Aydin's side.

I saw it as me standing on my own. "Will . . ."

"After everything you've done to us, you hesitated!" he yelled, his face twisted in anger.

Everyone surrounded us, standing silently, and I felt the heat of their eyes like I was a mouse and they were snakes circling me.

"What are you talking about?" Damon asked him. "What do you mean 'to us'? What did she do?"

I stared at Will, shaking my head slowly, begging him. *Not here. Please, not here. Not now.*

He straightened and drifted backward a couple of steps, finally having me trapped exactly where I deserved and savoring this moment.

"She's the reason we all went to jail seven years ago," he told them.

CHAPTER 32

EMORY

Seven Years Ago
A few months after the attack on Martin Scott

Hey," Thea called out, entering our room.

I looked up from my desk, seeing her whip off her Mia Wallace wig and toss it on our futon couch with the adrenaline needle she'd made me plaster to her chest earlier tonight. Her boyfriend was supposed to complete her *Pulp Fiction* theme by going as Vincent Vega, but they got in a fight an hour before, and I let her go to the party alone.

Like a jerk.

"Hey," I said, smiling at her makeup smeared everywhere. "Have fun?"

Judging from the lipstick across her cheek, Vincent must've found her and they made up.

But she just shrugged. "Eh, I don't remember."

I snorted as she skipped over to me, the beer on her breath hitting my nose. "But I thought of you." She held out a small jack-o'-lantern, already carved with a toothless happy face. "I stole it from in front of a frat house on my way home."

I laughed, taking it. "Thank you."

Man, I lucked out with roommates.

I shook my head, setting the pumpkin on my desk. After I'd

graduated last spring, I convinced Martin to use my college fund to put Grand-Mère in the nicest home money could buy because I didn't need it. With a scholarship thanks to my stunning designs around Thunder Bay, showcasing how you can make a ruin still functional while keeping its character, I didn't need my college fund. What I didn't cover with the scholarship, I got in loans. Screw it.

I had wanted to handle her myself, but he had power of attorney over her care, and that wasn't changing. He agreed when I outlined the perks of having the house to himself finally, plus the respect and admiration of people thinking he paid for her first-class care out of his modest, civil servant salary.

I called her every day, but I hadn't spoken to him since I'd left after graduation. I interned in San Francisco for the summer, snuck into town in late July to visit her, and then promptly left again to move into my dorm.

"You should've come," Thea said. "For once, just say . . . 'yes.'" And then she moaned loudly. "Yes, yes, yes!"

There were no shortages of parties and fun at Berkeley, but in the two months since school had started, adjusting to a new set of people and new surroundings proved harder than I thought it would be.

Which was stupid, because I didn't think anyone would agree I'd particularly adjusted to Thunder Bay, either, and I grew up there.

I was kind of homesick.

"I ruin the fun," I told her with a half smile. "Trust me."

I took out a pack of matches from my drawer and lit the tealight still inside the pumpkin, the warm glow peeking out of his eyes and mouth. We weren't supposed to be lighting anything in the dorms, but they'd never know.

I turned off my desk lamp, the darkness making the flickering candle a little spooky.

Thea undressed and then pulled on her robe, grabbing a towel and her shower caddy.

"Happy Halloween," she singsonged, leaving to take a shower.

But I spoke up. "Devil's Night."

"Huh?"

I turned my head, seeing her grip the door handle.

"Tomorrow is Halloween," I told her. "Tonight is Devil's Night."

"Like in *The Crow*?"

I broke out in a laugh. Devil's Night, Mischief Night, Cabbage Night . . . I forgot most of the world outside Thunder Bay—and maybe Detroit—had never heard of it before, other than in the movies.

She leaned over, looking at the clock on her own desk. "Well, it's after one," she said. "It's Halloween now."

She stuck out her tongue and then left, heading down the hall to take a shower.

Touché.

I took off my glasses and rubbed my eyes, closing my textbook for the night. Wrapping a rubber band around my flashcards, I tossed them on the desk and picked up the lid of the jack-o'-lantern and put it back on top.

I stared at its face. "Emory Scott loves Will Grayson," I murmured.

My throat ached with tears.

I'd never told him I loved him. Emptiness had spread through my insides over the months, and even though it made me feel stronger every time I looked away from him his last year at school—proud that I was surviving him and Martin and Thunder Bay—I never felt like I was winning.

The longing just grew, and if he walked in here right now, I'd let him pick me up, and I'd wrap my legs around him and not stop touching him the rest of the night.

My arms hummed with the need to hold him.

I looked up at the Godzilla on top of my supply drawers on my desktop. I'd done the right thing. Right? I hadn't wanted him to know what was happening in that house.

I had to cut him loose.

But I did regret not trusting him. Whatever I had to lose, I'd lost already. I should've told him I loved him, and it wasn't his fault, and maybe someday . . .

Maybe someday.

I dried my eyes and picked up my phone, tempted to call or text—maybe to apologize, I didn't know—but if nothing else, maybe he was in Thunder Bay tonight. Maybe he'd come back from Princeton to celebrate, even though he hadn't come back home last year while I was a senior.

Or maybe he wasn't home and everyone else carried on the tradition after the Horsemen had left for college.

I wanted to see home.

Logging on to Instagram, I searched #devilsnight and clicked on *Recent* for anything posted tonight and . . .

Images and videos assaulted me all at once, my heart starting to hammer as their faces popped up immediately, swarming the page.

I smiled, warm everywhere as I caught a glimpse of his smile in one square and his beautiful face, a little thinner than I remembered, with eyes piercing the camera in another.

I caught sight of Michael's red mask, Kai's silver one, Damon kissing some blonde in the shower, but then I spotted a video running in one of the squares, and my brother in the background.

I grabbed my glasses, putting them back on and holding the phone closer to my face to study the video.

What was this?

Guys in black hoodies and masks beat my brother as he hung by his hands in a dark room. The light from the camera phone shone on him, blood streaming down his face and his dark hair matted and sweaty.

My head spun. *No, no, no* . . .

I glanced at the door, worried Thea would be back, and grabbed my earbuds, plugging them into my phone and clicking the post, turning up the volume.

"Ah!" Martin growled, his face etched with pain.

One of the men in black approached him, and I perked my ears to try to hear, but all I heard was mumbling between them.

After a minute, I heard Martin's dark laugh, and I winced, remembering that sound.

This was from when my brother was attacked this past summer. He'd tried to tell me, but I'd refused to answer the phone, only hearing about it from my grandmother. He'd been hospitalized for more than a week, but I hadn't given a shit. He'd been lucky I wasn't praying for his death.

One of the men in black lost control, and I sucked in a breath as I watched him pummel Martin, bringing down his fist again and again, my brother's silver badge glinting in the light.

Jesus.

I didn't have to see his face to know who it was.

Another one came from behind the camera and started in, the first guy turning around, facing the camera, and . . .

My heart sank as I watched him lift his mask.

Will.

No.

He smirked and flipped off the camera, the bile rising up my throat as I scrolled the comments. So many. The video was everywhere.

It was everywhere. Everyone knew he'd done it.

Oh, my God, I mouthed.

Exiting out, I scrolled, seeing a video of Damon and Winter Ashby in a shower together, making out or something, and I clicked out of it and reported it to Instagram.

She was a minor. What the hell? Who'd posted this shit?

Had someone gotten a hold of their phone?

The first video was posted an hour ago from a ghost account, by the looks of it, and the only person I wasn't seeing was Michael in any of them.

I pulled out my earbuds, dialing Martin and checking the time. After one a.m. here, so it would be after four a.m. in Thunder Bay.

He didn't answer, so I called again, still getting no answer. I hesitated a moment and then tried Will.

Again, no answer.

God, he might not even be awake yet.

I sat there, my phone starting to buzz as the world back home started to wake with the news, and old classmates probably wanted to be the first to alert me about the video with Martin in it.

I inhaled and exhaled. It would be fine.

Right? They'd get out of this.

But even saying it, I knew it wasn't true. Whoever loaded the videos wanted a trial by public opinion. Even if they escaped without a charge, this could get them kicked out of their schools.

It would undoubtedly embarrass their families on a massive scale.

Michael.

Why wasn't Michael in any of them?

Whoever posted the videos had the phone. Michael would be on there. He was pretty much the leader.

And slowly, realization started to crystallize. Either it was Michael who'd posted them, or someone who didn't want him embarrassed.

Or his family embarrassed.

I barely breathed, too many thoughts trying to come up my throat all at once as my brain started to finally catch up.

If anyone had half a mind to, there would be no way to ignore their behavior if someone shared those videos in the right place, you know? Can you imagine the embarrassment?

Oh, no.

I closed my eyes, exhaling a single breath. "Fuck."

The cab crawled into Thunder Bay hours later, barely able to go more than twenty miles an hour with all the people cluttering the streets.

It looked like Mardi Gras, only no one was smiling.

Cameras, news crews . . . Will was going to be the center of this. His grandfather was a senator.

We entered the village where Sticks was packed with people and the sidewalks covered. Everyone wanted to be where the action was, and even kids were in the middle of it.

This was all my fault. God, what had I done?

After I'd failed to get a hold of anyone, I hadn't even stopped to throw anything into a bag. I just dressed and dragged Thea out of the shower to take me to the airport since she had a car.

I couldn't get a flight out until six a.m. my time, and it was now after six p.m. Thunder Bay time. I'd been able to see bits of pieces on my phone during my layover in Chicago.

They'd been arrested.

And Martin was probably in heaven.

I looked around, people I didn't even recognize walking the streets. I swallowed a few times, trying to generate some saliva, but I just wanted him out. Back at school where he belonged.

Will.

But then I smelled it.

The fire.

I turned my head, looking around, and my gaze stopped, seeing the yellow tape on the hill.

My stomach dropped.

"Stop," I breathed out.

The driver kept going.

"Stop!" I yelled, digging in my pocket for the cash.

The car halted, people talking and yelling outside the cab. I threw the money over the front seat and jumped out of the car, racing across the street, through the crowd.

I gazed up at it as I climbed the small incline—the wood charred, the roof collapsed, and debris everywhere.

My gazebo.

Why . . . who . . . ?

I spun in a circle, looking around the village and noticing the wood bolted over what used to be a display case at the front of Fane, the jewelry store.

What the hell happened here last night?

Tears wet my eyes, but I quickly wiped them away and charged back down the hill and across the street, pushing through the crowd of people until I felt like I couldn't breathe.

I'd built that. Nothing else seemed burned. Why that?

Like they had to erase me from the town.

I started running, taking a right down a quieter street and racing to the police station.

I swung the door open, pushed through all the people inside, and shoved my way through the partition, heading to the offices in the back.

"Emory!" someone barked.

But I ignored him, probably a cop to tell me I couldn't just barge in.

"Emmy!" another person shouted.

I dug in my heels, slamming my hands into the double doors and charging over to my brother's desk.

It was empty. I looked at Bryan Baker coming back to his desk with a coffee.

"Where is he?"

"In the john," he said, taking a sip. "Have a seat."

I set off, heading down the hall and charging into the men's room.

Sweat covered my back, and I breathed hard, about to explode. This wasn't his day. He wasn't going to win.

Martin stood at a urinal, the rest of the room apparently empty.

I glared at him as he turned his head slowly, looking me up and down.

But he didn't seem surprised to see me.

A scar stretched across his jaw as he spoke. "You disappoint me," he said, turning back around and finishing up. "Of all the things to drag your ass back to Thunder Bay for, you came back for this." He zipped up his pants and fastened his belt. "You didn't come back for me when they put me in the hospital last summer."

"Let them go," I demanded.

He just chuckled, turning around and heading to the sink.

Turning on the faucet, he pumped some soap and lathered his hands.

I stepped up. "The video is a fake," I stated, remaining calm. "Someone spliced in shots of their faces. After all, who would be dumb enough to show themselves committing such a heinous crime?"

He cocked an eyebrow, listening to the story I'd pieced together on the plane ride here.

I folded my arms over my chest. "I mean, why wear masks in the first place? The Graysons, Moris, and Torrances will pay for any expert you need to back up that story, and I'm sure they'll be very grateful for your willingness to show their families support."

He rinsed his hands, a smile playing on his lips. "And Griffin Ashby?" he pressed. "Am I supposed to ignore the justice he wants for his daughter?"

"She's sixteen," I growled in a low voice. "Not twelve. That law is laughable. Damon didn't force her."

No one thought he did. That video was evident.

Sure, he was kinda sleazy sometimes, and he was really good at coercion. Maybe he took advantage. She was blind, so . . .

My brother certainly wasn't anyone to ensure justice for young girls.

"These charges won't stand." I inched closer. "All you'll accomplish is making yourself the enemy."

Grabbing some paper towels, he dried his hands and listened, too at ease. Why was he so calm?

Even if he were confident, Martin didn't like me talking back to him. What was going on?

"The town is in shreds tonight," he mused, looking at me with a gleam in his eyes. "Have you seen the streets? Their heroes are dead. It's beautiful." He laughed again, tossing the towels into the trash. "I got each one of those little shits in a cell. Except Crist. My patience has paid off. I just need to be a little more patient."

What the hell did that mean? Did he know who posted the videos? Was he in on it?

"I'm going to tell everyone the truth," I said. "I'm going to tell them everything you did to me. Will Grayson and Kai Mori will be heroes."

He stepped closer, and I retreated a step, bracing myself, but then he said, "Come with me, Emory. I want to show you something."

He walked past me, out the men's room door, and I couldn't fucking swallow. Fear curdled in my gut.

Too calm. He was never this calm.

I spun around and followed him out the door and farther down the hall.

He didn't bat an eyelash at anything I'd said. Was he really going to charge a senator's grandson for giving him the beating he deserved?

Opening a door on the left, he walked into the dim room, and I stopped, looking inside.

There was a glass partition and a table on the other side, handcuffs wrapped around a set of fists.

I drifted in, Will coming into view in the next room as he sat secured to a table all by himself, Kai and Damon nowhere to be seen.

I rushed up to the glass, pressing my fingertips to it.

He looked like shit.

But that bergamot and blue cypress wafted over me as if it were yesterday and he were right next to me.

My chest shook, taking in the bags under his eyes and the smile that was no longer there.

"I'm going to tell everyone you're in love with him," Martin said. "You'd say anything to protect him. I'm sure I could find witnesses to corroborate a time or two you both were all over each other. The Cove. The school bus, was it?"

I stared at Will. I knew someone must've seen us that night racing through the parking lot.

"Do you have proof of *your* allegations?" Martin asked. "Witnesses? Photos?"

I curled my fingers into fists as Martin came to my side and looked at him, too.

"He burned down your gazebo, Em." His tone was steady. Planned. "He's been fucking everything with a skirt, snorting anything that'll fit up his nose, and drinking everything that promises him sweet oblivion for the past two years," he told me.

I clenched my teeth, locking my eyes on Will. *Look up.* Just let me see your eyes.

"And you still want to be his whore, you fucking sl—"

I growled. "Their lawyers will get them out of this," I said, cutting him off. "This entire town is on their side, and whoever isn't, is on their fathers' side. No one wants to see them pay."

He chuckled and then sighed. "It's the ones closest to them they can't trust the most."

"What do you mean?"

But he just kept staring through the glass.

What does he know? "Who uploaded the videos?" I demanded.

He just smiled to himself.

Something was going on. More than just some fuckup of someone getting a hold of that phone.

I looked at Will again. He sat back in his seat, staring at the table, something vacant in his gaze.

He burned down my gazebo.

He hated me. He didn't want to have to look at me anywhere in this town.

My eyes watered, but before I hardly had a chance to notice, Martin shoved an envelope at me.

I took it. "What is this?"

I opened it up and pulled out the document.

"I can't handle it anymore," he said. "She's yours now. You want to be free, you're free. Take her."

What? I skimmed the paperwork—my grandmother's power of attorney transferred to me, and all I had to do was sign.

This was the one thing he still had to hold over me. The only thing that kept me in his life. Why would he turn her over?

"Then give me my money, too," I told him.

I couldn't care for her without it.

But he just smirked. "I don't know what you're talking about."

I shook my head. Her nursing home was over seven grand a month. Even if I quit school and worked three jobs, I'd never be able to pay that and support myself.

And I didn't have the money to take him to court. God knows where he could've hidden the rest he hadn't used. It was gone.

Walking over to the table, he picked up another envelope, this one white. He ripped it open and pulled out whatever was inside, tossing it onto the table. Pictures spilled, fanning out, and I recognized the Polaroids instantly.

"Found your stash behind the coffee-table books."

He raised his eyes, meeting mine, and I stood there, squeezing the docs in my hand, because I couldn't squeeze his neck.

He picked up a photo of me, the one with the bruises on my ribs from when he'd kicked me when I was fifteen. "You know, it does make me feel a little badly," he said. "Looking at all of this together like this makes it look like you really went through hell."

I'd thought about taking the pictures with my phone. Indestructible with the cloud and easy to send and receive digitally.

But he checked my phone, so I documented the abuse for a rainy day with an old Polaroid camera for a while. In the beginning when I thought I was smart and I could use it if I had to run for my life.

I'd stopped keeping evidence by the time I was seventeen. By then, I just held on with every thread I could muster.

"I was aggravated at first . . . when I found these." He circled the table, picking up another and studying it. "But everything is an opportunity, isn't it?"

I narrowed my eyes, the papers crinkling in my fist.

"I'm not going to take your advice," he said, throwing the pic on the table and sliding his hands into his pockets. "They'll be charged, but the DA will suggest a plea bargain."

"Fuck you!" I gritted out. "They won't plea shit. They'll always win."

"I almost think you want them to."

Against him? Hell, yes. Whatever they did beyond that was none of my concern. I was leaving town tonight.

I wouldn't be able to keep Grand-Mère at Asprey Lodge, but I'd work hard enough to afford something decent in San Francisco. All that mattered was that we were free.

Martin approached me, pulling his phone out of his pocket and tapping a few buttons.

Then he handed it over, but I didn't take it as I looked down and watched someone in a white mask with a red stripe—Will—rear his arm back and launch a bottle of liquor affixed with a burning rag at my gazebo.

The camera shook, but I heard the glass break and then flames burst everywhere, the zoom coming back out to take in the whole scene as my work was consumed in fire.

I turned my eyes away, looking at Will through the glass.

"It's over," Martin said. "The end of an era. They'll plea. They won't fight the charges. And you're going to help me make sure they don't."

I shook my head. That would never happen.

"They'll go away for a couple years," he continued. "Just long enough for me and my associates to get a hold on this town, and then they can come home."

"And what makes you think they won't fight this?" I pressed, turning my gaze back on him. "You're fucking insane."

"Because if they do," he told me, inching in, "I'll be forced to air a much darker scandal. They victimized women in high school. Assaulted them. Beat on them. Forced them into the catacombs to satisfy their deviant desires. They're not boys. They're devils."

I laughed under my breath. He *was* insane. I'd be the first to admit they abused their power, but after helping one of them hide a body, I knew now that people were more complicated than that.

Everything used to be black-and-white until I realized that was just my perspective. I judged, because thinking was too hard.

They weren't evil.

"Not all the girls will come forward, but we have one on record." He walked to the table and spread out my selfies as if it were evidence. "And I'm confident more will follow."

I watched as he pushed a paper across the table and laid a pen on top of it.

I picked it up, reading it.

"She'll sign that paper, attesting to the validity of her claims," he instructed, and I stopped breathing, starting to understand. "Even if there are no findings, the accusations will be enough to ruin their lives."

I skimmed the statement, detailing how the guys "roughed me up" and forced me into the catacombs at St. Killian's and . . .

And hey, here were pictures to prove their abuse.

Oh, my God. He was going to pass my pictures off as evidence against *them*.

"I wish you would die," I said, tears filling my eyes.

"But I can make all this go away, Mr. Mori," he went on. "And

Mr. Torrance and Mr. Grayson. They fucked up. They're young. They'll serve some time, get out, and move on with their lives. It will be as if it never happened. The girl will be satisfied. I can keep her quiet. Perhaps with a small monetary donation to sweeten the deal?"

I forced down the lump in my throat. *No.* He could try it, but it would never happen. I'd never let him use me like this.

"I mean, this is actually a blessing," he continued. "If she's allowed to speak out, it could get so much worse for your sons."

"Fuck you."

"Sign it."

"Fuck you!"

He grabbed the back of my hair and shoved my head down to the paper, sticking the pen in my face.

I growled, pushing myself away from the table.

"Sign it, and you're free," he bit out as I backed up to the glass, my eyes burning. "You don't have to feel guilty. I mean, what's on those videos is only a small fraction of what they've done, Emory. How they've taken advantage of the people here. Let their money and family names save their asses time and again."

I whipped around, staring at Will still sitting at that table. Where was his lawyer?

I won't . . . I won't hurt you. I shook with sobs. I'll never hurt you again.

"Just think of all the women he's had," Martin pointed out. "All the life he's wasted as a burden on his family, never doing or living for anything important. For anything larger than himself. He's taken, Em. All he does is take. He fucks and screws and forgets about you."

I closed my eyes, about to cover my ears.

"They deserve some consequences. You know I'm right. They did commit crimes."

No. If it happened, it happened, but I wouldn't help Martin send them to jail.

"Those videos weren't the only ones on that phone, you know?" he pressed. "If they were poor, they would've been in jail a dozen times by now."

I stopped, my pulse ringing in my ears.

Phone . . .

"That's what they used to document their pranks, right?" he asked. "A cell phone?"

I looked over at him, my cheeks wet with tears.

He shrugged, feigning sympathy. "If more videos were to surface . . ." He tsked, continuing, "Arson, assault, robbery, grand theft auto, breaking and entering, sexual deviances . . . I can only imagine the videos lurking out there somewhere that haven't been posted yet."

My stomach sank, and I rose, standing up straight as I gaped at him. The vomit churned, and I almost dry-heaved.

No.

Pulling something off the table, he handed me one more piece of paper, and I read the check for over thirty-seven-thousand dollars made out to me.

"The balance of what's left," he told me. "And you have the power of attorney transferred to you. All you have to do is sign. You can take her, and we never have to see each other again. You'll be able to pay for top-notch care. And they won't even know it's you in the photos. Your full face isn't in them anyway, and it won't be on the unofficial statement I take to them."

I stared at the check.

He was giving me what I wanted. I could move my grandmother to somewhere close to me, pay for her care for however long she had left, and my education wouldn't be interrupted.

I set my palm on the glass, feeling warmth where everything else was cold.

He had a point, right? I'd heard that Will was messing up. Even his last year in high school, I heard he was getting high all the time. Would he clean up his act unless he were forced to?

I just wanted to go to school and take care of my grandma. I deserved for good things to happen, I'd fought long enough, and if I didn't give in and agree to this, he might go to jail anyway and for longer. What if Martin knew who uploaded the videos? What if he were telling the truth, and he could get them to upload more?

I clutched the thin piece of paper, everything I wanted one signature away.

One signature I'd never make.

"I want you to die," I whispered.

He stood there quietly. "You know what life is like inside of a one-star nursing home?" he finally asked.

I closed my eyes, seeing Damon Torrance with his hand wrapped around his mother's throat, and I could damn near feel it.

I wanted to know what that felt like.

"Sometimes the patients will have bruises they shouldn't have or they'll find the elderly lying in their own waste for hours," he went on. "She doesn't know what the fuck is going on half the time anyway, so she won't care."

My blood boiled, every muscle inside of me tightening.

"You're bluffing," I breathed out. "Even you wouldn't do that to her."

I saw him turn toward me out of the corner of my eye. "She was transferred this morning," he told me.

I whipped around to face him, and then I screamed, shoving him in the chest with both of my hands and then running in to knee him between the legs.

"Motherfucker!" I yelled.

He collapsed to the ground, and my body moved of its own accord. I couldn't stop it. I swung my leg back to kick him, but he launched up and grabbed it as it came in and yanked me down to the floor.

Gripping the back of my head, he grabbed a fistful of the flesh at my waist and crushed it in his hand. I cried out and dove in, biting his face.

He howled, and I swung, slamming him across his jaw before he grabbed me by the collar and slapped me across the face.

I whipped around, my body crashing back to the floor, and I coughed, scrambling to my feet as the sharp sting spread across my face.

Swinging my leg back, I kicked him in the head, not hesitating a moment before I did it again. And again.

The taste of copper filled my mouth as blood sputtered from his mouth, and he tried to sit up on his knees, but he just fell over again.

You'll never lay a hand on me again.

Unlike Damon, I knew how to really hide a dead body.

Pulling the chair out at the table, I sat down, silent tears blurring my eyes and blood coating my teeth as I reached over and grabbed the statement and then the pen.

Clicking the button at the top, I looked up, gazing at Will through the glass.

I could tell myself all sorts of things to make this okay.

If they weren't who they were, they'd go to jail anyway.

I was saving them, actually. More videos coming to light would increase the charges.

They did *commit crimes. And there were tons more no one knew about.*

But the bottom line was . . . this was wrong.

I scribbled my name at the bottom of the statement that would convince their families to accept the charges in order to not risk more charges. I shoved it across the table, stood up, and grabbed the check and power of attorney, walking to the window as shame made me look away from my reflection in the glass.

"Some of us will always be casualties," I whispered to him. "Rungs on a ladder that others climb."

He looked up suddenly, and it looked like he was looking right at me. Like he could see me.

"Some people can't stop what happens to them," I said. "They're just born in the wrong place, wrong time, with the wrong people."

Will deserved his vengeance.

I'd just thrown him under the bus to buy my grandmother's last days.

"I'll expect you," I whispered to him.

I felt my brother rise from the floor, sniffling and grunting.

I turned, not looking back as I walked for the door.

"Safe trip home," Martin choked out. "You'll never see me again."

I threw open the door, not bothering to clean up the blood on my face as I left the room.

I'll see you again. Will would be coming for both of us.

CHAPTER 33

WILL

Present

We put Rika and Winter through what we did for nothing!" I growled. "We spent years thinking it was about the fucking videos, and it was about you! *I* did that to my friends. *I* brought you into their lives."

I didn't give a shit about the story she'd just told us. I knew it wasn't her idea. I knew she had no beef with us.

She just didn't give a shit about me. How could she let anyone think I did those things to her?

I stepped closer. "Do you have any idea what prison feels like?" I said to her as Alex and I stood in our soaking clothes and Emmy dropped her eyes, her hair in her face. "You could've done anything. You could've come clean and told me what you did. You could've come to me before you signed that damn paper, and I would've had your grandmother sent to the best home in the country!" My voice grew harder again as I shouted. "My parents would've paid for your education. You never had to do anything alone!"

It had been years. If she felt badly about what she'd done, it would've eaten away at her enough by now that she would've owned up. But no. I'd found out through my grandfather who, of course, knew it was all bullshit. I couldn't believe he, my parents, and Kai's parents didn't tell us seven years ago, but they probably knew we'd battle it and just wanted us to take the lesser sentence instead of taking any chances.

Everyone stood around, silent as the train whistle rang in the air outside, and I watched her chin tremble and the lump in her throat move up and down.

"What, are you gonna cry now?" I taunted. "You gonna cry?" Again?

I'd fucking give her something to cry about. I could understand the position Martin put her in. I sympathized.

But my God, was she blind? All she had to do was tell me. Lean on me. Ask for help. That was all she ever had to do!

"Look at what you made of me," I said, inching forward and slapping my chest of tattoos that depicted home and all the life I'd lost even before I went to prison. "You made me into this." I screamed in her face. "You!"

She flinched, but just then, someone pushed my ass back, and I stumbled, looking up and meeting Micah's eyes.

He slipped in between us, Rory joining him and both of them inserting themselves between Emmy and me and staring at me like a warning.

What the hell? I tipped my chin up, glaring as my guys—*my guys*—now stood in front of her instead of behind me.

Unbelievable.

Peering between their shoulders, I met her eyes once more. "I reached for you," I told her. "In my head, all these years. Even after you dumped me like trash and I couldn't fall out of love with you no matter how much I drank and snorted, my brain reached for you always."

She remained frozen, not faltering as she stared at me.

"When nothing gave me a reason to get out of bed, my friends were falling in love, making babies, and I felt so alone . . ." I choked on the tears in my throat I wouldn't let loose. "What do you think was the only thing that made me keep breathing?" My tone hardened as I clenched my jaw. "In my brain, I reached for you. I never stopped reaching for you."

And she let her brother tell my family that, not only did I not love her, but I passed her around for my friends to abuse like she was nothing.

When she was everything.

I hardened my voice. "Get the fuck out of my face," I gritted out. "And it's fine if you want to get the fuck off the train, too. Go, run back to him."

I won't reach for you anymore.

She stood there a moment, her eyes darting around the people in the room and probably wondering something dumb like how she was going to save her pride or some shit.

But then . . .

She turned and walked away, still dressed in Aydin's T-shirt and boxers as she slid open the door and slipped into the next compartment.

As soon as she was gone, silence sat like a ten-ton weight in the room, no one speaking.

But then, after a few moments, someone spun me around and threw her arms around me, all of my friends crowding around me as Winter hugged me.

"Are you okay?" she asked. "What happened in there? Why was she there?"

I couldn't talk right now. I could barely draw in a breath.

Misha pulled me away and yanked me in next, squeezing me so tightly. "What can we do?" he asked. "What do you need?"

And then Damon. "You're sure you're okay?"

I held up my hands, sweat seeping out of my pores, and my stomach rolling with them so close. "I can't." I backed away, trying to get space. "Just . . . I can't right now, okay?"

But Michael grabbed me anyway. "Are you okay?"

I growled, yanking away. "Don't touch me." I shook my head, the room spinning. "Don't."

"All right," he breathed out, hands off. "I'm sorry."

They all stopped and stepped away, falling silent. I could feel their eyes on me and their looks between each other, because they didn't understand, and I couldn't get into it right now.

I rubbed my eyes, smelling the familiar scent of the cellar on my hands from the rope I'd tied Aydin up with.

Aydin.

I held my nose between my hands, breathing in the house.

I wasn't ready. I should still be there. I shouldn't have left.

"I gotta make some phone calls," I said, turning and heading for the door and leaving them. We were at least five cars from the engine. Hopefully Emmy was hiding her ass somewhere I wouldn't have to look at her, because I was so mad I could strangle her right now.

"Your name is on your cabin door," Ryen said, finally speaking up. "There's clothes in there."

I slid open the door, wind and the sounds of the wheels on the tracks rushing through, but then Winter spoke up before I could step through.

"Why would he do that?" she asked.

I stopped.

"Who?" Banks asked her.

"Martin Scott."

I let the door fall closed, quieting the room and remaining a moment.

Winter continued, "If what Emory said was true, why would he work so hard to make sure you all went to jail? Money does the walking in Thunder Bay. Your presence, or lack thereof, wouldn't make his career."

I listened, everyone silent as the words hung in the air.

Banks spoke up, figuring it out first. "Unless he's working with people who have power. People who wanted you in jail."

My stomach coiled tighter and tighter.

"You heard what she said," Kai chimed in. "He had plans for Michael, too. And then nothing. Michael never got fingered for anything."

"Because Trevor didn't want his family embarrassed," Misha said.

"Because Evans Crist didn't want his family embarrassed," Rika said instead.

I closed my eyes, not surprised at all. My friends picked up on things without missing a beat.

"Motherfucker," Michael said. "It wasn't about Will. Or his hatred of Will. His grandfather was coming up for reelection that year. He almost lost because of the bad press."

"And Kai and Damon?" Banks pressed.

No one said anything, and I finally spoke up, "Evans knew that Schraeder Fane accounted for Damon in his will." As executor of his estate, he would've known who Damon really was. "If he planned on marrying Rika to Trevor, he wouldn't want to share the fortune with Damon—and by extension, Gabriel."

"And Katsu Mori was forced to step down from the boards of Mitchell & Young and Stewart Banks," Rika explained. "Both of which helped finance Evans's real estate projects over the next several years."

"Which my father might not have been inclined to support if he'd still been on the boards, since he hates your dad," Kai said to Michael.

It had all come together. The past seven years spreading out before us in a maze that took all of us to complete, but finally made perfect sense once and for all.

The amount of people who had played us like puppets for their own end, and the amount of time I wasted being ignorant of all of it and floating with the current . . .

I almost wish I could go back to the nights at Delcour and fucking with Rika when we thought it was all her fault. How simple it was then.

"Alex?" Rika said. "You okay?"

I looked over my shoulder, realizing Alex hadn't spoken since we boarded. She leaned into the windows, arms folded across her chest and staring off.

After a moment, she nodded but didn't make eye contact, the usual square to her shoulders in an unnerving slump.

"Only three of you came on board," Damon said. "Where are the other two prisoners? Our research said there were five."

But neither Alex nor I answered.

I stared at the dazed look on her face, completely defeated.

She'd never see him again.

But just then, she pulled herself up straight, cleared her throat, and cracked her knuckles. "I need to spar. Now."

"Rika or me?" Banks asked.

She shot off, toward the door where I stood. "I'll take you both."

She passed me and left the car, followed quickly by the girls with Winter's hand locked in Rika's as they all followed Alex.

I hesitated only a moment before I opened the door again. "I need to make those calls," I said, leaving.

But Michael's voice rang out behind me. "Is anyone from that house coming for us?"

But I didn't turn back or answer. Aydin Khadir was problem six hundred fifty-three, and I was only on number four.

I ended my fourth call, setting the phone down as I rose from the chair. I was still in my semi-wet jeans, but instead of heading into the shower or changing into the suit laid out for me on the bed, I turned and stared out the window instead.

The night passed by quickly, the sea on the horizon calm and black as I ground my fist.

Martin Scott was dead meat. He deserved to rot in an unmarked grave in the middle of the woods where he'd be alone and forgotten.

The hell he put Emmy through . . .

I was angry and disappointed with her, and I'd never look at her again, but as much as I hated to admit it . . . maybe I understood how she thought she didn't have any other choice.

Her only unforgivable mistake was the years of silence since.

She should've stepped up and sought us out. How did anyone live like that?

I didn't want to make her suffer anymore. I just wanted her out of my life for good. It was obvious now that we weren't right and that she wasn't one of us.

I was ready to live.

A knock sounded on the door, and I tensed, hearing it immediately open behind me.

"Hey," Misha said, and I heard the door close.

I drew in a deep breath and exhaled, his presence making me feel like the walls were closing in. We were always close, despite the age difference, but I hated that he'd gotten tangled up in this. He never liked drama, and he hated my friends.

And I'd been without him a long time. Too long.

I turned and studied him, seeing the tail of a tattoo drift over his collarbone and his lip ring gleam in the small light.

He shifted on his feet. "I'm sorry it took us so long to find you," he said.

I crossed my arms over my chest and headed back to the desk, folding up the notes I'd taken from my calls and slipping the paper into my back pocket. "I wasn't waiting for a rescue or expecting one."

"Your fucking parents," he murmured. "They just . . ."

"They didn't send me there," I told him.

My parents would never do that. They were at their wits' ends, trying to figure out what to do with me, and they hid it from the rest of the family pretty well, but they wouldn't give up on me like that.

"Grandpa?" Misha guessed.

"It doesn't matter."

I wasn't ready to talk about Blackchurch and how I came to be there until I was sure my plan would work. I wasn't in the clear yet, and I didn't want to come clean until I was.

Misha stood there like they all stood there, because shit had changed, and it would be a while before we got back to normal. If ever.

He chuckled lightly. "I seem to remember your advice about not getting tattoos anywhere visible while wearing a suit?" he teased.

I met his eyes, seeing his gaze on my hands and the dark ink I'd added over the past year while I was gone.

I stood by my advice, but fuck it. I'd been bored there.

He approached, but I kept my gaze averted. "You were there for me—or tried to be as much as I would allow—when Annie died. I'm so sorry it took us so long."

His hands shook a little, and I could hear the sorrow in his voice.

It took a moment to get the words out. "I was always coming home," I assured him. "Don't worry about it."

He was going to be pissed when he found out who was really to blame. I didn't want him carrying any guilt.

"You're different," he said.

I nodded. "Yeah, I grew up."

"I wish you hadn't."

I stopped and looked up at him.

"You never did see how much everyone needed you." A smile crinkled the corners of his eyes. "You. Just the way you were."

No one needed me. I'd been useless.

But I wasn't anymore. Devil's Night was in three days, and Thunder Bay would be ours, free and clear, in four days if I had anything to say about it.

Misha looked like he wanted to hug me or something, which was strange, because he wasn't affectionate, but then he turned and walked for the cabin door, opening it to leave.

I wanted to go after him, but . . . I picked up the phone, getting ready to make another call instead.

Nothing was going to be normal for a while with any of them. I had to stay focused.

But then I heard Damon's voice. "I need to talk to him."

I shot my eyes up, seeing him loom over Misha and trying to squeeze past.

"I'm trying to fucking leave, if you would move," Misha spat out.

Damon pushed his way in, Misha stumbling into the hall, but I stalked over and grabbed the door before Damon could close it.

"I can't right now," I told him. "I'll talk later."

"No . . ."

"I can't." I pushed him out the door. "Please, man . . ."

My pulse raced, my blood boiled, and my brain was spiraling out of control. I had a chess board full of pieces, and I was playing both sides. I needed to think. There was no time to lose. He could ruffle my hair later.

"Dammit," Damon growled. "Are you fucking kidding me?"

"I'm not going anywhere," I assured him, hanging in the doorway as he glared at me from the corridor. "I'll see you tomorrow. I need to sleep."

Rolling his eyes, he gave in and spun around, heading off. "Fine."

But then guilt nipped at me. "Wait."

He stopped and turned, his white T-shirt wrinkled and his black pants stark against his pale, bare feet.

I felt a smile pull at the corners of my mouth. "So, what's his name?"

A gleam hit his eyes. "Ivarsen."

Ivarsen. My heart warmed a little. We had another boy running around. Kai's son, Madden.

Needles pricked my throat. I'd missed Winter giving birth.

"Next gen, huh?"

"Get your ass moving and catch up," he teased.

Yeah. I didn't see kids on my horizon any time soon, but . . . someday.

He started to leave, but I stopped him.

"Where are we?" I asked.

He met my eyes again. "North of the border," he said. "We're cruising the coast, and we'll pass under Deadlow Island and arrive home in the morning."

So, Canada, then. Where the hell had they gotten this train? And there was a tunnel underneath the seabed between Deadlow and Thunder Bay? No one ventured to the small island off the coast of our town, beyond Cold Point, because it was surrounded by an impassable reef.

It was deserted, or so I'd thought.

"Sorry it took us so long to get there," he told me. "We had to find a way in undetected, and some of the track was in bad shape."

It's fine. I didn't need them there any sooner, but I wouldn't tell him that.

"Just make sure . . ." I paused a moment. "Make sure she doesn't actually jump off the train, okay?"

She could be that stubborn, and I knew what I had said to her, but I was mad. I didn't want her dead.

And I definitely didn't want her to end up in Aydin's hands again. He'd had enough influence over her in five short days.

Damon struggled to hold back his smirk before he turned and left, and I closed my door, the phone in my hand forgotten.

Trailing over to the bed, I ran my hand over the black suit laid out, shivers running down my spine at the long-lost feel of good clothes.

Then I spotted my mask sitting on the bed, as well. I reached over and picked it up, the familiar texture filling me with memories and a charge of excitement in my veins at all the moments I wanted to keep, despite the ones I wanted to leave behind.

For a second, I felt like the old me, and I gazed at the white mask with the red stripe down the left side, suddenly ready for a thousand more adventures.

I smiled. Whatever was I going to do with Emory Scott when we got back to Thunder Bay?

CHAPTER 34

EMORY

Present

I knocked on the door, pretty sure she was going to slam it in my face, but I needed some clothes, and I didn't really know the other women enough to ask.

When there was no answer, I knocked again. "Alex," I called.

Her name was posted on the door.

But still, no answer.

She could be asleep. I hadn't located a clock, a phone, or a computer between hiding at a dark table in the empty dining car and now, so I had no idea what time it was, but it was still dark.

Twisting the handle, I entered her cabin, a shot of fear hitting me, and I didn't know why.

She might not be alone.

What if she was with Will?

Deep down, I knew that was ridiculous, but I couldn't help it.

Moonlight streamed through the windows, casting light onto the small space through the little curtains, and I looked around the empty room, closing the door behind me.

The coast was clear, so I didn't waste time. Stepping over to her closet, I opened it and pulled out some jeans, a flannel, and some sneakers.

I needed underwear and a bra too, and I almost blew it off, but I pulled open a small drawer in the cabinet, spotting lacy things.

A shot of heat rushed under my skin.

Setting my hand inside, I felt the black corset bra, kind of angry I'd never experimented more with clothes. When I lived at home, I didn't want my brother to see anything he wouldn't approve of, but in the years since I'd been gone, it never occurred to me to take an interest.

Without thinking about it, I pulled out the corset and some matching panties and donned them both before quickly pulling on the black jeans and buttoning up the blue plaid shirt.

The train whistle sounded again, and I looked out the window, squinting into the night. I wish I had my damn glasses.

I slipped on the shoes, tying them up, and then found Alex's brush and smoothed out the tangles in my hair. She had makeup and a little jewelry in there, always prepared for anything. I didn't know her like family, but I knew her well enough.

Closing the closet, I left the room and headed out of the sleeper car and down the train. I trailed through a corridor of more private cabins and crossed into another car with chairs facing the windows, and refrigeration units holding wine and champagne.

Darkness and the slight rocking under me were all that greeted me as I went from one car to another.

Where was everyone? I needed to find a phone to check in with the world.

As soon as I entered the next car, though, I looked up and saw some of the guys.

I stopped. The sconces on the dark wood walls barely lit the room, and I scanned their faces, a little hidden in shadow, but did not see Will, Misha, Micah, or Rory among them.

Michael sat in a chair, his eyes locked with mine as he lifted a glass to his lips, while Kai stood at the windows with his arms folded, and

Damon rested against the bar, holding a glass of something amber colored. I couldn't see his eyes, but I knew he was staring at me.

Next to Will, I was most sorry about him. I'd helped him bury a body that I'd watched him murder, and he never told anyone about my involvement. When we got back to Thunder Bay, he might have his own vengeance in mind for me.

"I didn't want to hurt him," I said. "I didn't want to hurt any of you. I just wanted to protect her."

They didn't move or speak, Michael taking another drink.

"I made a mistake," I told them, feeling naked as they glared at me like I was prey. "I thought I was alone."

My voice softened to a whisper, but no matter how much I hated this, and never in a million years dreamed I'd be groveling to them, it needed to be done. They deserved an apology. At the very least.

"I'm sorry," I murmured. "I am very sorry."

Kai turned and stepped toward me. "You think that erases anything?"

I shook my head. "No."

"You think we would ever trust you not to do something like that again?"

"No."

"You threw us to the wolves," he growled, and I could see his white teeth shining in the dark room. "You think your words mean anything to us? Your apologies? Your explanation? Your excuses?"

I forced the lump down my throat, keeping my spine straight, but my mouth shut.

"You're weak," Michael said. "There's no way we can trust you."

"You had years to come forward," Kai pointed out.

I nodded. *Yes. Yes, I did.*

"It was hard," Kai told me, and I could hear the tears in his throat. "We didn't deserve it."

My chin trembled, and I clenched my jaw to stop it.

"Will didn't deserve it," he continued.

I know. Just thinking about Will in a cell, surrounded by cruel people, locked up in gray walls . . .

"You're not good enough for him," Kai finally said.

I looked up, meeting his gaze despite my shoulders wanting to slump and the urge to fold in on myself.

I'd made a mistake. I wasn't a bad person.

I wasn't.

I turned to leave, but then I heard Damon's voice behind me.

"We set Rika's house on fire, Kai," he said.

I turned and looked at him as he stared at his friend.

"Stole all her money," he continued. "I kidnapped her, and you forced Banks to marry you. I tried to kill Will . . ."

"We made mistakes," Kai argued with him. "We would never do that again."

"Speak for yourself," Damon fired back. "The role of the villain is only determined by who's telling the story."

An electric current ran under my skin, and I almost smiled, grateful.

They got redemption, because they felt they had their reasons.

Damon and Kai looked at each other, and even though Kai was the one I could see myself connecting to in high school, because he was stubborn with a clear idea of right and wrong, Damon had been my savior on more than one occasion when life had proved there was so much gray.

They were like yin and yang, and I understood. I got it now.

"You'll make it up to us," Michael finally spoke up, meeting my eyes. "You'll stay at St. Killian's with Rika and me."

"No."

"Yes," he said.

He wanted to make sure I didn't skip town. What was he going to do? Lock me up?

And then I paused, remembering that he could. They lived at St.

Killian's. He had a whole dungeon at his disposal. No one would hear me scream.

"I have a place to stay," I told him. "In Thunder Bay."

His eyes thinned on me, probably not trusting me, but probably not wanting to deal with the hassle, either.

"You don't leave town," he ordered. "You will pay your debt."

I straightened. "I won't leave town."

He nodded once as Damon took a drink from his glass and Kai glared at me.

I shifted on my feet. "May I borrow someone's phone, please?"

But Michael just raised his glass to his mouth again, mumbling, "Borrow one from the girls. We're using ours."

I shifted on my feet, finally turning around and rolling my eyes as I left the car. I ventured back the way I came, trailing from one box to the next, past the kitchen, the dining car, the cabins, a room with William Grayson engraved on the door, and the lounge car.

They weren't using their phones, but at least he wasn't telling me I couldn't use one. For all he knew, I could be calling my brother and trying to get help.

But I wouldn't.

I might be safer if I jumped on a plane to California as soon as we arrived in Thunder Bay, but now that it was all on the table, I knew.

I was the one who hurt them. I needed to see this through.

For Will.

Even if he never wanted me again, I owed him this.

Leaving the empty lounge, I spotted movement through the window in the next railcar. I watched one of the girls inside, her dark locks hanging in her face as she held Alex in a headlock. I slid open the door and stepped inside the gym, noticing a couple of treadmills, weight machines, and a floor mat for sparring.

Erika Fane stood off to the left with her arms folded over her chest, while Winter Ashby straddled a bench off to my right.

As I let the door slide closed behind me, everyone turned their eyes, staring at me.

The black-haired one, poised over Alex, pierced me with her green eyes, and I saw Winter shift and turn her head to train her ears.

"Those are my clothes," Alex said, panting.

I chewed the corner of my mouth. "Yes, I know."

She hooded her eyes and pushed the other woman off, rising from her knees and standing up. Sweat made her skin glow, and her shorter hair was pulled back into a low ponytail as she walked to the treadmill and grabbed a towel.

Erika inched over, her arms still folded. "Alex filled us in." Her eyes fell down my body. "You're okay?"

I nodded. "Thank you for asking."

No one had yet.

Erika cast a glance at Alex, who was downing some water, and then back to me as she started to walk past. "We'll leave you two alone."

"Don't," Alex told her.

Erika stopped, and Alex capped the bottle and faced me.

Splotches of sweat darkened her white workout top, and she stepped toward me in her black yoga pants and bare feet, hands on her hips and fire in her eyes. "In the moment, you actually didn't know who you were going to choose down there, did you?"

I tipped my chin up. "Was it that I might've chosen Will or that I might have chosen Aydin that bothers you the most?"

Her eyebrows shot up, and I didn't quite feel satisfied that I'd annoyed her, but I didn't feel badly about it, either. She and Will still failed to understand that it wasn't a choice I was making between the two men in Aydin's bedroom.

It wasn't about them at all.

She approached, glaring at me like she was judge and jury. "You broke his heart."

"Don't sell yourself short," I retorted, remembering Will's taunts.

"I'm sure you provided loads of comfort to him all these years. 'In his bed, in the shower, on the beach, against the wall, on the hood of the car, and in his back seat.'"

She growled, coming right for me, but I shot out and caught her, pushing her away before she hit me. "I'm not going to fight you."

"You don't get to decide!"

She lunged into my face, and I pressed my palms to her chest, pushing her back again.

"And you're not going to fight me," I told her. "I'm tired of bleeding."

What had been happening in my head in that house was the same battle I'd always fought. A battle between how I always saw the world, and how I craved to see the world instead. I needed to change as much as I needed Will.

I needed to like myself as much as I loved him.

I stared at her, feeling the eyes of everyone else in the room, and while I kind of understood where she was coming from, because I felt the same jealousy thinking about her and Will as she did thinking about Aydin and me, her notions of who I was and what I deserved weren't my problem.

"I will make amends for my crime all those years ago," I told her, "but what goes on between Will and me is none of your business. I don't give a shit if you're his friend, his mom, or God. You're not entitled to a grudge against me. This isn't about you."

A glint hit her eyes, and then she cocked her head, silent for a moment.

"You sound just like him," she finally said, crossing her arms over her chest. "He got to you quick, I see."

He.

Aydin.

She shook her head. "Like a true, manipulative monster—"

"Like a father."

It wasn't at all like she was thinking. I barely knew Aydin, and I didn't want to sleep with him. She was taking something far more complicated and whittling it down to fit her own shallow perceptions of the world, so she could understand something she was determined not to ever comprehend.

I didn't want to fuck him.

I cast a glance at the others before turning my eyes back on her. "I thought I'd remember my parents better since I was almost twelve when they died," I told her. "I didn't realize what a burden it takes off your shoulders to have guidance. I didn't realize I'd missed it so much until I had it again."

Aydin Khadir had an agenda. He stole me, put me in a dangerous position, and manipulated me.

But people change people, and while he was no hero, I couldn't help but feel a little grateful. I'd been dying before I woke up in Blackchurch.

"I was safer in a house full of criminals than I was with my brother, because of Aydin," I gritted out, "so you may as well exhale, because I won't apologize for seeing something good in him. You did at one time, after all."

She stood there, silent with a glimmer in her eyes, but her jaw flexed, and she didn't budge.

Always strong. It was something I loved about her. He'd made her, too, after all. Even just a little.

"Now, may I please use someone's phone?" I asked.

After a moment, Erika reached over and plucked hers out of the cup holder of the stationary bike and handed it to me.

"Thank you," I said, backing out of the room and leaving them all alone again. "I'll bring it back within the hour."

I opened my eyes and stared up at the ceiling, blowing out a breath and shifting between the two huge bodies on both sides of me.

Too hot in here. Damn.

I looked over at Micah, seeing his face buried in his pillow, and then turned my head, seeing Rory. His blond hair covered his eyes, and his arm was pinned under his head. Both men were shirtless, but they'd thankfully kept their pants on.

After I'd found a room and made my call with Erika's phone, they pounded on the door, insisting to stay with me because the "pampered little know-it-alls who thought their shit didn't stink aren't getting a piece of you."

As if Micah and Rory weren't a little pampered themselves.

It was actually pretty adorable, though, and now we're all cramped in my bed as the moon shone outside and the train vibrated under us.

To hell with it. I'd take all the friends I could get right now. I liked them.

Sitting up, I climbed over Rory's body and gently stepped out of bed, looking down at the two beautiful guys and their sleeping forms. A serial killer on one side, and the son of a terrorist on the other. Man, my parents would be proud.

What were they both going to do after we got to Thunder Bay? They couldn't go home. Would someone be coming for them?

For Will?

Still in my jeans and shirt, I slipped on Alex's sneakers and tied them up.

I left the room, steam from the heaters fogging up the windows, but I could see the rain splattering on the outside.

I needed food. I couldn't remember the last time I ate, and now I wished I'd eaten that sandwich I'd made when I waited for the brownies to cook earlier today.

Or yesterday. It was probably after midnight now.

God, had I only made the brownies yesterday? Fixed the chandelier? Made love to Will in the shower? It seemed like so much had happened since then.

The kitchen was back by the bar car, and I still hadn't seen Will since the confrontation in there earlier. Not on my search for a phone, not when I returned it to Erika an hour later, and not tonight as I'd smelled food being wheeled down the corridor and past my room, not stopping at my door, unfortunately.

It was weird. I'd only made one phone call with Erika's phone. For some reason, I thought I'd have a lot to tend to, but after I called my firm and left a message, assuring them I was safe, I sat there at a loss of who else to contact.

I was of no concern to Martin, Grand-Mère was gone, and there was no one else. No friends, really. No pets to check in on. No man waiting for me.

I think I'd had a dentist appointment yesterday, maybe . . .

Heading down the next corridor, I approached the kitchen door, but heard a cry and halted for a moment.

"Oh," she moaned.

I didn't know if it was Erika, Winter, or one of the other girls, but hunger pangs wracked my stomach. I needed some food. Or a drink at the bar.

Tiptoeing down the passageway, I threw a quick glance through the kitchen door, seeing the naked back of Winter Ashby as she sat on the steel worktable in the dark kitchen, her arms around her husband.

"I love you," she whispered as he kissed her neck.

Taking his face in her hands, she pressed her lips to his mouth, lingering slow and gentle before moving her kisses to his cheeks, nose, forehead, and temples.

He closed his eyes and smiled, breathing that short, excited breathing like he was riding a roller coaster.

My body warmed, kind of intrigued to see him like that, but I didn't linger. Continuing past the door, I stopped at the end of the car, looking through the windows and seeing the bar full of people. Kai and his wife, Michael and Erika, and then Alex. Will and his cousin were still nowhere to be seen, as well as a couple of other men

I saw helping them when we were rescued. I believe Misha had a woman with him when we boarded the train, as well, but I didn't see her either.

The room was still dim, the cherry-colored sofas and chairs rich and warm against the wooden walls and the amber glow of the light.

Kai held his wife in his lap, smiling as she said something into his ear. Michael reached around Erika, making her a mixed drink and adding far too much tequila. She laughed.

My gaze dropped to Alex who was sitting in a chair with her legs pulled up. She nursed a glass and stared at nothing out the window.

I fisted my hands. Aydin could be dead.

She'd never admit it, but I knew that was where her mind was.

Someone approached my back, but I didn't have to turn around to smell the bergamot.

"Did you know about Aydin and Alex?" I asked Will, still staring at her.

"I knew what she told me," he said. "I knew of him. Not his name."

"He's in love with her."

"He can't have her."

I turned my head, tempted to meet his eyes, because the possessiveness of his words scared me.

But then he continued, "He's bad for her."

I looked at her again, seeing her how I never got to before. The couples surrounding her, in love, and despite the fact that she had Will to lean on, I'd never seen her so lost.

"And I'm bad for you, and you're bad for yourself," I went on, "and Damon's bad for the world, and Martin is bad for me . . ." I twisted the handle, crossing cars. "The world is only so big, Will."

We couldn't shut out every single person who'd disappointed us. Some of them were still worth fighting for.

I entered the bar car, eyes turning up at me as I walked in, Will following me. "We should go back," I told everyone. "To Blackchurch."

"What?" Kai blurted out.

Michael scowled. "Excuse me?"

The door slid closed, and I made eye contact with all of them. "We should go back and get the ones we left behind."

"We can't go back," Michael said.

"We can." I nodded. "The locomotive goes in reverse."

He rolled his eyes, and Kai stood up, his wife climbing off of him. "A security team will already be there. Going back puts Will at risk."

"First of all, Aydin and Taylor are loose ends," I told them. "You rescued Will under the assumption the other prisoners wouldn't care. They do. I promise. And second, Taylor Dinescu can go fuck himself, but Aydin would be a useful ally. We need him."

"You need him," Alex retorted. "Aydin Khadir doesn't deserve us. That's the difference between you and me, Em. I can sacrifice what I want for the good of others."

"And what do you think I did?" I fired back.

I wanted Will more than I'd ever wanted anything. I wanted it all.

I just didn't want him experiencing the stress of my life. I was embarrassed. And I needed to protect my grandma. I fucking sacrificed.

I held Alex's green eyes, seeing the pain in hers that I always felt in mine. She thought it was easy for me, because it was easier to believe that.

She knew better.

She pursed her lips, and I could see her trying to swallow, but she couldn't. After a moment, she downed the rest of her drink and swiveled in her chair, looking over at Michael and Erika as she set her empty glass on the table. "Do you remember that pool party Michael and the guys took you to when you first moved to Delcour?"

Erika nodded, hopping off the stool and walking over to sit in the chair next to Alex.

"Aydin was there that night," Alex told us. "He went to Yale with one of Michael's teammates, and we hadn't seen each other in a long time." She paused, and I could see the memory playing behind her eyes. "The more I drank, the more I hated him, and the braver I got."

Why did she hate him? I'd gotten pieces of a story at Black-church. He wanted her. He denied it, because of family pressure. She survived without him.

Alex looked over at me. "I was roommates with his girlfriend in college, you see?" she told me. "We played together one night while he watched us over Skype. That's how we met."

Played? I couldn't imagine that. I couldn't imagine Aydin in college. Experiencing youth like a real human.

I could see her, though. Performing for him. Taunting him.

"You should've seen his eyes." Alex closed hers for a moment as everyone listened. "It was like he was in pain or something. I could almost feel his breath and the heat in his arms." She opened her eyes, lost in thought. "And then a few nights later, he wanted me to himself, but when push came to shove, he couldn't step up, and he chose her."

I remained in my spot as Will dropped down into the sofa on my right.

Alex shrugged. "It was okay. He wasn't mine to begin with. I had no right."

Setting her glass down, she exhaled and continued, glancing at Erika. "The night of the pool party, I'd heard they weren't together anymore, and when he couldn't stop looking at me across the room, the stronger I got," she told us. "But I wasn't going to let him win. I wasn't a dog, sitting there waiting for his affection."

"What did you do?" I asked.

But it was Will's voice I heard next. "You let me take off your top in the pool."

Another man taking her top off in front of him . . .

"And he was watching," I said.

Alex tipped her chin up, the pride covering up the pain from a few moments ago. "Life goes on," she said, "and my bed wasn't cold. I wanted him to know he didn't matter, and I wasn't ashamed of anything I'd done. He didn't exist."

And Aydin couldn't look at her, but he didn't want his fiancée anymore, either. He got sent to Blackchurch over it.

She looked over at Will. "Everyone looked at me. Your hands on me."

"And then everyone else got naked in the pool," Will continued.

Alex's gaze drifted off. "And he watched me look at you and you look at me and knew that he'd lost."

"And what did you win?" I asked.

Believe me, I knew something about staying on your feet and not letting anyone get the better of you, but she'd been hiding behind Will to fend off the loneliness and despair.

Because when they enabled each other in their vices, they felt accepted and didn't have to face the harder road ahead.

That road was inevitable.

"Not everyone is born knowing their path is from point A to point B, Alex," I bit out. "You and Will are the same. You sit up there on your high horse, all 'love conquers all' and shit, and refuse to understand that there are impossible choices others have to make, but it doesn't mean we don't love."

My voice grew harder, and I glanced around the room and then back to Alex.

"Does it suck? Yes!" I yelled, feeling Will's eyes on me. "But do you understand it? I know you do. Sometimes the uncertainty seems like more of a risk than just staying with what's familiar. It takes time to grow that courage. Don't you understand that?"

They could all do whatever they wanted in high school, and now years later in Thunder Bay, because Damon was right. The villain was just a matter of perspective. It was as easy as pie for them to judge me, because on the rare occasion they weren't doing fucked-up shit themselves, they got these splendid little attacks of sanctimony when it came to anyone outside their little group.

"You're so self-righteous," I snarled, looking around the room. "All of you."

I lashed out and kicked the table so that the vase sitting on it toppled over. Alex tensed, a fire lighting in her eyes.

Will sat there like ice.

"You're not good enough for me," I told them and spun around, heading out of the room.

But then I heard a chair creak and Alex's voice behind me. "I want my shirt," she blurted out. "Now."

I twisted around, seeing her standing and challenging me with her hand out.

"And my sneakers," she said.

"Get fucked, Alex Palmer!" I bellowed, flipping her both of my middle fingers.

She started for me, but just then the lights went out, the train lurched, and the wheels underneath us screamed as I flew back into the wall and crashed to my ass.

I winced. What the hell?

Moonlight cast a soft glow in the car, and I saw Will jostle in his seat. Alex flew forward, landing on her hands and knees in front of me. One of the guys cursed, and a woman cried out.

I gasped, looking around the dark compartment, seeing Will still seated and righting himself, while Michael pushed himself to his feet and took out his phone.

"What was that?" Kai snapped.

"Everyone okay?" Erika asked.

The train had stopped, but I just looked up and met Alex's glare in the darkness as she looked at me like she wanted to kill me.

Right there in the darkness with everyone distracted.

Will's body ten feet away warmed my skin. Feeling his eyes

suddenly on us, my heart beat so hard in my chest I could hear it in my ears.

"What's wrong?" Michael asked.

He must be on the phone, but I didn't look away from Alex.

"Okay, got it," I heard Michael say in the distance. "Yes, we're all right. Send an attendant to check the rest of the cars. Thank you."

The V of Alex's gray T-shirt hung open as I gazed down the tunnel between her breasts. I dug my nails into the carpet.

"The trip stop engaged," someone said. "We were going too fast. It won't take long to get the railyard to throw the switch and get us going again."

But no one responded to him. Something pulled at me, and I looked over, seeing Will leaned back in his seat, arms slung over the back of the sofa, and his eyes locked on me.

Alex grabbed my foot, and I sucked in a breath, turning my eyes on her.

She stared at me, and then slowly . . . slid her other hand up my ankle, held my leg, and pulled her shoe off my body.

Heat rushed in my veins.

The eye of the storm. The eye of the storm.

I drew in a breath and gently exhaled, calming my breathing as I leaned back on my hands and let her take my other leg, pull it up, and slide off the other sneaker.

Rain hit the windows, the forest silent outside under the cover of night, and Michael lit a candle, everyone in the room looming in the background as the hairs on my body stood on end.

Everyone was silent.

There. Filling the room.

Watching us.

She gripped my ankle.

"I don't want to fight," I murmured.

But she retorted, "I still want my shirt."

Will didn't move, but I heard his intake of breath.

The pounding in my chest grew harder, and I felt his eyes and the heat pooling between my legs. I couldn't think about anything.

No fear. No doubt. Just the moment.

There was nothing about me to lose that I wanted to keep.

Slowly, I pushed off the floor, Alex rising with me, and I wasn't going to run.

I unbuttoned my shirt.

"Do you think he's dead?" Alex whispered, closing the distance between us.

"No." I moved my hands down, unfastening one button after another. "You know he's not."

Aydin had destroyed his life over her. He was too single-minded to die yet.

Slipping the shirt off my shoulders, I handed it to her, and she took it, letting it immediately drop to the floor.

"That's my favorite corset," she told me, not breaking eye contact.

I swallowed, my stomach dropping a little. I could feel six pairs of eyes all over the bare skin of my arms and chest.

With my gaze locked on her, I started unfastening the hooks, thinking about her bare chested at that party, and me feeling in front of Will right now what she would've felt in front of Aydin that night in the pool.

Others looking. Standing and not backing down.

If this made her feel stronger in front of her crew, I could take it.

Let's see how far she wanted to push this.

She dropped her head, her hair brushing my cheekbone as she ran her knuckles over the lace on my stomach. "You look good in it."

I unfastened the last hook, whispering, "It feels good."

Hesitating only a moment, maybe wondering if anyone was going to stop me as the fire of Will's gaze covered my skin, I opened the corset, baring myself, and slipped it off, holding her eyes as I held it out to her.

But she didn't take it. "And my pants?" she ordered next.

The air pricked my nipples, and my head swam. Michael Crist, Kai Mori, Erika Fane, Will Grayson all stared at me and . . .

Nine years ago, I wouldn't have given them the pleasure. Now, it was about my own.

Screw 'em. Alex and I had this coming.

I unbuttoned the jeans, and she slid down my body, dragging the pants with her. I breathed hard, closing my eyes as she helped me step out of them, and when she rose again, I pulled her in, hovering over her mouth and slipping my fingers just inside the hem of her pinstriped little boxers.

"You think so, huh?" she teased.

"Yeah. I think so."

I pushed them down her legs and then took her T-shirt, lifting it up.

She met my eyes, but before she could worry about me or what I was diving into, I pulled it over her head and then yanked her body into mine.

"Yes," I whispered over her mouth as I ran my hand over her face, down her neck, and back up to her jaw, squeezing it.

Threading my other hand up into the back of her scalp, I kissed the tip of her nose, her forehead, and ran my lips down her cheeks, tasting her soft, sweet skin, my stomach filling with this need that I knew I couldn't stop.

I dug my fingers into her, baring my teeth, and both of us panting hard as she whimpered, "Emmy."

But I didn't want to stop. I sank my mouth into hers, covering her lips and kissing her strong and hard. My nipples pressed into her own, and any protest she had died on her tongue as it tasted mine, sending a shockwave current right under my skin with its fucking wet touch.

I wanted to open my eyes and look. To see the look in Will's eyes, and know that he was traveling with me on this, but it was enough to know he was watching.

I nibbled her bottom lip, biting it with my teeth, and then flicked her top lip with my tongue, unable to stop kissing her.

Grabbing her hands, I forced her on me, peeling my panties down as I tugged at hers. Both of us naked, I pulled her into me again, nearly every inch of her body touching mine, and I couldn't think.

Gasping for air, I let my head fall back and closed my eyes, feeling her mouth graze all over my neck and fall down my chest.

I held her head to me. *God, I want this.* I wanted it all. I wanted Will to see me like I saw him in that wrestling room and know that I wanted to feel. I wasn't scared to fall with him, because he made me feel safe no matter how high we climbed.

I wanted him to see me, and I wanted it to be in her arms, and I wanted them to watch.

"Are you sure?" she asked.

I tipped my head forward again, caressing her face as her breath hit my lips.

I opened my mouth, but before I could tell her to keep going, I heard someone else instead.

"Don't stop," the other voice whispered.

My mouth dry and my body throbbing with need, I glanced over her shoulder to see Kai's wife sitting on the floor between his legs, staring at us and barely breathing. He leaned forward, his hand on her neck and his thumb caressing her jaw as they both watched us.

Michael held Erika in his lap, her leaning back against him and their gazes fixed on us, too. His hand rested inside her shirt.

And that was it. Any speck of hesitation or doubt completely drained out of me. I wanted to see me, too.

"Emmy . . ." Alex started.

But I grabbed the back of her neck and brought her in nose to nose as I stared at her mouth and reached down, stroking her pussy.

She whimpered. "Emmy, we should . . ."

"Don't talk," I growled low over her lips. "I want you."

She shivered under my touch, tears filling her eyes, and I pushed her back to the chaise. She crashed onto her back, her brown hair spilling over the upholstery as I came down on her, grazing my fingers over her cunt and reveling in how fucking soft she was.

She squirmed, grabbing my hand but not pulling me away, and I heard shifting in the room. Sharp breaths and groans coming from somewhere.

I refrained from looking at Will, not wanting my nerves to get the better of me, as Alex's and my hands roamed everywhere. Her hands gliding down my body and my hands caressing her face as I hovered over her and kissed her lips.

My breasts brushed hers, the hard flesh of her nipples sending a shiver up my spine, and I continued my light touches between her hot thighs.

"I'm going to lick you," I told her, working my fingers inside her and teasing her clit.

She shuddered. "No."

"Yes." I clasped the back of her neck and rolled my hips into her, the heat and sweat already too much to bear. "Open, Alex. Spread your legs for me."

I kissed her, dry humping her, our moans mixing with the other moans in the room, and her breath and tongue heating my mouth, so much so that I was almost ready to beg her for it. I wanted to suck on her so bad.

She remained still for a few moments, and then . . . Her thighs fell apart, and I smiled, arching my back as she pushed up and tugged my nipple with her teeth.

"Will?" I panted, keeping my eyes closed as she sucked. "I want to be in one of your videos."

Let me put it on the line like them right now, and no going back.

Alex groaned. "You sure?" she taunted. "You want a video of you fucking me?"

God, yes. I tipped my head down, capturing her lips, the taste of her boiling in my blood.

But then Will spoke up. "The train is already wired, baby," he said in a ragged voice. "Top right corner, behind you."

I looked over my shoulder, seeing the small black security camera near the ceiling, the glow from the candle reflecting in the lens. It was already recording all of this.

Alex licked her way up my neck, teasing my mouth. "Lick me now."

Yes, ma'am.

Grinning, I dove in for one more kiss, deep and so good, before I pushed her back down on the chaise and worked my way down her beautiful body.

I kissed her breast, tasting her skin with my tongue and sucking on her plump flesh. I moved to the other one, kneading her hips as I caught her nipple between my teeth and bit and sucked.

Gliding farther down, she scooted up for me, sitting against the back of the chaise as I laid on my stomach, bent my knees, crossed my ankles, and swung my feet into the air behind me, settling my head between her legs.

Hesitating only a moment for a glance, I spotted Kai's wife in his lap now, reverse cowgirl with his hand inside her panties and all of her other clothes gone as she watched us. Michael and Erika had moved, her ass planted on a bar stool as he stood between her legs, both of them watching us as he slowly peeled her panties down her thighs.

Will hadn't budged, his arms still draped over the sofa and his face hidden in shadow.

Fuck it. Fuck it all.

I glided my tongue up her silky slit, feeling the soft, supple skin of her pussy, and even though I wanted to feast, I wanted this to last forever. I wanted to taste her.

I sucked her clit into my mouth, drawing it out and feeling the little nub harden and rush with heat. I nibbled the sides, slipping my arms underneath her thighs and holding on as I flicked her with my tongue again and again, doing the same things to her that I liked Will doing to me.

Coming in hard, I sucked her into my mouth, French kissing her hot pussy, my own clit ringing like a damn bell.

God, I was wet.

I dove down, sinking my teeth into her thigh, kissing and biting her every damn place I could reach.

"Emmy," she cried, threading her fingers through my hair and grinding against my mouth.

I looked up at her, her tits pushed up and bobbing as she fucked my face, and I held on tight, feeling her body quiver as her orgasm crested.

Sweat glistened on her brow and between her breasts, and my head swam, so light and warm.

Everything was warm. A piece of fabric tore somewhere in the room, and I heard a cry and a groan, and I smiled, diving in and sucking her again so hard, she fisted my hair and threw her head back, belting out a hot, little moan.

"Ah!" She shook and panted, coming on my tongue, and I loved it. God, I loved it.

I had a heart. *I can dive and feel.* I knew that now.

I was free.

And now, it was my turn. Climbing up, I sucked her off my lips and lifted her leg, sliding my right one underneath it and putting my left foot next to her hip. Holding her leg with one hand and planting my other behind me for support, I started to rub my pussy against hers, grinding on her fast and feral, chasing the goddamn itch inside me.

"Oh, fuck," I heard Kai growl.

I leaned back, rolling my hips and turning to the side just a hair, so I could feel all of her as my breasts swayed with the ride.

I looked over at Kai and his wife, her eyes closed, her back against his chest, and his fingers deep inside her as she reached back and wrapped her arm around his neck.

He bit her ear, and she turned her head, sinking into his mouth.

Erika was naked, facing me with her fingers dug into the stool as Michael devoured her neck and slid inside of her from behind.

I let my head fall back as Alex and I scissored, my cunt growing wetter as I rolled my hips again and again, rubbing on her harder and harder.

Coming down from her orgasm, she gripped my thigh and started to ride me back, matching my rhythm, and I looked over, seeing Will still watching us, the heavy rise and fall of his chest the only sign that he was alive.

"He watches you like Aydin watched me," Alex said softly.

I squeezed her breast, possessive and hungry. "This isn't for him," I whispered.

This was about us. Her knowing that I saw her, and me knowing there was more to myself than I knew. That I could go to the edge.

I was more than I thought I was.

"Ah, Emmy," she moaned as our pace quickened. "Your cunt is so hot. Fuck me."

"Yeah," I whimpered.

My tits shook, and my hair tickled the small of my back as I fucked her pussy, and let the moans escape as I felt it coming and coming.

"Oh, Jesus," Michael growled.

Everyone watched us, Michael's and Erika's eyes zoned in, and Kai and his wife's gasping for air, piercing us with their desperate eyes as he finger-fucked her.

"I'm gonna come again," Alex said.

I shook my head. "Don't come yet."

"Oh, God." She squeezed her eyes shut. "Harder."

I rocked my hips harder, her clit rubbing against mine and making the blood rush in my legs as I let out cry after cry, unable to contain the pleasure.

"Fuck, fuck . . ." I screamed.

"Emmy!"

"Don't come," I demanded, grinding circles into her and feeling her heat mix with mine. "I want more. I'm not done with you. I'm not done."

I wanted to come all night.

But we were already there. Alex's body went rigid, every muscle tightening, and a trickle of sweat fell down my back as my orgasm exploded, lightning filling my body.

I cried out so loudly, I didn't care if the whole damn train heard. Shudders wracked through my body, and I slowed, locks of hair in my face, my skin damp, and a wave of contentment sweeping through my body.

God, that was hot. "Shit," I murmured.

"That didn't last long," I heard Michael say. "I'm sorry, babe."

Erika chuckled, out of breath. "It's okay. I came." And then some kissing sounds. "I love you."

"I love you, too," he said.

Opening my eyes, I looked down at Alex, her stomach rising and falling in heavy breaths, and I bent over, resting my forehead on her chest.

She ran her hands over my back, holding me tight.

In another moment, Kai's wife came, whimpering into the dark train car, and I almost smiled, but I didn't have the energy.

Never would I have imagined I'd do something like this, but I wasn't embarrassed. Not in the least. They followed us, all of us leaping over the edge, too.

I was about to rise back up and face Will, but just at that moment, something slipped around my neck and I was yanked up, an itchy rope squeezing my skin.

Will pulled me against his body, and I tipped my head back, looking up at him as he leaned down, his lips brushing my ear.

"Don't get too comfortable," he whispered in a raspy voice. "You haven't left prison yet."

He grabbed my breast, squeezing it like it was his property, and chills spread out over my body as the train started moving under us again.

His hot breath filled my ear. "It's time you saw the catacombs."

A shiver ran down my spine, and my nipples pebbled as I turned and looked at him. "I don't want to grow up anymore," I told him. "Take me back to Thunder Bay."

Back to Neverland.

I'm ready.

CHAPTER 35

WILL

Present

You gonna fight?" I said to her as David led her off the train.

She smirked, the rope I had around her neck last night tied around her wrists now. "I'll never stop," she taunted. "Promise."

A smile threatened, and I jerked my chin at David to get her out of here before she saw how much power she still had over me.

Last night was insane. What was she doing to me?

She was incredible. To see her like that, alive like she was in the greenhouse, too, and to know that the lies I carried around to make myself feel better about losing her all those years ago were completely untrue.

She fit with us.

She was *made* for us.

What wouldn't people do if they felt safe enough to dive in head-first? She did it. She didn't have to, but the best part about it was I didn't think she was thinking about it at all. She just let go.

I wanted to wrap my body around hers so badly I refrained, because I knew that I'd squeeze the life out of her, wanting her so much. My cock was so hard last night, watching them.

And Alex . . . The way Emmy took control of her was even more of a surprise, because I knew Alex wasn't used to it. It was beautiful to see her dominated and seduced and taken charge of, so she could just revel instead of feeling the pressure to give others pleasure when it was high time for her turn.

Luckily, Emmy hadn't seemed to wake up yet, even though nightfall had passed hours ago. The spell hadn't broken, and she was still . . . divine.

We arrived in Thunder Bay around eight this morning. Lev and David were instructed to take Emory to St. Killian's and they walked across the platform, followed by Misha and the girls. The guys stayed behind with me in the emptying car.

I spotted a courier outside and opened my mouth to tell the guys I'd see them in a while, but then, all of a sudden, a punch landed in my gut, and I hunched over, barely registering Damon moving to Kai, and then Michael next. He threw a punch across Kai's jaw and landed an uppercut right in Michael's stomach.

"Ugh!" Michael growled as I winced.

"Man, what the fuck?" Kai barked, rubbing his face.

I looked up at Damon, the pain in my abs like a knot tightening over and over again.

He inhaled a deep breath, fixing the lapels of his suit jacket. "I'd rather not walk in on my sisters in some weirdo, bacchanalian sex fest ever again," he stated. "Understand?"

He didn't wait for an answer. Spinning around with his lips tight, he stalked off the train as the rest of us tried to stand up straight again.

Shit. He saw that last night? Fuck.

"I keep forgetting those are his sisters," Michael said, rubbing his stomach.

Kai started laughing, shaking his head. "Crap . . ."

We all started laughing, an image of him walking in and then promptly back out replaying over and over again in my head. How had we not seen him?

Poor D.

I held out my hand to Kai. "Give me your keys," I told him. "Ride with Michael. I have a few things to do."

He nodded and dropped his keys into my palm, grabbing the back of my neck and bringing me in. "Welcome home," he said and then left the train.

It felt good to be home. *I think.*

"Take Emory with you," I told Michael. "Lock her up downstairs. I'll be back in a while."

"Okay."

Micah, Rory, and I headed off the train, and I grabbed the envelope from the courier as I passed, not stopping for anything as I ripped open the package and dug out a cell phone. Turning it on, I clicked to my keypad, my thumb hovering over the numbers, but . . .

I wasn't ready. I didn't want to face the world yet, and I wasn't sure what I was going to say to my parents if I did call them.

Or my grandfather, brothers, or other friends . . .

Slowly . . .

Clicking the key fob, I saw the taillights of a black Porsche Panamera light up, and the three of us climbed in, my body tingling at the feel of a car.

God, it had been so long. The leather seats grinded under my weight, and I inhaled the scent of the new vehicle, instant euphoria calming my brain.

Fuck, this felt good.

Starting it up, I hit the clutch, turned up the radio as some new song from Thousand Foot Krutch started playing, and punched the shift into reverse, hitting the gas.

We peeled out of the parking lot, the speed and music taking over as Rory let his head fall back and his eyes close, exhaling for the first time since I'd met him. Micah sat in the passenger seat next to me, his head tipped out the open window, smiling and sighing at the same time as the wind blew over his face.

How we'd missed the simple pleasures of speed and wind and freedom.

I just needed a decent cheeseburger now, and I was home.

We raced into town, past the Cove, past Cold Point, and through the neighborhoods, a for sale sign sitting on the lawn of Emmy's old house. The yard looked like shit, and I knew Martin Scott was spending more of his time in Meridian City as he moved up the ranks of public service, but I did a double take, not expecting to see that. Did Emmy know the house was for sale?

How long had it been on the market? It was a great house in a quaint little neighborhood. There would be interest soon, if not already.

Turning right, we passed the village and the cathedral, turning left up into the hills and past my old high school as we headed up to my parents' house.

I kind of wished I could put this off a while longer, especially since I wouldn't get out of there easily with my mom whining about how worried she'd been, and my dad grilling me about every detail until he was good and satisfied. But if they found out I was in town and hadn't touched base, it would be worse.

I wasn't sure why I'd brought Micah and Rory with me. Maybe I wanted them to see my life here. Or maybe it aggravated me they'd taken her side yesterday, and I wanted some time with them myself. I'd worked too long and too hard on them to lose them to my little usurper.

I did kind of appreciate their loyalty to her, though. That might be useful.

Climbing out of the car, we jogged up the steps of my house. Everything looked exactly the same as when I'd left more than a year ago. I had no idea where my keys or clothes were at this point, but I guessed the crew had kept my apartment at Delcour, so I should have a good supply of things still there.

I squeezed the handle, the door opening immediately, and I

smiled smelling the fresh flowers my mom always kept in the house as I stepped inside.

The foyer was grand and white, like Blackchurch, but my mom was a far better decorator. It was light and airy, and I smiled as the guys followed me, looking around themselves.

"Hello?" I heard Meredith's voice. "Who is that?"

The head housekeeper rounded the corner, drying her hands on a towel with her hair pulled back in a ponytail so tight her eyebrows nearly reached her hairline.

She smiled, seeing me. "Will!"

"Hey." I leaned in, giving her a peck on the cheek. "Any of my family home?"

I didn't want to give her a chance to ask questions.

She shook her head. "No. Your parents are in California for the week on business, and there's no one else here. Should I call Mr. and Mrs. Grayson?"

"No," I blurted out.

This was actually perfect. I missed them, but I had more pressing matters right now that were better dealt with with them out of the way.

"I'll surprise them," I told her.

She looked at Micah and Rory, and I could see she wanted to talk more, but knew it wasn't a good time for a chat. "Well, it's good to see you."

"Yeah, you, too."

"Do you want something to eat?"

"No," I lied, remembering how I loved her breakfast casseroles. "But I'll be back in the next few days. Just pass on the message to my parents when they get home that I'm in town, and I'm not going anywhere."

She grinned. "Good. Your mom needs her spin partner back."

I groaned inwardly before she winked and walked away.

"Spin partner?" Rory repeated.

"Shut up."

Micah snorted, and I rolled my eyes.

I looked around, intending to go to my room and pick up some things when I got here, but now I didn't feel up for it.

"You need clothes or something?" Micah asked.

I didn't answer. I walked to the small table on the wall, instead, and pulled open the drawer, taking out some car keys.

I tossed them to Micah. "Take the Audi and follow me."

We left the house, and they hopped in my father's car as I took Kai's, all of us jetting into the village and sliding into spots just along the curb in front of the theater. I had something to give them, and more business to take care of, but as soon as I grabbed the envelope and climbed out of the Porsche, I looked up and saw something new in the distance.

What . . . ?

The leaves rustled in the trees, the smell of pizza wafting out of Sticks hitting me, but I didn't even look when someone noticed me and called out, "Oh, my God. Will! You're back!"

I kept my eyes on the top of the small hill, in the center of the park, in the middle of the village.

Where the hell did that come from?

We jogged across the street, the guys following me into the park and up the incline, my heart pounding as I took in the massive, beautiful, wrought iron gazebo standing in the place of the one I'd burned down.

As if it had always been there. And Emmy's had not.

After the fire, the city had cleared away the debris, and a few years later I was out of jail, constantly avoiding the emptiness that loomed to my left every time I went into Sticks or the theater or the White Crow Tavern . . .

I'd only been away less than a year and a half this time, and someone had rebuilt a gazebo in the old one's place?

Someone had taken away my chance to make amends.

Not that I'd been rushing to do it myself, or even sure that I wanted to, still pissed at her constantly as I was, but . . . I didn't like the opportunity to decide for myself taken away from me now.

"This was the gazebo?" Micah asked. "I thought she said it was burned down."

I'd forgotten she'd mentioned it that night at the dinner table. I wasn't about to explain myself, especially when I had no idea who built this, but why wouldn't Michael or Kai stop them? They would anticipate I had plans of my own for a replacement someday. Or they'd anticipate that I'd *eventually* have plans of my own.

I gazed up at the black, circular structure with four sets of stairs, one each on the north, south, east, and west sides leading up to the landing, and the open roof, the beams coming from all sides to join at the top, letting in the falling leaves overhead and the rain during thunderstorms. Ivy wrapped around the railings, almost like the gazebo grew out of the land.

It was quite beautiful, actually. I wouldn't have done it better, so there was that consolation.

Well, shit . . .

Exhaling, I shook my head and turned away, facing the guys as I dug in the envelope. "The car is yours for now," I told them.

My parents wouldn't balk at me borrowing it for as long as I needed. They just didn't need to know it wasn't for me.

I handed Rory another key and pointed to our family's movie theater behind him. "There's an apartment at the top. Fully furnished, the fridge is stocked, and it's all yours."

My eyes shifted from him to Micah, and I handed them each a phone and a billfold.

Rory's brow knit in confusion as he opened the wallet and sifted through the license, the credit cards, and the cash, everything rush delivered this morning at the train station.

He looked up, pulling out the Black Card with his name on it. "You didn't have to do this."

"I didn't."

Micah's black eyebrows shot up, and he looked at Rory, and then at me. "Our parents?"

I didn't answer. I'd made lots of calls last night, but it wasn't as much of a miracle to arrange all of this on short notice as it probably seemed to them. I'd been planning all of this for a long time, and me and my little laptop in my attic room had started these wheels in motion a long time ago.

They had a car, a place to stay, money, and they didn't have to return to the families that had hidden them away in disgrace. It was the start of a new life, and it was the least they deserved.

"Do what you want," I told them. "Stay. Go. Flush the money and cards down the toilet."

I wanted them here, but they had to want it, too.

"Just give me the weekend," I said. "See if you want to build a life here."

They glanced at each other, knowing they could go anywhere, for at least a little while.

Their families only agreed to leave them alone, because my friends and I—Graymor Cristane, our company—came with the deal.

But I wasn't forcing them to do anything they didn't want to do.

"If you stay," I pointed out, "if you want to be a part of what we are, your parents will fund your buy-in to our resort. If not, no worries."

They could run on their own. Or they could run with us.

"Thunder Bay is where you don't have to hide," I told them.

We were a family. We'd had the rug pulled out from under us a long time ago, but we weren't changing. Everyone else would.

I just needed to hear a yes from them.

"I'll let you think about it. Let's head to Michael's house," I said, leading the way back to the cars. "We need food."

"I'm not arguing with that," Micah said. "I'm starving."

And I smiled to myself.

If they were willing to stay through breakfast, then that wasn't a no.

I didn't stay. I dropped them at St. Killian's where the cook had breakfast laid out, but then I saw the table bustling with everyone and parents and security and . . .

My heart plummeted, seeing little black heads of hair scurrying around the table.

Kids.

My chest cracked wide open, and I didn't know which one was Madden and which one was Ivarsen, but I couldn't stay.

I just . . . I couldn't. I bolted, jumping back into Kai's car and racing away, leaving my boys and Emmy behind, and spending the rest of the day taking care of the gazillion other things I had to do, so I didn't think about everything I'd missed while I was away.

I'd known that, though, right? Both Banks and Winter had been pregnant when I went to Blackchurch. I'd known what was happening at home.

It was so hard to see their sons for the first time. I should've been there.

I hadn't been there.

After burning a thousand calories at Hunter-Bailey where my membership was still current—thank you, Michael—I collected some clothes and belongings from Delcour, checked in with my bank and unfroze my accounts, made some more calls, took care of a couple of other minor tasks, and had a quick meeting at the White Crow.

The town was just as beautiful as ever. The Bell Tower still sat in ruins, the Cove was still standing quiet from a distance, and Edward McClanahan's grave was decorated with trinkets from the latest pilgrimage made by the current basketball team of Thunder Bay Prep. I drove around for a long time, past Emmy's old house repeatedly, our old school a few times, and completely avoided the bridge where I'd almost drowned two years ago.

It wasn't until my fifth pass through the neighborhoods surrounding the village, the sun setting and dusk rising, that I realized it was EverNight. "Man or a Monster" played on the radio as candles flickered in windows, the upstairs rooms that belonged to teenagers and children glowing bright with their offerings to Reverie Cross.

As night settled, and the chill seeped into my bones, I wanted warmth, and I wanted that scent I had on me last night.

Did her brother know we were in town? It wouldn't be hard for him to know where to find her.

I veered toward St. Killian's.

Climbing the cliffs, the sea air breezing through the car, I cruised down the blacktop road, past Damon's house, Banks's house, Michael's parents' house, and Rika's mother's house, speeding through the pillars with their gas lamps, and down the drive to St. Killian's.

Candles glowed in every window, and I saw movement through the drapes upstairs as a thatch of grass sat in the center of the driveway with a bowl of fire blazing high. Gravel crackled under the tires, and I pulled to a stop, exiting the car.

The drive in was gorgeous. This place was beautiful. They'd done a good job.

Music and laughter greeted me as soon as I opened the door, and I peered inside the dining room, the open floor plan pretty well preserved, except for the few walls they added here and there to give some rooms their privacy.

Winter sat in Damon's lap as she and Alex laughed at whatever Rika was saying, the table strewn with notes, magazines, tuxes—for the wedding, I presumed—snacks and flowers. Banks and Kai must've gone home, and Micah texted me earlier to let me know they were heading to the apartment for the night.

I had no idea where Misha and Ryen were, but they'd probably gone to his house or hers in Falcon's Well, not far from here. Michael walked in from the kitchen with a platter of sandwiches, devouring one as he walked.

But I slipped back and away before anyone saw me.

A coo drifted off behind me, a flutter hitting my stomach as I turned and crossed the foyer, into the ballroom.

The chandeliers dimmed and the chairs and sofas spread out around the room, and I looked over and saw a playpen with a spiky black head of hair sticking out the top.

Walking over, I looked down at the blue-eyed boy with his father's eyebrows and his mother's long lashes, my chin fucking quivering because he was so damn cute.

Reaching down, I picked him up and held him in my arms, his little body feeling lighter than air.

Laughter went off in the dining room. His awesome baby smell made me dizzy, and needles pricked my throat as tears welled in my eyes.

I shook with silent sobs, looking at his beautiful face as tears streamed down my own. Damon had done all this without me. He was doing so well—without me.

I should've been here when the kid was born. I should know Madden.

"I'm taking you trick-or-treating next year, okay?" I whispered down at him. "I'm taking you every year. I'm getting my own house, and I'm going to be at every one of Michael's games and every one of your mom's performances and I'll be giving you the biggest presents for every birthday." I leaned my cheek into his forehead, just sitting there. "I'll even blow off your bedtime when they leave you with me for date night."

Ivar, Mads, and the baby Winter was carrying now would never know that I was absent.

Setting him back in his bed, I pressed my lips to his head and handed him his stuffed snake, smiling to myself as I remembered the Godzilla that I got Em. I wondered if she still had it.

Heading to the back of the house, I descended the stairs into the catacombs, seeing Rika had talked Michael out of covering the uneven stone stairs with wooden ones.

How long had it been since I'd been here? The night Damon, Winter, and I went off the bridge?

I walked along the hardwood floors, fake flames flickering on the walls inside their sconces and knowing there were a dozen or so rooms down here. I wasn't exactly sure where they put her, but I tried the first room I came to and twisted the handle.

The door gave way, opening wide, and I stepped inside the dark room, light from the corridor spilling in and revealing the body on the bed, under the sheet.

"Will?" she said, turning over.

I looked down as she rubbed her eyes, seeing the lacy black bra under the jean overalls she wore, my pulse instantly pumping in my neck and my dick twitching with life.

Fuck. I loved her in overalls.

I gazed at her olive skin, and the brown hair on her head hanging down her arms. The plump chest and the pink lips.

And the rope that was around her wrists this morning back around her neck, the slack hanging between her breasts and inside her overalls.

I smiled.

Sitting up, she scooted over to me, and I stood in front of her, looking down at my Little Trouble who hadn't changed a bit from how badly she pissed me off and got me hard in high school.

"Micah and Rory are staying at an apartment in town." I reached over, caressing her cheek with the backs of my fingers. "You want to join them?"

She shook her head.

I moved to the other cheek, caressing what was mine and then taking her jaw, gently holding it.

"They've got food upstairs," I murmured. "You want food?"

Again, she shook her head.

I tipped her chin up, loving how she played. It pleased me.

"You want to stay with me?" I taunted.

Slowly, she nodded.

Reaching into my jacket, I took out a case and set it on the bedside table.

"I refilled your prescription for your glasses."

I was able to talk Dr. Lawrence here into contacting her doctor in California and getting her most recent prescription filled.

"Where'd you get the overalls?" I asked.

"Found them in Rika's closet."

"And you're down here alone, despite the door not being locked?"

She didn't move.

The outfit, the rope, the willing and waiting in bed . . . I wondered when the fight would come, because it would, but God, I loved that she wasn't rushing back to being my enemy. Fucking her in this bed tonight might be nice.

Pulling her up, I sat myself down in her place and pulled her into my lap, wrapping my arms around her.

Sweat cooled my pores, and I couldn't seem to catch my breath, the last year or so and everything in the last twenty-four hours making my head spin.

For five minutes, I needed something to hold on to.

I tightened my hold, smelling her hair and damn near tasting her. If she hadn't shown up at Blackchurch, would I really have sought my revenge? Would I have chased her down in California and made her pay?

And how would I have done it?

I'd learned about the pictures and the lies almost two years ago, after Damon's father was killed. Then it was six months of trying to chase away the rage with globe-trotting, running, and drinking before I knew what I had to do. That was when I went to Blackchurch.

I dreaded dealing with her, because even still—after the betrayal—I hadn't wanted to lose her.

"I should've come to you," she finally said. "I wish I had come to you and explained and faced you then."

I swallowed the lump in my throat, knowing it wasn't all her fault. I wasn't a passenger in all of this.

I should've stayed. When she walked off on me after the meeting in the dean's office, and I threatened her that I could get anyone—I should've stayed.

She hadn't needed a boyfriend. She'd needed a friend, and I'd been selfish and arrogant and spoiled. I should've been whatever she needed, whenever she needed me. She didn't owe me her heart just because I wanted it.

If I'd cared, I would've been more patient.

Throwing her to my side, I let her land on the bed and I shot off the mattress, walking out of the room.

"Will . . . ?"

I can't. I can't right now. I closed the door, grabbed the key off the wall, and locked it, keeping her safely inside.

"Will, no," she cried, banging on the other side of the door. "Don't go, please."

I tipped my forehead into the wood, desperate to have heard those words from her a million times in the past.

"Will," she called again. "Stay with me."

I squeezed my eyes shut, fighting the urge to rip the door open and climb into that bed with her.

"Stay with me," she said again.

I shook my head, trying to clear it.

"What will he do if he knows you're in town?" she asked.

I turned away and walked toward the stairs. "He already knows."

I was sick of this same story.

Sick of not having her. Sick of Martin Scott. Sick of not seizing the life I was meant for.

It was time to end this.

I was ready for new adventures.

I climbed the stairs and stepped back into the house, closing the door behind me as I headed for the dining room.

Rounding the corner, I looked at them all seated at the table, Damon stopping mid-sentence as everyone turned to me.

"You got a nanny here?" I asked Winter.

But Rika answered instead. "My mom is."

Good enough. "Put on something black," I told them, heading back out of the room. "Let's go."

"Why?" Alex called out. "What's going on?"

But I was already gone.

Heading out to Kai's car, I pulled a duffel out of the trunk and dug out a black sweater, pulling off my suit jacket and unbuttoning my shirt right there in the driveway. I pulled on the black top, stuffed my jacket and shirt into the trunk with the bag, and pulled on the black ski cap as I ran back into the house.

In minutes, I'd pulled Michael's old Mercedes G-Class out of the garage, loaded in the supplies I needed, called Kai and Banks and Micah and Rory, and stuffed a couple of sandwiches into my mouth as the rest of us made our way out to the cars.

"Winter not coming?" I asked Damon as he climbed into the passenger-side seat.

"Not pregnant, she's not," he said. "She's staying with . . ." And he waved his hand like he couldn't remember the name. "Christiane."

His mom. His birth mother, that was.

And Rika's.

It seemed he now tolerated her presence for the sake of the children, and for Rika, but there was still a grudge there that hadn't disappeared since I was last in town, apparently.

I sat down as Alex climbed into the back, and I fastened my seat belt, spotting Michael trying to get my attention from the window of his Jag.

I cut him off. "Just follow me!" I told him.

Not giving him a chance to argue, I sped off in his G-Class with the supplies, and with Alex and Damon, while Michael and Rika followed in his other car.

It didn't take us long to reach the warehouse, which was usually dormant the rest of the year, but now alive with activity as the famed Coldfield.

As it was otherwise known in October when it was transformed into a haunted theme park.

This was where we partied in high school, the abandoned factory a playground for kids who wanted some shelter from the weather for them and three hundred of their closest friends and a few kegs of beer.

This was where Misha came to write his songs and lose himself when the pain of Annie's death was too much to bear.

This was where Damon, Kai, and I beat up Emmy's brother, getting drunk and making my knuckles bleed until I couldn't feel anything else that night.

This was where I found out I had something to bring to the table. Something worth a damn to our future.

"What are we doing here?" Michael asked as we walked past the lines of patrons waiting to get inside.

Howls and creaky sound effects filled the air as fog hovered above the ground and "Pumped Up Kicks" by 3TEETH blasted over the speakers. The smell of hot dogs and popcorn drifted up my nostrils, and squeals went off behind me as the actors jumped up on a group of girls. Men and women in masks stood around, all creepy and frozen and shit, staring at people in the distance and trying to scare the crap out of them.

Kai and Banks jogged to catch up to us, and I looked past the gate, seeing Rory and Micah standing near the beverage cart.

I didn't stop. Heading into the warehouse, tarp and walls constructed to create various chambers hung around, creating a tunnel, and Micah and Rory fell in line, following.

The cold, wet dark hung everywhere, and we jetted past patrons laughing and screaming at the actors hanging in the rafters above and trying to grab for them.

I stepped into a room and dug a ring of fifteen-thousand keys out of my bag, finding the one that accessed the doors in the Mad Scientist section of the park. Passing the boiling vats of body parts and lava lamps of eyeballs, I fit the key into the door, opened it, and ushered everyone inside.

Michael stood back with his eyes narrowed on me. "*You* own Coldfield? You?"

I gave him a tight smile.

I paid for it. I helped design it. But I hired managers to handle everything else. I took part in it when I wanted to, but I knew I wasn't fit to deal with the business side there for a while, so I installed a seasonal team that would.

And good thing, too, since I was gone for a long time.

We entered the hallway, and I locked the door behind us, opening up another one and turning on the light inside.

Rock walls and steps, like the catacombs, burrowed into the ground, darkness consuming what lay beneath.

"What is this?" Rika asked me.

I half smiled. "*This* is Coldfield."

The real one.

Leading the way, I momentarily regretted not calling Misha for this, as I knew he'd love it, but I didn't want him involved. Not for this.

I descended the stairs, winding through the tunnels as electric-powered lanterns lit our way, and the rush of the river and the sea hit the walls all around us.

A track laid ahead, and I threw my bag into one of the cars with the containers of gasoline I'd had put here yesterday in one of the many calls I'd made.

Kai looked around at the rooms and tunnels forking off in different directions. "I can't believe we didn't know this was real."

"You knew about this?" Banks asked him.

But it was Damon who replied as he looked around, "A few whispers from the old-timers here and there, but I didn't know anyone who'd actually been here."

"What is this place?" Rika asked me.

I checked the supplies on the rail riders, making sure we had everything I'd instructed. "Remember how we learned the town was settled in the thirties?"

"Not true?" Rika teased.

I shook my head. "No."

That was either a lie or misinformation.

"Two hundred years ago, the river forked off into three streams instead of just one, and the settlers built bridges to cross them." I gestured to them to take their seats. "The arches of the bridges were rooted deep in the land, creating twenty-one chambers—or vaults—between the arches, underneath the ground."

Alex and Damon took a seat in the first car, while Kai and Banks took the second, Rika and Michael took the third, and Micah and Rory took the fourth.

"Merchants stored their goods down there, and there were even taverns and stores," I continued, checking their seat belts. "Over the years, it changed hands, popular among the smugglers, criminals, and pirates. They hid and lived down here, connecting all of the vaults under the three bridges with these tunnels, so they could get anywhere in town undetected."

"Shit," Damon murmured. "That's awesome."

"How did you find it?" Michael pressed.

"I looked for it."

Rory snorted as Micah smiled, looking excited about all of this.

"This is why you bought the warehouse," Alex guessed.

"One of the reasons." I took my seat in the first car with them and buckled in. "I also just like haunted houses."

"Are there other entrances, other than the one at the warehouse?" Damon called up from behind me.

I looked over my shoulder, grinning. "All over town. And there are even more underground vaults in Meridian City between Delcour and Whitehall."

"What the fuck?" Kai blurted out, but it sounded more like he was turned on than angry. His city house, the Pope, and Sensou were all in the Whitehall district and he'd have plenty of reason to use the underground transit system if he wanted. Especially if we, and the people who worked for us, were the only ones who knew about it.

"Shift the lever to three and press the green button," I yelled back. "After that, just enjoy the ride until you see my arm in the air. Then, start to bring the lever back down and engage the brakes."

A giggle escaped Alex as she shifted excitedly in the seat next to me. Emmy back in the catacombs drifted through my mind, but she didn't need to be here for this.

"Let's go," I called out.

Pushing the lever up to notch three, I pressed the button, the hydraulics hissing, and we shot off, cruising through the tunnels at about thirty miles an hour.

Normally, I'd go a little faster—kick it up to notch five—but this was their first time, and I didn't want anyone to lose me. Coasting left and then right, I felt the wind blow through our hair, and Alex laughed next to me as the tunnel ahead loomed black and haunting. The grips on the wheels hugged the track, no steering necessary, since I hadn't built track leading off anywhere else in town yet.

That was on my agenda, though.

"We should have helmets!" Damon called up.

Helmets? Pussy.

"For the kids, I mean!" he clarified. "You know they're going to use this a lot."

I nodded. Okay, that made sense. This was going to be a blast for the boys, and when they were teenagers, there was no way we were keeping them from it.

We cruised under the riverbed, past more dark vaults, under the village, across Old Pointe Road, and I spotted the fourth red light ahead, each one signaling a stop, and that one was ours.

I held up my arm, giving them a heads-up, and I grabbed the lever, slowing us down little by little, so Kai and Banks didn't rear-end me and cause a pileup.

Pulling to a stop, the brakes screeching under us, I yelled, "Hit the button again!" The railcars came to rest, and we all climbed out, everyone following my lead as we grabbed the red, plastic gasoline containers.

"Are we doing what I think we're doing?" Kai asked.

But I didn't answer. They wanted the Cove gone, and they wouldn't leave me to this on my own. Everyone won. They'd help.

Climbing up onto the platform, we headed through a door and into the tunnels underneath the theme park. When the place was in business, the workers used these tunnels to avoid the crowds if they needed to get across the park, and as ways to operate the animatronics, but everything had been abandoned for years.

I looked left and right, searching for any eyes to be sure. I didn't want any fatalities or witnesses. The place was empty, though.

"Hey, it's Rika," I heard Erika say behind me. "I need you to get to the fire station and borrow an engine. Bring it to the Cove and hook up the hoses. We'll need it. And hurry."

There was a pause as whoever on the other end answered her.

"Thank you," she said and hung up.

I shot a look back to our mayor.

"I can't commit arson *and* purposely put civil servants at risk, Will," she explained. "Lev and David will contain the fire."

I nodded once. *Good thinking.* Those two earned enough to do anything we asked them to.

Swinging myself around the railing, I jogged up the stairs and walked through the shop, papers and dust coating the floor as I exited into the park.

The stars dotted the night sky, the sea air tickling my nostrils as we strolled through the park and took in rotting paint and wood and the quiet bumper boats and Ferris wheel.

A lump filled my throat, and my heart pounded like it did when I had her in my truck that night after the game, and like that Devil's Night I torched all of her hard work and the only presence she had left to torture me with in this town.

I wasn't sure if she was going to forgive me for this, but I had to do it. I had to know if there was anything beyond this for us.

"Why are we doing this, Will?" Banks asked.

But I was done explaining myself. "Because I said so."

I was done living in the past. I had an ocean of tomorrows to get busy building, and I was ready to live.

I looked to Michael and Rika. "Take the west side." Then to Kai and Banks. "Past the swings."

The four of them ran off to douse as much as they could with the fuel they had, and I walked toward the coast, the pirate ship, and Cold Hill with Alex and Damon.

"Are you sure this isn't an impulse thing?" Alex asked.

"Are you sure he's sober?" Damon asked her instead.

"Shut up," I griped.

I realized that my life decisions could be characterized as questionable, but not every crazy thing I did was because I was drunk.

Just some things.

We all got busy emptying the containers on rides, game booths, and old food stands, keeping our eyes peeled for anyone who wasn't us, but I just wanted everyone to hurry. I wasn't going to stop myself.

I wanted the challenge of never being able to look back. I wanted the Cove gone.

But that didn't mean this wasn't painful.

I clenched my jaw, walking around Cold Hill and the cars, one of them that carried us one night where she let me touch and kiss her.

The pirate ship where she pealed with laughter, and I knew I was head over heels watching the light in her eyes.

Misha loved it here, too. Which was probably why I hadn't invited him tonight. He would try to stop this.

And I needed to do it.

"The last time we set a fire, we got arrested," Damon said.

The gazebo wasn't the last fire we or he set, but I supposed he chose to block out Rika's house and Sensou.

"I'm not going back to jail," I assured him.

I tossed him a couple of flares and one to Alex, tossing my gas can into the fray.

"Spread out and give one to Michael and Kai," I told him, raising my voice and shouting into the night. "We're going to light up the fucking sky, because Michael Crist is marrying Erika Fane in two days!"

I smiled, holding my hands to my mouth and howling into the night. Laughter and more howls went off around the park, and I heard Rika yelping with excitement.

I lit my flare and looked to Alex.

"Are you sure?" she asked, lighting hers. "I know what this place means to you."

"It was one night." I looked up at the Ferris wheel. "I need my life to be more than one night."

I launched the flare, watching it land on the platform, and all it took was a moment before a flame spouted and quickly spread.

The fire coursed up to the Ferris wheel, lighting the bottom car and its old leather seat on fire, the flames rising and rising, traveling from car to car as the whole park lit up in a glow so tremendous that I needed sunglasses.

The wind blew and the heat of the fire covered my face, and I closed my eyes, not sure if I wanted to cry or smile.

Michael Crist, Kai Mori, Damon Torrance, and Will Grayson were going to have their secluded, seaside resort, because we lasted, and we were going to build something that would, as well.

Heat rushed under my skin, and I couldn't hold it in anymore. I was home.

Tipping my head back, I belted out the loudest howl I could manage from deep in my stomach hearing the rest of them—the girls, too—join me as our fires spat and hissed around us, the whole fucking place going up in flames.

I looked over at Alex, seeing her eyes squeezed shut and her mouth in an O as she belted into the night air, and I laughed, hooking her neck and planting a slobbery kiss on her cheek.

She giggled, all of us looking up at the flames rising and spreading, and after a few more minutes, I looked right, seeing Lev and David arrive in the parking lot with the fire engine.

We'd let the fire do its job—just long enough for the place to be beyond repair—and then start putting it out.

"Wait," I heard someone call. "Hey, wait!"

I released Alex and looked around, seeing Rika staring off toward the back of the park.

"What is it?" I jogged over, stopping next to her.

She stared, bending to see around rides and into the distance. "I thought I saw something?" Then she looked at me. "Are you sure the place is empty?"

I thought it was. Just then, I saw the door to the shop we'd come through flapping in the wind, and if anyone were here, they'd be hiding there.

"The tunnels!" I told everyone. "Go!"

Everyone ran, heading back to the shop and toward the underground. We didn't have homeless in Thunder Bay, but there were no cars in the lot and there was nothing else within a couple miles from here. If someone were here, they were living here.

"We should've checked the place," Michael gritted out. "Dammit."

Scurrying down into the tunnels, we ran back toward the entrance to the track, and I opened the door, sending Alex, Damon, Kai, Banks, Micah, and Rory on their way.

"The seats swivel," I told them, out of breath. "Just turn around and go back the way we came like I taught you. It's the fourth red light down."

Kai nodded, everyone descending into Coldfield.

Damon looked back at me, but I shook my head, knowing what he was thinking. "Just go," I said. "I'll catch up."

I got ready to shove Rika and Michael in after them, but I looked back and they both were hanging by a room.

Closing the door, I approached. "What is it?"

I looked inside, seeing a bed, posters and graffiti on the walls, and a lamp turned on.

"Didn't Misha say he stayed down here for a while? After Annie?" Rika asked.

"Yeah."

She walked in, picking up a sandwich or something, half-eaten and laying on a wrapper. "Someone's here," she said, squeezing the fresh bread.

Either the light was off when we arrived, or the door was closed, because we passed this room on the way in and noticed nothing.

Shit.

"Dammit!" Michael growled.

We ran back up the stairs, the flames orange and bright outside the shop windows as we raced into the park, searching for who was here.

We couldn't let anyone be hurt.

And it would be fantastic if there were no witnesses.

"I know I saw someone," Rika said. "Maybe a girl."

"Like a little girl?" I asked.

She nodded.

"Shit! There!" Michael yelled, pointing.

We halted, sucking in air and looking through the swings and toward the fun house, seeing a small form standing way on top.

Jesus. She had to be thirty feet in the air.

Dressed in black, she had a long, blond braid draped over her shoulder and a beanie on her head, but I couldn't see well enough to know if I recognized her.

"You!" Michael yelled to her. "Come here!"

We ran and saw her spin around, disappearing off the roof.

She jumped down, the shoelaces of her ratty sneakers dragging across the ground.

"Get her!" Rika yelled.

Michael dug in his heels, shot toward the girl, and caught her arm just as she was rounding the corner.

"I got her!" he bellowed, sweeping her into his arms.

But then she bit his hand, and he dropped her, hissing.

"What the hell?" he barked.

She ran, slipping around the booths, past the roller coaster, and disappearing into the pitch-black forest.

"Shit!" Michael gritted out.

We stopped, breathing hard and knowing she was gone.

"Was she living down there?" Rika asked us. "She can't be more than eight."

I shot her a look. "Do you recognize her?"

"No." She shook her head. "She's not from around here."

I stared into the trees for another moment, hearing Lev and David start with the hoses and putting our shit out.

"Some mayor you are." I chuckled. "Little Newt from *Aliens* is squatting in your abandoned theme park, and you're trying on wedding dresses."

Rika slapped me in the stomach and then took Michael's hand, inspecting the bite.

"She's a fighter, huh?" she joked, grinning up at him.

He snarled. "She'll be back. Can't get far on foot."

And it almost sounded like he wasn't so worried about the little shit's safety and well-being, just itching for some payback.

Sirens pierced the air behind us, and I looked over my shoulder, seeing the oh-so-familiar lights of a police car racing into the lot.

That was fast.

I looked to Michael. "Go. Hurry."

He scowled at me.

"Go!" I whisper-yelled.

Don't worry about me. Not anymore.

He held my eyes, but before he could argue, I started walking toward the ticket booths and the parking lot.

A single police officer, dressed in black in a thick jacket for the chilly October evening, talked on his radio as he looked around the park and the flames.

He noticed me, stopped talking to whoever he was talking to, and I could almost see the sigh.

"Will Grayson," he said. "My favorite pyro."

I pulled off my hat and gave him a smile. "Baker. How's the family?"

"Growing." He nodded, stepping toward me as I stepped toward him. "The wife is on baby number three."

"Yours?"

He cocked an eyebrow, looking unamused.

I smiled wider.

"Are you going to make me handcuff you?" he asked.

I shook my head. "There are some people I wanted to say hi to anyway. Let's go."

CHAPTER 36

EMORY

Present

E mmy, wake up!" someone called, shaking my body.

My eyes popped open, and I startled, turning over. "What? Who is that?"

It wasn't Will's voice.

I sat up, rubbing my eyes as someone turned on the lamp, and I looked up, seeing Rory and Micah walking around my room.

I reached for my new glasses and slipped them on. "What are you guys doing?"

"Will's been arrested." Micah tossed me some clothes. "He started a fire at the Cove."

Huh? "The Cove?"

I held the clothes to my chest, trying to make sense out of what they were telling me, my chest slowly constricting.

He started a fire at the Cove? And he was now sitting in jail?

Son of a bitch. I growled, shooting off the bed. "One day! Not even one day back in town and he's back in a cell!" I unhooked my overalls and pulled on the black, long-sleeved shirt. "Ugh!"

They spun around, and I dropped the overalls, slipping into the jeans and pulling on Alex's sneakers before I tied up my hair into a ponytail.

In jail . . . Tears welled. *Not again.*

"Do you know who arrested him?" I asked.

"We don't know this town," Micah snapped, tossing me a jacket. "Damon is going to try to get him out, but we told him to wait. We wanted to get you."

I shook my head. "I'm going to kill him. What the hell is wrong with him?"

I zipped up the jacket and headed out of the room with them, jogging up the stairs.

I should let him sit there. This one was on him. An endless cycle of not being accountable or controlling his behavior. This wasn't a choice. It was a habit, and I didn't need this shit in my life.

He was a man? He was going to be a father someday? Yeah, right.

I kicked the door open. *Motherf—*

"Let's go," I told them, running out of the house and into the driveway.

Damon stood next to a G-Class that looked a lot like the one Michael drove in high school, and I had no idea where everyone else was, but he saw me and immediately straightened.

"No way in hell. She's not coming," he said.

I grabbed the keys out of his hand and walked around the front of the car. "She's driving, actually."

"Nah-uh. No."

I looked at him over the hood. "What are you going to do?" I challenged. "I sent him to jail. You tried to kill him. You really gonna argue with me right now?"

If I didn't have a right, then neither did he.

He twisted his lips to the side, giving me that eyes-falling-down-my-body-to-inspect-the-competition-with-a-side-of-judgment look, but he shut his damn mouth.

I wasn't any worse for Will than he was, so he could stow it.

We all climbed into the car, and I started it, punching the gas and swerving around the driveway.

Would Martin be there? I knew he didn't live or work in town anymore, but he still maintained a presence here, and if his police had Will Grayson in a cell, that would almost certainly get him out of bed at this hour.

Shit. I didn't want to see Martin. I didn't need to face him. We'd been done.

Will, you're such an asshole.

I raced through town as Micah filled me in on where they'd all gone tonight and what Will had decided to do. I was tempted to jerk the wheel right on over to the cathedral and disappear—stay somewhere he couldn't find me—but . . .

I should've gone to him years ago. I was going to show up for him once. At least once before this was over.

Stopping in front of the police station, I looked across the street, seeing a figure behind the desk inside, the neighborhood quiet and not another soul in sight.

"We need a distraction," I told Damon. "Any ideas?"

He stared out the front window, ignoring me, but then . . . He dropped his eyes and exhaled, giving in.

He turned his head, speaking to Micah and Rory. "Get out."

What?

"Hell no," Rory said. "We're going in."

"Get those cars started," Damon told Micah, turning and meeting his eyes and then pointing to the vehicles parked down the street behind him.

Micah's mouth dropped open. "Huh?"

But Damon didn't explain. Taking out his phone, he dialed and held it to his ear, the other line ringing.

"Mayor Fane?" he teased to Erika, I assumed. "Two idiots are drag racing around Thunder Bay. Can you call the station and tell all units to report to Delphi heading east?" he asked and then clarified. "Alllllll units."

I heard her voice on the other end. I couldn't tell what she was saying, but it sounded like an angry ferret.

"Don't be a douche," he said, picking at the cord of his hoodie. "What else do you do all day anyway?"

More angry chatter.

"Suck me," he mumbled, and then she said something else, and then he said, "Yeah, your mom . . ."

He hung up and then looked over his shoulder again at Micah.

"How did you know I was the one who knew how to hotwire a car?" Micah asked.

"Because you're the one with shit to prove to your loser old man," Damon retorted. "We can smell our own. Now, both of you, hurry up."

I glanced in my rearview mirror, seeing both of their mouths curl into grins. Yeah, who were they kidding? They liked trouble, too.

Damon withdrew a Slim Jim from under the seat and handed it to them, both of them hopping out of the car and running down the block.

In minutes, headlights illuminated behind us and both cars, a Mustang and a Jeep raced past, disappearing down the avenue.

"What's the plan?" Damon asked.

I stared at the officer inside the station house. "I don't know."

To my surprise, excitement bubbled up from my stomach, and I almost smiled. I had zero clue what the hell I was doing, but I felt like it would work.

"As soon as I get out of the car, slide into the driver's seat and make sure all doors are unlocked," I told him. "Got it?"

He nodded, and after a moment, we spotted two police cars exiting the lot from behind the station, their sirens activating as they pulled onto the street.

Erika made the call. Third shift was always light, unless it was Devil's Night.

"And here we go," I said.

They headed the opposite direction as Micah and Rory, toward Delphi, and I stepped out of the car, pulling up the hood of my jacket, but then I stopped, and yanked it back off again.

Martin would know I was here. No hiding.

Stuffing my hands into my pockets, I ran across the street and up the walkway, opening the door and diving inside the station.

The burly officer with a gray buzz cut and glasses looked up from the counter and immediately smiled, seeing me.

"Germaine." I greeted him first. "Hi."

"Emory Scott." He cocked his head, returning the grin. "Wow. How are you doing, honey?"

"Pretty decent," I told him. "Is my brother around?"

"Uh, no." He chuckled. "He maintains an office here, but he stays in Meridian City now. Did you not know he was appointed as police commissioner? He oversees all the departments in a hundred-mile radius. Most of his work keeps him in the city now." He slid some papers into a file folder and stuffed the folder into a drawer. "But he will be here first thing in the morning. He has a prisoner to attend to whom he's only too delighted to let sweat for the night."

I bit back my groan. So, he knew Will was here.

"Sounds like him," I teased, trying to hide my unease.

At least he hadn't dragged himself back to town tonight to deal with it. That worked for me.

"Okay, I'll try back in the morning." I sighed. "But just on the off chance I miss him, may I leave a note here for him?"

I reached for the message pad and the pen next to the computer, but he waved me off.

"Take it back yourself," he said. "You know the way."

My eyebrows shot up. Really? I thought I was going to have to try to sneak past him when he took the note back himself, but here I was, getting a hall pass.

I walked around the counter, toward the double doors. "Is he in the big office now?"

"Sounds like him, doesn't it?" Germaine grumbled.

Yeah. I didn't think Germaine thought much of my brother, either. Martin was only thirty-four, and he'd quickly risen through the ranks of Thunder Bay and then Meridian City, shrewd in playing his cards, but I suspected he had help and endorsements along the way. Germaine was easily in his fifties and still . . . manning the desk.

"Thanks," I called out. "It's good to see you."

"You, too."

I pushed through the doors, finding the entire precinct empty, a radio playing somewhere, and computers paused on screens.

Making my way toward the holding cells, I grabbed a ring of keys off Bruckheimer's desk and looked up, making direct eye contact with the camera in the corner of the ceiling.

I clenched my teeth. *This better work.* If he came after Will, he'd have to come after me, too, now that I'd been seen, and that would be embarrassing for him.

Pushing through the door, I saw Will standing in the cell, alone in the room with his arms draped through the bars.

I dropped my eyes, finding the key, my heart thundering in my chest. We just had to get out of here.

I didn't want to know if he had a cell to himself in prison, or if Kai or Damon had been with him. I just wanted him out.

I stuck the key in the lock, my hand shaking as he stared down at me, and I twisted it, yanking the door open.

But Will pulled it closed again. "What do you think you're doing?"

Dammit. I twisted the key again and pulled the door, but he grabbed the bars, holding it closed.

"I have a meeting with your brother in the morning," he stated.

What the hell? I shot my eyes up to him and fixed my glasses, wanting to yell at the jerk, but we needed to get the hell out of here.

I pulled at the door again, growling when it didn't give.

"Who let you out of your room?" he asked.

"Will!" I begged. "Please!"

We could talk later, for crying out loud.

I tried to pull at the door again, but he reached through the bars and grabbed me by my jeans instead, yanking me in. His mouth crashed down on mine, and for a moment, I was lost in how good he felt.

God.

My nerves were on fire. I wanted him out of here. I wanted him away from Martin.

I wanted him . . .

I wanted him.

I whimpered as his tongue caressed mine, and I barely even registered what he was doing until cool air hit my breasts and his hand slid down my jeans, between my legs.

He stroked me, his head dipping down and sucking my breast into his mouth through the fucking bars.

"We're going to get caught," I said.

He wasn't listening, though. He came back up, and I held his face as he hovered over my mouth and slipped his fingers over my clit.

"I'm glad you didn't visit me in prison," he whispered. "I wouldn't have been able to stand staring at this through a piece of fucking glass for over two years."

I kissed him, feeling the goddamn torture of the bars between us.

Never again.

"Breaking me out of jail?" he taunted. "He's going to hang you for this."

I kissed him again, panting, "He has to get through you first, right?"

He smiled, his ego liking the sound of that. "Yeah, he does."

"Please, baby." I pulled at the bars. "Please?"

I kissed him again, moaning, and finally, he released me. "Fuck him. Let's go."

I stumbled back, righting my clothes again, and he swung open the door, taking my hand and pulling me.

We ran back into the office area, and I tossed the keys back onto

Bruckheimer's desk as we raced through the rear door and out into the night.

Digging in our heels, we hurried across the street, darts of cold rain hitting my head as we made our way to the waiting car.

"Get in!" Damon yelled. "Hurry!"

We jumped into the back seat, slamming the door, and Damon hit the gas, speeding off down the road. I dove into the third-row bench seat, looking out the back window for any sign that we were seen, but there was no one coming after us. Lightning pierced the sky as droplets wet the ground.

I whipped around, no longer sad or soft or panting after Will. I was mad. "What the hell were you thinking?" I growled.

Damn him. I may have gotten caught up in that kiss inside, but sex was never our problem.

"I had a plan," he explained.

"Did you?"

He twisted around and looked at me. "I'm going to have to face him at some point, Emmy," he shouted. "May as well have fun while I'm at it."

"We still don't know who put you in Blackchurch!" I shouted, growing angrier. "If you get into any more trouble, who knows what will happen? You've learned nothing! Absolutely nothing. You don't have any idea how to plan your moves and keep your shit quiet until it's time to strike. You're like a bull in a china shop. When are you going to grow up? Demonstrate some patience?"

One fucking night back, and he was already in jail again.

I lost it. "This is why I don't love you!" I screamed.

And he turned on me, a scowl and piercing glare lighting him on fire.

He jumped into the back seat, pushing me down and coming down on top of me.

"Hell yeah, you love me," he said, sucking my lips into his mouth.

"You're crazy about me, and you may not be blonde or eighteen or named Heidi, but you're fucking mine, Little Trouble." He pushed up my shirt, yanked down my bra, and covered my nipple with his mouth, sucking hard. "And you can still walk my dogs someday if you want, but I'll for damn sure be peeling down your panties on my desk and letting you pretend like you don't love every second of it right before I write you that little check." He gripped my neck, his other hand trying to rip down my pants as he kissed me. "You're never getting free of me."

I pushed at him. "Will . . ."

"Never."

He thrust between my legs, sinking his tongue into my mouth, his hot body covering me and making the world spin.

I whimpered.

"Um . . ." someone said, and I blinked, noticing the car had stopped. "Okay, wow. I . . . um . . . I'd love to watch this, actually," Damon called out, "but Winter will consider it cheating if she's not here, too. I'll go ahead and walk home, and you fucking owe me, Will."

Damon opened the door, the rain coming down hard now, and got out, closing it again.

I shoved at Will, crawling out from underneath him. "I'm walking, too."

Opening the back door, I jumped out of the G-Class, seeing that we were in the village, and raced in the rain toward the cathedral.

"Oh, surprise, surprise," Will shouted behind me. "She's running again."

I spun around. "It's called being dumped, Grayson! Watch. I'll show you what it looks like again."

I ran harder, glancing up into the little park and noticing a new gazebo where mine once stood.

I narrowed my eyes. *What . . . ?*

But then arms caught me and whipped me around, Will picking

me up. I pounded his chest, feeling him lose his footing, and both of us fell to the ground, the pavement and our clothes soaking as the rain streamed down my face.

I swatted at him again, pushing my glasses up onto the top of my head. "You burned up the Cove!" I yelled.

How could he do that? The gazebo and now that? It was like he was determined to self-destruct and leave nothing of us to remember.

He hauled me into his lap right there in the middle of the street, people sitting under the awning of the White Crow Tavern gasping and rising from their seats to see what was going on.

He sat up, and I straddled him, gripping his collar.

But before I could fight, he said, "I still have the bus."

The bus.

Our bus?

I paused, looking down into his glistening, sea green eyes as he blinked up at me.

"I don't need the Cove," he said over the rain. "I need more memories with you."

I breathed hard, but I couldn't move as tears filled my eyes.

"Memories that aren't tainted with all the years apart right afterward," he explained.

Everyone watching us from a distance faded away, and I looked down at his hair matted to his scalp and temples, droplets cascading down his cheeks and over his lashes, and all I wanted in the world was to stare at him forever.

"I build with you now," he whispered to me, the heat of his mouth on my lips. "We make Thunder Bay together, Em. I love you."

I love you.

I closed my eyes, my face cracking and my eyes filling with tears. God, I was exhausted.

So tired that I longed for the days when Martin beat the shit out of me, because those were also the days I saw Will laughing at school and playing basketball with his friends.

The day he sat with me in the theater and joked around, and the night he took me to ride roller coasters and we were a couple, holding hands. For just a couple of hours.

Sliding off of him, I sat at his side, his words coursing their way through my heart as I wondered where the hell we were going to go from here.

"You came for me," he said.

Yes. Yes, I did.

I didn't need to search for an excuse. I knew why.

"I couldn't lose you anymore," I told him, staring at the street ahead.

I drew in a deep breath and tipped my head back, letting the rain cool my skin as I thought about my future and all of the things I thought were going to work out for me without him.

I fucking loved Will Grayson. I wanted to eat every meal with him, have that damn *Mission: Impossible* marathon with him, and let him knock me up as soon and as much as he wanted.

He stood up, standing over me. "I love you," he said again. "But I'll let you go."

He started to walk away, my heart ripping in two, and I shook my head.

No.

He couldn't let me go. He couldn't move on without me. Everything we'd been through—everything—meant something. It all meant something.

Didn't it?

This wasn't where we ended.

Nothing was over.

"Will you marry me?" I asked, breathing hard and my heart hammering.

Slowly, I climbed to my feet and turned to face him, seeing him stopped.

He stood there, frozen, not turning around, but that was okay. I wasn't sure I could do this if he looked at me.

God, my mouth was so dry I couldn't swallow.

"I love you," I said, and I could see people filming us with their phones out of the corner of my eye, but I didn't care. "I'm wild crazy for you, and I'm sure I'll kill you at some point, but . . . God, I love you so much, and I want you to marry me." More tears streamed down my face as I choked out the words. "Marry me, Will Grayson." I rushed up and hugged his back, wrapping my arms around him. "Can you marry me? Can I marry you?"

I held him, my cheek resting against his back and water catching between my lips.

He was going to laugh. He was probably freaked out or maybe angry I asked him instead of letting him ask me—if those were his intentions anyway.

Shit . . .

But then, he spun around, picked me up off my feet, and kissed me, pressing his lips to mine and backing me into a parked car.

Laughter went off around us, and I wrapped my arms and legs around him, reveling in his strong mouth and the warmth of his body.

I moaned, kissing him again and again. "Is that a yes?"

He chuckled and dropped me to my feet. I blinked against the rain, watching him dig into his pocket for something.

He pulled it out, pinching a vintage Victorian ring with a tear-drop diamond and a platinum band encrusted with more jewels, encased by an ornate setting above and below. It was almost like three rings in one, and nearly an inch in width.

"It's very old," Will said, slipping it onto my finger, his hand shaking.

"It's your family's?"

"It's yours now." He met my eyes. "It's been yours for nearly ten years."

I stared up at him, tears blurring my vision. He was going to ask me himself?

I took his face in my hands and looked into his eyes, our noses nearly touching as our life, up until this point, played through my head.

The pool at school and the feel of his body in the movie theater.

Dancing at Homecoming and him sweeping me into his arms and carrying me to his bed at Blackchurch.

The intoxicating scent of his truck, and the rain on the bus windows, hiding us inside.

There was so much more than the fights and the pain.

"I'm marrying you," I whispered.

He nodded. "'Bout time you caught up."

I started to laugh, diving in and kissing him, cheers going off at the tavern.

Will chuckled against my lips. "We need to get out of here," he said.

I took his hand, pulling him along. "Come on."

I knew just the place.

Running toward the cathedral, we splashed through puddles, turned right, and raced into the patch of grass between the church and the sidewalk.

"Where are we going?" he called out.

"Hiding us away."

The main doors would be closed now, but I'd found out years ago that Father Beir never really locked the basement door, so old Mr. Edgerton could sleep off the whisky here instead of facing his wife hammered.

We dove in, ran down the narrow hallways, and up another set of stairs, entering the nave of the main church. I led Will up to the gallery and hurried to the windowsill, prying up the piece of wood I'd nailed down years ago, picking out that old key with the thurible key chain.

"What is this?" Will asked, looking around for any sign of witnesses.

But I didn't answer him. I led him through the door, up the concrete stairs, and slipped the key in, opening the door to the Carfax Room.

I quickly looked around, inhaling the musty scent of rain and wood.

Dark, no sign of life, and the bed was still there. I didn't care about anything else.

Throwing the door closed, I dropped the key and wrapped my arms around Will, nibbling and sucking too fast, because I was too hungry.

"I love you," I panted, unbuttoning my jeans and pushing them down my legs.

He pulled off my shirt, my glasses dropping to the floor with it. "You better."

Not leaving his mouth, I stripped off my underwear and bra, completely naked as I pulled the rubber band out of my hair and he lifted me into his arms again.

I wrapped myself around him, my cold hair draping across my back as he walked us to the bed.

"Hurry," I begged.

I throbbed. I wanted him in me.

He let me fall to the bed, tore off his shirt, kicked off his shoes, and stripped off the rest of his clothes, his tight abs and black tattoos making my thighs rub together with need.

Mine.

He climbed onto the bed, coming down on top of me, and I just spread my legs as he reached between us, fit inside me and thrust, sheathing his cock. *No more waiting.*

"Ah," I moaned, arching my back.

"Don't sleep tonight." He gasped, pumping his hips and hovering over my mouth. "Don't break this. Don't break the spell."

I rolled into him, heat pooling in my belly as I devoured his shoulder, his neck, and his mouth, unable to get enough.

"I loved you last night," I told him. "And I loved you this morning. I'll still be here. I'll still be me tomorrow and every day after."

He lifted up, not breaking pace in the least as he stared down between us, watching himself enter me.

"I'm sorry about everything," I said.

"Me, too, baby." He kissed me. "I should've stayed. I'm sorry I walked away. I'm sorry I left you that day in the hallway at school."

He hit me deep inside, and my eyes started to roll into the back of my head.

"You and me against the world," he whispered, picking up speed and going harder.

"Always," I said.

And I held on as he slipped inside of me again and again, thrusting between my legs, both of us lost for the rest of the night in the warmth and frenzy of finally being together.

CHAPTER 37

EMORY

Present

Hours later, a ringing pierced the air, and I cracked open my eyelids, wincing at the light streaming through the windows.

"Hello?" I heard Will answer.

I rolled over and snuggled into his back, chasing the warmth of last night.

He'd been holding me all night in between spells of waking up to have sex, and I was going to kill whoever was bothering him this early. I had no plans to leave the Carfax Room today.

"Uh, just a minute," he said and turned over, pulling me into his chest. "Hey, sorry I woke you." He kissed my nose. "Rika's on the phone."

"For me?" I whined.

I felt the cell phone brush my hand as he tried to give it to me, and I kept my eyes closed, yawning as the warm jewelry on my ring finger tapped against the cell.

I smiled, remembering what happened last night.

"Hello?" I said.

"So, I hear you're engaged," she taunted.

I opened my eyes, narrowing my brows. "How . . . ?"

But then I stopped myself. The videos. People were filming on the street.

Fantastic.

"Can you meet me?" she asked. "Alone?"

Alone?

I glanced up at Will, his eyes were closed, but his thumb was rubbing circles on my shoulder.

"Where?" I asked.

"The Carriage House in Meridian City."

"Now?"

"An hour," she clarified.

I kissed the lines of one of the tattoos on Will's chest, unable to stop myself from grazing his soft skin with my lips.

"Two," I told her.

I couldn't leave him yet.

"See you soon," she said.

We hung up, and I smiled, climbing back on top of him and feeling his body stir to life underneath me as a grin spread across his lips.

Yeah, you know what's up. Come here.

Will tried to give me his car, but then I'd have to deal with parking, so I just took an Uber to Meridian City, instead.

I stepped down from the Jeep Cherokee, zipping up my brown leather jacket and looking up at the Carriage House sign, not even having to look through the windows to see the array of wedding dresses inside.

I knew what this place was. What did she want me for?

Asking someone to drive almost an hour to talk to you meant it was serious, and I'd really had enough drama to last a lifetime.

I was pretty sure she wasn't angry with me, since we'd all been naked in the same room night before last, but that didn't mean we were friends.

Yet.

The Jeep drove off, the sounds of the city behind me filling the air as horns honked in the distance, and pedestrians passed me from the left and right.

I looked down at my ring and couldn't help the smile at how it suited me perfectly. Like I'd always worn it.

Heading toward the shop entrance, I smoothed back my hair, pulled tightly into a high ponytail, and slipped my hands into my pockets to ward off the chill in the air.

After I'd gotten off the phone with Erika—and spent a little more time with my fiancé—I'd logged online and canceled my credit and debit cards, since I had no idea where my wallet dropped after I was taken in San Francisco. Then, I transferred some funds from my bank there to the nearly empty bank account I still had here and went to a store and bought clothes to get me through the next few days.

Thankfully, I didn't need replacement glasses because Will had thought of that. Now I could see Martin if he were coming for me, which he hadn't yet, strangely. I'd gone to the bank and shopping, all under the protection of Micah and Rory, of course, but it was like the jail break had never even happened.

Was he coming for us? Was Will ready?

I opened the door and stepped inside, the place appearing empty as I drifted around all the displays. I stepped into the dressing room, seeing Erika on the riser in a gorgeous gown of silk and sequins, the bodice tight and the sweetheart neckline complementing her body perfectly.

Her hair fell down her back as she looked at herself at all angles, and I inched in, seeing Winter speaking quietly into her phone as her fingers trailed over notes in her lap. I squinted, seeing the tips of her fingers move from left to right as she spoke.

Kai's wife slouched in a white cushioned chair, tapping away on her laptop. Where was Alex?

I cleared my throat. "Um, hi," I finally said.

They all looked up, Winter stopping her talking and turning toward my voice.

Erika spun around, her blue eyes bright. "Hey."

She was gorgeous—almost regal in how she wore the gown.

I walked in, approaching her as I gripped the phone in my pocket that Will had given me. I was kind of tempted to run. I didn't do well in groups of women. Erika Fane intimidated me, even in high school, and she had been two years behind me.

She stared down at me, and it took a moment to square my shoulders and hold her eyes.

"So . . ." she said, trailing off.

So . . .

But she just kept staring at me.

Jesus, what? My cheeks warmed, wondering if it was the train car sex, me sending her friends to prison, or me breaking Will out of jail last night that I was going to get grilled about first, but then she took my hand and looked down at my engagement ring, her own snowflake diamond setting gleaming in the light.

She was going to tell me I wasn't good enough for him.

She was going to tell me they couldn't trust me.

But instead, she asked, "You happy?"

Am I happy?

Confusion, and then relief, hit me, and then . . . a laugh filled my throat, and I couldn't keep it bottled up. I let out a chuckle, butterflies filling my stomach.

"That's all I wanted to know," Erika said, smiling at me. "Congratulations."

"Thanks."

Well, that was easy. She gazed at me with her warm eyes, and I heard the other two say, "Congratulations," as well.

"We've never been properly introduced." She held out her hand. "Erika Fane. You can call me Rika."

I took her hand. "Emory Scott."

Kai's wife set aside her laptop and stood up, offering me her hand. "Nikova Mori, but everyone calls me Banks."

"Banks," I repeated. But then I remembered. "Nikova," I said to myself. And then to her, "Nik? You're Damon's sister?"

She looked surprised, nodding. "That's right."

And then Rika chimed in again. "And so am I, actually."

Huh?

But she waved me off. "It's a long story. We'll explain later."

She and Banks weren't related, though, were they? Or else that train thingy was a whole lot weirder now.

"Winter Torrance." The other girl approached slowly, holding out both hands.

I took hers, shaking them. "It's good to meet you all."

"And you know Alex," Rika said, nodding behind me and then hopping back up onto the riser.

I glanced over my shoulder, seeing her lean against the wall, her bag hanging at her side as she gazed at us, almost looking like she was waiting for an invitation.

I hadn't seen her since we left the train, and I wasn't sure if she wanted to talk about anything.

Turning back to Rika, I told her, "You look really beautiful. Is that dress for a special occasion?"

"It's my wedding dress."

Her wedding dress?

Winter stepped up on the riser, running her hands down the fabric and then touching Rika's face.

"It's red." She smiled. "I can feel it."

The dress was strapless with red fabric, and a tight bodice featuring gold embroidery around the breasts. It hung on her like it grew out of her skin, and I loved her long blond hair hanging down her back with it.

It was an unconventional dress color, but why was I even surprised? Why shouldn't she do whatever she wanted?

Rika suddenly sucked in a breath and dropped her head, a couple of tears spilling down her face. "Best do this now and not down the aisle, I guess," she told us, laughing a little as she raised her eyes again, looking utterly lost in a way that made her finally seem real. "So many emotions. My stomach is swimming. He's never not done this to me, you know?"

I could relate. No matter how tough you thought you were, the one who owned your heart had the real power.

Banks spoke up, cooing, "Aw, that's so sweet. You love him so much he makes you nauseated."

I snorted, and Rika and Winter busted up with laughter. "To be frank, yes," Rika barked playfully at Banks.

She twirled on the riser, the gown fanning out and the train rustling on the floor.

"He's my life," she said, "and I couldn't be happier about that. Nothing is worth anything without him." Turning, she looked at us, taking Winter's hand as she gazed around the room. "I love you guys, you know? I love to fall, but I don't want to do it alone." Her chin trembled. "Thank you for being my family."

I wasn't so sure she loved me, having only recently met and all, but she was a little love drunk, so I took it. I hoped I was that happy on my wedding day.

She inhaled a deep breath and then clapped her hands. "All right, enough!" She wiped her eyes. "Champagne for everyone and bring in the dresses!"

"Huh?" Winter asked.

But before Rika could answer, two carts of gowns were wheeled in, and a tray of glasses filled with sparkling, golden champagne.

"What is this?" Banks asked Rika.

Some lady carried the tray to Rika, and she plucked a glass of champagne off. "Pick your favorite and go try it on, so she can fit it," Rika told us.

I looked at the racks, long dresses trailing to the floor in colors of black, silver, white, and gold.

Did this mean she wanted us in gowns, as well? Or . . . like bridesmaids?

"Rika, these are incredible," Banks said, guiding Winter to the dresses. "Are you sure?"

Rika didn't answer her, just dropped her eyes to me. "I hope you find something you like."

"I don't think—"

"Choose," she said, cutting off my protest.

Then she spun around with the glass in her hand as the tailor checked the fit.

I turned, watching Banks and Winter sift through the choices, smiling and giggling like teenage girls, even though I knew they were both mothers now.

What was Rika thinking? I couldn't be a bridesmaid, which I assumed that this was all about. She would only dress her bridal party, not the guests.

Still, though . . . I drifted over to the racks, seeing Banks pull out a black gown and Winter trailing her hands over the different fabrics.

I reached for a gold, sparkling A-line with long sleeves and a trim waist, but Alex cut me off, pulling a sheer silver off the rack with a V-neck, spaghetti straps, and dark gray embroidery on it.

"This," she told me.

I took it, not seeing how I could wear any underwear under this. It wasn't see-through, but it was thin and hugged nearly every curve.

Banks and Winter disappeared into dressing rooms. I asked Alex, "Shouldn't you be trying one on?"

"I have mine."

Taking the dress, she led me into a small room and unhooked the white drapes, pulling them closed on us.

In minutes, we had my clothes off, heels on, and I was stepping into the gown as Alex pulled it up my body and fastened the hooks in the back. Awareness pricked at my skin as she touched me, and I worried that she was worried.

About what, I had no idea. There were too many things to count right now, but I wanted to talk to her. There were still no repercussions concerning Blackchurch, and we hadn't heard a word about any survivors.

She hadn't had closure with him. He could be dead.

"Margaritas and pizza tonight?" I teased.

Will would freak if I disappeared on him, but he was fine. She wasn't.

"I'm working," she said in a low voice, fastening the last hook.

Working . . . It only took a moment to click.

She had a date.

"No," I said.

"There's nothing wrong with what I do, Emory."

"Is that what you told him when he tried to stop you?"

Her eyes shot up to mine, and I knew right then and there that I'd hit the nail on the head. Aydin should've fought harder, but he did try once, didn't he? He came for her.

She stood up straight, and I wrapped my ponytail around my fist, creating an updo as I looked at myself in the mirror.

"We're two of a kind, you know?" I told her. "Both too stubborn for our own good. He came after you, but your heart had steeled, and there was nothing to do except keep putting one foot in front of the other and never look back, right?"

I knew her because I knew myself. We were the same.

Tears welled in her eyes, and she shook her head to herself. "I would've liked to make love to him just once."

"So why didn't you?"

"Because he wouldn't pay for it," she shot back, her eyes full of pride.

Pain hit my heart.

I dropped my ponytail and wrapped my arms around her, squeezing her tight. Her body stayed frozen for a moment, but then I felt her melt and she released a quiet sob against my shoulder.

I squeezed her more, tucking my face into her neck as she wrapped her arms around me, too.

I'd wasted so much time being afraid of everything—holding a grudge, letting my pride lead me—but there was nothing to lose in going for it. This was it. We had one shot. They were destroying each other like Will and I did, but the worst of it was she might not have another chance with Aydin.

I got lucky.

We held each other for another minute, and then she sniffled and pulled back, wiping her tears.

"Shit," she whispered, looking up and down my body. "He's going to be hard in three seconds when he sees you in this, you know?"

I laughed, immediately seeing Will in my head getting a look at me dressed all hot for the first time ever. I might sit far away from him at this wedding and really let him suffer.

I turned and took in the fit as I envisioned my hair down with some curls. I felt beautiful.

"You and Will have been close," I told her. "Best friends."

"You have nothing to worry about, Em."

"I know." That wasn't what I was implying. "I trust you."

I met her eyes in the mirror as she fluffed the gown and checked the waist.

"I have to ask you to do something for me," I said.

She nodded. "I'm on it. What is it?"

I opened my mouth to tell her, but then I heard someone call me from outside of the dressing room. "Emory, are you okay?"

"Uh . . ." I looked to Alex and back toward the drapes, realizing we didn't have time for this right now. "We'll talk later," I told Alex. Then I shouted, "Yeah, coming."

We stepped out of the dressing room, Erika still on the riser, and

I gazed at Banks and Winter, both standing in their beautiful dresses fit for the Oscars.

Rika smiled at me. "It fits you perfectly."

"I'll take up the hem a little, I think," the tailor, with the brown bun on top of her head and a black blouse buttoned up to her neck, said.

"Do you have time?" Rika asked.

"I'll get it done."

Rika nodded at her, and I stepped closer, spinning around in front of the mirrors.

"Is this for the wedding?" I asked her.

"If you like it."

I definitely like it.

I beamed at her. "I love it."

Her excited eyes darted from me to Winter. "Does it feel good, Winter? Not too tight?"

The other girl, her almost white blond hair falling over one shoulder in beautiful waves grazed her fingers over the white feather gown, looking like a swan. "I love how it feels," she said, her voice wispy. "I almost don't want to wear it. He won't have patience for the buttons, and it'll end up in shreds on our bedroom floor."

Banks laughed, and I snorted. How does someone so soft and gentle fall in love with Damon Torrance, for crying out loud.

But . . . I guess after seeing him completely under her spell in the train kitchen, she was exactly his type.

Rika looked to Banks and Banks shrugged a little, apprehensive to admit that she liked her black gown with the off-the-shoulder straps and a bodice that made her breasts damn near bulge out of the top. She looked regal, though.

"It's perfect. You did perfect," she told Rika. "It's totally me."

"Good." Rika nodded, looking around at all of us with a mischievous smile playing on her lips. "Because I have an idea."

CHAPTER 38

WILL

Present

I'm gonna kill her. She'd had Emmy for the last thirty-six hours. No warning. No discussion. No explanation, other than some excuse about needing one last girls' night as a single woman.

I hadn't talked to Em, because Rika took all their cell phones, hiding with Alex, Banks, Winter, Emory, and Ryen at Delcour since yesterday morning.

I mean, what the fuck? I just got her back, and fear was nipping at the corner of my brain, worried that she'd change her mind about marrying me if I couldn't periodically remind her how hot I was.

Lev and David carried in six packs, handing them out as Kai shined his shoes, and Michael fixed his hair in front of the mirror.

We all loitered in the den of St. Killian's, the grandparents and parents shouting downstairs and trying to wrangle everyone as they piled into the limos, the sun setting outside as some old DMX played on the speaker next to me.

Micah pulled a bottle of bourbon out of Rory's hand, downing a shot, before Damon yanked Misha back in by the collar, fixing his tie and then grabbing his head, inspecting the stripe in his hair.

"What . . . ?" he barked. "Is this blue? Ughhh."

Misha slapped him away, and Damon shoved him off, grabbing a beer and rolling his eyes. "Watch your back," Damon told him.

Misha plopped down next to me, and I took a swig from my water bottle.

"You'll see her in an hour," he assured me.

I took another drink. "Rika could've warned us she was taking all the women overnight."

"It gives you a chance to miss her."

"I've missed her long enough," I retorted, watching Michael tie his shoes and then tip back the bottle of Kirin. "I'm done missing her."

"You think if you don't see her enough, she'll have time to change her mind?"

"No."

Yes. My cousin was smart.

I smirked at him, and he smiled, finishing his own bottle of beer.

Kai walked over, grabbing another for himself, but then he halted, eyeing me. "Does this bother you?" he asked. "We don't have to drink."

His hand was paused on the bottle, his eyes dropping to my water.

"No." I exhaled. "I want to be all here for her. I'm good."

He took the bottle and uncapped it, the sweat streaming down the sides looking like bliss at one time, but not this time. Bile rose up my throat, remembering the feeling when I drank. Of time moving too fast, of waking up feeling like hell, and feeling paranoid of saying the wrong thing or facing the music the next day after I'd done something stupid.

I could do so much more with myself. I was tired of who I used to be.

But I could have a vice.

If Damon got to drink in front of me, then I got to smoke in front of him. Shooting out of the chair, I dug a pack out of Rory's breast pocket with his lighter, and lit one up, waiting for a dirty look from Michael about smoking in his house.

But nothing. He was too busy smiling and laughing with Kai.

"That was fun last night," Micah said.

Em had filled me in on what it took to get me out of jail, and surprise, surprise, she was right. Her involvement at the station changed things, so whoever was in charge was keeping it quiet because of her. It still unnerved me that I hadn't heard a peep from Martin, though.

"As long as you don't get caught, it's a lot of fun," I replied.

Pulling over a duffel bag I had laid on the chair, I pulled out a green Army of Two mask, as well as a black one painted with white bandages to look like a mummy. I handed them each one.

Micah eyed me, looking confused.

"For later," I said. "It's Devil's Night."

Their eyes widened, remembering what Emmy had talked about, and they exchanged a look, laughing under their breaths.

"Seems like you and your friends are the law in Thunder Bay," Micah said.

"Just the opposite." I took a drag. "There are no bedtimes here."

Rory tossed his mask back on the chair. "Is anyone coming after us?"

"Undoubtedly."

Micah chuckled. "Oh, good."

Maybe not tonight, but someone was coming.

"You guys gassed up?" Michael called out, and I looked over to see him talking to David and Lev.

The other guys nodded. "Yeah."

Michael looked around to all of us. "Cell phones charged, everyone?"

We all replied in the affirmative.

"The kids?" he asked next.

"The nannies will meet us there," Damon answered.

Michael stood there, everything ready and all the ducks in a row, his shoulders tense.

"You ready?" I asked him.

He broke out in a smile and inhaled a deep breath, blowing it out slowly. "Yeah," he said. "Let's go."

We all jogged down the stairs, everyone laughing and chattering, our heavy footfalls reminding me of all the times we ran as a group—together and tight.

Diving out into the night air, "Let the Sparks Fly" started playing from someone's phone, and déjà vu hit me, thinking about the last time I heard that song. Rika was sixteen, in the car with us, and it was the last good night for a long time.

Rocks kicked up under our feet, bottles in everyone's hands as Kai tipped back his beer and we left the house behind.

"No cars?" I asked, noticing everyone just kept walking.

Michael shook his head. "I don't need to be carted to the altar," he announced. "I want to arrive in style with my friends. This is how it started, and this is how it continues."

Kai grabbed his shoulder as we stepped out onto the road. "Always."

David and Lev pulled out in two SUVs, going on ahead in case we needed transportation later, but the seven of us strolled down the black highway, the glow from the estates that we passed lighting our way.

Fires burned, the scent of wood and spice filled the air, and the Halloween decorations of every home lit up, the flickering flames inside the jack-o'-lanterns making me smile.

A howl pierced the air, and I looked over, seeing Michael holding his hands to his mouth, his roar carrying down the street and up into the trees.

"I'm marrying little Rika Fane, motherfuckers!" Michael yelled, and we all followed, belting our battle cry into the night.

"Whoo!" we all joined in.

Michael slapped my back. "Let's go get my girl."

Beers and bottles in hand, we strolled down the highway, spotting our neighbors loading into their cars and getting on their way, a Mercedes swerving past us as we took up most of the road.

"You're gonna be late!" Bryce laughed, hanging out the passenger-side window.

Michael held out his arms. "Like they can start without me!"

Bryce waved as they kept going, and I bobbed my head to the music, seeing the bottle of bourbon change hands from Micah to Rory, whispering between themselves and laughing.

"You know they might start without you if she wises up," I told him. "Remember when we kidnapped her mom, stole all her money, and burned down her house? That was good times."

"What the fuck?" Rory spat out. "You're not serious."

But Michael scoffed, defending himself. "Damon suffocated her with chloroform, threw her over his shoulder like a sack of flour, and took her to sea!"

"We were bonding," Damon retorted. "You're just jealous."

"I'm just glad your 'bonding' didn't go under the clothes before you knew she was your sister," I fired back. "Can you imagine?"

Damon hooked my neck, yanking me down, and I laughed as we play-fought for a moment.

"I'm starting to feel like we need to grab this girl and Emory and run," Micah mumbled to Rory.

I pushed Damon off and straightened, fixing my suit.

"We love the hell out of her," I assured my guys. "We'd die for her and each other. Erika Fane is a lucky woman."

"Yes, she is," Kai agreed. Then he looked at Michael. "You okay?"

We all glanced at Michael, a light sheen of sweat on his forehead and his breathing heavy.

"My heart's jackhammering," he panted, letting out a nervous chuckle, "like that day we walked into her math class and I saw her for the first time in months."

Kai grinned, squeezing his shoulder. "That's a good feeling."

Fuck, yeah, it is. It's an even better feeling when you know she feels the same way.

God, I missed Emmy already. She was all over me night before last, and it was like a new world opened up, and I could see decades of that ahead of us.

I knew she was the one for me.

Descending the hill, we headed into the village, Misha passing Damon the rest of his half-empty beer, and Damon happily swallowing the rest.

I loved watching their interactions the past couple of days. Misha was the only child now after Annie passed. Neither one of them had a brother, and if Misha's dad married Damon's estranged mother, they would be technically related.

They got in each other's faces a lot over the years, but a bond was forming. I guess the older you get, the more you realize how much you need others. It would be nice for Damon to have a brother.

People crowded the streets ahead, "Light Up the Sky" blasting from Sticks and no cars getting through as restaurants and the tavern swarmed with patrons. Vendors sold the best catered food on the streets, Graymor Cristane picking up the whole tab for everyone tonight.

People looked our way, seeing us coming, and we tossed our drinks into the trash bin, heading into the fray.

"Will!" Simon came up, grabbed my hand in a shake and my neck in a hug.

"Hey," I greeted, hugging him back.

"Congratulations," someone said to Michael.

"Thank you."

Food trucks lined the curbs, dealing dinner and drinks, bottles of champagne popped in every direction, and music played, the entire village lit up by just the gas lamps lining the sidewalks.

This was going to be an unconventional ceremony, I'd heard. They didn't want a lot of pomp. Just a good time and their town around them.

Making our way through the people, old friends and new residents, I spotted the current basketball team in their school jackets all piled on the roof and hood of a Hummer, the one in the front tipping his chin at me when I made eye contact. The captain, I assumed.

Kind of cute of them. Being here for this like we were every year for McClanahan. Someone was teaching the kids right.

The entire park was cleared, not a soul on the grass except the chairs placed for our immediate family as we made our way up to the gazebo. Misha veered off to join Ryen sitting in the second row, and Micah and Rory took the two seats reserved for them. Damon and Kai looked for their women, but I only spotted Ivarsen with Christiane, Matthew Grayson (Misha's dad and my uncle), sitting next to her. Madden was in Katsu Mori's arms as he sat next to his wife.

Michael's parents sat in the first row, his mother smiling ear to ear and blowing him a kiss as his father looked on, a coy smile on his face as if he was just biding his time.

Fucking hell.

But Michael knew what I was thinking and pulled me forward again. "Later," he said. "Not tonight."

"I know."

He and his dad had never gotten along. I didn't doubt Michael's loyalty and commitment to see this through to its end.

But that didn't mean I wasn't itching for it.

I did a quick scan of the crowd again. Where the hell was Emmy? I hadn't seen Winter or Banks, either, so hopefully that didn't mean anything.

We climbed the steps to the gazebo, and I looked around at the open roof, noticing crystals hanging from the leaves of the trees overhead.

The black, wrought iron circle stretched about fifteen feet in diameter as vines wound around the railings and beams, up to the roof that connected to a point. But where panels should've gone to keep out the sun and rain, it was open instead, the panels missing, so you could see up into the trees.

An officiant stood in the middle, a middle-aged judge with short brown hair and wine-colored lipstick.

I leaned over to Damon. "Who built this gazebo?"

But he just shrugged, not looking at me.

He didn't know? He'd been here the whole time. How could this go up without him knowing where it came from?

Michael moved to the center, in front of the judge as he fastened his tie, and we joined him, flanking his side and waiting for Rika and her entourage.

I couldn't wait to see Emmy. Rika always thought of everything, so I knew she'd handled a dress, but I kind of hoped they'd had fun, too. I wanted her to like my friends. They were family, and they were important to me.

"So, you gonna be a Crist?" Kai teased Michael. "Or a Fane?"

"Shut up," Michael snipped.

Kai and Damon snorted, laughing to themselves. What was that about?

But before I could catch up on the joke, the music died away, the crowd's chatter quieting a little, and we all looked around, the hair on my arms rising.

It was time.

"Michael," Kai whispered.

I looked to Kai, all of us following his gaze out toward the street and the start of the pathway leading up to the gazebo.

She stood there, and my throat swelled with a lump, and for some fucking reason, I was about to burst wide open.

Shit.

Rika looked up at Michael, dressed in her red gown, bold and on fire as she gazed up at him and he drifted to the edge of the stairs, looking down at her twenty-five yards away.

She'd turned into a beautiful woman. The skin of her bare shoulders glowed in the lamplight, her long blond hair cascading down her back in loose curls, and her red gown, layers of silk spilling over her waist and down her legs, making her look like the force she was. Gold embroidery decorated her bodice and fat, long gold earrings nearly reached her shoulders.

The crowd stood around her but left the path ahead clear.

A haunting piano tune with violins began playing, and without taking her eyes off Michael, she started walking to him.

I shot my eyes around, looking for Emmy, but the other three were still nowhere to be seen.

Michael stood frozen, his chest rising and falling hard as he watched her, looking almost in pain.

Her jaw flexed the closer she got, and I saw tears glisten in her eyes, because it was all too much.

Once upon a time, she was a kid who blew our minds and ran with us all night.

She hadn't changed.

She ascended the stairs, needing no one to lead her or give her away, and took Michael's hand, smiling up at him.

"Hey," she said.

And he dove in, his chest caving as he pressed his forehead to hers and hovered over her mouth.

But Kai pulled him back. "Soon, man."

Rika and Michael both laughed, Michael watching her lick her lips and struggling to take his eyes off her.

Clasping her hand, he walked with her to the judge, more than ready.

But I stepped up, stopping them. "Where are the girls?" I whispered.

Rika turned to me, smiling like she had a secret.

Then, her eyes flashed beyond the gazebo, and we followed her gaze, seeing the others all standing at the ends of the other three pathways leading up to the gazebo.

What . . . ?

I walked to the other side, Kai and Damon taking the other pathways, and I saw Emmy standing there in a silver gown, her dark hair spilling around, her eyes locked on mine.

Winter stood off to my left in a dress of white feathers, and Banks to my right, dressed in black.

What were they doing?

Was this . . . ?

And then . . . I stopped breathing, realization hitting me.

Shit.

"Is this okay?" I heard Rika murmur.

"Come here," Michael whispered, and I heard kissing. "I love you."

I remembered Rika planning to marry Michael at St. Killian's. At the cliffs under a midnight sky, she'd said.

Excitement coursed under my skin. I guess she had a better idea.

They all started walking, and Damon started off to meet Winter, but Rika stopped him. "She wants to do it herself, Damon."

He paused, all of them making their way down their paths toward us, Damon's body tense, but his eyes on her every step.

This was what Rika was planning. Why she took the girls.

I glanced over, seeing Alex seated with Kai's parents, dressed in midnight blue.

My heart pounded, smiling as Emmy climbed the stairs.

Was this for real? We were actually doing this?

Barely aware of anyone else as the world spun around, I held out my hand, helping her up the stairs.

"I was thinking you could kiss me this time," I heard Banks tell Kai.

And then Damon took Winter's hand. "You look so beautiful, it fucking hurts," he said.

But I couldn't swallow, my mouth was so dry.

Her dress, her body, every curve . . . What did the back look like? Holy shit . . .

"Are you up for this?" she asked in a quiet voice, looking hopeful.

I felt the ring on her finger, my eyes trailing over her breasts. *Emory Scott. What the . . . ?*

She took hold of my chin and forced my eyes back up, trying desperately to hold back her laugh. "Are you up for this?" she asked again.

I nodded. "Yeah, for like, ever now."

She took off her ring and handed it to me so I could marry her with it, and then she took my arm, all of us coming back to the middle.

Damon wrapped his arms around Winter, holding her to his body and not taking his eyes off her, while Banks held on to Kai, standing at his side.

They were the only ones actually married, but their first wedding was pretty tense. I was happy we were all here. It was perfect.

"Welcome," the officiant said as the music died down.

"Michael and Erika—"

But then . . . lights illuminated above us, and we all tipped our heads back as the crowd gasped and the judge fell silent.

The crystals above that I saw earlier were chandeliers. A dozen of them, hanging in the trees, coming to life and lighting up the leaves, their branches, and looking like a whole other world up there.

Emmy sucked in a breath, and I looked over at her, seeing her chin tremble and a tear hanging at the corner of her eye.

"Oh, my God," she murmured.

She seemed to love chandeliers, didn't she?

Reaching up, I wiped the tear, the lights glowing across her beautiful skin.

"Michael and Erika," the officiant started again. "Damon and Winter. Kai and Nikova. William and Emory."

We all looked at her, air filling my lungs and feeling Em's eyes on me.

"Are you happy?" the judge asked.

And I blew out my breath, breaking into a low chuckle, all of us laughing within a moment.

The judge nodded, needing no further answer. "I've been proud to watch you grow here, and I'm excited to see everything that comes next."

I clasped Emmy's hand.

"Rings, please?"

I held Emmy's, Michael held Rika's, and Damon and Kai took their women's back from them temporarily.

But then, all the girls opened their palms to reveal the bands they had for us.

I looked down at it to see silver rings emblazoned with a crest I didn't recognize. A skull hovering above a bed of grass where a snake laid. Antlers stretched out of the bone against a black background.

I looked around, kind of confused. Banks had the same ring for Kai, and I couldn't see Michael's or Damon's, but I assumed they were the same, too. I guess I'd missed something.

I liked it, though.

"What's wrong?" I heard Michael whisper.

"N . . . Nothing," Rika said. "I thought I saw something."

"Michael and Erika?" the officiant continued. "Do you promise that no matter what you do, you do it as one?"

They smiled at each other. "We do."

"Damon and Winter?" the judge asked next. "Do you promise to give your very best to each other?"

"We do," they said, their voices strong and sure.

"Kai and Nikova?"

My heart hammered inside me, and my pores cooled with sweat.

"Do you promise that the other will never be alone?" the judge asked.

"We do," they answered, and I could hear the smile in their voices.

"And William and Emory?"

I looked down, holding Em's eyes.

I was going to lose it, I was so nervous.

"Do you promise to believe in each other and stand together?"

I gulped.

Hell, yes.

"We do," we replied.

The officiant paused for a moment, then continued, "Do you promise to put the family first?"

"We do," we all answered.

"Do you promise to never break these promises?"

I grinned down at her. "We do."

We all slipped the rings on the other's hand, the band wrapping around me and my heart at the same fucking time.

"Michael and Erika, I now pronounce you husband and wife."

"Whoo!" I heard someone yelp, and we all laughed as Michael and Rika kissed.

"Damon and Winter?" the judge said. "I pronounce you husband and wife."

He took her face and kissed her, still going even after the judge moved on.

"Kai and Nikova, I pronounce you husband and wife."

"Come here," Kai said, crashing his mouth down on his wife's. She giggled.

Banks giggled. I shook my head.

The pulse in my neck pounded, readying myself and feeling like I was about to have a heart attack.

I looked into Em's eyes, whispering, "I love you, baby."

"Good," she told me. "Because I wasn't actually on the shot like I said I was in the greenhouse."

Huh? My eyes went wide, and I froze for a moment.

But then I snorted, diving down and kissing her before I was told.

Fuck yeah.

"William and Emory," the judge said, clearing her throat to try to give us a hint to stop kissing.

But before she could pronounce us husband and wife, thunder pierced the air in the distance, and I jerked, opening my eyes.

What the hell was that?

I pulled back from Emmy, hearing screams and shouting as all of us turned in circles, searching for where the sound came from.

And then we saw it. Beyond the cathedral, far into the black sky toward Cold Point—a cloud of fire and smoke rising into the air like an atomic bomb.

Oh, my God.

"What is that?" Damon yelled.

"It's near the Cove," I said. I knew exactly where it was, and the only thing that it could've been.

People started running, and I grabbed Em's hand, all of us racing out of the gazebo. I searched for the kids, Misha, Ryen, and Alex, but then something caught my attention, and I narrowed my eyes, spotting the little girl from the Cove the other night. Still dressed in her dirty black clothes and the beanie on her head. She was staring at us.

"What the hell?" I growled. "Michael!"

"What?"

I pointed toward the cars at the curb in front of Sticks. "Get her!"

Was that what Rika meant when she said she thought she saw something?

"Oh, shit," he exclaimed.

Keeping Emmy's hand in mine, I hurried with her through the crowd, the little girl spinning around and trying to get through the people as a car tried to exit the alley, and a food cart blocked her other way out.

She slipped through a patch in the chaos, but I lurched forward, catching her arm just in time.

I hauled her back to me, her arms flying out and trying to hit me.

"Let me go!" she yelled.

I wrapped my arms around her as she thrashed and kicked, and her head hit my nose, pain shooting up into my head.

Fuck.

"Hey, hey," Rika said, pulling her out of my arms. "It's okay. No one will hurt you."

She fell to her knees in her red gown, looking up at the little girl and taking her hands in hers.

"I promise," she told her. "No one will hurt you. We just want to make sure you're okay."

"I'm fine," she barked and tried to pull away. "Let me go!"

Damon grabbed her, keeping her there.

But Rika looked up at him. "Let her go."

He frowned but did it, and Rika smiled up at her, trying to soothe. "I saw you watching the wedding," she said as people ran every which way around us. "Did you like it? My mom says I should've worn white."

The little girl scowled but didn't move, her eyes trailing over Rika's earrings and hair.

I rubbed my hand over my face. *Jesus Christ.* We didn't have time for this. The Cove blew up, the townspeople were in a frenzy, most of them probably loading up to go check out the trouble for themselves, and this kid just happened to be there the other night and now here tonight? This was connected.

"I like red, though," Rika teased her. "Do you like red?"

The girl just stared at her, and after a moment, reached out and touched Rika's earring, enamored.

"Do you know what that was at the Cove, honey?" Rika asked.

The little girl looked around, fear etched in her eyes.

Rika tipped her chin at her. "It's okay."

The girl swallowed, finding her words. "No. I left the night you guys came and set the fire."

"I'm sorry about that," Rika told her. "We didn't know you lived there."

"I had already left my hiding spot when you got there," she explained. "When the men came through the tunnel from the sea a couple of hours before."

My eyes shot to Michael, seeing Micah, Rory, and everyone else join us.

"The men?" Rika asked.

The girl nodded.

"What did they look like?" Rory asked her.

"One looked like him." The kid pointed to Michael. "But with darker hair."

Darker hair and amber eyes.

Aydin.

"The other one was hurt," she said. "His hand."

Taylor.

"What's your name?" Rika asked.

But the kid took one more look around at all of us hovering over her and whipped out of Rika's hold, slipping between Alex and Em and diving into the crowd.

"Wait, no!" Rika called as Banks lunged for the kid.

But she was gone.

No matter.

I looked to Micah, Rory, and then Em. "Aydin and Taylor," I said.

They nodded.

The train went under Deadlow Island. I didn't know how they'd gotten that far, or if they had help, but the tunnel could've certainly connected to Coldfield and the Cove tunnels, as well.

Michael shook his head. "Two nights ago . . ."

They'd been here for two days.

Motherfucker.

"And they just announced their presence," Kai said, staring off at the black cloud dissipating into the air off the coast.

The town swarmed around us, people hopping into their cars, while others chatted wildly.

"Get out of your dresses," Michael told the girls. "Everyone meets at Coldfield in thirty minutes! Go!"

CHAPTER 39

EMORY

Present

Lev and David carted everyone home in the SUVs, and after we'd scrambled into new clothes, and the kids and grandmas were secure at Kai's parents' estate, safely under the care of Katsu and Vittoria, we raced down the black highway, pulling on jackets. I slipped on a pair of black leather gloves Banks lent to me, since it was chilly.

But I was pretty sure it was because she didn't want me leaving fingerprints.

I didn't argue. She'd had more experience in this. The girls had filled me in last night on everything I'd missed over the years— Delcour, the Pope, Pithom, Evans Crist, Gabriel Torrance, and everything the guys did wrong—and right—in their quests for vengeance.

And Trevor. I'd known he was dead but not the extent of his demise. It all should've scared me. It was a lot to take in.

But I couldn't help it. Something bubbled up inside me as Will drove, and I couldn't believe how running wasn't even an option. Even with the fear knotting my stomach, I didn't want to be anywhere else.

Sensing him staring at me, I pulled my black ski cap on and

glanced over at him in his black hoodie, and the veins in his tattooed hands bulging out as he gripped the wheel. His eyes flashed to me again, his mouth opening and closing.

"Stop looking at me," I said, facing forward. "I'm coming, and you're not stopping me."

I knew he was worried about the mess he'd gotten me into, but he was forgetting that this was all my mess, too. I didn't run anymore.

We pulled into Coldfield, the place swelling with a crowd, the explosion down on Old Pointe Road drawing people out of their houses instead of back in. Will didn't even bother looking for a parking spot. He pulled up behind two cars, blocking them in, and shut off the engine.

Another SUV pulled up behind us, and everyone climbed out of both cars.

Will and I walked to the rear of the vehicle and pulled open the hatchback. He dug in a duffel bag, handing everyone their mask, but no one put them on yet, simply hooked them onto their belts.

Misha and Ryen jogged up, dressed in street clothes and ready to rock.

Will narrowed his eyes at his cousin, pausing. "What are you doing?"

But Misha just reached down, pulling out a black mask with a blue stripe. "This belong to anybody?"

Will dropped his eyes. "You don't have to be here, man. You don't have to be involved."

Misha stared at him. "Yes, I do."

He strapped his mask onto his belt and dug back into the bag, pulling out a white one for Ryen.

Will gazed between them, a smile slowly forming at his cousin diving into the fray with us. "And my wolfpack, it grew," he said, choking on fake tears, "it grew by two."

"Shut up," Ryen told him.

Misha snorted, all three of them grinning ear to ear at *The Hangover* reference.

Misha and Ryen stepped away, and I didn't know much about them, but I knew Misha wasn't a Horseman and he wasn't the typical Thunder Bay rich boy. Will was family, though, and he was here for family.

Will grabbed one more mask out of the bag, a yellow one with blood around the mouth and eyes.

"They could be distracting us," Micah told him. "Drawing us out there, so they can destroy the town while we're running around in circles."

"They have nothing to gain," Will told him. "Their beef is with us. They want to confront us. They're not going to make it hard for us to find them."

Then he held the mask out to me.

"Real monsters don't wear masks," I teased.

He shrugged. "Real monsters might not care about being identified, either. No mask, no fun for you."

Aw, my man. Layin' down the law. God, it turned me on.

I reached in and pulled out a black one to match his white one instead, both with a thick red stripe down the left side.

"I like this one," I said.

He smiled and pulled his out, closing the back hatch and locking the car.

"Martin could be there," he told me as we all walked into Coldfield so we could sneak into the Cove undetected.

"Or he could not," I pointed out.

But he shook his head, leading the way through the crowd. "Somehow I don't think we're lucky enough that all of this isn't connected, Emory."

Connected . . .

I slowed, thinking about Martin, Evans Crist, Aydin . . .

Who put Will in Blackchurch? We still didn't know. Who had something to gain?

Aydin and Taylor had been in town two days. Why wait so long to make their presence known? What were they doing?

Like Micah and Rory, Aydin, Taylor, and their families would be useful allies to someone.

Evans knew Will had escaped, and now . . .

My chest caved. Evans put Will in Blackchurch.

Evans was connected to Martin.

It had been two days.

Two days.

I tipped my eyes up, looking around us, my face drifting from mask to mask to mask inside the haunted park.

Plenty of time to plan . . .

Shit.

"Wait," I called out, and then turned my head and raised my voice as everyone continued to drift ahead. "Wait!"

Everyone spun around and stared at me, and I rushed for them as Will rushed back to me.

"They've been here for two days," I said, everyone crowding around us. "Two days. What have they been doing? Taking in the sights?"

"They've been getting ready," Michael guessed.

"No," I told him, glancing around again for danger. "They're not alone."

Everyone gaped at me.

"They didn't come here without help," I clarified in a louder voice.

Blackchurch's caretakers would've sent them home or to another facility. They escaped and got here fast with someone's help.

A still figure caught my eye, and I did a double take, seeing him standing in the crowd and staring right at me as people bustled around him in a blur.

My whole body turned hot.

He wore a mask—a devil painted black—and I watched him as he watched me, my heart echoing in my ears.

Coldfield continued to rage like a party around us, people running, screaming, and laughing as "Highly Suspicious" played over the sound system.

"Their parents?" Rory threw the idea out there, and Micah shaking his head, not knowing.

But I answered for him. "No."

"What are you saying?" Alex asked, stepping in.

I looked to Will. "It's all connected. Evans Crist solicited Martin's help to cripple your parents by sending you all to prison, but he didn't anticipate that you'd get organized on your own when you got out. In time, you became a threat he needed to deal with, too."

"My father may have done shit," Michael chimed in, "for which he will pay, but he's been quiet for years."

"But mobile," I retorted. "What if he sent Will to Blackchurch to cripple you like he did to your parents all those years ago?" I looked around at all the guys. "You haven't moved forward with the resort in Will's absence, after all. It worked."

I shot my gaze to the right, seeing the figure again.

Or someone who looked exactly like him. He was also dressed in the same black jacket and black devil mask with the hood pulled up.

I darted my gaze back to the other one, noticing he still stood in the exact same spot. They were both staring at me.

"What if he knew the moment Will was broken out?" I asked Michael. "What if he enlisted the remaining prisoners and their families and had them brought here? What if Aydin and Taylor have been sleeping right down the road this whole time at your parents' house?"

No one spoke, the wheels turning in their heads as they exchanged looks. As they came to terms with the possibility that Aydin could win tonight.

"Aydin engages in nothing until he's sure he can win," Alex said in a quiet voice. "She's right. He's not alone."

I stepped in closer, our circle tightening. "They were probably at the wedding," I said, gesturing with my eyes to the crowd. "They've been following us the whole time."

I slid my eyes to the left, seeing another one. And then another one.

Slowly, the devils were all around us, slipping through the unknowing crowd and surrounding us like an army, and our crew averted their eyes, awareness finally written all over their faces that we were already caught.

"The masks," I murmured. "The devils. It's how their crew is identifying each other."

"Shit," Rika whispered, moving her gaze around the theme park.

We had enough to overcome Evans Crist with the eleven of us, plus Micah and Rory, but we might not now if Evans had Aydin's and Taylor's families behind him. And if he had Martin and a police force behind him?

We were screwed.

Rika grabbed my hand and pulled me toward the warehouse, everyone following as we piled inside, hurrying around a maze of dark tunnels, and slipping behind a prop wall, actors gasping as we found them sticking their hands through the holes to grab patrons and scare them.

Rika whipped off her hoodie and unhooked her mask. "Emmy, switch with me."

She took my mask and hooked it onto her belt.

"Alex, switch with Banks," she told her.

I remained still. "They're coming after all of us," I pointed out.

It was no use to hide my identity when she was in danger, too.

But she retorted, "Not Aydin and Taylor. They'll be after you two first."

Okay, maybe. And if Martin were here tonight, I would definitely be a target.

I slid off my jacket and tossed it to her, taking her hoodie and pulling it over my head as Alex and Banks did the same.

"Get to the underground," Will told everyone. "Em and Alex will go with Rika and Michael."

The underground?

But before I could ask questions, Ryen chimed in, "We shouldn't split up."

"We'll move faster and easier that way," he told her.

I grabbed his face and kissed him, out of breath already. "I want to go with you."

He caressed my cheek. "We'll meet at the Cove. I have to lead them away from the town. I just want to give you all a chance to get away before they catch up."

We pulled on our masks and yanked up our hoods to cover our hair.

"You two go with Kai and Banks," Will told Misha and Ryen. Then he jerked his chin at Rory and Micah. "And you both stick with Lev, Damon, and Winter."

They nodded, pulling on their new masks. I kind of wanted to smile. Will had thought of everything, hadn't he?

"Shake 'em," he instructed us. "I left the door unlocked. Get to the underground. Get to the Cove."

"Yup," everyone said, moving out into the maze again. Damon and Winter slipped through first to get a head start.

But before I could leave, Will grabbed me, pulled me into his arms, and lifted my mask, kissing me hard and deep, his tongue making me moan.

I love you.

"Don't get hurt," I whispered against his mouth.

I nodded.

He gazed into my eyes. "I'm marrying you."

And then he pulled down my mask and rushed me out of our hiding place.

Yeah, we hadn't exactly finished the ceremony, and I wanted all of it.

Rika grabbed my hand, pulling me after Michael and Alex, and I whipped my head around, seeing Will go the opposite direction.

He disappeared around a corner, and I sucked in a breath, an awful feeling curdling in my stomach.

Shit.

I didn't like this.

We headed through the haunted house, making our way for the Mad Scientist wing as Rika quickly filled me in on how Will owned Coldfield as a cover for . . . well, Coldfield, the underground transit system he'd discovered. I'd heard of the haunted theme park that had risen up in Thunder Bay over the past few years, but I'd never been here.

I couldn't wait to see the city underneath.

We moved as quickly as possible, trying not to draw attention, but I couldn't see where the others had gone until I spotted Damon grabbing a bloody sheet and throwing it over Winter, then sweeping her up into his arms like she was his latest victim.

She must've said something, because his lips moved, whispering back to her, and then he tickled her between her legs before they disappeared into a tunnel.

No one else was anywhere to be seen, and I kept my eyes peeled as we slinked through the life-size dollhouse portion, the fog drifting around our feet as the darkness loomed in the rafters above.

I passed mannequins with rotting green skin, fifties-style haircuts, and retro clothes, the joints of their bodies outlined in black to make them look like puppets, but as I slipped through, twisting my eyes from left to right, one came to life and jumped in my face. I screamed, raising my hands to hit her, but I stopped myself, running ahead instead.

I glanced over my shoulder, seeing her step back into place for the next victim, frozen in some creepy posture, but as soon as I whipped my gaze forward again, someone stepped into the pathway ahead of us, a dark form with a devil mask.

Alex, Rika, Michael, and I halted, seeing another one step into the path of our escape. I didn't think they knew where the entrance to Coldfield was because they wouldn't have been so keen to stop us if they knew where we were going and could follow, but there were a lot of them outside before, and probably more I didn't see.

"Let's go!" I yelled.

Twisting around, I raced between the houses, down a tunnel, and up the rickety stairwell, Alex and Rika jogging after me, and Michael keeping an eye on the rear.

I raced across the top floor and pushed through the door, stumbling onto the warehouse roof. Fog machines and strobe lights worked, pouring down on the party below while decorations, reapers, and evil angels blew in the wind, casting their foreboding doom over the courtyard.

Tall tents stood, protecting supplies from the rain, and I grabbed Alex's hand, Rika and Michael following as I bolted across the roof to the other side. If we could get back down the fire escape quickly enough, we could lose the tail and make it down to Coldfield.

I looked left, though, and immediately halted, breathing hard as I inched to the edge and peered into the dark expanse below.

"Emmy!" Michael barked. "What are you doing?"

I couldn't help but smile as I looked into the forest maze beyond, wolves howling and owls hooting over the speakers as a bus sat in the middle of all the activity behind the warehouse, a spooky red light glowing from inside.

Our bus. He'd been telling the truth. He had kept it.

My heart ached that he'd thought of it.

"Emory!" Michael growled again, and I startled, looking over to see him and Rika already at the fire escape, her descending first and then him climbing on after.

Alex ran over and took my hand, pulling me along, but then a dark figure swept around the tents, shoved me in the chest, and I flew back onto the ground, landing on my ass.

The world jumbled in my view, and it took a moment to draw in a breath. But then I blinked and found him struggling with Alex as he squeezed her neck.

"Hey!" I heard Michael bellow.

But I was already shooting off the ground as Alex whipped off his devil mask and Taylor faced her, her leg hooking around his and sweeping his leg out from underneath him, sending them both plummeting to the roof.

Taylor landed on his back, her body crashing down on top of his, and he grunted, rearing his hand back and slapping her across the face.

She gasped, tumbling to the side, but before he could climb on top of her, I shot my foot right between his legs.

He cried out, curling up, and I dropped down on him, his sweaty hair sticking to his forehead as I hit his face. He winced, trying to shield himself, and I bashed so hard, pain shot through my wrist and up my arm.

Someone lifted me off him, my breath filling my ears as I breathed inside my mask, and I almost took it off, but I knew the whole place was wired with cameras for security, so I obeyed Will and kept it on.

"Come on," Michael snapped, taking my hand and pulling me.

We all ran, heading over the side of the building, down the fire escape, and back onto the ground.

People rushed past, heading toward the stage as the announcer started the show, as "Devil Inside" boomed from the speakers.

I lifted my eyes, seeing masked devils heading over the side of the building, following us.

"Go!" I shouted.

But then my eyes caught something, and I stopped, spotting Martin.

He stood at the entrance, across the food court, dressed in jeans, a black pullover, and his dark hair perfectly coiffed.

He stared at me with his hand in his pocket. A smile reaching his eyes that he didn't give away across his lips.

My spine tingled, seeing the challenge in his gaze.

"Emmy!" Rika called. "Emmy, let's go!"

He stared at me.

I couldn't move.

My lungs constricted, one foot ready to retreat, and another wanting to charge over and beat him until my hands were bloody.

A cry lodged in my throat.

I can't move.

And then, a small hand slipped inside mine, the cold skin rough with dirt and grime.

I looked down, swallowing as I saw a little girl looking up at me. Who . . . ?

"Let's go," she whispered.

Blond hair and maybe eight or nine years old, she wore all black except for the white undershirt I saw poking out from the bottom of her sweater. A black cap on her head, and a braid hanging over her shoulder, she smiled and pulled me along. I followed, looking to Michael and Rika for an answer, but they just gaped at her, looking equally confused.

She let me go and shot ahead, dipping down and diving through the tarp covering the crawl space underneath the warehouse. "Through here!" she called.

We hesitated only a moment before following, Michael ushering us in her wake and then following us.

We crawled, digging on our hands and knees, the cold earth seeping through my jeans as the kid led the way under the floor, all of us glancing over our shoulders to see who was following us.

"You sure you know where you're going?" Michael asked.

"I own this town," she fired back.

He chuckled despite the rush we were in, but I had no time to wonder where the hell this kid came from, or if she was really leading us to safety.

Right now, we had no choice.

Stopping, she rose up and popped up a floorboard, all of us crawling up into the warehouse, and right into the Mad Scientist's wing again.

As soon as we were all inside and we knew where we were at, Michael picked up the kid, threw her over his shoulder, and ran, all of us following him.

"Oh, my God, I can walk." She raised up and held out her hands. "Dude!"

But he wouldn't stop as we raced into the lab, no one following us as we swung open the door and dived inside the room. Michael carried the kid down into the tunnel, followed by Rika and Alex, but I paused, sensing something.

Looking back over my shoulder, through the doorway and into the chem lab, I locked eyes on a group of figures draped in white in the other room. They stood like statues, black holes for the eyes and all of them looking like they were watching me.

Something crawled on my skin, fear snaking its way through me as my feet sprouted roots and dug into the ground.

Frozen, I stared at their faces, knowing.

I just knew.

And then . . . one turned his head, and my heart leapt into my throat. I screamed, knowing it might not be one of them, but it could be. Shit.

I slipped into the tunnel, closed the door, and raced after the others, tripping over a rock as I kept looking over my shoulder.

I stumbled, catching myself, and rushed up to the tracks.

Micah, Rory, and Lev were in the car ahead, already strapped in, and I barely had time to catch my breath before they sped off, their railcar zooming down the track.

There were only two cars left, so hopefully that meant that everyone else had already gotten out.

They got strapped in, Michael started the car, and I looked back, hearing the door creak open back down the tunnel.

Will . . .

But someone grabbed me and pushed me into the seat.

"Will!" I cried, feeling the seat belt strap onto me. "Michael, no!"

"Hurry," Rika yelled to him, the girl in her lap. "Go!"

The car shot off, my neck jerking back, and I twisted in my seat, seeing the lights behind grow smaller and smaller.

"No!" I cried.

There was only one car left. If someone saw where we went—if that ghost wasn't an actor and he saw where I was going—Will wouldn't get to the Cove.

I covered my face with my hands as the wind whipped across my body.

We shouldn't have split up.

Tears filled my eyes.

We coasted around a bend, and we must've gone under the river, because droplets of water hit me from above as we raced back up again, lights periodically marking our way.

Michael slowed, and I held on, seeing us approach a platform, and then he screeched to a stop, everyone ripping off their seat belts.

"Will," I called to them, unbuckling myself. "We left Will! Aydin was back there!"

I knew it was him in the lab.

I followed them, climbing out of the car and onto the platform.

"What if Will can't get past him?" I asked. "We have to go back."

Michael pulled Rika and the girl up. "Will wanted you out of there. We stick together."

"No!"

"He won't fail," Rika told me, looking at me dead-on. "He won't fail, Em. He'll be here."

I stilled, holding her eyes. I couldn't not go back for him.

I couldn't . . .

But the kid pulled my hand. "Come on!" she cried.

I dug in my heels, but before I could argue, Michael grabbed her and twisted her around by the shoulders. "Not so fast," he said. "Who are you? Tell me now and hurry."

She straightened, clamping her mouth shut.

"And why are you living here at the Cove?" he pressed.

She jerked, trying to run, but he caught her and held her tight.

I glanced down the tunnel, but I still didn't hear any other railcars approaching.

I'd never seen her before, but it seemed like they had.

"Athos," she finally answered. "My name is Athos."

Like the musketeer?

"And your last name?" Michael demanded.

"I don't have one."

He frowned. "You have one. You weren't born here, kid."

"Maybe I was beamed down to study your species."

Alex snorted, and we watched as the little girl took Rika's hand and backed up, hovering close to the woman and away from Michael with a scowl on her face.

He rose, scowling right back. "What?"

"I've seen what your species likes to do to women down at that cave on the beach," she told him.

Rika gasped, covering her mouth, but I caught the smile underneath as Alex laughed out loud.

"You saw that?" he asked, wide-eyed.

The little girl gave Michael a once-over up and down. "Hmph."

He shook his head and grabbed her, swinging her up and over his shoulder again. "Let's go!"

"Afraid I'll get away again?" she griped.

We ran through the dark tunnel, this one concrete with rooms and doors. Racing up the stairs, we came into an old shop, long since closed down with the Cove, and ran outside into the park with the Ferris wheel looming in the distance.

"We'll fight our way out of here," Michael told me as we ran, "search for my father, and take care of both him and Scott."

Take care of?

"You good with that?" he asked me.

I breathed hard, realizing I was going to have to take Alex up on her offer to train at Kai's dojo at some point to get in shape. "Like, murder him?"

He smiled. "I was thinking an island only accessible by train."

Blackchurch. He wanted to send my brother and his father to Blackchurch.

I grinned back. "I can live with that."

Damon, Winter, and everyone else jetted out from behind a game booth with a couple of other masked figures—extra security, I assumed—waiting for us, and I looked back to see both Damon and Banks holding Winter's hands as she ran with them.

"I got you, baby," he said.

"Where's Will?" Misha asked, looking around.

Not here, I knew that. I dug out my phone and unlocked the screen, ready to dial him, but then I noticed people ahead and slowed, seeing Martin and a team of men and women walking into the park, their eyes already on us.

Oh, no.

We all stopped as they blocked our way out, and I scanned the area again, still not finding Will among us. How did Martin get here so fast? How did he know where we were going?

"Move," I heard Michael tell him.

We were prepared to fight our way through Aydin and Taylor, but this?

Shit.

Michael stepped forward, everyone else behind him as he confronted Martin. I joined him, refusing to hide.

Martin gazed at me. "We never had to see each other again," he said, stepping toward me, a shoulder holster strapped around him and everyone in his ranks armed and dressed to run.

Memories washed over me, hearing almost the same words he last said to me all those years ago at the police station.

It seemed like yesterday.

He reached down and took my hand, Michael jerking and ready to pounce if he hurt me.

I clenched my teeth, the slime of his skin seeping into mine.

The eye of the storm. I remembered Aydin's words over and over.

Martin looked at my ring. "I wasn't invited."

I curled my fist and gently pulled away. "No, you weren't."

The eye of the storm . . .

"They know." I tipped my chin up. "It's too late."

Everyone here knew about our lie and his involvement in sending them to prison.

But he just broke into a smile and chuckled, a chill rising up my spine. "You think that scares me?" he asked. "That was small potatoes compared to the decisions I've made since. And I'm not the only one with shit to lose if I go down."

What did that mean? My gaze flashed behind him. *The cops?* I recognized a few of them.

"These officers know us," I said. "You think they'll really do this? All of them?"

Hurt Michael Crist, Kai Mori, Damon Torrance, and Will Grayson, not to mention Erika Fane?

He just tsked. "They're not officers at this hour, Emmy."

And I looked again, taking in the weapons and street clothes, not a badge in sight.

Footfalls hit the pavement behind us, and I whipped my head around, seeing Aydin coming through the park from where we entered. He looked at us, followed by a crew of people in devil masks, his black sweater zipped up to his chin, and his hair smooth and lying over his forehead.

Fire flashed in his gaze as he blocked us in from the back, and Martin blocked us in from the front.

"And I have so much more with me," Martin cooed and then called out. "Evans?"

I jerked back around, my eyes shooting from Martin to the figure coming through his crowd, seeing Evans Crist step forward in a three-piece navy suit, with his gray hair styled to the side.

Evans. Martin used to call him Mr. Crist, but since he was coming into power himself, it seemed he fancied himself his equal.

"Son of a bitch," Michael bit out.

Damon chimed in from behind. "We're ready whenever you are," he assured Michael.

Michael nodded, still facing his father, both men the same height.

Evans gazed at his oldest son, and I couldn't imagine what was going through Michael's head right now.

He'd killed Trevor. Was he going to kill his father, too?

"I didn't tell Trevor to post those videos when he found that phone," Evans told Michael. "But he told me after he did it. He knew it would serve me if Katsu, Gabriel, and the Graysons lost credibility with some orchestrated familial troubles." He smiled to himself. "Some of it worked in my favor, other things didn't."

Katsu lost his positions on two bank boards for a time, and Gabriel lost deals. But Will's grandfather remained senator, despite the bad press.

"But then we got powerful," Michael added.

Evans nodded. "Rika became mayor, Kai's been revitalizing Whitehall, Damon is Rika's heir, not to mention he's grooming Banks for national politics . . ." he listed off all of his concerns. "And Will discovered Coldfield, and now controls the underground transit system between Thunder Bay and Meridian City. I mean, if you had a playbook of how to make me sweat, that would be it." He chuckled. "I bow to you. You've impressed me, Michael. I wish I had you at my side."

"But that's not what you and I were made for," his son replied.

Evans shook his head. "No, you're right. But you are in over your head."

I took in the weapons and the sheer size of Aydin's and Martin's crews, knowing we were outmatched. We couldn't fight them with a sword and our fists.

This couldn't get that far.

I met Martin's eyes. "He influenced your career and helped you fly up a few ladders, but he's going down," I told him. "Save yourself."

"He had my father murdered," Rika pleaded, stepping in.

He wasn't getting away with it. Unless they killed us all, Martin was on the losing side.

But then Evans started laughing, looking to Martin, a knowing look passing between them both.

My stomach knotted.

"Who do you think cut the brake lines?" Evans asked Rika. "Altered the police report? Destroyed the vehicle before it could be inspected?"

She lunged for him, but Michael pulled her back, getting into his father's face. One of the guards shifted behind them, ready to grab for his weapon.

"I promise you," Michael said. "I won't tell my mother any of this after you're gone. She'll never have to know."

"It's not for you to protect me, Michael," someone spoke up.

Slowly, we turned around, the two masked figures I didn't recognize standing on both sides of Kai as they pulled off their masks and pushed down their hoods.

Christiane Fane stood on the left, tears filling her eyes, as Delia

Crist, Michael's mother, stood on the right, her light brown bangs hanging in her eyes.

Kai shrugged, looking apologetic. "The kids are safe," he assured. "I couldn't stop them. Sorry, man."

They must've cornered him at his mom and dad's house, and he snuck them past Michael.

Christiane stepped forward, not taking her eyes off Evans as she walked straight for him, her blond hair—like Rika's—pulled back in a low ponytail and her frail, quiet form looking too skinny to pick up a peanut.

She stopped in front of him, both of them locking eyes, and then . . . she whipped her hand across his face, sending him stumbling to the side.

The crew behind them tensed, and I balled my fists, ready.

He breathed hard, blinking and looking shocked, and then stood upright again, facing her.

She slapped him again, the same cheek, but the only part of him that moved this time was his head twisting to the side.

His jaw flexed, and I didn't even care she wasn't screaming at him for what he did to her husband and the years of torture since. She hit him again and again, and I almost smiled.

He grunted after the fifth one, sucking in angry air through his teeth. "Get the bitch off me," he finally growled to someone.

Martin hurried to grab her, and we stepped forward, but just as Christiane raised her hand to slap him again, Damon shoved Martin back, telling him, "Don't touch her." And then Will raced ahead, dived in, and caught Christiane by the wrist, stopping her.

My heart leapt. *Will.*

With his mask hooked onto his belt and his kind eyes cast down on Rika's mother, he said, "I'll tie him up later, and let you have some more fun, okay?"

She stared up at him, almost looking lost for a moment, but then she broke into a smile.

She turned around, the tears streaming down her face as she looked at the ground, and even though Damon, Michael, and I had so many problems with the people who raised us, not all of the parents were enemies.

Damon put his finger under her chin and pushed, forcing her to lift her eyes up.

"Chin up," he bit out. "And stop being a mouse. You're my mother, for Christ's sake."

He faced forward, but she gazed up at him, love and longing in her eyes as he took her hand and led her back to the group.

Depositing her next to Mrs. Crist, Michael's mother took her other hand, standing in solidarity.

Evans spit out blood and then stood up straight, fixing his tie and drawing in a deep breath. "That was always the real problem with you boys," Evans said. "No matter how smart you could be or how many occasions you proved yourselves shrewd and clever players, you ultimately always resorted to violence." He shifted his gaze from Michael to Will, Will's threat to tie him up still hanging in the air. "You never could keep your attention focused on the long game, could you? Friends and girls were more important, and the immediate gratification was what mattered most, when you should've always realized that you could trust no one. Crists don't build." He looked to Michael. "We win."

And they were going to win, too. We were vastly outnumbered. Evans and Martin could ship us all to Blackchurch tonight.

"Take your grandfather, for example," he told Will. "No grudges because we're not friends. We gain more this way. Together, we bought time to delay your resort project."

"His grandfather?" Kai repeated.

And just then, a puff of smoke drifted into the air, and we all looked through the cops to see Senator Grayson pushing off a ticket booth and strolling forward as he smoked a cigar.

I locked my jaw.

He wore a black, three-piece suit with a light blue shirt and the gold chain of a pocket watch draped over his vest.

I'd actually never seen him in real life before, which wasn't a feat, since he lived in DC almost around the clock for the past twenty years.

But I recognized him immediately.

He stopped behind Evans, drawing a puff off his cigar again, his cool expression unfazed.

Shit. I glanced to Will at my side, the stoic look on his face making me more nervous. If William Grayson, Sr., was here, in person, this was bad.

We were all going to Blackchurch.

Or worse.

"You two?" Michael asked, realization dawning.

"Old-timers . . ." Damon stepped forward. "You'll be dead before we will. Step down with dignity."

"Calm down," Kai grit out.

"Fuck calm," he barked. "I got rid of my parents, now they both do their part. Step up and deal with this, or else I'm ready to go *Children of the Corn* on this town."

I walked toward Senator Grayson a few steps. "You put Will in Blackchurch?"

"Mmm . . ."

My stomach coiled tightly as Evans grinned. I could see where Michael got his smile.

They were a team? They got rid of Will together?

"You bastards," Michael said.

Evans glanced over his shoulder at the senator. "You've been called worse."

"I have," he joked.

"I'm glad you came to me when you did," Evans said, turning back around, but still speaking to Senator Grayson. "I'm glad we could help each other."

"Me, too," Mr. Grayson said. "I learned a great deal."

"He's your grandson," I argued. "Why?"

The senator looked past me to Will. "He knows why."

I felt Will approach my side, he and his grandfather locked in a stare. "Because I liked my parties," Will said.

Mr. Grayson nodded. "You lack moderation, yes."

"And because I was going nowhere."

"And quite fast, too."

Will moved toward his grandfather slowly, the other man walking to meet him.

"Because I needed time to think," Will guessed.

"I hope you got it."

"And because I'm weak."

"As a kitten," the senator teased.

Will cocked his head, and Mr. Grayson rolled his eyes. "A puppy." Will stared at him.

"Okay, a small dog," the senator offered, placating his grandson.

I studied them, their banter almost warm. What was going on?

"Because I'm wild," Will cooed.

And Senator Grayson smiled, approaching his grandson. "Oh, beyond belief."

"And because I was an embarrassment."

Mr. Grayson peered at Will, his eyes thinning in skepticism. "Never," he answered.

I exhaled. "Then why did you put him in Blackchurch?"

For the fucking money? For the resort? To trip up Graymor Cristane? Why?

Senator Grayson smiled, looking lovingly at his grandson. "Because he asked me to," he said.

Will broke into a chuckle, both of them with the same bright green eyes as they dove in and embraced each other, laughing and smiling as they hugged.

My stomach dropped. What?

"What the hell?" Damon snapped.

Evans's face fell, watching the two men.

Will asked him to send him to Blackchurch? What?

"Missed you," Will said to his grandpa.

Senator Grayson held Will's face, taking him in after such a long time apart. "Missed you, too, kid."

CHAPTER 40

WILL

Present

I hugged Grandpa again, inhaling the scent of cigar and aftershave. Pain stretched my throat as I held my relief in check. Fuck, I'd missed him.

"What the hell is going on?" Damon snapped.

"Will!" Banks yelled next.

I pulled back from my grandpa, his presence always a comfort. Always.

He was a constant. As reliable as the tide, and even if I doubted whatever I was doing, I never doubted him. He was always right.

"You were gone too long," he told me.

"I know." I let him go. "We have lots to talk about."

He'd wanted me extracted from Blackchurch months ago, and again a month ago.

And again, a week ago.

I was his favorite. *No offense, Misha.*

He looked over his shoulder to the off-duty cops accompanying Martin. "Go home, gentlemen."

They nodded, some casting a quick look to their boss, but they knew a senator's protection trumped a police commissioner's threat.

"You son of a bitch," Evans growled as his officers drifted off, out of the park, only a couple of people remaining with the senator.

I looked over, seeing both Martin and Evans, the realization of how they'd been double-crossed playing in their eyes.

"Don't trust anyone, right?" Grandpa teased Evans.

I tried to wipe the smirk off my face as I gazed at Michael's father, but I couldn't. "Seems my long game was a little longer than yours, at least."

He thought my grandpa had teamed up with him, sent me to Blackchurch to screw over Graymor Cristane, and inserted himself to help protect all their financial legacy, but he failed to realize that I was my grandfather's legacy, and William Aaron Paine Grayson, Sr., would always choose family.

In truth, this plan of action had been set in motion long ago.

"What the hell is going on?" Michael charged up to us, eyeing my grandfather. "You knew? You knew about my father's role in everything?"

"Will knew," he replied.

I turned and looked at my friends, all of them staring at me with a mixture of fury, confusion, and unease.

I didn't want to look at Emmy, but I did, facing my almost-wife with the truth that I'd hidden since the moment she arrived at Blackchurch.

"I sent me to Blackchurch," I told her and then drifted my eyes around the group. "To make . . . friends. To see if I could find others just like us—sons needing a home and a fight to live for."

Micah, Rory, and Aydin loomed in my periphery, and I had no idea where Taylor was. By the time I'd made it to the tunnels, all the cars were gone, and I realized Aydin or someone must've followed them through the tunnels, either with a railcar or on foot. I jumped back in my SUV and raced here.

"And it didn't occur to you to let us in on the secret?" Winter charged. "We were worried."

"We thought you were gone," Damon added. "Maybe forever!"

I stared at all of them, knowing exactly what they were saying. I understood why they were mad. I would be, too.

But . . .

I dropped my eyes, the old doubts creeping back up. "I was afraid I would fail," I said in a quiet voice.

I couldn't commit to something, assuring all of them that I would succeed, when I knew it was entirely possible that I wouldn't. It wouldn't have shocked them. They would've expected me to fail.

And proving them right, I couldn't handle. Recruiting Micah and Rory wasn't the only hurdle at Blackchurch. I was also getting sober.

"You're all stronger than me." I raised my eyes. "You always were. I couldn't look you in the eyes anymore. I couldn't face you. So, when my grandfather told me about the pictures and the fake police report that forced us to plea down before we went to prison, I started digging. Why would Martin do that?" I cast a quick glare over my shoulder, seeing him still standing there, frozen. "Who was helping him that had everything to gain by us three getting sent away?"

I looked back to my friends, letting my eyes drift from Damon to Kai to Michael.

"I knew you'd help," I told them. "I knew you'd do anything I asked you to."

"So, you went to Blackchurch to recruit?" Kai asked, gesturing to Micah and Rory. "So you could bring them to the table?"

"So I could bring the table," I countered. "I needed to dry up, and I had to do something right all on my own. I had to go somewhere I could find powerful people who needed us, too." I met Michael's eyes. "We needed them. If we were going to go up against your father and Martin Scott and win."

"And yet," Evans chimed in, "I have Khadir and Dinescu."

"You have nothing," Aydin said, stepping forward. "I don't follow."

He snapped his fingers and his crew in the devil masks backed away, standing down.

He looked to Will. "I'm just here for the fun."

I held his eyes, knowing he was here to collect a lot more than that.

The immediate threat now equalized, Michael swept in, grabbed his father's collar, and reared his fist back, punching him right across the face. Evans stumbled to the side, tripping over his legs, but Michael held firm and pulled him back up, not letting him get away.

Damon laughed at my side.

Michael leaned into his father's face, growling low, "Someday, you and I are going to have a serious conversation," he told him. "I'll give you a few years to think about what you want to say to me. Now, walk to the car. Don't make my mother watch you be carried out."

Evans's chest rose and fell hard, fear etched across his face as I'm sure he wracked his brain to think about how he was going to get out of this.

But someone came up and grabbed him, force-walking him out of the park as the rest of the officers drifted with them.

"I'll take care of it from here," my grandfather told me. "Call Jack if you want the other one extracted, too."

"Thank you, Grandpa."

His assistant had been just as reliable as he had been, keeping in constant touch with me at Blackchurch and keeping my grandfather informed.

He stared at me and smiled. "Be safe. All of you," he said. "I'll be at the tavern if you need me."

I nodded, watching him, Evans, and all the officers leave the park. I turned, seeing only our crew, Aydin's, and Martin left to deal with.

Micah walked up to me. "You needed our families' power then?" he asked. "The protection of their connections and their investment into your resort? You used us for our families?"

"Wanna use me for mine?" I tossed back. "I asked you to give me till the end of the weekend. I chose you. Now, it's your turn to choose us."

We did need them, but I wasn't inviting anyone into the fold I didn't believe honestly belonged here. Micah Moreau and Rory Geardon were my friends, and in no time at all, I had every confidence that Michael and everyone else would consider them such, as well.

I turned to Aydin, squaring my shoulders. "Leave."

He glanced over my shoulder. "He could be useful to me."

Martin Scott?

Aydin Khadir had no interest in money, power, or business. His satisfaction in life came from playing people, and getting his hands on Scott would keep me engaged, Emmy prisoner, and Alex in his life as a result.

"I'll ask you one last time," I gritted out. "Leave."

Em walked over, standing at my side and facing him.

He'd used her at Blackchurch. But even so, he guided her when no one ever had.

For that, I'd let him walk out of here on his own two feet.

He met her eyes, a moment of something I couldn't place passing in his eyes. "Are you scared, Emory?" he asked her.

Her voice remained as still and calm as her body. "I'm the eye of the storm. You?"

He turned his head, looking at Alex, the longing stretching between them so strongly, I could almost feel it vibrating in the ground.

"I'm the storm," he murmured.

Alex stayed rooted, Aydin standing there, feeling like a ticking bomb, and I saw someone shift out of the corner of my eye, but before I could place it, Winter spoke up. "Gun," she said, sucking in a breath. "I heard someone chamber a round."

I darted my eyes to Aydin, the hint of a smile on his lips, and then Martin reached for his gun in his holster, and I spun around, knowing all hell was about to break loose.

"Lev, take the kid!" I yelled. "Now!"

Lev grabbed the little girl and ran, everyone fanning out as we faced Martin and Aydin, some whipping around to face Aydin's crew.

I looked to Em. "Hide."

"Are you kidding?" she yelled.

And then she ran, shooting out her foot right into Martin's chest, the gun knocking out of his hand as he fell back onto the ground.

The whole place descended into chaos.

Screams and shouts filled the air, someone taking Winter to the ground, and she kneed him right in the balls just as Damon got to her, pulling the guy off her.

Martin's gun clanked across the pavement, and he scrambled for it, but Em kicked it away. I was about to dive in, but she jumped on him, fury in her eyes as she wrapped her arms and legs around him and fought.

I turned to Aydin, who stood ready and willing.

"I'm leaving with one of them," he informed me.

I charged for him. "You're not leaving."

You had that chance.

I threw a fist across his face, taking him to the ground, everyone around us fighting and growling. Winter crossed my mind, and I wanted to make sure she was okay. Did anyone have a gun out and ready to use on us? Did Lev make it out with the kid?

Where were the moms? Jesus.

Aydin threw me over and climbed on top, pinning me to the ground, his fist landing on my jaw, and my teeth cutting the inside of my mouth.

Someone screamed and others cursed, Aydin's blood pouring down my hand where it seeped out of his nose.

We punched and fought, throwing kicks, and then he grabbed me by the collar, lifted me up, and slammed me into the pavement, my ears ringing and an ache coursing through my skull.

"Fuck," I grunted, whipping him off me.

Rising to my feet, I kicked him in the face, watching him fly backward, and then I dived in from behind and wrapped my arm around his neck.

Holding him tight, I glanced behind me, seeing Emmy on the ground, her hoodie in Martin's grasp as he slapped her.

No.

My hold loosened, and Aydin lurched forward, launching me over his body and onto the ground, coming around and throwing his kick across my face.

Fire exploded across my face, my vision blurring, and before I knew it, he kicked again and then again, straddling me and punching, again and again.

Blood filled my mouth, and I couldn't open my eyes, but I grabbed his sweater and yanked him to the side, both of us rolling over onto the ground, the fight a mess of fists and fingers digging into each other's necks.

But then something pierced the air, ringing in my ears, and I jumped, Aydin stopping, too.

Was that a . . . ? A gunshot?

Aydin stared up at me, his angry eyes turning shattered. He twisted his head, looking over, and I followed his line of sight, seeing Alex standing there.

Everything stopped.

The fighting halted, and the screams and growls fell silent as her black pullover darkened with something wet on her chest, and I spotted the hole in the fabric.

Everything broke inside me.

Oh, my God.

I jerked my eyes over to Martin, seeing the gun in his hand as he laid on the ground with it aimed at Alex, and Emmy lying on his back and reaching for it, but she couldn't stop him in time.

I shot off Aydin, dashed to Martin, and kicked the pistol out of his hand, and then brought down my boot, stomping his face.

I pulled Emmy up, starting off to Alex, but just then I saw Aydin racing over to her and catching her in his arms just as she fell.

Her eyes moved, but she wasn't blinking, like she was in shock.

A trickle of blood seeped out of her mouth, and I shot my hand to my hair, hoping that that blood came from the fight, and it hadn't hit her lungs.

"I'm calling an ambulance!" someone shouted.

Everyone rushed over to her as Aydin pressed his hand to her wound, applying pressure and breathing hard as tears filled his eyes and he cradled her.

"Look at me," he said as he ripped off part of his shirt to cover the wound. "Concentrate on my face."

The wound was between her shoulder and chest, near the joint of her arm.

"Tap a song with your fingers for me, okay?" he said, breathless.

"I'd rather just concentrate on your face," she whispered, reaching up and touching his cheek.

He slowed, unable to look at her as a tear dripped off his chin.

"Except your hair," she teased. "You look like you're in a K-Pop band, Aydin."

He shot his eyes to her, at a loss for words for once in his life.

Then he broke out into a chuckle. "I thought you hated the pompadour," he argued.

"I did."

He laughed again, tipping her head up. "You take me for a haircut, then," he said, dipping his head down and holding her close. "Whatever makes you happy. I'll do anything you want."

A sob escaped him, but he shook it off and tried to rise to his feet with her, but Kai shot down and swept her into his arms.

"Get off her," he said.

Kai carried her off, everyone following to the parking lot.

"Ambulance is on its way," Damon said.

"Wait." Aydin started after her.

But I whipped around and punched him, sending him flying back to the ground. "Fuck you!" I said.

I could hear Kai ahead. "You okay? Alex, talk to me. Stay with us."

Aydin's crew surrounded us, but he just stayed on the ground, not knocked out, but whatever fight he came in with was now gone. He just sat there, staring after her with blood dripping down his face.

I looked after my friends, everyone in one piece, although Banks was limping, and Misha carried Ryen, their lips locked together as they went off. Guilt washed over me.

I knew this wasn't our fault. We just wanted a piece of the pie. Evans sent us to jail with the help of Martin.

We didn't want this fight. We just wanted them both gone because we weren't safe otherwise.

But it still hurt. I didn't want Emmy, Misha, Ryen, or any of them in danger like this ever again.

I looked at her next to me, seeing a little blood on her face, and I quickly dabbed it, trying to get it off.

But she stopped me. "I had to fight back," she told me. "Now he knows. Now he knows it will never go unanswered again."

And I pulled her into me, squeezing her so tight.

She was like us. I would say the exact same thing, and even though I hated to risk losing her, she wasn't a flower.

And now I understood why Michael let Rika be at his side in everything they did. She wanted to feel this, too.

That didn't mean I couldn't defend her honor, though.

Now, it was my turn.

"Come here, motherfucker." I made my way for Martin, but when I turned, he was pushing off the ground and running.

Where the hell did he think he was going?

He raced for the entrance, but Damon spun around, quickly ushering Winter into Rika's care as he faced Martin, ready to stop him.

I ran for him, and Martin stopped, looking for a way out as he twisted toward me and then back to Damon, realizing he was trapped.

Going the only way he had left, because he was too stupid to give up, he dove between the Ferris wheel and the utility building, probably thinking he'd lose us under the cover of the rides and game booths.

Damon went left, I went right, both of us charging after him into the darkness with the coast looming beyond the cliffs. I rounded the Ferris wheel, looking left and right, and then saw him running along Cold Point in the pitch-black night.

I growled, digging in my heels and running so hard my muscles burned. I reached my hand out, only about four feet of clearance between me and the cliff dropping off into the sea, and pushed him, seeing him stumble to the ground before I came down on top of him. I punched him, we rolled, and he straddled me, climbing off and scurrying back.

I rose to my feet, the sea at my back, and he stared at me, turning his head and seeing Damon come up from behind, trapping him again.

His eyes shot to mine, and I could see it in his gaze.

The rage. The defiance.

I saw the moment his lips tightened, he inhaled, and his eyes sharpened, resolving what he had to do in his head, the decision made.

Oh, shit.

He charged, and I didn't have time to move out of the way before he rammed his body into mine, sending us both flying over the edge.

My heart jumped into my throat. *Emmy* . . .

Screams pierced the air above, and I stopped breathing, my mind paralyzed with so much fear I wanted to cry out.

No, no, no . . .

I almost closed my eyes, but I refused. I was going to look that fucker in the face, not giving him the satisfaction of my fear.

This was it.

We fell away from each other, but I kept my eyes locked on him.

I love you, Em. I love—

I crashed to the surface, white flashing behind my eyes and every nerve in my body sizzling like the end of an open wire. I floated, feeling the fade, the echoes quieting as I drifted further and further away.

White, white . . . and gone.

But then, all of a sudden, pain wracked through my body, my neck, and every joint, and I popped my eyes open, sucking in a huge breath.

It wasn't air I drew in. Water filled my mouth, and I thrashed, looking around and seeing the ocean—above, below, and all around.

We'd landed in the water. Not the rocks.

I started choking, and I didn't have time to take inventory of my limbs or where Martin was. I had to breathe.

Kicking my legs and crawling with my arms, I popped through the surface, sputtering water and coughing as I tried to clear my lungs. Finally, I took in one big gulp of air, hearing the wave behind me. I twisted around, and I didn't have time to take another breath before the wave crashed down on me.

I was pushed under the water, carried with the current, and I looked down, seeing the abyss below.

I tilted my eyes up, seeing the moon through the water.

A sob lodged in my chest, reaching for the surface, but I couldn't get to it. I knew this feeling.

The weight of the cinderblock around my ankle, feeling the slack stretch, and the sudden jerk as I was yanked down, and no matter how much I flailed and how hard I swam, I couldn't outpower it.

I swam and swam, fighting for the top before the waves pushed me into the rocks, but then something grabbed my foot, and I kicked, seeing Martin pull himself up and lock an arm around my neck.

Bubbles poured out of my mouth as I growled, feeling us sinking as the air expelled from our bodies.

I struggled and fought. What the hell was he doing?

But I knew.

He wasn't giving himself up, and he was taking me with him.

I twisted and thrashed, trying to pry his arms off me, but without any leverage to push off, we just kept falling.

I bit and hunched forward, trying to throw him away from me, but my lungs tightened and screamed, and I just wanted to open my mouth and take in air, but as I looked up, I couldn't see the moon anymore.

I couldn't see anything but the black as the cold covered us, swallowing us up.

Em.

I kept my eyes on the surface as it grew farther and farther away, my body part of the depths now. Too far gone to go back.

Just like the SUV filling up when we crashed into the river. Knowing it was only moments.

The air was gone, I could feel the fight in my chest for oxygen, and the cool comfort of the water.

I closed my eyes. *Do you still want to hold me?* she asked.

I could hear her in my head. *I love you, Will.*

No.

I popped my eyes open, fighting.

No.

I shot my head back, hitting his nose with my skull and swimming out of his grasp as he let go.

He grabbed me, and I climbed for the surface, but I couldn't get far as he held on tight. He clutched my arm, and I couldn't shake him off, the surface there if I could just get to it.

He had to let me go.

Sweeping behind him, I grabbed his face, his hand still clutching my arm and refusing to release me.

Fuck.

I dug my fingers into his skin, hesitating only a moment, and then . . . I twisted, feeling the neck snap in my hands.

They shook as his body went limp and fell out of my grasp, sinking to the bottom of the ocean as bubbles left his mouth.

I watched him go for a moment, making sure he was dead, and then I swam hard, one arm after another as I shot through the surface and sucked in a lungful of air.

I coughed, every inch of my body aching as I caught my breath and looked up at Cold Point.

I closed my eyes. "I survived," I panted, starting to laugh. "Holy shit."

How the hell was I going to get back up there?

I swam hard for the rocks, trying to beat the wave coming in, and climbed up onto a boulder, pulling myself up with my weakened arms.

I fisted my hands and tensed every muscle, making sure I was in one piece.

Looking up at the cliff, I noticed dark figures and flashlights beaming down, but then I saw something trailing down the cliff wall toward me.

I hopped over the rocks, making my way to the edge, and spotted a rope with knots for climbing.

Where did they get that?

I didn't wait, though. Glancing behind me and making sure Martin was still buried under the water, I started climbing, pinching each knot with my shoes and hands as I hiked myself up one rung after another.

Emmy.

Everything hurt, but nothing had ever felt better.

I smiled. It was over. *God, it was over.*

Nothing could stop me. Not my exhausted limbs or the cold or the bruises and cuts.

I won, and the first thing I was going to do with her when the weather warmed up was to take her out to sea on *Pithom*. I wanted to swim.

Reaching the top, Micah and Aydin pulled me over the edge and onto the ground, and I collapsed, trying to catch my breath.

The little girl from before—the one we caught here the other night—knelt beside me, smiling. I thought Lev had taken her out of here.

But I was glad she didn't go, after all.

"Was that your rope?" I panted.

She nodded, and I noticed she had two different colored eyes. One blue, one brown. "There's tons of caves down there that no one knows about. I explore sometimes."

Jesus. Who was she, and where did she come from? But then again, I was fine not knowing. It might've seemed weird to some people, but nothing seemed weird to me anymore. I liked mystery. Bring it.

I looked around at all the faces, Kai, Michael, Misha, and their girls probably having left to take Alex to the hospital.

"Where's Em?" I asked Damon.

He glanced around and shrugged.

I tensed. She was right next to me before I chased Martin. She wouldn't have left. I shot to my feet and pushed through them, rushing back into the park again and scanning the area for her.

Aydin was here. His people were here. Martin and Evans were gone.

Who . . .

Everyone hurried after me as realization dawned.

"Taylor," I said, looking to Micah and Rory. "Have you seen Taylor?"

I hadn't seen him, but the kid said she saw someone with an injured hand arrive two nights ago.

He had her.

I ran for the parking lot, everyone following me, but as soon as I got there, I saw a small group of men clad in black standing there with a convoy of cars, and I stopped.

Who the fuck was this now?

One of the men, built like a wrestler with muscles bulging out of his black shirt, stepped forward. His shiny black hair gleamed in the moonlight, the scruff on his cheek well-manicured. "Mr. Grayson?" he asked.

I opened my mouth to speak, but Micah walked to my side and put a hand on my chest, stopping me.

"How did you find us?" he asked the guy.

The burly one just smiled, looking coy. "Like he ever doesn't know where you are, Mr. Moreau."

Micah scoffed, looking away.

And then it hit me. Stalinz sent me backup. These were mine.

"Where do you need us?" the guy asked.

I walked over and opened the door of his car, climbing in. "Follow us. When I wave you past, cut off the car I'm trailing."

I started the engine, not wasting another moment. Damon, Micah, and Rory jumped in with me, and I sped off, out of the park, and turning left, toward Falcon's Well and the shortcut to Evans Crist's house. That was the only place I could think he'd go.

I slammed the steering wheel with my fist. No one—and I mean, no one—was coming between us again.

Not ever again.

I pushed the pedal to the floor, hanging right as Damon grabbed the dash for support, and headed up into the cliffs, speeding down the lane.

If he'd gotten inside the Crist gates, I was going to crash right through and into the fucking house to get her, dammit.

Two more of Moreau's SUVs trailed my ass like a convoy, and I rushed over dips in the highway, zooming past other cars and a truck full of kids out for Devil's Night.

And then I spotted taillights ahead, recognizing one of Evans's cars—a midnight blue Rover—racing down the road.

I smiled. Sticking my arm out the window, I waved the car behind me ahead and slowed just a little, so I didn't have to slam on the brakes in a moment.

Moreau's man sped past, raced ahead of the Rover, and jerked the wheel, screeching to a halt on the highway and blocking Taylor's path.

Taylor swerved, and my heart skipped a beat as he slammed into the ditch, the car bobbing up and down as he sank into the ground, the tires spinning under the halted vehicle.

I slammed on my brakes, pulling over to the side of the road, the gravel grinding under the tires as I stopped. Jumping out of the car, I raced over to the driver's side door, yanked it open, and pulled Taylor out, slamming a fist right across his face.

I watched him drop to the ground, knocked out. "Now it's over," I growled.

Ripping open the back door, I saw Emmy lying on the back seat, but trying to pull herself up as she rubbed her head.

"Ugh," she groaned. "He knocked me in the head."

She met my eyes, her own blinking and going wide when she saw me.

Alert, she jumped out of the car and threw her arms around me. "I saw you go over the Point," she cried.

I squeezed her tight, the scent of her hair in my nose, and my arms wrapped around her small body.

"I'm okay," I said.

She pulled back and gaped at me. "Okay?"

I almost laughed. She didn't know about Pithom or the crash in the river—both times I'd almost drowned seeming like some sort of destiny I was putting off or some shit.

But tonight, I won.

"Yeah." I nodded. "Going over was kind of a good thing, actually, but I'll explain later."

She hugged me again, and finally, I breathed a sigh of relief, peace washing over me that it was finally over.

"And Martin?" she asked.

I swallowed, holding her tighter. "I'm sorry, babe."

It was all I could say. I'd killed her brother. I wish I hadn't had to, but she wasn't his and he wasn't hers. We were her family now, and he was a threat.

It was him or me.

"I can't lose *you*," she said in my ear. "I need you."

And I buried my face in her neck, feeling everything start. My life. Our life.

We won.

CHAPTER 41

EMORY

Present

The police and Search and Rescue Unit brought up Martin's body, but as soon as they loaded him onto the gurney, I had to look away. Broken, dead, and small. *God, he looked so small.*

I wasn't sure what I was feeling, but I couldn't see him like that. I knew it was him or us. I didn't regret a thing, because he made his choices, and he forced me into a position where I had to choose, but after a lifetime of him, it wasn't a hard decision.

There was no choice.

It still muddled my brain, though, and all I saw when I looked down at his body was my parents' son. The brother I watched grow up.

I couldn't believe he was gone.

Taylor was arrested, and Jack Munro was in contact with his family, probably arranging for Taylor to join Evans on the transport to "another undisclosed location" since Blackchurch had burned down.

Micah and Rory stayed behind to give the police a statement, but we assured them we'd be at the station in the morning to fill in any details.

I had a feeling, with Will's grandfather present in town, we weren't going to be grilled too hard.

Aydin jogged behind us as we raced out of the elevator and down the corridor, spotting everyone loitering outside a glass hospital door with the curtain inside drawn.

"Hey, how is she?" I asked Michael as he, Damon, and Kai all stood in front of the door.

But Aydin nudged past us. "Move," he ordered them.

Michael crossed his arms, glaring down at him.

"I'm a physician," Aydin pointed out. "I can help."

"She has the best medical care money can buy," Michael told him. "You're not needed. Good night."

Aydin stood there as Damon and Kai flanked Michael, none of them budging.

I felt like stepping in and helping him, but part of me knew they were right. He cared, but did he care enough? How long would he stick around? She didn't need the hurt anymore.

Aydin's chest rose and fell, the wheels turning in his head as he came to terms with the fact that he wouldn't win in a fight against all four of them.

I stood back with the girls as Will joined his friends in shielding Alex.

Aydin turned around, looking ready to leave, but then he just stopped, letting out a breath. "And if I marry her?" he asked.

My heart skipped a beat, Rika and I straightening as my gaze flipped between him and the boys.

Aydin spun back around, facing them. "If I promise to marry her, will you let me in?"

Michael's gaze thinned. "No."

He didn't believe him.

"Still want to marry her?" he taunted.

Was Aydin just saying that to get in the door? Or was he absolutely serious?

Damon stepped in, grabbed Aydin's collar, and shot a fist right into his gut. I flinched, having had enough violence for one night.

Aydin lurched forward, bending in half and grunting, but Damon pulled him back up, straightening his shirt.

"Yes," Aydin gasped. "I still want to marry her."

I bit back my smile.

Kai reared back and threw a punch across Aydin's face, Aydin whipping around and wincing. "Fuck," he growled.

But after a moment, he turned and faced them again.

"Get out," Michael told him.

"No."

Michael grabbed his shirt, held him tight, and tossed another punch across his jaw. Aydin's arms stayed at his sides, his fists balled, but made no move to fight back.

Blood trickled out of the corner of his mouth as he breathed hard and let the pain course through him.

Slowly, he turned again and faced the guys, raising his chin and ready for more.

He knew what would happen to him if he broke her heart. He had to know that now, and he was still here.

I glanced at Michael.

"If she says yes," Michael told him, "and you don't come through, we will kill you."

I smiled to myself.

Kai cocked his head. "She deserves a huge wedding at your expense." He glared at Aydin. "You will invite everyone. You will give her the party of her life and honor her in front of the entire fucking world. Do you hear me?"

He nodded. No hiding her. No shame.

"She deserves a beautiful dress and flowers and a seated dinner with a band," Will advised, holding up his finger. "Not a DJ. I'm thinking a day wedding. In Boston Common, maybe."

"Oh, that sounds nice," Damon cooed, glancing from Will to Aydin. "I like that idea."

Banks snorted behind her hand, all of us amused at them planning the wedding for him.

"And a honeymoon," Kai added, "in a private bungalow in the Balinese jungle with first-class service."

"And you'll swim with her naked," Will demanded. "And have candlelit dinners."

"All right," Aydin growled, trying to shut them up.

"And you don't touch her until the wedding night," Michael told him.

Aydin's eyes shot up, his spine steeling. "What?"

They all remained silent, standing their ground.

Oh, boy.

"I've never even kissed her," Aydin gritted out. "I want to hold her. I want to—"

"When you're her husband," Michael clarified.

I pursed my lips to keep from laughing. They were adorable.

Aydin seethed, and I could tell this would be a far different story if it were just him and Michael. "Fine," he finally replied.

He started to move around Michael, but Damon spoke up. "And one more thing."

Aydin stopped. "Jesus, what?"

"Meet us at Sensou tomorrow night. 10 p.m.," Damon told him.

"Why?"

Damon smirked. "Having Alex means you're in the family, and there are two ways to get initiated into our gang. If you want to be in ours, you can either be beat in or—"

"Damon!" Rika barked.

The guys started laughing and Damon quieted, looking at Rika like a four-year-old saying, *What did I do?*

What? I looked around at all of them, lost. What was he going to say?

"I was just kidding," he told Rika.

I shook my head, making a mental note to get caught up on that joke later.

I pushed off the wall and slipped through the guys. "Us first," I told Aydin. "Wait your turn."

I stepped into the hospital room, a nurse tending to Alex's monitors, and my gaze fell onto the bed, seeing her as everyone trailed in behind me.

Her shoulder was bandaged up, her arm tucked into her, and her hospital gown and blankets keeping her warm.

She'd already been to surgery, as it had taken about two hours to get through the police and finding Martin's body.

I should take a picture. She was going to be really pissed when she saw her hair hanging all limp like that.

The girls and I crowded around the bed, seeing her eyes start to open, and I leaned down, hating how pale her lips were. Alex always had color there.

"Just a few minutes, everyone," the nurse warned and then left the room.

"How are you?" I asked as Will pulled the curtain closed from the night outside.

Alex's head bobbed a little. "I feel so good right now."

Rika laughed under her breath, leaning over from the other side. "A little high, are you?"

"Yeahhhhh," she said, sounding all satisfied about it.

"I think Aydin wants to be naked in this bed with you right now," I told her.

"He's sooooo adorable." She blinked, looking sleepy. "Did you see his muscles in that T-shirt? Shiverrrrrs."

"Jesus Christ," Damon grumbled, turning away.

"He wants to sit with you tonight, but we want to stay," I said. "He can see you tomorrow. If you want."

She didn't say anything, but after a few moments, her eyes opened and she took a deep breath, looking more alert.

"Let him in," she told us. "Go wake up that judge and finish that wedding."

I shook my head. "No, we can do that tomorrow."

"Tonight."

She met my eyes, and I pushed the hair out of her face, Rika diving in and kissing her temple.

"I'll see you later," she said.

But . . .

"Go," she ordered. "And don't leave each other . . . go for at least eight hours."

I chuckled, but I closed my mouth, not arguing any further. They had things to say to each other, at any rate. She needed to be alone with him.

"Send him in for me?" Alex asked as we all started to drift out.

"We're leaving Lev right outside," Michael called out.

"Why?" Alex inquired. "Am I in danger?"

"He's a . . ." I drifted off, searching for the words. "A chaperone, actually."

"Huh?"

"Night!" we singsonged, not bothering to explain.

We'd leave that for Aydin. They had a long evening ahead, especially since Michael's no-touch order completely depended on Lev's ability to take on Aydin by himself. I mean, he seemed like a scrapper, but I wasn't confident.

"Come in your pajamas, for all I care," Will said into the phone. "We'll be waiting at the gazebo."

I clutched his arm as he hung up with the judge, I assumed, and we all left the hospital, Rika talking to Michael close and quietly.

I knew she was concerned about the kid. She'd had David take the girl to St. Killian's for the night, while we wrapped up at the Cove and here, but if I knew her at all by now, an idea was already brewing.

Within ten minutes, the eight of us were back in front of the judge who wore her black robe over jeans this time, and I looked up at Will, blowing the lock of hair out of my face.

"You can still run," he taunted.

"Maybe after this." I did a little dance in my stained jeans and dirty face. "When you're legally required to come after me, that is."

Martin drifted through my mind, as well as my parents, Grand-Mère, and how I didn't have a single person of my own here whom I was bringing into this family.

I came alone, without much else to offer these people, but I was starting tomorrow with everything I ever wanted.

I had brothers who cared about me now. Aydin, Rory, and the beautiful Micah, his gentleness and presence that put me at ease at Blackchurch almost immediately.

I had a career, an education, and the Carfax Room. I also had Will behind me . . . and in front of me, willing to take a bullet if I were ever in danger.

I trusted myself now. I wasn't leaving, and I wasn't hiding.

Happy people don't fear death, because there's nothing more they want out of life than what they have right now.

I smiled because I didn't have any fear.

Finally, I was free.

"Okay," the judge said, all of us standing where we stood five hours ago, now dressed in street clothes with a little blood here and there.

"Michael and Erika," she said. "Damon and Winter. Kai and Nikova. William and Emory."

Will jerked his eyes to her. "We did this part," he told her. "Can you just finish where you left off?"

"Will . . ." I scolded under my breath.

He looked at me. "I have *Godzilla vs. Kong* at the theater waiting for us."

My mouth fell open. "Already? It doesn't release for a few weeks!"

He shot me a look, like *please.*

I snorted, glancing at the judge. "Yeah, hurry up."

I was going to like being a Grayson.

Laughter went off around the group, and the judge nodded. "Michael and Erika . . . I now pronounce you husband and wife," she told them.

They kissed, and the judge proceeded around the group.

"Damon and Winter? I pronounce you husband and wife."

I bit my lip, inching into Will and ready.

"Kai and Nikova?" she continued. "I pronounce you husband and wife."

Kai growled before kissing Banks hard.

"And William and Emory, I now pronounce you . . . husband and wife."

I dived in and kissed him deep, whimpering as he wrapped his arms around me, the ring on my finger solidifying what we should've known could never be stopped.

Not in the chem lab, the movie theater, or my first night at Blackchurch as he stood in the shadows of the kitchen.

"Live for your love," the judge said, "love your life, and raise hell."

I laughed against his lips, my stomach swarming with butterflies and my heart pitter-pattering a mile a minute.

Cheers and clapping went off around the village, crowds still loitering at Sticks and in the tavern as it was only about midnight still.

"Start your adventure," the judge told us.

"Thank you," I said, turning to her.

We all hugged each other, hugged the judge, and I spotted Misha, Ryen, Micah, and Rory head over to us as we descended the stairs. Will's grandfather left a group of men outside the White Crow as he pulled a cigar out of his mouth and headed over, as well.

I didn't realize he was still here.

"Congratulations," he said to Will, engulfing his grandson in a big hug.

"Thank you," Will told him.

Senator Grayson moved to me, taking my hand and kissing me on the cheek. "Congratulations, honey."

"Thank you, sir."

He looked to Will. "I'll let you get settled in and set up house and such. We'll talk in a couple of weeks, okay?"

"You got it."

They hugged again, Will telling him, "Thank you for everything."

"Hey, man," Micah called, gesturing Will over.

Will met my eyes, looking between me and his grandfather. "I'll be right back." He left a peck on my forehead.

I watched him head over to Micah, probably to check on how things went with the police.

I looked at the senator. "I kind of feel bad I sprung this on him," I said. "His parents weren't here."

It just seemed too perfect when Rika suggested it. But if he'd wanted his own wedding with all the trimmings, I would've loved that, too.

He shrugged a little. "My son and his wife love that boy to kingdom come," he teased. "I promise you they'll just be happy he's happy. And . . . you can always have another ceremony, of course. I can tell you right now, his mother won't be denied a proper reception, so get ready."

I laughed. That was fine. Sounded really nice, actually.

"Take care of him." He touched my arm, leaning in. "He's kind of my favorite."

"Ugh," Misha said, walking past us, clearly hearing.

I held back my snort. Mr. Grayson shot his other grandson a look. "That one's like me," he whispered. "Too much like me."

"So of course, you don't get along," I joked.

"Nope." He looked after Misha with a kind smile. "I do like his style, though. I had a pretty nice black leather jacket back in the day."

I could picture it. The man had to be eighty, but he looked fifty-five. Tall like Will, with amazing hair.

"Thank you for looking out for him, Senator Grayson," I said. "When I couldn't, I mean." I looked behind me, seeing Will shaking hands and smiling, surrounded by his friends and his town and all the possibilities to come. "At least he had his friends all those years, though. I used to pick on them in high school, but they really did start something incredible, didn't they? The first Horsemen will be a tough act to follow for future generations."

Lord help our kids, filling in those shoes, right?

But when he didn't say anything, I looked back to him, seeing a coy smile on his lips as he stared at me.

"They weren't the first," he said. "And please, call me A.P."

A.P.?

What?

Before I could react, he kissed my cheek again and turned around, walking back to the tavern. I stood there, frozen as I pieced together where I'd heard that name before.

A.P., A.P. . . .

Someone took my hand, and I walked over to Will, all of us setting up for a picture as my feet moved of their own volition.

And then it hit me. Reverie Cross. Edward McClanahan's best friend and Reverie Cross's boyfriend. The rumor that Reverie might not have jumped. The rumor that Edward or his friend or both of them . . .

Oh, my God.

I shot my eyes over to A.P., seeing him chat with Banks, both of them deep in discussion, and I turned to Will, wide-eyed. "A.P.?" I blurted out, gesturing to his grandfather.

William *Aaron Paine* Grayson, Sr.

The corner of Will's lips turned up. "Well, you'll never be bored with me, at least, right?"

I gaped at him, but then . . . a laugh escaped, not sure how to react to anything anymore, especially after the events of tonight.

Jesus Christ. After helping Damon bury a body, getting kidnapped, making the great train escape, and everything that went down tonight, I supposed a sixty-year-old murder mystery could sit for another evening or two more.

Bored, he'd said.

No, Will Grayson. That was one problem you and I would never have.

CHAPTER 42

EMORY

Present

"So, you want a honeymoon?" Will asked, caressing my arm as he held me in his arms.

"If you want."

His body shook under me with a laugh. "That sounds enthusiastic."

I grinned, slipping my hand up his shirt as we laid on a pile of canvas cloth on the floor behind the stage. The catwalk loomed above us, wires, ropes, and cords dangling every which way, and I couldn't even remember what the movie was about last night, because both times we tried to watch it, we just wanted to watch each other instead. I couldn't take my eyes off of him.

"I'm not in a hurry to leave again if you want to wait." I nestled into his warm body. "I just want you right now. The Eiffel Tower or the Mayan ruins or whatever you have planned would just go to waste on me when I only want this."

We'd been apart too long, and I was in need.

Sliding my leg over his body, my jeans somewhere on the floor and my bra who-knew-where, I climbed up his body as his hands slipped up my thighs and gripped my ass.

"Maybe stay here and take a tour of the Bell Tower and the cemetery," I taunted, kissing those tattoos on his arm and chest. "Do some climbing and have a tasting of the best cuisine Thunder Bay has to offer." I bit his nipple, tugging it and then licking it. "*Lots* of tastings."

He shivered and smiled, bringing me up and kissing my mouth. All I wanted to see in the world right now was him sweaty, him wet, him walking naked from our bed to the shower, him tied up underneath me . . .

He put his arms behind his head as I kissed his body and rubbed him everywhere.

"I'm putting a down payment on my old house," I told him, nibbling his neck and breaking the news while he was weak. "We don't have to live there. I'm just not ready to lose it yet."

When I saw it was for sale, I sent Alex to the realtor after the dress shop, so my brother wouldn't know it was me buying it. I still might sell it. I just didn't want to lose it before I was ready.

He stopped me, looking down as his thumbs rubbed circles on my face. "It has so many bad memories, Em."

I know. But . . .

"I'm not giving him that power," I told my husband. "That's my family's home. My grandmother grew up there. My mother and I did, as well."

That house was more than just Martin.

He gazed into my eyes, and after a moment, nodded. "Okay."

I dipped down and kissed him on the lips, soft, slow, and deep as I grinded on him through his jeans.

He gasped, chuckling. "Oh, baby. As much as I don't want you dressed, I need to eat." He groaned as I kept going. "Can you stay here? I'll go grab us some bagels and coffee or something?"

At the mention of bagels, my stomach growled.

Shit. Food would actually be good, but I didn't want him to leave me.

"I'll come with you," I said, looking down at him.

"Yeah?" He shot up and gave me a peck on the lips. "All right, let's go."

We threw on our clothes from last night, and I was kind of anxious to get to the hospital and check on Alex, and check in with the police to make sure there was nothing hanging over our heads regarding Martin.

It still hadn't hit me yet, except for the slight thump in my chest when I thought about them going over that cliff. I should be wrecked, right?

For some reason, I didn't hate him.

But there was that tear in the membrane again, my emotions muddled and confusing. His end wasn't going to go any other way.

We left the theater and locked up, Will taking my hand and leading me past Sticks toward the bagel shop, but I looked over toward the gazebo and saw Damon straddling the railing and disconnecting the lights they'd installed for the ceremony.

I stopped and looked at Will. "Can you grab us a table? I'll be there in a minute."

He followed my gaze, seeing his friend at the top of the hill and then back to me. "Sure."

He kissed me and left, and I pushed my hair behind my ear, crossing the street in a jog.

Orange and red leaves fell from the trees, and the chill in the air nipped at my nose, but there Damon was, black T-shirt and no jacket as the wind blew through his black hair.

Decorations hung from lampposts, and people walked to work dressed in costumes for Halloween.

I stopped, looking up at him and taking in the beautiful work, the solid build and foundation, and the jingles in the trees from the chandelier crystals rustling in the wind.

"I drew up blueprints for a gazebo just like this," I told him. "But with marble instead of wrought iron."

I gazed at him knowingly, and he just shot me a glance but kept silent.

"I like the wrought iron," I said. "It was a good choice."

He'd found my design and built it. The one I did after I lost my heart for the other gazebo and just forced the finish, instead of doing it right.

Hopping off the railing, he dipped down, picked something up, and tossed it over the side, into my arms.

I caught the coffee can, recognizing the mustard-yellow container.

"We found it when we were digging the new foundation," he told me.

I opened it up, finding what I knew I'd find. A plastic bag with the necktie, the Ride-All-Day bracelet, and the empty box of Milk Duds from Will's and my first date.

My throat swelled with a lump. "Thanks."

He descended the stairs and walked up next to me, both of us looking up at the beautiful work he'd done.

"Thank you for this. It's better than I imagined it."

"Well, let's face it," he replied. "That other gazebo was a freshman effort."

I chuckled. *Yeah, thanks.*

A smile played on his lips as he studied his work. "This is the one you had your heart in. I liked the idea for the chandeliers."

I wanted to ask him why he did it. Why he put in the time and effort, but I knew he'd only respond with a flippant remark. Maybe he felt he owed me something after I helped him that night in the cemetery, or maybe he felt guilty about the fire.

"I tried to stop him," he told me, looking down at me. "Kind of, anyway. Sorry."

Honestly, it was the least of the pain Will and I had caused each other. I loved the new gazebo.

I recapped the container, too afraid to raise my eyes as I said, "You gave me the key to the Carfax Room, didn't you?"

The BMW we left the cemetery in was the same one outside my house that night I received the key. That was where I left the blueprints for the new gazebo. He'd found them there.

Finally, he nodded. "As someone gave it to me once."

"How did you know I'd figure it out?"

He could've left a note directing me to the cathedral.

But he just shrugged. "I was in the church every Wednesday. I saw you hang out sometimes." He looked over at me. "After I saw the bruises in the shower, I figured fate was trying to tell me something."

So he passed it on when he no longer needed it. As I should've done. Nine years later, and I still had the key in my possession.

Being privy to that one mystery in Thunder Bay kept me a part of this town long after I'd left. I couldn't give it up.

Maybe now I could.

"It helped those last couple of years at home," I murmured. "Thank you."

I might not have survived if I didn't have that one place where I knew I'd be safe. Even if I rarely used it.

He started to walk away, but I stopped him. "I have to tell Will about that night," I said. "I just wanted to warn you."

His back went rigid, and he didn't turn to look at me, but he knew what I was talking about. I couldn't keep the fact that I'd helped conceal a body from Will.

Damon sighed. "I appreciate the heads-up. I'll be waiting for the beating."

I laughed. "Just keep Winter close. He won't hit you with a pregnant woman nearby."

He shook his head and kept walking. "He'll just get her to hit me for him," he grumbled.

After a splendid month of squatting in my old house with a mattress on the floor and take-out Chinese food where we were completely happy, barely leaving bed or seeing anyone but each other, we finally took over Christiane Fane's house up on the cliffs.

She moved in with Matthew Grayson, and even though we didn't need that much space, Will made some good points. Enemies seemed to be an occupational hazard of Graymor Cristane, and our family needed more protection than a neighborhood Victorian offered.

Not to mention, our children someday would want to be close to their friends. Kai and Banks had the Torrance house when they were in town, Damon and Winter had the old Ashby house, Michael and Rika had St. Killian's, and we were in her old house, the company buying it and turning over the deed to Will free and clear. We were all on the same road up in the quiet, haunting sea cliffs of Thunder Bay.

I was happy, and over the months of celebrating the holidays and the snow and the first warm day of spring, I couldn't stop smiling, the pain of the past there but no longer hard.

Micah and Rory decided to laugh in the face of danger, however, and took over my house in town, Micah absolutely loving the simple life. His and Rory's families were more than happy with the capital their sons were now good for, and left them the hell alone.

"Baby, I need you!" Will called from downstairs.

I bit my bottom lip to stifle the smile as my hand shook.

I looked down at the third pregnancy test I'd taken this morning, the plus sign big and bold and pink.

It was no wonder I'd gotten knocked up, and I was surprised it didn't happen sooner with as much as he was on top of me.

Wrapping it in toilet paper, I stuffed it in the garbage can and looked up, fluffing my hair in the mirror and unable to hide the huge-ass smile.

William Grayson IV.

I squealed and then clamped a hand over my mouth, not ready to let the cat out of the bag. Winter had gone into labor a couple of hours ago, and Will was trying to wrangle Ivarsen and Madden from their naps so we could get to the hospital. We'd been babysitting overnight to give the parents a break.

"Please, baby!" he shouted, sounding stressed.

I laughed to myself, hopping out of the bathroom and down the stairs, Will's beagle, Diablo, scampering after me. I found Will in the foyer and watched him grab Ivar's foot and pull him back so he could get his sock on.

I snorted. The twenty-month-old giggled, finding it all so funny as Madden stood nearby and watched the action.

I slung my purse over my head, grabbed the diaper bags that we'd already filled with snacks, drinks, and toys, and picked up Madden, leaving the house and loading him into the car. Will could deal with Ivar. I swore the kid knew Will owed him for lost time and loved yanking his uncle's chain constantly.

I buckled Madden into his car seat, giving him an attack of kisses as Will carried Ivar out, the kid kicking and squealing, full of smiles.

Fruit punch stained Will's button-down shirt, and he looked like he was going to punch Damon when he got a hold of him, because Ivar's sense of mischief was entirely his fault, and not Winter's.

I climbed into the driver's seat, picking up Will's textbooks off the passenger seat and dumping them onto the floor behind me.

In addition to the company's real estate ventures, breaking ground on the resort, and helping Winter with her humanitarian organization, Will had started college.

He didn't want to go back to school or be with people younger than him, but he wanted to do something more with his life outside of what he had with the guys.

So, he bit the bullet.

And I loved him for it. I wasn't sure if he wanted to be a lawyer or a veterinarian or what, but I kind of saw him running a publishing company someday.

Which was going to come in handy, because I wasn't helping William IV with his lit homework. That stuff came easily to Will.

He finished with Ivar and opened the passenger side door, sliding into his seat.

"What are you smiling about?" he asked, buckling up.

I eighty-sixed the grin. "I'm sorry. I'll stop."

He chuckled, and I ran my hand over his hair, soothing him. The boys had taken a lot out of us the past twenty-four hours.

"Fuck, baby," he groaned at the feel of my hands.

But then we heard Ivar shout behind us. "Buck!"

And it sounded a lot like . . .

Shit, Will mouthed, looking behind him as both of us went wide-eyed.

I frowned. "Oh, come on. You know he already got that from his father."

We didn't teach him bad language.

"And when Mads says it to Kai?" Will retorted, worrying about Banks and Kai losing their shit.

I just shook my head. *Oh, well.* "If you don't act like it's a big deal, then it's not."

Kids tended not to repeat behavior they didn't get a reaction for. And it wasn't like we were going to be able to protect the children from Damon Torrance forever.

We raced to the hospital, maybe a little over the speed limit, Will introducing the boys to the band Disturbed for the first time. Ivar banged his head, rocking out to the music, but ever-calm Mads sat there and observed, so much like his dad in his poise.

It would be interesting to see what a girl would bring to the new family, since Damon was convinced the newborn was female, even though they didn't find out the sex yet.

Grabbing the boys and the bags, we hurried into the hospital and up to the third floor, finding a hallway full of family as Winter screeched from inside the room.

I winced, realizing I was no longer a spectator in her plight. I'd be doing what she was doing next fall if my calculations were correct.

"Ah!" she growled from inside the room, the door just cracked enough to hear.

"How's it going?" I asked, handing off Mads to his mom as Rika took Ivar from Will.

Another scream pierced the air, and a nurse ran past us, entering the room.

"Should be soon," Alex said, the rock on her hand gleaming as she held her phone to her ear.

Aydin had to rush to Chicago this morning for a meeting, but he was supposed to be flying back now. He and Alex had taken over most of Evans Crist's responsibilities, both of them in Meridian City most of the time and loving it. They liked the noise and the hustle and bustle.

Michael sat on a chair next to Athos, enthralled as he watched her play some game on her phone while she wore huge headphones over her ears.

He pointed to something and she shoved him off, not wanting help. "Daddy, stop it."

He smiled, watching her now instead of the game.

They had told her when they adopted her this past winter that she could call them whatever she felt comfortable calling them, but it only took a few weeks for her to love the fact that these were her parents. She wanted everyone to know Michael and Rika were her mom and dad.

And who wouldn't love it? She had everything she could ever want in life, and she certainly knew that.

They were the lucky ones, though. They'd all found each other.

"What?" Damon shouted from inside the room.

We all stopped, looking at each other.

"It's a boy?" he blurted out. "Are you sure?"

We leaned in, and I folded my lips between my teeth to contain the laughter.

A baby cried, there was some shuffling, and then we heard Damon's playful little growl. "Ugh, what am I going to do with you?"

"Damon!" Winter growled. "I'm going to kill you. You better love him. You do, right?"

There was a pause, and I met Alex's wide eyes with my own.

Drama . . .

Damon and I ran the construction business together now, him building and me designing, so I'd gotten used to his . . . brand of humor.

Finally, he answered. "Y—yeah," he stuttered, not sounding convincing. "Yeah, of course, baby. But, like, are you sure there aren't any more in there or something?"

"Damon!"

Will collapsed against the wall, shaking with laughter, and I shook my head, reaching over and taking the squirming Ivar out of Rika's arms.

I set him down on the floor, holding his hand as we walked and Will followed.

Another boy. Fun, fun.

I looked over at Will, amusement written all over his face, but I could tell the wheels were turning.

"You sad?" I asked.

"Why would I be sad?"

I shrugged, leaning against the wall as Ivar reached for me and I picked him up. "He's got two kids on you now."

"It's not a contest, Emmy." Will leaned next to me as he let Ivar wrap his little hand around his finger. "I'm fine. I'm in school right now, anyway. We've got plenty of time. We'll have our family and fill all those rooms. Whether it's in three years or five or ten."

"Or eight months," I offered, a tingle fluttering under my skin. "Eight-ish. Give or take."

He stood there silently for a moment, and when I finally looked up, he was staring at me and not breathing.

"Are you serious?" he murmured.

I couldn't contain the excitement. "Are you ready?"

He grabbed me and kissed me, laughing against my lips. "I am never not ready for anything with you."

And with the long, hard road it took to get us here, I'd never trusted any other words more. I kissed him, nothing clouding my happiness with him for another second ever again.

This was always our story.

We want what we want.

NIGHTFALL BONUS SCENE

The four Horsemen have an incredible bond that survived, endured, and flourished against all the odds and only grew stronger as they became men. Let's see how it started . . .

KAI

I bet you couldn't cut the tension in this car with a chain saw.

God, this sucks.

"I don't agree with your reasoning," I finally say, glaring at the side of my dad's face as he drives. "And the education is inferior," I point out in another pathetic attempt to prove him wrong. My tone is somewhere between a grumble and growl, not really bitchy but definitely not pleasant. It's the most disrespect I would ever show Katsu Mori, especially with my mother in the car. "I would like to continue on to St. Andrew's for high school like the rest of my friends."

There. I stated my position.

His reply is simple. "I don't like your friends."

But he says it in Japanese. *Watashi wa anata no tomodachi ga sukide wa arimasen.*

And I know the conversation is over. When he speaks in a language my Italian-American mother can barely understand, it means he's going to say things he doesn't want her to hear. And that's not a good sign for me.

We coast through the village and up to the cliffs, on the other side of town, but even though Thunder Bay is small, I can't say I know anyone here well. Now that I'm going into high school, my parents recently told me they'd allow me to go to parties and community activities, but I haven't taken advantage of the privilege yet. All of my friends are in the city.

That's where they'll stay, now that my mom and dad have decided that the opportunities for culture and diversity that originally prompted them to shuttle me nearly an hour back and forth twice a day for my education are now overshadowed by the fast scenes of drugs, clubs, and sex that some of my friends are enjoying. They didn't take into account that Catholic schoolkids know how to break a rule more than most.

I attended Holy Ghost for elementary, but when I got to middle school, I started asking if I could stay in the city on the weekends, too.

What did they expect? My life wasn't here anymore. My classes, sports teams, study groups, girls I was interested in . . . I wanted to be around my friends more.

Nevertheless, I'm now home every day. I shouldn't have snuck out last May to go to that party in Whitehall. That was stupid. And not even worth it.

I sit there silently as my father cruises down a long driveway with trees lining both sides. People in suits and women in heels wander around the lawn. We pull into a parking lot off to the side, and I take in the grounds of bright green lawns, trees that look like lollipops, and an occasional spray of bushes, the perfect backdrop for my photo on graduation day. Mom on one side. Dad on the other. Right there, in front of three hedges, a dense collection of trees in the background. Me, in the center, smiling. I guarantee it.

I inhale, smelling the leather of my father's seats, but it doesn't feel like there's any air at all. I clench my jaw, pushing open my door as my parents climb out and draw in the cool breeze, clearing my nostrils.

Clusters of three—parents with their student—flow toward the school, tents spread out over the lawn to the left of the building. We follow the crowd, seeing white linen tablecloths draped underneath spreads of hors d'oeuvres and light dishes of pasta and salads. Champagne cocktails are deftly passed off to adults, while punch the color of blood oranges gushes from a silver fountain.

A white cake sits on a side table, round with trim in the school colors of navy blue and forest green. Pieces are already being doled out to students as moms and dads talk and laugh.

An orientation at St. Andrew's—my preferred high school choice in Meridian City—would be much the same, but we'd all be in uniform. Thunder Bay has uniforms, too, starting the first day of school.

Everyone drifts, and I lock eyes with every boy and girl I see, hyperaware that I'll know all of them soon enough. One of them will be my best friend. Maybe one of them will be my girlfriend.

Maybe one of them will give me a lot of trouble.

Or maybe nothing will ever happen here. I'm already counting the days till college.

"Charles." My mom smiles and holds out her hand, heading up to a man in a three-piece black pinstripe suit with a white shirt, and forest green tie.

He takes her hand, and she dips in, pressing her cheek to his briefly.

He pulls back, smiling, and turns to my father, immediately shaking his hand. *Good man.* He didn't linger too long. My dad doesn't like it when men linger too long with my mom, because he loves her a lot. They have a really good marriage. It's a lot of pressure to be raised by people who never make mistakes.

"How are you?" my dad asks him.

"I'm well," Charles replies. "You?"

My dad simply nods.

This must be the headmaster, Charles Kincaid. I take in the chain of the gold pocket watch and matching tie pin, my mind drifting to the old gray tweed my last headmaster wore.

"This is our son," my dad says, turning to me. "Kai."

I meet the man's eyes, and immediately square my shoulders, holding out my hand.

Mr. Kincaid takes it. "Kai," he says. "Nice to meet you. Your transcripts from Holy Ghost are impressive." He glances to my father, a sparkle hitting his eye. "I suspect your teachers are presently preparing new ways to challenge you."

I smile tight-lipped. "Well, I'd hate to make their jobs harder," I tease, but not really, as I throw my father a look.

One of his eyebrows simply darts up, and I take my hand back from Mr. Kincaid, settling back into my quiet position.

My mom wraps an arm around me. "We're excited to keep Kai close to home for high school."

"Absolutely," Mr. Kincaid adds, eyeing me. "This is your community. These bonds will last a lifetime because we always come home."

I remain silent, not willing to admit that might've sounded like a pearl of wisdom that's actually true whether or not I want it to be.

I look to my parents. "I'd like to look around if that's okay."

My dad nods, and my mother smiles, looking a little relieved as she takes my father's arm. At least if I'm not next to her, visibly uncomfortable the entire afternoon, she can hold out hope that I'll embrace this decision eventually.

I step around a dad carrying a plate of food and turn my head, letting my eyes wander from group to group. Boys congregate in clusters or pairs, already familiar with each other from middle school, while a group of girls stand in a circle, whispering and laughing together and looking like mini versions of their moms. A safe assumption because they look like mini versions of mine. They giggle, their hands covering their mouths, doing that thing people do to act like they're trying not to let you see they're laughing at you, but all it does is draw more attention to their amusement, which is really their goal. It doesn't hurt my feelings. A girl in a friend group is always performing for someone.

But now it does hit me that there aren't any other Asian students here. Not even half Asians like me.

I step slowly, moving around the party when I hear someone say, "Hi, Emmy."

I look over, seeing a kid in a black suit with dark brown hair, standing in front of a dark-haired girl in glasses. He holds a plate, looking hopeful as he gazes down at her. "Would you like some cake?"

He shoves the plate at her, but she simply looks at him, fiddling with her cuffs.

"Come on," he urges, taking her wrist to put the plate in her hand.

But a little cry escapes her, and she yanks her arm away, quickly pulling her cuff down over her wrist. I think I see a bruise.

The guy doesn't linger too long, though. Some other boys grab him and drag him away. He drops the plate on the buffet table, looking back at her as they lead him off.

He looks like he has a lot of friends. That either means he's trouble or he's connected. Either way, he seemed nice. Something about his voice.

I stroll toward the trees, toward the school, and I smell the cigarette smoke about three-eighths of a second before I know exactly who it is.

I look up, seeing Damon Torrance.

I exhale. *Great.*

I don't say it out loud, but it doesn't matter. He hears me.

Blowing out smoke, he holds up his hand, pinches the cigarette between his fingers, and flicks it in my direction, missing me by a couple of feet.

Awesome.

I keep going, ignoring his smirk and heading through the hedges. I guess I will know one person here, after all. We won't be friends, though. The priest who oversaw our catechism classes the past two years used a lot of Lucifer references when dealing with Damon.

I traipse over the lawn, the lush grass as soft as hair under my leather shoes. Maple trees that will rain down red and gold leaves in a month or so rise high, giving shade, and I draw in a deep breath, the wind blowing in off the sea rustling my hair.

A stone building rises beyond the gathering, every window on the upper floors a series of three large panes, some of them open like little doors to let in the fresh air. Above each one is a square window separated by wrought iron into four smaller sections. Sun shines on the glass, slowly dimming when a cloud interrupts its rays.

I turn in a circle, seeing the spires of an old cathedral, St. Killian's, in the distance.

"It's not bad, is it?" my father says.

I open my eyes, just realizing they were closed. He steps up to my side, and I stand a little straighter. "It's peaceful," I admit.

He nods, liking that I have something positive to say. "No city noise. Less distractions."

He's quiet for a moment, and I know he's about to tell me things he wants to make sure I understand. "This is when you start thinking about the man you want to be," he tells me.

I lower my eyes and nod. "I know."

"Places like this are as much about networking as they are about education." He gestures around us. "All of these students will be important someday. You can choose your friends. People who encourage you to level up."

Everything he tells me sounds smart, and I've been good, compared to my friends in the city who were always looking for excitement.

But I think sometimes that my father sees me as part two of him. A clone to whom he can input all of his knowledge, because let's not waste time on mistakes he already made.

"Your mother and I have made many sacrifices to arrive here."

I nod again.

"You'll understand me better someday," he tells me. "Right now, all you have to do is trust me."

Don't explore. Don't discover. Ignore anything and everyone that calls you off course. Just do this and live the life we want for you.

"You should introduce yourself," he says. "Maybe to the football or swim coach. You need to compete in a sport."

I inhale a lungful of air and glance at him. "Just give me a minute."

He smiles and walks away. I can't even be mad at him, really, because he loves me.

I can never be too honest with him, though. I'll have to keep secrets.

"Would you get off my back?" someone suddenly barks.

I peer around a hedge, seeing a basketball court about twenty yards away. A guy my age dribbles a basketball in place, glaring at someone I can't see. I move closer until the court comes into view.

"Not here," a woman begs in a quiet voice as she comes into view. She's beautiful. Tight, white dress with short sleeves and a thin, black belt. She looks like him, and I assume it's his mother, but an older man moves in, ignoring her plea and getting in the kid's face.

"I'm not doing this with a fucking fourteen-year-old," he growls. "Get serious or I'm not paying for this. You can go rough it in a public school, because your entire education has been a waste of money up until this point."

I blink. *Jesus.* My parents would never say the F-word around me.

But the guy is unfazed. "Why?" he claps back. "Because I didn't learn the only thing you ever wanted me to, which was to keep my mouth shut."

I can't help smiling a little, the shock and amusement coming at once.

"Oh, yes, you know everything," his father spits back. "Always so fucking smart." He backs away, throwing the woman a look. "Maybe he's my son, after all."

And he charges away, leaving his wife and son on the basketball court.

Damn. Compared to that, my dad and I are best friends. Does he talk to his kid like that all the time?

The woman comes around to face the kid. "You're his son, Michael."

"Could you *not* ruin the fantasy, please?" he teases back.

His mother tries to bite back her smile. She pinches his chin, forcing him to look at her. "I love you."

A smile curls the corners of his mouth, but he's too cool to say it back to her out loud. He starts dribbling again, and she leaves him to it.

The ball bounces again and again, smacking against the pavement harder and faster as he moves in a circle. Then, all of a sudden, he shoots off down the court, his strides getting smaller and tighter just before he leaps up and dunks the ball. It sinks into the net, not even grazing the rim. Smooth. Like ice.

I step a little closer, sliding my hands into my pockets as he recovers the ball and lifts it to his nose. I stop and watch him smell it. Like it's a bit of peace.

I would hate for my father to treat me that way. Like I'm his employee. But I envy his ease in handling it. Like he's on his own and has no problem with that.

He takes off his jacket and continues running around the court, the ball slipping through the basket a dozen times, but I don't even think he's counting. He barely seems to notice anything in front him. He looks, but there's no reaction. No tension. No exhaustion. No pause. He jogs, shoots, recovers, and then again. It's all as easy as breathing, and I wish I had calm like that in doing anything.

Some music starts behind me at the party, but my father is forgotten. Removing my jacket, I head over and grab a basketball from the full cart. He glances up, but puts his head back down, carrying on.

He jogs for the other end of the court, while I move up to the three-point line on this end and shoot the ball. It hits the backboard with a loud thud and bounces right back off, not even touching the net or the rim. Heat covers my back, and I can't help a glance over my shoulder. He catches the ball as it falls out of the net and dribbles, his eyes meeting mine again.

I hear myself swallow.

I'm good at swimming. And martial arts and running and golf. I'm not really sure why I avoided team sports, but my dad says it will help develop skills for the workplace, so I'm supposed to find one to join in high school.

Michael, as his mother called him, jogs back toward me, the ball bouncing from his left hand to his right and back again. Shoulders relaxed and at ease, he shoots from the center circle. I watch his feet as he leaps high, no more than shoulder width apart and one foot slightly ahead of the other. I narrow my eyes, noting it's the foot on the same side as the hand he shoots with. Elbow straight, the power seeming to come more from his shoulders than his arms.

He retrieves the ball, moves away, and I dribble up to the free throw circle, trying again. It skids off the rim, but it's closer.

We continue in silence for the next ten minutes, and I steal glances, absorbing his posture, stance, and how he aims his shot. There's always one foot, one hand, and one eye in line every time.

I mimic, watching him, and after a few minutes, it's like we're in unison. He's at one end of the court, I'm at the other, and then we switch. Passing each other en route. I shoot, he shoots, both balls sink through the nets, and then we go again until he stops in the center. I halt in the center, as well, breathing hard and watching him shoot. I turn and do the same, my ball slipping through right after his. I resist smiling.

I'm about to chase after my ball, but he doesn't move, so neither do I. He breathes hard, and I feel a little pride, because he wasn't out of breath before.

He turns his head, finally looking me in the eyes. "Not bad," he says. "How's your footwork?"

He doesn't wait for a reply, though. He points to the sideline as he grabs another ball from the container and moves to the other side. He sends the ball across the court, bouncing once between us before I catch. He sweeps to the side, moving down the sideline, and I follow. Sending the ball to him, we keep skidding down the edges, moving it back and forth between each other.

Catching the ball, he shoots it back to me and moves in, and I follow without instruction. I dribble, and he guards, both of us swaying back and forth. We switch, and I block him, both of us in sync, before I snatch the ball mid-dribble and brush past him, accidentally slamming him in the shoulder.

He stumbles, hitting the ground, and I stop, the ball rolling away. *Shit.*

He looks up at me. "Yeah, so that's football," he jokes. "But not bad."

I laugh, reach out and offering my hand. "Sorry," I say, helping him off the ground. "I'm Kai Mori."

We shake.

"I know," he says. "I've seen you around town with your parents." He releases my hand. "Michael Crist."

Oh, so that makes sense then. His father must be Evans Crist. My dad doesn't like him. I've never met him, but if my father doesn't like another adult, it's a moral issue, and after what I just saw, my dad is undoubtedly correct in his assessment.

"You should try out for the team," Michael tells me.

I walk over, getting another ball out of the bin. "Will you?"

"Yeah, but I'll be varsity," he says, snatching the ball from me. "The only freshman."

I tease back. "Maybe."

He's clearly good, but I'll be good, too, with practice.

"And I'll get to start," he points out. "You don't want to ride a bench until you're needed, do you? You're better off in JV where you'll get some play time."

I snatch the ball back. "Scared?"

I run, he runs. I shoot, and he retrieves the ball after it falls through the net. He moves toward me, dribbling, and I scurry back, staying in front of him. My heart beats hard, blood hot in my legs. He raises the ball, bends his knees, about to leap, but I slap the ball out of his hands. It flies behind him, he scowls, and I gape at him. "Was that legal?"

"Hell yeah, it's legal!" he barks, sounding angry and pleased at the same time. "Keep going!"

I race after it, shoot, score, and grab the ball again. I try to take a shot, but Michael snatches the ball. He moves for the other end of the court, stepping backward, and I'm on his back, because I know he's going to spin around to shoot.

But he fakes me out. Maneuvering left and then right, he bumps me and sends me to the ground as he leaps up and fires the ball.

My ass lands on the court, and I hear the ball spill through the net.

I exhale hard, collapsing completely. Sweat glides down my back, my hair sticks to my temples, and I'm afraid to look at the state of my pants and white shirt. I yank my tie loose, the collar of my shirt chafing my skin.

Michael comes to stand over me, the ball safely under his arm. His hair is wet with sweat, too.

He stares at me with an unreadable expression, like he's intrigued and confused at the same time.

"You know where my house is?" he asks.

I nod. Everyone knows where the Crist house is.

He helps me to my feet. "I have a court. You want to come over to play tomorrow?"

My heart skips a beat, and I don't know why. "What time?"

"Six a.m."

In the morning?

But I don't say that out loud. I dust the dirt off my clothes and run my fingers through my hair, straightening it. "Just us?"

He shrugs, moving for the edge of the court. I follow. "We could invite some guys if you want," he says. "Get a game going." He jerks his chin to the grassy area. "He's tall. Who is that?"

I follow his gaze, seeing Damon.

"Gabriel Torrance's son, right?" he asks. "What's his name?"

But I shake my head. "The only thing he's interested in is trouble. Trust me." I turn to Michael. "I'd rather you show me some stuff on my own first anyway."

I want to get good before I play anyone else.

He shoots the ball into the storage bin, and I reach down, picking up another one and doing the same.

"I'm not showing you everything," he retorts. "You're not taking my spot on varsity."

I just look at him. "Can't they open up two spots?"

He smiles for the first time, and we head back to the party side by side, grabbing our jackets off the ground as we go.

WILL

One Month Later

"In 1945, the US dropped two atomic bombs on Japan." The teacher patrols a lane between desks. "Why?"

My arms grow warm.

"Miss Cornish?" he calls.

I release my breath.

She quickly replies, "To avoid a costly invasion and end the war."

"Did it work?" he continues, pointing at the next student. "Mr. Meyer?"

"Yes."

"No," Mr. Albrecht retorts. "Mr. Mori?" He snaps his fingers at the kid in front of me.

Kai Mori replies, "Emperor Hirohito was also threatened by a declaration of war from the Soviet Union."

I blink rapidly. Was that in the book? I don't remember that.

"Yes." Mr. Albrecht navigates around the student in back with his hands behind his back as he strolls down the next lane. "That and the bombs compelled his surrender."

I scratch my neck.

"After the war," he goes on, "Germany was divided between the Soviet Union and . . . Mr. Grayson?"

I look over my shoulder, up at him. "Russia?"

Everyone laughs, Jay Vanger patting me on the back like I made a joke. Did I?

The teacher simply arches a brow and then turns to the guy sitting at his side. "Mr. Hood?" he asks instead.

"Between the Soviet Union and the Western Allies," Hood responds.

"Correct."

I wipe the sweat off my forehead.

The onslaught continues. "The Soviet Union developed its own design for atomic weapons based on plans stolen frommmm . . ." he quizzes. "Miss Salazar?"

"The Manhattan Project," she calls out.

"Correct. Which effectively kicked off the . . ." He shoots out his arm and points to the kid in the front right corner. "Mr. Merluzzi?"

"Uh," the kid stammers for a second. "The Nuclear Arms Race."

"Correct!"

No one talks. No one plays on their phones. No one has time.

"The US tested its first hydrogen bomb on . . ."

I wince.

"Mr. Grayson?"

Shit.

I meet his eyes again. "Hawaii?"

Another round of laughter, my friend Brace Salinger smirks at my side and gives me a nod of approval.

Mr. Albrecht simply turns his attention to someone else. "Miss Stonehouse?"

"On November 1, 1952, Mr. Albrecht."

I turn back around. Oh, he wanted a date.

He goes on. "Korea was divided into North and South as the result of . . . Miss Gaudin?"

I sit there, trying to keep my shoulders squared. Damon Torrance glances at me out of the corner of his eye.

"As the result of Japan losing control after the war," she promptly calls out, like she's got the lines in front of her.

Like we're all in some play with assigned parts, and I didn't get the script.

"The US and Soviet Union," she continues, "divided the territories like they did in Germany."

"Correct," he announces. "Which resulted in what, Mr. Crist?"

"Uh," Michael starts, somewhere behind me. "Communist government formed in the north, they invaded the south, and the US stepped in to help, starting a proxy war between the US and USSR."

"Correct!" The teacher moves faster. "The Cold War escalated further with technological aspirations to launch a missile into space capable of carrying nuclear weapons. In October 1957, the Soviet Union . . . Mr. Drake?"

"Launched Sputnik!" the guy singsongs.

I pull at my collar, my necktie feeling like it's lined with silver spikes. The bell rings, class ends, and I filter toward the door with everyone else.

I pass Albrecht's desk. "No more jokes," he warns. "Your last warning."

I nod as I walk out of the room.

I don't stop at my locker. I carry my book, with my pencil stuck between the pages, and head down the stairs, to the right, and through the door. Once outside, I exhale hard and jerk my head, cracking my neck.

I hate that goddamn class. And it's the last one of the day, so I have hours to dread it as soon as I walk into the school every morning. I can't think that fast.

I'm not stupid. But . . .

How does everyone else recall answers so quickly? I don't even remember half of that shit in the reading, but it had to be there, because everyone knew it except for me. And he does that every damn day. I'm sweating before I even walk into class. It's like a firing squad. Luckily, people think I'm just making jokes. I think they're even looking forward to what I'll say next. I've never been funny before, but they all think I'm hilarious.

I keep walking.

I should go back inside and collect my stuff from my locker, but I will in a minute. I never walk home right after school.

I traipse through the parking lot, the chain-link fence to my left stretching down the football field. Bushes rise high in front of it, and I keep walking, waiting.

And then, finally, she comes into view.

Surrounded by the rest of her bandmates, Emory Scott drops her backpack on a sideline bench and opens her flute case. Cymbals clatter as everyone gathers, but I don't see anything else but her. Not the trumpets or the trombones. Not the grass or the sun. Just the way her hair, wisps that escaped from her ponytail, flies in the breeze, and how she has to push her glasses up the bridge of her nose when she stands back upright. No one talks to her. She doesn't talk to them.

I wish she'd talk to me.

Cigarette smoke hits my nostrils, and I look up, seeing a cloud of smoke pour out of the tree above me.

I arch my neck, spotting Damon Torrance through the branches as he sits and leans against the trunk. He looks down at me, a ciga-rette burning between his fingers.

"Why doesn't he ever call on you?" I shout up to him.

"Believe me, he does not want me to respond."

I don't know what he means exactly, but I have an idea. Damon Torrance was like a ghost in Thunder Bay up until now. We heard things, and sometimes you'd see him around town.

And then there'd be months where you didn't catch glimpses of him at all, and you'd wonder if what you saw was real. It's not easy to disappear in a small town like Thunder Bay. I was actually surprised when he showed up the first day of school, and he was my age. The way people whispered about him, I imagined he had to be older.

I glance back at Emmy as she gets into formation with the rest of the band and look back up at Torrance, gesturing to his cigarette. "Can I have one?"

He holds my eyes for a second, finally digging inside his school jacket for his pack. I leap up onto the tree trunk, launching myself to the branch opposite him and pull up. Straddling the branch, I gaze over at the field, finding her again before I turn back to Damon.

I pull a cigarette out of the pack he offers. "I'm Will."

"Yeah, I know."

He slips the pack back into his pocket and takes out his lighter, handing it to me.

I fiddle with the cigarette, hesitating. I've never smoked before, and we're not that hidden. Teachers leaving for the day might smell it as they head through the parking lot.

I deflect. "Where'd you go before here?" I ask him.

He inhales, the end of his cigarette burning orange. "A few places." He exhales, the smoke hitting my clothes and drifting away. "Before I got kicked out anyway. Mostly tutors at home the past cou-ple of years."

"Really?" I can't help but sound impressed. "That's lucky. I'd love to stay home."

"I hate being home."

His reply is quick, and it makes me pause for a second.

He flicks the ash off the cigarette, the sudden anger fading from his eyes. "I like school," is all he adds.

I feel like I should ask him about it.

But I don't. What if he tells me?

Everyone knows his father. My dad doesn't like Mr. Torrance, and my mom isn't friends with his mom. And my mom loves everyone.

If Damon doesn't like his parents, I think they'll like him.

Emmy marches down the field, and I can just make out the sun reflecting in her glasses and her gray sneakers that used to be white. She doesn't smile a lot, and I don't know why I like stern people. My grandpa is the same way. A little scary, but if you have his heart, you have it forever.

I want Emory to smile at me.

"So, which one is it?"

I startle at Damon's question. I quickly turn back around, looking down as I stick the cigarette in my mouth and light it.

I suck in a little, smoke filling my mouth. I blow it out, the taste of dirt, burning newspaper, and something like the tailpipe of a car all mixed together. I run my tongue over the roof of my mouth. *Gross.*

Damon lets out a quiet laugh, and I try again, drawing the smoke into my lungs. I blow out, meeting his eyes, and resisting the need to cough up the bristle brush in my throat.

"So, come on, which one?" he asks again.

I haven't told my friends how much I like Emory Scott yet. They'd just make fun of her.

But I like that he's honest. Most people are just polite.

I gesture behind me. "Third row. Second from us. She has a flute."

He cranes his neck, looking over my shoulder, then comes back to rest against the trunk. "Do you jerk off to her?"

My face falls. *Seriously . . .* I take another drag of the cigarette.

"Have you even touched her?" he scoffs.

I narrow my eyes. "Well, what have you done?" I charge.

Smoke comes out of his mouth in bursts as he chuckles. "Not even half of what I'm gonna do over the next four years here," he tells me. "I'll be infamous."

Infamous . . .

For some reason, every hair on my arms feels like it's being pulled from the inside. Not an entirely unpleasant feeling actually.

I like him. He's not trying to be anyone else.

I suck on the cigarette again. "What do you do for fun?"

I blow out the smoke.

His eyes are black, but when they gleam, they seem a little blue around the iris. "I thought I'd ask them . . ." He jerks his chin over my opposite shoulder this time. ". . . if they want to go to the Cove this weekend."

I follow his gaze, seeing three girls, two blondes and one redhead, smiling and chatting next to a Mini Cooper convertible.

I laugh at him. "They're sophomores."

We're freshmen.

He just shrugs like nothing is out of his reach.

"Haven't you been there a million times?" I press. "I have."

It's just a few miles away, down the road between Thunder Bay and Falcon's Well. I became less excited about it after I got a season pass from my grandma every Christmas between the ages of eight and twelve.

But Damon tells me, "Oh, there's more to see if you know where to look." He pauses, his eyes falling and then rising again. "Wanna go?"

The question surprises me.

I do want to go. Kind of. I have a feeling he's going to get me into trouble, though, and I kind of like my parents.

Someone bounces a basketball, and I look down, seeing Kai Mori and Michael Crist dribble as they carry their duffel bags to the old gym across the parking lot.

The band plays at basketball games.

I dart my eyes up, spotting Emory.

They play at football games, too, but no one gives a shit about football here. Basketball is more important than anything at this school. My grandfather and his friends ruled back in the day, and no one has seen anything like it since.

I call down, shouting, "Hey, are tryouts today?"

Mori looks up, recognizing me. We've met a couple times. "Yeah," he replies. "Hurry up if you're coming."

I smile before hearing Damon next to me. "Kai," he taunts. "You haven't said 'hi' to me."

"I know," Kai says, continuing to bounce the ball next to Michael as they head for the gym.

Damon breathes out smoke. "Prick."

I nod at him. "Want to try out?"

"No." He looks at me like I'm crazy. "Why would you? They're just going to make you sweat for free."

I start to climb down from the tree. "She's going to be playing at all the sporting events," I tell him, unable to stop smiling as I slide down the trunk. "Away games, bus rides, pep rallies . . . She'll be forced to watch me."

I'm almost laughing, jumping to the ground and racing off, without telling him goodbye. I fly across the lawn and dive into the old gym, which is only in use anymore when absolutely needed. Fall is a busy time, so if the main gym isn't occupied by the football team or the cheer team, I'm guessing there's some kind of extracurricular fair, CPR training, or used book sale in there right now.

I like the brown-tiled walls, old wooden bleachers, and the scents of leather, sweat, and winter wool. Probably trapped forever in the old championship banners hanging around the entire court, high up on the walls.

This was the gym my grandfather used. He practiced here. He played here. Scouts watched him here. And some years later, he returned as one of the alumni who helped pay for the renovations on the school with the agreement that no changes would be made to this gym. He wouldn't even let them repair the basement when it flooded years ago. He hired his own crew. I remember. My dad was pissed because it had cost so much.

I jog to where everyone stands, not bothering to change into gym clothes.

"Five minutes!" Coach Lerner shouts. "Warm up!"

He turns to a couple of dads standing nearby, the sound of basketballs filling the court, and I look around for what to do. Simon Ulrich and Brace Salinger nod at me, and I jog over. Whipping off my jacket, I toss it to the side and loosen my tie. They pass the ball to me, and we spread out on the edges of the lane.

"Flick Pass Drill," Ulrich calls.

No idea what he means, but I go with it. But I spare a glance, seeing Mori and Crist dribbling around orange cones, and I freeze for a minute.

They both move down their individual rows, dribbling left to right and back again as they move through the little course, but every time they do it, the ball bounces through their legs. One hand sends it through, the other catches it in behind them, and then they swing it around the front to send it back through again.

My face falls. *What the fuck?* I'm never going to make this team.

"Let's go!" Salinger says.

We sidestep down the lane, shooting the ball back and forth, and I watch my friends, mimicking their movements. How the pads of their fingers manage the ball. Their footwork. The flick in their wrists.

But after a minute, my attention keeps getting drawn to Crist and Mori. How Crist seems to know how he's going to react before Mori even moves. How the latter always passes off to his left hand and back to his right the moment before he shoots the ball.

Salinger, Ulrich, and I move across the court, closer, and when

Crist's ball ricochets off the rim and bounces off the floor, I catch the rebound and leap up, dunking it into the basket.

Crist looks at me, his chest rising and falling fast. "Good job," he says.

The ball dances across the floor, and he takes it, throwing a look to his friend who says nothing before Crist turns back and tosses it to me.

I can't hold back the grin at the invitation. I go, driving the ball to the other end of the court. They chase, Mori easily racing in and stealing the ball away, running it back to the far end of the court. He shoots from the three-point line before I even get to him, scoring. I retrieve the ball, walking as I dribble and taking it slower this time. Michael faces off with me, his eyes falling to my feet every once in a while, and I watch how he favors his left side. Which is my right.

He dives in, and just like I knew it was coming, I escape to my left and race around him, barreling for the other end of the court. I shoot, the ball dipping through the basket.

Others have stopped moving on the court, but Michael and Kai haven't stopped, so I don't, either.

Kai smiles as he recovers the ball, and I jump up two times high, the adrenaline pumping and too much. But God, it feels good, too.

Kai coasts for the other end, Michael shouting, "Open!"

I keep my eyes on the ball, waiting for it.

"Here!" Michael shouts at him.

The court has gone quiet, but I can't stop to see long enough to see what's happening.

Kai passes the ball, Michael catches it, and when he spins left (because that's the side he favors) I'm there. He dribbles, trying to gauge his next move before finally catching the ball in both hands, leaping high, and firing. He scores, and I keep going, snatching up the ball and running at top speed as I dribble it down the court. I shoot, it skates off the rim, and I growl in frustration.

But it never touches the ground. Damon Torrance appears, jumps up, and catches it as soon as it spills over the rim. He dunks it.

I laugh, hearing someone shout, "Nice!"

A few claps go off around us.

The basketball bounces over to me, and I send it flying over to Kai. He moves the ball smoothly down the sideline.

"Where are you going?" I hear Damon ask him.

He jogs alongside Kai, getting up in his grill as Kai stops to lay out his shot.

"Huh? Huh?" he taunts him. "You wanna be sorry? Take the shot. You'll be sorry. You can't do it. You're a lousy fucking shot." He sways in front of Kai as Kai tries to move the ball from left to right and get around Damon. "You can't even see the net right now, can you? All you see is me."

I chuckle to myself.

Kai shoots, the ball slipping through the net, and I grab it, passing it to Damon as Kai races after him. Damon stops at the free throw line, positions the ball in his hands, and jumps up.

But the next thing I know, Kai is falling to the ground, a hand over one of his eyes. "Shit!" he barks.

Damon leaps up again, shoots and scores.

A whistle blows, and I hear Lerner yell at us. "All right, that's enough!"

I stare at Kai on the ground, all of us out of breath. What the hell just happened? Did Torrance elbow him in the eye? I didn't even see it.

Kai glares up at Damon, sweat covering his neck as he breathes hard. I almost head over to help him up, but Crist is there, offering a hand.

Damon just stares down at Kai.

"So what the hell was that?" Lerner asks, sounding out of breath as he charges over. He stops, the four of us spread out in front of him. "What was all that?"

I don't say a word. What does he mean? Damon pushing Mori to the ground? It's not legal, but it happens. The coach can't be surprised.

"What?" Michael finally asks.

"You three." The coach steps closer, eyeing Kai, Michael, and me. "You ever play together before?"

I glance at them, their gazes catching mine.

"No." Michael shakes his head. "Not really."

I've seen him and Kai together the past few weeks, but I don't think they've ever played on a team together.

The coach approaches me, and I stand up straight. "You anticipate them," he says.

I do?

He narrows his eyes on me. "That's good instinct."

"Yeah," Michael adds. "Kai and I move the ball easily together, and Grayson's reflexes are incredible."

Lerner nods, the wheels in his head looking like they're spinning. He backs up, oblivious to Torrance standing just off to the side.

"You three stay together," Coach tells us. "I want to see more later."

Michael and Kai share a smile, Kai still rubbing his eye.

The coach moves away, clapping loudly. "All right, everyone! Let's line up for warm-ups. Three rows of six!"

Damon grabs his jacket off the court and pulls it on as he leaves.

"You okay?" Michael asks Kai.

But Kai just gestures to Damon who pushes through the heavy double doors. "I told you, man," he blurts out to Michael. "He's trouble."

"No," Michael quickly retorts, looking in the direction Damon left. "He's an *enforcer*, Kai."

His friend stares at him.

"And every team needs one," Michael adds, dropping the basketball into Kai's hands. "Tell the coach I'll be right back."

He follows Damon out the same door, and I know he's going to bring him back, because he's right. My grandfather wasn't a great player, but his presence on the court did enough to intimidate the other team. He talked shit, got rebounds, protected his teammates . . . Enforcers know how to foul and hide it. Like Damon just did.

Every team has ruthless players. We need one, too.

My grandfather and his friends ruled back in the day, and no one has seen anything like it since . . .

"The four Horsemen . . ." I murmur, remembering their nickname.

"What?"

I blink, remembering Kai next to me. I simply smile.

Crist, Mori, Grayson . . . and Torrance.

"Do you know what Devil's Night is?" I ask him.

DAMON

The Next Summer

"Damon."

I jerk my head up, water spilling in a stream from my hair down the bridge of my nose.

Kai?

"Get out," I snap at him.

I slam the lever, turning off my shower and grabbing the towel hanging over the door.

"You missed practice," he calls out.

I run the towel over my hair and quickly wrap it around my waist. Small puddles of blood pool on the shower floor. *Fuck.* I growl, "I don't like people in my room, Kai!"

Nik had better be hiding. Goddammit. The door is usually locked.

I open the shower door with one hand, holding the towel closed with the other. Kai stands across from me, in front of the broken mirror, and I glance at him long enough to see his eyes drop to my feet and the blood I'm tracking on the rug.

"Jesus Christ . . ."

"Oh, what do you care?" I bark, grabbing clean jeans off the chair just inside my bedroom and pulling them on.

Bloody footprints paint the floor under me, and I whip off the towel, fastening my pants. Why is he even here? *Practice. That's right.* At Michael's insistence, so we don't get out of shape over the summer.

"What the hell, Damon?" he barks louder, rushing to me. "What did you do?"

But I push him away. "Leave it." The cuts on the pads of my feet sting as I force myself to walk to the sink, the pain making every-thing that happened last night fade. "Some assholes jumped me at Sticks," I tell him. "Then I came home drunk."

"Bullshit."

I lean over the sink, turning on the cold water and splashing my face.

"You don't go anywhere without us," he says.

God, I fucking hate Kai. At least Michael lets me lie.

He grabs my arm, shoving me toward the edge of the tub. "Sit down."

I fall to the edge, vile words for him on the tip of my tongue, but I'm so fucking tired. All I mutter is, "It's fine."

Kai yanks a towel off the rack and kneels in front of me, lifting my right leg under the ankle. I forget how many times I sliced into my skin last night. I like to do it in places people don't see. My feet, between my toes, my scalp, under my arms . . .

I glance to the right, into my room. A shadow floats just slightly on the wall up the short stairwell to the little tower attached to my room.

Kai presses the towel to my foot, applying pressure. "Someone said your mom left town this morning." He looks around the bath-room, surveying the damage. "Servants talk. Are you okay?"

He shifts his attention to the other foot, but when I don't answer, he lifts his gaze.

"Don't mention her ever again," I whisper. "Do you understand?"

My mother will never come back, because now she knows what will happen if she does. Not all of the blood on the floor is mine.

Movement flashes in the corner of my eye, and I see my sister peeking around the corner as she stands at the bottom of the stairs. She sees me, I narrow my eyes, and she promptly disappears back behind the wall.

I look down at Kai as he inspects the cuts, but there's no need. I never do it deep enough to need stitches.

"Don't worry," I say, my voice raspy around my clenched teeth. "I'll be able to play this fall."

"I don't give a shit about that."

A smile pulls at one corner of my lips. That's why I love Kai. He's good. He pisses me off, but he has my back.

Out of the four of us, I'm closest to Will. There are no problems with him, and I need one person in my life who's easy to be around. There are no expectations. No pressure. He never pushes back, and he always shows up. He would never let me jump off a building. By myself anyway.

But I can't tell him things. He has happy parents and a happy life, and he thinks we all do. I can't ruin him. I need him pure. I'm glad it was Kai who came looking for me today instead of him. I'm not sure what he would've done if he'd found me like this.

Kai is the exact opposite of Will. He's in my fucking face all the time to keep my grades up, or I'll get kicked off the team. Not to mouth off to a teacher, or I'll get kicked off the team. Not to fuck someone's daughter, or I'll get kicked off the team.

But times like right now, when he knows something is very wrong, and he's letting his façade slip enough to show that he's scared for me . . . that's when my heart thunders in my chest and warmth spreads down my arms and into my head. All of a sudden, there is no pain, and I know I would never want another life. I have Nik. I have Will, Kai, and Michael. They're all mine and no one else's. And if being in this town and in this house with parents who deserve to die is the price, I'd endure it forever. No one will take the four of them away from me.

I reach behind him, pulling open the drawer and handing him the gauze. He takes it, biting the end of the roll between his teeth, and ripping off a portion of it. He starts wrapping my foot, from the ball to the arch.

"Where are Will and Michael?" I ask him, glancing at the stairwell again. I know Nik is listening, but she knows not to be seen. She better.

"Will's in the kitchen, mooching off your cook," Kai replies, "and Michael is at Schraeder Fane's funeral with our parents."

Our parents?

"My dad went?"

"That's what Marina told me when I made sure the coast was clear," he says.

My dad hates the Fanes. I guess he had to be seen at the funeral, though. They're important in the community.

I'm surprised he's not more preoccupied with my mother leaving.

Then again, I'm not surprised, either. He valued her presence for social gatherings and running his house, but everyone is replaceable, and my father has had a lot of experience explaining the sudden disappearance of an employee. A wife is the same thing.

I blow out a breath. "I need a cigarette."

"No."

I glare down at him. "Fuck, Kai."

I rake my hand through my wet hair.

He bites off the end of the wrap and fastens it to the rest of the bandage. "You need a fucking detox," he bites out. "No drinking, no smoking, and no sex. Dammit. You need sleep." He wraps the other foot. "*Only* sleep. You understand?"

Sleep . . .

I glance up at the bathroom counter that fucking subhuman piece of shit tried to get me to fuck her on last night. I don't need sleep. Sleep is time. Sleep is thoughts. Sleep is lonely. And quiet. Too quiet.

I grind the palm of my hand into my thigh, still feeling her hair in my fist as I smashed her face into the mirror.

I want to hurt her more. I would. I wish she was still here because I would. I'd stab her. I'd like to feel a blade pierce her rib cage.

One pain at a time . . .

The room spins, my head lulls to one side, and my eyelids flutter. *We can only feel one pain at a time.*

Kai stands me up and leads me over to the sink. The water comes on, and he pushes my head down, dropping palmfuls of cold water over the back of my neck. "Kai . . ." I whisper, but I don't know what I want to say.

"You trust me, so trust me," he says. "You need to cool down."

He holds me around the waist, my knees about to buckle.

"Just a rough night." My voice shakes. "I'll be okay."

"I know you will."

I give a weak smile, but he can't see it. "Drinking, smoking, and sex are the only things that make me feel good."

"No," he says, resolute. "They don't. They distract you. And when they're over, you feel even worse than you did before they made you forget for five minutes."

I let the cold water cascade over my neck and into my hair, bringing me back down to the ground.

"Don't you understand?" he asks me. "When we do bad, we feel bad. That's it. That's all there is. I don't know why one follows the other or what guilt and conscience are or where they come from, but I do know that's the only religion I understand."

That's the only thing Kai and I have in common. We knew each other before high school. Before Michael and Will knew either of us. We attended catechism classes together as kids.

And the more we were taught, the less we understood. Kai ended up simplifying his doctrine. I wrote my own.

"Who's to say what's bad?" I ask.

"You tell me," he fires back. "How are you feeling lately?"

Finally, I chuckle. *Prick*.

He's got a point, I guess. All my vices simply keep me running like a rat on a wheel.

But I do know something else that felt good and got the result I wanted. I open and close my fist, noticing a long black hair stretching like a fishing line between my fingers.

He shoves a glass in front of me. "Drink this."

I take the water and sit back on the edge of the tub.

"Drink all of it," he says.

I gulp down the water and hand it back to him, but he refills it and hands it back. "More."

I take it. "Jesus Christ."

But I down the second glass in four gulps.

Kai thinks every problem can be solved with sleep and hydration. I have to give him something if I want him off my back.

Banks peeks around the wall, and I shove the glass back at Kai. "Go wait for me in your car," I tell him.

"You should sleep."

"Go."

I'm not fucking sleeping. It's not even dark out yet.

He sets the glass down and walks out, and I follow, slamming the door shut behind him as I head right up to my sister as she comes down the stairs. I back her into the wall, seeing the fear rise in her eyes as I pin my forehead to hers.

She wanted him to see her.

And she knows I know.

Slowly, her arms snake around my waist, and she presses her cheek into my chest, hugging me tightly. So tightly, I can't not feel her devotion. She knows I better feel it.

The irony doesn't escape me. Commanding her love. Keeping her hidden away from everyone else like my possession. Scaring her into obeying me. Controlling her food. Denying her an education. She wears my clothes and owns nothing I don't buy her.

She may smash *my* face into a mirror someday.

But with her arms around me like a belt, the muscles in my legs tighten, the steel in my spine straightens, and my lungs draw in a tank of air. Finally. Everything releases, the wrong stuff is tapped down and the right stuff warms. I close my eyes, exhaling long and slow, smelling my shampoo in her hair. I wrap her in my arms, kissing the top of her head. "I'll be home late."

I let her go. In two minutes, I'm dressed and pulling on a hoodie as I hear the lock click behind me on my way out of the room.

I leave the house, climb into Kai's car, with Will in the back seat, and slam the door shut. Kai starts the engine and my warning comes before he takes off. "Don't come in my room again," I say.

Rain taps the windshield so light and sporadic that Kai's wipers don't intervene for several minutes. A shadow moves west across his dashboard, erasing the sun as a cloud moves in, and we race down into the village.

Kai hangs right, sliding into a spot in front of Sticks, and we all get out.

Drops of water hit my wet hair, the summer breeze chilly tonight. I inhale through my nose. Fall is coming.

Mischief. Wind. Basketball. School. Longer nights. Sweet things.

Will introduced us to Devil's Night last year. I'd heard about it. The stories from the old days. The rumors. But he told us how his grandfather did it, and we all picked a prank. I liked it, but I liked it more because we did it together. I wonder if we'll up our game this year.

I head for Sticks. One of the bartenders puts whisky in our Cokes. Just ours.

But Kai's voice is stern behind me. "No. Food," he says, pointing to the deli a couple of doors down.

"No."

"Now," he barks.

I widen my eyes. Is he fucking serious?

He steps up on the sidewalk, veering right, and Will looks at me, sympathy in his gaze, but he backs away from me, trailing after Kai.

Heaving a sigh, I traipse after them.

The smell of roasted turkey and steak fills the store, and I head for the deli counter, seeing K.O. Knox behind the counter. He tips his chin at me.

My stomach growls. I am pretty fucking starving actually.

"What do you want?" I ask Will as he heads for the coolers.

"Philly."

I meet Kai's eyes.

"The one that tastes like Thanksgiving," he tells me.

I turn back to K.O. "You heard that?"

He nods, chuckling to himself. I don't know what the sandwich is called, either.

"And I'll take the shaved steak one," I tell him.

One by one, he slaps a sandwich wrapped in a layer of butcher paper underneath a layer of tin foil onto the counter in front of me, while Kai grabs other snacks and Will gets drinks.

Then a gentle voice catches my attention. "It's okay, honey," someone says. "You can bring me the money next time you come in."

Simone Tinsbury leans over the register, trying to keep her voice small as she speaks to a little girl.

"No, I have it," the kid says in a voice that's just a notch above a whisper.

I take the sandwiches and walk up to pay, standing behind little Erika Fane as she holds an ice cream cone in one hand and digs in her pocket, pulling out coins with the other. She places them on the counter, counting out what she needs and dips her hand back in, because it's not enough.

I stare down at the back of her little head. Long blond hair. Small shoulders. Black leather shoes. Black coat.

Schraeder Fane. *Funeral*, Kai said.

She buried her father today.

"Rika, it's okay," Simone tells her.

People have stopped to look at her. I turn my glare on one of them, and he quickly leaves my line of sight.

What the hell is she doing in town alone? On a day like today?

"I'm sorry," she says quickly, her ice cream cone switching hands as she digs into her other pocket. "I almost have it."

Winter would be her age, I think. About thirteen now.

Holding the sandwiches in one arm, I pull out some cash and flip open my folded-up bills with one hand. I drop a five on the counter, and Rika's head pops up, her eyes going big and round at seeing me.

I jerk my chin at Simone, and she takes the cash, getting change. Rika steps away, ice cream dripping over her hand, her gaze frozen on me.

I hold her eyes.

No thank-you. No smile. No protest like she pulled with Simone. She's just fucking standing there, looking at me like I'm the grim reaper. We've never spoken, that I can remember anyway, but she knows who I am.

At least it certainly looks like it.

I dump the sandwiches on the counter and swipe all of her coins onto the floor, not sparing her another glance. She rears back, and out of the corner of my eye, I see the top scoop of her ice cream spill to the floor.

Simone casts a look at me, anger piercing her gaze, but she won't scold me, because I can be a lot worse than this.

I hear Kai behind me. "Damon, Jesus . . ."

He and Will try to pick up the coins, but Rika runs out of the store with her one scoop before they can help her.

I hold back my smile. *Sorry, Kai, but that felt a lot better than trying to be a hero.*

I pay for the sandwiches, Kai grabbing our drinks and an extra one for Michael.

"Warehouse tonight?"

I glance, seeing Simon Ulrich approach us, two girls with him. I start to grab one of the bags, but I stop, looking back at Stevie Marlowe.

She wears a tight brown vest that might've been from a three-piece suit of her brother's when he was younger, but what catches my eyes is the long black shoestring circling her neck three times before it's tied into a little bow in front. Each end is adorned with a gold aglet, both of which rest between her breasts.

"Yeah," Will answers.

But I shake my head. "No."

The word slips from my tongue before I even know why I said it. But as soon as I do, I know what I want.

When I step up to Stevie, her face falls a little, her brown ponytail swaying as she looks to Simon. For what? I don't know. He's not going to interfere.

Pulling one end of the shoestring, I remove it from her body and reach around her, securing her wrists behind her back. Her breath shudders against me as I hold her eyes and tie her up.

"Damon . . ."

"Kai," I spit back, not taking my eyes off of her.

He can reel me in when I know I need it, but I need something else right now.

Not sex. Not yet anyway. But something definitely sexual. I clench my teeth, hearing a whimper she tries to hold back.

"Blink once if this is okay," Kai asks her, everyone else as silent as ice. "Blink twice if it's not."

Stevie looks up at me, and I hold my breath, finally seeing her blink. Just once.

I lift the corner of my mouth in a smile. "Follow us."

I give her back to her friends, Simon grinning as he nods.

"Call everyone," I tell him.

"And where are we going?" he asks.

But I don't say just yet. Kai pulls out his keys, and I snatch them. "I'll drive."

We grab our food and leave, tossing it into the car.

I'm not hungry anymore.

I speed out of the village, texting Michael with one hand and steering with the other as we race back up to the cliffs, past our houses. I toss a glance to the Ashby house, always thinking I'll see something, but I never do.

Kai's Jeep drifts into the other lane, and I quickly jerk the wheel as I glance up and down between the road and my phone. Kai clears his throat, louder than necessary, and I tap out the last two letters and press send. Then I stick my phone in my pocket.

Michael will like where we're going.

Simon's headlights appear in my rearview mirror, but I want to get there before they do. I shift into fourth, gas it, and then shift into fifth, hearing a curse leave Kai's mouth. I smile a little, Simon disappearing behind me.

We fly past Michael's house, the Fane house, and I slow, knowing the driveway to the old cathedral on the left is unmarked and overgrown. Easy to miss.

I spot a reflector and press the brakes just enough to make the turn. Will sits behind Kai but holds his headrest, looking over Kai's shoulder as the massive stone cathedral, abandoned decades ago rises out of the trees. It's not dark yet, but the clouds flash with lightning, like a melody skipping across the sky.

"What are we doing here?" Kai asks me.

I can't explain it to him. He has to see.

We climb out of the Jeep, and I lead them back to his tailgate. I open it up and start pulling out all of the supplies a well-prepared man always travels with. We grab two flashlights, some matches, and . . . I grab a handful of orange LED disks.

I look at Kai. "Road flares?" I tease. "God, I love you."

He chuckles. "It makes my mother feel better."

At the mention of "mother," my smile falls, and he sees it. He looks down, suddenly somber, probably thinking he was being inconsiderate, but I'm not sad mine skipped town last night. And they'll never know why. There will only be pain because of *me* now. I found out how to handle my mother.

I wouldn't mind handling his, too. She's fucking beautiful.

We take all the shit up to the church, but Kai and Will head for the steps to the front door.

"This way," I tell him, jerking my head. "There's a side door that works."

Kai looks at me, skeptical, but they won't be able to get through those locks.

We trail down the side of the cathedral, dry leaves rustling under our shoes and whatever glass that spilled from the broken stained glass windows is long since buried after years of rain, snow, and falling foliage.

Two steps lead to a side door near the rear, and I grab the circular handle, twisting, and kicking the door open.

One step inside, and the air hits me, instantly feeling different.

I remember when Michael showed me this place. It was just us that night. Spring break last year. Kai was in Japan, visiting his father's family, and Will was in Cabo with his parents. Michael and I didn't go anywhere, so we hung out, and he was forced to walk a casserole or some shit to the Fanes' for dinner, so I went with him.

I stayed back by the gate, little Rika's drugged-up mother staring at me from a second-floor window, but he didn't want to go home after that so we kept walking. Into the woods, farther and farther away from light until we came upon this place. We all knew it was here, but I never gave it a second thought before he wanted to go inside.

My feet keep moving, Kai and Will following as we step into the transept, the sanctuary on our right and the nave on our left.

Most of the pews are ripped up, piles of wood spread out across the floor, and I look around, dim light spilling through broken orange, blue, red, and yellow windows.

The air is thicker inside, wet and heavy with dirt and granite and dried hay. And something sweet, too. I inhale again. *Apples*. Raindrops in through the broken roof, soft and light.

Michael and I walked around a little that night, but it got dark and we were unprepared. He still didn't want to leave.

I press the power button on the LED flare, its bright glow spreading over my hands. I drop it on the ground before illuminating another and leaving a trail.

"My family's been in this town the longest," I tell Kai and Will. "There are pictures of this place when it was in its prime. There were masses, celebrations, funerals . . ." I look at them over my shoulder. "And the underground."

"The catacombs," Michael calls out, walking in behind Kai and Will.

He tips his chin over my shoulder, and I follow his gaze. A large, wooden door with an arched top sits in the corner of the sanctuary, and I don't waste time. Dropping another flare, I yank on the handle, but it's not budging. Will grabs it with me, and we pull, years of dirt and grime grinding in the hinges as the heavy door creaks open.

Leaving the door ajar, I turn on a flashlight, Kai flipping on the other one, and we descend the stone stairs into the pitch-black tunnels underneath the cathedral.

"Damn . . ." I hear Will whisper.

We come to the bottom, Will leaving another flare to light up the area, and Kai and I swing around our flashlights, taking in the pathways and the numerous doorways cut into the walls. Rooms. So many rooms.

"It's huge," Will says. "I wonder if my grandfather ever explored this back in the day."

"It's not cold." Michael's eyes float between all of us, looking puzzled. "Shouldn't it be?"

It's a little chilly outside, as New England can be anytime of the year when the sun goes down. But he's right. We're must've come down twenty or thirty feet on those stairs. And no sunlight. It should be considerably cooler.

We stand there—the four of us—hearing noise above, music and laughter as Simon, the girls, and some others arrive. We could burn one of those piles of wood up there for a bonfire.

"We need to install some kind of light down here," Kai says.

And I like that he wants to come back.

"But not too much light," I add.

Everyone looks around, and I turn off my flashlight.

We stand there silently with only Kai's flashlight on, none of us moving as the seconds pass, gazing at each other's faces, unable to see the eyes.

I'm not sure what's being said, but it gets louder the longer we all stay rooted.

Everyone feels it.

"Not too much light," Michael echoes after me.

Followed by Will. "Not too much."

The music pounds upstairs, and I can feel every inch of my clothes that touches my skin. I listen to their music. Their laughter. We can hear them, yet, it's so quiet down here.

I'd like to imagine hell like this. A realm so much closer than we realize.

"Hello?" a girl calls, sounding like she's at the top of the stairs.

No one moves. *Stevie.*

I see her shadow against the rock wall as she makes her way down.

I can't see the guys' faces, but we're looking at each other.

I take a step back, and so does Michael. I don't breathe for a second, waiting, and then . . . Kai and Will follow, each one of us backing down a separate tunnel, sinking into the darkness of the catacombs. I see Will pull off his T-shirt just before he disappears, his smiling swallowed up by the dark.

"Simon says you have to be the ones to untie me," she calls out, standing at the bottom in the dim light that filters down from the stairs.

She rolls her wrists inside her bindings, and I hope she's still up for fun, because I might like to see that thing back on her neck tonight.

Staying in place, she peers down each pathway, unable to see what lurks just beyond the darkness. Her voice is so small. "Hello?"

I draw in a deep breath. *Pick a tunnel, honey. See what you find.*

MICHAEL

Two Months Later

"Mori catches the rebound . . ." the announcer bellows, ". . . passing it off to Grayson!"

I run down the sideline, my eyes on Will, and his eyes on Ulrich as the crowd full of parents and students cheers.

"Grayson moves down the court . . ."

But then Will stops dribbling, catches the ball in both hands, and passes it over to me.

". . . and slipping it over to Crist . . ."

He didn't even look when he passed it. Smooth, clean, cold. Will always knows where I am.

I catch it, hearing his mom scream "Good job, honey!" and I

know he's shaking his head and chuckling. I jog, leap up, and shoot over the guard, the ball riding the rim. I hold my breath for a second before it finally sinks into the basket. *Fuck that was close.*

"Shoots and scores!" one of the live streamers calls out. "Meara couldn't get around Torrance."

We move, Kai throwing me a look. I don't ever come that close to missing when shooting from the top of the key.

I turn away, looking back down the court. But all I see are his parents sitting next to Will's in the stands. It's a rare occasion Katsu Mori doesn't make one of his son's games. But Kai's mom is at every game. Will's parents, too.

That's Damon's and my common ground. Our fathers are never here.

Falcon's Well gets the ball, and I hang back, watching Damon get in Meara's face. I can't hear what he says, but I know he's in the guy's head. That's his job. Meara shifts right to left, but his feet stutter like he doesn't know what to do.

"One player got around him once," the commentator continues. "He took the ball home as a souvenir."

"And it has never been seen since," the other one jokes. "I think we all know Torrance got it back."

"No proof, no proof . . ." they go on, joking.

Jesus, shut up.

Damon gets the ball, shoots it to Anderson, but he gets blocked in. He passes the ball to me, it bounces once on the court, and I try to shoot from the left baseline, but Devon Benedict slaps it out of my hands. The crowd goes wild, and I stand there, completely fucking frozen.

Shouts of anger and screams from my coach pierce my ears like needles, and I feel the eyes of scouts on me. Scouts, and I still have three years of high school. And they're here to see me.

"Don't pay attention to it," Kai yells, coming up to me over the roar of the crowd.

I jog away. "I'm not."

"Your head isn't in this game!" he shouts. "What are you doing?"

What does he care? We don't need this. Our college educations are paid for already. Why am I even putting myself through this? No one gives a shit. I'm sick of this.

"Michael!"

I look up, Will passing to me, and I'm going to miss. I pass it off to Kai, but Chase Williams intercepts it, Kai's eyes going wide at me, because that wasn't the play.

Boos hit the air, reverberating through the gymnasium, and I bite my teeth together.

But then Damon smacks the ball out of Williams's hand, catching it and holding it over his head.

A clear foul.

The whistle blows, the referee issuing Damon with his second penalty of the game, and I exhale, hearing the coach call a time-out.

Damon winks at me, and if I weren't so fucking pissed at myself, I'd smile.

"No one is here to see this," my coach yells at me.

Kai grabs my arm, telling the coach. "I got it. Just give me a minute."

"I don't coach shit shows!" the coach barks as Kai pulls me away from everyone else.

The crowd pounds their feet against the bleachers, the sound deafening as everyone laughs as Damon continues taunting Williams, talking shit.

"Goddammit," the coach cries to Will. "Get him off the court!"

Kai knocks my head. "Look at me!"

I meet his eyes, my own starting to burn as I breathe hard. I can't be here.

"Open the box," he says. "Put it all in one by one."

"I can't stow it away like you can."

I can't believe my fucking chin is trembling. My head is splitting.

No one cares if I'm here. He doesn't know what this feels like. He always has someone here for him. Why do I give a shit?

But he just shrugs. "Fine. Let's just get out of here then."

What?

He continues, "Go get in our cars that our dads bought us, spend the money they gave us, get drunk, and find a girl to have some fun."

My chin stops shaking. I narrow my eyes.

"Be fucking losers who take rewards they didn't earn," he spits out.

I lock my jaw.

He steps up to me. "The weak are meat . . . the strong eat."

I breathe hard.

"The weak are meat . . . the strong eat," he grits out.

I clench my fists, both of us reciting in unison. "The weak are meat . . . the strong eat. The weak are meat . . . the strong eat."

I can't fucking send him home like this.

I can't wake up tomorrow like that.

A minute later, we're back on the court, the words rolling in my head, putting muscle on my heart. *The weak are meat . . . the strong eat, the weak are meat . . . the strong eat . . .*

"I'm open!" Ulrich calls out.

Will passes to him, he tries to shoot, but passes to Kai. Kai halts at the top of the key and shoots, but the ball skids off the rim. I grab it. *The strong eat . . .*

"Go, go, go!" Damon shouts at me.

I shoot, sinking the ball into the net, and cheers erupt.

I tip my head back and breathe out.

Eight minutes later, I stand on the court, the band playing our school song as Will lets his mom hug him. His dad congratulates him on the win, but I see people looking at me and knowing the slim four-point lead is my fault.

Damon stands next to me, Kai's parents stepping onto the court and waiting for their son. Damon pulls off his jersey, some students ogling him and whispering to each other as they leave the stands.

"Go," I tell him, forcing a half smile. "They're waiting for you."

"They'll wait forever for me."

I love his confidence.

Although, it's more of a fact than just self-assurance. The worse the stories are about Damon, the more people want his personal attention in a dark room somewhere.

"Besides," he says. "I'm saving my energy for next week."

"Got plans for us?"

He smiles, walking off. "I like Devil's Night, don't you?"

He heads over to a group, Will following him because it positions him just a few rows down from where Emory Scott stands with her flute, so she'll see him.

Yeah, I like Devil's Night, too. *Thanks, Will.*

And I liked the catacombs. *Damon's idea.*

I picked friends with imagination. I guess I can say I did one thing right.

Kai stops at my side. "Come to dinner with us."

He gestures to his parents. I know he feels pressure from his father, but Kai is also smart. He knows it also feels good to be worth his father's time. I wish I didn't care about the things I care about.

"Not tonight," I say quietly.

I walk off, toward the locker room.

"Will I see you later?" he calls after me.

But I don't answer, itching to get out of here as quickly as possible.

I carry my duffel bag to my car, the parking lot crowded with people, parents, and the opposing team's bus. I feel their stares and ignore others calling to me as I veer around a kid hanging at the fence and climb into my car.

It feels like we lost. They know I flaked. It's the one thing I have that's all mine—that he didn't give me—and I almost couldn't keep it.

I race home, neither of my parents' cars in the driveaway. I drop my bag on the stairs but head into the kitchen. Pulling out a plate, I start to make a sandwich.

But I'm not really hungry. Like everything else, I go through the motions. If my family didn't have money, I'd wish I had some, but on the other side of that, it also makes things too easy. I know I'll go to college. I can afford it. I won't be left to figure it out or take chances. I will never have to fight for anything.

Look at me. So privileged.

And I'm fucking starving.

"Hi, sweetie." My mom walks into the kitchen, setting down her handbag. "Sorry we missed the game."

"But I didn't want to go," Trevor adds, trailing in behind her.

I ignore my brother, twisting the cap back on the peanut butter.

"No," my mom answers for him. "He had swim lessons, and he can't drive himself yet. You understand."

"It's fine," I murmur.

She does come to a lot of games. Just her, but she's there sometimes.

I wish my dad didn't hate me.

"But I checked online." She smiles big. "You won. That's great."

"Of course, they won," Trevor spits out, opening the fridge. "They win every time. You know why?" He pulls out a soda and slams the door. "Because no team they play can afford the best coaches, private lessons, and home basketball courts constantly at their disposal." He scoffs, taunting me. "Oh, if everyone had the opportunities you have. Would you still be the best?"

God, he's a little shit.

But touché. He's right.

"Where's Rika?" my mom asks me.

"How should I know?"

"You didn't see her? She was at the game."

I halt, looking up. She was?

"She wanted to cheer for you," Trevor says in a mocking tone.

And then it hits me. The kid. By the fence. *Shit*. The one who turned and looked up at me when I left the locker room. I didn't even make eye contact. She was at the game by herself?

"Oh, there you are," my mom says.

I look up, seeing Rika enter the kitchen. Her gaze flashes to me really quickly and then to my mom.

"Why didn't you wait for Michael?" Mom asks her.

Rika climbs up onto the stool at the island. "I wanted to walk."

I look back down at the sandwich, the fucking cherry on top of a shitty day. A thirteen-year-old is covering for me.

My mom pours her a chocolate milk, and I zone in on the scar on her neck as she smiles at my mom. She got the stitches out several weeks ago, but the injury will be there in the mirror forever. Part of me envies her. I can't explain why, but I feel like the world will change a lot for her someday.

I pass her the peanut butter sandwich and snatch her chocolate milk, downing half of it. She takes a bite, not protesting, as if this is our routine, and I almost feel like smiling.

But then Trevor pulls at her. "Come on, Rika."

Her eyes meet mine, and I almost start to tell him to leave her alone. She's eating. He never fucking lets her be.

I need to get out of here anyway.

I grab my keys and leave the kitchen, looking back over my shoulder, her eyes following me like an elastic band stretching and about to snap the farther away I get.

When I slam the front door shut and climb in my car, the passenger-side door immediately opens.

I jerk my eyes, seeing Kai hop in. Looking behind me, I spot his black Jeep parked in the driveway.

"What are you doing?" I watch him close his door. "You're supposed to be at dinner."

"I was thinking we should go to the city."

He's dressed in a hoodie, definitely not for dinner with his parents.

"They opened this new paintball place," he tells me. "Damon and Will are ready to go whenever."

"I don't want to shoot paintballs."

I start the car, hoping that'll signal him to get out.

But he turns in his seat. Did he blow off dinner for me?

"Look," he tells me. "Damon and I don't agree on most things, but a little healthy violence goes a long way. You need to blow off some steam. Come on, you won't hurt me."

"I don't want to hurt anyone but m—"

I stop, facing forward again.

I just need to be alone. I don't want him here.

"What were you going to say next?" he asks me.

"Nothing."

He's staring at me. I see him in my peripheral, and I know he knows. I don't want to talk about it.

"Let's go." He sits back in his seat. "I'll text them to meet us there."

I shake my head. "You should get out of the car."

My voice is calm, patient.

"I need to be alone now," I tell him. "Please get out of the car."

He doesn't.

In a moment, I hear the *click* of his seat belt, and I shift into gear, taking off away from my house.

I turn left, heading to where the only things are St. Killian's, the Bell Tower, the cemetery, and the highway. No one. No people.

I punch the gas, my odometer rising past thirty, forty, and then fifty.

"Do you want to hurt yourself instead?" he asks quietly.

"No."

"Then what do you want?"

I race around a curve, feeling my body pull with the momentum.

"I don't know," I whisper.

"You're not alone." His voice grows stronger. "What do you want?"

I squeeze the steering wheel. "I don't know."

I want . . . I shake my head. We coast down a small incline onto a flat stretch under the cover of trees. I loosen my grip, feeling the wheel tug a little to the left.

"I want to feel my heart in my throat," I say under my breath.

He stays quiet.

"I want to be someone else," I tell him. "I'd like to have secrets. To be somewhere I'm not supposed to be. I'd like to play, and fuck, I'd love to not know what's next for once, Kai." I turn back to the road. "I'd love anything in life to be mysterious. I want to be curious. I want someone to whisper my name." I pause, staring at the road racing toward us. "I want to let go of the steering wheel."

I expect him to talk me down, but he doesn't.

"I don't need anything," I say. "I don't need food, money, clothes, cars . . . I need nothing, and my heart never races, because I'm not desperate for anything."

One hand drops from the wheel, my other lightly resting on the bottom.

I draw in a breath. "I wish you'd get out of the car."

"I'm not getting out of the car."

I turn my eyes on him, a gleam rising in his gaze like he dares me. "Kai . . ."

But he simply shifts his gaze slowly back out the front windshield, chin up.

He's going to have to let me go at some point. Like all dead weight.

"Let go of the wheel," he says.

My pulse throbs in my ears.

His chest rises slowly. "Let go . . ." he whispers.

Eyes burning, I face forward, the long black highway spread out in front of me. I slide my hand off the wheel, my stomach sinking.

I press the gas a little more, and the car charges ahead, the empty road swaying in front me as my mind tilts. I almost grab the wheel again.

But my heart beats so fast, and it feels fucking good.

The wheel shifts left and right just a hair, the uneven lane guiding the tires off center, and I see Kai's fingers curl into his thigh.

More.

I press the gas harder, the dial moving to sixty, sixty-five, seventy, every second closer. *Closer.*

The car veers to the right and then to the left, taking us into the opposing lane, and my breath catches in my throat, feeling it.

Fuck.

Come on, come on, come on . . .

My heart swells in my chest, and I feel like I'm on a roller coaster.

Except any moment, it'll be too late to stop it.

It'll end. I'll go off the road. Into another car. Into a tree. Rolling. One minute. Or maybe in three seconds. Just . . . a . . . matter . . . of . . . time.

Headlights come over the hill, speeding toward us.

It'll happen. It's about to happen. Everything's going to change.

They honk, laying on the horn hard, and I don't blink.

I don't blink.

And then I hear it.

Kai's sudden intake of breath.

I squeeze my eyes shut, my heart swelling and my stomach rising. *No.*

I gasp, grabbing the wheel and yanking it right. We swing back into our lane, over the shoulder, onto the grass, and into the trees. I slam on the brakes, the other car racing by, and we skid to a halt, my hands tight on the wheel as my car stops just in front of a tree trunk.

I breathe hard, my knuckles aching as I hold my arms straight, braced against the wheel.

I hear Kai's seat belt unfastening, and the next thing I know is he's up, leaning over me and pushing me back in my seat. I release the wheel as he looks down at me, holding his fingers to the pulse in my neck.

"You felt that," he teases.

I expected him to be fucking mad.

"I wasn't scared," he says. "I knew you didn't want to die."

"I don't want you to die," I retort. "There's a difference."

My heart is already slowing down. As stupid as what I just did was, I liked the feeling of my stomach in my throat.

"You think I want to see your end, either?" he asks.

"You didn't try to stop me."

His eyes soften, his voice just above a whisper. "I'll never stop you from doing anything, Michael." A small smile pulls at his mouth. "The first day I met you, I knew . . . when I became a man, I would keep secrets, but I wouldn't have to keep them alone. You're my stairway."

I shake my head. "No one needs me, Kai. What the fuck do I do?" I ask him. "I'm not honorable like Will. I'm not clever like you. I'm not dangerous like Damon. Who the fuck am I?"

But without hesitation, he answers as if I should already know. "You're the dreamer, Michael."

I narrow my eyes.

"The visionary," he explains.

No.

I'm not.

"My mom gave me this poetry book when I was, like, twelve," he tells me, laughter in his voice. "And I don't know why, because I wasn't into poetry, and all I ever read was the first poem. But I read it so much that I memorized it. It was called *The Builders*. It talks about how we all have a role to play. We're all beams in a building, and if one beam is missing, the structure won't stand."

A Longfellow poem. I remember it from middle school.

He stares at me. "You saw what Damon was capable of before I did," he says. "You saw that we needed him, and now we know that we needed him in more ways than one. You knew Will needed to be a part of something bigger than himself. That no matter where we turned, he would be there for us. And we've been best friends since that day at orientation because you didn't see a rival. You saw, before I did, what we were going to be. And what we'll still be. You see the future."

My eyes start to burn, and I look down so he doesn't see.

"We're all together, because of you," he says. "You're the one I follow to the edge, because you make every thought that goes through my head okay."

My insides crack, everything in pain, and I fucking wish all of that was true. To know that I picked my family without even knowing it, and my dad doesn't matter. That I have brothers. Three who don't share my blood, but we found each other all the same.

"I mean, can you imagine . . ." he says, joking. "Damon and I left to our own devices? Will would be constantly cleaning up the blood."

I break into a laugh, and he smiles, satisfied. "Come on." He sits back in his seat. "Let's go to the city."

I start the car again and grab the wheel, but I stop and put on my seat belt. Pulling out, I drive us back toward Thunder Bay and past it, on to Meridian City. I blast music, so we don't have to talk about what just happened.

Or that I still feel like shit.

I love him, though. I can't hurt him. I'll never do that again.

I don't want to die. I just want to remember why I want to live.

Everything I said was true. I would like to not know what's next. I'd love to leave my skin once in a while, and I don't know how to do that.

And I still want to let go of the wheel. To feel that in one second, everything could change forever.

He's right, though. No matter what, I'll never have to go it alone.

I walk around the paintball shop as Kai sets us up at the counter.

Will and Damon try on vests, and I really don't want to fucking do this tonight, but I can't be home, either.

I gaze at the masks on the wall, only half looking at them as something knocks in the corner of my brain.

Would I have swerved if Kai hadn't been in the car?

Would I have saved myself so soon? I didn't want that feeling to end.

I walk, eyes on the floor, but I look up and stop. I don't move. Reaching out, I pull a mask off the wall, hanging there among a dozen others, but I like red. I gaze down at the skull with black eyes and claw marks marring the thin flesh, and my heart skips a beat.

I run my hand over the gashes in the face, laughing at myself on the inside, because when I said I wanted to be someone else, I never would've thought I wanted to be a monster.

I see a mirror in front of me and pull the mask on, over my face.

Damon comes up, removing a matching black one off the wall.

"They have some to rent," Will tells us. "Unless you think we'll be doing this enough to need our own."

I stare at myself in the mirror, slowly pulling the hood of my sweatshirt up and covering my hair.

Fuck.

It's the strangest feeling, isn't it? Like looking at the world through different eyes.

Like I don't have to talk in order to speak.

Fear . . .

"What are you thinking?" Kai asks me.

I shake my head, removing the skull. "I don't know." It's on the tip of my brain, but I still can't see it clearly. "But what the hell . . ." I tell him, grinning. "I'm getting it."

I hear Damon breathe out a laugh, holding his, as Will picks out a white one with a red stripe.

Kai finally shrugs, grabbing a silver skull. "All right, then. Let's all get one."

Thank you for reading *Nightfall* and for supporting these characters! If you'd like to read a series epilogue set ten years after the end of *Nightfall*, head to my website, pendouglas.com/bonus-scenes/devils-night-bonus-scenes/devils-night-series-epilogue/!

xx Pen

ACKNOWLEDGMENTS

To the readers—I want to thank you so much for all the help and support over the years. I love being online with you, having fun and socializing, but social media has a funny way of sucking me in, and before I know it, it's noon! Not that it's time wasted, by any means, but I realized that I'm more successful about reaching my goals and staying organized the more disciplined I am about how my time is spent. Thank you to those of you who put up with my long spells offline. You understand that just because someone isn't constantly posting doesn't mean that great things aren't happening.

Thank you also to everyone who emailed this spring while I was offline writing to just say how much they like my stories and how much they "love my brain" lol. It makes me smile and helps me stay creative. I can't wait to show you what's next.

To my family—my husband for taking over so much in the past year. Seriously. Roles have certainly changed between us since we met, and I'm grateful you're here to handle so much, so I can make good use of my time to do the work I love. It's probably ridiculous I still have no idea how to run the dishwasher that we bought four months ago, so just to let you know . . . You can start making me clear my own plates now. The book is done!

And to AydanCakes—my daughter, my girl with powerhouse kicks and weird dance moves just like her mom . . . I love you so much. Thank you for being amazing during this time at home through quarantine, cooperating for online schooling, and letting me win Uno once in a while. You'll never beat me at Scrabble, though, because I'm the WRITER in the family. Boo-yah.

To Dystel, Goderich & Bourret LLC—thank you for being so readily available and helping me grow every day. I couldn't be happier.

To the PenDragons—gosh, I've missed you all. There were so many days, especially a month into quarantine, that I was desperate to spend some time with you. I needed people, and I really appreciate that you're my guaranteed happy place. Thanks for giving me a tribe and validating the stories I love.

To Adrienne Ambrose, Tabitha Russell, Tiffany Rhyne, Kristi Grimes, Lee Tenaglia, and Claudia Alfaro—the amazing Facebook group admins! Not enough can be said about the time and energy you give freely to make a community for the readers and me. You're selfless, amazing, patient, and needed. Thank you.

To Vibeke Courtney—my indie editor who goes over every move I make with a fine-toothed comb. Thank you for teaching me how to write and laying it down straight.

To Charlene Tillit—thank you for being available to check my French! You were a huge help.

To all the wonderful readers, especially on Instagram, who make art for the books and keep us all excited, motivated, and inspired . . . thank you for everything! I love your vision, and I apologize if I miss things while I'm offline.

To all of the bloggers and bookstagrammers—there are too many to name, but I know who you are. I see the posts and the tags, and all the hard work you do. You spend your free time reading, reviewing, and promoting, and you do it for free. You are the life's blood of the book world, and who knows what we would do without you. Thank you for your tireless efforts. You do it out of passion, which makes it all the more incredible.

To every author and aspiring author—thank you for the stories you've shared, many of which have made me a happy reader in search of a wonderful escape, and a better writer, trying to live up to your standards. Write and create, and don't ever stop. Your voice is important, and as long as it comes from your heart, it is right and good.

Copyright © Penelope Douglas

Penelope Douglas is a *New York Times*, *USA Today*, and *Wall Street Journal* bestselling author. Their books have been translated into twenty languages and include the Fall Away series, the Hellbent series, the Devil's Night series, and the stand-alones *Misconduct*, *Punk 57*, *Birthday Girl*, *Credence*, and *Tryst Six Venom*.

VISIT PENELOPE DOUGLAS ONLINE

PenDouglas.com
 PenelopeDouglasAuthor
 PenDouglas
 Penelope.Douglas

LEARN MORE ABOUT THIS BOOK
AND OTHER TITLES FROM
NEW YORK TIMES BESTSELLING AUTHOR

PENELOPE DOUGLAS

SCAN ME

or visit
prh.com/penelopedouglas

By scanning, I acknowledge that I have read and agree to Penguin Random House's
Privacy Policy (prh.com/privacy) and Terms of Use (prh.com/terms) and understand
that Penguin Random House collects certain categories of personal information for
the purposes listed in that policy, discloses, sells, or shares certain personal information
and retains personal information in accordance with the policy located here:
prh.com/privacy. You can opt-out of the sale or sharing of personal information
anytime from prh.com/privacy/right-to-opt-out-of-sale-form.